"THE STARS ARE HIGH..."

"We are a tough and resourceful lot; our descendants will have to be tougher and more resourceful still.

"The odds are all against them. The stars are high, life is short, and the house always takes a percentage. But Man himself is so unlikely that if he did not exist, his possibility would not be worth discussing.

"Heinlein's money is on Man; and I have a hunch that the next century will prove him right."

from the **INTRODUCTION** by

DAMON KNIGHT

Robert A. Heinlein

Future History Stories

The Past Through Tomorrow

BERKLEY BOOKS, NEW YORK

For GINNY

This Berkley book contains the complete
text of the original hardcover edition.
It has been completely reset in a typeface
designed for easy reading and was printed
from new film.

THE PAST THROUGH TOMORROW

A Berkley Book / published by arrangement with
G. P. Putnam's Sons

PRINTING HISTORY
G. P. Putnam's Sons edition published 1967
Berkley edition / January 1975
Fifteenth printing / March 1983
Sixteenth printing / August 1983
Seventeenth printing / October 1984
Eighteenth printing / January 1986
Nineteenth printing / November 1986

ISBN: 0-425-10223-8

A BERKLEY BOOK ® TM 757,375
Berkley Books are published by The Berkley Publishing Group,
200 Madison Avenue, New York, New York 10016.
The name "BERKLEY" and the stylized "B" with design
are trademarks belonging to Berkley Publishing Corporation.

PRINTED IN THE UNITED STATES OF AMERICA

CONTENTS

Introduction by Damon Knight

THE YEAR is 1967, and in Carmel, California, a retired admiral named Robert A. Heinlein is tending his garden. Commissioned in 1929, he served through World War II with distinction, taught aeronautical engineering for a few years, then became a partner in a modestly successful electronics firm. Aside from his neighbors, his business associates and Navy friends, no one has ever heard of him.

This is a likely story, but not true. What really happened is much less probable: six years after graduation from the Naval Academy, while serving on a destroyer, Heinlein contracted tuberculosis. He spent a couple of years in bed, then was retired at the age of 27.

Like the consumptive Robert Louis Stevenson, like Mark Twain, whose career as a river-boat pilot was swept away by the war, Heinlein turned to writing almost at random, because he could not lead the more active life he would have preferred. Cut adrift from the Navy and from the life-line that would have led him to that rose garden in Carmel, he took graduate courses in physics and mathematics, intending to pursue his old dream of becoming an astronomer, but was again forced to drop out because of poor health. He tried his hand at silver mining, politics, real estate, without conspicuous success.

Then, in 1939, he happened across the announcement of an amateur short-story contest in a magazine called *Thrilling Wonder Stories*. The prize was $50, not a fortune, but not to be sneezed at. Heinlein wrote a story, called it "Life-Line," and submitted it, not to the contest editor, but to John W. Campbell, editor of *Astounding Science-Fiction*. Campbell bought it, and the next one, and the next. Heinlein's reaction was, "How long has this been going on? And why didn't anybody ever tell me?" Except for the war years, which he spent at the Naval Air Experimental Station in Philadelphia in "the necessary tedium of aviation engineering," he never did anything else for a living again.

In the February, 1941, issue of *Astounding*, in which two

9

Heinlein stories appeared (one under the pseudonym Anson MacDonald), the editor wrote:

"Robert A. Heinlein's back again next month with the cover story, 'Logic of Empire.' This story is, as usual with Heinlein's material, a soundly worked out, fast-moving yarn, more than able to stand on its own feet. But in connection with it, I'd like to mention something that may or may not have been noticed by the regular readers of *Astounding*: all Heinlein's science-fiction is laid against a common background of a proposed future history of the world and of the United States. Heinlein's worked the thing out in detail that grows with each story; he has an outlined and graphed history of the future with characters, dates of major discoveries, et cetera, plotted in. I'm trying to get him to let me have a photostat of that history chart; if I lay hands on it, I'm going to publish it."

He published the chart three months later—the same chart, with some modifications and additions, that appears in this book. Heinlein had the cover of that issue, too, with a story called "Universe."

"Future History" is Campbell's phrase, not Heinlein's, and the author has sometimes been mildly embarrassed by it. This connected series of stories does not pretend to be prophetic. It is a history, not of *the* future, but of *a* future—an alternate-probability world (perhaps the same one in which the retired Rear Admiral is tending his roses) which is logically self-consistent, dramatic, and recognizably an offshoot of our own past. The stories really do not form a linear series at all —they are more like a pyramid, in which earlier stories provide a solid base for later ones to rest on.

Partly because of this pyramiding of background and partly because of the author's broad knowledge—about which more in a moment—Heinlein's readers find themselves in a world which is clearly our own, only projected a few years or decades into the future. There have been changes, naturally, but they are things you feel you could adjust to without much trouble. People are still people: they read *Time* magazine, are worried about money, smoke Luckies, argue with their wives.

It is easy to say what the ideal science fiction writer would be like. He would be a talented and imaginative writer, trained in the physical and social sciences and in engineering, with a broad and varied experience of people—not only scientists and engineers, but secretaries, lawyers, labor leaders, admen, newspapermen, politicians, businessmen. The trouble is that no one in his senses would spend the time to acquire all this training and background merely in order to write science fiction. But Heinlein had it all.

Far more of Heinlein's work comes out of his own experience than most people realize. When he doesn't know something himself, he is too conscientious a workman to guess at it: he goes and finds out. His stories are full of precisely right details, the product of painstaking research. But many of the things he writes about, including some that strain the reader's credulity, are from his own life. A few examples, out of many:

The elaborate discussion of the problems of linkages in designing household robots, in *The Door Into Summer*. Heinlein was an engineer, specializing in linkages.

The hand-to-hand combat skills of the heroes of such stories as *Gulf* and *Glory Road*. Heinlein himself is an expert marksman, swordsman and rough-and-tumble fighter.

The redheaded and improbably multi-skilled heroine of *The Puppet Masters* and other Heinlein stories. Heinlein's redheaded wife Ginny is a chemist, biochemist, aviation test engineer, experimental horticulturist; she earned varsity letters at N.Y.U. in swimming, diving, basketball and field hockey, and became a competitive figure skater after graduation; she speaks seven languages so far, and is starting on an eighth.

The longevity of the "Families" in *Methuselah's Children*. Five of Heinlein's six brothers and sisters are still living. So is his mother: she is 87, "frail, but very much alive and mentally active." All the returns are not in yet.

Even the improbably talented families that appear in *The Rolling Stones* and elsewhere are not wild inventions: Heinlein himself played chess before he could read. Of his three brothers, one is a professor of electrical engineering, one a professor of political science, and the third is a retired major general who "made it the hard way—i.e., from private right up through every rank without any college education at all."

Like Mark Twain, Heinlein is from Missouri. It shows in his skepticism, his rich appreciation of human absurdity, and in an occasional turn of phrase—a taste for gaudily embellished understatement. He has the Missourian admiration for competence of any kind, for those who can get things done—

even (or perhaps especially) if they bend a few rules in the process. (Heinlein: "I stood quite high at the Naval Academy and would have stood much higher save for a tendency to collect 'Black N's'—major offenses against military discipline.") Unlike most modern novelists, he has no patience with the unskilled and incompetent. Those who contribute most to the world, Heinlein thinks, are also those who have the most fun. Those who contribute nothing are objects of pity; and pity for the self-pitying is not high on Heinlein's list of virtues.

This tough-mindedness is an altogether different thing from the cynicism of other writers. Heinlein is a moralist to the core; he devoutly believes in courage, honor, self-discipline, self-sacrifice for love or duty. Above all, he is a libertarian. "When any government, or any church for that matter, undertakes to say to its subjects, 'This you may not read, this you must not see, this you are forbidden to know,' the end result is tyranny and oppression, no matter how holy the motives. Mighty little force is needed to control a man whose mind has been hoodwinked; contrariwise, no amount of force can control a free man, a man whose mind is free. No, not the rack, not fission bombs, not anything—you can't conquer a free man; the most you can do is kill him."

The author himself has often denied that the stories in this book are prophecy. Yet it is apparent that some of Heinlein's fictional forecasts have already come true—not literally but symbolically. "The Roads Must Roll" predicts urban sprawl, and anticipates Jimmy Hoffa's threat of a nationwide transport strike. The 1969 newspaper headlines in *Methuselah's Children*, illustrating the character of "The Crazy Years"—Heinlein's term for the present era—seem less fantastic now than they did in 1941.

"Blowups Happen," written and published five years before the Bomb, is based on a series of shrewd guesses that turned out to be wrong. The specific dilemma of that story never became real; nevertheless, it mirrors the real, agonizing dilemma of atomic power with which we have been living since 1945.

Some of these stories are minor entertainments, but one, at least, is a major work of art: "The Man Who Sold the Moon." Written with deceptive ease and simplicity, it functions brilliantly on half a dozen levels at once. It is a story of man's conquest of the Moon, a penetrating essay on robber-baron capitalism, and a warm, utterly convincing and human portrait of an extraordinary man.

As for the still-unfolding future, there are guideposts and warnings here. Heinlein continually reminds us that history is a process, not something dead and embalmed in textbooks. The ultimate problem is man's control of his own inventions—not only the minor ones, like the crossbow and the atom bomb, but the major inventions—language, culture and technology. We are a tough and resourceful lot, all things considered; our descendants will need to be tougher and more resourceful still.

The odds are all against them. The stars are high, life is short, and the house always takes a percentage. But Man himself is so unlikely that if he did not exist, his possibility would not be worth discussing. Heinlein's money is on Man; and I have a hunch that the next century will prove him right.

The Anchorage
Milford, Pennsylvania

Life-Line

THE CHAIRMAN rapped loudly for order. Gradually the catcalls and boos died away as several self-appointed sergeants-at-arms persuaded a few hotheaded individuals to sit down. The speaker on the rostrum by the chairman seemed unaware of the disturbance. His bland, faintly insolent face was impassive. The chairman turned to the speaker, and addressed him, in a voice in which anger and annoyance were barely restrained.

"Doctor Pinero,"—the "Doctor" was faintly stressed—"I must apologize to you for the unseemly outburst during your remarks. I am surprised that my colleagues should so far forget the dignity proper to men of science as to interrupt a speaker, no matter," he paused and set his mouth, "no matter how great the provocation." Pinero smiled in his face, a smile that was in some way an open insult. The chairman visibly controlled his temper and continued, "I am anxious that the program be concluded decently and in order. I want you to finish your remarks. Nevertheless, I must ask you to refrain from affronting our intelligence with ideas that any educated man knows to be fallacious. Please confine yourself to your discovery—if you have made one."

Pinero spread his fat white hands, palms down. "How can I possibly put a new idea into your heads, if I do not first remove your delusions?"

The audience stirred and muttered. Someone shouted from the rear of the hall, "Throw the charlatan out! We've had enough." The chairman pounded his gavel.

"Gentlemen! Please!" Then to Pinero, "Must I remind you that you are not a member of this body, and that we did not invite you?"

Pinero's eyebrows lifted. "So? I seem to remember an invitation on the letterhead of the Academy?"

The chairman chewed his lower lip before replying. "True. I wrote that invitation myself. But it was at the request of one of the trustees—a fine public-spirited gentleman, but not a scientist, not a member of the Academy."

Pinero smiled his irritating smile. "So? I should have guessed. Old Bidwell, not so, of Amalgamated Life Insurance? And he wanted his trained seals to expose me as a fraud, yes? For if I can tell a man the day of his own death, no one will buy his pretty policies. But how can you expose me, if you will not listen to me first? Even supposing you had the wit to understand me? Bah! He has sent jackals to tear down a lion." He deliberately turned his back on them. The muttering of the crowd swelled and took on a vicious tone. The chairman cried vainly for order. There arose a figure in the front row.

"Mister Chairman!"

The chairman grasped the opening and shouted, "Gentlemen! Doctor Van RheinSmitt has the floor." The commotion died away.

The doctor cleared his throat, smoothed the forelock. of his beautiful white hair, and thrust one hand into a side pocket of his smartly tailored trousers. He assumed his women's-club manner.

"Mister Chairman, fellow members of the Academy of Science, let us have tolerance. Even a murderer has the right to say his say before the state exacts its tribute. Shall we do less? Even though one may be intellectually certain of the verdict? I grant Doctor Pinero every consideration that should be given by this august body to any unaffiliated colleague, even though"—he bowed slightly in Pinero's direction—"we may not be familiar with the university which bestowed his degree. If what he has to say is false, it can not harm us. If what he has to say is true, we should know it." His mellow cultivated voice rolled on, soothing and calming. "If the eminent doctor's manner appears a trifle inurbane for our tastes, we must bear in mind that the doctor may be from a place, or a stratum, not so meticulous in these little matters. Now our good friend and benefactor has asked us to hear this person and carefully assess the merit of his claims. Let us do so with dignity and decorum."

He sat down to a rumble of applause, comfortably aware that he had enhanced his reputation as an intellectual leader. Tomorrow the papers would again mention the good sense and persuasive personality of "America's Handsomest University President". Who knew? Perhaps old Bidwell would come through with that swimming pool donation.

When the applause had ceased, the chairman turned to

where the center of the disturbance sat, hands folded over his little round belly, face serene.

"Will you continue, Doctor Pinero?"

"Why should I?"

The chairman shrugged his shoulders. "You came for that purpose."

Pinero arose. "So true. So very true. But was I wise to come? Is there anyone here who has an open mind, who can stare a bare fact in the face without blushing? I think not. Even that so beautiful gentleman who asked you to hear me out has already judged me and condemned me. He seeks order, not truth. Suppose truth defies order, will he accept it? Will you? I think not. Still, if I do not speak, you will win your point by default. The little man in the street will think that you little men have exposed me, Pinero, as a hoaxer, a pretender. That does not suit my plans. I will speak.

"I will repeat my discovery. In simple language I have invented a technique to tell how long a man will live. I can give you advance billing of the Angel of Death. I can tell you when the Black Camel will kneel at your door. In five minutes time with my apparatus I can tell any of you how many grains of sand are still left in your hourglass." He paused and folded his arms across his chest. For a moment no one spoke. The audience grew restless. Finally the chairman intervened.

"You aren't finished, Doctor Pinero?"

"What more is there to say?"

"You haven't told us how your discovery works."

Pinero's eyebrows shot up. "You suggest that I should turn over the fruits of my work for children to play with. This is dangerous knowledge, my friend. I keep it for the man who understands it, myself." He tapped his chest.

"How are we to know that you have anything back of your wild claims?"

"So simple. You send a committee to watch me demonstrate. If it works, fine. You admit it and tell the world so. If it does not work, I am discredited, and will apologize. Even I, Pinero, will apologize."

A slender stoop-shouldered man stood up in the back of the hall. The chair recognized him and he spoke:

"Mr. Chairman, how can the eminent doctor seriously propose such a course? Does he expect us to wait around for twenty or thirty years for some one to die and prove his claims?"

Pinero ignored the chair and answered directly:

"Pfui! Such nonsense! Are you so ignorant of statistics that you do not know that in any large group there is at least one who will die in the immediate future? I make you a proposition; let me test each one of you in this room and I will name the man who will die within the fortnight, yes, and the day and hour of his death." He glanced fiercely around the room. "Do you accept?"

Another figure got to his feet, a portly man who spoke in measured syllables. "I, for one, can not countenance such an experiment. As a medical man, I have noted with sorrow the plain marks of serious heart trouble in many of our elder colleagues. If Doctor Pinero knows those symptoms, as he may, and were he to select as his victim one of their number, the man so selected would be likely to die on schedule, whether the distinguished speaker's mechanical egg-timer works or not."

Another speaker backed him up at once. "Doctor Shepard is right. Why should we waste time on voodoo tricks? It is my belief that this person who calls himself *Doctor* Pinero wants to use this body to give his statements authority. If we participate in this farce, we play into his hands. I don't know what his racket is, but you can bet that he has figured out some way to use us for advertising for his schemes. I move, Mister Chairman, that we proceed with our regular business."

The motion carried by acclamation, but Pinero did not sit down. Amidst cries of "Order! Order!" he shook his untidy head at them, and had his say:

"Barbarians! Imbeciles! Stupid dolts! Your kind have blocked the recognition of every great discovery since time began. Such ignorant canaille are enough to start Galileo spinning in his grave. That fat fool down there twiddling his elk's tooth calls himself a medical man. Witch doctor would be a better term! That little bald-headed runt over there— You! You style yourself a philosopher, and prate about life and time in your neat categories. What do you know of either one? How can you ever learn when you won't examine the truth when you have a chance? Bah!" He spat upon the stage. "You call this an Academy of Science. I call it an undertaker's convention, interested only in embalming the ideas of your red-blooded predecessors."

He paused for breath and was grasped on each side by two members of the platform committee and rushed out the wings. Several reporters arose hastily from the press table and followed him. The chairman declared the meeting adjourned.

The newspapermen caught up with him as he was going out by the stage door. He walked with a light springy step, and whistled a little tune. There was no trace of the belligerence he had shown a moment before. They crowded about him. "—How about an interview, doc?" "What dyu think of Modern Education?" "You certainly told 'em. What are your views on Life after Death?" "Take off your hat, doc, and look at the birdie."

He grinned at them all. "One at a time, boys, and not so fast. I used to be a newspaperman myself. How about coming up to my place, and we'll talk about it?"

A few minutes later they were trying to find places to sit down in Pinero's messy bed-living-room, and lighting his cigars. Pinero looked around and beamed. "What'll it be, boys? Scotch, or Bourbon?" When that was taken care of he got down to business. "Now, boys, what do you want to know?"

"Lay it on the line, doc. Have you got something, or haven't you?"

"Most assuredly I have something, my young friend."

"Then tell us how it works. That guff you handed the profs won't get you anywhere now."

"Please, my dear fellow. It is my invention. I expect to make some money with it. Would you have me give it away to the first person who asks for it?"

"See here, doc, you've got to give us something if you expect to get a break in the morning papers. What do you use? A crystal ball?"

"No, not quite. Would you like to see my apparatus?"

"Sure. Now we are getting somewhere."

He ushered them into an adjoining room, and waved his hand. "There it is, boys." The mass of equipment that met their eyes vaguely resembled a medico's office x-ray gear. Beyond the obvious fact that it used electrical power, and that some of the dials were calibrated in familiar terms, a casual inspection gave no clue to its actual use.

"What's the principle, doc?"

Pinero pursed his lips and considered. "No doubt you are all familiar with the truism that life is electrical in nature? Well, that truism isn't worth a damn, but it will help to give you an idea of the principle. You have also been told that time is a fourth dimension. Maybe you believe it, perhaps not.

It has been said so many times that it has ceased to have any meaning. It is simply a cliché that windbags use to impress fools. But I want you to try to visualize it now and try to feel it emotionally."

He stepped up to one of the reporters. "Suppose we take you as an example. Your name is Rogers, is it not? Very well, Rogers, you are a space-time event having duration four ways. You are not quite six feet tall, you are about twenty inches wide and perhaps ten inches thick. In time, there stretches behind you more of this space-time event reaching to perhaps nineteen-sixteen, of which we see a cross-section here at right angles to the time axis, and as thick as the present. At the far end is a baby, smelling of sour milk and drooling its breakfast on its bib. At the other end lies, perhaps, an old man someplace in the nineteen-eighties. Imagine this space-time event which we call Rogers as a long pink worm, continuous through the years, one end at his mother's womb, the other at the grave. It stretches past us here and the cross-section we see appears as a single discrete body. But that is illusion. There is physical continuity to this pink worm, enduring through the years. As a matter of fact there is physical continuity in this concept to the entire race, for these pink worms branch off from other pink worms. In this fashion the race is like a vine whose branches intertwine and send out shoots. Only by taking a cross-section of the vine would we fall into the error of believing that the shootlets were discrete individuals."

He paused and looked around at their faces. One of them, a dour hardbitten chap, put in a word.

"That's all very pretty, Pinero, if true, but where does that get you?"

Pinero favored him with an unresentful smile. "Patience, my friend. I asked you to think of life as electrical. Now think of our long pink worm as a conductor of electricity. You have heard, perhaps, of the fact that electrical engineers can, b certain measurements, predict the exact location of a break in a trans-Atlantic cable without ever leaving the shore. I do the same with our pink worms. By applying my instruments to the cross-section here in this room I can tell where the break occurs, that is to say, when death takes place. Or, if you like, I can reverse the connections and tell you the date of your birth. But that is uninteresting; you already know it."

The dour individual sneered. "I've caught you, doc. If what you said about the race being like a vine of pink worms is true, you can't tell birthdays because the connection with the race is continuous at birth. Your electrical conductor reaches on back through the mother into a man's remotest ancestors."

Pinero beamed. "True, and clever, my friend. But you have pushed the analogy too far. It is not done in the precise manner in which one measures the length of an electrical conductor. In some ways it is more like measuring the length of a long corridor by bouncing an echo off the far end. At birth there is a sort of twist in the corridor, and, by proper calibration, I can detect the echo from that twist. There is just one case in which I can get no determinant reading; when a woman is actually carrying a child, I can't sort out her life-line from that of the unborn infant."

"Let's see you prove it."

"Certainly, my dear friend. Will you be a subject?"

One of the others spoke up. "He's called your bluff, Luke. Put up, or shut up."

"I'm game. What do I do?"

"First write the date of your birth on a sheet of paper, and hand it to one of your colleagues."

Luke complied. "Now what?"

"Remove your outer clothing and step upon these scales. Now tell me, were you ever very much thinner, or very much fatter, than you are now. No? What did you weigh at birth? Ten pounds? A fine bouncing baby boy. They don't come so big any more."

"What is all this flubdubbery?"

"I am trying to approximate the average cross-section of our long pink conductor, my dear Luke. Now will you seat yourself here. Then place this electrode in your mouth. No, it will not hurt you; the voltage is quite low, less than one micro-volt, but I must have a good connection." The doctor left him and went behind his apparatus, where he lowered a hood over his head before touching his controls. Some of the exposed dials came to life and a low humming came from the machine. It stopped and the doctor popped out of his little hide-away.

"I get sometime in February, nineteen-twelve. Who has the piece of paper with the date?"

It was produced and unfolded. The custodian read, "February 22nd, 1912."

The stillness that followed was broken by a voice from the edge of the little group. "Doc, can I have another drink?"

The tension relaxed, and several spoke at once, "Try it on me, doc." "Me first, doc, I'm an orphan and really want to know." "How about it, doc. Give us all a little loose play."

He smilingly complied, ducking in and out of the hood like a gopher from its hole. When they all had twin slips of paper to prove the doctor's skill, Luke broke a long silence:

"How about showing how you predict death, Pinero."

"If you wish. Who will try it?"

No one answered. Several of them nudged Luke forward. "Go ahead, smart guy. You asked for it." He allowed himself to be seated in the chair. Pinero changed some of the switches, then entered the hood. When the humming ceased, he came out, rubbing his hands briskly together.

"Well, that's all there is to see, boys. Got enough for a story?"

"Hey, what about the prediction? When does Luke get his 'thirty'?"

Luke faced him. "Yes, how about it? What's your answer?"

Pinero looked pained. "Gentlemen, I am surprised at you. I give that information for a fee. Besides, it is a professional confidence. I never tell anyone but the client who consults me."

"I don't mind. Go ahead and tell them."

"I am very sorry. I really must refuse. I agreed only to show you how, not to give the results."

Luke ground the butt of his cigaret into the floor. "It's a hoax, boys. He probably looked up the age of every reporter in town just to be ready to pull this. It won't wash, Pinero."

Pinero gazed at him sadly. "Are you married, my friend?"

"No."

"Do you have any one dependent on you? Any close relatives?"

"No. Why, do you want to adopt me?"

Pinero shook his head sadly. "I am very sorry for you, my dear Luke. You will die before tomorrow."

"SCIENCE MEET ENDS IN RIOT"
"SAVANTS SAPS SAYS SEER"
"DEATH PUNCHES TIMECLOCK"
"SCRIBE DIES PER DOC'S DOPE"
" 'HOAX' CLAIMS SCIENCE HEAD"

". . . within twenty minutes of Pinero's strange prediction, Timons was struck by a falling sign while walking down Broadway toward the offices of the *Daily Herald* where he was employed.

"Doctor Pinero declined to comment but confirmed the story that he had predicted Timons' death by means of his so-called chronovitameter. Chief of Police Roy . . ."

Legal Notice

To whom it may concern, greetings; I, John Cabot Winthrop III, of the firm Winthrop, Winthrop, Ditmars & Winthrop, Attorneys-at-Law, do affirm that Hugo Pinero of this city did hand to me ten thousand dollars in lawful money of the United States, and instruct me to place it in escrow with a chartered bank of my selection with escrow instructions as follows:

The entire bond shall be forfeit, and shall forthwith be paid to the first client of Hugo Pinero and/or Sands of Time, Inc. who shall exceed his life tenure as predicted by Hugo Pinero by one per centum, or to the estate of the first client who shall fail of such predicted tenure in a like amount, whichever occurs first in point of time.

I do further affirm that I have this day placed this bond in escrow with the above related instructions with the Equitable-First National Bank of this city.

Subscribed and sworn,
John Cabot Winthrop III

Subscribed and sworn to before me
this 2nd day of April, 1951.
    Albert M. Swanson
Notary Public in and for this county and state
My commission expires June 17, 1951.

"Good evening Mr. and Mrs. Radio Audience, let's go to Press! Flash! Hugo Pinero, The Miracle Man from Nowhere, has made his thousandth death prediction without a claimant for the reward he posted for anyone who catches him failing to call the turn. With thirteen of his clients already dead it is mathematically certain that he has a private line to the main office of the Old Man with the Scythe. That is one piece of news I don't want to know before it happens. Your Coast-to-Coast Correspondent will *not* be a client of Prophet Pinero. . . ."

The judge's watery baritone cut through the stale air of the courtroom. "Please, Mr. Weems, let us return to our muttons. This court granted your prayer for a temporary restraining order, and now you ask that it be made permanent. In rebuttal, Mr. Pinero claims that you have presented no cause and asks that the injunction be lifted, and that I order your client to cease from attempts to interfere with what Pinero describes as a simple lawful business. As you are not addressing a jury, please omit the rhetoric and tell me in plain language why I should not grant his prayer."

Mr. Weems jerked his chin nervously, making his flabby grey dewlap drag across his high stiff collar, and resumed:

"May it please the honorable court, I represent the public—"

"Just a moment. I thought you were appearing for Amalgamated Life Insurance."

"I am, Your Honor, in a formal sense. In a wider sense I represent several other of the major assurance, fiduciary, and financial institutions; their stockholders, and policy holders, who constitute a majority of the citizenry. In addition we feel that we protect the interests of the entire population; unorganized, inarticulate, and otherwise unprotected."

"I thought that I represented the public," observed the judge drily. "I am afraid I must regard you as appearing for your client-of-record. But continue; what is your thesis?"

The elderly barrister attempted to swallow his Adam's apple, then began again. "Your Honor, we contend that there are two separate reasons why this injunction should be made permanent, and, further, that each reason is sufficient alone. In the first place, this person is engaged in the practice of soothsaying, an occupation proscribed both in common law and statute. He is a common fortune teller, a vagabond charlatan who preys on the gullibility of the public. He is cleverer than the ordinary gypsy palm-reader, astrologer, or table tipper, and to the same extent more dangerous. He makes false claims of modern scientific methods to give a spurious dignity to his thaumaturgy. We have here in court leading representatives of the Academy of Science to give expert witness as to the absurdity of his claims.

"In the second place, even if this person's claims were true —granting for the sake of argument such an absurdity"——Mr. Weems permitted himself a thin-lipped smile—"we contend that his activities are contrary to the public interest in general, and unlawfully injurious to the interests of my client in particular. We are prepared to produce numerous exhibits with the legal custodians to prove that this person did publish, or cause to have published, utterances urging the public to dispense with the priceless boon of life insurance to the great detriment of their welfare and to the financial damage of my client."

Pinero arose in his place. "Your Honor, may I say a few words?"

"What is it?"

"I believe I can simplify the situation if permitted to make a brief analysis."

"Your Honor," cut in Weems, "this is most irregular."

"Patience, Mr. Weems. Your interests will be protected. It seems to me that we need more light and less noise in this matter. If Dr. Pinero can shorten the proceedings by speaking at this time, I am inclined to let him. Proceed, Dr. Pinero."

"Thank you, Your Honor. Taking the last of Mr. Weems' points first, I am prepared to stipulate that I published the utterances he speaks of—"

."One moment, Doctor. You have chosen to act as your own attorney. Are you sure you are competent to protect your own interests?"

"I am prepared to chance it, Your Honor. Our friends here can easily prove what I stipulate."

"Very well. You may proceed."

"I will stipulate that many persons have cancelled life insurance policies as a result thereof, but I challenge them to show that anyone so doing has suffered any loss or damage therefrom. It is true that the Amalgamated has lost business through my activities, but that is the natural result of my discovery, which has made their policies as obsolete as the bow and arrow. If an injunction is granted on that ground, I shall set up a coal oil lamp factory, then ask for an injunction against the Edison and General Electric companies to forbid them to manufacture incandescent bulbs.

"I will stipulate that I am engaged in the business of making predictions of death, but I deny that I am practicing magic, black, white, or rainbow colored. If to make predictions by methods of scientific accuracy is illegal, then the actuaries of the Amalgamated have been guilty for years in that they predict the exact percentage that will die each year in any given large group. I predict death retail; the Amalgamated predicts it wholesale. If their actions are legal, how can mine be illegal?

"I admit that it makes a difference whether I can do what I claim, or not; and I will stipulate that the so-called expert witnesses from the Academy of Science will testify that I cannot. But they know nothing of my method and cannot give truly expert testimony on it—"

"Just a moment, Doctor. Mr. Weems, is it true that your expert witnesses are not conversant with Dr. Pinero's theory and methods?"

Mr. Weems looked worried. He drummed on the table top, then answered, "Will the Court grant me a few moments indulgence?"

"Certainly."

Mr. Weems held a hurried whispered consultation with his cohorts, then faced the bench. "We have a procedure to suggest, Your Honor. If Dr. Pinero will take the stand and explain the theory and practice of his alleged method, then these distinguished scientists will be able to advise the Court as to the validity of his claims."

The judge looked inquiringly at Pinero, who responded, "I will not willingly agree to that. Whether my process is true or false, it would be dangerous to let it fall into the hands of fools and quacks—" he waved his hand at the group of professors seated in the front row, paused and smiled maliciously "—as these gentlemen know quite well. Furthermore it is not necessary to know the process in order to prove that it will work. Is it necessary to understand the complex miracle of biological reproduction in order to observe that a hen lays eggs? Is it necessary for me to re-educate this entire body of self-appointed custodians of wisdom—cure them of their ingrown superstitions—in order to prove that my predictions are correct? There are but two ways of forming an opinion in science. One is the scientific method; the other, the scholastic. One can judge from experiment, or one can blindly accept authority. To the scientific mind, experimental proof is all important and theory is merely a convenience in description, to be junked when it no longer fits. To the academic mind, authority is everything and facts are junked when they do not fit theory laid down by authority.

"It is this point of view—academic minds clinging like oysters to disproved theories—that has blocked every advance of knowledge in history. I am prepared to prove my method by experiment, and, like Galileo in another court, I insist, 'It still moves!'

"Once before I offered such proof to this same body of self-styled experts, and they rejected it. I renew my offer; let me measure the life lengths of the members of the Academy of Science. Let them appoint a committee to judge the results. I will seal my findings in two sets of envelopes; on the outside of each envelope in one set will appear the name of a member, on the inside the date of his death. In the other envelopes I will place names, on the outside I will place dates. Let the committee place the envelopes in a vault, then meet from time to time to open the appropriate envelopes. In such a large body of men some deaths may be expected, if Amalgamated actuaries can be trusted, every week or two. In such a fashion they will accumulate data very rapidly to prove that Pinero is a liar, or no."

He stopped, and pushed out his little chest until it almost caught up with his little round belly. He glared at the sweating savants. "Well?"

The judge raised his eyebrows, and caught Mr. Weems' eye. "Do you accept?"

"Your Honor, I think the proposal highly improper—"

The judge cut him short. "I warn you that I shall rule against you if you do not accept, or propose an equally reasonable method of arriving at the truth."

Weems opened his mouth, changed his mind, looked up and down the faces of learned witnesses, and faced the bench. "We accept, Your Honor."

"Very well. Arrange the details between you. The temporary injunction is lifted, and Dr. Pinero must not be molested in the pursuit of his business. Decision on the petition for permanent injunction is reserved without prejudice pending the accumulation of evidence. Before we leave this matter I wish to comment on the theory implied by you, Mr. Weems, when you claimed damage to your client. There has grown up in the minds of certain groups in this country the notion that because a man or corporation has made a profit out of the public for a number of years, the government and the courts are charged with the duty of guaranteeing such profit in the future, even in the face of changing circumstances and contrary public interest. This strange doctrine is not supported by statute nor common law. Neither individuals nor corporations have any right to come into court and ask that the clock of history be stopped, or turned back, for their private benefit. That is all."

Bidwell grunted in annoyance. "Weems, if you can't think up anything better than that, Amalgamated is going to need a new chief attorney. It's been ten weeks since you lost the injunction, and that little wart is coining money hand over fist. Meantime every insurance firm in the country is going broke. Hoskins, what's our loss ratio?"

"It's hard to say, Mr. Bidwell. It gets worse every day. We've paid off thirteen big policies this week; all of them taken out since Pinero started operations."

A spare little man spoke up. "I say, Bidwell, we aren't accepting any new applications for United until we have time to check and be sure that they have not consulted Pinero. Can't we afford to wait until the scientists show him up?"

Bidwell snorted. "You blasted optimist! They won't show him up. Aldrich, can't you face a fact? The fat little blister has got something; how I don't know. This is a fight to the finish. If we wait, we're licked." He threw his cigar into a cuspidor, and bit savagely into a fresh one. "Clear out of here, all of you! I'll handle this my own way. You too, Aldrich. United may wait, but Amalgamated won't."

Weems cleared his throat apprehensively. "Mr. Bidwell, I trust you will consult with me before embarking on any major change in policy?"

Bidwell grunted. They filed out. When they were all gone and the door closed, Bidwell snapped the switch of the interoffice announcer. "O.K.; send him in."

The outer door opened; a slight dapper figure stood for a moment at the threshold. His small dark eyes glanced quickly about the room before he entered, then he moved up to Bidwell with a quick soft tread. He spoke to Bidwell in a flat emotionless voice. His face remained impassive except for the live animal eyes. "You wanted to talk to me?"

"Yes."

"What's the proposition?"

"Sit down, and we'll talk."

Pinero met the young couple at the door of his inner office.

"Come in, my dears, come in. Sit down. Make yourselves at home. Now tell me, what do you want of Pinero? Surely such young people are not anxious about the final roll call?"

The boy's honest young face showed slight confusion. "Well, you see, Dr. Pinero, I'm Ed Hartley and this is my wife, Betty. We're going to have—that is, Betty is expecting a baby and, well—"

Pinero smiled benignly. "I understand. You want to know how long you will live in order to make the best possible provision for the youngster. Quite wise. Do you both want readings, or just yourself?"

The girl answered, "Both of us, we think."

Pinero beamed at her. "Quite so. I agree. Your reading presents certain technical difficulties at this time, but I can give you some information now, and more later after your baby arrives. Now come into my laboratory, my dears, and we'll commence." He rang for their case histories, then showed them into his workshop. "Mrs. Hartley first, please. If you will go behind that screen and remove your shoes and your outer clothing, please. Remember, I am an old man, whom you are consulting as you would a physician."

He turned away and made some minor adjustments of his

apparatus. Ed nodded to his wife who slipped behind the screen and reappeared almost at once, clothed in two wisps of silk. Pinero glanced up, noted her fresh young prettiness and her touching shyness.

"This way, my dear. First we must weigh you. There. Now take your place on the stand. This electrode in your mouth. No, Ed, you mustn't touch her while she is in the circuit. It won't take a minute. Remain quite."

He dove under the machine's hood and the dials sprang into life. Very shortly he came out with a perturbed look on his face. "Ed, did you touch her?"

"No, Doctor." Pinero ducked back again, remained a little longer. When he came out this time, he told the girl to get down and dress. He turned to her husband.

"Ed, make yourself ready."

"What's Betty's reading, Doctor?"

"There is a little difficulty. I want to test you first."

When he came out from taking the youth's reading, his face was more troubled than ever. Ed inquired as to his trouble. Pinero shrugged his shoulders, and brought a smile to his lips.

"Nothing to concern you, my boy. A little mechanical mis-adjustment, I think. But I shan't be able to give you two your readings today. I shall need to overhaul my machine. Can you come back tomorrow?"

"Why, I think so. Say, I'm sorry about your machine. I hope it isn't serious."

"It isn't, I'm sure. Will you come back into my office, and visit for a bit?"

"Thank you, Doctor. You are very kind."

"But Ed, I've got to meet Ellen."

Pinero turned the full force of his personality on her. "Won't you grant me a few moments, my dear young lady? I am old and like the sparkle of young folk's company. I get very little of it. Please." He nudged them gently into his office, and seated them. Then he ordered lemonade and cookies sent in, offered them cigarets, and lit a cigar.

Forty minutes later Ed listened entranced, while Betty was quite evidently acutely nervous and anxious to leave, as the doctor spun out a story concerning his adventures as a young man in Tierra del Fuego. When the doctor stopped to relight his cigar, she stood up.

"Doctor, we really must leave. Couldn't we hear the rest tomorrow?"

"Tomorrow? There will not be time tomorrow."

"But you haven't time today either. Your secretary has rung five times."

"Couldn't you spare me just a few more minutes?"

"I really can't today, doctor. I have an appointment. There is someone waiting for me."

"There is no way to induce you?"

"I'm afraid not. Come, Ed."

After they had gone, the doctor stepped to the window and stared out over the city. Presently he picked out two tiny figures as they left the office building. He watched them hurry to the corner, wait for the lights to change, then start across the street. When they were part way across, there came the scream of a siren. The two little figures hesitated, started back, stopped, and turned. Then the car was upon them. As the car slammed to a stop, they showed up from beneath it, no longer two figures, but simply a limp unorganized heap of clothing.

Presently the doctor turned away from the window. Then he picked up his phone, and spoke to his secretary.

"Cancel my appointments for the rest of the day. . . . No . . . No one . . . I don't care; cancel them."

Then he sat down in his chair. His cigar went out. Long after dark he held it, still unlighted.

Pinero sat down at his dining table and contemplated the gourmet's luncheon spread before him. He had ordered this meal with particular care, and had come home a little early in order to enjoy it fully.

Somewhat later he let a few drops of Fiori d'Alpini roll around his tongue and trickle down his throat. The heavy fragrant syrup warmed his mouth, and reminded him of the little mountain flowers for which it was named. He sighed. It had been a good meal, an exquisite meal and had justified the exotic liqueur. His musing was interrupted by a disturbance at the front door. The voice of his elderly maidservant was raised in remonstrance. A heavy male voice interrupted her. The commotion moved down the hall and the dining room door was pushed open.

"Madonna! Non si puo entrare! The Master is eating!"

"Never mind, Angela. I have time to see these gentlemen. You may go." Pinero faced the surly-faced spokesman of the intruders. "You have business with me; yes?"

"You bet we have. Decent people have had enough of your damned nonsense."

"And so?"

The caller did not answer at once. A small dapper individual moved out from behind him and faced Pinero.

"We might as well begin." The chairman of the committee placed a key in the lock-box and opened it. "Wenzell, will you help me pick out today's envelopes?" He was interrupted by a touch on his arm.

"Dr. Baird, you are wanted on the telephone."

"Very well. Bring the instrument here."

When it was fetched he placed the receiver to his ear. "Hello. . . . Yes; speaking. . . . What? . . . No, we have heard nothing. . . . Destroyed the machine, you say. . . . Dead! How? . . . No! No statement. None at all. . . . Call me later. . . ."

He slammed the instrument down and pushed it from him.

"What's up?"—"Who's dead now?"

Baird held up one hand. "Quiet, gentlemen, please! Pinero was murdered a few moments ago at his home."

"Murdered?!"

"That isn't all. About the same time vandals broke into his office and smashed his apparatus."

No one spoke at first. The committee members glanced around at each other. No one seemed anxious to be the first to comment.

Finally one spoke up. "Get it out."

"Get what out?"

"Pinero's envelope. It's in there too. I've seen it."

Baird located it and slowly tore it open. He unfolded the single sheet of paper, and scanned it.

"Well? Out with it!"

"One thirteen p.m.—today."

They took this in silence.

Their dynamic calm was broken by a member across the table from Baird reaching for the lock-box. Baird interposed a hand.

"What do you want?"

"My prediction—it's in there—we're all in there."

"Yes, yes. We're all in here. Let's have them."

Baird placed both hands over the box. He held the eye of the man opposite him but did not speak. He licked his lips. The corner of his mouth twitched. His hands shook. Still he did not speak. The man opposite relaxed back into his chair.

"You're right, of course," he said.

"Bring me that waste basket." Baird's voice was low and strained but steady.

He accepted it and dumped the litter on the rug. He placed the tin basket on the table before him. He tore half a dozen envelopes across, set a match to them, and dropped them in the basket. Then he started tearing a double handful at a time, and fed the fire steadily. The smoke made him cough, and tears ran out of his smarting eyes. Someone got up and opened a window. When he was through, he pushed the basket away from him, looked down, and spoke.

"I'm afraid I've ruined this table top."

The Roads Must Roll

"WHO MAKES THE ROADS ROLL?"

The speaker stood still on the rostrum and waited for his audience to answer him. The reply came in scattered shouts that cut through the ominous, discontented murmur of the crowd.

"We do!"—"We do!"—"Damn right!"

"Who does the dirty work 'down inside'—so that Joe Public can ride at his ease?"

This time it was a single roar, "We do!"

The speaker pressed his advantage, his words tumbling out in a rasping torrent. He leaned toward the crowd, his eyes picking out individuals at whom to fling his words. "What makes business? The roads! How do they move the food they eat? The roads! How do they get to work? The roads! How do they get home to their wives? The roads!" He paused for effect, then lowered his voice. "Where would the public be if you boys didn't keep them roads rolling?—Behind the eight ball and everybody knows it. But do they appreciate it? Pfui! Did we ask for too much? Were our demands unreasonable? 'The right to resign whenever we want to.' Every working stiff in other lines of work has that. 'The same pay as the engineers.' Why not? Who are the real engineers around here? D'yuh have to be a cadet in a funny little hat before you can learn to wipe a bearing, or jack down a rotor? Who earns his keep: The 'gentlemen' in the control offices, or the boys 'down inside'? What else do we ask? 'The right to elect our own engineers.' Why the hell not? Who's competent to pick engineers? The technicians?—or some damn, dumb examining board that's never been 'down inside', and couldn't tell a rotor bearing from a field coil?"

He changed his pace with natural art, and lowered his voice still further. "I tell you, brother, it's time we quit fiddlin' around with petitions to the Transport Commission, and use a little direct action. Let 'em yammer about democracy; that's a lot of eye wash—we've got the power, and we're the men that count!"

A man had risen in the back of the hall while the speaker was haranguing. He spoke up as the speaker paused. "Brother Chairman," he drawled, "may I stick in a couple of words?"

"You are recognized, Brother Harvey."

"What I ask is: what's all the shootin' for? We've .got the highest hourly rate of pay of any mechanical guild, full insurance and retirement, and safe working conditions, barring the chance of going deaf." He pushed his anti-noise helmet further back from his ears. He was still in dungarees, apparently just up from standing watch. "Of course we have to give ninety days notice to quit a job, but, cripes, we knew that when we signed up. The roads have got to roll—they can't stop every time some lazy punk gets bored with his billet.

"And now Soapy—" The crack of the gavel cut him short. "Pardon me, I mean *Brother* Soapy—tells us how powerful we are, and how we should go in for direct action. Rats! Sure we could tie up the roads, and play hell with the whole community—but so could any screwball with a can of nitroglycerine, and he wouldn't have to be a technician to do it, neither.

"We aren't the only frogs in the puddle. Our jobs are important, sure, but where would we be without the farmers —or the steel workers—or a dozen other trades and professions?"

He was interrupted by a sallow little man with protruding upper teeth, who said, "Just a minute, Brother Chairman, I'd like to ask Brother Harvey a question," then turned to Harvey and inquired in a sly voice, "Are you speaking for the guild, Brother—or just for yourself? Maybe you don't believe in the guild? You wouldn't by any chance be"—he stopped and slid his eyes up and down Harvey's lank frame—"a *spotter,* would you?"

Harvey looked over his questioner as if he had found something filthy in a plate of food. "Sikes," he told him, "if you weren't a runt, I'd stuff your store teeth down your throat. I helped found this guild. I was on strike in 'seventy-six. Where were you in 'seventy-six? With the finks?"

The chairman's gavel pounded "There's been enough of this," he said. "Nobody who knows anything about the history of this guild doubts the loyalty of Brother Harvey. We'll continue with the regular order of business." He stopped to clear his throat. "Ordinarily we don't open our floor to outsiders, and some of you boys have expressed a distaste for some of the engineers we work under, but there is one engineer we always like to listen to whenever he can get away from his pressing duties. I guess maybe it's because he's had dirt under his nails the same as us. Anyhow, I present at this time Mr. Shorty Van Kleeck—"

A shout from the floor stopped him. "*Brother* Van Kleeck!"

"O.K.—*Brother* Van Kleeck, Chief Deputy Engineer of this road-town."

"Thanks, Brother Chairman." The guest speaker came briskly forward, and grinned expansively at the crowd, seeming to swell under their approval. "Thanks, Brothers. I guess our chairman is right. I always feel more comfortable here in the Guild Hall of the Sacramento Sector—or any guild hall, for that matter—than I do in the engineers' clubhouse. Those young punk cadet engineers get in my hair. Maybe I should have gone to one of the fancy technical institutes, so I'd have the proper point of view, instead of coming up from 'down inside'.

"Now about those demands of yours that the Transport Commission just threw back in your face— Can I speak freely?"

"Sure you can, Shorty!"—"You can trust us!"

"Well, of course I shouldn't say anything, but I can't help but understand how you feel. The roads are the big show these days, and you are the men that make them roll. It's the natural order of things that your opinions should be listened to, and your desires met. One would think that even politicians would be bright enough to see that. Sometimes, lying awake at night, I wonder why we technicians don't just take things over, and—"

"Your wife is calling, Mr. Gaines."

"Very well." He picked up the handset and turned to the visor screen.

"Yes, darling, I know I promised, but . . . You're perfectly right, darling, but Washington has especially requested that we show Mr. Blekinsop anything he wants to see. I didn't know he was arriving today. . . . No, I can't turn him over to a subordinate. It wouldn't be courteous. He's Minister of Transport for Australia. I told you that. . . . Yes, darling, I know that courtesy begins at home, but the roads must roll.

It's my job; you knew that when you married me. And this is part of my job. . . . That's a good girl. We'll positively have breakfast together. Tell you what, order horses and a breakfast pack and we'll make it a picnic. I'll meet you in Bakersfield—usual place. . . . Goodbye, darling. Kiss Junior goodnight for me."

He replaced the handset on the desk whereupon the pretty, but indignant, features of his wife faded from the visor screen. A young woman came into his office. As she opened the door she exposed momentarily the words printed on its outer side; "DIEGO-RENO ROADTOWN, Office of the Chief Engineer." He gave her a harassed glance.

"Oh, it's you. Don't marry an engineer, Dolores, marry an artist. They have more home life."

"Yes, Mr. Gaines. Mr. Blekinsop is here, Mr. Gaines."

"Already? I didn't expect him so soon. The Antipodes ship must have grounded early."

"Yes, Mr. Gaines."

"Dolores, don't you ever have any emotions?"

"Yes, Mr. Gaines."

"Hmmm, it seems incredible, but you are never mistaken. Show Mr. Blekinsop in."

"Very good, Mr. Gaines."

Larry Gaines got up to greet his visitor. Not a particularly impressive little·guy, he thought, as they shook hands and exchanged formal amenities. The rolled umbrella, the bowler hat were almost too good to be true. An Oxford accent partially masked the underlying clipped, flat, nasal twang of the native Australian.

"It's a pleasure to have you here, Mr. Blekinsop, and I hope we can make your stay enjoyable."

The little man smiled. "I'm sure it will be. This is my first visit to your wonderful country. I feel at home already. The eucalyptus trees, you know, and the brown hills—"

"But your trip is primarily business?"

"Yes, yes. My primary purpose is to study your roadcities, and report to my government on the advisability of trying to adapt your startling American methods to our social problems Down Under. I thought you understood that such was the reason I was sent to you."

"Yes, I did, in a general way. I don't know just what it is that you wish to find out. I suppose that you have heard

about our road towns, how they came about, how they operate, and so forth."

"I've read a good bit, true, but I am not a technical man,
Mr. Gaines, not an engineer. My field is social and political. I
want to see how this remarkable technical change has affected
your people. Suppose you tell me about the roads as if I were
entirely ignorant. And I will ask questions."

"That seems a practical plan. By the way, how many are
there in your party?"

"Just myself. I sent my secretary on to Washington."

"I see." Gaines glanced at his wrist watch. "It's nearly dinner time. Suppose we run up to the Stockton strip for dinner.
There is a good Chinese restaurant up there that I'm partial
to. It will take us about an hour and you can see the ways in
operation while we ride."

"Excellent."

Gaines pressed a button on his desk, and a picture formed
on a large visor screen mounted on the opposite wall. It
showed a strong-boned, angular young man seated at a semi-
circular control desk, which was backed by a complex instrument board. A cigaret was tucked in one corner of his mouth.

The young man glanced up, grinned, and waved from the
screen. "Greetings and salutations, Chief. What can I do for
you?"

"Hi, Dave. You've got the evening watch, eh? I'm running
up to the Stockton sector for dinner. Where's Van Kleeck?"

"Gone to a meeting somewhere. He didn't say."

"Anything to report?"

"No, sir. The roads are rolling, and all the little people are
going ridey-ridey home to their dinners."

"O.K.—keep 'em rolling."

"They'll roll, Chief."

Gaines snapped off the connection and turned to Blekinsop.
"Van Kleeck is my chief deputy. I wish he'd spend more time
on the road and less on politics. Davidson can handle things,
however. Shall we go?"

They glided down an electric staircase, and debouched on
the walkway which bordered the northbound five-mile-an-
hour strip. After skirting a stairway trunk marked OVER-
PASS TO SOUTHBOUND ROAD, they paused at the edge
of the first strip. "Have you ever ridden a conveyor strip
before?" Gaines inquired. "It's quite simple. Just remember to
face against the motion of the strip as you get on."

They threaded their way through homeward-bound throngs, passing from strip to strip. Down the center of the twenty-mile-an-hour strip ran a glassite partition which reached nearly to the spreading roof. The Honorable Mister Blekinsop raised his eyebrows inquiringly as he looked at it.

"Oh, that?" Gaines answered the unspoken inquiry as he slid back a panel door and ushered his guest through. "That's a wind break. If we didn't have some way of separating the air currents over the strips of different speeds, the wind would tear our clothes off on the hundred-mile-an-hour strip." He bent his head to Blekinsop's as he spoke, in order to cut through the rush of air against the road surfaces, the noise of the crowd, and the muted roar of the driving mechanism concealed beneath the moving strips. The combination of noises inhibited further conversation as they proceeded toward the middle of the roadway. After passing through three more wind screens located at the forty, sixty, and eighty-mile-an-hour strips respectively, they finally reached the maximum speed strip, the hundred-mile-an-hour strip, which made the round trip, San Diego to Reno and back, in twelve hours.

Blekinsop found himself on a walkway twenty feet wide facing another partition. Immediately opposite him an illuminated show window proclaimed:

JAKE'S STEAK HOUSE No. 4
The Fastest Meal on the Fastest Road!
"To dine on the fly
Makes the miles roll by!!"

"Amazing!" said Mr. Blekinsop. "It would be like dining in a tram. Is this really a proper restaurant?"

"One of the best. Not fancy, but sound."

"Oh, I say, could we—"

Gaines smiled at him. "You'd like to try it, wouldn't you, sir?"

"I don't wish to interfere with your plans—"

"Quite all right. I'm hungry myself, and Stockton is a long hour away. Let's go in."

Gaines greeted the manageress as an old friend. "Hello, Mrs. McCoy. How are you tonight?"

"If it isn't the chief himself! It's a long time since we've had the pleasure of seeing your face." She led them to a booth

somewhat detached from the crowd of dining commuters.
"And will you and your friend be having dinner?"

"Yes, Mrs. McCoy—suppose you order for us—but be sure
it includes one of your steaks."

"Two inches thick—from a steer that died happy." She
glided away, moving her fat frame with surprising grace.

With sophisticated foreknowledge of the chief engineer's
needs, Mrs. McCoy had left a portable telephone at the table.
Gaines plugged it in to an accommodation jack at the side of
the booth, and dialed a number. "Hello—Davidson? Dave,
this is the chief. I'm in Jake's beanery number four for supper. You can reach me by calling ten-L-six-six."

He replaced the handset, and Blekinsop inquired politely:
"Is it necessary for you to be available at all times?"

"Not strictly necessary," Gaines told him, "but I feel safer
when I am in touch. Either Van Kleeck, or myself, should be
where the senior engineer of the watch—that's Davidson this
shift—can get hold of us in a pinch. If it's a real emergency,
I want to be there, naturally."

"What would constitute a real emergency?"

"Two things, principally. A power failure on the rotors
would bring the road to a standstill, and possibly strand millions of people a hundred miles, or more, from their homes.
If it happened during a rush hour we would have to evacuate
those millions from the road—not too easy to do."

"You say millions—as many as that?"

"Yes, indeed. There are twelve million people dependent on
this roadway, living and working in the buildings adjacent to
it, or within five miles of each side."

The Age of Power blends into the Age of Transportation
almost imperceptibly, but two events stand out as landmarks
in the change: the achievement of cheap sun power and the
installation of the first mechanized road. The power resources
of oil and coal of the United States had—save for a few sporadic outbreaks of common sense—been shamefully wasted in
their development all through the first half of the twentieth
century. Simultaneously, the automobile, from its humble
start as a one-lunged horseless carriage, grew into a steel-
bodied monster of over a hundred horsepower and capable of
making more than a hundred miles an hour. They boiled over
the countryside, like yeast in ferment. In 1955 it was esti-

mated that there was a motor vehicle for every two persons in the United States.

They contained the seeds of their own destruction. Eighty million steel juggernauts, operated by imperfect human beings at high speeds, are more destructive than war. In the same reference year the premiums paid for compulsory liability and property damage insurance by automobile owners exceeded in amount the sum paid that year to purchase automobiles. Safe driving campaigns were chronic phenomena, but were mere pious attempts to put Humpty-Dumpty together again. It was not physically possible to drive safely in those crowded metropolises. Pedestrians were sardonically divided into two classes, the quick, and the dead.

But a pedestrian could be defined as a man who had found a place to park his car. The automobile made possible huge cities, then choked those same cities to death with their numbers. In 1900 Herbert George Wells pointed out that the saturation point in the size of a city might be mathematically predicted in terms of its transportation facilities. From a standpoint of speed alone the automobile made possible cities two hundred miles in diameter, but traffic congestion, and the inescapable, inherent danger of high-powered, individually operated vehicles cancelled out the possibility.

In 1955 Federal Highway #66 from Los Angeles to Chicago, "The Main Street of America", was transformed into a superhighway for motor vehicles, with an underspeed limit of sixty miles per hour. It was planned as a public works project to stimulate heavy industry; it had an unexpected by-product. The great cities of Chicago and St. Louis stretched out urban pseudopods toward each other, until they met near Bloomington, Illinois. The two parent cities actually shrunk in population.

That same year the city of San Francisco replaced its antiquated cable cars with moving stairways, powered with the Douglas-Martin Solar Reception Screens. The largest number of automobile licenses in history had been issued that calendar year, but the end of the automobile era was in sight, and the National Defense Act of 1957 gave fair warning.

This act, one of the most bitterly debated ever to be brought out of committee, declared petroleum to be an essential and limited material of war. The armed forces had first call on all oil, above or below the ground, and eighty million civilian vehicles faced short and expensive rations. The "temporary" conditions during World War II had become permanent.

Take the superhighways of the period, urban throughout their length. Add the mechanized streets of San Francisco's hills. Heat to boiling point with an imminent shortage of gasoline. Flavor with Yankee ingenuity. The first mechanized road was opened in 1960 between Cincinnati and Cleveland.

It was, as one would expect, comparatively primitive in design, being based on the ore belt conveyors of ten years earlier. The fastest strip moved only thirty miles per hour, and was quite narrow, for no one had thought of the possibility of locating retail trade on the strips themselves. Nevertheless, it was a prototype of social pattern which was to dominate the American scene within the next two decades—neither rural, nor urban, but partaking equally of both, and based on rapid, safe, cheap, convenient transportation.

Factories—wide, low buildings whose roofs were covered with solar power screens of the same type that drove the road —lined the roadway on each side. Back of them and interspersed among them were commercial hotels, retail stores, theatres, apartment houses. Beyond this long, thin, narrow strip was the open country-side, where the bulk of the population lived. Their homes dotted the hills, hung on the banks of creeks, and nestled between the farms. They worked in the "city" but lived in the "country"—and the two were not ten minutes apart.

Mrs. McCoy served the chief and his guest in person. They checked their conversation at the sight of the magnificent steaks.

Up and down the six hundred mile line, Sector Engineers of the Watch were getting in their hourly reports from their subsector technicians. "Subsector one—check!" "Subsector two—check!" Tensionometer readings, voltage, load, bearing temperatures, synchrotachometer readings—"Subsector seven —check!" Hardbitten, able men in dungarees, who lived much of their lives 'down inside' amidst the unmuted roar of the hundred mile strip, the shrill whine of driving rotors, and the complaint of the relay rollers.

Davidson studied the moving model of the road, spread out before him in the main control room at Fresno Sector. He watched the barely perceptible crawl of the miniature hundred mile strip and subconsciously noted the reference number on it which located Jake's Steak House No. 4. The chief would be getting in to Stockton soon; he'd give him a ring after the hourly reports were in. Everything was quiet; traffic tonnage normal for rush hour; he would be sleepy before this watch was over. He turned to his Cadet Engineer of the Watch. "Mr. Barnes."

"Yes, sir."

"I think we could use some coffee."

"Good idea, sir. I'll order some as soon as the hourlies are in."

The minute hand of the control board chronometer reached twelve. The cadet watch officer threw a switch. "All sectors, report!" he said, in crisp, self-conscious tones.

The faces of two men flicked into view on the visor screen. The younger answered him with the same air of acting under supervision. "Diego Circle—rolling!"

They were at once replaced by two more. "Angeles Sector —rolling!"

Then: "Bakersfield Sector—rolling!"

And: "Fresno Sector—rolling!"

Finally, when Reno Circle had reported, the cadet turned to Davidson and reported: "Rolling, sir."

"Very well—keep them rolling!"

The visor screen flashed on once more. "Sacramento Sector; supplementary report."

"Proceed."

"Cadet Guenther, while on visual inspection as cadet sector engineer of the watch, found Cadet Alec Jeans, on watch as cadet subsector technician, and R. J. Ross, technician second class, on watch as technician for the same subsector, engaged in playing cards. It was not possible to tell with any accuracy how long they had neglected to patrol their subsector."

"Any damage?"

"One rotor running hot, but still synchronized. It was jacked down, and replaced."

"Very well. Have the paymaster give Ross his time, and turn him over to the civil authorities. Place Cadet Jeans under arrest and order him to report to me."

"Very well, sir."

"Keep them rolling!"

Davidson turned back to the control desk and dialled Chief Engineer Gaines' temporary number.

"You mentioned that there were two things that could cause major trouble on the road, Mr. Gaines, but you spoke only of power failure to the rotors."

Gaines pursued an elusive bit of salad before answering. "There really isn't a second major trouble—it won't happen. However—we are travelling along here at one hundred miles per hour. Can you visualize what would happen if this strip under us should break?"

Mr. Blekinsop shifted nervously in his chair. "Hmm—rather a disconcerting idea, don't you think? I mean to say, one is hardly aware that one is travelling at high speed, here in this snug room. What *would* the result be?"

"Don't let it worry you; the strip can't part. It is built up of overlapping sections in such a fashion that it has a safety factor of better than twelve to one. Several miles of rotors would have to shut down all at once, and the circuit breakers for the rest of the line fail to trip out before there could possibly be sufficient tension on the strip to cause it to part.

"But it happened once, on the Philadelphia-Jersey City Road, and we aren't likely to forget it. It was one of the earliest high speed roads, carrying a tremendous passenger traffic, as well as heavy freight, since it serviced a heavily industrialized area. The strip was hardly more than a conveyor belt, and no one had foreseen the weight it would carry. It happened under maximum load, naturally, when the high speed way was crowded. The part of the strip behind the break buckled for miles, crushing passengers against the roof at eighty miles per hour. The section forward of the break cracked like a whip, spilling passengers onto the slower ways, dropping them on the exposed rollers and rotors down inside, and snapping them up against the roof.

"Over three thousand people were killed in that one accident, and there was much agitation to abolish the roads. They were even shut down for a week by presidential order, but he was forced to reopen them again. There was no alternative."

"Really? Why not?"

"The country had become economically dependent on the roads. They were the principal means of transportation in the industrial areas—the only means of economic importance. Factories were shut down; food didn't move; people got hungry—and the President was forced to let them roll again. It was the only thing that could be done; the social pattern had crystallized in one form, and it couldn't be changed overnight. A large, industrialized population must have large-scale transportation, not only for people, but for trade."

Mr. Blekinsop fussed with his napkin, and rather diffidently suggested, "Mr. Gaines, I do not intend to disparage the ingenious accomplishments of your great people, but isn't it possible that you may have put too many eggs in one basket in allowing your whole economy to become dependent on the functioning of one type of machinery?"

Gaines considered this soberly. "I see your point. Yes—and no. Every civilization above the peasant-and-village type is dependent on some key type of machinery. The old South was based on the cotton gin. Imperial England was made possible by the steam engine. Large populations have to have machines for power, for transportation, and for manufacturing in order to live. Had it not been for machinery the large populations could never have grown up. That's not a fault of the machine; that's its virtue.

"But it is true that whenever we develop machinery to the point where it will support large populations at a high standard of living we are then bound to keep that machinery running, or suffer the consequences. But the real hazard in that is not the machinery, but the men who run the machinery. These roads, as machines, are all right. They are strong and safe and will do everything they were designed to do. No, it's not the machines, it's the men.

"When a population is dependent on a machine, they are hostages of the men who tend the machines. If their morale is high, their sense of duty strong—"

Someone up near the front of the restaurant had turned up the volume control of the radio, letting out a blast of music that drowned out Gaines' words. When the sound had been tapered down to a more nearly bearable volume, he was saying:

"Listen to that. It illustrates my point."

Blekinsop turned an ear to the music. It was a swinging march of compelling rhythm, with a modern interpretive arrangement. One could hear the roar of machinery, the repetitive clatter of mechanisms. A pleased smile of recognition spread over the Australian's face. "It's your Field Artillery Song, *The Roll of the Caissons*, isn't it? But I don't see the connection."

"You're right; it *was* the *Roll of the Caissons*, but we

adapted it to our own purposes. It's the *Road Song of the Transport Cadets.* Wait."

The persistent throb of the march continued, and seemed to blend with the vibration of the roadway underneath into a single tympany. Then a male chorus took up the verse:

"Hear them hum!
Watch them run!
Oh, our job is never done,
For our roadways go rolling along!
While you ride;
While you glide;
We are watching 'down inside',
So your roadways keep rolling along!

"Oh, it's Hie! Hie! Hee!
The rotor men are we—
Check off the sectors loud and strong! (spoken) *One!*
Two! Three!
Anywhere you go
You are bound to know
That your roadways are rolling along!
(Shouted) *KEEP THEM ROLLING!*
That your roadways are rolling along!"

"See?" said Gaines, with more animation in his voice. "See? That is the real purpose of the United States Academy of Transport. That is the reason why the transport engineers are a semi-military profession, with strict discipline. We are the bottle neck, the *sine qua non,* of all industry, all economic life. Other industries can go on strike, and only create temporary and partial dislocations. Crops can fail here and there, and the country takes up the slack. But if the roads stop rolling, everything else much stop; the effect would be the same as a general strike—with this important difference: It takes a majority of the population, fired by a real feeling of grievance, to create a general strike; but the men that run the roads, few as they are, can create the same complete paralysis.

"We had just one strike on the roads, back in 'seventy-six. It was justified, I think, and it corrected a lot of real abuses—but it mustn't happen again."

"But what is to prevent it happening again, Mr. Gaines?"

"Morale—*esprit de corps*. The technicians in the road service are indoctrinated constantly with the idea that their job is a sacred trust. Besides which we do everything we can to build up their social position. But even more important is the Academy. We try to turn out graduate engineers imbued with the same loyalty, the same iron self-discipline, and determination to perform their duty to the community at any cost, that Annapolis and West Point and Goddard are so successful in inculcating in their graduates."

"Goddard? Oh, yes, the rocket field. And have you been successful, do you think?"

"Not entirely, perhaps, but we will be. It takes time to build up a tradition. When the oldest engineer is a man who entered the Academy in his 'teens, we can afford to relax a little and treat it as a solved problem."

"I suppose you are a graduate?"

Gaines grinned. "You flatter me—I must look younger than I am. No, I'm a carry-over from the army. You see, the Department of Defense operated the roads for some three months during reorganization after the strike in 'seventy-six. I served on the conciliation board that awarded pay increases and adjusted working conditions, then I was assigned—"

The signal light of the portable telephone glowed red. Gaines said, "Excuse me," and picked up the handset. "Yes?"

Blekinsop could overhear the voice at the other end. "This is Davidson, Chief. The roads are rolling."

"Very well. Keep them rolling!"

"Had another trouble report from the Sacramento Sector."

"Again? What this time?"

Before Davidson could reply he was cut off. As Gaines reached out to dial him back, his coffee cup, half full, landed in his lap. Blekinsop was aware, even as he was rocked against the edge of the table, of a disquieting change in the hum of the roadway.

"What has happened, Mr. Gaines?"

"Don't know. Emergency stop—God knows why." He was dialling furiously. Shortly he flung the phone down, without bothering to return the handset to its cradle. "Phones are out. Come on! No— You'll be safe here. Wait."

"Must I?"

"Well, come along then, and stick close to me." He turned away, having dismissed the Australian cabinet minister from his mind. The strip ground slowly to a stop, the giant rotors and myriad rollers acting as fly wheels in preventing a disastrous sudden stop. Already a little knot of commuters, disturbed at their evening meal, were attempting to crowd out the door of the restaurant.

"Halt!"

There is something about a command issued by one who is used to being obeyed which enforces compliance. It may be intonation, or possibly a more esoteric power, such as animal tamers are reputed to be able to exercise in controlling ferocious beasts. But it does exist, and can be used to compel even those not habituated to obedience.

The commuters stopped in their tracks.

Gaines continued, "Remain in the restaurant until we are ready to evacuate you. I am the Chief Engineer. You will be in no danger here. You!" He pointed to a big fellow near the door. "You're deputized. Don't let anyone leave without proper authority. Mrs. McCoy, resume serving dinner."

Gaines strode out the door, Blekinsop tagging along. The situation outside permitted no such simple measures. The hundred mile strip alone had stopped; a few feet away the next strip flew by at an unchecked ninety-five miles an hour. The passengers on it flickered past, unreal cardboard figures.

The twenty-foot walkway of the maximum speed strip had been crowded when the breakdown occurred. Now the customers of shops, of lunchstands, and of other places of business, the occupants of lounges, of television theatres—all came crowding out onto the walkway to see what had happened. The first disaster struck almost immediately.

The crowd surged, and pushed against a middle-aged woman on its outer edge. In attempting to recover her balance she put one foot over the edge of the flashing ninety-five mile strip. She realized her gruesome error, for she screamed before her foot touched the ribbon.

She spun around and landed heavily on the moving strip, and was rolled by it, as the strip attempted to impart to her mass, at one blow, a velocity of ninety-five miles per hour—one hundred and thirty-nine feet per second. As she rolled she mowed down some of the cardboard figures as a sickle strikes a stand of grass. Quickly, she was out of sight, her identity, her injuries, and her fate undetermined, and already remote.

But the consequences of her mishap were not done with. One of the flickering cardboard figures bowled over by her relative momentum fell toward the hundred mile strip, slammed into the shockbound crowd, and suddenly appeared as a live man—but broken and bleeding, amidst the luckless, fallen victims whose bodies had checked his wild flight.

Even there it did not end. The disaster spread from its source, each hapless human ninepin more like than not to knock down others so that they fell over the danger-laden boundary, and in turn ricocheted to a dearly bought equilibrium.

But the focus of calamity sped out of sight, and Blekinsop could see no more. His active mind, accustomed to dealing with large numbers of individual human beings, multiplied the tragic sequence he had witnessed by twelve hundred miles of thronged conveyor strip, and his stomach chilled.

To Blekinsop's surprise, Gaines made no effort to succor the fallen, nor to quell the fear-infected mob, but turned an expressionless face back to the restaurant. When Blekinsop saw that he was actually re-entering the restaurant, he plucked at his sleeve. "Aren't we going to help those poor people?"

The cold planes of the face of the man who answered him bore no resemblance to his genial, rather boyish, host of a few minutes before. "No. Bystanders can help them—I've got the whole road to think of. Don't bother me."

Crushed, and somewhat indignant, the politician did as he was ordered. Rationally, he knew that the Chief Engineer was right—a man responsible for the safety of millions cannot turn aside from his duty to render personal service to one—but the cold detachment of such viewpoint was repugnant to him.

Gaines was back in the restaurant. "Mrs. McCoy, where is your get-away?"

"In the pantry, sir."

Gaines hurried there, Bleksinop at his heels. A nervous Filipino salad boy shrank out of his way as he casually swept a supply of prepared green stuffs onto the floor and stepped up on the counter where they had rested. Directly above his head and within reach was a circular manhole, counterweighted and operated by a handwheel set in its center. A short steel ladder, hinged to the edge of the opening, was swung up flat to ceiling and secured by a hook.

Blekinsop lost his hat in his endeavor to clamber quickly enough up the ladder after Gaines. When he emerged on the roof of the building, Gaines was searching the ceiling of the roadway with a pocket flashlight. He was shuffling along, stooped double in the awkward four feet of space between the roof underfoot and ceiling.

He found what he sought, some fifty feet away—another manhole similar to the one they had used to escape from below. He spun the wheel of the lock and stood up in the space, then rested his hands on the sides of the opening and with a single lithe movement vaulted to the roof of the roadways. His companion followed him with more difficulty.

They stood in darkness, a fine, cold rain feeling at their faces. But underfoot, and stretching beyond sight on each hand, the sun power screens glowed with a faint opalescent radiance, their slight percentage of inefficiency as transformers of radiant sun power to available electrical power being evidenced as a mild phosphorescence. The effect was not illumination, but rather like the ghostly sheen of a snow covered plain seen by starlight.

The glow picked out the path they must follow to reach the rain-obscured wall of buildings bordering the ways. The path was a narrow black stripe which arched away into the darkness over the low curve of the roof. They started away on this path at a dog trot, making as much speed as the slippery footing and the dark permitted, while Blekinsop's mind still fretted at the problem of Gaines' apparently callous detachment. Although possessed of a keen intelligence his nature was dominated by a warm, human sympathy, without which no politician, irrespective of other virtues or shortcomings, is long successful.

Because of this trait he distrusted instinctively any mind which was guided by logic alone. He was aware that, from a standpoint of strict logic, no reasonable case could be made out for the continued existence of the human race, still less for the human values he served.

Had he been able to pierce the preoccupation of his companion, he would have been reassured. On the surface Gaines' exceptionally intelligent mind was clicking along with the facile ease of an electronic integrator—arranging data at hand, making tentative decisions, postponing judgments without prejudice until necessary data were available, exploring alternatives. Underneath, in a compartment insulated by stern self-discipline from the acting theatre of his mind, his emotions were a torturing storm of self-reproach. He was heartsick at suffering he had seen, and which he knew too well was duplicated up and down the line. Although he was not aware of any personal omission, nevertheless, the fault was somehow his, for authority creates responsibility.

He had carried too long the superhuman burden of kingship—which no sane mind can carry light-heartedly—and was at this moment perilously close to the frame of mind which sends captains down with their ships. Only the need for immediate, constructive action sustained him.

But no trace of this conflict reached his features.

At the wall of buildings glowed a green line of arrows, pointing to the left. Over them, at the terminus of the narrow path, shone a sign: "ACCESS DOWN." They pursued this, Blekinsop puffing in Gaines' wake, to a door let in the wall, which gave into a narrow stairway lighted by a single glowtube. Gaines plunged down this, still followed, and they emerged on the crowded, noisy, stationary walkway adjoining the northbound road.

Immediately adjacent to the stairway, on the right, was a public telebooth. Through the glassite door they could see a portly, well-dressed man speaking earnestly to his female equivalent, mirrored in the visor screen. Three other citizens were waiting outside the booth.

Gaines pushed past them, flung open the door, grasped the bewildered and indignant man by the shoulders, and hustled him outside, kicking the door closed after him. He cleared the visor screen with one sweep of his hand, before the matron pictured therein could protest, and pressed the *emergency-priority* button.

He dialed his private code number, and was shortly looking into the troubled face of his Engineer of the Watch, Davidson.

"Report!"

"It's you, Chief! Thank God! Where are you?" Davidson's relief was pathetic.

"Report!"

The Senior Watch Officer repressed his emotion and complied in direct, clipped phrases, "At seven-oh-nine p.m. the consolidated tension reading. strip twenty, Sacramento Sector, climbed suddenly. Before action could be taken. tension on strip twenty passed emergency level: the interlocks acted, and power to subject strip cut out. Cause of failure unknown. Direct communication to Sacramento control office has failed. They do not answer the auxiliary, nor the commercial line.

Effort to re-establish communication continues. Messenger dispatched from Stockton Subsector Ten.

"No casualties reported. Warning broadcast by public announcement circuit to keep clear of strip nineteen. Evacuation has commenced."

"There are casualties," Gaines cut in. "Police and hospital emergency routine. Move!"

"Yes, sir!" Davidson snapped back, and hooked a thumb over his shoulder—but his Cadet Officer of the Watch had already jumped to comply. "Shall I cut out the rest of the road, Chief?"

"No. No more casualties are likely after the first disorder. Keep up the broadcast warnings. Keep those other strips rolling, or we will have a traffic jam the devil himself couldn't untangle."—Gaines had in mind the impossibility of bringing the strips up to speed under load. The rotors were not powerful enough to do this. If the entire road was stopped, he would have to evacuate every strip, correct the trouble on strip twenty, bring all strips up to speed, and then move the accumulated peak load traffic. In the meantime, over five million stranded passengers would constitute a tremendous police problem. It was simpler to evacuate passengers on strip twenty over the roof, and allow them to return home via the remaining strips. "Notify the Mayor and the Governor that I have assumed emergency authority. Same to the Chief of Police and place him under your orders. Tell the Commandant to arm all cadets available and await orders. Move!"

"Yes, sir. Shall I recall technicians off watch?"

"No. This isn't an engineering failure. Take a look at your readings; that entire sector went out simultaneously— Somebody cut out those rotors by hand. Place off-watch technicians on standby status—but don't arm them, and don't send them down inside. Tell the Commandant to rush all available senior-class cadets to Stockton Subsector Office number ten to report to me. I want them equipped with tumblebugs, pistols, and sleepy bombs."

"Yes, sir." A clerk leaned over Davidson's shoulder and said something in his ear. "The Governor wants to talk to you, Chief."

"Can't do it—nor can you. Who's your relief? Have you sent for him?"

"Hubbard—he's just come in."

"Have him talk to the Governor, the Mayor, the press—

anybody that calls—even the White House. You stick to your watch. I'm cutting off. I'll be back in communication as quickly as I can locate a reconnaissance car." He was out of the booth almost before the screen cleared.

Blekinsop did not venture to speak, but followed him out to the northbound twenty-mile strip. There Gaines stopped, short of the wind break, turned, and kept his eyes on the wall beyond the stationary walkway. He picked out some landmark, or sign—not apparent to his companion—and did an Eliza-crossing-the-ice back to the walkway, so rapidly that Blekinsop was carried some hundred feet beyond him, and almost failed to follow when Gaines ducked into a doorway and ran down a flight of stairs.

They came out on a narrow lower walkway, 'down inside'. The pervading din claimed them, beat upon their bodies as well as their ears. Dimly, Blekinsop perceived their surroundings, as he struggled to face that wall of sound. Facing him, illuminated by the yellow monochrome of a sodium arc, was one of the rotors that drove the five-mile strip, its great, drum-shaped armature revolving slowly around the stationary field coils in its core. The upper surface of the drum pressed against the under side of the moving way and imparted to it its stately progress.

To the left and right, a hundred yards each way, and beyond at similar intervals, farther than he could see, were other rotors. Bridging the gaps between the rotors were the slender rollers, crowded together like cigars in a box, in order that the strip might have a continuous rolling support The rollers were supported by steel girder arches through the gaps of which he saw row after row of rotors in staggered succession, the rotors in each succeeding row turning over more rapidly than the last.

Separated from the narrow walkway by a line of supporting steel pillars, and lying parallel to it on the side away from the rotors, ran a shallow paved causeway, joined to the walk at this point by a ramp. Gaines peered up and down this tunnel in evident annoyance. Blekinsop started to ask him what troubled him, but found his voice snuffed out by the sound. He could not cut through the roar of thousands of rotors and the whine of hundreds of thousands of rollers.

Gaines saw his lips move and guessed at the question. He cupped his hands around Blekinsop's right ear, and shouted, "No car—I expected to find a car here."

The Australian, wishing to be helpful, grasped Gaines' arm and pointed back into the jungle of machinery. Gaines' eye followed the direction indicated and picked out something that he had missed in his preoccupation—a half dozen men working around a rotor several strips away. They had jacked down a rotor until it was no longer in contact with the road surface and were preparing to replace it in toto. The replacement rotor was standing by on a low, heavy truck.

The Chief Engineer gave a quick smile of acknowledgment and thanks and aimed his flashlight at the group, the beam focused down to a slender, intense needle of light. One of the technicians looked up, and Gaines snapped the light on and off in a repeated, irregular pattern. A figure detached itself from the group, and ran toward them.

It was a slender young man, dressed in dungarees and topped off with earpads and an incongruous, pillbox cap, bright with gold braid and insignia. He recognized the Chief Engineer and saluted, his face falling into humorless, boyish intentness.

Gaines stuffed his torch into a pocket and commenced to gesticulate rapidly with both hands—clear, clean gestures, as involved and as meaningful as deaf-mute language. Blekinsop dug into his own dilettante knowledge of anthropology and decided that it was most like American Indian sign language, with some of the finger movements of hula. But it was necessarily almost entirely strange, being adapted for a particular terminology.

The cadet answered him in kind, stepped to the edge of the causeway, and flashed his torch to the south. He picked out a car, still some distance away, but approaching at headlong speed. It braked, and came to a stop alongside them.

It was a small affair, ovoid in shape, and poised on two centerline wheels. The forward, upper surface swung up and disclosed the driver, another cadet. Gaines addressed him briefly in sign language, then hustled Blekinsop ahead of him into the cramped passenger compartment.

As the glassite hood was being swung back into place, a blast of wind smote them, and the Australian looked up in time to glimpse the last of three much larger vehicles hurtle past them. They were headed north, at a speed of not less than two hundred miles per hour. Blekinsop thought that he had made out the little hats of cadets through the windows of the last of the three, but he could not be sure.

He had no time to wonder, so violent was the driver's get-away. Gaines ignored the accelerating surge; he was already calling Davidson on the built-in communicator. Comparative silence had settled down once the car was closed. The face of a female operator at the relay station showed on the screen.

"Get me Davidson—Senior Watch Office!"

"Oh! It's Mr. Gaines! The Mayor wants to talk to you, Mr. Gaines."

"Refer him—and get me Davidson. Move!"

"Yes, sir!"

"And see here—leave this circuit hooked in to Davidson's board until I tell you personally to cut it."

"Right." Her face gave way to the Watch Officer.

"That you, Chief? We're moving—progress O.K.—no change."

"Very well. You'll be able to raise me on this circuit, or at Subsector Ten office. Clearing now." Davidson's face gave way to the relay operator.

"Your wife is calling, Mr. Gaines. Will you take it?"

Gaines muttered something not quite gallant, and answered, "Yes."

Mrs. Gaines flashed into facsimile. He burst into speech before she could open her mouth. "Darling I'm all right don't worry I'll be home when I get there I've got to go now." It was all out in one breath, and he slapped the control that cleared the screen.

They slammed to a breath-taking stop alongside the stair leading to the watch office of Subsector Ten, and piled out. Three big lorries were drawn up on the ramp, and three platoons of cadets were ranged in restless ranks alongside them.

A cadet trotted up to Gaines, and saluted. "Lindsay, sir—Cadet Engineer of the Watch. The Engineer of the Watch requests that you come at once to the control room."

The Engineer of the Watch looked up as they came in. "Chief—Van Kleeck is calling you."

"Put him on."

When Van Kleeck appeared in the big visor, Gaines greeted him with, "Hello, Van. Where are you?"

"Sacramento Office. Now, listen—"

"Sacramento? That's good! Report."

Van Kleeck looked disgruntled. "Report, hell! I'm not your deputy any more, Gaines. Now, you—"

"What the hell are you talking about?"

"Listen, and don't interrupt me, and you'll find out. You're through, Gaines. I've been picked as Director of the Provisional Control Committee for the New Order."

"Van, have you gone off your rocker? What do you mean —the 'New Order'?"

"You'll find out. This is it—the functionalist revolution. We're in; you're out. We stopped strip twenty just to give you a little taste of what we can do."

Concerning Function: A Treatise on the Natural Order in Society, the bible of the functionalist movement, was first published in 1930. It claimed to be a scientifically accurate theory of social relations. The author, Paul Decker, disclaimed the "outworn and futile" ideas of democracy and human equality, and substituted a system in which human beings were evaluated "functionally"—that is to say, by the role each filled in the economic sequence. The underlying thesis was that it was right and proper for a man to exercise over his fellows whatever power was inherent in his function, and that any other form of social organization was silly, visionary, and contrary to the "natural order."

The complete interdependence of modern economic life seems to have escaped him entirely.

His ideas were dressed up with a glib mechanistic pseudo-psychology based on the observed orders of precedence among barnyard fowls, and on the famous Pavlov conditioned-reflex experiments on dogs. He failed to note that human beings are neither dogs, nor chickens. Old Doctor Pavlov ignored him entirely, as he had ignored so many others who had blindly and unscientifically dogmatized about the meaning of his important, but strictly limited, experiments.

Functionalism did not take hold at once—during the 'thirties almost everyone, from truckdriver to hatcheck girl, had a scheme for setting the world right in six easy lessons; and a surprising percentage managed to get their schemes published. But it gradually spread. Functionalism was particularly popular among little people everywhere who could persuade themselves that their particular jobs were the indispensable ones, and that, therefore, under the "natural order" they would be top dog. With so many different functions actually indispensable such self-persuasion was easy.

Gaines stared at Van Kleeck for a moment before replying. "Van," he said slowly, "you don't really think you can get away with this, do you?"

The little man puffed out his chest. "Why not? We *have* gotten away with it. You can't start strip twenty until I am ready to let you, and I can stop the whole road, if necessary."

Gaines was becoming uncomfortably aware that he was dealing with unreasonable conceit, and held himself patiently in check. "Sure you can, Van—but how about the rest of the country? Do you think the United States Army will sit quietly by and let you run California as your private kingdom?"

Van Kleeck looked sly. "I've planned for that. I've just finished broadcasting a manifesto to all the road technicians in the country, telling them what we have done, and telling them to arise, and claim their rights. With every road in the country stopped, and people getting hungry, I reckon the President will think twice before sending the army to tangle with us. Oh, he could send a force to capture, or kill me—I'm not afraid to die!—but he doesn't dare start shooting down road technicians as a class, because the country can't get along without us—consequently, he'll have to get along with us—on our terms!"

There was much bitter truth in what he said. If an uprising of the road technicians became general, the government could no more attempt to settle it by force than a man could afford to cure a headache by blowing out his brains. But was the uprising general?

"Why do you think that the technicians in the rest of the country will follow your lead?"

"Why not? It's the natural order of things. This is an age of machinery; the real power everywhere is in the technicians, but they have been kidded into not using their power with a lot of obsolete catch-phrases. And of all the classes of technicians, the most important, the absolutely essential, are the road technicians. From now on they run the show—it's the natural order of things!" He turned away for a moment, and fussed with some papers on the desk before him, then he added, "That's all for now, Gaines—I've got to call the White House, and let the President know how things stand. You carry on, and behave yourself, and you won't get hurt."

Gaines sat quite still for some minutes after the screen cleared. So that's how it was. He wondered what effect, if any, Van Kleeck's invitation to strike had had on road technicians elsewhere. None, he thought—but then he had not dreamed that it could happen among his own technicians. Perhaps he had made a mistake in refusing to take time to talk to anyone outside the road. No—if he had stopped to talk to the Governor, or the newspapermen, he would still be talking. Still—

He dialled Davidson.

"Any trouble in any other sectors, Dave?"

"No, Chief."

"Or on any other road?"

"None reported."

"Did you hear my talk with Van Kleeck?"

"I was cut in—yes."

"Good. Have Hubbard call the President and the Governor, and tell them that I am strongly opposed to the use of military force as long as the outbreak is limited to this road. Tell them that I will not be responsible if they move in before I ask for help."

Davidson looked dubious. "Do you think that is wise, Chief?"

"I do! If we try to blast Van and his red-hots out of their position, we may set off a real, country-wide uprising. Furthermore, he could wreck the road so that God himself couldn't put it back together. What's your rolling tonnage now?"

"Fifty-three percent under evening peak."

"How about strip twenty?"

"Almost evacuated."

"Good. Get the road clear of all traffic as fast as possible. Better have the Chief of Police place a guard on all entrances to the road to keep out new traffic. Van may stop all strips any time—or I may need to, myself. Here is my plan: I'm going 'down inside' with these armed cadets. We will work north, overcoming any resistance we meet. You arrange for watch technicians and maintenance crews to follow immediately behind us. Each rotor, as they come to it, is to be cut out, then hooked into the Stockton control board. It will be a haywire rig, with no safety interlocks, so use enough watch technicians to be able to catch trouble before it happens.

"If this scheme works, we can move control of the Sacramento Sector right out from under Van's feet, and he can stay in this Sacramento control office until he gets hungry enough to be reasonable."

He cut off and turned to the Subsector Engineer of the Watch. "Edmunds, give me a helmet—and a pistol."

"Yes, sir." He opened a drawer, and handed his chief a

slender, deadly looking weapon. Gaines belted it on, and accepted a helmet, into which he crammed his head, leaving the anti-noise ear flaps up. Blekinsop cleared his throat.

"May—uh—may I have one of those helmets?" he inquired.

"What?" Gaines focused his attention. "Oh— You won't need one, Mr. Blekinsop. I want you to remain right here until you hear from me."

"But—" The Australian statesman started to speak, thought better of it, and subsided.

From the doorway the Cadet Engineer of the Watch demanded the Chief Engineer's attention. "Mr. Gaines, there is a technician out here who insists on seeing you—a man named Harvey."

"Can't do it."

"He's from the Sacramento Sector, sir."

"Oh!—send him in."

Harvey quickly advised Gaines of what he had seen and heard at the guild meeting that afternoon. "I got disgusted and left while they were still jawin', Chief. I didn't think any more about it until twenty stopped rolling. Then I heard that the trouble was in Sacramento Sector, and decided to look you up."

"How long has this been building up?"

"Quite some time, I guess. You know how it is—there are a few soreheads everywhere and a lot of them are functionalists. But you can't refuse to work with a man just because he holds different political views. It's a free country."

"You should have come to me before, Harvey." Harvey looked stubborn. Gaines studied his face. "No, I guess you are right. It's my business to keep tab on your mates, not yours. As you say, it's a free country. Anything else?"

"Well—now that it has come to this, I thought maybe I could help you pick out the ringleaders."

"Thanks. You stick with me. We're going 'down inside' and try to clear up this mess."

The office door opened suddenly, and a technician and a cadet appeared, lugging a burden between them. They deposited it on the floor, and waited.

It was a young man, quite evidently dead. The front of his dungaree jacket was soggy with blood. Gaines looked at the watch officer. "Who is he?"

Edmunds broke his stare and answered, "Cadet Hughes—
he's the messenger I sent to Sacramento when communication
failed. When he didn't report, I sent Marston and Cadet Jenkins after him."

Gaines muttered something to himself, and turned away.
"Come along, Harvey."

The cadets waiting below had changed in mood. Gaines
noted that the boyish intentness for excitement had been replaced by something uglier. There was much exchange of
hand signals and several appeared to be checking the loading
of their pistols.

He sized them up, then signalled to the cadet leader. There
was a short interchange of signals. The cadet saluted, turned
to his men, gesticulated briefly, and brought his arm down
smartly. They filed upstairs and into an empty standby room,
Gaines following.

Once inside, and the noise shut out, he addressed them,
"You saw Hughes brought in—how many of you want a
chance to kill the louse that did it?"

Three of the cadets reacted almost at once, breaking ranks
and striding forward. Gaines looked at them coldly. "Very
well. You three turn in your weapons, and return to your
quarters. Any of the rest of you that think this is a matter of
private revenge, or a hunting party, may join them." He permitted a short silence to endure before continuing. "Sacramento Sector has been seized by unauthorized persons. We are
going to retake it—if possible, without loss of life on either
side, and, if possible, without stopping the roads. The plan is
to take over 'down inside', rotor by rotor, and cross connect
through Stockton. The task assignment of this group is to proceed north 'down inside', locating and overpowering all persons in your path. You will bear in mind the probability that
most of the persons you will arrest are completely innocent.
Consequently, you will favor the use of sleep gas bombs, and
will shoot to kill only as a last resort.

"Cadet Captain, assign your men in squads of ten each,
with squad leader. Each squad is to form a skirmish line
across 'down inside', mounted on tumblebugs, and will proceed north at fifteen miles per hour. Leave an interval of one
hundred yards between successive waves of skirmishers.
Whenever a man is sighted, the entire leading wave will con-
verge on him, arrest him, and deliver him to a transport car

and then fall in as the last wave. You will assign the transports that delivered you here to receive prisoners. Instruct the drivers to keep abreast of the second wave.

"You will assign an attack group to recapture subsector control offices, but no office is to be attacked until its subsector has been crossconnected with Stockton. Arrange liaison accordingly.

"Any questions?" He let his eyes run over the faces of the young men. When no one spoke up, he turned back to the cadet in charge. "Very well, sir. Carry out your orders!"

By the time the dispositions had been completed, the follow-up crew of technicians had arrived, and Gaines had given the engineer in charge his instructions. The cadets "stood to horse" alongside their poised tumblebugs. The Cadet Captain looked expectantly at Gaines. He nodded, the cadet brought his arm down smartly, and the first wave mounted and moved off.

Gaines and Harvey mounted tumblebugs, and kept abreast of the Cadet Captain, some twenty-five yards behind the leading wave. It had been a long time since the Chief Engineer had ridden one of these silly-looking little vehicles, and he felt awkward. A tumblebug does not give a man dignity, since it is about the size and shape of a kitchen stool, gyro-stabilized on a single wheel. But it is perfectly adapted to patrolling the maze of machinery 'down inside', since it can go through an opening the width of a man's shoulders, is easily controlled, and will stand patiently upright, waiting, should its rider dismount.

The little reconnaissance car followed Gaines at a short interval, weaving in and out among the rotors, while the television and audio communicator inside continued as Gaines' link to his other manifold responsibilities.

The first two hundred yards of the Sacramento Sector passed without incident, then one of the skirmishers sighted a tumblebug parked by a rotor. The technician it served was checking the gauges at the rotor's base, and did not see them approach. He was unarmed and made no resistance, but seemed surprised and indignant, as well as very bewildered.

The little command group dropped back and permitted the new leading wave to overtake them.

Three miles farther along the score stood thirty-seven men

arrested, none killed. Two of the cadets had received minor wounds, and had been directed to retire. Only four of the prisoners had been armed, one of these Harvey had been able to identify definitely as a ringleader. Harvey expressed a desire to attempt to parley with the outlaws, if any occasion arose. Gaines agreed tentatively. He knew of Harvey's long and honorable record as a labor leader, and was willing to try anything that offered a hope of success with a minimum of violence.

Shortly thereafter the first wave flushed another technician. He was on the far side of a rotor; they were almost on him before he was seen. He did not attempt to resist, although he was armed, and the incident would not have been worth recording, had he not been talking into a hush-a-phone which he had plugged into the telephone jack at the base of the rotor.

Gaines reached the group as the capture was being effected. He snatched at the soft rubber mask of the 'phone, jerking it away from the man's mouth so violently that he could feel the bone-conduction receiver grate between the man's teeth. The prisoner spat out a piece of broken tooth and glared, but ignored attempts to question him.

Swift as Gaines had been, it was highly probable that they had lost the advantage of surprise. It was necessary to assume that the prisoner had succeeded in reporting the attack going on beneath the ways. Word was passed down the line to proceed with increased caution.

Gaines' pessimism was justified shortly. Riding toward them appeared a group of men, as yet several hundred feet away. There were at least a score, but their exact strength could not be determined, as they took advantage of the rotors for cover as they advanced. Harvey looked at Gaines, who nodded, and signalled the Cadet Captain to halt his forces.

Harvey went on ahead, unarmed, his hands held high above his head, and steering by balancing the weight of his body. The outlaw party checked its speed uncertainly, and finally stopped. Harvey approached within a couple of rods of them and stopped likewise. One of them, apparently the leader, spoke to him in sign language, to which he replied.

They were too far away and the yellow light too uncertain to follow the discussion. It continued for several minutes, then ensued a pause. The leader seemed uncertain what to do. One of his party rolled forward, returned his pistol to its holster, and conversed with the leader. The leader shook his head at the man's violent gestures.

The man renewed his argument, but met the same negative response. With a final disgusted wave of his hands, he desisted, drew his pistol, and shot at Harvey. Harvey grabbed at his middle and leaned forward. The man shot again; Harvey jerked, and slid to the ground.

The Cadet Captain beat Gaines to the draw. The killer looked up as the bullet hit him. He looked as if he were puzzled by some strange occurrence—being too freshly dead to be aware of it.

The cadets came in shooting. Although the first wave was outnumbered better than two to one, they were helped by the comparative demoralization of the enemy. The odds were nearly even after the first ragged volley. Less than thirty seconds after the first treacherous shot all of the insurgent party were dead, wounded, or under arrest. Gaines' losses were two dead (including the murder of Harvey) and two wounded.

Gaines modified his tactics to suit the changed conditions. Now that secrecy was gone, speed and striking power were of first importance. The second wave was directed to close in practically to the heels of the first. The third wave was brought up to within twenty-five yards of the second. These three waves were to ignore unarmed men, leaving them to be picked up by the fourth wave, but they were directed to shoot on sight any person carrying arms.

Gaines cautioned them to shoot to wound, rather than to kill, but he realized that his admonishment was almost impossible to obey. There would be killing. Well—he had not wanted it, but he felt that he had no choice. Any armed outlaw was a potential killer—he could not, in fairness to his own men, lay too many restrictions on them.

When the arrangements for the new marching order were completed, he signed the Cadet Captain to go ahead, and the first and second waves started off together at the top speed of which the tumblebugs were capable—not quite eighteen miles per hour. Gaines followed them.

He swerved to avoid Harvey's body, glancing involuntarily down as he did so. The face was an ugly jaundiced yellow under the sodium arc, but it was set in a death mask of rugged beauty in which the strong fibre of the dead man's character was evident. Seeing this, Gaines did not regret so much his order to shoot, but the deep sense of loss of personal honor lay more heavily on him than before.

They passed several technicians during the next few minutes, but had no occasion to shoot. Gaines was beginning to feel somewhat hopeful of a reasonably bloodless victory, when he noticed a change in the pervading throb of machinery which penetrated even through the heavy anti-noise pads of his helmet. He lifted an ear pad in time to hear the end of a rumbling diminuendo as the rotors and rollers slowed to rest.

The road was stopped.

He shouted, "Halt your men!" to the Cadet Captain. His words echoed hollowly in the unreal silence.

The top of the reconnaissance car swung up as he turned and hurried to it. "Chief!" the cadet within called out, "relay station calling you."

The girl in the visor screen gave way to Davidson as soon as she recognized Gaines' face. "Chief," Davidson said at once, "Van Kleeck's calling you."

"Who stopped the road?"

"He did."

"Any other major change in the situation?"

"No—the road was practically empty when he stopped it."

"Good. Give me Van Kleeck."

The chief conspirator's face was livid with uncurbed anger when he identified Gaines. He burst into speech.

"So! You thought I was fooling, eh? What do you think now, Mister Chief Engineer Gaines?"

Gaines fought down an impulse to tell him exactly what he thought, particularly about Van Kleeck. Everything about the short man's manner affected him like a squeaking slate pencil.

But he could not afford the luxury of speaking his mind. He strove to get just the proper tone into his voice which would soothe the other man's vanity. "I've got to admit that you've won this trick, Van—the roadway is stopped—but don't think I didn't take you seriously. I've watched your work too long to underrate you. I know you mean what you say."

Van Kleeck was pleased by the tribute, but tried not to show it. "Then why don't you get smart, and give up?" he demanded belligerently. "You can't win."

"Maybe not, Van, but you know I've got to try. Besides,"

he went on, "why can't I win? You said yourself that I could call on the whole United States Army."

Van Kleeck grinned triumphantly. "You see that?" He held up a pear-shaped electric push button, attached to a long cord. "If I push that, it will blow a path right straight across the ways—blow it to Kingdom Come. And just for good measure I'll take an ax, and wreck this control station before I leave."

Gaines wished wholeheartedly that he knew more about psychiatry. Well—he'd just have to do his best, and trust to horse sense to give him the right answers. "That's pretty drastic, Van, but I don't see how we can give up."

"No? You'd better have another think. If you force me to blow up the road, how about all the people that will be blown up along with it?"

Gaines thought furiously. He did not doubt that Van Kleeck would carry out his threat; his very phraseology, the childish petulance of "If you force me to do this—" betrayed the dangerous irrationality of his mental processes. And such an explosion anywhere in the thickly populated Sacramento Sector would be likely to wreck one, or more, apartment houses, and would be certain to kill shopkeepers on the included segment of strip twenty, as well as chance bystanders. Van was absolutely right; he dare not risk the lives of bystanders who were not aware of the issue and had not consented to the hazard—even if the road never rolled again.

For that matter, he did not relish chancing major damage to the road itself—but it was the danger to innocent life that left him helpless.

A tune ran through his head—"*Hear them hum; watch them run. Oh, our work is never done—*" What to do? What to do? "*While you ride; while you glide; we are—*" This wasn't getting anyplace.

He turned back to the screen. "Look, Van, you don't want to blow up the road unless you have to, I'm sure. Neither do I. Suppose I come up to your headquarters, and we talk this thing over. Two reasonable men ought to be able to make a settlement."

Van Kleeck was suspicious. "Is this some sort of a trick?"

"How can it be? I'll come alone, and unarmed, just as fast as my car can get there."

"How about your men?"

"They will sit where they are until I'm back. You can put out observers to make sure of it."

Van Kleeck stalled for a moment, caught between the fear of a trap, and the pleasure of having his erstwhile superior come to him to sue for terms. At last he grudgingly consented.

Gaines left his instructions and told Davidson what he intended to do. "If I'm not back within an hour, you're on your own, Dave."

"Be careful, Chief."

"I will."

He evicted the cadet driver from the reconnaissance car and ran it down the ramp into the causeway, then headed north and gave it the gun. Now he would have a chance to collect his thoughts, even at two hundred miles per hour. Suppose he pulled off this trick—there would still have to be some changes made. Two lessons stood out like sore thumbs: First, the strips must be cross-connected with safety interlocks so that adjacent strips would slow down, or stop, if a strip's speed became dangerously different from those adjacent. No repetition of what happened on twenty!

But that was elementary, a mere mechanical detail. The real failure had been in men. Well, the psychological classification tests must be improved to insure that the roads employed only conscientious, reliable men. But hell's bells—that was just exactly what the present classification tests were supposed to insure beyond question. To the best of his knowledge there had never been a failure from the improved Humm-Wadsworth-Burton method—not until today in the Sacramento Sector. How had Van Kleeck gotten one whole sector of temperament-classified men to revolt?

It didn't make sense.

Personnel did not behave erratically without a reason. One man might be unpredictable, but in large numbers they were as dependable as machines, or figures. They could be measured, examined, classified. His inner eye automatically pictured the personnel office, with its rows of filing cabinets, its clerks— He'd got it! He'd got it! Van Kleeck, as Chief Deputy, was ex officio *personnel officer for the entire road!*

It was the only solution that covered all the facts. The personnel officer alone had the perfect opportunity to pick out all the bad apples and concentrate them in one barrel. Gaines was convinced beyond any reasonable doubt that there had been skulduggery, perhaps for years, with the temperament classification tests, and that Van Kleeck had deliberately transferred the kind of men he needed to one sector, after falsifying their records.

And that taught another lesson—tighter tests for officers, and no officer to be trusted with classification and assignment without close supervision and inspection. Even he, Gaines, should be watched in that respect. *Qui custodiet ipsos custodes?* Who will guard those selfsame guardians? Latin might be obsolete, but those old Romans weren't dummies.

He at last knew wherein he had failed, and he derived melancholy pleasure from the knowledge. Supervision and inspection, check and re-check, was the answer. It would be cumbersome and inefficient, but it seemed that adequate safeguards always involved some loss of efficiency.

He should not have entrusted so much authority to Van Kleeck without knowing more about him. He still should know more about him— He touched the emergency-stop button, and brought the car to a dizzying halt. "Relay station! See if you can raise my office."

Dolores' face looked out from the screen. "You're still there—good!" he told her. "I was afraid you'd gone home."

"I came back, Mr. Gaines."

"Good girl. Get me Van Kleeck's personal file jacket. I want to see his classification record."

She was back with it in exceptionally short order and read from it the symbols and percentages. He nodded repeatedly as the data checked his hunches—masked introvert—inferiority complex. It checked.

"'Comment of the Board:'" she read, "'In spite of the potential instability shown by maxima A and D on the consolidated profile curve, the Board is convinced that this officer is, nevertheless, fitted for duty. He has an exceptionally fine record, and is especially adept in handling men. He is, therefore, recommended for retention and promotion.'"

"That's all, Dolores. Thanks."

"Yes, Mr. Gaines."

"I'm off for a showdown. Keep your fingers crossed."

"But Mr. Gaines—" Back in Fresno, Dolores stared wide-eyed at an empty screen.

"Take me to Mr. Van Kleeck!"

The man addressed took his gun out of Gaines' ribs—reluctantly, Gaines thought—and indicated that the Chief Engineer should precede him up the stairs. Gaines climbed out of the car, and complied.

Van Kleeck had set himself up in the sector control room proper, rather than the administrative office. With him were half a dozen men, all armed.

"Good evening, Director Van Kleeck." The little man swelled visibly at Gaines' acknowledgment of his assumed rank.

"We don't go in much around here for titles," he said, with ostentatious casualness. "Just call me Van. Sit down, Gaines."

Gaines did so. It was necessary to get those other men out. He looked at them with an expression of bored amusement. "Can't you handle one unarmed man by yourself, Van? Or don't the functionalists trust each other?"

Van Kleeck's face showed his annoyance, but Gaines' smile was undaunted. Finally the smaller man picked up a pistol from his desk, and motioned toward the door. "Get out, you guys."

"But Van—"

"Get out, I said!"

When they were alone, Van Kleeck picked up the electric push button which Gaines had seen in the visor screen, and pointed his pistol at his former chief. "O.K.," he growled, "try any funny stuff, and off it goes! What's your proposition?"

Gaines' irritating smile grew broader. Van Kleeck scowled. "What's so damn funny?" he said.

Gaines granted him an answer. "You are, Van—honest, this is rich. You start a functionalist revolution, and the only function you can think of to perform is to blow up the road that justifies your title. Tell me," he went on, "what is it you are so scared of?"

"I am not afraid!"

"Not afraid? You? Sitting there, ready to commit hara-kiri with that toy push button, and you tell me that you aren't afraid. If your buddies knew how near you are to throwing away what they've fought for, they'd shoot you in a second. You're afraid of them, too, aren't you?"

Van Kleeck thrust the push button away from him, and stood up. "I am not afraid!" he screamed, and came around the desk toward Gaines.

Gaines sat where he was, and laughed. "But you are! You're afraid of me, this minute. You're afraid I'll have you on the carpet for the way you do your job. You're afraid the cadets won't salute you. You're afraid they are laughing behind your back. You're afraid of using the wrong fork at dinner. You're afraid people are looking at you—and you are afraid that they won't notice you."

"I am not!" he protested. "You— You dirty, stuckup snob! Just because you went to a high-hat school you think you're better than anybody." He choked, and became incoherent, fighting to keep back tears of rage. "You, and your nasty little cadets—"

Gaines eyed him cautiously. The weakness in the man's character was evident now—he wondered why he had not seen it before. He recalled how ungracious Van Kleeck had been one time when he had offered to help him with an intricate piece of figuring.

The problem now was to play on his weakness, to keep him so preoccupied that he would not remember the peril-laden push button. He must be caused to center the venom of his twisted outlook on Gaines, to the exclusion of every other thought.

But he must not goad him too carelessly, or a shot from across the room might put an end to Gaines, and to any chance of avoiding a bloody, wasteful struggle for control of the road.

Gaines chuckled. "Van," he said, "you are a pathetic little shrimp. That was a dead give-away. I understand you perfectly; you're a third-rater, Van, and all your life you've been afraid that someone would see through you, and send you back to the foot of the class. Director—pfui! If you are the best the functionalists can offer, we can afford to ignore them —they'll fold up from their own rotten inefficiency." He swung around in his chair, deliberately turning his back on Van Kleeck and his gun.

Van Kleeck advanced on his tormentor, halted a few feet away, and shouted: "You—I'll show you—I'll put a bullet in you; that's what I'll do!"

Gaines swung back around, got up, and walked steadily toward him. "Put that popgun down before you hurt yourself."

Van Kleeck retreated a step. "Don't you come near me!" he screamed. "Don't you come near me—or I'll shoot you— see if I don't!"

This is it, thought Gaines, and dived.

The pistol went off alongside his ear. Well, that one didn't get him. They were on the floor. Van Kleeck was hard to hold, for a little man. Where was the gun? There! He had it. He broke away.

Van Kleeck did not get up. He lay sprawled on the floor, tears streaming out of his closed eyes, blubbering like a frustrated child.

Gaines looked at him with something like compassion in his eyes, and hit him carefully behind the ear with the butt of the pistol. He walked over to the door, and listened for a moment, then locked it cautiously.

The cord from the push button led to the control board. He examined the hookup, and disconnected it carefully. That done, he turned to the televisor at the control desk, and called Fresno.

"Okay, Dave," he said, "let 'em attack now—and for the love of Pete, hurry!" Then he cleared the screen, not wishing his watch officer to see how he was shaking.

Back in Fresno the next morning Gaines paced around the Main Control Room with a fair degree of contentment in his heart. The roads were rolling—before long they would be up to speed again. It had been a long night. Every engineer, every available cadet, had been needed to make the inch-by-inch inspection of Sacramento Sector which he had required. Then they had to cross-connect around two wrecked subsector control boards. But the roads were rolling—he could feel their rhythm up through the floor.

He stopped beside a haggard, stubbly-bearded man. "Why don't you go home, Dave?" he asked. "McPherson can carry on from here."

"How about yourself, Chief? You don't look like a June bride."

"Oh, I'll catch a nap in my office after a bit. I called my wife, and told her I couldn't make it. She's coming down here to meet me."

"Was she sore?"

"Not very. You know how women are." He turned back to the instrument board, and watched the clicking 'busy-bodies' assembling the data from six sectors. San Diego Circle, Angeles Sector, Bakersfield Sector, Fresno Sector, Stockton—Stockton? Stockton! Good grief!—Blekinsop! He had left a cabinet minister of Australia cooling his heels in the Stockton office all night long!

He started for the door, while calling over his shoulder, "Dave, will you order a car for me? Make it a fast one!" He was across the hall, and had his head inside his private office before Davidson could acknowledge the order.

"Dolores!"

"Yes, Mr. Gaines."

"Call my wife, and tell her I had to go to Stockton. If she's already left home, just have her wait here. And Dolores—"

"Yes, Mr. Gaines?"

"Calm her down."

She bit her lip, but her face was impassive. "Yes, Mr. Gaines."

"That's a good girl." He was out and started down the stairway. When he reached road level, the sight of the rolling strips warmed him inside and made him feel almost cheerful.

He strode briskly away toward a door marked ACCESS DOWN, whistling softly to himself. He opened the door, and the rumbling, roaring rhythm from 'down inside' seemed to pick up the tune even as it drowned out the sound of his whistling.

> "Hie! Hie! Hee!
> The rotor men are we—
> Check off the sectors loud and strong! One! Two! Three!
> Anywhere you go
> You are bound to know
> That your roadways are rolling along!"

Blowups Happen

"PUT DOWN that wrench!"

The man addressed turned slowly around and faced the speaker. His expression was hidden by a grotesque helmet, part of a heavy, lead-and-cadmium armor which shielded his entire body, but the tone of voice in which he answered showed nervous exasperation.

"What the hell's eating on you, doc?" He made no move to replace the tool in question.

They faced each other like two helmeted, arrayed fencers, watching for an opening. The first speaker's voice came from behind his mask a shade higher in key and more peremptory in tone. "You heard me, Harper. Put down that wrench at once, and come away from that 'trigger'. Erickson!"

A third armored figure came from the far end of the control room. "What 'cha want, doc?"

"Harper is relieved from watch. You take over as engineer-of-the-watch. Send for the standby engineer."

"Very well." His voice and manner were phlegmatic, as he accepted the situation without comment. The atomic engineer whom he had just relieved glanced from one to the other, then carefully replaced the wrench in its rack.

"Just as you say, _Doctor_ Silard—but send for your relief, too. I shall demand an immediate hearing!" Harper swept indignantly out, his lead-sheathed boots clumping on the floorplates.

Doctor Silard waited unhappily for the ensuing twenty minutes until his own relief arrived. Perhaps he had been hasty. Maybe he was wrong in thinking that Harper had at last broken under the strain of tending the most dangerous machine in the world—the atomic breeder plant. But if he had made a mistake, it had to be on the safe side—slips _must not happen_ in this business; not when a slip might result in atomic detonation of nearly ten tons of uranium-238, U-235, and plutonium.

He tried to visualize what that would mean, and failed. He had been told that uranium was potentially twenty million times as explosive as T.N.T. The figure was meaningless that way. He thought of the pile instead as a hundred million tons of high explosive, or as a thousand Hiroshimas. It still did not mean anything. He had once seen an A-bomb dropped, when he had been serving as a temperament analyst for the Air Forces. He could not imagine the explosion of a thousand such bombs; his brain balked.

Perhaps these atomic engineers could. Perhaps, with their greater mathematical ability and closer comprehension of what actually went on inside the nuclear fission chamber, they had some vivid glimpse of the mind-shattering horror locked up beyond that shield. If so, no wonder they tended to blow up—

He sighed. Erickson looked away from the controls of the linear resonant accelerator on which he had been making some adjustment. "What's the trouble, doc?"

"Nothing. I'm sorry I had to relieve Harper."

Silard could feel the shrewd glance of the big Scandinavian. "Not getting the jitters yourself, are you, doc? Sometimes you squirrel-sleuths blow up, too—"

"Me? I don't think so. I'm scared of that thing in there— I'd be crazy if I weren't."

"So am I," Erickson told him soberly, and went back to his work at the controls of the accelerator. The accelerator proper lay beyond another shielding barrier; its snout disappeared in the final shield between it and the pile and fed a steady stream of terrifically speeded up sub-atomic bullets to the beryllium target located within the pile itself. The tortured beryllium yielded up neutrons, which shot out in all directions through the uranium mass. Some of these neutrons struck uranium atoms squarely on their nuclei and split them in two. The fragments were new elements, barium, xenon, rubidium—depending on the proportions in which each atom split. The new elements were usually unstable isotopes and broke down into a dozen more elements by radioactive disintegration in a progressive reaction.

But these second transmutations were comparatively safe; it was the original splitting of the uranium nucleus, with the release of the awe-inspiring energy that bound it together—an incredible two hundred million electron-volts—that was important—and perilous.

For, while uranium was used to breed other fuels by bombarding it with neutrons, the splitting itself gives up more neutrons which in turn may land in other uranium nuclei and split them. If conditions are favorable to a progressively increasing reaction of this sort, it may get out of hand, build up in an unmeasurable fraction of a micro-second into a complete atomic explosion—an explosion which would dwarf an atom bomb to pop-gun size; an explosion so far beyond all human experience as to be as completely incomprehensible as the idea of personal death. It could be feared, but not understood.

But a self-perpetuating sequence of nuclear splitting, *just under the level of complete explosion*, was necessary to the operation of the breeder plant. To split the first uranium nucleus by bombarding it with neutrons from the beryllium target took more power than the death of the atom gave up. In order that the breeder pile continue to operate it was imperative that each atom split by a neutron from the beryllium target should cause the splitting of many more.

It was equally imperative that this chain of · reactions should always tend to dampen, to die out. It must not build up, or the uranium mass would explode within a time interval too short to be measured by any means whatsoever.

Nor would there be anyone left to measure it.

The atomic engineer on duty at the pile could control this reaction by means of the "trigger", a term the engineers used to include the linear resonant accelerator, the beryllium target, the cadmium damping rods, and adjacent controls, instrument board, and power sources. That is to say he could vary the bombardment on the beryllium target to increase or decrease the level of operation of the plant, he could change the "effective mass" of the pile with the cadmium dampers, and he could tell from his instruments that the internal reaction was dampened—or, rather, that it had been dampened the split second before. He could not possibly know what was actually happening *now* within the pile—sub-atomic speeds are too great and the time intervals too small. He was like the bird that flew backward; he could see where he had been, but he never knew where he was going.

Nevertheless, it was his responsibility, and his alone, not only to maintain the pile at a high efficiency, but to see that the reaction never passed the critical point and progressed into mass explosion.

But that was impossible. He could not be sure; he could never be sure.

He could bring to the job all of the skill and learning of the finest technical education, and use it to reduce the hazard to the lowest mathematical probability, but the blind laws of chance which appear to rule in sub-atomic action might turn up a royal flush against him and defeat his most skillful play.

And each atomic engineer knew it, knew that he gambled not only with his own life, but with the lives of countless others, perhaps with the lives of every human being on the planet. Nobody knew quite what such an explosion would do. A conservative estimate assumed that, in addition to destroying the plant and its personnel completely, it would tear a chunk out of the populous and heavily traveled Los Angeles-Oklahoma Road-City a hundred miles to the north.

The official, optimistic viewpoint on which the plant had been authorized by the Atomic Energy Commission was based on mathematics which predicted that such a mass of uranium would itself be disrupted on a molar scale, and thereby limit the area of destruction, before progressive and accelerated atomic explosion could infect the entire mass.

The atomic engineers, by and large, did not place faith in the official theory. They judged theoretical mathematical prediction for what it was worth—precisely nothing, until confirmed by experiment.

But even from the official viewpoint, each atomic engineer while on watch carried not only his own life in his hands, but the lives of many others—how many, it was better not to think about. No pilot, no general, no surgeon ever carried such a daily, inescapable, ever present weight of responsibility for the lives of others as these men carried every time they went on watch, every time they touched a vernier screw, or read a dial.

They were selected not alone for their intelligence and technical training, but quite as much for their characters and sense of social responsibility. Sensitive men were needed— men who could fully appreciate the importance of the charge entrusted to them; no other sort would do. But the burden of responsibility was too great to be borne indefinitely by a sensitive man.

It was, of necessity, a psychologically unstable condition. Insanity was an occupational disease.

Doctor Cummings appeared, still buckling the straps of the armor worn to guard against stray radiation. "What's up?" he asked Silard.

"I had to relieve Harper."

"So I guessed. I met him coming up. He was sore as hell— just glared at me."

"I know. He wants an immediate hearing. That's why I had to send for you."

Cummings grunted, then nodded toward the engineer, anonymous in all-enclosing armor. "Who'd I draw?"

"Erickson."

"Good enough. Squareheads can't go crazy—eh, Gus?"

Erickson looked up momentarily, and answered, "That's your problem," and returned to his work. Cummings turned back to Silard, and commented, "Psychiatrists don't seem very popular around here. O.K.—I relieve you, sir."

"Very well, sir."

Silard threaded his way through the zig-zag in the outer shield which surrounded the control room. Once outside this outer shield, he divested himself of the cumbersome armor, disposed of it in the locker room provided, and hurried to a lift. He left the lift at the tube station, underground, and looked around for an unoccupied capsule. Finding one, he strapped himself in, sealed the gasketed door, and settled the back of his head into the rest against the expected surge of acceleration.

Five minutes later he knocked at the door of the office of the general superintendent, twenty miles away.

The breeder plant proper was located in a bowl of desert hills on the Arizona plateau. Everything not necessary to the immediate operation of the plant—administrative offices, television station, and so forth—lay beyond the hills. The buildings housing these auxiliary functions were of the most durable construction technical ingenuity could devise. It was hoped that, if *der tag* ever came, occupants would stand approximately the chance of survival of a man going over Niagara Falls in a barrel.

Silard knocked again. He was greeted by a male secretary, Steinke. Silard recalled reading his case history. Formerly one of the most brilliant of the young engineers, he had suffered a blanking out of the ability to handle mathematical operations. A plain case of *fugue*, but there had been nothing that the poor devil could do about it—he had been anxious enough with his conscious mind to stay on duty. He had been rehabilitated as an office worker.

Steinke ushered him into the superintendent's private office. Harper was there before him, and returned his greeting with icy politeness. The superintendent was cordial, but Silard thought he looked tired, as if the twenty-four-hour-a-day strain was too much for him.

"Come in, Doctor, come in. Sit down. Now tell me about this. I'm a little surprised. I thought Harper was one of my steadiest men."

"I don't say he isn't, sir."

"Well?"

"He may be perfectly all right, but your instructions to me are not to take any chances."

"Quite right." The superintendent gave the engineer, silent and tense in his chair, a troubled glance, then returned his attention to Silard. "Suppose you tell me about it."

Silard took a deep breath. "While on watch as psychological observer at the control station I noticed that the engineer of the watch seemed preoccupied and less responsive to stimuli than usual. During my off-watch observation of this case, over a period of the past several days, I have suspected an increasing lack of attention. For example, while playing contract bridge, he now occasionally asks for a review of the bidding, which is contrary to his former behavior pattern.

"Other similar data are available. To cut it short, at 3:11 today, while on watch, I saw Harper, with no apparent reasonable purpose in mind, pick up a wrench used only for operating the valves of the water shield and approach the trigger. I relieved him of duty, and sent him out of the control room."

"Chief!" Harper calmed himself somewhat and continued, "If this witch-doctor knew a wrench from an oscillator, he 'ud know what I was doing. The wrench was on the wrong rack. I noticed it, and picked it up to return it to its proper place. On the way, I stopped to check the readings!"

The superintendent turned inquiringly to Doctor Silard.

"That may be true— Granting that it is true," answered the psychiatrist doggedly, "my diagnosis still stands. Your behavior pattern has altered; your present actions are unpredictable, and I can't approve you for responsible work without a complete check-up."

General Superintendent King drummed on the desk top, and sighed. Then he spoke slowly to Harper, "Cal, you're a good boy, and, believe me, I know how you feel. But there is no way to avoid it—you've got to go up for the psychometricals, and accept whatever disposition the board makes of you." He paused, but Harper maintained an expressionless silence. "Tell you what, son—why don't you take a few days' leave? Then, when you come back, you can go up before the board, or transfer to another department away from the bomb, whichever you prefer." He looked to Silard for approval, and received a nod.

But Harper was not mollified. "No, chief," he protested. "It won't do. Can't you see what's wrong? It's this constant supervision. Somebody always watching the back of your neck, *expecting* you to go crazy. A man can't even shave in private. We're jumpy about the most innocent acts, for fear some head doctor, half batty himself, will see it and decide it's a sign we're slipping—good grief, what do you expect!" His outburst having run its course, he subsided into a flippant cynicism that did not quite jell. "O.K.—never mind the strait jacket; I'll go quietly. You're a good Joe in spite of it, chief," he added, "and I'm glad to have worked under you. Goodbye."

King kept the pain in his eyes out of his voice. "Wait a minute, Cal—you're not through here. Let's forget about the vacation. I'm transferring you to the radiation laboratory. You belong in research anyhow; I'd never have spared you from it to stand watches if I hadn't been short on number-one men.

"As for the constant psychological observation, I hate it as much as you do. I don't suppose you know that they watch me about twice as hard as they watch you duty engineers." Harper showed his surprise, but Silard nodded in sober confirmation. "But we have to have this supervision . . . Do you remember Manning? No, he was before your time. We didn't have psychological observers then. Manning was able and brilliant. Furthermore, he was always cheerful; nothing seemed to bother him.

"I was glad to have him on the pile, for he was always alert, and never seemed nervous about working with it—in fact he grew more buoyant and cheerful the longer he stood control watches. I should have known that was a very bad sign, but I didn't, and there was no observer to tell me so.

"His technician had to slug him one night . . . He found

him dismounting the safety interlocks on the cadmium assembly. Poor old Manning never pulled out of it—he's been violently insane ever since. After Manning cracked up, we worked out the present system of two qualified engineers and an observer for every watch. It seemed the only thing to do."

"I suppose so, chief," Harper mused, his face no longer sullen, but still unhappy. "It's a hell of a situation just the same."

"That's putting it mildly." He got up and put out his hand. "Cal, unless you're dead set on leaving us, I'll expect to see you at the radiation laboratory tomorrow. Another thing—I don't often recommend this, but it might do you good to get drunk tonight."

King had signed to Silard to remain after the young man left. Once the door was closed he turned back to the psychiatrist. "There goes another one—and one of the best. Doctor, what am I going to do?"

Silard pulled at his cheek. "I don't know," he admitted. "The hell of it is, Harper's absolutely right. It does increase the strain on them to know that they are being watched . . . and yet they have to be watched. Your psychiatric staff isn't doing too well, either. It makes us nervous to be around the Big Bomb . . . the more so because we don't understand it. And it's a strain on us to be hated and despised as we are. Scientific detachment is difficult under such conditions; I'm getting jumpy myself."

King ceased pacing the floor and faced the doctor. "But there must be *some* solution—" he insisted.

Silard shook his head. "It's beyond me, Superintendent. I see no solution from the standpoint of psychology."

"No? Hmm—Doctor, who is the top man in your field?"

"Eh?"

"Who is the recognized number-one man in handling this sort of thing?"

"Why, that's hard to say. Naturally, there isn't any one leading psychiatrist in the world; we specialize too much. I know what you mean, though. You don't want the best industrial temperament psychometrician; you want the best all-around man for psychoses non-lesional and situational. That would be Lentz."

"Go on."

"Well— He covers the whole field of environmental adjustment. He's the man that correlated the theory of optimum tonicity with the relaxation technique that Korzybski had developed empirically. He actually worked under Korzybski himself, when he was a young student—it's the only thing he's vain about."

"He did? Then he must be pretty old; Korzybski died in— What year did he die?"

"I started to say that you must know his work in symbology—theory of abstraction and calculus of statement, all that sort of thing—because of its applications to engineering and mathematical physics."

"*That* Lentz—yes, of course. But I had never thought of him as a psychiatrist."

"No, you wouldn't, in your field. Nevertheless, we are inclined to credit him with having done as much to check and reduce the pandemic neuroses of the Crazy Years as any other man, and more than any man left alive."

"Where is he?"

"Why, Chicago, I suppose. At the Institute."

"Get him here."

"Eh?"

"Get him down here. Get on that visiphone and locate him. Then have Steinke call the Port of Chicago, and hire a stratocar to stand by for him. I want to see him as soon as possible —before the day is out." King sat up in his chair with the air of a man who is once more master of himself and the situation. His spirit knew that warming replenishment that comes only with reaching a decision. The harassed expression was gone.

Silard looked dumbfounded. "But, superintendent," he expostulated, "you can't ring for Doctor Lentz as if he were a junior clerk. He's—he's *Lentz*."

"Certainly—that's why I want him. But I'm not a neurotic clubwoman looking for sympathy, either. He'll come. If necessary, turn on the heat from Washington. Have the White House call him. But get him here at once. Move!" King strode out of the office.

When Erickson came off watch he inquired around and found that Harper had left for town. Accordingly, he dispensed with dinner at the base, shifted into "drinkin' clothes", and allowed himself to be dispatched via tube to Paradise.

Paradise, Arizona, was a hard little boom town, which owed its existence to the breeder plant. It was dedicated exclusively to the serious business of detaching the personnel of the plant from their inordinate salaries. In this worthy project they received much cooperation from the plant personnel themselves, each of whom was receiving from twice to ten times as much money each pay day as he had ever received in any other job, and none of whom was certain of living long enough to justify saving for old age. Besides, the company carried a sinking fund in Manhattan for their dependents; why be stingy?

It was claimed, with some truth, that any entertainment or luxury obtainable in New York City could be purchased in Paradise. The local chamber of commerce had appropriated the slogan of Reno, Nevada, "Biggest Little City in the World." The Reno boosters retaliated by claiming that, while any town that close to the atomic breeder plant undeniably brought thoughts of death and the hereafter, Hell's Gates would be a more appropriate name.

Erickson started making the rounds. There were twenty-seven places licensed to sell liquor in the six blocks of the main street of Paradise. He expected to find Harper in one of them, and, knowing the man's habits and tastes, he expected to find him in the first two or three he tried.

He was not mistaken. He found Harper sitting alone at a table in the rear of deLancey's Sans Souci Bar. DeLancey's was a favorite of both of them. There was an old-fashioned comfort about its chrome-plated bar and red leather furniture that appealed to them more than did the spectacular fittings of the up-to-the-minute places. DeLancey was conservative; he stuck to indirect lighting and soft music; his hostesses were required to be fully clothed, even in the evening.

The fifth of Scotch in front of Harper was about two-thirds full. Erickson shoved three fingers in front of Harper's face and demanded, "Count!"

"Three," announced Harper. "Sit down, Gus."

"That's correct," Erickson agreed, sliding his big frame into a low-slung chair. "You'll do—for now. What was the outcome?"

"Have a drink. Not," he went on, "that this Scotch is any good. I think Lance has taken to watering it. I surrendered, horse and foot."

"Lance wouldn't do that—stick to that theory and you'll sink in the sidewalk up to your knees. How come you capitulated? I thought you planned to beat 'em about the head and shoulders, at least."

"I did," mourned Harper, "but, cripes, Gus. the chief is right. If a brain mechanic says you're punchy, he has *got* to back him up, and take you off the watch list. The chief can't afford to take a chance."

"Yeah, the chief's all right, but I can't learn to love our dear psychiatrists. Tell you what—let's find us one, and see if he can feel pain. I'll hold him while you slug 'im."

"Oh, forget it, Gus. Have a drink."

"A pious thought—but not Scotch. I'm going to have a martini; we ought to eat pretty soon."

"I'll have one, too."

"Do you good." Erickson lifted his blond head and bellowed, "Israfel!"

A large, black person appeared at his elbow. "Mistuh Erickson! Yes, suh!"

"Izzy, fetch two martinis. Make mine with Italian." He turned back to Harper. "What are you going to do now, Cal?"

"Radiation laboratory."

"Well, that's not so bad. I'd like to have a go at the matter of rocket fuels myself. I've got some ideas."

Harper looked mildly amused. "You mean atomic fuel for interplanetary flight? That problem's pretty well exhausted. No, son, the ionosphere is the ceiling until we think up something better than rockets. Of course, you *could* mount a pile in a ship, and figure out some jury rig to convert some of its output into push, but where does that get you? You would still have a terrible mass-ratio because of the shielding and I'm betting you couldn't convert one percent into thrust. That's disregarding the question of getting the company to lend you a power pile for anything that doesn't pay dividends."

Erickson looked balky. "I don't concede that you've covered all the alternatives. What have we got? The early rocket boys went right ahead trying to build better rockets, serene in the belief that, by the time they could build rockets good enough to fly to the moon, a fuel would be perfected that would do the trick. And they did build ships that were good enough—you could take any ship that makes the Antipodes run, and refit it for the moon—*if* you had a fuel that was adequate. But they haven't got it.

"And why not? Because we let 'em down, that's why. Because they're still depending on molecular energy, on chemical reactions, with atomic power sitting right here in our laps. It's not their fault—old D. D. Harriman had Rockets Consolidated underwrite the whole first issue of Antarctic Pitchblende, and took a big slice of it himself, in the expectation that we would produce something usable in the way of a concentrated rocket fuel. Did we do it? Like hell! The company went hog-wild for immediate commercial exploitation, and there's no atomic rocket fuel yet."

"But you haven't stated it properly," Harper objected. "There are just two forms of atomic power available, radioactivity and atomic disintegration. The first is too slow; the energy is there, but you can't wait years for it to come out—not in a rocket ship. The second we can only manage in a large power plant. There you are—stymied."

"We haven't really tried," Erickson answered. "The power is there; we ought to give 'em a decent fuel."

"What would you call a 'decent fuel'?"

Erickson ticked it off. "A small enough critical mass so that all, or almost all, the energy could be taken up as heat by the reaction mass—I'd like the reaction mass to be ordinary water. Shielding that would have to be no more than a lead and cadmium jacket. And the whole thing controllable to a fine point."

Harper laughed. "Ask for Angel's wings and be done with it. You couldn't store such fuel in a rocket; it would set itself off before it reached the jet chamber."

Erickson's Scandinavian stubbornness was just gathering for another try at the argument when the waiter arrived with the drinks. He set them down with a triumphant flourish. "There you are, suh!"

"Want to roll for them, Izzy?" Harper inquired.

"Don' mind if I do."

The Negro produced a leather dice cup and Harper rolled. He selected his combinations with care and managed to get four aces and jack in three rolls. Israfel took the cup. He rolled in the grand manner with a backwards twist to his wrist. His score finished at five kings, and he courteously accepted the price of six drinks. Harper stirred the engraved cubes with his forefinger.

"Izzy," he asked, "are these the same dice I rolled with?"

"Why, Mistuh Harper!" The black's expression was pained.

"Skip it," Harper conceded. "I should know better than to

gamble with you. I haven't won a roll from you in six weeks. What did you start to say, Gus?"

"I was just going to say that there ought to be a better way to get energy out of—"

But they were joined again, this time by something very seductive in an evening gown that appeared to have been sprayed on her lush figure. She was young, perhaps nineteen or twenty. "You boys lonely?" she asked as she flowed into a chair.

"Nice of you to ask, but we're not," Erickson denied with patient politeness. He jerked a thumb at a solitary figure seated across the room. "Go talk to Hannigan; he's not busy."

She followed his gesture with her eyes, and answered with faint scorn, "Him? He's no use. He's been like that for three weeks—hasn't spoken to a soul. If you ask me, I'd say that he was cracking up."

"That so?" he observed noncommittally. "Here—" He fished out a five-dollar bill and handed it to her. "Buy yourself a drink. Maybe we'll look you up later."

"Thanks, boys." The money disappeared under her clothing, and she stood up. "Just ask for Edith."

"Hannigan does look bad," Harper considered, noting the brooding stare and apathetic attitude, "and he has been awfully stand-offish lately, for him. Do you suppose we're obliged to report him?"

"Don't let it worry you," advised Erickson, "there's a spotter on the job now. Look." Harper followed his companion's eyes and recognized Dr. Mott of the psychological staff. He was leaning against the far end of the bar and nursing a tall glass, which gave him protective coloration. But his stance was such that his field of vision included not only Hannigan, but Erickson and Harper as well.

"Yeah, and he's studying us as well," Harper added. "Damn it to hell, why does it make my back hair rise just to lay eyes on one of them?"

The question was rhetorical, Erickson ignored it. "Let's get out of here," he suggested, "and have dinner somewhere else."

"O.K."

DeLancey himself waited on them as they left. "Going so soon, gentlemen?" he asked, in a voice that implied that their departure would leave him no reason to stay open. "Beautiful lobster thermidor tonight. If you do not like it, you need not pay." He smiled brightly.

"No sea food, Lance," Harper told him, "not tonight. Tell me—why do you stick around here when you know that the pile is bound to get you in the long run? Aren't you afraid of it?"

The tavernkeeper's eyebrows shot up. "Afraid of the pile? But it is my friend!"

"Makes you money, eh?"

"Oh, I do not mean that." He leaned toward them confidentially. "Five years ago I come here to make some money quickly for my family before my cancer of the stomach, it kills me. At the clinic, with the wonderful new radiants you gentlemen make with the aid of the Big Bomb, I am cured—I live again. No, I am not afraid of the pile; it is my good friend."

"Suppose it blows up?"

"When the good Lord needs me, he will take me." He crossed himself quickly.

As they turned away, Erickson commented in a low voice to Harper, "There's your answer, Cal—if all us engineers had his faith, the job wouldn't get us down."

Harper was unconvinced. "I don't know," he mused. "I don't think it's faith; I think it's lack of imagination—and knowledge."

Notwithstanding King's confidence, Lentz did not show up until the next day. The superintendent was subconsciously a little surprised at his visitor's appearance. He had pictured a master psychologist as wearing flowing hair, an imperial, and having piercing black eyes. But this man was not overly tall, was heavy in his framework, and fat—almost gross. He might have been a butcher. Little, piggy, faded-blue eyes peered merrily out from beneath shaggy blond brows. There was no hair anywhere else on the enormous skull, and the ape-like jaw was smooth and pink. He was dressed in mussed pajamas of unbleached linen. A long cigaret holder jutted permanently from one corner of a wide mouth, widened still more by a smile which suggested unmalicious amusement at the worst that life, or men, could do. He had gusto.

King found him remarkably easy to talk to.

At Lentz' suggestion the Superintendent went first into the

history of atomic power plants, how the fission of the uranium atom by Dr. Otto Hahn in December, 1938, had opened up the way to atomic power. The door was opened just a crack; the process to be self perpetuating and commercially usable required an enormously greater knowledge than there was available in the entire civilized world at that time.

In 1938 the amount of separated uranium-235 in the world was not the mass of the head of a pin. Plutonium was unheard of. Atomic power was abstruse theory and a single, esoteric laboratory experiment. World War II, the Manhattan Project, and Hiroshima changed that; by late 1945 prophets were rushing into print with predictions of atomic power, cheap, almost free atomic power, for everyone in a year or two.

It did not work out that way. The Manhattan Project had been run with the single-minded purpose of making weapons; the engineering of atomc power was still in the future.

The far future, so it seemed. The uranium piles used to make the atom bomb were literally no good for commercial power; they were designed to throw away power as a useless byproduct, nor could the design of a pile, once in operation, be changed. A design—on paper—for an economic, commercial power pile could be made, but it had two serious hitches. The first was that such a pile would give off energy with such fury, if operated at a commercially satisfactory level, that there was no known way of accepting that energy and putting it to work.

This problem was solved first. A modification of the Douglas-Martin power screens, originally designed to turn the radiant energy of the sun (a natural atomic power pile itself) directly into electrical power, was used to receive the radiant fury of uranium fission and carry it away as electrical current.

The second hitch seemed to be no hitch at all. An "enriched" pile—one in which U-235 or plutonium had been added to natural uranium—was a quite satisfactory source of commercial power. We knew how to get U-235 and plutonium; that was the primary accomplishment of the Manhattan Project.

Or did we know how? Hanford produced plutonium; Oak Ridge extracted U-235, true—but the Hanford piles used more U-235 than they produced plutonium and Oak Ridge produced nothing but merely separated out the 7/10 of one percent of U-235 in natural uranium and "threw away" the 99%-plus of the energy which was still locked in the discarded U-238. Commercially ridiculous, economically fantastic!

But there was another way to breed plutonium, by means of a high-energy, unmoderated pile of natural uranium somewhat enriched. At a million electron volts or more U-238 will fission; at somewhat lower energies it turns to plutonium. Such a pile supplies its own "fire" and produces more "fuel" than it uses; it could breed fuel for many other power piles of the usual moderated sort.

But an unmoderated power pile is almost by definition an atom bomb.

The very name "pile" comes from the pile of graphite bricks and uranium slugs set up in a squash court at the University of Chicago at the very beginning of the Manhattan Project. Such a pile, moderated by graphite or heavy water *cannot* explode.

Nobody knew what an unmoderated, high-energy pile might do. It would breed plutonium in great quantities—but would it explode? Explode with such violence as to make the Nagasaki bomb seem like a popgun?

Nobody knew.

In the meantime the power-hungry technology of the United States grew still more demanding. The Douglas-Martin sunpower screens met the immediate crisis when oil became too scarce to be wasted as fuel, but sunpower was limited to about one horsepower per square yard and was at the mercy of the weather.

Atomic power was needed—demanded.

Atomic engineers lived through the period in an agony of indecision. Perhaps a breeder pile could be controlled. Or perhaps if it did go out of control it would simply blow itself apart and thus extinguish its own fires. Perhaps it would explode like several atom bombs but with low efficiency. But it might—it just might—explode its whole mass of many tons of uranium at once and destroy the human race in the process.

There is an old story, not true, which tells of a scientist who had made a machine which would instantly destroy the world, so he believed, if he closed one switch. He wanted to know whether or not he was right. So he closed the switch—and never found out.

The atomic engineers were afraid to close the switch.

"It was Destry's mechanics of infinitesimals that showed

a way out of the dilemma," King went on. "His equations appeared to predict that such an atomic explosion, once started, would disrupt the molar mass enclosing it so rapidly that neutron loss through the outer surface of the fragments would dampen the progression of the atomic explosion to zero before complete explosion could be reached. In an atom bomb such damping actually occurs.

"For the mass we use in the pile, his equations predict a possible force of explosion one-seventh of one percent of the force of complete explosion. That alone, of course, would be incomprehensibly destructive—enough to wreck this end of the state. Personally, I've never been sure that is all that would happen."

"Then why did you accept this job?" inquired Lentz.

King fiddled with items on his desk before replying. "I couldn't turn it down, doctor—I *couldn't*. If I had refused, they would have gotten someone else—and it was an opportunity that comes to a physicist once in history."

Lentz nodded. "And probably they would have gotten someone not as competent. I understand, Dr. King—you were compelled by the 'truth-tropism' of the scientist. He must go where the data is to be found, even if it kills him. But about this fellow Destry, I've never liked his mathematics; he postulates too much."

King looked up in quick surprise, then recalled that this was the man who had refined and given rigor to the calculus of statement. "That's just the hitch," he agreed. "His work is brilliant, but I've never been sure that his predictions were worth the paper they were written on. Nor, apparently," he added bitterly, "do my junior engineers."

He told the psychiatrist of the difficulties they had had with personnel, of how the most carefully selected men would, sooner or later, crack under the strain. "At first I thought it might be some degenerating effect from the neutron radiation that leaks out through the shielding, so we improved the screening and the personal armor. But it didn't help. One young fellow who had joined us after the new screening was installed became violent at dinner one night, and insisted that a pork chop was about to explode. I hate to think of what might have happened if he had been on duty at the pile when he blew up."

The inauguration of the system of constant psychological observation had greatly reduced the probability of acute danger resulting from a watch engineer cracking up, but King was forced to admit that the system was not a success; there had actually been a marked increase in psychoneuroses, dating from that time.

"And that's the picture, Dr. Lentz. It gets worse all the time. It's getting me now. The strain is telling on me; I can't sleep, and I don't think my judgment is as good as it used to be—I have trouble making up my mind, or coming to a decision. Do you think you can do anything for us?"

But Lentz had no immediate relief for his anxiety. "Not so fast, superintendent," he countered. "You have given me the background, but I have no real data as yet. I must look around for a while, smell out the situation for myself, talk to your engineers, perhaps have a few drinks with them, and get acquainted. That is possible, is it not? Then in a few days, maybe, we know where we stand."

King had no alternative but to agree.

"And it is well that your young men do not know what I am here for. Suppose I am your old friend, a visiting physicist, eh?"

"Why, yes—of course. I can see to it that that idea gets around. But say—" King was reminded again of something that had bothered him from the time Silard had first suggested Lentz' name. "May I ask a personal question?"

The merry eyes were undisturbed. "Go ahead."

"I can't help but be surprised that one man should attain eminence in two such widely differing fields as psychology and mathematics. And right now I'm perfectly convinced of your ability to pass yourself off as a physicist. I don't understand it."

The smile was more amused, without being in the least patronizing, nor offensive. "Same subject," he answered.

"Eh? How's that—"

"Or rather, both mathematical physics and psychology are branches of the same subject, symbology. You are a specialist; it would not necessarily come to your attention."

"I still don't follow you."

"No? Man lives in a world of ideas. Any phenomenon is so complex that he cannot possibly grasp the whole of it. He abstracts certain characteristics of a given phenomenon as an idea, then represents that idea as a symbol, be it a word or a mathematical sign. Human reaction is almost entirely reaction to symbols, and only negligibly to phenomena. As a matter of fact," he continued, removing the cigaret holder from his mouth and settling into his subject, "it can be demonstrated that the human mind can think only in terms of symbols.

"When we think, we let symbols operate on other symbols in certain, set fashions—rules of logic, or rules of mathematics. If the symbols have been abstracted so that they are structurally similar to the phenomena they stand for, and if the symbol operations are similar in structure and order to the operations of phenomena in the real world, we think sanely. If our logic-mathematics, or our word-symbols, have been poorly chosen, we think not-sanely.

"In mathematical physics you are concerned with making your symbology fit physical phenomena. In psychiatry I am concerned with precisely the same thing, except that I am more immediately concerned with the man who does the thinking than with the phenomena he is thinking about. But the same subject, always the same subject."

"We're not getting anyplace, Gus." Harper put down his slide rule and frowned.

"Seems like it, Cal," Erickson grudgingly admitted. "Damn it, though—there ought to be some reasonable way of tackling the problem. What do we need? Some form of concentrated, controllable power for rocket fuel. What have we got? Power galore through fission. There must be some way to bottle that power, and serve it out when we need it—and the answer is some place in one of the radioactive series. I *know* it." He stared glumly around the laboratory as if expecting to find the answer written somewhere on the lead-sheathed walls.

"Don't be so down in the mouth about it. You've got me convinced there is an answer; let's figure out how to find it. In the first place the three natural radioactive series are out, aren't they?"

"Yes . . . at least we had agreed that all that ground had been fully covered before."

"Okay; we have to assume that previous investigators have done what their notes show they have done—otherwise we might as well not believe anything, and start checking on everybody from Archimedes to date. Maybe that is indicated, but Methuselah himself couldn't carry out such an assignment. What have we got left?"

"Artificial radioactives."

"All right. Let's set up a list of them, both those that have been made up to now, and those that might possibly be made in the future. Call that our group or rather, field, if you want to be pedantic about definitions. There are a limited number of operations that can be performed on each member of the group, and on the members taken in combination. Set it up."

Erickson did so, using the curious curlicues of the calculus of statement. Harper nodded. "All right—expand it."

Erickson looked up after a few moments, and asked, "Cal, have you any idea how many terms there are in the expansion?"

"No . . . hundreds, maybe thousands, I suppose."

"You're conservative. It reaches four figures without considering possible new radioactives. We couldn't finish such a research in a century." He chucked his pencil down and looked morose.

Cal Harper looked at him curiously, but with sympathy. "Gus," he said gently, "the job isn't getting you, too, is it?"

"I don't think so. Why?"

"I never saw you so willing to give up anything before. Naturally you and I will never finish any such job, but at the very worst we will have eliminated a lot of wrong answers for somebody else. Look at Edison—sixty years of experimenting, twenty hours a day, yet he never found out the one thing he was most interested in knowing. I guess if he could take it, we can."

Erickson pulled out of his funk to some extent. "I suppose so," he agreed. "Anyhow, maybe we could work out some techniques for carrying a lot of experiments simultaneously."

Harper slapped him on the shoulder. "That's the ol' fight. Besides—we may not need to finish the research, or anything like it, to find a satisfactory fuel. The way I see it, there are probably a dozen, maybe a hundred, right answers. We may run across one of them any day. Anyhow, since you're willing to give me a hand with it in your off-watch time, I'm game to peck away at it till hell freezes."

Lentz puttered around the plant and the administration center for several days, until he was known to everyone by sight. He made himself pleasant and asked questions. He was soon regarded as a harmless nuisance, to be tolerated because he was a friend of the superintendent. He even poked his nose into the commercial power end of the plant, and had the radiation-to-electric-power sequence explained to him in detail. This alone would have been sufficient to disarm any suspicion that he might be a psychiatrist, for the staff psychiatrists paid no attention to the hard-bitten technicians of the power-conversion unit. There was no need to; mental instability on their part could not affect the pile, nor were they subject to the mankilling strain of social responsibility. Theirs was simply a job personally dangerous, a type of strain strong men have been inured to since the jungle.

In due course he got around to the unit of the radiation laboratory set aside for Calvin Harper's use. He rang the bell and waited. Harper answered the door, his anti-radiation helmet shoved back from his face like some grotesque sunbonnet. "What is it?" he asked. "Oh—it's you, Doctor Lentz. Did you want to see me?"

"Why, yes, and no," the older man answered, "I was just looking around the experimental station and wondered what you do in here. Will I be in the way?"

"Not at all. Come in. Gus!"

Erickson got up from where he had been fussing over the power leads to their trigger—a modified betatron rather than a resonant accelerator. "Hello."

"Gus, this is Doctor Lentz—Gus Erickson."

"We've met," said Erickson, pulling off his gauntlet to shake hands. He had had a couple of drinks with Lentz in town and considered him a "nice old duck." "You're just between shows, but stick around and we'll start another run—not that there is much to see."

While Erickson continued with the set-up, Harper conducted Lentz around the laboratory, explaining the line of research they were conducting, as happy as a father showing off twins. The psychiatrist listened with one ear and made appropriate comments while he studied the young scientist for signs of the instability he had noted to be recorded against him.

"You see," Harper explained, oblivious to the interest in himself, "we are testing radioactive materials to see if we can produce disintegration of the sort that takes place in the pile, but in a minute, almost microscopic, mass. If we are successful, we can use the breeder pile to make a safe, convenient, atomic fuel for rockets—or for anything else." He went on to explain their schedule of experimentation.

"I see," Lentz observed politely. "What element are you examining now?"

Harper told him. "But it's not a case of examining one element—we've finished Isotope II of this element with negative results. Our schedule calls next for running the same test on Isotope V. Like this." He hauled out a lead capsule, and showed the label to Lentz. He hurried away to the shield around the target of the betatron, left open by Erickson. Lentz saw that he had opened the capsule, and was performing some operation on it with a long pair of tongs in a gingerly manner, having first lowered his helmet. Then he closed and clamped the target shield.

"Okay, Gus?" he called out. "Ready to roll?"

"Yeah, I guess so," Erickson assured him, coming around from behind the ponderous apparatus, and rejoining them. They crowded behind a thick metal and concrete shield that cut them off from direct sight of the set-up.

"Will I need to put on armor?" inquired Lentz.

"No," Erickson reassured him, "we wear it because we are around the stuff day in and day out. You just stay behind the shield and you'll be all right."

Erickson glanced at Harper, who nodded, and fixed his eyes on a panel of instruments mounted behind the shield. Lentz saw Erickson press a push button at the top of the board, then heard a series of relays click on the far side of the shield. There was a short moment of silence.

The floor slapped his feet like some incredible bastinado. The concussion that beat on his ears was so intense that it paralyzed the auditory nerve almost before it could be recorded as sound. The air-conducted concussion wave flailed every inch of his body with a single, stinging, numbing blow. As he picked himself up, he found he was trembling uncontrollably and realized, for the first time, that he was getting old.

Harper was seated on the floor and had commenced to bleed from the nose. Erickson had gotten up, his cheek was cut. He touched a hand to the wound, then stood there, regarding the blood on his fingers with a puzzled expression on his face.

"Are you hurt?" Lentz inquired inanely. "What happened?"

Harper cut in. "Gus, we've done it! We've done it! Isotope Five has turned the trick!"

Erickson looked still more bemused. "Five?" he said stupidly, "—but that wasn't Five, that was Isotope II. I put it in myself."

"*You* put it in? *I* put it in! It was Five, I tell you!"

They stood staring at each other, still confused by the explosion, and each a little annoyed at the boneheaded stupidity the other displayed in the face of the obvious. Lentz diffidently interceded.

"Wait a minute, boys," he suggested, "maybe there's a reason— Gus, you placed a quantity of the second isotope in the receiver?"

"Why, yes, certainly. I wasn't satisfied with the last run, and I wanted to check it."

Lentz nodded. "It's my fault, gentlemen," he admitted ruefully. "I came in, disturbed your routine, and both of you charged the receiver. I know Harper did, for I saw him do it —with Isotope V. I'm sorry."

Understanding broke over Harper's face, and he slapped the older man on the shoulder. "Don't be sorry," he laughed; "you can come around to our lab and help us make mistakes any time you feel in the mood— Can't he, Gus? This is the answer, Doctor Lentz, this is it!"

"But," the psychiatrist pointed out, "you don't know which isotope blew up."

"Nor care," Harper supplemented. "Maybe it was both, taken together. But we *will* know—this business is cracked now; we'll soon have it open." He gazed happily around at the wreckage.

In spite of Superintendent King's anxiety, Lentz refused to be hurried in passing judgment on the situation. Consequently, when he did present himself at King's office, and announced that he was ready to report, King was pleasantly surprised as well as relieved. "Well, I'm delighted," he said. "Sit down, doctor, sit down. Have a cigar. What do we do about it?"

But Lentz stuck to his perennial cigaret, and refused to be hurried. "I must have some information first: how important," he demanded, "is the power from your plant?"

King understood the implication at once. "If you are thinking about shutting down the plant for more than a limited period, it can't be done."

"Why not? If the figures supplied me are correct, your power output is less than thirteen percent of the total power used in the country."

"Yes, that is true, but we also supply another thirteen percent second hand through the plutonium we breed here—

and you haven't analyzed the items that make up the balance. A lot of it is domestic power which householders get from sunscreens located on their roofs. Another big slice is power for the moving roadways—that's sunpower again. The portion we provide here directly or indirectly is the main power source for most of the heavy industries—steel, plastics, lithics, all kinds of manufacturing and processing. You might as well cut the heart out of a man—"

"But the food industry isn't basically dependent on you?" Lentz persisted.

"No . . . Food isn't basically a power industry—although we do supply a certain percentage of the power used in processing. I see your point, and will go on, and concede that transportation, that is to say, distribution of food, could get along without us. But good heavens, Doctor, you can't stop atomic power without causing the biggest panic this country has ever seen. It's the keystone of our whole industrial system."

"The country has lived through panics before, and we got past the oil shortage safely."

"Yes—because sunpower and atomic power came along to take the place of oil. You don't realize what this would mean, Doctor. It would be worse than a war; in a system like ours, one thing depends on another. If you cut off the heavy industries all at once, everything else stops, too."

"Nevertheless, you had better dump the pile." The uranium in the pile was molten, its temperature being greater than twenty-four hundred degrees centigrade. The pile could be dumped into a group of small containers, when it was desired to shut it down. The mass into any one container would be too small to maintain progressive atomic disintegration.

King glanced involuntarily at the glass-enclosed relay mounted on his office wall, by which he, as well as the engineer on duty, could dump the pile, if need be. "But I couldn't do that . . . or rather, if I did, the plant wouldn't stay shut down. The directors would simply replace me with someone who *would* operate it."

"You're right, of course." Lentz silently considered the situation for some time, then said, "Superintendent, will you order a car to fly me back to Chicago?"

"You're going, doctor?"

"Yes." He took the cigaret holder from his face, and, for once, the smile of Olympian detachment was gone completely. His entire manner was sober, even tragic. "Short of shutting down the plant, there is no solution to your problem —none whatsoever!

"I owe you a full explanation," he continued, presently. "You are confronted here with recurring instances of situational psychoneurosis. Roughly, the symptoms manifest themselves as anxiety neurosis, or some form of hysteria. The partial amnesia of your secretary, Steinke, is a good example of the latter. He might be cured with shock technique, but it would hardly be a kindness, as he has achieved a stable adjustment which puts him beyond the reach of the strain he could not stand.

"That other young fellow, Harper, whose blowup was the immediate cause of you sending for me, is an anxiety case. When the cause of the anxiety was eliminated from his matrix, he at once regained full sanity. But keep a close watch on his friend, Erickson—

"However, it is the cause, and prevention, of situational psychoneurosis we are concerned with here, rather than the forms in which it is manifested. In plain language, psychoneurosis situational simply refers to the common fact that, if you put a man in a situation that worries him more than he can stand, in time he blows up, one way or another.

"That is precisely the situation here. You take sensitive, intelligent young men, impress them with the fact that a single slip on their part, or even some fortuitous circumstance beyond their control, will result in the death of God knows how many other people, and then expect them to remain sane. It's ridiculous—impossible!"

"But good heavens, doctor!—there must be some answer— There must!" He got up and paced around the room. Lentz noted, with pity, that King himself was riding the ragged edge of the very condition they were discussing.

"No," he said slowly. "No . . . let me explain. You don't dare entrust control to less sensitive, less socially conscious men. You might as well turn the controls over to a mindless idiot. And to psychoneurosis situational there are but two cures. The first obtains when the psychosis results from a misevaluation of environment. That cure calls for semantic readjustment. One assists the patient to evaluate correctly his environment. The worry disappears because there never was a real reason for worry in the situation itself, but simply in the wrong meaning the patient's mind had assigned to it.

"The second case is when the patient has correctly evaluated the situation, and rightly finds in it cause for extreme worry. His worry is perfectly sane and proper, but he cannot stand up under it indefinitely; it drives him crazy. The only possible cure is to change the situation. I have stayed here long enough to assure myself that such is the condition here. You engineers have correctly evaluated the public danger of this thing, and it will, with dreadful certainty, drive all of you crazy!

"The only possible solution is to dump the pile—and leave it dumped."

King had continued his nervous pacing of the floor, as if the walls of the room itself were the cage of his dilemma. Now he stopped and appealed once more to the psychiatrist. "Isn't there *anything* I can do?"

"Nothing to cure. To alleviate—well, possibly."

"How?"

"Situational psychosis results from adrenalin exhaustion. When a man is placed under a nervous strain, his adrenal glands increase their secretion to help compensate for the strain. If the strain is too great and lasts too long, the adrenals aren't equal to the task, and he cracks. That is what you have here. Adrenalin therapy might stave off a mental breakdown, but it most assuredly would hasten a physical breakdown. But that would be safer from a viewpoint of public welfare—even though it assumes that physicists are expendable!

"Another thing occurs to me: If you selected any new watch engineers from the membership of churches that practice the confessional, it would increase the length of their usefulness."

King was plainly surprised. "I don't follow you."

"The patient unloads most of his worry on his confessor, who is not himself actually confronted by the situation, and can stand it. That is simply an ameliorative, however. I am convinced that, in this situation, eventual insanity is inevitable. But there is a lot of good sense in the confessional," he mused. "It fills a basic human need. I think that is why the early psychoanalysts were so surprisingly successful, for all their limited knowledge." He fell silent for a while, then added, "If you will be so kind as to order a stratocab for me—"

"You've nothing more to suggest?"

"No. You had better turn your psychological staff loose on means of alleviation; they're able men, all of them."

King pressed a switch, and spoke briefly to Steinke. Turning back to Lentz, he said, "You'll wait here until your car is ready?"

Lentz judged correctly that King desired it, and agreed.

Presently the tube delivery on King's desk went "Ping!" The superintendent removed a small white pasteboard, a calling card. He studied it with surprise and passed it over to Lentz. "I can't imagine why he should be calling on me," he observed, and added, "Would you like to meet him?"

Lentz read:

> THOMAS P. HARRINGTON
> Captain (Mathematics)
> United States Navy
>
> Director,
> U.S. Naval Observatory

"But I do know him," he said. "I'd be very pleased to see him."

Harrington was a man with something on his mind. He seemed relieved when Steinke had finished ushering him in and had returned to the outer office. He commenced to speak at once, turning to Lentz, who was nearer to him than King. "You're King? Why, Doctor Lentz! What are you doing here?"

"Visiting," answered Lentz, accurately but incompletely, as he shook hands. "This is Superintendent King over here. Superintendent King—Captain Harrington."

"How do you do, Captain—it's a pleasure to have you here."

"It's an honor to be here, sir."

"Sit down?"

"Thanks." He accepted a chair, and laid a briefcase on a corner of King's desk. "Superintendent, you are entitled to an explanation as to why I have broken in on you like this—"

"Glad to have you." In fact, the routine of formal politeness was an anodyne to King's frayed nerves.

"That's kind of you, but— That secretary chap, the one that

brought me in here, would it be too much to ask for you to tell him to forget my name? I know it seems strange—"

"Not at all." King was mystified, but willing to grant any reasonable request of a distinguished colleague in science. He summoned Steinke to the interoffice visiphone and gave him his orders.

Lentz stood up, and indicated that he was about to leave. He caught Harrington's eye. "I think you want a private palaver, Captain."

King looked from Harrington to Lentz, and back to Harrington. The astronomer showed momentary indecision, then protested, "I have no objection at all myself; it's up to Doctor King. As a matter of fact," he added, "it might be a very good thing if you did sit in on it."

"I don't know what it is, Captain," observed King, "that you want to see me about, but Doctor Lentz is already here in a confidential capacity."

"Good! Then that's settled . . . I'll get right down to business. Doctor King, you know Destry's mechanics of infinitesimals?"

"Naturally." Lentz cocked a brow at King, who chose to ignore it.

"Yes, of course. Do you remember theorem six, and the transformation between equations thirteen and fourteen?"

"I think so, but I'd want to see them." King got up and went over to a bookcase. Harrington stayed him with a hand.

"Don't bother. I have them here." He hauled out a key, unlocked his briefcase, and drew out a large, much-thumbed, loose-leaf notebook. "Here. You, too, Doctor Lentz. Are you familiar with this development?"

Lentz nodded. "I've had occasion to look into them."

"Good—I think it's agreed that the step between thirteen and fourteen is the key to the whole matter. Now the change from thirteen to fourteen looks perfectly valid—and would be, in some fields. But suppose we expand it to show every possible phase of the matter, every link in the chain of reasoning."

He turned a page, and showed them the same two equations broken down into nine intermediate equations. He placed a finger under an associated group of mathematic symbols. "Do you see that? Do you see what that implies?" He peered anxiously at their faces.

King studied it, his lips moving. "Yes. . . . I believe I do see. Odd . . . I never looked at it just that way before—yet I've studied those equations until I've dreamed about them." He turned to Lentz. "Do you agree, Doctor?"

Lentz nodded slowly. "I believe so . . . Yes, I think I may say so."

Harrington should have been pleased; he wasn't. "I had hoped you could tell me I was wrong," he said, almost petulantly, "but I'm afraid there is no further doubt about it. Doctor Destry included an assumption valid in molar physics, but for which we have absolutely no assurance in atomic physics. I suppose you realize what this means to you, Doctor King?"

King's voice was a dry whisper. "Yes," he said, "yes . . . It means that if the Big Bomb out there ever blows up, we must assume that it will all go up all at once, rather than the way Destry predicted . . . and God help the human race!"

Captain Harrington cleared his throat to break the silence that followed. "Superintendent," he said, "I would not have ventured to call had it been simply a matter of disagreement as to interpretation of theoretical predictions—"

"You have something more to go on?"

"Yes, and no. Probably you gentlemen think of the Naval Observatory as being exclusively preoccupied with ephmerides and tide tables. In a way you would be right—but we still have some time to devote to research as long as it doesn't cut into the appropriation. My special interest has always been lunar theory.

"I don't mean lunar ballistics," he continued, "I mean the much more interesting problem of its origin and history, the problem the younger Darwin struggled with, as well as my illustrious predecessor, Captain T. J. J. See. I think that it is obvious that any theory of lunar origin and history must take into account the surface features of the moon—especially the mountains, the craters, that mark its face so prominently."

He paused momentarily, and Superintendent King put in, "Just a minute, Captain—I may be stupid, or perhaps I missed something, but—is there a connection between what we were discussing before and lunar theory?"

"Bear with me for a few moments, Doctor King," Harrington apologized; "there is a connection—at least, I'm *afraid* there is a connection—but I would rather present my points in their proper order before making my conclusions." They granted him an alert silence; he went on:

"Although we are in the habit of referring to the 'craters' of the moon, we know they are not volcanic craters. Superficially, they follow none of the rules of terrestrial volcanoes in appearance or distribution, but when Rutter came out in 1952 with his monograph on the dynamics of vulcanology, he proved rather conclusively that the lunar craters could not be caused by anything that we know as volcanic action.

"That left the bombardment theory as the simplest hypothesis. It looks good, on the face of it, and a few minutes spent throwing pebbles in to a patch of mud will convince anyone that the lunar craters could have been formed by falling meteors.

"But there are difficulties. If the moon was struck so repeatedly, why not the earth? It hardly seems necessary to mention that the earth's atmosphere would be no protection against masses big enough to form craters like Endymion, or Plato. And if they fell after the moon was a dead world while the earth was still young enough to change its face and erase the marks of bombardment, why did the meteors avoid so nearly completely the great dry basins we call the seas?

"I want to cut this short; you'll find the data and the mathematical investigations from the data here in my notes. There is one other major objection to the meteor-bombardment theory: the great rays that spread from Tycho across almost the entire surface of the moon. It makes the moon look like a crystal ball that had been struck with a hammer, and impact from outside seems evident, but there are difficulties. The striking mass, our hypothetical meteor, must have been smaller than the present crater of Tycho, but it must have the mass and speed to crack an entire planet.

"Work it out for yourself—you must either postulate a chunk out of the core of a dwarf star, or speeds such as we have never observed within the system. It's conceivable but a far-fetched explanation."

He turned to King. "Doctor, does anything occur to you that might account for a phenomenon like Tycho?"

The Superintendent grasped the arms of his chair, then glanced at his palms. He fumbled for a handkerchief, and wiped them. "Go ahead," he said, almost inaudibly.

"Very well then—" Harrington drew out of his briefcase a large photograph of the moon—a beautiful full-moon portrait made at Lick. "I want you to imagine the moon as she might have been sometime in the past. The dark areas we call the 'Seas' are actual oceans. It has an atmosphere, perhaps a heavier gas than oxygen and nitrogen, but an active gas, capable of supporting some conceivable form of life.

"For this is an inhabited planet, inhabited by intelligent beings, beings capable of discovering atomic power and exploiting it!"

He pointed out on the photograph, near the southern limb, the lime-white circle of Tycho, with its shining, incredible, thousand-mile-long rays spreading, thrusting, jutting out from it. "Here . . . here at Tycho was located their main atomic plant." He moved his finger to a point near the equator, and somewhat east of meridian—the point where three great dark areas merged, *Mare Nubium, Mare Imbrium, Oceanus Procellarum*—and picked out two bright splotches surrounded also by rays, but shorter, less distinct, and wavy. "And here at Copernicus and at Kepler, on islands at the middle of a great ocean, were secondary power stations."

He paused, and interpolated soberly, "Perhaps they knew the danger they ran, but wanted power so badly that they were willing to gamble the life of their race. Perhaps they were ignorant of the ruinous possibilities of their little machines, or perhaps their mathematicians assured them that it could not happen.

"But we will never know . . . no one can ever know. For it blew up, and killed them—and it killed their planet.

"It whisked off the gassy envelope and blew it into outer space. It may even have set up a chain reaction in that atmosphere. It blasted great chunks of the planet's crust. Perhaps some of that escaped completely, too, but all that did not reach the speed of escape fell back down in time and splashed great ring-shaped craters in the land.

"The oceans cushioned the shock; only the more massive fragments formed craters through the water. Perhaps some life still remained in those ocean depths. If so, it was doomed to die—for the water, unprotected by atmospheric pressure, could not remain liquid and must inevitably escape in time to outer space. Its life blood drained away. The planet was dead —dead by suicide!"

He met the grave eyes of his two silent listeners with an expression almost of appeal. "Gentlemen—this is only a theory, I realize . . . only a theory, a dream, a nightmare— But it has kept me awake so many nights that I had to come tell you about it, and see if you saw it the same way I do. As for the mechanics of it, it's all in there, in my notes. You can check it —and I pray that you find some error! But it is the only lunar theory I have examined which included all of the known data, and accounted for all of them."

He appeared to have finished; Lentz spoke up. "Suppose, Captain, suppose we check your mathematics and find no flaw —what then?"

Harrington flung out his hands. "That's what I came here to find out!"

Although Lentz had asked the question, Harrington directed the appeal to King. The superintendent looked up; his eyes met the astronomer's, wavered, and dropped again. "There's nothing to be done," he said dully, "nothing at all."

Harrington stared at him in open amazement. "But good God, man!" he burst out. "Don't you see it? That pile has *got* to be disassembled—at once!"

"Take it easy, Captain." Lentz's calm voice was a spray of cold water. "And don't be too harsh on poor King—this worries him even more than it does you. What he means is this; we're not faced with a problem in physics, but with a political and economic situation. Let's put it this way: King can no more dump his plant than a peasant with a vineyard on the slopes of Mount Vesuvius can abandon his holdings and pauperize his family simply because there will be an eruption someday.

"King doesn't own that plant out there; he's only the custodian. If he dumps it against the wishes of the legal owners, they'll simply oust him and put in someone more amenable. No, we have to convince the owners."

"The President could make them do it," suggested Harrington. "I could get to the President—"

"No doubt you could, through your department. And you might even convince him. But could he help much?"

"Why, of course he could. He's the *President!*"

"Wait a minute. You're Director of the Naval Observatory; suppose you took a sledge hammer and tried to smash the big telescope—how far would you get?"

"Not very far," Harrington conceded. "We guard the big fellow pretty closely."

"Nor can the President act in an arbitrary manner," Lentz persisted. "He's not an unlimited monarch. If he shuts down this plant without due process of law, the federal courts will tie him in knots. I admit that Congress isn't helpless, since the Atomic Energy Commission takes orders from it, but—would you like to try to give a congressional committee a course in the mechanics of infinitesimals?"

Harrington readily stipulated the point. "But there is another way," he pointed out. "Congress is responsive to public opinion. What we need to do is to convince the public that the pile is a menace to everybody. That could be done without ever trying to explain things in terms of higher mathematics."

"Certainly it could," Lentz agreed. "You could go on the air with it and scare everybody half to death. You could create the damnedest panic this slightly slug-nutty country has ever seen. No, thank you. I, for one, would rather have us all take the chance of being quietly killed than bring on a mass psychosis that would destroy the culture we are building up. I think one taste of the Crazy Years is enough."

"Well, then, what do *you* suggest?"

Lentz considered shortly, then answered, "All I see is a forlorn hope. We've got to work on the Board of Directors and try to beat some sense in their heads."

King, who had been following the discussion with attention in spite of his tired despondency, interjected a remark. "How would you go about that?"

"I don't know," Lentz admitted. "It will take some thinking. But it seems the most fruitful line of approach. If it doesn't work, we can always fall back on Harrington's notion of publicity—I don't insist that the world commit suicide to satisfy my criteria of evaluation."

Harrington glanced at his wrist watch—a bulky affair—and whistled. "Good heavens," he exclaimed, "I forgot the time! I'm supposed officially to be at the Flagstaff Observatory."

King had automatically noted the time shown by the Captain's watch as it was displayed. "But it can't be that late," he had objected. Harrington looked puzzled, then laughed.

"It isn't—not by two hours. We are in zone plus-seven; this shows zone plus-five—it's radio-synchronized with the master clock at Washington."

"Did you say radio-synchronized?"

"Yes. Clever, isn't it?" He held it out for inspection. "I call

it a telechronometer; it's the only one of its sort to date. My
nephew designed it for me. He's a bright one, that boy. He'll
go far. That is"—his face clouded, as if the little interlude
had only served to emphasize the tragedy that hung over
them—"if any of us live that long!"

A signal light glowed at King's desk, and Steinke's face
showed on the communicator screen. King answered him,
then said, "Your car is ready, Doctor Lentz."

"Let Captain Harrington have it."

"Then you're not going back to Chicago?"

"No. The situation has changed. If you want me, I'm
stringing along."

The following Friday Steinke ushered Lentz into King's
office. King looked almost happy as he shook hands. "When
did you ground, Doctor? I didn't expect you back for another
hour, or so."

"Just now. I hired a cab instead of waiting for the shuttle."

"Any luck?" King demanded.

"None. The same answer they gave you: 'The Company is
assured by independent experts that Destry's mechanics is
valid, and sees no reason to encourage an hysterical attitude
among its employees.' "

King tapped on his desk top, his eyes unfocused. Then,
hitching himself around to face Lentz directly, he said, "Do
you suppose the Chairman is right?"

"How?"

"Could the three of us, you, me, and Harrington, have gone
off the deep end, slipped mentally?"

"No."

"You're sure?"

"Certain. I looked up some independent experts of my
own, not retained by the Company, and had them check Harrington's work. It checks." Lentz purposely neglected to mention that he had done so partly because he was none too sure
of King's present mental stability.

King sat up briskly, reached out and stabbed a push button.
"I am going to make one more try," he explained, "to see if I
can't throw a scare into Dixon's thick head. Steinke," he said
to the communicator, "get me Mr. Dixon on the screen."

"Yes, sir."

In about two minutes the visiphone screen came to life and
showed the features of Chairman Dixon. He was transmitting,

not from his office, but from the boardroom of the power syndicate in Jersey City. "Yes?" he said. "What is it, Superintendent?" His manner was somehow both querulous and affable.

"Mr. Dixon," King began, "I've called to try to impress on you the seriousness of the Company's action. I stake my scientific reputation that Harrington has proved completely——"

"Oh, that? Mr. King, I thought you understood that that was a closed matter."

"But Mr. Dixon——"

"Superintendent, please! If there was any possible legitimate cause to fear do you think I would hesitate? I have children you know, and grandchildren."

"That is just why——"

"We try to conduct the affairs of the Company with reasonable wisdom, and in the public interest. But we have other responsibilities, too. There are hundreds of thousands of little stockholders who expect us to show a reasonable return on their investment. You must not expect us to jettison a billion-dollar corporation just because you've taken up astrology. Moon theory!" He sniffed.

"Very well, Mister Chairman." King's tone was stiff.

"Don't take it that way, Mr. King. I'm glad you called—the Board has just adjourned a special meeting. They have decided to accept you for retirement—with full pay, of course."

"I did not apply for retirement!"

"I know, Mr. King, but the Board feels that——"

"I understand. Goodbye!"

"Mr. King——"

"Goodbye!" He switched him off, and turned to Lentz. " '—with full pay,' " he quoted, "which I can enjoy in any way that I like for the rest of my life—just as happy as a man in the deathhouse!"

"Exactly," Lentz agreed. "Well, we've tried our way. I suppose we should call up Harrington now and let him try the political and publicity method."

"I suppose so," King seconded absent-mindedly. "Will you be leaving for Chicago now?"

"No . . ." said Lentz. "No. . . . I think I will catch the shuttle for Los Angeles and take the evening rocket for the Antipodes."

King looked surprised, but said nothing. Lentz answered

the unspoken comment. "Perhaps some of us on the other side of the earth will survive. I've done all that I can here. I would rather be a live sheepherder in Australia than a dead psychiatrist in Chicago."

King nodded vigorously. "That shows horse sense. For two cents, I'd dump the pile now, and go with you."

"Not horse sense, my friend—a horse will run back into a burning barn, which is exactly what I plan *not* to do. Why don't you do it and come along. If you did, it would help Harrington to scare 'em to death."

"I believe I will!"

Steinke's face appeared again on the screen. "Harper and Erickson are here, Chief."

"I'm busy."

"They are pretty urgent about seeing you."

"Oh—all right," King said in a tired voice, "show them in. It doesn't matter."

They breezed in, Harper in the van. He commenced talking at once, oblivious to the superintendent's morose preoccupation. "We've got it, Chief, we've got it!—and it all checks out to the umpteenth decimal!"

"You've got what? Speak English."

Harper grinned. He was enjoying his moment of triumph, and was stretching it out to savor it. "Chief, do you remember a few weeks back when I asked for an additional allotment—a special one without specifying how I was going to spend it?"

"Yes. Come on—get to the point."

"You kicked at first, but finally granted it. Remember? Well, we've got something to show for it, all tied up in pink ribbon. It's the greatest advance in radioactivity since Hahn split the nucleus. Atomic fuel, Chief, atomic fuel, safe, concentrated, and controllable. Suitable for rockets, for power plants, for any damn thing you care to use it for."

King showed alert interest for the first time. "You mean a power source that doesn't require a pile?"

"Oh, no, I didn't say that. You use the breeder pile to make the fuel, then you use the fuel anywhere and anyhow you like, with something like ninety-two percent recovery of energy. But you could junk the power sequence, if you wanted to."

King's first wild hope of a way out of his dilemma was dashed; he subsided. "Go ahead. Tell me about it."

"Well—it's a matter of artificial radioactives. Just before I asked for that special research allotment, Erickson and I—Doctor Lentz had a finger in it too," he acknowledged with an appreciative nod to the psychiatrist, "—found two isotopes that seemed to be mutually antagonistic. That is, when we goosed 'em in the presence of each other they gave up their latent energy all at once—blew all to hell. The important point is we were using just a gnat's whisker of mass of each—the reaction didn't require a big mass to maintain it."

"I don't see," objected King, "how that could—"

"Neither do we, quite—but it works. We've kept it quiet until we were sure. We checked on what we had, and we found a dozen other fuels. Probably we'll be able to tailor-make fuels for any desired purpose. But here it is." He handed him a bound sheaf of typewritten notes which he had been carrying under his arm. "That's your copy. Look it over."

King started to do so. Lentz joined him, after a look that was a silent request for permission, which Erickson had answered with his only verbal contribution, "Sure, doc."

As King read, the troubled feelings of an acutely harassed executive left him. His dominant personality took charge, that of the scientist. He enjoyed the controlled and cerebral ecstasy of the impersonal seeker for the elusive truth. The emotions felt in his throbbing thalamus were permitted only to form a sensuous obbligato for the cold flame of cortical activity. For the time being, he was sane, more nearly completely sane than most men ever achieve at any time.

For a long period there was only an occasional grunt, the clatter of turned pages, a nod of approval. At last he put it down.

"It's the stuff," he said. "You've done it, boys. It's great; I'm proud of you."

Erickson glowed a bright pink, and swallowed. Harper's small, tense figure gave the ghost of a wriggle, reminiscent of a wire-haired terrier receiving approval. "That's fine, Chief. We'd rather hear you say that than get the Nobel Prize."

"I think you'll probably get it. However"—the proud light in his eyes died down—"I'm not going to take any action in this matter."

"Why not, Chief?" His tone was bewildered.

"I'm being retired. My successor will take over in the near future; this is too big a matter to start just before a change in administration."

"*You* being *retired!* What the hell?"

"About the same reason I took you off watch—at least, the directors think so."

"But that's nonsense! You were right to take me off the watchlist; I *was* getting jumpy. But you're another matter—we all depend on you."

"Thanks, Cal—but that's how it is; there's nothing to be done about it." He turned to Lentz. "I think this is the last ironical touch needed to make the whole thing pure farce," he observed bitterly. "This thing is big, bigger than we can guess at this stage—and I have to give it a miss."

"Well," Harper burst out, "I can think of something to do about it!" He strode over to King's desk and snatched up the manuscript. "Either you superintend the exploitation, or the Company can damn well get along without our discovery!" Erickson concurred belligerently.

"Wait a minute." Lentz had the floor. "Doctor Harper, . . . have you already achieved a practical rocket fuel?"

"I said so. We've got it on hand now."

"An escape-speed fuel?" They understood his verbal shorthand—a fuel that would lift a rocket free of the earth's gravitational pull.

"Sure. Why, you could take any of the *Clipper* rockets, refit them a trifle, and have breakfast on the moon."

"Very well. Bear with me. . . ." He obtained a sheet of paper from King, and commenced to write. They watched in mystified impatience. He continued briskly for some minutes, hesitating only momentarily. Presently he stopped, and spun the paper over to King. "Solve it!" he demanded.

King studied the paper. Lentz had assigned symbols to a great number of factors, some social, some psychological, some physical, some economic. He had thrown them together into a structural relationship, using the symbols of calculus of statement. King understood the paramathematical operations indicated by the symbols, but he was not as used to them as he was to the symbols and operations of mathematical physics. He plowed through the equations, moving his lips slightly in subconscious vocalization.

He accepted a pencil from Lentz, and completed the solution. It required several more lines, a few more equations, before they cancelled out, or rearranged themselves, into a definite answer.

He stared at this answer while puzzlement gave way to dawning comprehension and delight.

He looked up. "Erickson! Harper!" he rapped out. "We will take your new fuel, refit a large rocket, install the breeder pile in it, and throw it into an orbit around the earth, far out in space. There we will use it to make more fuel, safe fuel, for use on earth, with the danger from the Big Bomb itself limited to the operators actually on watch!"

There was no applause. It was not that sort of an idea; their minds were still struggling with the complex implications.

"But Chief," Harper finally managed, "how about your retirement? We're still not going to stand for it."

"Don't worry," King assured him. "It's all in there, implicit in those equations, you two, me, Lentz, the Board of Directors—and just what we all have to do about it to accomplish it."

"All except the matter of time," Lentz cautioned.

"Eh?"

"You'll note that elapsed time appears in your answer as an undetermined unknown."

"Yes . . . yes, of course. That's the chance we have to take. Let's get busy!"

Chairman Dixon called the Board of Directors to order. "This being a special meeting we'll dispense with minutes and reports," he announced. "As set forth in the call we have agreed to give the retiring superintendent two hours of our time."

"Mr. Chairman—"

"Yes, Mr. Strong?"

"I thought we had settled that matter."

"We have, Mr. Strong, but in view of Superintendent King's long and distinguished service, if he asks a hearing, we are honor bound to grant it. You have the floor, Doctor King."

King got up, and stated briefly, "Doctor Lentz will speak for me." He sat down.

Lentz had to wait for coughing, throat-clearing, and scraping of chairs to subside. It was evident that the Board resented the outsider.

Lentz ran quickly over the main points in the argument which contended that the bomb presented an intolerable danger anywhere on the face of the earth. He moved on at once to the alternative proposal that the bomb should be located in a rocket ship, an artificial moonlet flying in a free orbit around the earth at a convenient distance—say fifteen thousand miles—while secondary power stations on earth burned a safe fuel manufactured by the bomb.

He announced the discovery of the Harper-Erickson technique and dwelt on what it meant to them commercially. Each point was presented as persuasively as possible, with the full power of his engaging personality. Then he paused and waited for them to blow off steam.

They did. "Visionary—" "Unproved—" "No essential change in the situation—" The substance of it was that they were very happy to hear of the new fuel, but not particularly impressed by it. Perhaps in another twenty years, after it had been thoroughly tested and proved commercially, they might consider setting up another breeder pile outside the atmosphere. In the meantime there was no hurry. Only one director supported the scheme and he was quite evidently unpopular.

Lentz patiently and politely dealt with their objections. He emphasized the increasing incidence of occupational psychoneurosis among the engineers and the grave danger to everyone near the bomb even under the orthodox theory. He reminded them of their insurance and indemnity bond costs, and of the "squeeze" they paid state politicians.

Then he changed his tone and let them have it directly and brutally. "Gentlemen," he said, "we believe that we are fighting for our lives . . . our own lives, our families, and every life on the globe. If you refuse this compromise, we will fight as fiercely and with as little regard for fair play as any cornered animal." With that he made his first move in attack.

It was quite simple. He offered for their inspection the outline of a propaganda campaign on a national scale, such as any major advertising firm could carry out as a matter of routine. It was complete to the last detail, television broadcasts, spot plugs, newspaper and magazine coverage with planted editorials, dummy "citizens' committees," and—most important—a supporting whispering campaign and a letters-to-Congress organization. Every business man there knew from experience how such things worked.

But its object was to stir up fear of the Arizona pile and to direct that fear, not into panic, but into rage against the Board of Directors personally, and into a demand that the Atomic Energy Commission take action to have the Big Bomb removed to outer space.

"This is blackmail! We'll stop you!"

"I think not," Lentz replied gently. "You may be able to keep us out of some of the newspapers, but you can't stop the rest of it. You can't even keep us off the air—ask the Federal Communications Commission." It was true. Harrington had handled the political end and had performed his assignment well; the President was convinced.

Tempers were snapping on all sides; Dixon had to pound for order. "Doctor Lentz," he said, his own temper under taut control, "you plan to make every one of us appear a black-hearted scoundrel with no other thought than personal profit, even at the expense of the lives of others. You know that is not true; this is a simple difference of opinion as to what is wise."

"I did not say it was true," Lentz admitted blandly, "but you will admit that I can convince the public that you are deliberate villains. As to it being a difference of opinion . . . you are none of you atomic physicists; you are not entitled to hold opinions in this matter.

"As a matter of fact," he went on callously, "the only doubt in my mind is whether or not an enraged public will destroy your precious plant before Congress has time to exercise eminent domain and take it away from you!"

Before they had time to think up arguments in answer and ways of circumventing him, before their hot indignation had cooled and set as stubborn resistance, he offered his gambit. He produced another lay-out for a propaganda campaign—an entirely different sort.

This time the Board of Directors was to be built up, not torn down. All of the same techniques were to be used; behind-the-scenes feature articles with plenty of human interest would describe the functions of the Company, describe it as a great public trust, administered by patriotic, unselfish statesmen of the business world. At the proper point in the campaign, the Harper-Erickson fuel would be announced, not as a semi-accidental result of the initiative of two employees, but as the long-expected end product of years of systematic research conducted under a fixed policy of the Board of Directors, a policy growing naturally out of their humane determination to remove forever the menace of explosion from even the sparsely settled Arizona desert.

No mention was to be made of the danger of complete, planet-embracing catastrophe.

Lentz discussed it. He dwelt on the appreciation that would be due them from a grateful world. He invited them to make a noble sacrifice, and, with subtle misdirection, tempted them to think of themselves as heroes. He deliberately played on one of the most deep-rooted of simian instincts, the desire for approval from one's kind, deserved or not.

All the while he was playing for time, as he directed his attention from one hard case, one resistant mind, to another. He soothed and he tickled and he played on personal foibles. For the benefit of the timorous and the devoted family men, he again painted a picture of the suffering, death, and destruction that might result from their well-meant reliance on the unproved and highly questionable predictions of Destry's mathematics. Then he described in glowing detail a picture of a world free from worry but granted almost unlimited power, safe power from an invention which was theirs for this one small concession.

It worked. They did not reverse themselves all at once, but a committee was appointed to investigate the feasibility of the proposed spaceship power plant. By sheer brass Lentz suggested names for the committee and Dixon confirmed his nominations, not because he wished to, particularly, but because he was caught off guard and could not think of a reason to refuse without affronting those colleagues. Lentz was careful to include his one supporter in the list.

The impending retirement of King was not mentioned by either side. Privately, Lentz felt sure that it never would be mentioned.

It worked, but there was left much to do. For the first few days, after the victory in committee, King felt much elated by the prospect of an early release from the soul-killing worry. He was buoyed up by pleasant demands of manifold new administrative duties. Harper and Erickson were detached to Goddard Field to collaborate with the rocket engineers there in design of firing chambers, nozzles, fuel stowage, fuel metering, and the like. A schedule had to be worked out with the business office to permit as much use of the pile as possible to be diverted to making atomic fuel, and a giant combustion chamber for atomic fuel had to be designed and ordered to replace the pile itself during the interim between the time it was shut down on earth and the later time when sufficient local, smaller plants could be built to carry the commercial load. He was busy.

When the first activity had died down and they were settled in a new routine, pending the shutting down of the plant and its removal to outer space, King suffered an emotional reaction. There was, by then, nothing to do but wait, and tend the pile, until the crew at Goddard Field smoothed out the bugs and produced a space-worthy rocket ship.

At Goddard they ran into difficulties, overcame them, and came across more difficulties. They had never used such high reaction velocities; it took many trials to find a nozzle shape that would give reasonably high efficiency. When that was solved, and success seemed in sight, the jets burned out on a time-trial ground test. They were stalemated for weeks over that hitch.

There was another problem quite separate from the rocket problem: what to do with the power generated by the breeder pile when relocated in a satellite rocket? It was solved drastically by planning to place the pile proper *outside* the satellite, unshielded, and let it waste its radiant energy. It would be a tiny artificial star, shining in the vacuum of space. In the meantime research would go on for a means to harness it again and beam the power back to Earth. But only its power would be wasted; plutonium and the newer atomic fuels would be recovered and rocketed back to Earth.

Back at the power plant Superintendent King could do nothing but chew his nails and wait. He had not even the release of running over to Goddard Field to watch the progress of the research, for, urgently as he desired to, he felt an even stronger, an overpowering compulsion to watch over the pile more lest it—heartbreakingly!—blow up at the last minute.

He took to hanging around the control room. He had to stop that; his unease communicated itself to his watch engineers; two of them cracked up in a single day—one of them on watch.

He must face the fact—there had been a grave upswing in psychoneurosis among his engineers since the period of watchful waiting had commenced. At first, they had tried to keep the essential facts of the plan a close secret, but it had leaked out, perhaps through some member of the investigating committee. He admitted to himself now that it had been a mistake ever to try to keep it secret—Lentz had advised against it, and the engineers not actually engaged in the change-over were bound to know that something was up.

He took all of the engineers into confidence at last, under oath of secrecy. That had helped for a week or more, a week in which they were all given a spiritual lift by the knowledge, as he had been. Then it had worn off, the reaction had set in, and the psychological observers had started disqualifying engineers for duty almost daily. They were even reporting each other as mentally unstable with great frequency; he might even be faced with a shortage of psychiatrists if that kept up, he thought to himself with bitter amusement. His engineers were already standing four hours in every sixteen. If one more dropped out, he'd put himself on watch. That would be a relief, to tell himself the truth.

Somehow some of the civilians around about and the non-technical employees were catching on to the secret. That mustn't go on—if it spread any further there might be a nationwide panic. But how the hell could he stop it? He couldn't.

He turned over in bed, rearranged his pillow, and tried once more to get to sleep. No good. His head ached, his eyes were balls of pain, and his brain was a ceaseless grind of useless, repetitive activity, like a disc recording stuck in one groove.

God! This was unbearable! He wondered if he were cracking up—if he already had cracked up. This was worse, many times worse, than the old routine when he had simply acknowledged the danger and tried to forget it as much as possible. Not that the pile was any different—it was this five-minutes-to-armistice feeling, this waiting for the curtain to go up, this race against time with nothing to do to help.

He sat up, switched on his bed lamp, and looked at the clock. Three-thirty. Not so good. He got up, went into his bathroom, and dissolved a sleeping powder in a glass of whisky and water, half and half. He gulped it down and went back to bed. Presently he dozed off.

He was running, fleeing down a long corridor. At the end lay safety—he knew that, but he was so utterly exhausted that he doubted his ability to finish the race. The thing pursuing him was catching up; he forced his leaden, aching legs into greater activity. The thing behind him increased its pace, and actually touched him. His heart stopped, then pounded again. He became aware that he was screaming, shrieking in mortal terror.

But he had to reach the end of that corridor, more depended on it than just himself. He had to. He had to— *He had to!*

Then the flash came and he realized that he had lost, realized it with utter despair and utter, bitter defeat. He had failed; the pile had blown up.

The flash was his bed lamp coming on automatically; it was seven o'clock. His pajamas were soaked, dripping with sweat, and his heart still pounded. Every ragged nerve throughout his body screamed for release. It would take more than a cold shower to cure this case of the shakes.

He got to the office before the janitor was out of it. He sat there, doing nothing, until Lentz walked in on him, two hours later. The psychiatrist came in just as he was taking two small tablets from a box in his desk.

"Easy . . . easy, old man," Lentz said in a slow voice. "What have you there?" He came around and gently took possession of the box.

"Just a sedative."

Lentz studied the inscription on the cover. "How many have you had today?"

"Just two, so far."

"You don't need barbiturates; you need a walk in the fresh air. Come take one with me."

"You're a fine one to talk—you're smoking a cigaret that isn't lighted!"

"Me? Why, so I am! We both need that walk. Come."

Harper arrived less than ten minutes after they had left the office. Steinke was not in the outer office. He walked on through and pounded on the door of King's private office, then waited with the man who accompanied him—a hard young chap with an easy confidence to his bearing. Steinke let them in.

Harper brushed on past him with a casual greeting, then checked himself when he saw that there was no one else inside.

"Where's the chief?" he demanded.

"Out. He'll be back soon."

"I'll wait. Oh—Steinke, this is Greene. Greene—Steinke."

The two shook hands. "What brings you back, Cal?" Steinke asked, turning back to Harper.

"Well. . . . I guess it's all right to tell you—"

The communicator screen flashed into sudden activity, and cut him short. A face filled most of the frame. It was apparently too close to the pickup, as it was badly out of focus. "Superintendent!" it yelled in an agonized voice. "The pile—!"

A shadow flashed across the screen, they heard a dull "Smack!", and the face slid out of the screen. As it fell it revealed the control room behind it. Someone was down on the floor plates, a nameless heap. Another figure ran across the field of pickup and disappeared.

Harper snapped into action first. "That was Silard!" he shouted, "—in the control room! Come on, Steinke!" He was already in motion himself.

Steinke went dead white, but hesitated only an unmeasurable instant. He pounded sharp on Harper's heels. Greene followed without invitation, in a steady run that kept easy pace with them.

They had to wait for a capsule to unload at the tube station. Then all three of them tried to crowd into a two-passenger capsule. It refused to start and moments were lost before Greene piled out and claimed another car.

The four minute trip at heavy acceleration seemed an interminable crawl. Harper was convinced that the system had broken down, when the familiar click and sigh announced their arrival at the station under the plant. They jammed each other trying to get out at the same time.

The lift was up; they did not wait for it. That was unwise; they gained no time by it, and arrived at the control level out of breath. Nevertheless, they speeded up when they reached the top, zig-zagged frantically around the outer shield, and burst into the control room.

The limp figure was still on the floor, and another, also inert, was near it.

A third figure was bending over the trigger. He looked up as they came in, and charged them. They hit him together, and all three went down. It was two to one, but they got in each other's way. His heavy armor protected him from the force of their blows. He fought with senseless, savage violence.

Harper felt a bright, sharp pain; his right arm went limp

and useless. The armored figure was struggling free of them. There was a shout from somewhere behind them: "Hold still!"

He saw a flash with the corner of one eye, a deafening crack hurried on top of it, and re-echoed painfully in the restricted space.

The armored figure dropped back to his knees, balanced there, and then fell heavily on his face. Greene stood in the entrance, a service pistol balanced in his hand.

Harper got up and went over to the trigger. He tried to reduce the power-level adjustment, but his right hand wouldn't carry out his orders, and his left was too clumsy. "Steinke," he called, "come here! Take over."

Steinke hurried up, nodded as he glanced at the readings, and set busily to work.

It was thus that King found them when he bolted in a very few minutes later.

"Harper!" he shouted, while his quick glance was still taking in the situation. "What's happened?"

Harper told him briefly. He nodded. "I saw the tail end of the fight from my office— Steinke!" He seemed to grasp for the first time who was on the trigger. "He can't manage the controls—" He hurried toward him.

Steinke looked up at his approach. "Chief!" he called out, "Chief! *I've got my mathematics back!*"

King looked bewildered, then nodded vaguely, and let him be. He turned back to Harper. "How does it happen you're here?"

"Me? I'm here to report—we've done it, Chief!"

"Eh?"

"We've finished; it's all done. Erickson stayed behind to complete the power plant installation on the big ship. I came over in the ship we'll use to shuttle between Earth and the big ship, the power plant. Four minutes from Goddard Field to here in her. That's the pilot over there." He pointed to the door, where Greene's solid form partially hid Lentz.

"Wait a minute. You say that everything is ready to install the pile in the ship? You're *sure?*"

"Positive. The big ship has already flown with our fuel— longer and faster than she will have to fly to reach station in her orbit; I was in it—out in space, Chief! We're all set, six ways from zero."

King stared at the dumping switch, mounted behind glass

at the top of the instrument board. "There's fuel enough," he said softly, as if he were alone and speaking only to himself, "there's been fuel enough for weeks."

He walked swiftly over to the switch, smashed the glass with his fist, and pulled it.

The room rumbled and shivered as tons of molten, massive metal, heavier than gold, coursed down channels, struck against baffles, split into a dozen dozen streams, and plunged to rest in leaden receivers—to rest, safe and harmless, until it should be reassembled far out in space.

The Man Who Sold the Moon

"YOU'VE GOT to be a believer!"

George Strong snorted at his partner's declaration. "Delos, why don't you give up? You've been singing this tune for years. Maybe someday men will get to the Moon, though I doubt it. In any case, you and I will never live to see it. The loss of the power satellite washes the matter up for our generation."

D. D. Harriman grunted. "We won't see it if we sit on our fat behinds and don't do anything to make it happen. But we can make it happen."

"Question number one: how? Question number two: why?"

" 'Why?' The man asks 'why.' George, isn't there anything in your soul but discounts, and dividends? Didn't you ever sit with a girl on a soft summer night and stare up at the Moon and wonder what was there?"

"Yeah, I did once. I caught a cold."

Harriman asked the Almighty why he had been delivered into the hands of the Philistines. He then turned back to his partner. "I could tell you why, the real 'why,' but you wouldn't understand me. You want to know why in terms of cash, don't you? You want to know how Harriman & Strong and Harriman Enterprises can show a profit, don't you?"

"Yes," admitted Strong, "and don't give me any guff about tourist trade and fabulous lunar jewels. I've had it."

"You ask me to show figures on a brand-new type of enterprise, knowing I can't. It's like asking the Wright brothers at Kitty Hawk to estimate how much money Curtiss-Wright Corporation would someday make out of building airplanes. I'll put it another way. You didn't want us to go into plastic houses, did you? If you had had your way we would still be back in Kansas City, subdividing cow pastures and showing rentals."

Strong shrugged.

"How much has New World Homes made to date?"

Strong looked absent-minded while exercising the talent he brought to the partnership. "Uh . . . $172,946,004.62, after taxes, to the end of the last fiscal year. The running estimate to date is—"

"Never mind. What was our share in the take?"

"Well, uh, the partnership, exclusive of the piece you took personally and then sold to me later, has benefited from New World Homes during the same period by $13,010,437.20, ahead of personal taxes. Delos, this double taxation has got to stop. Penalizing thrift is a sure way to run this country straight into—"

"Forget it, forget it! How much have we made out of Skyblast Freight and Antipodes Transways?"

Strong told him.

"And yet I had to threaten you with bodily harm to get you to put up a dime to buy control of the injector patent. You said rockets were a passing fad."

"We were lucky," objected Strong. "You had no way of knowing that there would be a big uranium strike in Australia. Without it, the Skyways group would have left us in the red. For that matter New World Homes would have failed, too, if the roadtowns hadn't come along and given us a market out from under local building codes."

"Nuts on both points. Fast transportation will pay; it always has. As for New World, when ten million families need new houses and we can sell 'em cheap, they'll buy. They won't let building codes stop them, not permanently. We gambled on a certainty. Think back, George: what ventures have we lost money on and what ones have paid off? Every one of my crack-brain ideas has made money, hasn't it? And the only times we've lost our ante was on conservative, blue-chip investments."

"But we've made money on some conservative deals, too," protested Strong.

"Not enough to pay for your yacht. Be fair about it, George; the Andes Development Company, the integrating pantograph patent, every one of my wildcat schemes I've had to drag you into—and every one of them paid."

"I've had to sweat blood to make them pay," Strong grumbled.

"That's why we are partners. I get a wildcat by the tail: you harness him and put him to work. Now we go to the Moon—and you'll make it pay."

"Speak for yourself. I'm not going to the Moon."

"I am."

"Hummph! Delos, granting that we have gotten rich by speculating on your hunches, it's a steel-clad fact that if you keep on gambling you lose your shirt. There's an old saw about the pitcher that went once too often to the well."

"Damn it, George—I'm going to the Moon! If you won't back me up, let's liquidate and I'll do it alone."

Strong drummed on his desk top. "Now, Delos, nobody said anything about not backing you up."

"Fish or cut bait. Now is the opportunity and my mind's made up. I'm going to be the Man in the Moon."

"Well . . . let's get going. We'll be late to the meeting."

As they left their joint office, Strong, always penny conscious, was careful to switch off the light. Harriman had seen him do so a thousand times; this time he commented. "George, how about a light switch that turns off automatically when you leave a room?"

"Hmm—but suppose someone were left in the room?"

"Well . . . hitch it to stay on only when someone was *in* the room—key the switch to the human body's heat radiation, maybe."

"Too expensive and too complicated."

"Needn't be. I'll turn the idea over to Ferguson to fiddle with. It should be no larger than the present light switch and cheap enough so that the power saved in a year will pay for it."

"How would it work?" asked Strong.

"How should I know? I'm no engineer; that's for Ferguson and the other educated laddies."

Strong objected, "It's no good commercially. Switching off a light when you leave a room is a matter of temperament. I've got it; you haven't. If a man hasn't got it, you can't interest him in such a switch."

"You can if power continues to be rationed. There is a power shortage now; and there will be a bigger one."

"Just temporary. This meeting will straighten it out."

"George, there is nothing in this world so permanent as a temporary emergency. The switch will sell."

Strong took out a notebook and stylus. "I'll call Ferguson in about it tomorrow."

Harriman forgot the matter, never to think of it again. They had reached the roof; he waved to a taxi, then turned to Strong. "How much could we realize if we unloaded our holdings in Roadways and in Belt Transport Corporation—yes, and in New World Homes?"

"Huh? Have you gone crazy?"

"Probably. But I'm going to need all the cash you can shake loose for me. Roadways and Belt Transport are no good anyhow; we should have unloaded earlier."

"You *are* crazy! It's the one really conservative venture you've sponsored."

"But it wasn't conservative when I sponsored it. Believe me, George, roadtowns are on their way out. They are growing moribund, just as the railroads did. In a hundred years there won't be a one left on the continent. What's the formula for making money, George?"

"Buy low and sell high."

"That's only half of it . . . *your* half. We've got to guess which way things are moving, give them a boost, and see that we are cut in on the ground floor. Liquidate that stuff, George; I'll need money to operate." The taxi landed; they got in and took off.

The taxi delivered them to the roof of the Hemisphere Power Building; they went to the power syndicate's board room, as far below ground as the landing platform was above —in those days, despite years of peace, tycoons habitually came to rest at spots relatively immune to atom bombs. The room did not seem like a bomb shelter; it appeared to be a chamber in a luxurious penthouse, for a "view window" back of the chairman's end of the table looked out high above the city, in convincing, live stereo, relayed from the roof.

The other directors were there before them. Dixon nodded as they came in, glanced at his watch finger and said, "Well, gentlemen, our bad boy is here, we may as well begin." He took the chairman's seat and rapped for order.

"The minutes of the last meeting are on your pads as usual. Signal when ready." Harriman glanced at the summary before him and at once flipped a switch on the table top; a small green light flashed on at his place. Most of the directors did the same.

"Who's holding up the procession?" inquired Harriman, looking around. "Oh—you, George. Get a move on."

"I like to check the figures," his partner answered testily, then flipped his own switch. A larger green light showed in front of Chairman Dixon, who then pressed a button; a transparency, sticking an inch or two above the table top in front of him lit up with the word RECORDING.

"Operations report," said Dixon and touched another switch. A female voice came out from nowhere. Harriman followed the report from the next sheet of paper at his place. Thirteen Curie-type power piles were now in operation, up five from the last meeting. The Susquehanna and Charleston piles had taken over the load previously borrowed from Atlantic Roadcity and the roadways of that city were now up to normal speed. It was expected that the Chicago-Angeles road could be restored to speed during the next fortnight. Power would continue to be rationed but the crisis was over.

All very interesting but of no direct interest to Harriman. The power crisis that had been caused by the explosion of the power satellite was being satisfactorily met—very good, but Harriman's interest in it lay in the fact that the cause of interplanetary travel had thereby received a setback from which it might not recover.

When the Harper-Erickson isotopic artificial fuels had been developed three years before it had seemed that, in addition to solving the dilemma of an impossibly dangerous power source which was also utterly necessary to the economic life of the continent, an easy means had been found to achieve interplanetary travel.

The Arizona power pile had been installed in one of the largest of the Antipodes rockets, the rocket powered with isotopic fuel created in the power pile itself, and the whole thing was placed in an orbit around the Earth. A much smaller rocket had shuttled between satellite and Earth, carrying supplies to the staff of the power pile, bringing back synthetic radioactive fuel for the power-hungry technology of Earth.

As a director of the power syndicate Harriman had backed the power satellite—with a private ax to grind: he expected to power a Moon ship with fuel manufactured in the power satellite and thus to achieve the first trip to the Moon almost at once. He had not even attempted to stir the Department of Defense out of its sleep; he wanted no government subsidy—the job was a cinch; anybody could do it—and Harriman *would* do it. He had the ship; shortly he would have the fuel.

The ship had been a freighter of his own Antipodes line, her chem-fuel motors replaced, her wings removed. She still waited, ready for fuel—the recommissioned *Santa Maria*, nee *City of Brisbane*.

But the fuel was slow in coming. Fuel had to be earmarked for the shuttle rocket; the power needs of a rationed continent came next—and those needs grew faster than the power satellite could turn out fuel. Far from being ready to supply him for a "useless" Moon trip, the syndicate had seized on the safe but less efficient low temperature uranium-salts and heavy water, Curie-type power piles as a means of using uranium directly to meet the ever growing need for power, rather than build and launch more satellites.

Unfortunately the Curie piles did not provide the fierce star-interior conditions necessary to breeding the isotopic fuels needed for an atom-powered rocket. Harriman had reluctantly come around to the notion that he would have to use political pressure to squeeze the necessary priority for the fuels he wanted for the *Santa Maria*.

Then the power satellite had blown up.

Harriman was stirred out of his brown study by Dixon's voice. "The operations report seems satisfactory, gentlemen. If there is no objection, it will be recorded as accepted. You will note that in the next ninety days we will be back up to the power level which existed before we were forced to close down the Arizona pile."

"But with no provision for future needs," pointed out Harriman. "There have been a lot of babies born while we have been sitting here."

"Is that an objection to accepting the report, D. D.?"

"No."

"Very well. Now the public relations report—let me call attention to the first item, gentlemen. The vice-president in charge recommends a schedule of annuities, benefits, scholarships and so forth for dependents of the staff of the power satellite and of the pilot of the *Charon:* see appendix 'C'."

A director across from Harriman—Phineas Morgan, chairman of the food trust, Cuisine, Incorporated—protested, "What is this, Ed? Too bad they were killed of course, but we paid them sky-high wages and carried their insurance to boot. Why the charity?"

Harriman grunted. "Pay it—I so move. It's peanuts. 'Do not bind the mouths of the kine who tread the grain.'"

"I wouldn't call better than nine hundred thousand 'peanuts,'" protested Morgan.

"Just a minute, gentlemen—" It was the vice-president in charge of public relations, himself a director. "If you'll look at the breakdown, Mr. Morgan, you will see that eighty-five percent of the appropriation will be used to publicize the gifts."

Morgan squinted at the figures. "Oh—why didn't you say so? Well, I suppose the gifts can be considered unavoidable overhead, but it's a bad precedent."

"Without them we have nothing to publicize."

"Yes, but—"

Dixon rapped smartly. "Mr. Harriman has moved acceptance. Please signal your desires." The tally board glowed green; even Morgan, after hesitation, okayed the allotment. "We have a related item next," said Dixon. "A Mrs.—uh, Garfield, through her attorneys, alleges that we are responsible for the congenital crippled condition of her fourth child. The putative facts are that her child was being born just as the satellite exploded and that Mrs. Garfield was then on the meridian underneath the satellite. She wants the court to award her half a million."

Morgan looked at Harriman. "Delos, I suppose that *you* will say to settle out of court."

"Don't be silly. We fight it."

Dixon looked around, surprised. "Why, D. D.? It's my guess we could settle for ten or fifteen thousand—and that was what I was about to recommend. I'm surprised that the legal department referred it to publicity."

"It's obvious why; it's loaded with high explosive. But we should fight, regardless of bad publicity. It's not like the last case; Mrs. Garfield and her brat are not our people. And any dumb fool knows you can't mark a baby by radioactivity at birth; you have to get at the germ plasm of the previous generation at least. In the third place, if we let this get by, we'll be sued for every double-yolked egg that's laid from now on. This calls for an open allotment for defense and not one damned cent for compromise."

"It might be very expensive," observed Dixon.

"It'll be more expensive not to fight. If we have to, we should buy the judge."

The public relations chief whispered to Dixon, then

announced, "I support Mr. Harriman's view. That's my department's recommendation."

It was approved. "The next item," Dixon went on, "is a whole sheaf of suits arising out of slowing down the road-cities to divert power during the crisis. They allegè loss of business, loss of time, loss of this and that, but they are all based on the same issue. The most touchy, perhaps, is a stockholder's suit which claims that Roadways and this company are so interlocked that the decision to divert the power was not done in the interests of the stockholders of Roadways. Delos, this is your pidgin; want to speak on it?"

"Forget it."

"Why?"

"Those are shotgun suits. This corporation is not responsible; I saw to it that Roadways volunteered to sell the power because I anticipated this. And the directorates don't interlock; not on paper, they don't. That's why dummies were born. Forget it—for every suit you've got there, Roadways has a dozen. We'll beat them."

"What makes you so sure?"

"Well—" Harriman lounged back and hung a knee over the arm of his chair. "—a good many years ago I was a Western Union messenger boy. While waiting around the office I read everything I could lay hands on, including the contract on the back of the telegram forms. Remember those? They used to come in big pads of yellow paper; by writing a message on the face of the form you accepted the contract in the fine print on the back—only most people didn't realize that. Do you know what that contract obligated the company to do?"

"Send a telegram, I suppose."

"It didn't promise a durn thing. The company offered to *attempt* to deliver the message, by camel caravan or snail back, or some equally streamlined method, if convenient, but in event of failure, the company was not responsible. I read that fine print until I knew it by heart. It was the loveliest piece of prose I had ever seen. Since then all my contracts have been worded on the same principle. Anybody who sues Roadways will find that Roadways can't be sued on the element of time, because time is not of the essence. In the event of complete non-performance—which hasn't happened yet—Roadways is financially responsible only for freight charges or the price of the personal transportation tickets. So forget it."

Morgan sat up. "D. D., suppose I decided to run up to my

country place tonight, by the roadway, and there was a failure of some sort so that I didn't get there until tomorrow? You mean to say Roadways is not liable?"

Harriman grinned. "Roadways is not liable even if you starve to death on the trip. Better use your copter." He turned back to Dixon. "I move that we stall these suits and let Roadways carry the ball for us."

"The regular agenda being completed," Dixon announced later, "time is allotted for our colleague, Mr. Harriman, to speak on a subject of his own choosing. He has not listed a subject in advance, but we will listen until it is your pleasure to adjourn."

Morgan looked sourly at Harriman. "I move we adjourn."

Harriman grinned. "For two cents I'd second that and let you die of curiosity." The motion failed for want of a second. Harriman stood up.

"Mr. Chairman, friends—" He then looked at Morgan. "—and associates. As you know, I am interested in space travel."

Dixon looked at him sharply. "Not that again, Delos! If I weren't in the chair, I'd move to adjourn myself."

" 'That again'," agreed Harriman. "Now and forever. Hear me out. Three years ago, when we were crowded into moving the Arizona power pile out into space, it looked as if we had a bonus in the shape of interplanetary travel. Some of you here joined with me in forming Spaceways, Incorporated, for experimentation, exploration—and exploitation.

"Space was conquered; rockets that could establish orbits around the globe could be modified to get to the Moon—and from there, anywhere! It was just a matter of doing it. The problems remaining were financial—and political.

"In fact, the real engineering problems of space travel have been solved since World War II. Conquering space has long been a matter of money and politics. But it did seem that the Harper-Erickson process, with its concomitant of a round-the-globe rocket and a practical economical rocket fuel, had at last made it a very present thing, so close indeed that I did not object when the early allotments of fuel from the satellite were earmarked for industrial power."

He looked around. "I shouldn't have kept quiet. I should have squawked and brought pressure and made a hairy nuisance of myself until you allotted fuel to get rid of me. For now we have missed our best chance. The satellite is gone; the source of fuel is gone. Even the shuttle rocket is gone. We are back where we were in 1950. Therefore—"

He paused again. "Therefore—I propose that we build a space ship and send it to the Moon!"

Dixon broke the silence. "Delos, have you come unzipped? You just said that it was no longer possible. Now you say to build one."

"I didn't say it was impossible; I said we had missed our best chance. The time is overripe for space travel. This globe grows more crowded every day. In spite of technical advances the daily food intake on this planet is lower than it was thirty years ago—and we get 46 new babies every minute, 65,000 every day, 25,000,000 every year. Our race is about to burst forth to the planets; if we've got the initiative God promised an oyster we will help it along!

"Yes, we missed our best chance—but the engineering details can be solved. The real question is who's going to foot the bill? That is why I address you gentlemen, for right here in this room is the financial capital of this planet."

Morgan stood up. "Mr. Chairman, if all *company* business is finished, I ask to be excused."

Dixon nodded. Harriman said, "So long, Phineas. Don't let me keep you. Now, as I was saying, it's a money problem and here is where the money is. I move we finance a trip to the Moon."

The proposal produced no special excitement; these men knew Harriman. Presently Dixon said, "Is there a second to D. D.'s proposal?"

"Just a minute, Mr. Chairman—" It was Jack Entenza, president of Two-Continents Amusement Corporation. "I want to ask Delos some questions." He turned to Harriman. "D. D., you know I strung along when you set up Spaceways. It seemed like a cheap venture and possibly profitable in educational and scientific values—I never did fall for space liners plying between planets; that's fantastic. I don't mind playing along with your dreams to a moderate extent, but how do you propose to get to the Moon? As you say, you are fresh out of fuel."

Harriman was still grinning. "Don't kid me, Jack, I know why you came along. You weren't interested in science;

you've never contributed a dime to science. You expected a monopoly on pix and television for your chain. Well, you'll get 'em, if you stick with me—otherwise I'll sign up 'Recreations, Unlimited'; they'll pay just to have you in the eye."

Entenza looked at him suspiciously. "What will it cost me?"

"Your other shirt, your eye teeth, and your wife's wedding ring—unless 'Recreations' will pay more."

"Damn you, Delos, you're crookeder than a dog's hind leg."

"From you, Jack, that's a compliment. We'll do business. Now as to how I'm going to get to the Moon, that's a silly question. There's not a man in here who can cope with anything more complicated in the way of machinery than a knife and fork. You can't tell a left-handed monkey wrench from a reaction engine, yet you ask me for blue prints of a space ship.

"Well, I'll tell you how I'll get to the Moon. I'll hire the proper brain boys, give them everything they want, see to it that they have all the money they can use, sweet talk them into long hours—then stand back and watch them produce. I'll run it like the Manhattan Project—most of you remember the A-bomb job; shucks, some of you can remember the Mississippi Bubble. The chap that headed up the Manhattan Project didn't know a neutron from Uncle George—but he got results. They solved that trick *four ways*. That's why I'm not worried about fuel; we'll get a fuel. We'll get several fuels."

Dixon said, "Suppose it works? Seems to me you're asking us to bankrupt the company for an exploit with no real value, aside from pure science, and a one-shot entertainment exploitation. I'm not against you—I wouldn't mind putting in ten, fifteen thousand to support a worthy venture—but I can't see the thing as a business proposition."

Harriman leaned on his fingertips and stared down the long table. "Ten or fifteen thousand gum drops! Dan, I mean to get into you for a couple of megabucks *at least*—and before we're through you'll be hollering for more stock. This is the greatest real estate venture since the Pope carved up the New World. Don't ask me what we'll make a profit on; I can't itemize the assets—but I can lump them. The assets are a planet—a *whole planet,* Dan, that's never been touched. And more planets beyond it. If we can't figure out ways to swindle a few fast bucks out of a sweet set-up like that then you and

I had better both go on relief. It's like having Manhattan Island offered to you for twenty-four dollars and a case of whiskey."

Dixon grunted. "You make it sound like the chance of a lifetime."

"Chance of a lifetime, nuts! This is the greatest chance in all history. It's raining soup; grab yourself a bucket."

Next to Entenza sat Gaston P. Jones, director of Trans-America and half a dozen other banks, one of the richest men in the room. He carefully removed two inches of cigar ash, then said dryly, "Mr. Harriman, I will sell you all of my interest in the Moon, present and future, for fifty cents."

Harriman looked delighted. "Sold!"

Entenza had been pulling at his lower lip and listening with a brooding expression on his face. Now he spoke up. "Just a minute, Mr. Jones—I'll give you a dollar for it."

"Dollar fifty," answered Harriman.

"Two dollars," Entenza answered slowly.

"Five!"

They edged each other up. At ten dollars Entenza let Harriman have it and sat back, still looking thoughtful. Harriman looked happily around. "Which one of you thieves is a lawyer?" he demanded. The remark was rhetorical; out of seventeen directors the normal percentage—eleven, to be exact—were lawyers. "Hey, Tony," he continued, "draw me up an instrument right *now* that will tie down this transaction so that it couldn't be broken before the Throne of God. All of Mr. Jones' interests, rights, title, natural interest, future interests, interests held directly or through ownership of stock, presently held or to be acquired, and so forth and so forth. Put lots of Latin in it. The idea is that every interest in the Moon that Mr. Jones now has or may acquire is mine—for a ten spot, cash in hand paid." Harriman slapped a bill down on the table. "That right, Mr. Jones?"

Jones smiled briefly. "That's right, young fellow." He pocketed the bill. "I'll frame this for my grandchildren—to show them how easy it is to make money." Entenza's eyes darted from Jones to Harriman.

"Good!" said Harriman. "Gentlemen, Mr. Jones has set a market price for one human being's interest in our satellite. With around three billion persons on this globe that sets a price on the Moon of thirty billion dollars." He hauled out a wad of money. "Any more suckers? I'm buying every share that's offered, ten bucks a copy."

"I'll pay twenty!" Entenza rapped out.

Harriman looked at him sorrowfully. "Jack—don't do that! We're on the same team. Let's take the shares together, at ten."

Dixon pounded for order. "Gentlemen, please conduct such transactions after the meeting is adjourned. Is there a second to Mr. Harriman's motion?"

Gaston Jones said, "I owe it to Mr. Harriman to second his motion, without prejudice. Let's get on with a vote."

No one objected; the vote was taken. It went eleven to three against Harriman—Harriman, Strong, and Entenza for; all others against. Harriman popped up before anyone could move to adjourn and said, "I expected that. My real purpose is this: since the company is no longer interested in space travel, will it do me the courtesy of selling me what I may need of patents, processes, facilities, and so forth now held by the company but relating to space travel and not relating to the production of power on this planet? Our brief honeymoon with the power satellite built up a backlog; I want to use it. Nothing formal—just a vote that it is the policy of the company to assist me in any way not inconsistent with the primary interests of the company. How about it, gentlemen? It'll get me out of your hair."

Jones studied his cigar again. "I see no reason why we should not accommodate him, gentlemen . . . and I speak as the perfect disinterested party."

"I think we can do it, Delos," agreed Dixon, "only we won't sell you anything, we'll *lend* it to you. Then, if you happen to hit the jackpot, the company still retains an interest. Has anyone any objection?" he said to the room at large.

There was none; the matter was recorded as company policy and the meeting was adjourned. Harriman stopped to whisper with Entenza and, finally, to make an appointment. Gaston Jones stood near the door, speaking privately with Chairman Dixon. He beckoned to Strong, Harriman's partner. "George, may I ask a personal question?"

"I don't guarantee to answer. Go ahead."

"You've always struck me as a level-headed man. Tell me —why do you string along with Harriman? Why, the man's mad as a hatter."

Strong looked sheepish. "I ought to deny that, he's my friend . . . but I can't. But dawggone it! every time Delos has a wild hunch, it turns out to be the real thing. I hate to string along—it makes me nervous—but I've learned to trust his hunches rather than another man's sworn financial report."

Jones cocked one brow. "The Midas touch, eh?"

"You could call it that."

"Well, remember what happened to King Midas—in the long run. Good day, gentlemen."

Harriman had left Entenza; Strong joined him. Dixon stood staring at them, his face very thoughtful.

2

HARRIMAN'S HOME had been built at the time when everyone who could was decentralizing and going underground. Above ground there was a perfect little Cape Cod cottage—the clapboards of which concealed armor plate—and most delightful, skillfully landscaped grounds; below ground there was four or five times as much floorspace, immune to anything but a direct hit and possessing an independent air supply with reserves for one thousand hours. During the Crazy Years the conventional wall surrounding the grounds had been replaced by a wall which looked the same but which would stop anything short of a broaching tank—nor were the gates weak points; their gadgets were as personally loyal as a well-trained dog.

Despite its fortress-like character the house was comfortable. It was also very expensive to keep up.

Harriman did not mind the expense; Charlotte liked the house and it gave her something to do. When they were first married she had lived uncomplainingly in a cramped flat over a grocery store; if Charlotte now liked to play house in a castle, Harriman did not mind.

But he was again starting a shoe-string venture; the few thousand per month of ready cash represented by the household expenses might, at some point in the game, mean the difference between success and the sheriff's bailiffs. That night at dinner, after the servants fetched the coffee and port, he took up the matter.

"My dear, I've been wondering how you would like a few months in Florida."

His wife stared at him. "Florida? Delos, is your mind wandering? Florida is unbearable at this time of the year."

"Switzerland, then. Pick your own spot. Take a real vacation, as long as you like."

"Delos, you are up to something."

Harriman sighed. Being "up to something" was the unnameable and unforgivable crime for which any American male could be indicted, tried, convicted, and sentenced in one breath. He wondered how things had gotten rigged so that the male half of the race must always behave to suit feminine rules and feminine logic, like a snotty-nosed school boy in front of a stern teacher.

"In a way, perhaps. We've both agreed that this house is a bit of a white elephant. I was thinking of closing it, possibly even of disposing of the land—it's worth more now than when we bought it. Then, when we get around to it, we could build something more modern and a little less like a bomb-proof."

Mrs. Harriman was temporarily diverted. "Well, I *have* thought it might be nice to build another place, Delos—say a little chalet tucked away in the mountains, nothing ostentatious, not more than two servants, or three. But we won't close this place until it's built, Delos—after all, one must live somewhere."

"I was not thinking of building right away," he answered cautiously.

"Why not? We're not getting any younger, Delos; if we are to enjoy the good things of life we had better not make delays. You needn't worry about it; I'll manage everything."

Harriman turned over in his mind the possibility of letting her build to keep her busy. If he earmarked the cash for her "little chalet," she would live in a hotel nearby wherever she decided to build it—and he could sell this monstrosity they were sitting in. With the nearest roadcity now less than ten miles away, the land should bring more than Charlotte's new house would cost and he would be rid of the monthly drain on his pocketbook.

"Perhaps you are right," he agreed. "But suppose you do

build at once; you won't be living here; you'll be supervising every detail of the new place. I say we should unload this place; it's eating its head off in taxes, upkeep, and running expenses."

She shook her head. "Utterly out of the question, Delos. This is my home."

He ground out an almost unsmoked cigar. "I'm sorry, Charlotte, but you can't have it both ways. If you build, you can't stay here. If you stay here, we'll close these below-ground catacombs, fire about a dozen of the parasites I keep stumbling over, and live in the cottage on the surface. I'm cutting expenses."

"Discharge the servants? Delos, if you think that I will undertake to make a home for you without a proper staff, you can just—"

"Stop it." He stood up and threw his napkin down. "It doesn't take a squad of servants to make a home. When we were first married you had *no* servants—and you washed and ironed my shirts in the bargain. But we had a home then. This place is owned by that staff you speak of. Well, we're getting rid of them, all but the cook and a handy man."

She did not seem to hear him. "Delos! sit down and behave yourself. Now what's all this about cutting expenses? Are you in some sort of trouble? Are you? Answer me!"

He sat down wearily and answered, "Does a man have to be in trouble to want to cut out unnecessary expenses?"

"In your case, yes. Now what is it? Don't try to evade me."

"Now see here, Charlotte, we agreed a long time ago that I would keep business matters in the office. As for the house, we simply don't need a house this size. It isn't as if we had a passel of kids to fill up—"

"*Oh!* Blaming me for *that* again!"

"Now see here, Charlotte," he wearily began again, "I never did blame you and I'm not blaming you now. All I ever did was suggest that we both see a doctor and find out what the trouble was we didn't have any kids. And for twenty years you've been making me pay for that one remark. But that's all over and done with now; I was simply making the point that two people don't fill up twenty-two rooms. I'll pay a reasonable price for a new house, if you want it, and give you an ample household allowance." He started to say how much, then decided not to. "Or you can close this place and live in the cottage above. It's just that we are going to quit squandering money—for a while."

She grabbed the last phrase. " 'For a while.' What's going on, Delos? What are *you* going to squander money on?" When he did not answer she went on, "Very well, if you won't tell me, I'll call George. He will tell me."

"Don't do that, Charlotte. I'm warning you. I'll—"

"You'll what!" She studied his face. "I don't need to talk to George; I can tell by looking at you. You've got the same look on your face you had when you came home and told me that you had sunk all our money in those crazy rockets."

"Charlotte, that's not fair. Skyways paid off. It's made us a mint of money."

"That's beside the point. I know why you're acting so strangely; you've got that old trip-to-the-Moon madness again. Well, I won't stand for it, do you hear? I'll stop you; I don't have to put up with it. I'm going right down in the morning and see Mr. Kamens and find out what has to be done to make you behave yourself." The cords of her neck jerked as she spoke.

He waited, gathering his temper before going on. "Charlotte, you have no real cause for complaint. No matter what happens to me, your future is taken care of."

"Do you think I want to be a widow?"

He looked thoughtfully at her. "I wonder."

"Why— Why, you heartless *beast*." She stood up. "We'll say no more about it; do you mind?" She left without waiting for an answer.

His "man" was waiting for him when he got to his room. Jenkins got up hastily and started drawing Harriman's bath. "Beat it," Harriman grunted. "I can undress myself."

"You require nothing more tonight, sir?"

"Nothing. But don't go unless you feel like it. Sit down and pour yourself a drink. Ed, how long you been married?"

"Don't mind if I do." The servant helped himself. "Twenty-three years, come May, sir."

"How's it been, if you don't mind me asking?"

"Not bad. Of course there have been times—"

"I know what you mean. Ed, if you weren't working for me, what would you be doing?"

"Well, the wife and I have talked many times of opening a little restaurant, nothing pretentious, but good. A place where a gentleman could enjoy a quiet meal of good food."

"Stag, eh?"

"No, not entirely, sir—but there would be a parlor for gentlemen only. Not even waitresses, I'd tend that room myself."

"Better look around for locations, Ed. You're practically in business."

3

STRONG ENTERED their joint offices the next morning at a precise nine o'clock, as usual. He was startled to find Harriman there before him. For Harriman to fail to show up at all meant nothing; for him to beat the clerks in was significant.

Harriman was busy with a terrestrial globe and a book—the current Nautical Almanac, Strong observed. Harriman barely glanced up. "Morning, George. Say, who've we got a line to in Brazil?"

"Why?"

"I need some trained seals who speak Portuguese, that's why. And some who speak Spanish, too. Not to mention three or four dozen scattered around in this country. I've come across something very, very interesting. Look here . . . according to these tables the Moon only swings about twenty-eight, just short of twenty-nine degrees north and south of the equator." He held a pencil against the globe and spun it. "Like that. That suggest anything?"

"No. Except that you're getting pencil marks on a sixty dollar globe."

"And you an old real estate operator! What does a man own when he buys a parcel of land?"

"That depends on the deed. Usually mineral rights and other subsurface rights are—"

"Never mind that. Suppose he buys the works, without splitting the rights: how far down does he own? How far up does he own?"

"Well, he owns a wedge down to the center of the Earth. That was settled in the slant-drilling and off-set oil lease cases. Theoretically he used to own the space above the land, too, out indefinitely, but that was modified by a series of cases after the commercial airlines came in—and a good thing, for us, too, or we would have to pay tolls every time one of our rockets took off for Australia."

"No, no, no, George! you didn't read those cases right. Right of passage was established—but *ownership* of the space above the land remained unchanged. And even right of passage was not absolute; you can build a thousand-foot tower on your own land right where airplanes, or rockets, or whatever, have been in the habit of passing and the ships will thereafter have to go above it, with no kick back on you. Remember how we had to lease the air south of Hughes Field to insure that our approach wasn't built up?"

Strong looked thoughtful. "Yes. I see your point. The ancient principle of land ownership remains undisturbed—down to the center of the Earth, up to infinity. But what of it? It's a purely theoretical matter. You're not planning to pay tolls to operate those spaceships you're always talking about, are you?" He grudged a smile at his own wit.

"Not on your tintype. Another matter entirely. George— *who owns the Moon?*"

Strong's jaw dropped, literally. "Delos, you're joking."

"I am not. I'll ask you again: if basic law says that a man owns the wedge of sky above his farm out to infinity, *who owns the Moon?* Take a look at this globe and tell me."

Strong looked. "But it can't mean anything, Delos. Earth laws wouldn't apply to the Moon."

"They apply here and that's where I am worrying about it. The Moon stays constantly over a slice of Earth bounded by latitude twenty-nine north and the same distance south; if one man owned all that belt of Earth—it's roughly the tropical zone—then he'd own the Moon, too, wouldn't he? By all the theories of real property ownership that our courts pay any attention to. And, by direct derivation, according to the sort of logic that lawyers like, the various owners of that belt of land have title—good vendable title—to the Moon somehow lodged collectively in them. The fact that the distribution of the title is a little vague wouldn't bother a lawyer; they grow fat on just such distributed titles every time a will is probated."

"It's fantastic!"

"George, when are you going to learn that 'fantastic' is a notion that doesn't bother a lawyer?"

"You're not planning to try to buy the entire tropical zone —that's what you would have to do."

"No," Harriman said slowly, "but it might not be a bad idea to buy right, title and interest in the Moon, as it may appear, from each of the sovereign countries in that belt. If I thought I could keep it quiet and not run the market up, I might try it. You can buy a thing awful cheap from a man if he thinks it's worthless and wants to sell before you regain your senses.

"But that's not the plan," he went on. "George, I want corporations—local corporations—in every one of those countries. I want the legislatures of each of those countries to grant franchises to its local corporation for lunar exploration, exploitation, et cetera, and the right to claim lunar soil on behalf of the country—with fee simple, naturally, being handed on a silver platter to the patriotic corporation that thought up the idea. And I want all this done quietly, so that the bribes won't go too high. We'll own the corporations, of course, which is why I need a flock of trained seals. There is going to be one hell of a fight one of these days over who owns the Moon; I want the deck stacked so that we win no matter how the cards are dealt."

"It will be ridiculously expensive, Delos. And you don't even know that you will ever get to the Moon, much less that it will be worth anything after you get there."

"We'll get there! It'll be more expensive not to establish these claims. Anyhow it need not be very expensive; the proper use of bribe money is a homeopathic art—you use it as a catalyst. Back in the middle of the last century four men went from California to Washington with $40,000; it was all they had. A few weeks later they were broke—but Congress had awarded them a billion dollars worth of railroad right of way. The trick is not to run up the market."

Strong shook his head. "Your title wouldn't be any good anyhow. The Moon doesn't stay in one place; it passes *over* owned land certainly—but so does a migrating goose."

"And nobody has title to a migrating bird. I get your point —but the Moon *always* stays over that one belt. If you move a boulder in your garden, do you lose title to it? Is it still real estate? Do the title laws still stand? This is like that group of real estate cases involving wandering islands in the Mississippi, George—the land moved as the river cut new channels, *but somebody always owned it*. In this case I plan to see to it that we are the 'somebody'."

Strong puckered his brow. "I seem to recall that some of

those island-and-riparian cases were decided one way and some another."

"We'll pick the decisions that suit us. That's why lawyers' wives have mink coats. Come on, George; let's get busy."

"On what?"

"Raising the money."

"Oh." Strong looked relieved. "I thought you were planning to use *our* money."

"I am. But it won't be nearly enough. We'll use our money for the senior financing to get things moving; in the meantime we've got to work out ways to keep the money rolling in." He pressed a switch at his desk; the face of Saul Kamens, their legal chief of staff, sprang out at him. "Hey, Saul, can you slide in for a powwow?"

"Whatever it is, just tell them 'no,' " answered the attorney. "I'll fix it."

"Good. Now come on in—they're moving Hell and I've got an option on the first ten loads."

. Kamens showed up in his own good time. Some minutes later Harriman had explained his notion for claiming the Moon ahead of setting foot on it. "Besides those dummy corporations," he went on, "we need an agency that can receive contributions without having to admit any financial interest on the part of the contributor—like the National Geographic Society."

Kamens shook his head. "You can't buy the National Geographic Society."

"Damn it, who said we were going to? We'll set up our own."

"That's what I started to say."

"Good. As I see it, we need at least one tax-free, non-profit corporation headed up by the right people—we'll hang on to voting control, of course. We'll probably need more than one; we'll set them up as we need them. And we've got to have at least one new ordinary corporation, *not* tax-free—but it won't show a profit until we are ready. The idea is to let the non-profit corporations have all of the prestige and all of the publicity—and the other gets all of the profits, if and when. We swap assets around between corporations, always for perfectly valid reasons, so that the non-profit corporations pay the expenses as we go along. Come to think about it, we had better have at least two ordinary corporations, so that we can let one of them go through bankruptcy if we find it necessary to shake out the water. That's the general sketch. Get busy and fix it up so that it's legal, will you?"

Kamens said, "You know, Delos, it would be a lot more honest if you did it at the point of a gun."

"A lawyer talks to me of honesty! Never mind, Saul; I'm not actually going to cheat anyone—"

"Hmmph!"

"—and I'm just going to make a trip to the Moon. That's what everybody will be paying for; that's what they'll get. Now fix it up so that it's legal, that's a good boy."

"I'm reminded of something the elder Vanderbilt's lawyer said to the old man under similar circumstances: 'It's beautiful the way it is; why spoil it by making it legal?' Okeh, brother gonoph, I'll rig your trap. Anything else?"

"Sure. Stick around, you might have some ideas. George, ask Montgomery to come in, will you?" Montgomery, Harriman's publicity chief, had two virtues in his employer's eyes: he was personally loyal to Harriman, and, secondly, he was quite capable of planning a campaign to convince the public that Lady Godiva wore a *Caresse*-brand girdle during her famous ride . . . or that Hercules attributed his strength to Crunchies for breakfast.

He arrived with a large portfolio under his arm. "Glad you sent for me, Chief. Get a load of this—" He spread the folder open on Harriman's desk and began displaying sketches and layouts. "Kinsky's work—is that boy hot!"

Harriman closed the portfolio. "What outfit is it for?"

"Huh? New World Homes."

"I don't want to see it; we're dumping New World Homes. Wait a minute—don't start to bawl. Have the boys go through with it; I want the price kept up while we unload. But open your ears to another matter." He explained rapidly the new enterprise.

Presently Montgomery was nodding. "When do we start and how much do we spend?"

"Right away and spend what you need to. Don't get chicken about expenses; this is the biggest thing we've ever tackled." Strong flinched; Harriman went on, "Have insomnia over it tonight; see me tomorrow and we'll kick it around."

"Wait a sec, Chief. How are you going to sew up all those franchises from the, uh—the Moon states, those countries the Moon passes over, while a big publicity campaign is going on about a trip to the Moon and how big a thing it is for everybody? Aren't you about to paint yourself into a corner?"

"Do I look stupid? We'll get the franchises *before* you hand out so much as a filler—*you*'ll get 'em, you and Kamens. That's your first job."

"Hmmm. . . ." Montgomery chewed a thumb nail. "Well, all right—I can see some angles. How soon do we have to sew it up?"

"I give you six weeks. Otherwise just mail your resignation in, written on the skin off your back."

"I'll write it right now, if you'll help me by holding a mirror."

"Damn it, Monty, I know you can't do it in six weeks. But make it fast; we can't take a cent in to keep the thing going until you sew up those franchises. If you dilly-dally, we'll all starve—and we won't get to the Moon, either."

Strong said, "D. D., why fiddle with these trick claims from a bunch of moth-eaten tropical countries? If you are dead set on going to the Moon, let's call Ferguson in and get on with the matter."

"I like your direct approach, George," Harriman said, frowning. "Mmmm. . . . back about 1845 or '46 an eager-beaver American army officer captured California. You know what the State Department did?"

"No."

"They made him hand it back. Seems he hadn't touched second base, or something. So they had to go to the trouble of capturing it all over again a few months later. Now I don't want that to happen to us. It's not enough just to set foot on the Moon and claim it; we've got to validate that claim in terrestrial courts—or we're in for a peck of trouble. Eh, Saul?"

Kamens nodded. "Remember what happened to Columbus."

"Exactly. We aren't going to let ourselves be rooked the way Coumbus was."

Montgomery spat out some thumb nail. "But, Chief—you know damn well those banana-state claims won't be worth two cents after I do tie them up. Why not get a franchise right from the U. N. and settle the matter? I'd as lief tackle that as tackle two dozen cockeyed legislatures. In fact I've got an angle already—we work it through the Security Council and—"

"Keep working on that angle; we'll use it later. You don't appreciate the full mechanics of the scheme, Monty. Of course those claims are worth nothing—except nuisance value. But their nuisance value is all important. Listen: we get to the Moon, or appear about to. Every one of those countries puts up a squawk; we goose them into it through the dummy corporations they have enfranchised. Where do they squawk? To the U. N., of course. Now the big countries on this globe, the rich and important ones, are all in the northern temperate zone. They see what the claims are based on and they take a frenzied look at the globe. Sure enough, the Moon does not pass over a one of them. The biggest country of all—Russia—doesn't own a spadeful of dirt south of twenty-nine north. So they reject all the claims.

"Or do they?" Harriman went on. "The U. S. balks. *The Moon passes over Florida and the southern part of Texas.* Washington is in a tizzy. Should they back up the tropical countries and support the traditional theory of land title or should they throw their weight to the idea that the Moon belongs to everyone? Or should the United States try to claim the whole thing, seeing as how it was Americans who actually got there first?

"At this point we creep out from under cover. It seems that the Moon ship was owned and the expenses paid by a non-profit corporation chartered by the U. N. itself—"

"Hold it," interrupted Strong. "I didn't know that the U. N. could create corporations?"

"You'll find it can," his partner answered. "How about it, Saul?" Kamens nodded. "Anyway," Harriman continued, "I've already got the corporation. I had it set up several years ago. It can do most anything of an educational or scientific nature—and, brother, that covers a lot of ground! Back to the point—this corporation, this creature of the U. N., asks its parent to declare the lunar colony autonomous territory, under the protection of the U. N. We won't ask for outright membership at first because we want to keep it simple—"

"Simple, he calls it!" said Montgomery.

"Simple. This new colony will be a *de facto* sovereign state, holding title to the entire Moon, and—listen closely!—capable of buying, selling, passing laws, issuing title to land, setting up monopolies, collecting tariffs, et cetera without end. *And we own it!*

"The reason we get all this is because the major states in the U. N. can't think up a claim that sounds as legal as the claim made by the tropical states, they can't agree among themselves as to how to split up the swag if they were to attempt brute force and the other major states aren't willing to see the United States claim the whole thing. They'll take the easy way out of their dilemma by appearing to retain title in the U. N. itself. The real title, the title controlling all economic and legal matters, will revert to us. Now do you see my point, Monty?"

Montgomery grinned. "Damned if I know if it's necessary, Chief, but I love it. It's beautiful."

"Well, I don't think so," Strong grumbled. "Delos, I've seen you rig some complicated deals—some of them so devious that they turned even my stomach—but this one is the worst yet. I think you've been carried away by the pleasure you get out of cooking up involved deals in which somebody gets double-crossed."

Harriman puffed hard on his cigar before answering, "I don't give a damn, George. Call it chicanery, call it anything you want to. *I'm going to the Moon!* If I have to manipulate a million people to accomplish it, I'll do it."

"But it's not necessary to do it this way."

"Well, how would you do it?"

"Me? I'd set up a straightforward corporation. I'd get a resolution in Congress making my corporation the chosen instrument of the United States—"

"Bribery?"

"Not necessarily. Influence and pressure ought to be enough. Then I would set about raising the money and make the trip."

"And the United States would then own the Moon?"

"Naturally," Strong answered a little stiffly.

Harriman got up and began pacing. "You don't see it, George, you don't see it. The Moon was not meant to be owned by a single country, even the United States."

"It was meant to be owned by *you,* I suppose."

"Well, if I own it—for a short while—I won't misuse it and I'll take care that others don't. Damnation, nationalism should stop at the stratosphere. Can you see what would happen if the United States lays claim to the Moon? The other nations won't recognize the claim. It will become a permanent bone of contention in the Security council—just when we were beginning to get straightened out to the point where a man could do business planning without having his elbow jogged by a war every few years. The other nations—

quite rightfully—will be scared to death of the United States. They will be able to look up in the sky any night and see the main atom-bomb rocket base of the United States staring down the backs of their necks. Are they going to hold still for it? No, sirree—they are going to try to clip off a piece of the Moon for their own national use. The Moon is too big to hold, all at once. There will be other bases established there and presently there will be the God-damnedest war this planet has ever seen—and we'll be to blame.

"No, it's got to be an arrangement that everybody will hold still for—and that's why we've got to plan it, think of all the angles, and be devious about it until we are in a position to make it work.

"Anyhow, George, if we claim it in the name of the United States, do you know where we will be, as business men?"

"In the driver's seat," answered Strong.

"In a pig's eye! We'll be dealt right out of the game. The Department of National Defense will say, 'Thank you, Mr. Harriman. Thank you, Mr. Strong. We are taking over in the interests of national security; you can go home now.' And that's just what we would have to do—go home and wait for the next atom war.

"I'm not going to do it, George. I'm not going to let the brass hats muscle in. I'm going to set up a lunar colony and then nurse it along until it is big enough to stand on its own feet. I'm telling you—all of you!—this is the biggest thing for the human race since the discovery of fire. Handled right, it can mean a new and braver world. Handle it wrong and it's a one-way ticket to Armageddon. It's coming, it's coming soon, whether we touch it or not. But I plan to be the Man in the Moon myself—and give it my personal attention to see that it's handled right."

He paused. Strong said, "Through with your sermon, Delos?"

"No, I'm not," Harriman denied testily. "You don't see this thing the right way. Do you know what we may find up there?" He swung his arm in an arc toward the ceiling. *"People!"*

"On the *Moon?*" said Kamens.

"Why not on the Moon?" whispered Montgomery to Strong.

"No, not on the Moon—at least I'd be amazed if we dug down and found anybody under that airless shell. The Moon has had its day; I was speaking of the other planets—Mars and Venus and the satellites of Jupiter. Even maybe out at the stars themselves. Suppose we do find people? Think what it will mean to us. We've been alone, all alone, the only intelligent race in the only world we know. We haven't even been able to talk with dogs or apes. Any answers we got we had to think up by ourselves, like deserted orphans. But suppose we find *people,* intelligent people, who have done some thinking in their own way. *We wouldn't be alone any more!* We could look up at the stars and never be afraid again."

He finished, seeming a little tired and even a little ashamed of his outburst, like a man surprised in a private act. He stood facing them, searching their faces.

"Gee whiz, Chief," said Montgomery, "I can use that. How about it?"

"Think you can remember it?"

"Don't need to—I flipped on your 'silent steno.' "

"Well, damn your eyes!"

"We'll put it on video—in a play I think."

Harriman smiled almost boyishly. "I've never acted, but if you think it'll do any good, I'm game."

"Oh, no, not you, Chief," Montgomery answered in horrified tones. "You're not the type. I'll use Basil Wilkes-Booth, I think. With his organ-like voice and that beautiful archangel face, he'll really send 'em."

Harriman glanced down at his paunch and said gruffly, "O.K.—back to business. Now about money. In the first place we can go after straight donations to one of the non-profit corporations, just like endowments for colleges. Hit the upper brackets, where tax deductions really matter. How much do you think we can raise that way?"

"Very little," Strong opined. "That cow is about milked dry."

"It's never milked dry, as long as there are rich men around who would rather make gifts than pay taxes. How much will a man pay to have a crater on the Moon named after him?"

"I thought they all had names?" remarked the lawyer.

"Lots of them don't—and we have the whole back face that's not touched yet. We won't try to put down an estimate today; we'll just list it. Monty, I want an angle to squeeze dimes out of the school kids, too. Forty million school kids at a dime a head is $4,000,000.00—we can use that."

"Why stop at a dime?" asked Monty. "If you get a kid really interested he'll scrape together a dollar."

"Yes, but what do we offer him for it? Aside from the honor of taking part in a noble venture and so forth?"

"Mmmm. . . ." Montgomery used up more thumb nail. "Suppose we go after both the dimes and·the dollars. For a dime he gets a card saying that he's a member of the Moonbeam club—"

"No, the 'Junior Spacemen'."

"O.K., the Moonbeams will be girls—and don't forget to rope the Boy Scouts and the Girl Scouts into it, too. We give each kid a card; when he kicks in another dime, we punch it. When he's punched out a dollar, we give him a certificate, suitable for framing, with his name and some process engraving, and on the back a picture of the Moon."

"On the *front*," answered Harriman. "Do it in one print job; it's cheaper and it'll look better. We give him something else, too, a steelclad guarantee that his name will be on the rolls of the Junior Pioneers of the Moon, which same will be placed in a monument to be erected on the Moon at the landing site of the first Moon ship—in microfilm, of course; we have to watch weight."

"Fine!" agreed Montgomery. "Want to swap jobs, Chief? When he gets up to ten dollars we give him a genuine, solid gold-plated shooting star pin and he's a senior Pioneer, with the right to vote or something or other. And his name goes *outside* of the monument—microengraved on a platinum strip."

Strong looked as if he had bitten a lemon. "What happens when he reaches a hundred dollars?" he asked.

"Why, then," Montgomery answered happily, "we give him another card and he can start over. Don't worry about it, Mr. Strong—if any kid goes that high, he'll have his reward. Probably we will take him on an inspection tour of the ship before it takes off and give him, absolutely free, a picture of himself standing in front of it, with the pilot's own signature signed across the bottom by some female clerk."

"Chiseling from kids. Bah!"

"Not at all," answered Montgomery in hurt tones. "Intangibles are the most honest merchandise anyone can sell. They are always worth whatever you are willing to pay for them and they never wear out. You can take them to your grave untarnished."

"Hmmmph!"

Harriman listened to this, smiling and saying nothing. Kamens cleared his throat. "If you two ghouls are through cannibalizing the youth of the land, I've another idea."

"Spill it."

"George, you collect stamps, don't you?"

"Yes."

"How much would a cover be worth which had been to the Moon and been cancelled there?"

"Huh? But you couldn't, you know."

"I think we could get our Moon ship declared a legal post office substation without too much trouble. What would it be worth?"

"Uh, that depends on how rare they are."

"There must be some optimum number which will fetch a maximum return. Can you estimate it?"

Strong got a faraway look in his eye, then took out an old-fashioned pencil and commenced to figure. Harriman went on, "Saul, my minor success in buying a share in the Moon from Jones went to my head. How about selling building lots on the Moon?"

"Let's keep this serious, Delos. You can't do that until you've landed there."

"I am serious. I know you are thinking of that ruling back in the 'forties that such land would have to be staked out and accurately described. I want to sell land on the Moon. You figure out a way to make it legal. I'll sell the whole Moon, if I can—surface rights, mineral rights, anything."

"Suppose they want to occupy it?"

"Fine. The more the merrier. I'd like to point out, too, that we'll be in a position to assess taxes on what we have sold. If they don't use it and won't pay taxes, it reverts to us. Now you figure out how to offer it, without going to jail. You may have to advertise it abroad, then plan to peddle it personally in this country, like Irish Sweepstakes tickets."

Kamens looked thoughtful. "We could incorporate the land company in Panama and advertise by video and radio from Mexico. Do you really think you can sell the stuff?"

"You can sell snowballs in Greenland," put in Montgomery. "It's a matter of promotion."

Harriman added. "Did you ever read about the Florida land boom, Saul? People bought lots they had never seen and sold them at tripled prices without ever having laid eyes on

them. Sometimes a parcel would change hands a dozen times
before anyone got around to finding out that the stuff was
ten-foot deep in water. We can offer bargains better than that
—an acre, a guaranteed dry acre with plenty of sunshine, for
maybe ten dollars—or a thousand acres at a dollar an acre.
Who's going to turn down a bargain like that? Particularly
after the rumor gets around that the Moon is believed to be
loaded with uranium?"

"Is it?"

"How should I know? When the boom sags a little we will
announce the selected location of Luna City—and it will just
happen to work out that the land around the site is still available for sale. Don't worry, Saul, if it's real estate, George and
I can sell it. Why, down in the Ozarks, where the land stands
on edge, we used to sell both sides of the same acre." Harriman looked thoughtful. "I think we'll reserve mineral rights—
there just might actually be uranium there!"

Kamens chuckled. "Delos, you are a kid at heart. Just a
great big, overgrown, lovable—juvenile delinquent."

Strong straightened up. "I make it half a million," he said.

"Half a million what?" asked Harriman.

"For the cancelled philatelic covers, of course. That's what
we were talking about. Five thousand is my best estimate of
the number that could be placed with serious collectors and
with dealers. Even then we will have to discount them to a
syndicate and hold back until the ship is built and the trip
looks like a probability."

"Okay," agreed Harriman. "You handle it. I'll just note
that we can tap you for an extra half million toward the end."

"Don't I get a commission?" asked Kamens. "I thought of
it."

"You get a rising vote of thanks—and ten acres on the
Moon. Now what other sources of revenue can we hit?"

"Don't you plan to sell stock?" asked Kamens.

"I was coming to that. Of course—but no preferred stock;
we don't want to be forced through a reorganization. Partici-
pating common, non-voting—"

"Sounds like another banana-state corporation to me."

"Naturally—but I want some of it on the New York Exchange, and you'll have to work that out with the Securities
Exchange Commission somehow. Not too much of it—that's
our show case and we'll have to keep it active and moving
up."

"Wouldn't you rather I swam the Hellespont?"

"Don't be like that, Saul. It beats chasing ambulances, doesn't it?"

"I'm not sure."

"Well, that's what I want you—wups!" The screen on Harriman's desk had come to life. A girl said, "Mr. Harriman, Mr. Dixon is here. He has no appointment but he says that you want to see him."

"I thought I had that thing shut off," muttered Harriman, then pressed his key and said, "O.K., show him in."

"Very well, sir—oh, Mr. Harriman, Mr. Entenza came in just this second."

"Send them both in." Harriman disconnected and turned back to his associates. "Zip your lips, gang, and hold on to your wallets."

"Look who's talking," said Kamens.

Dixon came in with Entenza behind him. He sat down, looked around, started to speak, then checked himself. He looked around again, especially at Entenza.

"Go ahead, Dan," Harriman encouraged him. "'Tain't nobody here at all but just us chickens."

Dixon made up his mind. "I've decided to come in with you, D. D.," he announced. "As an act of faith I went to the trouble of getting this." He took a formal-looking instrument from his pocket and displayed it. It was a sale of lunar rights, from Phineas Morgan to Dixon, phrased in exactly the same fashion as that which Jones had granted to Harriman.

Entenza looked startled, then dipped into his own inner coat pocket. Out came three more sales contracts of the same sort, each from a director of the power syndicate. Harriman cocked an eyebrow at them. "Jack sees you and raises you two, Dan. You want to call?"

Dixon smiled ruefully. "I can just see him." He added two more to the pile, grinned and offered his hand to Entenza.

"Looks like a stand off." Harriman decided to say nothing just yet about seven telestated contracts now locked in his desk—after going to bed the night before he had been quite busy on the phone almost till midnight. "Jack, how much did you pay for those things?"

"Standish held out for a thousand; the others were cheap."

"Damn it, I warned you not to run the price up. Standish will gossip. How about you, Dan?"

"I got them at satisfactory prices."

"So you won't talk, eh? Never mind—gentlemen, how serious are you about this? How much money did you bring with you?"

Entenza looked to Dixon, who answered, "How much does it take?"

"How much can you raise?" demanded Harriman.

Dixon shrugged. "We're getting no place. Let's use figures. A hundred thousand."

Harriman sniffed. "I take it what you really want is to reserve a seat on the first regularly scheduled Moon ship. I'll sell it to you at that price."

"Let's quit sparring, Delos. How much?"

Harriman's face remained calm but he thought furiously. He was caught short, with too little information—he had not even talked figures with his chief engineer as yet. Confound it! why had he left that phone hooked in? "Dan, as I warned you, it will cost you at least a million just to sit down in this game."

"So I thought. How much will it take to *stay* in the game?"

"All you've got."

"Don't be silly, Delos. I've got more than you have."

Harriman lit a cigar, his only sign of agitation. "Suppose you match us, dollar for dollar."

"For which I get two shares?"

"Okay, okay, you chuck in a buck whenever each of us does—share and share alike. But I run things."

"You run the operations," agreed Dixon. "Very well, I'll put up a million now and match you as necessary. You have no objection to me having my own auditor, of course."

"When have I ever cheated you, Dan?"

"Never and there is no need to start."

"Have it your own way—but be damned sure you send a man who can keep his mouth shut."

"He'll keep quiet. I keep his heart in a jar in my safe."

Harriman was thinking about the extent of Dixon's assets. "We just might let you buy in with a second share later, Dan. This operation will be expensive."

Dixon fitted his finger tips carefully together. "We'll meet that question when we come to it. I don't believe in letting an enterprise fold up for lack of capital."

"Good." Harriman turned to Entenza. "You heard what Dan had to say, Jack. Do you like the terms?"

Entenza's forehead was covered with sweat. "I can't raise a million that fast."

"That's all right, Jack. We don't need it this morning. Your note is good; you can take your time liquidating."

"But you said a million is just the beginning. I can't match you indefinitely; you've got to place a limit on it. I've got my family to consider."

"No annuities, Jack? No monies transferred in an irrevocable trust?"

"That's not the point. You'll be able to squeeze me—freeze me out."

Harriman waited for Dixon to say something. Dixon finally said, "We wouldn't squeeze you, Jack—as long as you could prove you had converted every asset you hold. We would let you stay in on a pro rata basis."

Harriman nodded. "That's right, Jack." He was thinking that any shrinkage in Entenza's share would give himself and Strong a clear voting majority.

Strong had been thinking of something of the same nature, for he spoke up suddenly, "I don't like this. Four equal partners—we can be deadlocked too easily."

Dixon shrugged. "I refuse to worry about it. I am in this because I am betting that Delos can manage to make it profitable."

"We'll get to the Moon, Dan!"

"I didn't say that. I am betting that you will show a profit whether we get to the Moon or not. Yesterday evening I spent looking over the public records of several of your companies; they were very interesting. I suggest we resolve any possible deadlock by giving the Director—that's you, Delos—the power to settle ties. Satisfactory, Entenza?"

"Oh, sure!"

Harriman was worried but tried not to show it. He did not trust Dixon, even bearing gifts. He stood up suddenly. "I've got to run, gentlemen. I leave you to Mr. Strong and Mr. Kamens. Come along, Monty." Kamens, he was sure, would not spill anything prematurely, even to nominal full partners. As for Strong—George, he knew, had not even let his left hand know how many fingers there were on his right.

He dismissed Montgomery outside the door of the partners' personal office and went across the hall. Andrew Ferguson, chief engineer of Harriman Enterprises, looked up as he came in. "Howdy, Boss. Say, Mr. Strong gave me an interesting idea for a light switch this morning. It did not seem practical at first but—"

"Skip it. Let one of the boys have it and forget it. You know the line we are on now."

"There have been rumors," Ferguson answered cautiously.

"Fire the man that brought you the rumor. No—send him on a special mission to Tibet and keep him there until we are through. Well, let's get on with it. I want you to build a Moon ship as quickly as possible."

Ferguson threw one leg over the arm of his chair, took out a pen knife and began grooming his nails. "You say that like it was an order to build a privy."

"Why not? There have been theoretically adequate fuels since way back in '49. You get together the team to design it and the gang to build it; you build it—I pay the bills. What could be simpler?"

Ferguson stared at the ceiling. " 'Adequate fuels—' " he repeated dreamily.

"So I said. The figures show that hydrogen and oxygen are enough to get a step rocket to the Moon and back—it's just a matter of proper design."

" 'Proper design,' he says," Ferguson went on in the same gentle voice, then suddenly swung around, jabbed the knife into the scarred desk top and bellowed, "What do you know about proper design? Where do I get the steels? What do I use for a throat liner? How in the hell do I burn enough tons of your crazy mix per second to keep from wasting all my power breaking loose? How can I get a decent mass-ratio with a step rocket? Why in the hell didn't you let me build a proper ship when we had the fuel?"

Harriman waited for him to quiet down, then said, "What do we do about it, Andy?"

"Hmmm. . . . I was thinking about it as I lay abed last night—and my old lady is sore as hell at you; I had to finish the night on the couch. In the first place, Mr. Harriman, the proper way to tackle this is to get a research appropriation from the Department of National Defense. Then you—"

"Damn it, Andy, you stick to engineering and let me handle the political and financial end of it. I don't want your advice."

"Damn it, Delos, don't go off half-cocked. This *is* engineering I'm talking about. The government owns a whole mass of former art about rocketry—all classified. Without a government contract you can't even get a peek at it."

"It can't amount to very much. What can a government rocket do that a Skyways rocket can't do? You told me yourself that Federal rocketry no longer amounted to anything."

Ferguson looked supercilious. "I am afraid I can't explain it in lay terms. You will have to take it for granted that we need those government research reports. There's no sense in spending thousands of dollars in doing work that has already been done."

"Spend the thousands."

"Maybe millions."

"Spend the millions. Don't be afraid to spend money. Andy, I don't want this to be a military job." He considered elaborating to the engineer the involved politics back of his decision, thought better of it. "How bad do you actually need that government stuff? Can't you get the same results by hiring engineers who used to work for the government? Or even hire them away from the government right now?"

Ferguson pursed his lips. "If you insist on hampering me, how can you expect me to get results?"

"I am not hampering you. I am telling you that this is not a government project. If you won't attempt to cope with it on those terms, let me know now, so that I can find somebody who will."

Ferguson started playing mumblety-peg on his desk top. When he got to "noses"—and missed—he said quietly, "I mind a boy who used to work for the government at White Sands. He was a very smart lad indeed—design chief of section."

"You mean he might head up your team?"

"That was the notion."

"What's his name? Where is he? Who's he working for?"

"Well, as it happened, when the government closed down White Sands, it seemed a shame to me that a good boy should be out of a job, so I placed him with Skyways. He's maintenance chief engineer out on the Coast."

"Maintenance? What a hell of a job for a creative man! But you mean he's working for us now? Get him on the screen. No—call the coast and have them send him here in a special rocket; we'll all have lunch together."

"As it happens," Ferguson said quietly, "I got up last night and called him—that's what annoyed the Missus. He's waiting outside. Coster—Bob Coster."

A slow grin spread over Harriman's face. "Andy! You black-hearted old scoundrel, why did you pretend to balk?"

"I wasn't pretending. I like it here, Mr. Harriman. Just as long as you don't interfere, I'll do my job. Now my notion is this: we'll make young Coster chief engineer of the project and give him his head. I won't joggle his elbow; I'll just read the reports. Then you leave him alone, d'you hear me? Nothing makes a good technical man angrier than to have some incompetent nitwit with a check book telling him how to do his job."

"Suits. And I don't want a penny-pinching old fool slowing him down, either. Mind you don't interfere with him, either, or I'll jerk the rug out from under you. Do we understand each other?"

"I think we do."

"Then get him in here."

Apparently Ferguson's concept of a "lad" was about age thirty-five, for such Harriman judged Coster to be. He was tall, lean, and quietly eager. Harriman braced him immediately after shaking hands with, "Bob, can you build a rocket that will go to the Moon?"

Coster took it without blinking. "Do you have a source of X-fuel?" he countered, giving the rocket man's usual shorthand for the isotope fuel formerly produced by the power satellite.

"No."

Coster remained perfectly quiet for several seconds, then answered, "I can put an unmanned messenger rocket on the face of the Moon."

"Not good enough. I want it to go there, land, and come back. Whether it lands here under power or by atmosphere braking is unimportant."

It appeared that Coster never answered promptly; Harriman had the fancy that he could hear wheels turning over in the man's head. "That would be a very expensive job."

"Who asked you how much it would cost? Can you do it?"

"I could try."

"Try, hell. Do you think you can *do* it? Would you bet your shirt on it? Would you be willing to risk your neck in the attempt? If you don't believe in yourself, man, you'll always lose."

"How much will *you* risk, sir? I told you this would be expensive—and I doubt if you have any idea how expensive."

"And I told you not to worry about money. Spend what you need; it's my job to pay the bills. Can you do it?"

"I can do it. I'll let you know later how much it will cost and how long it will take."

"Good. Start getting your team together. Where are we going to do this, Andy?" he added, turning to Ferguson. "Australia?"

"No." It was Coster who answered. "It can't be Australia; I want a mountain catapult. That will save us one step-combination."

"How big a mountain?" asked Harriman. "Will Pikes Peak do?"

"It ought to be in the Andes," objected Ferguson. "The mountains are taller and closer to the equator. After all, we own facilities there—or the Andes Development Company does."

"Do as you like, Bob," Harriman told Coster. "I would prefer Pikes Peak, but it's up to you." He was thinking that there were tremendous business advantages to locating Earth's space port #1 inside the United States—and he could visualize the advertising advantage of having Moon ships blast off from the top of Pikes Peak, in plain view of everyone for hundreds of miles to the East.

"I'll let you know."

"Now about salary. Forget whatever it was we were paying you; how much do you want?"

Coster actually gestured, waving the subject away. "I'll work for coffee and cakes."

"Don't be silly."

"Let me finish. Coffee and cakes and one other thing: I get to make the trip."

Harriman blinked. "Well, I can understand that," he said slowly. "In the meantime I'll put you on a drawing account." He added, "Better calculate for a three-man ship, unless you are a pilot."

"I'm not."

"Three men, then. You see, I'm going along, too."

4

"A GOOD THING you decided to come in, Dan," Harriman was saying, "or you would find yourself out of a job. I'm going to put an awful crimp in the power company before I'm through with this."

Dixon buttered a roll. "Really? How?"

"We'll set up high-temperature piles, like the Arizona job, just like the one that blew up, around the corner on the far face of the Moon. We'll remote-control them; if one explodes it won't matter. And I'll breed more X-fuel in a week than the company turned out in three months. Nothing personal about it; it's just that I want a source of fuel for interplanetary liners. If we can't get good stuff here, we'll have to make it on the Moon."

"Interesting. But where do you propose to get the uranium for six piles? The last I heard the Atomic Energy Commission had the prospective supply earmarked twenty years ahead."

"Uranium? Don't be silly; we'll get it on the Moon."

"On the Moon? Is there uranium on the Moon?"

"Didn't you know? I thought that was why you decided to join up with me?"

"No, I didn't know," Dixon said deliberately. "What proof have you?"

"Me? I'm no scientist, but it's a well-understood fact. Spectroscopy, or something. Catch one of the professors. But don't go showing too much interest; we aren't ready to show our hand." Harriman stood up. "I've got to run, or I'll miss the shuttle for Rotterdam. Thanks for the lunch." He grabbed his hat and left.

Harriman stood up. "Suit yourself, Mynheer van der Velde. I'm giving you and your colleagues a chance to hedge your bets. Your geologists all agree that diamonds result from volcanic action. What do you think we will find *there?*" He dropped a large photograph of the Moon on the Hollander's desk.

The diamond merchant looked impassively at the pictured

planet, pockmarked by a thousand giant craters. "If you get there, Mr. Harriman."

Harriman swept up the picture. "We'll get there. And we'll find diamonds—though I would be the first to admit that it may be twenty years or even forty before there is a big enough strike to matter. I've come to you because I believe that the worst villain in our social body is the man who introduces a major new economic factor without planning his innovation in such a way as to permit peaceful adjustment. I don't like panics. But all I can do is warn you. Good day."

"Sit down, Mr. Harriman. I'm always confused when a man explains how he is going to do *me* good. Suppose you tell me instead how this is going to do *you* good? Then we can discuss how to protect the world market against a sudden influx of diamonds from the Moon."

Harriman sat down.

Harriman liked the Low Countries. He was delighted to locate a dog-drawn milk cart whose young master wore real wooden shoes; he happily took pictures and tipped the child heavily, unaware that the set-up was arranged for tourists. He visited several other diamond merchants but without speaking of the Moon. Among other purchases he found a brooch for Charlotte—a peace offering.

Then he took a taxi to London, planted a story with the representatives of the diamond syndicate there, arranged with his London solicitors to be insured by Lloyd's of London through a dummy, *against* a successful Moon flight, and called his home office. He listened to numerous reports, especially those concerning Montgomery, and found that Montgomery was in New Delhi. He called him there, spoke with him at length, then hurried to the port just in time to catch his ship. He was in Colorado the next morning.

At Peterson Field, east of Colorado Springs, he had trouble getting through the gate, even though it was now his domain, under lease. Of course he could have called Coster and gotten it straightened out at once, but he wanted to look around before seeing Coster. Fortunately the head guard knew him by sight; he got in and wandered around for an hour or more, a tri-colored badge pinned to his coat to give him freedom.

The machine shop was moderately busy, so was the foundry . . . but most of the shops were almost deserted. Harriman left the shops, went into the main engineering building. The drafting room and the loft were fairly active, as was the computation section. But there were unoccupied desks in the structures group and a churchlike quiet in the metals group and in the adjoining metallurgical laboratory. He was about to cross over into the chemicals and materials annex when Coster suddenly showed up.

"Mr. Harriman! I just heard you were here."

"Spies everywhere," remarked Harriman. "I didn't want to disturb you."

"Not at all. Let's go up to my office."

Settled there a few moments later Harriman asked, "Well —how's it going?"

Coster frowned. "All right, I guess."

Harriman noted that the engineer's desk baskets were piled high with papers which spilled over onto the desk. Before Harriman could answer, Coster's desk phone lit up and a feminine voice said sweetly, "Mr. Coster—Mr. Morgenstern is calling."

"Tell him I'm busy."

After a short wait the girl answered in a troubled voice, "He says he's just got to speak to you, sir."

Coster looked annoyed. "Excuse me a moment, Mr. Harriman—O.K., put him on."

The girl was replaced by a man who said, "Oh, there you are—what was the hold up? Look, Chief, we're in a jam about these trucks. Every one of them that we leased needs an overhaul and now it turns out that the White Fleet company won't do anything about it—they're sticking to the fine print in the contract. Now the way I see it, we'd do better to cancel the contract and do business with Peak City Transport. They have a scheme that looks good to me. They guarantee to—"

"Take care of it," snapped Coster. "You made the contract and you have authority to cancel. You know that."

"Yes, but Chief, I figured this would be something you would want to pass on personally. It involves policy and—"

"Take care of it! I don't give a damn what you do as long as we have transportation when we need it." He switched off.

"Who is that man?" inquired Harriman.

"Who? Oh, that's Morgenstern, Claude Morgenstern."

"Not his name—what does he do?"

"He's one of my assistants—buildings, grounds, and transportation."

"Fire him!"

Coster looked stubborn. Before he could answer a secretary came in and stood insistently at his elbow with a sheaf of papers. He frowned, initialed them, and sent her out.

"Oh, I don't mean that as an order," Harriman added, "but I do mean it as serious advice. I won't give orders in your backyard,—but will you listen to a few minutes of advice?"

"Naturally," Coster agreed stiffly.

"Mmm . . . this your first job as top boss?"

Coster hesitated, then admitted it.

"I hired you on Ferguson's belief that you were the engineer most likely to build a successful Moon ship. I've had no reason to change my mind. But top administration ain't engineering, and maybe I can show you a few tricks there, if you'll let me." He waited. "I'm not criticizing," he added. "Top bossing is like sex; until you've had it, you don't know about it." Harriman had the mental reservation that if the boy would not take advice, he would suddenly be out of a job, whether Ferguson liked it or not.

Coster drummed on his desk. "I don't know what's wrong and that's a fact. It seems as if I can't turn anything over to anybody and have it done properly. I feel as if I were swimming in quicksand."

"Done much engineering lately?"

"I try to." Coster waved at another desk in the corner. "I work there, late at night."

"That's no good. I hired you as an engineer. Bob, this set-up is all wrong. The joint ought to be jumping—and it's not. Your office ought to be quiet as a grave. Instead your office is jumping and the plant looks like a graveyard."

Coster buried his face in his hands, then looked up. "I know it. I know what needs to be done—but every time I try to tackle a technical problem some bloody fool wants me to make a decision about trucks—or telephones—or some damn thing. I'm sorry, Mr. Harriman. I thought I could do it."

Harriman said very gently, "Don't let it throw you, Bob. You haven't had much sleep lately, have you? Tell you what —we'll put over a fast one on Ferguson. I'll take that desk you're at for a few days and build you a set-up to protect you against such things. I want that brain of yours thinking about reaction vectors and fuel efficiencies and design stresses, not about contracts for trucks." Harriman stepped to the door, looked around the outer office and spotted a man who might or might not be the office's chief clerk. "Hey, you! C'mere."

The man looked startled, got up, came to the door and said, "Yes?"

"I want that desk in the corner and all the stuff that's on it moved to an empty office on this floor, right away."

The clerk raised his eyebrows. "And who are you, if I may ask?"

"God damn it—"

"Do as he tells you, Weber," Coster put in.

"I want it done inside of twenty minutes," added Harriman. "Jump!"

He turned back to Coster's other desk, punched the phone, and presently was speaking to the main offices of Skyways. "Jim, is your boy Jock Berkeley around? Put him on leave and send him to me, at Peterson Field, right away, special trip. I want the ship he comes in to raise ground ten minutes after we sign off. Send his gear after him." Harriman listened for a moment, then answered, "No, your organization won't fall apart if you lose Jock—or, if it does, maybe we've been paying the wrong man the top salary . . . okay, okay, you're entitled to one swift kick at my tail the next time you catch up with me, but send Jock. So long."

He supervised getting Coster and his other desk moved into another office, saw to it that the phone in the new office was disconnected, and, as an afterthought, had a couch moved in there, too. "We'll install a projector, and a drafting machine and bookcases and other junk like that tonight," he told Coster. "Just make a list of anything you need—to work on *engineering*. And call me if you want anything." He went back to the nominal chief-engineer's office and got happily to work trying to figure where the organization stood and what was wrong with it.

Some four hours later he took Berkeley in to meet Coster. The chief engineer was asleep at his desk, head cradled on his arms. Harriman started to back out, but Coster roused. "Oh! Sorry," he said, blushing, "I must have dozed off."

"That's why I brought you the couch," said Harriman. "It's more restful. Bob, meet Jock Berkeley. He's your new slave. You remain chief engineer and top, undisputed boss. Jock is Lord High Everything Else. From now on you've got absolutely nothing to worry about—except for the little detail of building a Moon ship."

They shook hands. "Just one thing I ask, Mr. Coster," Berkeley said seriously, "bypass me all you want to—you'll have to run the technical show—but for God's sake record it so I'll know what's going on. I'm going to have a switch placed on your desk that will operate a sealed recorder at my desk."

"Fine!" Coster was looking, Harriman thought, younger already.

"And if you want something that is not technical, don't do it yourself. Just flip a switch and whistle; it'll get done!" Berkeley glanced at Harriman. "The Boss says he wants to talk with you about the real job. I'll leave you and get busy." He left.

Harriman sat down; Coster followed suit and said, "Whew!"

"Feel better?"

"I like the looks of that fellow Berkeley."

"That's good; he's your twin brother from now on. Stop worrying; I've used him before. You'll think you're living in a well-run hospital. By the way, where do you live?"

"At a boarding house in the Springs."

"That's ridiculous. And you don't even have a place here to sleep?" Harriman reached over to Coster's desk, got through to Berkeley. "Jock—get a suite for Mr. Coster at the Broadmoor, under a phoney name."

"Right."

"And have this stretch along here adjacent to his office fitted out as an apartment."

"Right. Tonight."

"Now, Bob, about the Moon ship. Where do we stand?"

They spent the next two hours contentedly running over the details of the problem, as Coster had laid them out. Admittedly very little work had been done since the field was leased but Coster had accomplished considerable theoretical work and computation before he had gotten swamped in administrative details. Harriman, though no engineer and certainly not a mathematician outside the primitive arithmetic of money, had for so long devoured everything he could find about space travel that he was able to follow most of what Coster showed him.

"I don't see anything here about your mountain catapult," he said presently.

Coster looked vexed. "Oh, that! Mr. Harriman, I spoke too quickly."

"Huh? How come? I've had Montgomery's boys drawing up beautiful pictures of what things will look like when we are running regular trips. I intend to make Colorado Springs the spaceport capital of the world. We hold the franchise of the old cog railroad now; what's the hitch?"

"Well, it's both time and money."

"Forget money. That's my pidgin."

"Time then. I still think an electric gun is the best way to get the initial acceleration for a chem-powered ship. Like this—" He began to sketch rapidly. "It enables you to omit the first step-rocket stage, which is bigger than all the others put together and is terribly inefficient, as it has such a poor mass-ratio. But what do you have to do to get it? You can't build a tower, not a tower a couple of miles high, strong enough to take the thrusts—not this year, anyway. So you have to use a mountain. Pikes Peak is as good as any; it's accessible, at least.

"But what do you have to do to use it? First, a tunnel in through the side, from Manitou to just under the peak, and big enough to take the loaded ship—"

"Lower it down from the top," suggested Harriman.

Coster answered, "I thought of that. Elevators two miles high for loaded space ships aren't exactly built out of string, in fact they aren't built out of any available materials. It's possible to gimmick the catapult itself so that the accelerating coils can be reversed and timed differently to do the job, but believe me, Mr. Harriman, it will throw you into other engineering problems quite as great . . . such as a giant railroad up to the top of the ship. And it still leaves you with the shaft of the catapult itself to be dug. It can't be as small as the ship, not like a gun barrel for a bullet. It's got to be considerably larger; you don't compress a column of air two miles high with impunity. Oh, a mountain catapult could be built, but it might take ten years—or longer."

"Then forget it. We'll build it for the future but not for this flight. No, wait—how about a *surface* catapult. We scoot up the side of the mountain and curve it up at the end?"

"Quite frankly, I think something like that is what will eventually be used. But, as of today, it just creates new problems. Even if we could devise an electric gun in which you could make that last curve—we can't, at present—the ship would have to be designed for terrific side stresses and all the additional weight would be parasitic so far as our main purpose is concerned, the design of a rocket ship."

"Well, Bob, what *is* your solution?"

Coster frowned. "Go back to what we know how to do—build a step rocket."

5

"MONTY—"

"Yeah, Chief?"

"Have you ever heard this song?" Harriman hummed, *"The Moon belongs to everyone; the best things in life are free—,"* then sang it, badly off key.

"Can't say as I ever have."

"It was before your time. I want it dug out again. I want it revived, plugged until Hell wouldn't ·have it, and on everybody's lips."

"O.K." Montgomery took out his memorandum pad. "When do you want it to reach its top?"

Harriman considered. "In, say, about three months. Then I want the first phrase picked up and used in advertising slogans."

"A cinch."

"How are things in Florida, Monty?"

"I thought we were going to have to buy the whole damned legislature until we got the rumor spread around that Los Angeles had contracted to have a City-Limits-of-Los-Angeles sign planted on the Moon for publicity pix. Then they came around."

"Good." Harriman pondered. "You know, that's not a bad idea. How much do you think the Chamber of Commerce of Los Angeles would pay for such a picture?"

Montgomery made another note. "I'll look into it."

"I suppose you are about ready to crank up Texas, now that Florida is loaded?"

"Most any time now. We're spreading a few snide rumors first."

Headline from Dallas-Fort Worth *Banner*:

"THE MOON BELONGS TO TEXAS!!!"

"—and that's all for tonight, kiddies. Don't forget to send in those box tops, or reasonable facsimiles. Remember—first prize is a thousand-acre ranch on the Moon itself, free and clear; the second prize is a six-foot scale model of the actual Moon ship, and there are fifty, count them, fifty third prizes, each a saddle-trained Shetland pony. Your hundred word composition 'Why I want to go to the Moon' will be judged for sincerity and originality, not on literary merit. Send those box-tops to Uncle Taffy, Box 214, Juarez, Old Mexico."

Harriman was shown into the office of the president of the Moka-Coka Company ("Only a Moke is truly a coke"—"Drink the Cola drink with the Lift"). He paused at the door, some twenty feet from the president's desk and quickly pinned a two-inch wide button to his lapel.

Patterson Griggs looked up. "Well, this is really an honor, D. D. Do come in and—" The soft-drink executive stopped suddenly, his expression changed. "What are you doing wearing *that*?" he snapped. "Trying to annoy me?"

"That" was the two-inch disc; Harriman unpinned it and put it in his pocket. It was a celluloid advertising pin, in plain yellow; printed on it in black, almost covering it, was a simple

(6 +), the trademark of Moka-Coka's only serious rival.

"No," answered Harriman, "though I don't blame you for being irritated. I see half the school kids in the country wearing these silly buttons. But I came to give a friendly tip, not to annoy you."

"What do you mean?"

"When I paused at your door that pin on my lapel was just the size—to you, standing at your desk—as the full Moon looks when you are standing in your garden, looking up at it. You didn't have any trouble reading what was on the pin, did you? I know you didn't; you yelled at me before either one of us stirred."

"What about it?"

"How would you feel—and what would the effect be on your sales—if there was 'six-plus' written across the face of the Moon instead of just on a school kid's sweater?"

Griggs thought about it, then said, "D. D., don't make poor jokes. I've had a bad day."

"I'm not joking. As you have probably heard around the Street, I'm behind this Moon trip venture. Between ourselves, Pat, it's quite an expensive undertaking, even for me. A few days ago a man came to me—you'll pardon me if I don't mention names? You can figure it out. Anyhow, this man represented a client who wanted to buy the advertising concession for the Moon. He knew we weren't sure of success; but he said his client would take the risk.

"At first I couldn't figure out what he was talking about; he set me straight. Then I thought he was kidding. Then I was shocked. Look at this—" Harriman took out a large sheet of paper and spread it on Griggs' desk. "You see the equipment is set up anywhere near the center of the Moon, as we see it. Eighteen pyrotechnics rockets shoot out in eighteen directions, like the spokes of a wheel, but to carefully calculated distances. They hit and the bombs they carry go off, spreading finely divided carbon black for calculated distances. There's no air on the Moon, you know, Pat—a fine powder will throw just as easily as a javelin. Here's your result." He turned the paper over; on the back there was a picture of the Moon, printed lightly. Overlaying it, in black, heavy print

was: (6 +)

"So it *is* that outfit—those poisoners!"

"No, no, I didn't say so! But it illustrates the point; six-plus is only two symbols; it can be spread large enough to be read on the face of the Moon."

Griggs stared at the horrid advertisement. "I don't believe it will work!"

"A reliable pyrotechnics firm has guaranteed that it will—provided I can deliver their equipment to the spot. After all, Pat, it doesn't take much of a pyrotechnics rocket to go a long distance on the Moon. Why, you could throw a baseball a couple of miles yourself—low gravity, you know."

"People would never stand for it. It's sacrilege!"

Harriman looked sad. "I wish you were right. But they stand for sky-writing—and video commercials."

Griggs chewed his lip. "Well, I don't see why you come to me with it," he exploded. "You know damn well the name of my product won't go on the face of the Moon. The letters would be too small to be read."

Harriman nodded. "That's exactly why I came to you. Pat, this isn't just a business venture to me; it's my heart and soul. It just made me sick to think of somebody actually wanting to use the face of the Moon for advertising. As you say, it's sacrilege. But somehow, these jackals found out I was pressed for cash. They came to me when they knew I would have to listen.

"I put them off. I promised them an answer on Thursday. Then I went home and lay awake about it. After a while I thought of you."

"Me?"

"You. You and your company. After all, you've got a good product and you need legitimate advertising for it. It occurred to me that there are more ways to use the Moon in advertising than by defacing it. Now just suppose that your company bought the same concession, but with the public-spirited promise of never letting it be used. Suppose you featured that fact in your ads? Suppose you ran pictures of a boy and girl, sitting out under the Moon, sharing a bottle of Moke? Suppose Moke was the only soft drink carried on the first trip to the Moon? But I don't have to tell you how to do it." He glanced at his watch finger. "I've got to run and I don't want to rush you. If you want to do business, just leave word at my office by noon tomorrow and I'll have our man Montgomery get in touch with your advertising chief."

The head of the big newspaper chain kept him waiting the minimum time reserved for tycoons and cabinet members. Again Harriman stopped at the threshold of a large office and fixed a disc to his lapel.

"Howdy, Delos," the publisher said, "how's the traffic in green cheese today?" He then caught sight of the button and frowned. "If that is a joke, it is in poor taste."

Harriman pocketed the disc; it displayed not $(6+)$, but the hammer-and-sickle.

"No," he said, "it's not a joke; it's a nightmare. Colonel, you and I are among the few people in this country who realize that communism is still a menace."

Sometime later they were talking as chummily as if the Colonel's chain had not obstructed the Moon venture since its inception. The publisher waved a cigar at his desk. "How did you come by those plans? Steal them?"

"They were copied," Harriman answered with narrow truth. "But they aren't important. The important thing is to get there first; we can't risk having an enemy rocket base on the Moon. For years I've had a recurrent nightmare of waking up and seeing headlines that the Russians had landed on the Moon and declared the Lunar Soviet—say thirteen men and two female scientists—and had petitioned for entrance into the U.S.S.R.—and that the petition had, of course, been graciously granted by the Supreme Soviet. I used to wake up and tremble. I don't know that they would actually go through with painting a hammer and sickle on the face of the Moon, but it's consistent with their psychology. Look at those enormous posters they are always hanging up."

The publisher bit down hard on his cigar. "We'll see what we can work out. Is there any way you can speed up your take-off?"

6

"MR. HARRIMAN?"

"Yes?"

"That Mr. LeCroix is here again."

"Tell him I can't see him."

"Yes, sir—uh, Mr. Harriman, he did not mention it the other day but he says he is a rocket pilot."

"Damn it, send him around to Skyways. I don't hire pilots."

A man's face crowded into the screen, displacing Harriman's reception secretary. "Mr. Harriman—I'm Leslie Le-Croix, relief pilot of the *Charon*."

"I don't care if you are the Angel Gab— Did you say *Charon*?"

"I said *Charon*. And I've got to talk to you."

"Come in."

Harriman greeted his visitor, offered him tobacco, then looked him over with interest. The *Charon*, shuttle rocket to the lost power satellite, had been the nearest thing to a space ship the world had yet seen. Its pilot, lost in the same explosion that had destroyed the satellite and the *Charon* had been the first, in a way, of the coming breed of spacemen.

Harriman wondered how it had escaped his attention that the *Charon* had alternating pilots. He had known it, of course —but somehow he had forgotten to take the fact into account. He had written off the power satellite, its shuttle rocket and everything about it, ceased to think about them. He now looked at LeCroix with curiosity.

He saw a small, neat man with a thin, intelligent face, and the big, competent hands of a jockey. LeCroix returned his inspection without embarrassment. He seemed calm and utterly sure of himself.

"Well, Captain LeCroix?"

"You are building a Moon ship."

"Who says so?"

"A Moon ship is being built. The boys all say you are behind it."

"Yes?"

"I want to pilot it."

"Why should you?"

"I'm the best man for it."

Harriman paused to let out a cloud of tobacco smoke. "If you can prove that, the billet is yours."

"It's a deal." LeCroix stood up. "I'll leave my name and address outside."

"Wait a minute. I said 'if.' Let's talk. I'm going along on this trip myself; I want to know more about you before I trust my neck to you."

They discussed Moon flight, interplanetary travel, rocketry, what they might find on the Moon. Gradually Harriman warmed up, as he found another spirit so like his own, so obsessed with the Wonderful Dream. Subconsciously he had already accepted LeCroix; the conversation began to assume that it would be a joint venture.

After a long time Harriman said, "This is fun, Les, but I've got to do a few chores yet today, or none of us will get to the Moon. You go on out to Peterson Field and get acquainted with Bob Coster—I'll call him. If the pair of you can manage to get along, we'll talk contract." He scribbled a chit and handed it to LeCroix. "Give this to Miss Perkins as you go out and she'll put you on the payroll."

"That can wait."

"Man's got to eat."

LeCroix accepted it but did not leave. "There's one thing I don't understand, Mr. Harriman."

"Huh?"

"Why are you planning on a chemically powered ship? Not that I object; I'll herd her. But why do it the hard way? I know you had the *City of Brisbane* refitted for X-fuel—"

Harriman stared at him. "Are you off your nut, Les? You're asking why pigs don't have wings—there isn't any X-fuel and there won't be any more until we make some ourselves—on the Moon."

"Who told you that?"

"What do you mean?"

"The way I heard it, the Atomic Energy Commission allocated X-fuel, under treaty, to several other countries—and some of them weren't prepared to make use of it. But they got it just the same. What happened to it?"

"Oh, *that!* Sure, Les, several of the little outfits in Central America and South America were cut in for a slice of pie for political reasons, even though they had no way to eat it. A good thing, too—we bought it back and used it to ease the immediate power shortage." Harriman frowned. "You're right, though. I should have grabbed some of the stuff then."

"Are you *sure* it's all gone?"

"Why, of course, I'm— No, I'm not. I'll look into it. G'bye, Les."

His contacts were able to account for every pound of X-fuel in short order—save for Costa Rica's allotment. That nation had declined to sell back its supply because its power plant, suitable for X-fuel, had been almost finished at the time of the disaster. Another inquiry disclosed that the power plant had never been finished.

Montgomery was even then in Managua; Nicaragua had had a change in administration and Montgomery was making certain that the special position of the local Moon corporation was protected. Harriman sent him a coded message to proceed to San José, locate X-fuel, buy it and ship it back—at any cost. He then went to see the chairman of the Atomic Energy Commission.

That official was apparently glad to see him and anxious to be affable. Harriman got around to explaining that he wanted a license to do experimental work in isotopes—X-fuel, to be precise.

"This should be brought up through the usual channels, Mr. Harriman."

"It will be. This is a preliminary inquiry. I want to know your reactions."

"After all, I am not the only commissioner . . . and we almost always follow the recommendations of our technical branch."

"Don't fence with me, Carl. You know dern well you control a working majority. Off the record, what do you say?"

"Well, D. D.—off the record—you can't get any X-fuel, so why get a license?"

"Let me worry about that."

"Mmmm . . . we weren't required by law to follow every millicurie of X-fuel, since it isn't classed as potentially suitable for mass weapons. Just the same, we knew what happened to it. There's none available."

Harriman kept quiet.

"In the second place, you can have an X-fuel license, if you wish—for any purpose but rocket fuel."

"Why the restriction?"

"You are building a Moon ship, aren't you?"

"Me?"

"Don't *you* fence with me, D. D. It's my business to know things. You can't use X-fuel for rockets, even if you can find it—which you can't." The chairman went to a vault back of his desk and returned with a quarto volume, which he laid in front of Harriman. It was titled: *Theoretical Investigation into the Stability of Several Radioisotopic Fuels—With Notes on the* Charon-*Power-Satellite Disaster*. The cover had a serial number and was stamped: *SECRET*.

Harriman pushed it away. "I've got no business looking at that—and I wouldn't understand it if I did."

The chairman grinned. "Very well, I'll tell you what's in it. I'm deliberately tying your hands, D. D., by trusting you with a defense secret—"

"I won't have it, I tell you!"

"Don't try to power a space ship with X-fuel, D. D. It's a lovely fuel—but it may go off like a firecracker anywhere out in space. That report tells why."

"Confound it, we ran the *Charon* for nearly three years!"

"You were lucky. It is the official—but utterly confidential —opinion of the government that the *Charon* set off the power satellite, rather than the satellite setting off the *Charon*. We had thought it was the other way around at first, and of course it could have been, but there was the disturbing matter of the radar records. It seemed as if the ship had gone up a split second before the satellite. So we made an intensive theoretical investigation. X-fuel is too dangerous for rockets."

"That's ridiculous! For every pound burned in the *Charon* there were at least a hundred pounds used in power plants on the surface. How come *they* didn't explode?"

"It's a matter of shielding. A rocket necessarily uses less shielding than a stationary plant, but the worst feature is that it operates out in space. The disaster is presumed to have been triggered by primary cosmic radiation. If you like, I'll call in one of the mathematical physicists to elucidate."

Harriman shook his head. "You know I don't speak the language." He considered. "I suppose that's all there is to it?"

"I'm afraid so. I'm really sorry." Harriman got up to leave. "Uh, one more thing, D. D.—you weren't thinking of approaching any of my subordinate colleagues, were you?"

"Of course not. Why should I?"

"I'm glad to hear it. You know, Mr. Harriman, some of our staff may not be the most brilliant scientists in the world —it's very hard to keep a first-class scientist happy in the conditions of government service. But there is one thing I am sure of; all of them are utterly incorruptible. Knowing that, I would take it as a personal affront if anyone tried to influence one of my people—a very personal affront."

"So?"

"Yes. By the way, I used to box light-heavyweight in college. I've kept it up."

"Hmmm . . . well, I never went to college. But I play a fair game of poker." Harriman suddenly grinned. "I won't tamper with your boys, Carl. It would be too much like offering a bribe to a starving man. Well, so long."

When Harriman got back to his office he called in one of his confidential clerks. "Take another coded message to Mr. Montgomery. Tell him to ship the stuff to Panama City, rather than to the States." He started to dictate another message to Coster, intending to tell him to stop work on the *Pioneer*, whose skeleton was already reaching skyward on the Colorado prairie, and shift to the *Santa Maria*, formerly the *City of Brisbane*.

He thought better of it. Take-off would have to be outside the United States; with the Atomic Energy Commission acting stuffy, it would not do to try to move the *Santa Maria:* it would give the show away.

Nor could she be moved without refitting her for chem-powered flight. No, he would have another ship of the *Brisbane* class taken out of service and sent to Panama, and the power plant of the *Santa Maria* could be disassembled and shipped there, too. Coster could have the new ship ready in six weeks, maybe sooner . . . and he, Coster, and LeCroix would start for the Moon!

The devil with worries over primary cosmic rays! The *Charon* operated for three years, didn't she? They would make the trip, they would prove it could be done, then, if safer fuels were needed, there would be the incentive to dig them out. The important thing was to do it, make the trip. If Columbus had waited for decent ships, we'd all still be in Europe. A man had to take some chances or he never got anywhere.

Contentedly he started drafting the messages that would get the new scheme underway.

He was interrupted by a secretary. "Mr. Harriman, Mr. Montgomery wants to speak to you."

"Eh? Has he gotten my code already?"

"I don't know, sir."

"Well, put him on."

Montgomery had not received the second message. But he had news for Harriman: Costa Rica had sold all its X-fuel to the English Ministry of Power, soon after the disaster. There was not an ounce of it left, neither in Costa Rica, nor in England.

Harriman sat and moped for several minutes after Montgomery had cleared the screen. Then he called Coster. "Bob? Is LeCroix there?"

"Right here—we were about to go out to dinner together. Here he is, now."

"Howdy, Les. Les, that was a good brain storm of yours, but it didn't work. Somebody stole the baby."

"Eh? Oh, I get you, I'm sorry."

"Don't ever waste time being sorry. We'll go ahead as originally planned. We'll get there!"

"Sure we will."

7

FROM THE JUNE ISSUE of *Popular Technics* magazine: "URANIUM PROSPECTING ON THE MOON—a Fact Article about a soon-to-come Major Industry"

From HOLIDAY: "*Honeymoon on the Moon*—A Discussion of the Miracle Resort that your children will enjoy, as told to our travel editor."

From the *American Sunday Magazine*: "DIAMONDS ON THE MOON?—A World Famous Scientist Shows Why Diamonds Must Be Common As Pebbles in the Lunar Craters"

"Of course, Clem, I don't know anything about electronics, but here is the way it was explained to me. You can hold the beam of a television broadcast down to a degree or so these days, can't you?"

"Yes—if you use a big enough reflector."

"You'll have plenty of elbow room. Now Earth covers a space two degrees wide, as seen from the Moon. Sure, it's quite a distance away, but you'd have no power losses and absolutely perfect and unchanging conditions for transmission. Once you made your set-up, it wouldn't be any more expensive than broadcasting from the top of a mountain here, and a derned sight less expensive than keeping copters in the air from coast to coast, the way you're having to do now."

"It's a fantastic scheme, Delos."

"What's fantastic about it? Getting to the Moon is my worry, not yours. Once we are there, there's going to be television back to Earth, you can bet your shirt on that. It's a natural set-up for line-of-sight transmission. If you aren't interested, I'll have to find someone who is."

"I didn't say I wasn't interested."

"Well, make up your mind. Here's another thing, Clem—I don't want to go sticking my nose into your business, but haven't you had a certain amount of trouble since you lost the use of the power satellite as a relay station?"

"You know the answer; don't needle me. Expenses have gone out of sight without any improvement in revenue."

"That wasn't quite what I meant. How about censorship?"

The television executive threw up his hands. "Don't say that word! How anybody expects a man to stay in business with every two-bit wowser in the country claiming a veto over what we can say and can't say and what we can show and what we can't show—it's enough to make you throw up. The whole principle is wrong; it's like demanding that grown men live on skim milk because the baby can't eat steak. If I were able to lay my hands on those confounded, prurient-minded, slimy—"

"Easy! Easy!" Harriman interrupted. "Did it ever occur to you that there is absolutely no way to interfere with a telecast from the Moon—and that boards of censorship on Earth won't have jurisdiction in any case?"

"What? Say that again."

"'LIFE goes to the Moon.' LIFE-TIME Inc. is proud to announce that arrangements have been completed to bring LIFE's readers a personally conducted tour of the first trip to our satellite. In place of the usual weekly feature 'LIFE Goes to a Party' there will commence, immediately after the return of the first successful—"

"ASSURANCE FOR THE NEW AGE"

(An excerpt from an advertisement of the North Atlantic Mutual Insurance and Liability Company)

"—the same looking-to-the-future that protected our policyholders after the Chicago Fire, after the San Francisco Fire, after every disaster since the War of 1812, now reaches out to insure you from unexpected loss *even on the Moon*—"

"THE UNBOUNDED FRONTIERS OF TECHNOLOGY"

"When the Moon ship *Pioneer* climbs skyward on a ladder of flame, twenty-seven essential devices in her 'innards' will be powered by especially-engineered *DELTA* batteries—"

"Mr. Harriman, could you come out to the field?"

"What's up, Bob?"

"Trouble," Coster answered briefly.

"What sort of trouble?"

Coster hesitated. "I'd rather not talk about it by screen. If you can't come, maybe Les and I had better come there."

"I'll be there this evening."

When Harriman got there he saw that LeCroix's impassive face concealed bitterness, Coster looked stubborn and defensive. He waited until the three were alone in Coster's workroom before he spoke. "Let's have it, boys."

LeCroix looked at Coster. The engineer chewed his lip and said, "Mr. Harriman, you know the stages this design has been through."

"More or less."

"We had to give up the catapult idea. Then we had this—" Coster rummaged on his desk, pulled out a perspective treatment of a four-step rocket, large but rather graceful. "Theoretically it was a possibility; practically it cut things too fine. By the time the stress group boys and the auxiliary group and the control group got through adding things we were forced to come to this—" He hauled out another sketch; it was basically like the first, but squattier, almost pyramidal. "We added a fifth stage as a ring around the fourth stage. We even managed to save some weight by using most of the auxiliary and control equipment for the fourth stage to control the fifth stage. And it still had enough sectional density to punch through the atmosphere with no important drag, even if it was clumsy."

Harriman nodded. "You know, Bob, we're going to have to get away from the step rocket idea before we set up a scheduled run to the Moon."

"I don't see how you can avoid it with chem-powered rockets."

"If you had a decent catapult you could put a single-stage chem-powered rocket into an orbit around the Earth, couldn't you?"

"Sure."

"That's what we'll do. Then it will refuel in that orbit."

"The old space-station set-up. I suppose that makes sense—in fact I know it does. Only the ship wouldn't refuel and continue on to the Moon. The economical thing would be to have special ships that never landed anywhere make the jump from there to another fueling station around the Moon. Then—"

Le Croix displayed a most unusual impatience. "All that doesn't mean anything now. Get on with the story, Bob."

"Right," agreed Harriman.

"Well, this model should have done it. And, damn it, it still should do it."

Harriman looked puzzled. "But, Bob, that's the approved design, isn't it? That's what you've got two-thirds built right out there on the field."

"Yes." Coster looked stricken. "But it won't do it. It won't work."

"Why not?"

"Because I've had to add in too much dead weight, that's why. Mr. Harriman, you aren't an engineer; you've no idea how fast the performance falls off when you have to clutter up a ship with anything but fuel and power plant. Take the landing arrangements for the fifth-stage power ring. You use that stage for a minute and a half, then you throw it away. But you don't dare take a chance of it falling on Wichita or Kansas City. We have to include a parachute sequence. Even then we have to plan on tracking it by radar and cutting the shrouds by radio control when it's over empty countryside and not too high. That means more weight, besides the parachute. By the time we are through, we don't get a net addition of a mile a second out of that stage. It's not enough."

Harriman stirred in his chair. "Looks like we made a mistake in trying to launch it from the States. Suppose we took off from someplace unpopulated, say the Brazil coast, and let the booster stages fall in the Atlantic; how much would that save you?"

Coster looked off in the distance, then took out a slide rule. "Might work."

"How much of a chore will it be to move the ship, at this stage?"

"Well . . . it would have to be disassembled completely; nothing less would do. I can't give you a cost estimate off hand, but it would be expensive."

"How long would it take?"

"Hmm . . . shucks, Mr. Harriman, I can't answer off hand. Two years—eighteen months, with luck. We'd have to prepare a site. We'd have to build shops."

Harriman thought about it, although he knew the answer in his heart. His shoe string, big as it was, was stretched to the danger point. He couldn't keep up the promotion, on talk alone, for another two years; he *had* to have a successful flight and soon—or the whole jerry-built financial structure would burst. "No good, Bob."

"I was afraid of that. Well. I tried to add still a sixth stage." He held up another sketch. "You see that monstrosity? I reached the point of diminishing returns. The final effective velocity is actually less with this abortion than with the five-step job."

"Does that mean you are whipped, Bob? You can't build a Moon ship?"

"No. I—"

LeCroix said suddenly, "Clear out Kansas."

"Eh?" asked Harriman.

"Clear everybody out of Kansas and Eastern Colorado. Let the fifth and fourth sections fall anywhere in that area. The third section falls in the Atlantic; the second section goes into a permanent orbit—and the ship itself goes on to the Moon. You could do it if you didn't have to waste weight on the parachuting of the fifth and fourth sections. Ask Bob."

"So? How about it, Bob?"

"That's what I said before. It was the parasitic penalties that whipped us. The basic design is all right."

"Hmmm . . . somebody hand me an Atlas." Harriman looked up Kansas and Colorado, did some rough figuring. He stared off into space, looking surprisingly, for the moment, as Coster did when the engineer was thinking about his own work. Finally he said, "It won't work."

"Why not?"

"Money. I told you not to worry about money—for the ship. But it would cost upward of six or seven million dollars to evacuate that area even for a day. We'd have to settle nuisance suits out of hand; we couldn't wait. And there would be a few die-hards who just couldn't move anyhow."

LeCroix said savagely, "If the crazy fools won't move, let them take their chances."

"I know how you feel, Les. But this project is too big to hide and too big to move. Unless we protect the bystanders we'll be shut down by court order and force. I can't buy all the judges in two states. Some of them wouldn't be for sale."

"It was a nice try, Les," consoled Coster.

"I thought it might be an answer for all of us," the pilot answered.

Harriman said, "You were starting to mention another solution, Bob?"

Coster looked embarrassed. "You know the plans for the ship itself—a three-man job, space and supplies for three."

"Yes. What are you driving at?"

"It doesn't have to be three men. Split the first step into two parts, cut the ship down to the bare minimum for one man and jettison the remainder. That's the only way I see to make this basic design work." He got out another sketch. "See? One man and supplies for less than a week. No airlock —the pilot stays in his pressure suit. No galley. No bunks. The bare minimum to keep one man alive for a maximum of two hundred hours. It will work."

"It will work," repeated LeCroix, looking at Coster.

Harriman looked at the sketch with an odd, sick feeling at his stomach. Yes, no doubt it would work—and for the purposes of the promotion it did not matter whether one man or three went to the Moon and returned. Just to do it was enough; he was dead certain that one successful flight would cause money to roll in so that there would be capital to develop to the point of practical, passenger-carrying ships.

The Wright brothers had started with less.

"If that is what I have to put up with, I suppose I have to," he said slowly.

Coster looked relieved. "Fine! But there is one more hitch. You know the conditions under which I agreed to tackle this job—I was to go along. Now Les here waves a contract under my nose and says *he* has to be the pilot."

"It's not just that," LeCroix countered. "You're no pilot, Bob. You'll kill yourself and ruin the whole enterprise, just through bull-headed stubbornness."

"I'll learn to fly it. After all, I designed it. Look here, Mr. Harriman, I hate to let you in for a suit—Les says he will sue —but my contract antedates his. I intend to enforce it."

"Don't listen to him, Mr. Harriman. Let him do the suing. I'll fly that ship and bring her back. He'll wreck it."

"Either I go or I don't build the ship," Coster said flatly.

Harriman motioned both of them to keep quiet. "Easy, easy, both of you. You can both sue me if it gives you any pleasure. Bob, don't talk nonsense; at this stage I can hire other engineers to finish the job. You tell me it has to be just one man."

"That's right."

"You're looking at him."

They both stared.

"Shut your jaws," Harriman snapped. "What's funny about that? You both knew I meant to go. You don't think I went to all this trouble just to give you two a ride to the Moon, do you? *I intend to go.* What's wrong with me as a pilot? I'm in good health, my eyesight is all right, I'm still smart enough to learn what I have to learn. If I have to drive my own buggy, I'll do it. I won't step aside for anybody, not anybody, d'you hear me?"

Coster got his breath first. "Boss, you don't know what you are saying."

Two hours later they were still wrangling. Most of the time Harriman had stubbornly sat still, refusing to answer their arguments. At last he went out of the room for a few minutes, on the usual pretext. When he came back in he said, "Bob, what do you weigh?"

"Me? A little over two hundred."

"Close to two twenty, I'd judge. Les, what do you weigh?"

"One twenty-six."

"Bob, design the ship for a net load of one hundred and twenty-six pounds."

"Huh? Now wait a minute, Mr. Harriman—"

"Shut up! If I can't learn to be a pilot in six weeks, neither can you."

"But I've got the mathematics and the basic knowledge to—"

"Shut up I said! Les has spent as long learning his profession as you have learning yours. Can he become an engineer in six weeks? Then what gave you the conceit to think that you can learn his job in that time? I'm not going to have you wrecking my ship to satisfy your swollen ego. Anyhow, you gave out the real key to it when you were discussing the design. The real limiting factor is the actual weight of the passenger or passengers, isn't it? Everything—*everything* works in proportion to that one mass. Right?"

"Yes, but—"

"Right or wrong?"

"Well . . . yes, that's right. I just wanted—"

"The smaller man can live on less water, he breathes less air, he occupies less space. Les goes." Harriman walked over and put a hand on Coster's shoulder. "Don't take it hard, son. It can't be any worse on you than it is on me. This trip has got to succeed—and that means you and I have got to give up the honor of being the first man on the Moon. But I promise you this: we'll go on the second trip, we'll go with Les as our private chauffeur. It will be the first of a lot of passenger trips.

Look, Bob—you can be a big man in this game, if you'll play along now. How would you like to be chief engineer of the first lunar colony?"

Coster managed to grin. "It might not be so bad."

"You'd like it. Living on the Moon will be an engineering problem; you and I have talked about it. How'd you like to put your theories to work? Build the first city? Build the big observatory we'll found there? Look around and know that you were the man who had done it?"

Coster was definitely adjusting himself to it. "You make it sound good. Say, what will *you* be doing?"

"Me? Well, maybe I'll be the first mayor of Luna City." It was a new thought to him; he savored it. "The Honorable Delos David Harriman, Mayor of Luna City. Say, I like that! You know, I've never held any sort of public office; I've just owned things." He looked around. "Everything settled?"

"I guess so," Coster said slowly. Suddenly he stuck his hand out at LeCroix. "You fly her, Les; I'll build her."

LeCroix grabbed his hand. "It's a deal. And you and the Boss get busy and start making plans for the next job—big enough for all of us."

"Right!"

Harriman put his hand on top of theirs. "That's the way I like to hear you talk. We'll stick together and we'll found Luna City together."

"I think we ought to call it 'Harriman,' " LeCroix said seriously.

"Nope, I've thought of it as Luna City ever since I was a kid; Luna City it's going to be. Maybe we'll put Harriman Square in the middle of it," he added.

"I'll mark it that way in the plans," agreed Coster.

Harriman left at once. Despite the solution he was terribly depressed and did not want his two colleagues to see it. It had been a Pyrrhic victory; he had saved the enterprise but he felt like an animal who has gnawed off his own leg to escape a trap.

8

STRONG WAS ALONE in the offices of the partnership when he got a call from Dixon. "George, I was looking for D. D. Is he there?"

"No, he's back in Washington—something about clearances. I expect him back soon."

"Hmmm. . . . Entenza and I want to see him. We're coming over."

They arrived shortly. Entenza was quite evidently very much worked up over something; Dixon looked sleekly impassive as usual. After greetings Dixon waited a moment, then said, "Jack, you had some business to transact, didn't you?"

Entenza jumped, then snatched a draft from his pocket. "Oh, yes! George, I'm not going to have to pro-rate after all. Here's my payment to bring my share up to full payment to date."

Strong accepted it. "I know that Delos will be pleased." He tucked it in a drawer.

"Well," said Dixon sharply, "aren't you going to receipt for it?"

"If Jack wants a receipt. The cancelled draft will serve." However, Strong wrote out a receipt without further comment; Entenza accepted it.

They waited a while. Presently Dixon said, "George, you're in this pretty deep, aren't you?"

"Possibly."

"Want to hedge your bets?"

"How?"

"Well, candidly, I want to protect myself. Want to sell one half of one percent of your share?"

Strong thought about it. In fact he was worried—worried sick. The presence of Dixon's auditor had forced them to keep on a cash basis—and only Strong knew how close to the line that had forced the partners. "Why do you want it?"

"Oh, I wouldn't use it to interfere with Delos's operations. He's our man; we're backing him. But I would feel a lot safer if I had the right to call a halt if he tried to commit us to something we couldn't pay for. You know Delos; he's an incurable optimist. We ought to have some sort of a brake on him."

Strong thought about it. The thing that hurt him was that he agreed with everything Dixon said; he had stood by and watched while Delos dissipated two fortunes, painfully built up through the years. D. D. no longer seemed to care. Why, only this morning he had refused even to look at a report on the H & S automatic household switch—after dumping it on Strong.

Dixon leaned forward. "Name a price, George. I'll be generous."

Strong squared his stooped shoulders. "I'll sell—"

"Good!"

"—if Delos okays it. Not otherwise."

Dixon muttered something. Entenza snorted. The conversation might have gone acrimoniously further, had not Harriman walked in.

No one said anything about the proposal to Strong. Strong inquired about the trip; Harriman pressed a thumb and finger together. "All in the groove! But it gets more expensive to do business in Washington every day." He turned to the others. "How's tricks? Any special meaning to the assemblage? Are we in executive session?"

Dixon turned to Entenza. "Tell him, Jack."

Entenza faced Harriman. "What do you mean by selling television rights?"

Harriman cocked a brow. "And why not?"

"Because you promised them to me, that's why. That's the original agreement; I've got it in writing."

"Better take another look at the agreement, Jack. And don't go off half-cocked. You have the exploitation rights for radio, television, and other amusement and special feature ventures in connection with the first trip to the Moon. You've still got 'em. Including broadcasts from the ship, provided we are able to make any." He decided that this was not a good time to mention that weight considerations had already made the latter impossible; the *Pioneer* would carry no electronic equipment of any sort not needed in astrogation. "What I sold was the franchise to erect a television station on the Moon, later. By the way, it wasn't even an exclusive franchise, although Clem Haggerty thinks it is. If you want to buy one yourself, we can accommodate you."

"*Buy* it! Why, you—"

"Wups! Or you can have it free, if you can get Dixon and George to agree that you are entitled to it. I won't be a tightwad. Anything else?"

Dixon cut in. "Just where do we stand now, Delos?"

"Gentlemen, you can take it for granted that the *Pioneer* will leave on schedule—next Wednesday. And now, if you will excuse me, I'm on my way to Peterson Field."

After he had left his three associates sat in silence for some time, Entenza muttering to himself, Dixon apparently thinking, and Strong just waiting. Presently Dixon said, "How about that fractional share, George?"

"You didn't see fit to mention it to Delos."

"I see." Dixon carefully deposited an ash. "He's a strange man, isn't he?"

Strong shifted around. "Yes."

"How long have you known him?"

"Let me see—he came to work for me in—"

"*He* worked for *you?*"

"For several months. Then we set up our first company." Strong thought back about it. "I suppose he had a power complex, even then."

"No," Dixon said carefully. "No, I wouldn't call it a power complex. It's more of a Messiah complex."

Entenza looked up. "He's a crooked son of a bitch, that's what he is!"

Strong looked at him mildly. "I'd rather you wouldn't talk about him that way. I'd really rather you wouldn't."

"Stow it, Jack," ordered Dixon. "You might force George to take a poke at you. One of the odd things about him," went on Dixon, "is that he seems to be able to inspire an almost feudal loyalty. Take yourself. I know you are cleaned out, George—yet you won't let me rescue you. That goes beyond logic; it's personal."

Strong nodded. "He's an odd man. Sometimes I think he's the last of the Robber Barons."

Dixon shook his head. "Not the last. The last of them opened up the American West. He's the first of the *new* Robber Barons—and you and I won't see the end of it. Do you ever read Carlyle?"

Strong nodded again. "I see what you mean, the 'Hero' theory, but I don't necessarily agree with it."

"There's something to it, though," Dixon answered. "Truthfully, I don't think Delos knows what he is doing. He's setting up a new imperialism. There'll be hell to pay before it's cleaned up." He stood up. "Maybe we should have waited. Maybe we should have balked him—*if* we could have. Well, it's done. We're on the merry-go-round and we can't get off. I hope we enjoy the ride. Come on, Jack."

9

THE COLORADO PRAIRIE was growing dusky. The Sun was behind the peak and the broad white face of Luna, full and round, was rising in the east. In the middle of Peterson Field the *Pioneer* thrust toward the sky. A barbed-wire fence, a thousand yards from its base in all directions, held back the crowds. Just inside the barrier guards patrolled restlessly. More guards circulated through the crowd. Inside the fence, close to it, trunks and trailers for camera, sound, and television equipment were parked and, at the far ends of cables, remote-control pick-ups were located both near and far from the ship on all sides. There were other trucks near the ship and a stir of organized activity.

Harriman waited in Coster's office; Coster himself was out on the field, and Dixon and Entenza had a room to themselves. LeCroix, still in a drugged sleep, was in the bedroom of Coster's on-the-job living quarters.

There was a stir and a challenge outside the door. Harriman opened it a crack. "If that's another reporter, tell him 'no.' Send him to Mr. Montgomery across the way. Captain LeCroix will grant no unauthorized interviews."

"Delos! Let me in."

"Oh—you, George. Come in. We've been hounded to death."

Strong came in and handed Harriman a large and heavy handbag. "Here it is."

"Here is what?"

"The cancelled covers for the philatelic syndicate. You forgot them. That's half a million dollars, Delos," he complained. "If I hadn't noticed them in your coat locker we'd have been in the soup."

Harriman composed his features. "George, you're a brick, that's what you are."

"Shall I put them in the ship myself?" Strong said anxiously.

"Huh? No, no. Les will handle them." He glanced at his watch. "We're about to waken him. I'll take charge of the covers." He took the bag and added, "Don't come in now. You'll have a chance to say goodbye on the field."

Harriman went next door, shut the door behind him, waited for the nurse to give the sleeping pilot a counteracting stimulant by injection, then chased her out. When he turned around the pilot was sitting up, rubbing his eyes. "How do you feel, Les?"

"Fine. So this is it."

"Yup. And we're all rooting for you, boy. Look, you've got to go out and face them in a couple of minutes. Everything is ready—but I've got a couple of things I've got to say to you."

"Yes?"

"See this bag?" Harriman rapidly explained what it was and what it signified.

LeCroix looked dismayed. "But I *can't* take it, Delos. It's all figured to the last ounce."

"Who said you were going to take it? Of course you can't; it must weigh sixty, seventy pounds. I just plain forgot it. Now here's what we do: for the time being I'll just hide it in here—" Harriman stuffed the bag far back into a clothes closet. "When you land, I'll be right on your tail. Then we pull a sleight-of-hand trick and you fetch it out of the ship."

LeCroix shook his head ruefully. "Delos, you beat me. Well, I'm in no mood to argue."

"I'm glad you're not; otherwise I'd go to jail for a measly half million dollars. We've already spent that money. Anyhow, it doesn't matter," he went on. "Nobody but you and me will know it—and the stamp collectors will get their money's worth." He looked at the younger man as if anxious for his approval.

"Okay, okay," LeCroix answered. "Why should I care what happens to a stamp collector—tonight? Let's get going."

"One more thing," said Harriman and took out a small cloth bag. "This you take with you—and the weight *has* been figured in. I saw to it. Now here is what you do with it." He gave detailed and very earnest instructions.

LeCroix was puzzled. "Do I hear you straight? I let it be found- then I tell the exact truth about what happened?"

"That's right."

"Okay." LeCroix zipped the little bag into a pocket of his coveralls. "Let's get out to the field. H-hour minus twenty-one minutes already."

Strong joined Harriman in the control blockhouse after Le-Croix had gone up inside the ship. "Did they get aboard?" he demanded anxiously. "LeCroix wasn't carrying anything."

"Oh, sure," said Harriman. "I sent them ahead. Better take your place. The ready flare has already gone up."

Dixon, Entenza, the Governor of Colorado, the Vice-President of the United States, and a round dozen of V.I.P.'s were already seated at periscopes, mounted in slits, on a balcony above the control level. Strong and Harriman climbed a ladder and took the two remaining chairs.

Harriman began to sweat and realized he was trembling. Through his periscope out in front he could see the ship; from below he could hear Coster's voice, nervously checking departure station reports. Muted through a speaker by him was a running commentary of one of the newscasters reporting the show. Harriman himself was the—well, the admiral, he decided—of the operation, but there was nothing more he could do, but wait, watch, and try to pray.

A second flare arched up in the sky, burst into red and green. Five minutes.

The seconds oozed away. At minus two minutes Harriman realized that he could not stand to watch through a tiny slit; he had to be outside, take part in it himself—he had to. He climbed down, hurried to the exit of the blockhouse. Coster glanced around, looked startled, but did not try to stop him; Coster could not leave his post no matter what happened. Harriman elbowed the guard aside and went outdoors.

To the east the ship towered skyward, her slender pyramid sharp black against the full Moon. He waited.

And waited.

What had gone wrong? There had remained less than two minutes when he had come out; he was sure of that—yet there she stood, silent, dark, unmoving. There was not a sound, save the distant ululation of sirens warning the spectators behind the distant fence. Harriman felt his own heart stop, his breath dry up in his throat. Something had failed. Failure.

A single flare rocket burst from the top of the blockhouse; a flame licked at the base of the ship.

It spread, there was a pad of white fire around the base. Slowly, almost lumberingly, the *Pioneer* lifted, seemed to hover for a moment, balanced on a pillar of fire—then reached for the sky with acceleration so great that she was above him almost at once, overhead at the zenith, a dazzling circle of flame. So quickly was she above, rather than out in front, that it seemed as if she were arching back over him and must surely fall on him. Instinctively and futilely he threw a hand in front of his face.

The sound reached him.

Not as sound—it was a white noise, a roar in all frequencies, sonic, subsonic, supersonic, so incredibly loaded with energy that it struck him in the chest. He heard it with his teeth and with his bones as well as with his ears. He crouched his knees, bracing against it.

Following the sound at the snail's pace of a hurricane came the backwash of the splash. It ripped at his clothing, tore his breath from his lips. He stumbled blindly back, trying to reach the lee of the concrete building, was knocked down.

He picked himself up coughing and strangling and remembered to look at the sky. Straight overhead was a dwindling star. Then it was gone.

He went into the blockhouse.

The room was a babble of high-tension, purposeful confusion. Harriman's ears, still ringing, heard a speaker blare, "Spot One! Spot One to blockhouse! Step five loose on schedule—ship and step five showing separate blips—" and Coster's voice, high and angry, cutting in with, "Get Track One! Have they picked up step five yet? Are they tracking it?"

In the background the news commentator was still blowing his top. "A great day, folks, a great day! The mighty *Pioneer*, climbing like an angel of the Lord, flaming sword at hand, is even now on her glorious way to our sister planet. Most of you have seen her departure on your screens; I wish you could have seen it as I did, arching up into the evening sky, bearing her precious load of—"

"Shut that damn thing off!" ordered Coster, then to the visitors on the observation platform, "And pipe down up there! Quiet!"

The Vice-President of the United States jerked his head around, closed his mouth. He remembered to smile. The other V.I.P.'s shut up, then resumed again in muted whispers. A girl's voice cut through the silence, "Track One to Blockhouse

—step five tracking high, plus two." There was a stir in the corner. There a large canvas hood shielded a heavy sheet of Plexiglass from direct light. The sheet was mounted vertically and was edge-lighted; it displayed a coordinate map of Colorado and Kansas in fine white lines; the cities and towns glowed red. Unevacuated farms were tiny warning dots of red light.

A man behind the transparent map touched it with a grease pencil; the reported location of step five shone out. In front of the map screen a youngish man sat quietly in a chair, a pear-shaped switch in his hand, his thumb lightly resting on the button. He was a bombardier, borrowed from the Air Forces; when he pressed the switch, a radio-controlled circuit in step five should cause the shrouds of step five's landing 'chute to be cut and let it plummet to Earth. He was working from radar reports alone with no fancy computing bombsight to think for him. He was working almost by instinct—or, rather, by the accumulated subconscious knowledge of his trade, integrating in his brain the meager data spread before him, deciding where the tons of step five would land if he were to press his switch at any particular instant. He seemed unworried.

"Spot One to Blockhouse!" came a man's voice again. "Step four free on schedule," and almost immediately following, a deeper voice echoed, "Track Two, tracking step four, instantaneous altitude nine-five-one miles, predicted vector."

No one paid any attention to Harriman.

Under the hood the observed trajectory of step five grew in shining dots of grease, near to, but not on, the dotted line of its predicted path. Reaching out from each location dot was drawn a line at right angles, the reported altitude for that location.

The quiet man watching the display suddenly pressed down hard on his switch. He then stood up, stretched, and said, "Anybody got a cigaret?" "Track Two!" he was answered. "Step four—first impact prediction—forty miles west of Charleston, South Carolina."

"Repeat!" yelled Coster.

The speaker blared out again without pause, "Correction, correction—forty miles east, repeat *east*."

Coster sighed. The sigh was cut short by a report: "Spot One to Blockhouse—step three free, minus five seconds," and a talker at Coster's control desk called out, "Mr. Coster, *Mister Coster*—Palomar Observatory wants to talk to you."

"Tell 'em to go—no, tell 'em to wait." Immediately another voice cut in with, "Track One, auxiliary range Fox—Step one about to strike near Dodge City, Kansas."

"How near!"

There was no answer. Presently the voice of Track One proper said, "Impact reported approximately fifteen miles southwest of Dodge City."

"Casualties?"

Spot One broke in before Track One could answer, "Step two free, step two free—the ship is now on its own."

"Mr. Coster—*please*, Mr. Coster—"

And a totally new voice: "Spot Two to Blockhouse—we are now tracking the ship. Stand by for reported distances and bearings. Stand by—"

"Track Two to Blockhouse—step four will definitely land in Atlantic, estimated point of impact oh-five-seven miles east of Charleston bearing oh-nine-three. I will repeat—"

Coster looked around irritably. "Isn't there any drinking water anywhere in this dump?"

"Mr. Coster, please—Palomar says they've just *got* to talk to you."

Harriman eased over to the door and stepped out. He suddenly felt very much let down, utterly weary, and depressed.

The field looked strange without the ship. He had watched it grow; now suddenly it was gone. The Moon, still rising, seemed oblivious—and space travel was as remote a dream as it had been in his boyhood.

There were several tiny figures prowling around the flash apron where the ship had stood—souvenior hunters, he thought contemptuously. Someone came up to him in the gloom. "Mr. Harriman?"

"Eh?"

"Hopkins—with the A.P. How about a statement?"

"Uh? No, no comment. I'm bushed."

"Oh, now, just a word. How does it feel to have backed the first successful Moon flight—if it is successful."

"It will be successful." He thought a moment, then squared his tired shoulders and said, "Tell them that this is the beginning of the human race's greatest era. Tell them that every one of them will have a chance to follow in Captain LeCroix's footsteps, seek out new planets, wrest a home for them-

selves in new lands. Tell them that this means new frontiers, a
shot in the arm for prosperity. It means—" He ran down.
"That's all tonight. I'm whipped, son. Leave me alone, will
you?"

Presently Coster came out, followed by the V.I.P.'s. Harriman went up to Coster. "Everything all right?"

"Sure. Why shouldn't it be? Track three followed him out
to the limit of range—all in the groove." Coster added, "Step
five killed a cow when it grounded."

"Forget it—we'll have steak for breakfast." Harriman then
had to make conversation with the Governor and the Vice-
President, had to escort them out to their ship. Dixon and Entenza left together, less formally; at last Coster and Harriman
were alone save for subordinates too junior to constitute a
strain and for guards to protect them from the crowds.
"Where you headed, Bob?"

"Up to the Broadmoor and about a week's sleep. How
about you?"

"If you don't mind, I'll doss down in your apartment."

"Help yourself. Sleepy pills in the bathroom."

"I won't need them." They had a drink together in Coster's
quarters, talked aimlessly, then Coster ordered a copter cab
and went to the hotel. Harriman went to bed, got up, read a
day-old copy of the Denver *Post* filled with pictures of the *Pioneer,* finally gave up and took two of Coster's sleeping cap-
sules.

10

SOMEONE WAS SHAKING HIM. "Mr. Harriman! Wake up—Mr.
Coster is on the screen."

"Huh? Wazza? Oh, all right." He got up and padded to the
phone. Coster was looking tousle-headed and excited. "Hey,
Boss—*he made it!*"

"Huh? What do you mean?"

"Palomar just called me. They saw his mark and now
they've spotted the ship itself. He—"

"Wait a minute, Bob. Slow up. He *can't* be there yet. He
just left last night."

Coster looked disconcerted. "What's the matter, Mr. Harriman? Don't you feel well? He left Wednesday."

Vaguely, Harriman began to be oriented. No, the take-off had not been the night before—fuzzily he recalled a drive up into the mountains, a day spent dozing in the sun, some sort of a party at which he had drunk too much. What day was today? He didn't know. If LeCroix had landed on the Moon, then—never mind. "It's all right, Bob—I was half asleep. I guess I dreamed the take-off all over again. Now tell me the news, slowly."

Coster started over. "LeCroix has landed, just west of Archimedes crater. They can see his ship, from Palomar. Say that was a great stunt you thought up, marking the spot with carbon black. Les must have covered two acres with it. They say it shines out like a billboard, through the Big Eye."

"Maybe we ought to run down and have a look. No—later," he amended. "We'll be busy."

"I don't see what more we can do, Mr. Harriman. We've got twelve of our best ballistic computers calculating possible routes for you now."

Harriman started to tell the man to put on another twelve, switched off the screen instead. He was still at Peterson Field, with one of Skyways' best stratoships waiting for him outside, waiting to take him to whatever point on the globe LeCroix might ground. LeCroix was in the upper stratosphere, had been there for more than twenty-four hours. The pilot was slowly, cautiously wearing out his terminal velocity, dissipating the incredible kinetic energy as shock wave and radiant heat.

They had tracked him by radar around the globe and around again—and again . . . yet there was no way of knowing just where and what sort of landing the pilot would choose to risk. Harriman listened to the running radar reports and cursed the fact that they had elected to save the weight of radio equipment.

The radar figures started coming closer together. The voice broke off and started again: "He's in his landing glide!"

"Tell the field to get ready!" shouted Harriman. He held his breath and waited. After endless seconds another voice cut in with, "The Moon ship is now landing. It will ground somewhere west of Chihuahua in Old Mexico."

Harriman started for the door at a run.

Coached by radio en route, Harriman's pilot spotted the *Pioneer* incredibly small against the desert sand. He put his own ship quite close to it, in a beautiful landing. Harriman was fumbling at the cabin door before the ship was fairly stopped.

LeCroix was sitting on the ground, resting his back against a skid of his ship and enjoying the shade of its stubby triangular wings. A paisano sheepherder stood facing him, open-mouthed. As Harriman trotted out and lumbered toward him LeCroix stood up, flipped a cigaret butt away and said, "Hi, Boss!"

"Les!" The older man threw his arms around the younger. "It's good to see you, boy."

"It's good to see *you*. Pedro here doesn't speak my language." LeCroix glanced around; there was no one else nearby but the pilot of Harriman's ship. "Where's the gang? Where's Bob?"

"I didn't wait. They'll surely be along in a few minutes—hey, there they come now!" It was another stratoship, plunging in to a landing. Harriman turned to his pilot. "Bill—go over and meet them."

"Huh? They'll come, never fear."

"Do as I say."

"You're the doctor." The pilot trudged through the sand, his back expressing disapproval. LeCroix looked puzzled. "Quick, Les—help me with this."

"This" was the five thousand cancelled envelopes which were supposed to have been to the Moon. They got them out of Harriman's stratoship and into the Moon ship, there to be stowed in an empty food locker, while their actions were still shielded from the later arrivals by the bulk of the stratoship. "Whew!" said Harriman. "That was close. Half a million dollars. We need it, Les."

"Sure, but look, Mr. Harriman, the di—"

"Sssh! The others are coming. How about the other business? Ready with your act?"

"Yes. But I was trying to tell you—"

"Quiet!"

It was not their colleagues; it was a shipload of reporters, camera men, mike men, commentators, technicians. They swarmed over them.

Harriman waved to them jauntily. "Help yourselves, boys. Get a lot of pictures. Climb through the ship. Make yourselves at home. Look at anything you want to. But go easy on Captain LeCroix—he's tired."

Another ship had landed, this time with Coster, Dixon and Strong. Entenza showed up in his own chartered ship and began bossing the TV, pix, and radio men, in the course of which he almost had a fight with an unauthorized camera crew. A large copter transport grounded and spilled out nearly a platoon of khaki-clad Mexican troops. From somewhere— out of the sand apparently—several dozen native peasants showed up. Harriman broke away from reporters, held a quick and expensive discussion with the captain of the local troops and a degree of order was restored in time to save the *Pioneer* from being picked to pieces.

"Just let that be!" It was LeCroix's voice, from inside the *Pioneer*. Harriman waited and listened. "None of your business!" the pilot's voice went on, rising higher, "and put them back!"

Harriman pushed his way to the door of the ship. "What's the trouble, Les?"

Inside the cramped cabin, hardly large enough for a TV booth, three men stood, LeCroix and two reporters. All three men looked angry. "What's the trouble, Les?" Harriman repeated.

LeCroix was holding a small cloth bag which appeared to be empty. Scattered on the pilot's acceleration rest between him and the reporters were several small, dully brilliant stones. A reporter held one such stone up to the light.

"These guys were poking their noses into things that didn't concern them," LeCroix said angrily.

The reporter looked at the stone and said, "You told us to look at what we liked, didn't you, Mr. Harriman?"

"Yes."

"Your pilot here—" He jerked a thumb at LeCroix. "—apparently didn't expect us to find these. He had them hidden in the pads of his chair."

"What of it?"

"They're diamonds."

"What makes you think so?"

"They're diamonds all right."

Harriman stopped and unwrapped a cigar. Presently he said, "Those diamonds were where you found them because I put them there."

A flashlight went off behind Harriman; a voice said, "Hold the rock up higher, Jeff."

The reporter called Jeff obliged, then said, "That seems an odd thing to do, Mr. Harriman."

"I was interested in the effect of outer space radiations on raw diamonds. On my orders Captain LeCroix placed that sack of diamonds in the ship."

Jeff whistled thoughtfully. "You know, Mr. Harriman, if you did not have that explanation, I'd think LeCroix had found the rocks on the Moon and was trying to hold out on you."

"Print that and you will be sued for libel. I have every confidence in Captain LeCroix. Now give me the diamonds."

Jeff's eyebrows went up. "But not confidence enough in him to let him keep them, maybe?"

"Give me the stones. Then get out."

Harriman got LeCroix away from the reporters as quickly as possible and into Harriman's own ship. "That's all for now," he told the news and pictures people. "See us at Peterson Field."

Once the ship raised ground he turned to LeCroix. "You did a beautiful job, Les."

"That reporter named Jeff must be sort of confused."

"Eh? Oh, *that*. No, I mean the flight. You did it. You're head man on this planet."

LeCroix shrugged it off. "Bob built a good ship. It was a cinch. Now about those diamonds—"

"Forget the diamonds. You've done your part. We placed those rocks in the ship; now we tell everybody we did—truthful as can be. It's not our fault if they don't believe us."

"But Mr. Harriman—"

"What?"

LeCroix unzipped a pocket in his coveralls, hauled out a soiled handkerchief, knotted into a bag. He untied it—and spilled into Harriman's hands many more diamonds than had been displayed in the ship—larger, finer diamonds.

Harriman stared at them. He began to chuckle.

Presently he shoved them back at LeCroix. "Keep them."

"I figure they belong to all of us."

"Well, keep them for us, then. And keep your mouth shut about them. No, wait." He picked out two large stones. "I'll have rings made from these two, one for you, one for me. But keep your mouth shut, or they won't be worth anything, except as curiosities."

It was quite true, he thought. Long ago the diamond syndicate had realized that diamonds in plentiful supply were worth little more than glass, except for industrial uses. Earth had more than enough for that, more than enough for jewels. If Moon diamonds were literally "common as pebbles" then they were just that—pebbles.

Not worth the expense of bringing them to earth.

But now take uranium. If that were plentiful—

Harriman sat back and indulged in daydreaming.

Presently LeCroix said softly, "You know, Boss, it's wonderful there."

"Eh? Where?"

"Why, on the Moon of course. I'm going back. I'm going back just as soon as I can. We've got to get busy on the new ship."

"Sure, sure! And this time we'll build one big enough for all of us. This time I go, too!"

"You bet."

"Les—" The older man spoke almost diffidently. "What does it look like when you look back and see the Earth?"

"Huh? It looks like— It looks—" LeCroix stopped. "Hell's bells, Boss, there isn't any way to tell you. It's wonderful, that's all. The sky is black and—well, wait until you see the pictures I took. Better yet, wait and see it yourself."

Harriman nodded. "But it's hard to wait."

11

"FIELDS OF DIAMONDS ON THE MOON!!!"

"BILLIONAIRE BACKER DENIES DIAMOND STORY
Says Jewels Taken Into Space for Science Reasons"

"MOON DIAMONDS: HOAX OR FACT?"

"—but consider this, friends of the invisible audience: why would anyone take diamonds *to* the moon? Every ounce of that ship and its cargo was calculated; diamonds would not be taken along without reason. Many scientific authorities have pronounced Mr. Harriman's professed reason an absurdity. It is easy to guess that diamonds might be taken along for the purpose of 'salting' the Moon, so to speak, with earthly jewels, with the intention of convincing us that diamonds exist on the Moon—but Mr. Harriman, his pilot Captain LeCroix, and everyone connected with the enterprise have sworn from the beginning that the diamonds *did not* come from the Moon. But it is an absolute certainty that the diamonds were in the space ship when it landed. Cut it how you will; this reporter is going to try to buy some lunar diamond mining stock—"

Strong was, as usual, already in the office when Harriman came in. Before the partners could speak, the screen called out, "Mr. Harriman, Rotterdam calling."

"Tell them to go plant a tulip."

"Mr. van der Velde is waiting, Mr. Harriman."

"Okay."

Harriman let the Hollander talk, then said, "Mr. van der Velde, the statements attributed to me are absolutely correct. I put those diamonds the reporters saw into the ship before it took off. They were mined right here on Earth. In fact I bought them when I came over to see you; I can prove it."

"But Mr. Harriman—"

"Suit yourself. There may be more diamonds on the Moon than you can run and jump over. I don't guarantee it. But I do guarantee that those diamonds the newspapers are talking about came from Earth."

"Mr. Harriman, why would you send diamonds to the Moon? Perhaps you intended to fool us, no?"

"Have it your own way. But I've said all along that those diamonds came from Earth. Now see here: you took an option —an option on an option, so to speak. If you want to make the second payment on that option and keep it in force, the deadline is nine o'clock Thursday, New York time, as specified in the contract. Make up your mind."

He switched off and found his partner looking at him sourly. "What's eating you?"

"I wondered about those diamonds, too, Delos. So I've been looking through the weight schedule of the *Pioneer*."

"Didn't know you were interested in engineering."

"I can read figures."

"Well, you found it, didn't you? Schedule F-17-c, two ounces, allocated to me personally."

"I found it. It sticks out like a sore thumb. But I didn't find something else."

Harriman felt a cold chill in his stomach. "What?"

"I didn't find a schedule for the canceled covers." Strong stared at him.

"It must be there. Let me see that weight schedule."

"It's not there, Delos. You know, I thought it was funny when you insisted on going to meet Captain LeCroix by yourself. What happened, Delos. Did you sneak them aboard?" He continued to stare while Harriman fidgeted. "We've put over some sharp business deals—but this will be the first time that anyone can say that the firm of Harriman and Strong has cheated."

"Damn it, George—I would cheat, lie, steal, beg, bribe— do *anything* to accomplish what we have accomplished."

Harriman got up and paced the room. "We *had* to have that money, or the ship would never have taken off. We're cleaned out. You know that, don't you?"

Strong nodded. "But those covers should have gone to the Moon. That's what we contracted to do."

"Damn it, I just forgot it. Then it was too late to figure the weight in. But it doesn't matter. I figured that if the trip was a failure, if LeCroix cracked up, nobody would know or care that the covers hadn't gone. And I knew if he made it, it wouldn't matter; we'd have plenty of money. And we will, George, we will!"

"We've got to pay the money back."

"Now? Give me time, George. Everybody concerned is happy the way it is. Wait until we recover our stake; then I'll buy every one of those covers back—out of my own pocket. That's a promise."

Strong continued to sit. Harriman stopped in front of him. "I ask you, George, is it worth while to wreck an enterprise of this size for a purely theoretical point?"

Strong sighed and said, "When the time comes, use the firm's money."

"That's the spirit! But I'll use my own, I promise you."

"No, the firm's money. If we're in it together, we're in it together."

"O.K., if that's the way you want it."

Harriman turned back to his desk. Neither of the two partners had anything to say for a long while. Presently Dixon and Entenza were announced.

"Well, Jack," said Harriman. "Feel better now?"

"No thanks to you. I had to fight for what I did put on the air—and some of it was pirated as it was. Delos, there should have been a television pick-up in the ship."

"Don't fret about it. As I told you, we couldn't spare the

weight this time. But there will be the next trip, and the next. Your concession is going to be worth a pile of money."

Dixon cleared his throat. "That's what we came to see you about, Delos. What are your plans?"

"Plans? We go right ahead. Les and Coster and I make the next trip. We set up a permanent base. Maybe Coster stays behind. The third trip we send a real colony—nuclear engineers, miners, hydroponics experts, communications engineers. We'll found Luna City, first city on another planet."

Dixon looked thoughtful. "And when does this begin to pay off?"

"What do you mean by 'pay off'? Do you want your capital back, or do you want to begin to see some return on your investment? I can cut it either way."

Entenza was about to say that he wanted his investment back; Dixon cut in first, "Profits, naturally. The investment is already made."

"Fine!"

"But I don't see how you expect profits. Certainly, LeCroix made the trip and got back safely. There is honor for all of us. But where are the royalties?"

"Give the crop time to ripen, Dan. Do I look worried? What are our assets?" Harriman ticked them off on his fingers. "Royalties on pictures, television, radio—"

"Those things go to Jack."

"Take a look at the agreement. He has the concession, but he pays the firm—that's all of us—for them."

Dixon said, "Shut up, Jack!" before Entenza could speak, then added, "What else? That won't pull us out of the red."

"Endorsements galore. Monty's boys are working on that. Royalties from the greatest best seller yet—I've got a ghost writer and a stenographer following LeCroix around this very minute. A franchise for the first and only space line—"

"From whom?"

"We'll get it. Kamens and Montgomery are in Paris now, working on it. I'm joining them this afternoon. And we'll tie down that franchise with a franchise from *the other end,* just as soon as we can get a permanent colony there, no matter how small. It will be the autonomous state of Luna, under the protection of the United Nations—and no ship will land or take off in its territory without its permission. Besides that we'll have the right to franchise a dozen other companies for various purposes—and tax them, too—just as soon as we set up the Municipal Corporation of the City of Luna under the laws of the State of Luna. We'll sell everything but vacuum—we'll even sell vacuum, for experimental purposes. And don't forget—we'll still have a big chunk of real estate, sovereign title in us—as a state—and not yet sold. The Moon is *big*."

"Your ideas are rather big, too, Delos," Dixon said dryly. "But what actually happens next?"

"First we get title confirmed by the U. N. The Security Council is now in secret session; the Assembly meets tonight. Things will be popping; that's why I've got to be there. When the United Nations decides—as it will!—that it's own non-profit corporation has the only real claim to the Moon, then I get busy. The poor little weak non-profit corporation is going to grant a number of things to some real honest-to-god corporations with hair on their chests—in return for help in setting up a physics research lab, an astronomical observatory, a lunography institute and some other perfectly proper non-profit enterprises. That's our interim pitch until we get a permanent colony with its own laws. Then we—"

Dixon gestured impatiently. "Never mind the legal shenanigans, Delos. I've known you long enough to know that you can figure out such angles. What do we actually have to *do* next?"

"Huh? We've got to build another ship, a bigger one. Not actually bigger, but effectively bigger. Coster has started the design of a surface catapult—it will reach from Manitou Springs to the top of Pikes Peak. With it we can put a ship in free orbit around the Earth. Then we'll use such a ship to fuel more ships—it amounts to a space station, like the power station. It adds up to a way to get there on chemical power without having to throw away nine-tenths of your ship to do it."

"Sounds expensive."

"It will be. But don't worry; we've got a couple of dozen piddling little things to keep the money coming in while we get set up on a commerical basis, then we sell stock. We sold stock before; now we'll sell a thousand dollars worth where we sold ten before."

"And you think that will carry you through until the enterprise as a whole is on a paying basis? Face it, Delos, the thing as a whole doesn't pay off until you have ships plying between here and the Moon on a paying basis, figured in freight and passenger charges. That means customers, with cash. What is there on the Moon to ship—and who pays for it?"

"Dan, don't you believe there will be? If not, why are you here?"

"I believe in it, Delos—or I believe in you. But what's your time schedule? What's your budget? What's your prospective commodity? And please don't mention diamonds; I think I understand that caper."

Harriman chewed his cigar for a few moments. "There's one valuable commodity we'll start shipping at once."

"What?"

"Knowledge."

Entenza snorted. Strong looked puzzled. Dixon nodded. "I'll buy that. Knowledge is always worth something—to the man who knows how to exploit it. And I'll agree that the Moon is a place to find new knowledge. I'll assume that you can make the next trip pay off. What's your budget and your time table for that?"

Harriman did not answer. Strong searched his face closely. To him Harriman's poker face was as revealing as large print—he decided that his partner had been crowded into a corner. He waited, nervous but ready to back Harriman's play. Dixon went on, "From the way you describe it, Delos, I judge that you don't have money enough for your next step—and you don't know where you will get it. I believe in you, Delos—and I told you at the start that I did not believe in letting a new business die of anemia. I'm ready to buy in with a fifth share."

Harriman stared. "Look," he said bluntly, "you own Jack's share now, don't you?"

"I wouldn't say that."

"You vote it. It sticks out all over."

Entenza said, "That's not true. I'm independent. I—"

"Jack, you're a damn liar," Harriman said dispassionately. "Dan, you've got fifty percent now. Under the present rules I decide deadlocks, which gives me control as long as George sticks by me. If we sell you another share, you vote three-fifths—and are boss. Is that the deal you are looking for?"

"Delos, as I told you, I have confidence in you."

"But you'd feel happier with the whip hand. Well, I won't do it. I'll let space travel—*real* space travel, with established runs—wait another twenty years before I'll turn loose. I'll let us all go broke and let us live on glory before I'll turn loose. You'll have to think up another scheme."

Dixon said nothing. Harriman got up and began to pace. He stopped in front of Dixon. "Dan, if you really understood what this is all about, I'd let you have control. But you don't. You see this as just another way to money and to power. I'm perfectly willing to let you vultures get rich—but I keep control. I'm going to see this thing developed, not milked. The human race is heading out to the stars—and this adventure is going to present new problems compared with which atomic power was a kid's toy. The race is about as prepared for it as an innocent virgin is prepared for sex. Unless the whole matter is handled carefully, it will be bitched up. *You*'ll bitch it up, Dan, if I let you have the deciding vote in it—because you don't understand it."

He caught his breath and went on, "Take safety for instance. Do you know *why* I let LeCroix take that ship out instead of taking it myself? Do you think I was afraid? No! I wanted it to come back—*safely*. I didn't want space travel getting another set-back. Do you know why we have to have a monopoly, for a few years at least? Because every so-and-so and his brother is going to want to build a Moon ship, now that they know it can be done. Remember the first days of ocean flying? After Lindbergh did it, every so-called pilot who could lay hands on a crate took off for some over-water point. Some of them even took their kids along. And most of them landed in the drink. Airplanes got a reputation for being dangerous. A few years after that the airlines got so hungry for quick money in a highly competitive field that you couldn't pick up a paper without seeing headlines about another airliner crash.

"That's not going to happen to space travel! I'm not going to let it happen. Space ships are too big and too expensive; if they get a reputation for being unsafe as well, we might as well have stayed in bed. I run things."

He stopped. Dixon waited and then said, "I said I believed in you, Delos. How much money do you need?"

"Eh? On what terms?"

"Your note."

"My note? Did you say *my note*?"

"I'd want security, of course."

Harriman swore. "I knew there was a hitch in it. Dan, you know damn well everything I've got is tied up in this venture."

"You have insurance. You have quite a lot of insurance, I know."

"Yes, but that's all made out to my wife."

"I seem to have heard you say something about that sort of thing to Jack Entenza," Dixon said. "Come, now—if I know your tax-happy sort, you have at least one irrevocable trust, or paid-up annuities, or something, to keep Mrs. Harriman out of the poor house."

Harriman thought fiercely about it. "When's the call date on this note?"

"In the sweet bye and bye. I want a no-bankruptcy clause, of course."

"Why? Such a clause has no legal validity."

"It would be valid with *you*, wouldn't it?"

"Mmm . . . yes. Yes, it would."

"Then get out your policies and see how big a note you can write."

Harriman looked at him, turned abruptly and went to his safe. He came back with quite a stack of long, stiff folders. They added them up together; it was an amazingly large sum —for those days. Dixon then consulted a memorandum taken from his pocket and said, "One seems to be missing—a rather large one. A North Atlantic Mutual policy, I think."

Harriman glared at him. "Damn you, am I going to have to fire every confidential clerk in my force?"

"No," Dixon said mildly, "I don't get my information from your staff."

Harriman went back to the safe, got the policy and added it to the pile. Strong spoke up, "Do you want mine, Mr. Dixon?"

"No," answered Dixon, "that won't be necessary." He started stuffing the policies in his pocket. "I'll keep these, Delos, and attend to keeping up the premiums. I'll bill you of course. You can send the note and the change-of-beneficiary forms to my office. Here's your draft." He took out another slip of paper; it was the draft—already made out in the amount of the policies.

Harriman looked at it. "Sometimes," he said slowly, "I wonder who's kidding who?" He tossed the draft over to Strong. "O.K., George, take care of it. I'm off to Paris, boys. Wish me luck." He strode out as jauntily as a fox terrier.

Strong looked from the closed door to Dixon, then at the note. "I ought to tear this thing up!"

"Don't do it," advised Dixon. "You see, I really do believe in him." He added, "Ever read Carl Sandburg, George?"

"I'm not much of a reader."

"Try him some time. He tells a story about a man who started a rumor that they had struck oil in hell. Pretty soon everybody has left for hell, to get in on the boom. The man who started the rumor watches them all go, then scratches his head and says to himself that there just *might* be something in it, after all. So he left for hell, too."

Strong waited, finally said, "I don't get the point."

"The point is that I just want to be ready to protect myself if necessary, George—and so should you. Delos might begin believing his own rumors. Diamonds! Come, Jack."

12

THE ENSUING MONTHS were as busy as the period before the flight of the *Pioneer* (now honorably retired to the Smithsonian Institution). One engineering staff and great gangs of men were working on the catapult; two more staffs were busy with two new ships; the *Mayflower*, and the *Colonial;* a third ship was on the drafting tables. Ferguson was chief engineer for all of this; Coster, still buffered by Jock Berkeley, was engineering consultant, working where and as he chose. Colorado Springs was a boom town; the Denver-Trinidad roadcity settlements spread out at the Springs until they surrounded Peterson Field.

Harriman was as busy as a cat with two tails. The constantly expanding exploitation and promotion took eight full days a week of his time, but, by working Kamens and Montgomery almost to ulcers and by doing without sleep himself, he created frequent opportunities to run out to Colorado and talk things over with Coster.

Luna City, it was decided, would be founded on the very next trip. The *Mayflower* was planned for a pay-load not only of seven passengers, but with air, water and food to carry four of them over to the next trip; they would live in an aluminum Quonset-type hut, sealed, pressurized, and buried under the loose soil of Luna until—and assuming—they were succored.

The choice of the four estra passengers gave rise to another contest, another publicity exploitation—and more sale of stock. Harriman insisted that they be two married couples, over the united objections of scientific organizations everywhere. He gave in only to the extent of agreeing that there was no objection to all four being scientists, providing they constituted two married couples. This gave rise to several hasty marriages—and some divorces, after the choices were announced.

The *Mayflower* was the maximum size that calculations showed would be capable of getting into a free orbit around the Earth from the boost of the catapult, plus the blast of her own engines. Before she took off, four other ships, quite as large, would precede her. But they were not space ships; they were mere tankers—nameless. The most finicky of ballistic calculations, the most precise of launchings, would place them in the same orbit at the same spot. There the *Mayflower* would rendezvous and accept their remaining fuel.

This was the trickiest part of the entire project. If the four tankers could be placed close enough together, LeCroix, using a tiny maneuvering reserve, could bring his new ship to them. If not—well, it gets very lonely out in space.

Serious thought was given to placing pilots in the tankers and accepting as a penalty the use of enough fuel from one tanker to permit a get-away boat, a life boat with wings, to decelerate, reach the atmosphere and brake to a landing. Coster found a cheaper way.

A radar pilot, whose ancestor was the proximity fuse and whose immediate parents could be found in the homing devices of guided missiles, was given the task of bringing the tankers together. The first tanker would not be so equipped, but the second tanker through its robot would smell out the first and home on it with a pint-sized rocket engine, using the smallest of vectors to bring them together. The third would home on the first two and the fourth on the group.

LeCroix should have no trouble—if the scheme worked.

13

STRONG WANTED to show Harriman the sales reports on the H&S automatic household switch; Harriman brushed them aside.

Strong shoved them back under his nose. "You'd better start taking an interest in such things, Delos. *Somebody* around this office had better start seeing to it that some money comes in—some money that belongs to us, personally —or you'll be selling apples on a street corner."

Harriman leaned back and clasped his hands back of his head. "George, how can you talk that way on a day like this? Is there no poetry in your soul? Didn't you hear what I said when I came in? *The rendezvous worked.* Tankers one and two are as close together as Siamese twins. We'll be leaving within the week."

"That's as may be. Business has to go on."

"You keep it going; I've got a date. When did Dixon say he would be over?"

"He's due now."

"Good!" Harriman bit the end off a cigar and went on, "You know, George, I'm not sorry I didn't get to make the first trip. Now I've still got it to do. I'm as expectant as a bridegroom—and as happy." He started to hum.

Dixon came in without Entenza, a situation that had obtained since the day Dixon had dropped the pretence that he controlled only one share. He shook hands. "You heard the news, Dan?"

"George told me."

"This is it—or almost. A week from now, more or less, I'll be on the Moon. I can hardly believe it."

Dixon sat down silently. Harriman went on, "Aren't you even going to congratulate me? Man, this is a great day!"

Dixon said, "D. D., why are you going?"

"Huh? Don't ask foolish questions. This is what I have been working toward."

"It's not a foolish question. I asked why *you* were going. The four colonists have an obvious reason, and each is a selected specialist observer as well. LeCroix is the pilot. Coster is the man who is designing the permanent colony. But why are *you* going? What's your function?"

"My function? Why, I'm the guy who runs things. Shucks, I'm going to run for mayor when I get there. Have a cigar, friend—the name's Harriman. Don't forget to vote." He grinned.

Dixon did not smile. "I did not know you planned on staying."

Harriman looked sheepish. "Well, that's still up in the air.

If we get the shelter built in a hurry, we may save enough in the way of supplies to let me sort of lay over until the next trip. You wouldn't begrudge me that, would you?"

Dixon looked him in the eye. "Delos, I can't let you go at all."

Harriman was too startled to talk at first. At last he managed to say, "Don't joke, Dan. I'm going. You can't stop me. Nothing on Earth can stop me."

Dixon shook his head. "I can't permit it, Delos. I've got too much sunk in this. If you go and anything happens to you, I lose it all."

"That's silly. You and George would just carry on, that's all."

"Ask George."

Strong had nothing to say. He did not seem anxious to meet Harriman's eyes. Dixon went on, "Don't try to kid your way out of it, Delos. This venture is you and you are this venture. If you get killed, the whole thing folds up. I don't say space travel folds up; I think you've already given that a boost that will carry it along even with lesser men in your shoes. But as for this venture—our company—it will fold up. George and I will have to liquidate at about half a cent on the dollar. It would take sale of patent rights to get that much. The tangible assets aren't worth anything."

"Damn it, it's the intangibles we sell. You knew that all along."

"You are the intangible asset, Delos. You are the goose that lays the golden eggs. I want you to stick around until you've laid them. You must not risk your neck in space flight until you have this thing on a profit-making basis, so that any competent manager, such as George or myself, thereafter can keep it solvent. I mean it, Delos. I've got too much in it to see you risk it in a joy ride."

Harriman stood up and pressed his fingers down on the edge of his desk. He was breathing hard. "You can't stop me!" he said slowly and forcefully. "You knew all along that I meant to go. You can't stop me now. Not all the forces of heaven or hell can stop me."

Dixon answered quietly, "I'm sorry, Delos. But I can stop you and I will. I can tie up that ship out there."

"Try it! I own as many lawyers as you do—and better ones!"

"I think you will find that you are not as popular in American courts as you once were—not since the United States found out it didn't own the Moon after all."

"Try it, I tell you. I'll break you and I'll take your shares away from you, too."

"Easy, Delos! I've no doubt you have some scheme whereby you could milk the basic company right away from George and me if you decided to. But it won't be necessary. Nor will it be necessary to tie up the ship. I want that flight to take place as much as you do. But you won't be on it, because you will decide not to go."

"I will, eh? Do I look crazy from where you sit?"

"No, on the contrary."

"Then why won't I go?"

"Because of your note that I hold. I want to collect it."

"What? There's no due date."

"No. But I want to be sure to collect it."

"Why, you dumb fool, if I get killed you collect it sooner than ever."

"Do I? You are mistaken, Delos. If you are killed—on a flight to the Moon—I collect nothing. I know; I've checked with every one of the companies underwriting you. Most of them have escape clauses covering experimental vehicles that date back to early aviation. In any case all of them will cancel and fight it out in court if you set foot inside that ship."

"You put them up to this!"

"Calm down, Delos. You'll be bursting a blood vessel. Certainly I queried them, but I was legitimately looking after my own interests. I don't want to collect on that note—not now, not by your death. I want you to pay it back out of your own earnings, by staying here and nursing this company through till it's stable."

Harriman chucked his cigar, almost unsmoked and badly chewed, at a waste basket. He missed. "I don't give a hoot if you lose on it. If you hadn't stirred them up, they'd have paid without a quiver."

"But it did dig up a weak point in your plans, Delos. If space travel is to be a success, insurance will have to reach out and cover the insured anywhere."

"Damn it, one of them does now—N. A. Mutual."

"I've seen their ad and I've looked over what they claim to offer. It's just window dressing, with the usual escape clause. No, insurance will have to be revamped, all sorts of insurance."

Harriman looked thoughtful. "I'll look into it. George, call Kamens. Maybe we'll have to float our own company."

"Never mind Kamens," objected Dixon. "The point is you can't go on this trip. You have too many details of that sort to watch and plan for and nurse along."

Harriman looked back at him. "You haven't gotten it through your head, Dan, that *I'm going!* Tie up the ship if you can. If you put sheriffs around it, I'll have goons there to toss them aside."

Dixon looked pained. "I hate to mention this point, Delos, but I am afraid you will be stopped even if I drop dead."

"How?"

"Your wife."

"What's she got to do with it?"

"She's ready to sue for separate maintenance right now— she's found out about this insurance thing. When she hears about this present plan, she'll force you into court and force an accounting of your assets."

"You put her up to it!"

Dixon hesitated. He knew that Entenza had spilled the beans to Mrs. Harriman—maliciously. Yet there seemed no point in adding to a personal feud. "She's bright enough to have done some investigating on her own account. I won't deny I've talked to her—but she sent for me."

"I'll fight both of you!" Harriman stomped to a window, stood looking out—it was a real window; he liked to look at the sky.

Dixon came over and put a hand on his shoulder, saying softly, "Don't take it this way, Delos. Nobody's trying to keep you from your dream. But you can't go just yet; you can't let us down. We've stuck with you this far; you owe it to us to stick with us until it's done."

Harriman did not answer; Dixon went on, "If you don't feel any loyalty toward me, how about George? He's stuck with you *against* me, when it hurt him, when he thought you were ruining him—and you surely were, unless you finish this job. How about George, Delos? Are you going to let him down, too?"

Harriman swung around, ignoring Dixon and facing Strong. "What about it, George? Do you think I should stay behind?"

Strong rubbed his hands and chewed his lip. Finally he

looked up. "It's all right with me, Delos. You do what you think is best."

Harriman stood looking at him for a long moment, his face working as if he were going to cry. Then he said huskily, "Okay, you bastards. Okay. I'll stay behind."

14

IT WAS ONE of those glorious evenings so common in the Pikes Peak region, after a day in which the sky has been well scrubbed by thunderstorms. The track of the catapult crawled in a straight line up the face of the mountain, whole shoulders having been carved away to permit it. At the temporary space port, still raw from construction, Harriman, in company with visiting notables, was saying good-bye to the passengers and crew of the *Mayflower*.

The crowds came right up to the rail of the catapult. There was no need to keep them back from the ship; the jets would not blast until she was high over the peak. Only the ship itself was guarded, the ship and the gleaming rails.

Dixon and Strong, together for company and mutual support, hung back at the edge of the area roped off for passengers and officials. They watched Harriman jollying those about to leave: "Good-bye, Doctor. Keep an eye on him, Janet. Don't let him go looking for Moon Maidens." They saw him engage Coster in private conversation, then clap the younger man on the back.

"Keeps his chin up, doesn't he?" whispered Dixon.

"Maybe we should have let him go," answered Strong.

"Eh? Nonsense! We've got to have him. Anyway, his place in history is secure."

"He doesn't care about history," Strong answered seriously, "he just wants to go to the Moon."

"Well, confound it—he can go to the Moon . . . as soon as he gets his job done. After all, it's his job. He made it."

"I know."

Harriman turned around, saw them, started toward them. They shut up. "Don't duck," he said jovially. "It's all right. I'll

go on the next trip. By then I plan to have it running itself.
You'll see." He turned back toward the *Mayflower*. "Quite a
sight, isn't she?"

The outer door was closed; ready lights winked along the
track and from the control tower. A siren sounded.

Harriman moved a step or two closer.

"There she goes!"

It was a shout from the whole crowd. The great ship
started slowly, softly up the track, gathered speed, and shot
toward the distant peak. She was already tiny by the time she
curved up the face and burst into the sky.

She hung there a split second, then a plume of light exploded from her tail. Her jets had fired.

Then she was a shining light in the sky, a ball of flame,
then—nothing. She was gone, upward and outward, to her
rendezvous with her tankers.

The crowd had pushed to the west end of the platform as
the ship swarmed up the mountain. Harriman had stayed
where he was, nor had Dixon and Strong followed the crowd.
The three were alone, Harriman most alone for he did not
seem aware that the others were near him. He was watching
the sky.

Strong was watching him. Presently Strong barely whispered to Dixon, "Do you read the Bible?"

"Some."

"He looks as Moses must have looked, when he gazed out
over the promised land."

Harriman dropped his eyes from the sky and saw them.
"You guys still here?" he said. "Come on—there's work to be
done."

Delilah and the Space-Rigger

SURE, WE HAD TROUBLE building Space Station One—but the trouble was people.

Not that building a station twenty-two thousand three hundred miles out in space is a breeze. It was an engineering feat bigger than the Panama Canal or the Pyramids—or even the Susquehanna Power Pile. But "Tiny" Larsen built her—and a job Tiny tackles gets built.

I first saw Tiny playing guard on a semi-pro team, working his way through Oppenheimer Tech. He worked summers for me thereafter till he graduated. He stayed in construction and eventually I went to work for him.

Tiny wouldn't touch a job unless he was satisfied with the engineering. The Station had jobs designed into it that called for six-armed monkeys instead of grown men in space suits. Tiny spotted such boners; not a ton of material went into the sky until the specs and drawings suited him.

But it was people that gave us the headaches. We had a sprinkling of married men, but the rest were wild kids, attracted by high pay and adventure. Some were busted spacemen. Some were specialists, like electricians and instrument men. About half were deep-sea divers, used to working in pressure suits. There were sandhogs and riggers and welders and shipfitters and two circus acrobats.

We fired four of them for being drunk on the job; Tiny had to break one stiff's arm before he would stay fired. What worried us was where did they get it? Turned out a shipfitter had rigged a heatless still, using the vacuum around us. He was making vodka from potatoes swiped from the commissary. I hated to let him go, but he was too smart.

Since we were falling free in a 24-hour circular orbit, with everything weightless and floating, you'd think that shooting craps was impossible. But a radioman named Peters figured a dodge to substitute steel dice and a magnetic field. He also eliminated the element of chance, so we fired him.

We planned to ship him back in the next supply ship, the R. S. *Half Moon*. I was in Tiny's office when she blasted to match our orbit. Tiny swam to the view port. "Send for Peters, Dad," he said, "and give him the old heave ho. Who's his relief?"

"Party named G. Brooks McNye," I told him.

A line came snaking over from the ship. Tiny said, "I don't believe she's matched." He buzzed the radio shack for the ship's motion relative to the Station. The answer didn't please him and he told them to call the *Half Moon*.

Tiny waited until the TV screen showed the rocket ship's C.O. "Good morning, Captain. Why have you placed a line on us?"

"For cargo, naturally. Get your hopheads over here. I want to blast off before we enter the shadow." The Station spent about an hour and a quarter each day passing through Earth's shadow; we worked two eleven-hour shifts and skipped the dark period, to avoid rigging lights and heating suits.

Tiny shook his head. "Not until you've matched course and speed with us."

"I *am* matched!"

"Not to specification, by my instruments."

"Have a heart, Tiny! I'm short on maneuvering fuel. If I juggle this entire ship to make a minor correction on a few lousy tons of cargo, I'll be so late I'll have to put down on a secondary field. I may even have to make a dead-stick landing." In those days all ships had landing wings.

"Look, Captain," Tiny said sharply, "the only purpose of your lift was to match orbits for those same few lousy tons. I don't care if you land in Little America on a pogo stick. The first load here was placed with loving care in the proper orbit and I'm making every other load match. Get that covered wagon into the groove."

"Very well, Superintendent!" Captain Shields said stiffly.

"Don't be sore, Don," Tiny said softly. "By the way, you've got a passenger for me?"

"Oh, yes, so I have!" Shields' face broke out in a grin.

"Well, keep him aboard until we unload. Maybe we can beat the shadow yet."

"Fine, fine! After all, why should I add to your troubles?" The skipper switched off, leaving my boss looking puzzled.

We didn't have time to wonder at his words. Shields whipped his ship around on gyros, blasted a second or two, and put her dead in space with us pronto—and used very little fuel, despite his bellyaching. I grabbed every man we could spare and managed to get the cargo clear before we swung into Earth's shadow. Weightlessness is an unbelievable advantage in handling freight; we gutted the *Half Moon*—by hand, mind you—in fifty-four minutes.

The stuff was oxygen tanks, loaded, and aluminum mirrors to shield them, panels of outer skin—sandwich stuff of titanium alloy sheet with foamed glass filling—and cases of jato units to spin the living quarters. Once it was all out and snapped to our cargo line I sent the men back by the same line—I won't let a man work outside without a line no matter how space happy he figures he is. Then I told Shields to send over the passenger and cast off.

This little guy came out the ship's air lock, and hooked on to the ship's line. Handling himself like he was used to space, he set his feet and dived, straight along the stretched line, his snap hook running free. I hurried back and motioned him to follow me. Tiny, the new man, and I reached the air locks together.

Besides the usual cargo lock we had three G. E. Kwikloks. A Kwiklok is an Iron Maiden without spikes; it fits a man in a suit, leaving just a few pints of air to scavenge, and cycles automatically. A big time saver in changing shifts. I passed through the middlesized one; Tiny, of course, used the big one. Without hesitation the new man pulled himself into the small one.

We went into Tiny's office. Tiny strapped down, and pushed his helmet back. "Well, McNye," he said. "Glad to have you with us."

The new radio tech opened his helmet. I heard a low, pleasant voice answer, "Thank you."

I stared and didn't say anything. From where I was I could see that the radio tech was wearing a hair ribbon.

I thought Tiny would explode. He didn't need to see the hair ribbon; with the helmet up it was clear that the new "man" was as female as Venus de Milo. Tiny sputtered, then he was unstrapped and diving for the view port. "Dad!" he yelled. "Get the radio shack. Stop that ship!"

But the *Half Moon* was already a ball of fire in the distance. Tiny looked dazed. "Dad," he said, "who else knows about this?"

"Nobody, so far as I know."

He thought a bit. "We've got to keep her out of sight.

That's it—we keep her locked up and out of sight until the next ship matches in." He didn't look at her.

"What in the world are you talking about?" McNye's voice was higher and no longer pleasant.

Tiny glared. "You, that's what. What are you—a stow-away?"

"Don't be silly! I'm G. B. McNye, electronics engineer. Don't you have my papers?"

Tiny turned to me. "Dad, this is your fault. How in Chr— pardon me, Miss. How did you let them send you a woman? Didn't you even read the advance report on her?"

"Me?" I said. "Now see here, you big squarehead! those forms don't show sex; the Fair Employment Commission won't allow it except where it's pertinent to the job."

"You're telling *me* it's not pertinent to the job *here?*"

"Not by job classification it ain't. There's lots of female radio and radar men, back Earthside."

"This isn't Earthside." He had something. He was thinking of those two-legged wolves swarming over the job outside. And G. B. McNye was pretty. Maybe eight months of no women at all affected my judgment, but she would pass.

"I've even heard of female rocket pilots," I added, for spite.

"I don't care if you've heard of female archangels; I'll have no women here!"

"Just a minute!" If I was riled, *she* was plain sore. "You're the construction superintendent, are you not?"

"Yes," Tiny admitted.

"Very well, then, how do *you* know what sex I am?"

"Are you trying to deny that you are a woman?"

"Hardly! I'm proud of it. But officially you don't know what sex G. Brooks McNye is. That's why I use 'G' instead of Gloria. I don't ask favors."

Tiny grunted. "You won't get any. I don't know how you sneaked in, but get this, McNye, or Gloria, or whatever— you're fired. You go back on the next ship. Meanwhile we'll try to keep the men from knowing we've got a woman aboard."

I could see her count ten. "May I speak," she said finally, "or does your Captain Bligh act extend to that, too?"

"Say your say."

"I didn't sneak in. I am on the permanent staff of the Station, Chief Communications Engineer. I took this vacancy myself to get to know the equipment while it was being installed. I'll live here eventually; I see no reason not to start now."

Tiny waved it away. "There'll be men and women both here—some day. Even kids. Right now it's stag and it'll stay that way."

"We'll see. Anyhow, you can't fire me; radio personnel don't work for you." She had a point; communicators and some other specialists were lent to the contractors, Five Companies, Incorporated, by Harriman Enterprises.

Tiny snorted. "Maybe I can't fire you; I can send you home. 'Requisitioned personnel must be satisfactory to the contractor.'—meaning me. Paragraph Seven, clause M; I wrote that clause myself."

"Then you know that if requisitioned personnel are refused without cause the contractor bears the replacement cost."

"I'll risk paying your fare home, but I won't have you here."

"You are most unreasonable!"

"Perhaps, but I'll decide what's good for the job. I'd rather have a dope peddler than have a woman sniffing around my boys!"

She gasped. Tiny knew he had said too much; he added, "Sorry, Miss. But that's it. You'll stay under cover until I can get rid of you."

Before she could speak I cut in. "Tiny—look behind you!"

Staring in the port was one of the riggers, his eyes bugged out. Three or four more floated up and joined him.

Then Tiny zoomed up to the port and they scattered like minnows. He scared them almost out of their suits; I thought he was going to shove his fists through the quartz.

He came back looking whipped. "Miss," he said, pointing, "wait in my room." When she was gone he added, "Dad, what'll we do?"

I said, "I thought you had made up your mind, Tiny."

"I have," he answered peevishly. "Ask the Chief Inspector to come in, will you?"

That showed how far gone he was. The inspection gang belonged to Harriman Enterprises, not to us, and Tiny rated them mere nuisances. Besides, Tiny was an Oppenheimer graduate; Dalrymple was from M.I.T.

He came in, brash and cheerful. "Good morning, Superintendent. Morning, Mr. Witherspoon. What can I do for you?"

Glumly, Tiny told the story. Dalrymple looked smug. "She's right, old man. You can send her back and even specify a male relief. But I can hardly endorse 'for proper cause' now, can I?"

"Damnation. Dalrymple, we can't have a woman around here!"

"A moot point. Not covered by contract, y'know."

"If your office hadn't sent us a crooked gambler as her predecessor I wouldn't be in this jam!"

"There, there! Remember the old blood pressure. Suppose we leave the endorsement open and arbitrate the cost. That's fair, eh?"

"I suppose so. Thanks."

"Not at all. But consider this: when you rushed Peters off before interviewing the newcomer, you cut yourself down to one operator. Hammond can't stand watch twenty-four hours a day."

"He can sleep in the shack. The alarm will wake him."

"I can't accept that. The home office and ships' frequencies must be guarded at all times. Harriman Enterprises has supplied a qualified operator; I am afraid you must use her for the time being."

Tiny will always cooperate with the inevitable; he said quietly, "Dad, she'll take first shift. Better put the married men on that shift."

Then he called her in. "Go to the radio shack and start makee-learnee, so that Hammond can go off watch soon. Mind what he tells you. He's a good man."

"I know," she said briskly. "I trained him."

Tiny bit his lip. The C.I. said, "The Superintendent doesn't bother with trivia—I'm Robert Dalrymple, Chief Inspector. He probably didn't introduce his assistant either—Mr. Witherspoon."

"Call me Dad," I said.

She smiled and said, "Howdy, Dad." I felt warm clear through. She went on to Dalrymple, "Odd that we haven't met before."

Tiny butted in. "McNye, you'll sleep in my room—"

She raised her eyebrows; he went on angrily, "Oh, I'll get my stuff out—at once. And get this: keep the door locked, off shift."

"You're darn tootin' I will!"

Tiny blushed.

I was too busy to see much of Miss Gloria. There was cargo to stow, the new tanks to install and shield. That left the most worrisome task of all: putting spin on the living quarters. Even the optimists didn't expect much interplanetary traffic for some years; nevertheless Harriman Enterprises wanted to get some activities moved in and paying rent against their enormous investment.

I.T.&T. had leased space for a microwave relay station—several million a year from television alone. The Weather Bureau was itching to set up its hemispheric integrating station; Palomar Observatory had a concession (Harriman Enterprises donated that space); the Security Council had some hush-hush project; Fermi Physical Labs and Kettering Institute each had space—a dozen tenants wanted to move in now, or sooner, even if we never completed accommodations for tourists and travelers.

There were time bonuses in it for Five Companies, Incorporated—and their help. So we were in a hurry to get spin on the quarters.

People who have never been out have trouble getting through their heads—at least I had—that there is no feeling of weight, no up and down, in a free orbit in space. There's Earth, round and beautiful, only twenty-odd thousand miles away, close enough to brush your sleeve. You know it's pulling you towards it. Yet you feel no weight, absolutely none. You float.

Floating is fine for some types of work, but when it's time to eat, or play cards, or bathe, it's good to feel weight on your feet. Your dinner stays quiet and you feel more natural.

You've seen pictures of the Station—a huge cylinder, like a bass drum, with ships' nose pockets dimpling its sides. Imagine a snare drum, spinning around inside the bass drum; that's the living quarters, with centrifugal force pinch-hitting for gravity. We could have spun the whole Station but you can't berth a ship against a whirling dervish.

So we built a spinning part for creature comfort and an outer, stationary part for docking, tanks, storerooms, and the like. You pass from one to the other at the hub. When Miss Gloria joined us the inner part was closed in and pressurized, but the rest was a skeleton of girders.

Mighty pretty though, a great network of shiny struts and ties against black sky and stars—titanium alloy 1403, light, strong, and non-corrodible. The Station is flimsy compared with a ship, since it doesn't have to take blastoff stresses. That meant we didn't dare put on spin by violent means—which is where jato units come in.

"Jato"—*Jet Assisted Take-Off*—rocket units invented to give airplanes a boost. Now we use them wherever a controlled push is needed, say to get a truck out of the mud on a dam job. We mounted four thousand of them around the frame of the living quarters, each one placed just so. They were wired up and ready to fire when Tiny came to me looking worried. "Dad," he said, "let's drop everything and finish compartment D-113."

"Okay," I said. D-113 was in the non-spin part.

"Rig an air lock and stock it with two weeks supplies."

"That'll change your mass distribution for spin," I suggested.

"I'll refigure it next dark period. Then we'll shift jatos."

When Dalrymple heard about it he came charging around. It meant a delay in making rental space available. "What's the idea?"

Tiny stared at him. They had been cooler than ordinary lately; Dalrymple had been finding excuses to seek out Miss Gloria. He had to pass through Tiny's office to reach her temporary room, and Tiny had finally told him to get out and stay out. "The idea," Tiny said slowly, "is to have a pup tent in case the house burns."

"What do you mean?"

"Suppose we fire up the jatos and the structure cracks? Want to hang around in a space suit until a ship happens by?"

"That's silly. The stresses have been calculated."

"That's what the man said when the bridge fell. We'll do it my way."

Dalrymple stormed off.

Tiny's efforts to keep Gloria fenced up were sort of pitiful. In the first place, the radio tech's biggest job was repairing suit walkie-talkies, done on watch. A rash of such troubles broke out—on her shift. I made some shift transfers and docked a few for costs, too; it's not proper maintenance when a man deliberately busts his aerial.

There were other symptoms. It became stylish to shave. Men started wearing shirts around quarters and bathing increased to where I thought I would have to rig another water still.

Came the shift when D-113 was ready and the jatos readjusted. I don't mind saying I was nervous. All hands were ordered out of the quarters and into suits. They perched around the girders and waited.

Men in space suits all look alike; we used numbers and colored armbands. Supervisors had two antennas, one for a gang frequency, one for the supervisors' circuit. With Tiny and me the second antenna hooked back through the radio shack and to all the gang frequencies—a broadcast.

The supervisors had reported their men clear of the fireworks and I was about to give Tiny the word, when this figure came climbing through the girders, inside the danger zone. No safety line. No armband. One antenna.

Miss Gloria, of course. Tiny hauled her out of the blast zone, and anchored her with his own safety line. I heard his voice, harsh in my helmet: "Who do you think you are? A sidewalk superintendent?"

And her voice: "What do you expect me to do? Go park on a star?"

"I told you to stay away from the job. If you can't obey orders, I'll lock you up."

I reached him, switched off my radio and touched helmets. "Boss! Boss!" I said. "You're broadcasting!"

"Oh—" he says, switches off, and touches helmets with her. We could still hear her; she didn't switch off. "Why, you big baboon, I came outside because you sent a search party to clear everybody out," and, "How would I know about a safety line rule? You've kept me penned up." And finally, "We'll see!"

I dragged him away and he told the boss electrician to go ahead. Then we forgot the row for we were looking at the prettiest fireworks ever seen, a giant St. Catherine's wheel, rockets blasting all over it. Utterly soundless, out there in space—but beautiful beyond compare.

The blasts died away and there was the living quarters, spinning true as a flywheel—Tiny and I both let out sighs of relief. We all went back inside then to see what weight tasted like.

It tasted funny. I went through the shaft and started down the ladders, feeling myself gain weight as I neared the rim. I felt seasick, like the first time I experienced no weight. I could hardly walk and my calves cramped.

We inspected throughout, then went to the office and sat down. It felt good, just right for comfort, one-third gravity at the rim. Tiny rubbed his chair arms and grinned, "Beats being penned up in D-113."

"Speaking of being penned up," Miss Gloria said, walking in, "may I have a word with you, Mr. Larsen?"

"Uh? Why, certainly. Matter of fact, I wanted to see you. I owe you an apology, Miss McNye. I was—"

"Forget it," she cut in. "You were on edge. But I want to know this: how long are you going to keep up this nonsense of trying to chaperone me?"

He studied her. "Not long. Just till your relief arrives."

"So? Who is the shop steward around here?"

"A shipfitter named McAndrews. But you can't use him. You're a staff member."

"Not in the job I'm filling. I am going to talk to him. You're discriminating against me, and in my off time at that."

"Perhaps, but you will find I have the authority. Legally I'm a ship's captain, while on this job. A captain in space has wide discriminatory powers."

"Then you should use them with discrimination!"

He grinned. "Isn't that what you just said I was doing?"

We didn't hear from the shop steward, but Miss Gloria started doing as she pleased. She showed up at the movies, next off shift, with Dalrymple. Tiny left in the middle—good show, too; *Lysistrata Goes to Town*, relayed up from New York.

As she was coming back alone he stopped her, having seen to it that I was present. "Umm—Miss McNye. . . ."

"Yes?"

"I think you should know, uh, well . . . Chief Inspector Dalrymple is a married man."

"Are you suggesting that my conduct has been improper?"

"No, but—"

"Then mind your own business!" Before he could answer she added, "It might interest you that he told me about your four children."

Tiny sputtered. "Why . . . why, I'm not even married!"

"So? That makes it worse, doesn't it?" She swept out.

Tiny quit trying to keep her in her room, but told her to notify him whenever she left it. It kept him busy riding herd on her. I refrained from suggesting that he get Dalrymple to spell him.

But I was surprised when he told me to put through the

order dismissing her. I had been pretty sure he was going to drop it.

"What's the charge?" I asked.

"Insubordination!"

I kept mum. He said, "Well, she won't take orders."

"She does her work okay. You give her orders you wouldn't give to one of the men—and that a man wouldn't take."

"You disagree with my orders?"

"That's not the point. You can't prove the charge, Tiny."

"Well, charge her with being female! I can prove *that*."

I didn't say anything. "Dad," he added wheedlingly, "you know how to write it. 'No personal animus against Miss McNye, but it is felt that as a matter of policy, and so forth and so on.' "

I wrote it and gave it to Hammond privately. Radio techs are sworn to secrecy but it didn't surprise me when I was stopped by O'Connor, one of our best metalsmiths. "Look, Dad, is it true that the Old Man is getting rid of Brooksie?"

"Brooksie?"

"Brooksie McNye—she says to call her Brooks. Is it true?"

I admitted it, then went on, wondering if I should have lied.

It takes four hours, about, for a ship to lift from Earth. The shift before the *Pole Star* was due, with Miss Gloria's relief, the timekeeper brought me two separation slips. Two men were nothing; we averaged more each ship. An hour later he reached me by supervisors' circuit, and asked me to come to the time office. I was out on the rim, inspecting a weld job; I said no. "*Please*, Mr. Witherspoon," he begged, "you've *got* to." When one of the boys doesn't call me 'Dad,' it means something. I went.

There was a queue like mail call outside his door; I went in and he shut the door on them. He handed me a double handful of separation slips. "What in the great depths of night is this?" I asked.

"There's dozens more I ain't had time to write up yet."

None of the slips had any reason given—just "own choice." "Look, Jimmie—what goes on here?"

"Can't you dope it out, Dad? Shucks, I'm turning in one, too."

I told him my guess and he admitted it. So I took the slips, called Tiny and told him for the love of Heaven to come to his office.

Tiny chewed his lip considerable. "But, Dad, they *can't* strike. It's a non-strike contract with bonds from every union concerned."

"It's no strike, Tiny. You can't stop a man from quitting."

"They'll pay their own fares back, so help me!"

"Guess again. Most of 'em have worked long enough for the free ride."

"We'll have to hire others quick, or we'll miss our date."

"Worse than that, Tiny—we won't finish. By next dark period you won't even have a maintenance crew."

"I've never had a gang of men quit me. I'll talk to them."

"No good, Tiny. You're up against something too strong for you."

"*You*'re against me, Dad?"

"I'm never against you, Tiny."

He said, "Dad, you think I'm pig-headed, but I'm *right*. You can't have one woman among several hundred men. It drives 'em nutty."

I didn't say it affected him the same way; I said, "Is that bad?"

"Of course. I can't let the job be ruined to humor one woman."

"Tiny, have you looked at the progress charts lately?"

"I've hardly had time to—what about them?"

I knew why he hadn't had time. "You'll have trouble proving Miss Gloria interfered with the job. We're ahead of schedule."

"We *are?*"

While he was studying the charts I put an arm around his shoulder. "Look, son," I said, "sex has been around our planet a long time. Earthside, they never get away from it, yet some pretty big jobs get built anyhow. Maybe we'll just have to learn to live with it here, too. Matter of fact, you had the answer a minute ago."

"I did? I sure didn't know it."

"You said, 'You can't have *one* woman among several hundred men.' Get me?"

"Huh? No, I don't. Wait a minute! Maybe I do."

"Ever tried jiu jitsu? Sometimes you win by relaxing."

"Yes. Yes!"

"When you can't beat 'em, you jine 'em."

He buzzed the radio shack. "Have Hammond relieve you, McNye, and come to my office."

He did it handsomely, stood up and made a speech—he'd been wrong, taken him a long time to see it, hoped there were no hard feelings, etc. He was instructing the home office to see how many jobs could be filled at once with female help. "Don't forget married couples," I put in mildly, "and better ask for some older women, too."

"I'll do that," Tiny agreed. "Have I missed anything, Dad?"

"Guess not. We'll have to rig quarters, but there's time."

"Okay. I'm telling them to hold the *Pole Star,* Gloria, so they can send us a few this trip."

"That's fine!" She looked really happy.

He chewed his lip. "I've a feeling I've missed something. Hmm—I've got it. Dad, tell them to send up a chaplain for the Station, as soon as possible. Under the new policy we may need one anytime." I thought so, too.

Space Jockey

JUST AS THEY WERE LEAVING the telephone called his name. "Don't answer it," she pleaded. "We'll miss the curtain."

"Who is it?" he called out. The viewplate lighted; he recognized Olga Pierce, and behind her the Colorado Springs office of Trans-Lunar Transit.

"Calling Mr. Pemberton. Calling—Oh, it's you, Jake. You're on. Flight 27, Supra-New York to Space Terminal. I'll have a copter pick you up in twenty minutes."

"How come?" he protested. "I'm fourth down on the call board."

"You *were* fourth down. Now you are standby pilot to Hicks—and he just got a psycho down-check."

"Hicks got psychoed? That's silly!"

"Happens to the best, chum. Be ready. 'Bye now."

His wife was twisting sixteen dollars worth of lace handkerchief to a shapeless mass. "Jake, this is ridiculous. For three months I haven't seen enough of you to know what you look like."

"Sorry, kid. Take Helen to the show."

"Oh, Jake, I don't care about the show; I wanted to get you where they couldn't reach you for once."

"They would have called me at the theater."

"Oh, no! I wiped out the record you'd left."

"Phyllis! Are you trying to get me fired?"

"Don't look at me that way." She waited, hoping that he would speak, regretting the side issue, and wondering how to tell him that her own fretfulness was caused, not by disappointment, but by gnawing worry for his safety every time he went out into space.

She went on desperately, "You don't have to take this flight, darling; you've been on Earth less than the time limit. Please, Jake!"

He was peeling off his tux. "I've told you a thousand times: a pilot doesn't get a regular run by playing space-lawyer with the rule book. Wiping out my follow-up message—why did you do it, Phyllis? Trying to ground me?"

227

"No, darling, but I thought just this once—"

"When they offer me a flight I take it." He walked stiffly out of the room.

He came back ten minutes later, dressed for space and apparently in good humor; he was whistling: "—the caller called Casey at ha' past four; he kissed his—" He broke off when he saw her face, and set his mouth. "Where's my coverall?"

"I'll get it. Let me fix you something to eat."

"You know I can't take high acceleration on a full stomach. And why lose thirty bucks to lift another pound?"

Dressed as he was, in shorts, singlet, sandals, and pocket belt, he was already good for about minus-fifty pounds in weight bonus; she started to tell him the weight penalty on a sandwich and a cup of coffee did not matter to them, but it was just one more possible cause for misunderstanding.

Neither of them said much until the taxicab clumped on the roof. He kissed her goodbye and told her not to come outside. She obeyed—until she heard the helicopter take off. Then she climbed to the roof and watched it out of sight.

The traveling-public gripes at the lack of direct Earth-to-Moon service, but it takes three types of rocket ships and two space-station changes to make a fiddling quarter-million-mile jump for a good reason: Money.

The Commerce Commission has set the charges for the present three-stage lift from here to the Moon at thirty dollars a pound. Would direct service be cheaper?—a ship designed to blast off from Earth, make an airless landing on the Moon, return and make an atmosphere landing, would be so cluttered up with heavy special equipment used only once in the trip that it could not show a profit at a thousand dollars a pound! Imagine combining a ferry boat, a subway train, and an express elevator—

So Trans-Lunar uses rockets braced for catapulting, and winged for landing on return to Earth to make the terrific lift from Earth to our satellite station Supra-New York. The long middle lap, from there to where Space Terminal circles the Moon, calls for comfort—but no landing gear. The *Flying Dutchman* and the *Philip Nolan* never land; they were even assembled in space, and they resemble winged rockets like the *Skysprite* and the *Firefly* as little as a Pullman train resembles a parachute.

The *Moonbat* and the *Gremlin* are good only for the jump from Space Terminal down to Luna . . . no wings, cocoon-like acceleration-and-crash hammocks, fractional controls on their enormous jets.

The change-over points would not have to be more than air-conditioned tanks. Of course Space Terminal is quite a city, what with the Mars and Venus traffic, but even today Supra-New York is still rather primitive, hardly more than a fueling point and a restaurant-waiting room. It has only been the past five years that it has even been equipped to offer the comfort of one-gravity centrifuge service to passengers with queasy stomachs.

Pemberton weighed in at the spaceport office, then hurried over to where the *Skysprite* stood cradled in the catapult. He shucked off his coverall, shivered as he handed it to the gate-man, and ducked inside. He went to his acceleration ham-mock and went to sleep; the lift to Supra-New York was not his worry—his job was deep space.

He woke at the surge of the catapult and the nerve-tingling rush up the face of Pikes Peak. When the *Skysprite* went into free flight, flung straight up above the Peak, Pemberton held his breath; if the rocket jets failed to fire, the ground-to-space pilot must try to wrestle her into a glide and bring her down, on her wings.

The rockets roared on time; Jake went back to sleep.

When the *Skysprite* locked in with Supra-New York, Pemberton went to the station's stellar navigation room. He was pleased to find Shorty Weinstein, the computer, on duty. Jake trusted Shorty's computations—a good thing when your ship, your passengers, and your own skin depend thereon. Pemberton had to be a better than average mathematician himself in order to be a pilot; his own limited talent made him appreci-ate the genius of those who computed the orbits.

"Hot Pilot Pemberton, the Scourge of the Spaceways—Hi!" Weinstein handed him a sheet of paper.

Jake looked at it, then looked amazed. "Hey, Shorty—you've made a mistake."

"Huh? Impossible. Mabel can't make mistakes." Weinstein gestured at the giant astrogation computer filling the far wall.

"*You* made a mistake. You gave me an easy fix—'Vega, Antares, Regulus.' You make things easy for the pilot and your guild'll chuck you out." Weinstein looked sheepish but pleased. "I see I don't blast off for seventeen hours. I could have taken the morning freight." Jake's thoughts went back to Phyllis.

"UN canceled the morning trip."

"Oh—" Jake shut up, for he knew Weinstein knew as little as he did. Perhaps the flight would have passed too close to an A-bomb rocket, circling the globe like a policeman. The General Staff of the Security Council did not give out information about the top secrets guarding the peace of the planet.

Pemberton shrugged. "Well, if I'm asleep, call me three hours minus."

"Right. Your tape will be ready."

While he slept, the *Flying Dutchman* nosed gently into her slip, sealed her airlocks to the Station, discharged passengers and freight from Luna City. When he woke, her holds were filling, her fuel replenished, and passengers boarding. He stopped by the post office radio desk, looking for a letter from Phyllis. Finding none, he told himself that she would have sent it to Terminal. He went on into the restaurant, bought the facsimile *Herald-Tribune*, and settled down grimly to enjoy the comics and his breakfast.

A man sat down opposite him and proceeded to plague him with silly questions about rocketry, topping it by misinterpreting the insignia embroidered on Pemberton's singlet and miscalling him "Captain." Jake hurried through breakfast to escape him, then picked up the tape from his automatic pilot, and went aboard the *Flying Dutchman*.

After reporting to the Captain he went to the control room, floating and pulling himself along by the handgrips. He buckled himself into the pilot's chair and started his check off.

Captain Kelly drifted in and took the other chair as Pemberton was finishing his checking runs on the ballistic tracker. "Have a Camel, Jake."

"I'll take a rain check." He continued; Kelly watched him with a slight frown. Like captains and pilots on Mark Twain's Mississippi—and for the same reasons—a spaceship captain bosses his ship, his crew, his cargo, and his passengers, but the pilot is the final, legal, and unquestioned boss of how the ship is handled from blast-off to the end of the trip. A captain may turn down a given pilot—nothing more. Kelly fingered a slip of paper tucked in his pouch and turned over in his mind the words with which the Company psychiatrist on duty had handed it to him.

"I'm giving this pilot clearance, Captain, but you need not accept it."

"Pemberton's a good man. What's wrong?"

The psychiatrist thought over what he had observed while posing as a silly tourist bothering a stranger at breakfast. "He's a little more anti-social than his past record shows. Something on his mind. Whatever it is, he can tolerate it for the present. We'll keep an eye on him."

Kelly had answered, "Will you come along with him as pilot?"

"If you wish."

"Don't bother—I'll take him. No need to lift a deadhead."

Pemberton fed Weinstein's tape into the robot-pilot, then turned to Kelly. "Control ready, sir."

"Blast when ready, Pilot." Kelly felt relieved when he heard himself make the irrevocable decision.

Pemberton signaled the Station to cast loose. The great ship was nudged out by an expanding pneumatic ram until she swam in space a thousand feet away, secured by a single line. He then turned the ship to its blast-off direction by causing a flywheel, mounted on gymbals at the ship's center of gravity, to spin rapidly. The ship spun slowly in the opposite direction, by grace of Newton's Third Law of Motion.

Guided by the tape, the robot-pilot tilted prisms of the pilot's periscope so that Vega, Antares, and Regulus would shine as one image when the ship was headed right; Pemberton nursed the ship to that heading . . . fussily; a mistake of one minute of arc here meant two hundred miles at destination.

When the three images made a pinpoint, he stopped the flywheels and locked in the gyros. He then checked the heading of his ship by direct observation of each of the stars, just as a salt-water skipper uses a sextant, but with incomparably more accurate instruments. This told him nothing about the correctness of the course Weinstein had ordered—he had to take that as Gospel—but it assured him that the robot and its tape were behaving as planned. Satisfied, he cast off the last line.

Seven minutes to go—Pemberton flipped the switch permitting the robot-pilot to blast away when its clock told it to. He waited, hands poised over the manual controls, ready to take over if the robot failed, and felt the old, inescapable sick excitement building up inside him.

Even as adrenalin poured into him, stretching his time sense, throbbing in his ears, his mind kept turning back to Phyllis.

He admitted she had a kick coming—spacemen shouldn't marry. Not that she'd starve if he messed up a landing, but a gal doesn't want insurance; she wants a husband—minus six minutes.

If he got a regular run she could live in Space Terminal.

No good—idle women at Space Terminal went bad. Oh, Phyllis wouldn't become a tramp or a rum bum; she'd just go bats.

Five minutes more—he didn't care much for Space Terminal himself. Nor for space! "The Romance of Interplanetary Travel"—it looked well in print, but he knew what it was: A job. Monotony. No scenery. Bursts of work, tedious waits. No home life.

Why didn't he get an honest job and stay home nights?

He knew! Because he was a space jockey and too old to change.

What chance has a thirty-year-old married man, used to important money, to change his racket? (Four minutes) He'd look good trying to sell helicopters on commission, now, wouldn't he?

Maybe he could buy a piece of irrigated land and— Be your age, chum! You know as much about farming as a cow knows about cube root! No, he had made his bed when he picked rockets during his training hitch. If he had bucked for the electronics branch, or taken a GI scholarship—too late now. Straight from the service into Harriman's Lunar Exploitations, hopping ore on Luna. That had torn it.

"How's it going, Doc?" Kelly's voice was edgy.

"Minus two minutes some seconds." Damnation—Kelly knew better than to talk to the pilot on minus time.

He caught a last look through the periscope. Antares seemed to have drifted. He unclutched the gyro, tilted and spun the flywheel, braking it savagely to a stop a moment later. The image was again a pinpoint. He could not have explained what he did: it was virtuosity, exact juggling, beyond textbook and classroom.

Twenty seconds . . . across the chronometer's face beads of light trickled the seconds away while he tensed, ready to fire by hand, or even to disconnect and refuse the trip if his judgment told him to. A too-cautious decision might cause Lloyds' to cancel his bond; a reckless decision could cost his license or even his life—and others.

But he was not thinking of underwriters and licenses, nor

even of lives. In truth he was not thinking at all; he was feeling, feeling his ship, as if his nerve ends extended into every part of her. Five seconds . . . the safety disconnects clicked out. Four seconds . . . three seconds . . . two seconds . . . . one——

He was stabbing at the hand-fire button when the roar hit him.

Kelly relaxed to the pseudo-gravity of the blast and watched. Pemberton was soberly busy, scanning dials, noting time, checking his progress by radar bounced off Supra-New York. Weinstein's figures, robot-pilot, the ship itself, all were clicking together.

Minutes later, the critical instant neared when the robot should cut the jets. Pemberton poised a finger over the hand cut-off, while splitting his attention among radarscope, accelerometer, periscope, and chronometer. One instant they were roaring along on the jets; the next split second the ship was in free orbit, plunging silently toward the Moon. So perfectly matched were human and robot that Pemberton himself did not know which had cut the power.

He glanced again at the board, then unbuckled. "How about that cigarette, Captain? And you can let your passengers unstrap."

No co-pilot is needed in space and most pilots would rather share a toothbrush than a control room. The pilot works about an hour at blast off, about the same before contact, and loafs during free flight, save for routine checks and corrections. Pemberton prepared to spend one hundred and four hours eating, reading, writing letters, and sleeping—especially sleeping.

When the alarm woke him, he checked the ship's position, then wrote to his wife. "Phyllis my dear," he began, "I don't blame you for being upset at missing your night out. I was disappointed, too. But bear with me, darling, I should be on a regular run before long. In less than ten years I'll be up for retirement and we'll have a chance to catch up on bridge and golf and things like that. I know it's pretty hard to—"

The voice circuit cut in. "Oh, Jake—put on your company face. I'm bringing a visitor to the control room."

"No visitors in the control room, Captain."

"Now, Jake. This lunkhead has a letter from Old Man Harriman himself. 'Every possible courtesy—' and so forth."

Pemberton thought quickly. He could refuse—but there was no sense in offending the big boss. "Okay, Captain. Make it short."

The visitor was a man, jovial, oversize—Jake figured him for an eighty pound weight penalty. Behind him a thirteen-year-old male counterpart came zipping through the door and lunged for the control console. Pemberton snagged him by the arm and forced himself to speak pleasantly. "Just hang on to that bracket, youngster. I don't want you to bump your head."

"Leggo me! Pop—make him let go."

Kelly cut in. "I think he had best hang on, Judge."

"Umm, uh—very well. Do as the Captain says, Junior."

"Aw, gee, Pop!"

"Judge Schacht, this is First Pilot Pemberton," Kelly said rapidly. "He'll show you around."

"Glad to know you, Pilot. Kind of you, and all that."

"What would you like to see, Judge?" Jake said carefully.

"Oh, this and that. It's for the boy—his first trip. I'm an old spacehound myself—probably more hours than half your crew." He laughed. Pemberton did not.

"There's not much to see in free flight."

"Quite all right. We'll just make ourselves at home—eh, Captain?"

"I wanna sit in the control seat," Schacht Junior announced.

Pemberton winced. Kelly said urgently, "Jake, would you mind outlining the control system for the boy? Then we'll go."

"He doesn't have to show me anything. I know all about it. I'm a Junior Rocketeer of America—see my button?" The boy shoved himself toward the control desk.

Pemberton grabbed him, steered him into the pilot's chair, and strapped him in. He then flipped the board's disconnect.

"Whatcha doing?"

"I cut off power to the controls so I could explain them."

"Aintcha gonna fire the jets?"

"No." Jake started a rapid description of the use and purpose of each button, dial, switch, meter, gimmick, and scope.

Junior squirmed. "How about meteors?" he demanded.

"Oh, that—maybe one collision in half a million Earth-Moon trips. Meteors are scarce."

"So what? Say you hit the jackpot? You're in the soup."

"Not at all. The anti-collision radar guards all directions

five hundred miles out. If anything holds a steady bearing for three seconds, a direct hook-up starts the jets. First a warning gong so that everybody can grab something solid, then one second later—*Boom!*—We get out of there fast."

"Sounds corny to me. Lookee, I'll show you how Commodore Cartwright did it in *The Comet Busters*—"

"Don't touch those controls!"

"You don't own this ship. My pop says—"

"Oh, Jake!" Hearing his name, Pemberton twisted, fish-like, to face Kelly.

"Jake, Judge Schacht would like to know—" From the corner of his eye Jake saw the boy reach for the board. He turned, started to shout—acceleration caught him, while the jets roared in his ear.

An old spacehand can usually recover, catlike, in an unexpected change from weightlessness to acceleration. But Jake had been grabbing for the boy, instead of for anchorage. He fell back and down, twisted to try to avoid Schacht, banged his head on the frame of the open air-tight door below, and fetched up on the next deck, out cold.

Kelly was shaking him. "You all right, Jake?"

He sat up. "Yeah. Sure." He became aware of the thunder, the shivering deckplates. "The jets! Cut the power!"

He shoved Kelly aside and swarmed up into the control room, jabbed at the cut-off button. In sudden ringing silence, they were again weightless.

Jake turned, unstrapped Schacht Junior, and hustled him to Kelly. "Captain, please remove this menace from my control room."

"Leggo! Pop—he's gonna hurt me!"

The elder Schacht bristled at once. "What's the meaning of this? Let go of my son!"

"Your precious son cut in the jets."

"Junior—did you do that?"

The boy shifted his eyes. "No, Pop. It . . . it was a meteor."

Schacht looked puzzled. Pemberton snorted. "I had just told him how the radar-guard can blast to miss a meteor. He's lying."

Schacht ran through the process he called "making up his mind", then answered, "Junior never lies. Shame on you, a grown man, to try to put the blame on a helpless boy. I shall report you, sir. Come, Junior."

Jake grabbed his arm. "Captain, I want those controls photographed for fingerprints before this man leaves the room. It was not a meteor; the controls were dead, until this boy switched them on. Furthermore the anti-collision circuit sounds an alarm."

Schacht looked wary. "This is ridiculous. I simply objected to the slur on my son's character. No harm has been done."

"No harm, eh? How about broken arms—or necks? And wasted fuel, with more to waste before we're back in the groove. Do you know, Mister 'Old Spacehound,' just how precious a little fuel will be when we try to match orbits with Space Terminal—if we haven't got it? We may have to dump cargo to save the ship, cargo at $60,000 a ton on freight charges alone. Fingerprints will show the Commerce Commission whom to nick for it."

When they were alone again Kelly asked anxiously, "You won't really have to jettison? You've got a maneuvering reserve."

"Maybe we can't even get to Terminal. How long did she blast?"

Kelly scratched his head. "I was woozy myself."

"We'll open the accelerograph and take a look."

Kelly brightened. "Oh, sure! If the brat didn't waste too much, then we just swing ship and blast back the same length of time."

Jake shook his head. "You forgot the changed mass-ratio."

"Oh . . . oh, yes!" Kelly looked embarrassed. Mass-ratio . . . under power, the ship lost the weight of fuel burned. The thrust remained constant; the mass it pushed shrank. Getting back to proper position, course, and speed became a complicated problem in the calculus of ballistics. "But you can do it, can't you?"

"I'll have to. But I sure wish I had Weinstein here."

Kelly left to see about his passengers; Jake got to work. He checked his situation by astronomical observation and by radar. Radar gave him all three factors quickly but with limited accuracy. Sights taken of Sun, Moon, and Earth gave him position, but told nothing of course and speed, at that time—nor could he afford to wait to take a second group of sights for the purpose.

Dead reckoning gave him an estimated situation, by adding Weinstein's predictions to the calculated effect of young Schacht's meddling. This checked fairly well with the radar and visual observations, but still he had no notion of whether or not he could get back in the groove and reach his destination; it was now necessary to calculate what it would take and whether or not the remaining fuel would be enough to brake his speed and match orbits.

In space, it does no good to reach your journey's end if you flash on past at miles per second, or even crawling along at a few hundred miles per hour. To catch an egg on a plate—don't bump!

He started doggedly to work to compute how to do it using the least fuel, but his little Marchant electronic calculator was no match for the tons of IBM computer at Supra-New York, nor was he Weinstein. Three hours later he had an answer of sorts. He called Kelly. "Captain? You can start by jettisoning Schacht & Son."

"I'd like to. No way out, Jake?"

"I can't promise to get your ship in safely without dumping. Better dump now, before we blast. It's cheaper."

Kelly hesitated; he would as cheerfully lose a leg. "Give me time to pick out what to dump."

"Okay." Pemberton returned sadly to his figures, hoping to find a saving mistake, then thought better of it. He called the radio room. "Get me Weinstein at Supra-New York."

"Out of normal range."

"I know that. This is the Pilot. Safety priority—urgent. Get a tight beam on them and nurse it."

"Uh . . . aye aye, sir. I'll try."

Weinstein was doubtful. "Cripes, Jake, I can't pilot you."

"Dammit, you can work problems for me!"

"What good is seven-place accuracy with bum data?"

"Sure, sure. But you know what instruments I've got; you know about how well I can handle them. Get me a better answer."

"I'll try." Weinstein called back four hours later. "Jake? Here's the dope: You planned to blast back to match your predicted speed, then made side corrections for position. Orthodox but uneconomical. Instead I had Mabel solve for it as one maneuver."

"Good!"

"Not so fast. It saves fuel but not enough. You can't possibly get back in your old groove and then match Terminal without dumping."

Pemberton let it sink in, then said, "I'll tell Kelly."

"Wait a minute, Jake. Try this. Start from scratch."

"Huh?"

"Treat it as a brand-new problem. Forget about the orbit on your tape. With your present course, speed, and position, compute the cheapest orbit to match with Terminal's. Pick a new groove."

Pemberton felt foolish. "I never thought of that."

"Of course not. With the ship's little one-lung calculator it'd take you three weeks to solve it. You set to record?"

"Sure."

"Here's your data." Weinstein started calling it off.

When they had checked it, Jake said, "That'll get me there?"

"Maybe. *If* the data you gave me is up to your limit of accuracy; *if* you can follow instructions as exactly as a robot, *if* you can blast off and make contact so precisely that you don't need side corrections, then you might squeeze home. Maybe. Good luck, anyhow." The wavering reception muffled their goodbyes.

Jake signaled Kelly. "Don't jettison, Captain. Have your passengers strap down. Stand by to blast. Minus fourteen minutes."

"Very well, Pilot."

The new departure made and checked, he again had time to spare. He took out his unfinished letter, read it, then tore it up.

"Dearest Phyllis," he started again, "I've been doing some hard thinking this trip and have decided that I've just been stubborn. What am I doing way out here? I like my home. I like to see my wife.

"Why should I risk my neck and your peace of mind to herd junk through the sky? Why hang around a telephone waiting to chaperon fatheads to the Moon—numbskulls who couldn't pilot a rowboat and should have stayed at home in the first place?

"Money, of course. I've been afraid to risk a change. I won't find another job that will pay half as well, but, if you are game, I'll ground myself and we'll start over. All my love,

"Jake"

He put it away and went to sleep, to dream that an entire troop of Junior Rocketeers had been quartered in his control room.

The closeup view of the Moon is second only to the space-side view of the Earth as a tourist attraction; nevertheless Pemberton insisted that all passengers strap down during the swing around to Terminal. With precious little fuel for the matching maneuver, he refused to hobble his movements to please sightseers.

Around the bulge of the Moon, Terminal came into sight—by radar only, for the ship was tail foremost. After each short braking blast Pemberton caught a new radar fix, then compared his approach with a curve he had plotted from Weinstein's figures—with one eye on the time, another on the 'scope, a third on the plot, and a fourth on his fuel gages.

"Well, Jake?" Kelly fretted. "Do we make it?"

"How should I know? You be ready to dump." They had agreed on liquid oxygen as the cargo to dump, since it could be let boil out through the outer valves, without handling.

"Don't say it, Jake."

"Damn it—I won't if I don't have to." He was fingering his controls again; the blast chopped off his words. When it stopped, the radio maneuvering circuit was calling him.

"*Flying Dutchman*, Pilot speaking," Jake shouted back.

"Terminal Control—Supro reports you short on fuel."

"Right."

"Don't approach. Match speeds outside us. We'll send a transfer ship to refuel you and pick up passengers."

"I think I can make it."

"Don't try it. Wait for refueling."

"Quit telling me how to pilot my ship!" Pemberton switched off the circuit, then stared at the board, whistling morosely. Kelly filled in the words in his mind: *"Casey said to the fireman, 'Boy, you better jump, cause two locomotives are agoing to bump!'"*

"You going in the slip anyhow, Jake?"

"Mmm—no, blast it. I can't take a chance of caving in the side of Terminal, not with passengers aboard. But I'm not going to match speeds fifty miles outside and wait for a piggyback."

He aimed for a near miss just outside Terminal's orbit, conning by instinct, for Weinstein's figures meant nothing by now. His aim was good; he did not have to waste his hoarded fuel on last minute side corrections to keep from hitting Terminal. When at last he was sure of sliding safely on past if unchecked, he braked once more. Then, as he started to cut off the power, the jets coughed, sputtered, and quit.

The *Flying Dutchman* floated in space, five hundred yards outside Terminal, speeds matched.

Jake switched on the radio. "Terminal—stand by for my line. I'll warp her in."

He had filed his report, showered, and was headed for the post office to radiostat his letter, when the bullhorn summoned him to the Commodore-Pilot's office. Oh, oh, he told himself, Schacht has kicked the Brass—I wonder just how much stock that bliffy owns? And there's that other matter— getting snotty with Control.

He reported stiffly. "First Pilot Pemberton, sir."

Commodore Soames looked up. "Pemberton—oh, yes. You hold two ratings, space-to-space and airless-landing."

Let's not stall around, Jake told himself. Aloud he said, "I have no excuses for anything this last trip. If the Commodore does not approve the way I run my control room, he may have my resignation."

"What are you talking about?"

"I, well—don't you have a passenger complaint on me?"

"Oh, that!" Soames brushed it aside. "Yes, he's been here. But I have Kelly's report, too—and your chief jetman's, and a special from Supra-New York. That was crack piloting, Pemberton."

"You mean there's no beef from the Company?"

"When have I failed to back up my pilots? You were perfectly right; I would have stuffed him out the air lock. Let's get down to business: You're on the space-to-space board, but I want to send a special to Luna City. Will you take it, as a favor to me?"

Pemberton hesitated; Soames went on, "That oxygen you saved is for the Cosmic Research Project. They blew the seals on the north tunnel and lost tons of the stuff. The work is stopped—about $130,000 a day in overhead, wages, and penalties. The *Gremlin* is here, but no pilot until the *Moonbat* gets in—except you. Well?"

"But I—look, Commodore, you can't risk people's necks on

a jet landing of mine. I'm rusty; I need a refresher and a
check-out."

"No passengers, no crew, no captain—your neck alone."

"I'll take her."

Twenty-eight minutes later, with the ugly, powerful hull of
the *Gremlin* around him, he blasted away. One strong shove
to kill her orbital speed and let her fall toward the Moon,
then no more worries until it came time to "ride 'er down on
her tail".

He felt good—until he hauled out two letters, the one he
had failed to send, and one from Phyllis, delivered at Terminal.

The letter from Phyllis was affectionate—and superficial.
She did not mention his sudden departure; she ignored his
profession completely. The letter was a model of correctness,
but it worried him.

He tore up both letters and started another. It said, in part:
"—never said so outright, but you resent my job.

"I have to work to support us. You've got a job, too. It's an
old, old job that women have been doing a long time—crossing the plains in covered wagons, waiting for ships to come
back from China, or waiting around a mine head after an explosion—kiss him goodbye with a smile, take care of him at
home.

"You married a spaceman, so part of your job is to accept
my job cheerfully. I think you can do it, when you realize it.
I hope so, for the way things have been going won't do for either of us.

                              Believe me, I love you.
                                        Jake"

He brooded on it until time to bend the ship down for his
approach. From twenty miles altitude down to one mile he let
the robot brake her, then shifted to manual while still falling
slowly. A perfect airless-landing would be the reverse of the
take-off of a war rocket—free fall, then one long blast of the
jets, ending with the ship stopped dead as she touches the
ground. In practice a pilot must feel his way down, not too
slowly; a ship could burn all the fuel this side of Venus
fighting gravity too long.

Forty seconds later, falling a little more than 140 miles per
hour, he picked up in his periscopes the thousand-foot static

towers. At 300 feet he blasted five gravities for more than a second, cut it, and caught her with a one-sixth gravity, Moon-normal blast. Slowly he eased this off, feeling happy.

The *Gremlin* hovered, her bright jet splashing the soil of the Moon, then settled with dignity to land without a jar.

The ground crew took over; a sealed runabout jeeped Pemberton to the tunnel entrance. Inside Luna City, he found himself paged before he finished filing his report. When he took the call, Soames smiled at him from the viewplate. "I saw that landing from the field pick-up, Pemberton. You don't need a refresher course."

Jake blushed. "Thank you, sir."

"Unless you are dead set on space-to-space, I can use you on the regular Luna City run. Quarters here or Luna City? Want it?"

He heard himself saying, "Luna City. I'll take it."

He tore up his third letter as he walked into Luna City post office. At the telephone desk he spoke to a blonde in a blue moonsuit. "Get me Mrs. Jake Pemberton, Suburb six-four-oh-three, Dodge City, Kansas, please."

She looked him over. "You pilots sure spend money."

"Sometimes phone calls are cheap. Hurry it, will you?"

Phyllis was trying to phrase the letter she felt she should have written before. It was easier to say in writing that she was not complaining of loneliness nor lack of fun, but that she could not stand the strain of worrying about his safety. But then she found herself quite unable to state the logical conclusion. Was she prepared to face giving him up entirely if he would not give up space? She truly did not know . . . the phone call was a welcome interruption.

The viewplate stayed blank. "Long distance," came a thin voice. "Luna City calling."

Fear jerked at her heart. "Phyllis Pemberton speaking."

An interminable delay—she knew it took nearly three seconds for radio waves to make the Earth-Moon round trip, but she did not remember it and it would not have reassured her. All she could see was a broken home, herself a widow, and Jake, beloved Jake, dead in space.

"Mrs. Jake Pemberton?"

"Yes, yes! Go ahead." Another wait—had she sent him

away in a bad temper, reckless, his judgment affected? Had he died out there, remembering only that she fussed at him for leaving her to go to work? Had she failed him when he needed her? She knew that her Jake could not be tied to apron strings; men—grown-up men, not mammas' boys—had to break away from mother's apron strings. Then why had she tried to tie him to hers?—she had known better; her own mother had warned her not to try it.

She prayed.

Then another voice, one that weakened her knees with relief: "That you, honey?"

"Yes, darling, yes! What are you doing on the Moon?"

"It's a long story. At a dollar a second it will keep. What I want to know is—are you willing to come to Luna City?"

It was Jake's turn to suffer from the inevitable lag in reply. He wondered if Phyllis were stalling, unable to make up her mind. At last he heard her say, "Of course, darling. When do I leave?"

"When—say, don't you even want to know *why?*"

She started to say that it did not matter, then said, "Yes, tell me." The lag was still present but neither of them cared. He told her the news, then added, "Run over to the Springs and get Olga Pierce to straighten out the red tape for you. Need my help to pack?"

She thought rapidly. Had he meant to come back anyhow, he would not have asked. "No. I can manage."

"Good girl. I'll radiostat you a long letter about what to bring and so forth. I love you. 'Bye now!"

"Oh, I love you, too. Goodbye, darling."

Pemberton came out of the booth whistling. Good girl, Phyllis. Staunch. He wondered why he had ever doubted her.

Requiem

On a high hill in Samoa there is a grave. Inscribed on the marker are these words:

> *"Under the wide and starry sky*
> *Dig the grave and let me lie*
> *Glad did I live and gladly die*
> *And I laid me down with a will!*

> *"This be the verse you grave for me:*
> *'Here he lies where he longed to be,*
> *Home is the sailor, home from the sea,*
> *And the hunter home from the hill.'"*

These lines appear another place—scrawled on a shipping tag torn from a compressed-air container, and pinned to the ground with a knife.

It wasn't much of a fair, as fairs go. The trottin' races didn't promise much excitement, even though several entries claimed the blood of the immortal Dan Patch. The tents and concession booths barely covered the circus grounds, and the pitchmen seemed discouraged.

D. D. Harriman's chauffeur could not see any reason for stopping. They were due in Kansas City for a directors' meeting, that is to say, Harriman was. The chauffeur had private reasons for promptness, reasons involving darktown society on Eighteenth Street. But the Boss not only stopped, but hung around.

Bunting and a canvas arch made the entrance to a large enclosure beyond the race track. Red and gold letters announced:

This way to the
MOON ROCKET!!!!
See it in actual flight!
Public Demonstration Flights
Twice Daily

This is the ACTUAL TYPE used by the
First Man to Reach the MOON!!!
YOU can ride in it!!—$50.00

A boy, nine or ten years old, hung around the entrance and
stared at the posters.

"Want to see the ship, son?"

The kid's eyes shone. "Gee, mister. I sure would."

"So would I. Come on." Harriman paid out a dollar for
two pink tickets which entitled them to enter the enclosure
and examine the rocket ship. The kid took his and ran on
ahead with the single-mindedness of youth. Harriman looked
over the stubby curved lines of the ovoid body. He noted with
a professional eye that she was a single-jet type with fractional controls around her midriff. He squinted through his
glasses at the name painted in gold on the carnival red of the
body, *Care Free*. He paid another quarter to enter the control
cabin.

When his eyes had adjusted to the gloom caused by the
strong ray filters of the ports he let them rest lovingly on the
keys of the console and the semi-circle of dials above. Each
beloved gadget was in its proper place. He knew them—
graven in his heart.

While he mused over the instrument board, with the warm
liquid of content soaking through his body, the pilot entered
and touched his arm.

"Sorry, sir. We've got to cast loose for the flight."

"Eh?" Harriman started, then looked at the speaker. Hand-
some devil, with a good skull and strong shoulders—reckless
eyes and a self-indulgent mouth, but a firm chin. "Oh, excuse
me, Captain."

"Quite all right."

"Oh, I say, Captain, er, uh—"

"McIntyre."

"Captain McIntyre, could you take a passenger this trip?"
The old man leaned eagerly toward him.

"Why, yes, if you wish. Come along with me." He ushered
Harriman into a shed marked OFFICE which stood near the
gate. "Passenger for a check over, doc."

Harriman looked startled but permitted the medico to run
a stethoscope over his thin chest, and to strap a rubber bandage around his arm. Presently he unstrapped it, glanced at
McIntyre, and shook his head.

"No go, doc?"

"That's right, Captain."

Harriman looked from face to face. "My heart's all right—that's just a flutter."

The physician's brows shot up. "Is it? But it's not just your heart; at your age your bones are brittle, too brittle to risk a take-off."

"Sorry, sir," added the pilot, "but the Bates County Fair Association pays the doctor here to see to it that I don't take anyone up who might be hurt by the acceleration."

The old man's shoulders drooped miserably. "I rather expected it."

"Sorry, sir." McIntyre turned to go, but Harriman followed him out.

"Excuse me, Captain—"

"Yes?"

"Could you and your, uh, engineer have dinner with me after your flight?"

The pilot looked at him quizzically. "I don't see why not. Thanks."

"Captain McIntyre, it is difficult for me to see why anyone would quit the Earth-Moon run." Fried chicken and hot biscuits in a private dining room of the best hotel the little town of Butler afforded, three-star Hennessey and Corona-Coronas had produced a friendly atmosphere in which three men could talk freely.

"Well, I didn't like it."

"Aw, don't give him that, Mac—you know damn well it was Rule G that got you." McIntyre's mechanic poured himself another brandy as he spoke.

McIntyre looked sullen. "Well, what if I did take a couple o' drinks? Anyhow, I could have squared that—it was the damn persnickety regulations that got me fed up. Who are you to talk?—Smuggler!"

"Sure I smuggled! Who wouldn't with all those beautiful rocks just aching to be taken back to Earth. I had a diamond once as big as. . . . But if I hadn't been caught I'd be in Luna City tonight. And so would you, you drunken blaster . . . with the boys buying us drinks, and the girls smiling and making suggestions. . . ." He put his face down and began to weep quietly.

McIntyre shook him. "He's drunk."

"Never mind." Harriman interposed a hand. "Tell me, are you really satisfied not to be on the run any more?"

McIntyre chewed his lip. "No—he's right of course. This barnstorming isn't what it's all cracked up to be. We've been hopping junk at every pumpkin doin's up and down the Mississippi valley—sleeping in tourist camps, and eating at greaseburners. Half the time the sheriff has an attachment on the ship, the other half the Society for the Prevention of Something or Other gets an injunction to keep us on the ground. It's no sort of a life for a rocket man."

"Would it help any for you to get to the Moon?"

"Well . . . Yes. I couldn't get back on the Earth-Moon run, but if I was in Luna City, I could get a job hopping ore for the Company—they're always short of rocket pilots for that, and they wouldn't mind my record. If I kept my nose clean, they might even put me back on the run, in time."

Harriman fiddled with a spoon, then looked up. "Would you young gentlemen be open to a business proposition?"

"Perhaps. What is it?"

"You own the *Care Free*?"

"Yeah. That is, Charlie and I do—barring a couple of liens against her. What about it?"

"I want to charter her . . . for you and Charlie to take me to the Moon!"

Charlie sat up with a jerk. "D'joo hear what he said, Mac? He wants us to fly that old heap to the Moon!"

McIntyre shook his head. "Can't do it, Mister Harriman. The old boat's worn out. You couldn't convert to escape fuel. We don't even use standard juice in her—just gasoline and liquid air. Charlie spends all of his time tinkering with her at that. She's going to blow up some day."

"Say, Mister Harriman," put in Charlie, "what's the matter with getting an excursion permit and going in a Company ship?"

"No, son," the old man replied, "I can't do that. You know the conditions under which the U. N. granted the Company a monopoly on lunar exploitation—no one to enter space who was not physically qualified to stand up under it. Company to take full responsibility for the safety and health of all citizens beyond the stratosphere. The official reason for granting the franchise was to avoid unnecessary loss of life during the first few years of space travel."

"And you can't pass the physical exam?"

Harriman shook his head.

"Well, what the hell—if you can afford to hire us, why don't you just bribe yourself a brace of Company docs? It's been done before."

Harriman smiled ruefully. "I know it has, Charlie, but it won't work for me. You see, I'm a little too prominent. My full name is Delos D. Harriman."

"What? *You* are old D. D.? But hell's bells, you own a big slice of the Company yourself—you practically *are* the Company; you ought to be able to do anything you like, rules or no rules."

"That is a not unusual opinion, son, but it is incorrect. Rich men aren't more free than other men; they are less free, a good deal less free. I tried to do what you suggest, but the other directors would not permit me. They are afraid of losing their franchise. It costs them a good deal in—uh—political contact expenses to retain it, as it is."

"Well, I'll be a— Can you tie that, Mac? A guy with lots of dough, and he can't spend it the way he wants to."

McIntyre did not answer, but waited for Harriman to continue.

"Captain McIntyre, if you had a ship, would you take me?"

McIntyre rubbed his chin. "It's against the law."

"I'd make it worth your while."

"Sure he would, Mr. Harriman. Of course you would, Mac. Luna City! Oh, baby!"

"Why do you want to go to the Moon so badly, Mister Harriman?"

"Captain, it's the one thing I've really wanted to do all my life—ever since I was a young boy. I don't know whether I can explain it to you, or not. You young fellows have grown up to rocket travel the way I grew up to aviation. I'm a great deal older than you are, at least fifty years older. When I was a kid practically nobody believed that men would ever reach the Moon. You've seen rockets all your lives, and the first to reach the Moon got there before you were a young boy. When I was a boy they laughed at the idea.

"But I believed—I believed. I read Verne, and Wells, and Smith, and I believed that we could do it—that we *would* do it. I set my heart on being one of the men to walk the surface of the Moon, to see her other side, and to look back on the face of the Earth, hanging in the sky.

"I used to go without my lunches to pay my dues in the

American Rocket Society, because I wanted to believe that I was helping to bring the day nearer when we would reach the Moon. I was already an old man when that day arrived. I've lived longer than I should, but I would not let myself die . . . I will not!—until I have set foot on the Moon."

McIntyre stood up and put out his hand. "You find a ship, Mister Harriman. I'll drive 'er."

"Atta' boy, Mac! I told you he would, Mister Harriman."

Harriman mused and dozed during the half-hour run to the north into Kansas City, dozed in the light troubled sleep of old age. Incidents out of a long life ran through his mind in vagrant dreams. There was that time . . . oh, yes, 1910 . . . A little boy on a warm spring night; "What's that, Daddy?"—"That's Halley's comet, Sonny."—"Where did it come from?" —"I don't know, Son. From way out in the sky somewhere." —"It's *beyoooootiful*, Daddy. I want to touch it."—" 'Fraid not, Son."

"Delos, do you mean to stand there and tell me you put the money we had saved for the house into that crazy rocket company?"—"Now, Charlotte, please! It's not crazy; it's a sound business investment. Someday soon rockets will fill the sky. Ships and trains will be obsolete. Look what happened to the men that had the foresight to invest in Henry Ford."— "We've been all over this before."—"Charlotte, the day will come when men will rise up off the Earth and visit the Moon, even the planets. This is the beginning."—"Must you shout?" —"I'm sorry, but—"—"I feel a headache coming on. Please try to be a little quiet when you come to bed."

He hadn't gone to bed. He had sat out on the veranda all night long, watching the full Moon move across the sky. There would be the devil to pay in the morning, the devil and a thin-lipped silence. But he'd stick by his guns. He'd given in on most things, but not on this. But the night was his. Tonight he'd be alone with his old friend. He searched her face. Where was Mare Crisium? Funny, he couldn't make it out. He used to be able to see it plainly when he was a boy. Probably needed new glasses—this constant office work wasn't good for his eyes.

But he didn't need to see, he knew where they all were; Crisium, Mare Fecunditatis, Mare Tranquilitatis—that one had a satisfying roll!—the Apennines, the Carpathians, old Tycho with its mysterious rays.

Two hundred and forty thousand miles—ten times around the Earth. Surely men could bridge a little gap like that. Why, he could almost reach out and touch it, nodding there behind the elm trees.

Not that he could help. He hadn't the education.

"Son, I want to have a little serious talk with you."—"Yes, Mother."—"I know you had hoped to go to college next year —" (Hoped! He had lived for it. The University of Chicago to study under Moulton, then on to the Yerkes Observatory to work under the eye of Dr. Frost himself)—"and I had hoped so too. But with your father gone, and the girls growing up, it's harder to make ends meet. You've been a good boy, and worked hard to help out. I know you'll understand."—"Yes, Mother."

"Extra! Extra! STRATOSPHERE ROCKET REACHES PARIS. Read aaaaallllll about 't." The thin little man in the bifocals snatched at the paper and hurried back to the office. —"Look at this, George."—"Huh? Hmm, interesting, but what of it?"—"Can't you see? The next stage is to the Moon!" —"God, but you're a sucker, Delos. The trouble with you is, you read too many of those trashy magazines. Now I caught my boy reading one of 'em just last week, *Stunning Stories*, or some such title, and dressed him down proper. Your folks should have done you the same favor."—Harriman squared his narrow, middle-aged shoulders. "They will so reach the Moon!"—His partner laughed. "Have it your own way. If baby wants the Moon, papa bring it for him. But you stick to your discounts and commissions; that's where the money is."

The big car droned down the Paseo, and turned off on Armour Boulevard. Old Harriman stirred uneasily in his sleep and muttered to himself.

"But Mister Harriman—" The young man with the notebook was plainly perturbed. The old man grunted.

"You heard me. Sell 'em. I want every share I own realized in cash as rapidly as possible; Spaceways, Spaceways Provisioning Company, Artemis Mines, Luna City Recreations, the whole lot of them."

"It will depress the market. You won't realize the full value of your holdings."

"Don't you think I know that? I can afford it."

"What about the shares you had earmarked for Richardson Observatory, and for the Harriman Scholarships?"

"Oh, yes. Don't sell those. Set up a trust. Should have done it long ago. Tell young Kamens to draw up the papers. He knows what I want."

The interoffice visor flashed into life. "The gentlemen are here, Mr. Harriman."

"Send 'em in. That's all, Ashley. Get busy." Ashley went out as McIntyre and Charlie entered. Harriman got up and trotted forward to greet them.

"Come in, boys, come in. I'm so glad to see you. Sit down. Sit down. Have a cigar."

"Mighty pleased to see you, Mr. Harriman," acknowledged Charlie. "In fact, you might say we need to see you."

"Some trouble, gentlemen?" Harriman glanced from face to face. McIntyre answered him.

"You still mean that about a job for us, Mr. Harriman?"

"Mean it? Certainly, I do. You're not backing out on me?"

"Not at all. We need that job now. You see the *Care Free* is lying in the middle of the Osage River, with her jet split clear back to the injector."

"Dear me! You weren't hurt?"

"No, aside from sprains and bruises. We jumped."

Charlie chortled. "I caught a catfish with my bare teeth."

In short order they got down to business. "You two will have to buy a ship for me. I can't do it openly; my colleagues would figure out what I mean to do and stop me. I'll supply you with all the cash you need. You go out and locate some sort of a ship that can be refitted for the trip. Work up some good story about how you are buying it for some playboy as a stratosphere yacht, or that you plan to establish an arctic-antarctic tourist route. Anything as long as no one suspects that she is being outfitted for space flight.

"Then, after the Department of Transport licenses her for strato flight, you move out to a piece of desert out west—I'll find a likely parcel of land and buy it—and then I'll join you. Then we'll install the escape-fuel tanks, change the injectors, and timers, and so forth, to fit her for the hop. How about it?"

McIntyre looked dubious. "It'll take a lot of doing. Charlie, do you think you can accomplish that change-over without a dockyard and shops?"

"Me? Sure I can—with your thick-fingered help. Just give me the tools and materials I want, and don't hurry me too much. Of course, it won't be fancy—"

"Nobody wants it to be fancy. I just want a ship that won't blow when I start slapping the keys. Isotope fuel is no joke."

"It won't blow, Mac."

"That's what you thought about the *Care Free*."

"That ain't fair, Mac. I ask you, Mr. Harriman— That heap was junk, and we knew it. This'll be different. We're going to spend some dough and do it right. Ain't we, Mr. Harriman?"

Harriman patted him on the shoulder. "Certainly we are, Charlie. You can have all the money you want. That's the least of our worries. Now do the salaries and bonuses I mentioned suit you? I don't want you to be short."

"—as you know, my clients are his nearest relatives and have his interests at heart. We contend that Mr. Harriman's conduct for the past several weeks, as shown by the evidence here adduced, gives clear indication that a mind, once brilliant in the world of finance, has become senile. It is, therefore, with the deepest regret that we pray this honorable court, if it pleases, to declare Mr. Harriman incompetent and to assign a conservator to protect his financial interests and those of his future heirs and assigns." The attorney sat down, pleased with himself.

Mr. Kamens took the floor. "May it please the court, if my esteemed friend is *quite* through, may I suggest that in his last few words he gave away his entire thesis. '—the financial interests of future heirs and assigns.' It is evident that the petitioners believe that my client should conduct his affairs in such a fashion as to insure that his nieces and nephews, and their issue, will be supported in unearned luxury for the rest of their lives. My client's wife has passed on, he has no children. It is admitted that he has provided generously for his sisters and their children in times past, and that he has established annuities for such near kin as are without means of support.

"But now like vultures, worse than vultures, for they are not content to let him die in peace, they would prevent my client from enjoying his wealth in whatever manner best suits him for the few remaining years of his life. It is true that he has sold his holdings; is it strange that an elderly man should wish to retire? It is true that he suffered some paper losses in liquidation. 'The value of a thing is what that thing will bring.' He was retiring and demanded cash. Is there anything strange about that?

"It is admitted that he refused to discuss his actions with his so-loving kinfolk. What law, or principle, requires a man to consult with his nephews on anything?

"Therefore, we pray that this court will confirm my client in his right to do what he likes with his own, deny this petition, and send these meddlers about their business."

The judge took off his spectacles and polished them thoughtfully.

"Mr. Kamens, this court has as high a regard for individual liberty as you have, and you may rest assured that any action taken will be solely in the interests of your client. Nevertheless, men do grow old, men do become senile, and in such cases must be protected.

"I shall take this matter under advisement until tomorrow. Court is adjourned."

From the *Kansas City Star*:
"ECCENTRIC MILLIONAIRE DISAPPEARS"
"—failed to appear for the adjourned hearing. The bailiffs returned from a search of places usually frequented by Harriman with the report that he had not been seen since the previous day. A bench warrant under contempt proceedings has been issued and—"

A desert sunset is a better stimulant for the appetite than a hot dance orchestra. Charlie testified to this by polishing the last of the ham gravy with a piece of bread. Harriman handed each of the younger men cigars and took one himself.

"My doctor claims that these weeds are bad for my heart condition," he remarked as he lighted it, "but I've felt so much better since I joined you boys here on the ranch that I am inclined to doubt him." He exhaled a cloud of blue-grey smoke and resumed. "I don't think a man's health depends so much on what he does as on whether he wants to do it. I'm doing what I want to do."

"That's all a man can ask of life," agreed McIntyre.

"How does the work look now, boys?"

"My end's in pretty good shape," Charlie answered. "We finished the second pressure tests on the new tanks and the fuel lines today. The ground tests are all done, except the calibration runs. Those won't take long—just the four hours to make the runs if I don't run into some bugs. How about you, Mac?"

McIntyre ticked them off on his fingers. "Food supplies and water on board. Three vacuum suits, a spare, and service kits. Medical supplies. The buggy already had all the standard equipment for strato flight. The late lunar ephemerides haven't arrived as yet."

"When do you expect them?"

"Any time—they should be here now. Not that it matters. This guff about how hard it is to navigate from here to the Moon is hokum to impress the public. After all you can *see* your destination—it's not like ocean navigation. Gimme a sextant and a good radar and I'll set you down anyplace on the Moon you like, without cracking an almanac or a star table, just from a general knowledge of the relative speeds involved."

"Never mind the personal buildup, Columbus," Charlie told him, "we'll admit you can hit the floor with your hat. The general idea is, you're ready to go now. Is that right?"

"That's it."

"That being the case, I *could* run those tests tonight. I'm getting jumpy—things have been going too smoothly. If you'll give me a hand, we ought to be in bed by midnight."

"O.K., when I finish this cigar."

They smoked in silence for a while, each thinking about the coming trip and what it meant to him. Old Harriman tried to repress the excitement that possessed him at the prospect of immediate realization of his life-long dream.

"Mr. Harriman—"

"Eh? What is it, Charlie?"

"How does a guy go about getting rich, like you did?"

"Getting rich? I can't say; I never tried to get rich. I never wanted to be rich, or well known, or anything like that."

"Huh?"

"No, I just wanted to live a long time and see it all happen. I wasn't unusual; there were lots of boys like me—radio hams, they were, and telescope builders, and airplane amateurs. We had science clubs, and basement laboratories, and science-fiction leagues—the kind of boys who thought there was more romance in one issue of the *Electrical Experimenter* than in all the books Dumas ever wrote. We didn't want to be one of Horatio Alger's Get-Rich heroes either, we wanted to build space ships. Well, some of us did."

"Jeez, Pop, you make it sound exciting."

"It was exciting, Charlie. This has been a wonderful, romantic century, for all of its bad points. And it's grown more wonderful and more exciting every year. No, I didn't want to be rich; I just wanted to live long enough to see men rise up to the stars, and, if God was good to me, to go as far as the Moon myself." He carefully deposited an inch of white ash in a saucer. "It has been a good life. I haven't any complaints."

McIntyre pushed back his chair. "Come on, Charlie, if you're ready."

"O.K."

They all got up. Harriman started to speak, then grabbed at his chest, his face a dead grey-white.

"Catch him, Mac!"

"Where's his medicine?"

"In his vest pocket."

They eased him over to a couch, broke a small glass capsule in a handkerchief, and held it under his nose. The volatile released by the capsule seemed to bring a little color into his face. They did what little they could for him, then waited for him to regain consciousness.

Charlie broke the uneasy silence. "Mac, we ain't going through with this."

"Why not?"

"It's murder. He'll never stand up under the initial acceleration."

"Maybe not, but it's what he wants to do. You heard him."

"But we oughtn't to let him."

"Why not. It's neither your business, nor the business of this damn paternalistic government, to tell a man not to risk his life doing what he really wants to do."

"All the same, I don't feel right about it. He's such a swell old duck."

"Then what d'yuh want to do with him—send him back to Kansas City so those old harpies can shut him up in a laughing academy till he dies of a broken heart?"

"N-no-o-o—not that."

"Get out there, and make your set-up for those test runs. I'll be along."

A wide-tired desert runabout rolled in the ranch yard gate the next morning and stopped in front of the house. A heavy-set man with a firm, but kindly, face climbed out and spoke to McIntyre, who approached to meet him.

"You James McIntyre?"

"What about it?"

"I'm the deputy federal marshal hereabouts. I got a warrant for your arrest."

"What's the charge?"

"Conspiracy to violate the Space Precautionary Act."

Charlie joined the pair. "What's up, Mac?"

The deputy answered. "You'd be Charles Cummings, I guess. Warrant here for you. Got one for a man named Harriman, too, and a court order to put seals on your space ship."

"We've no space ship."

"What d'yuh keep in that big shed?"

"Strato yacht."

"So? Well, I'll put seals on her until a space ship comes along. Where's Harriman?"

"Right in there." Charlie obliged by pointing, ignoring McIntyre's scowl.

The deputy turned his head. Charlie couldn't have missed the button by a fraction of an inch for the deputy collapsed quietly to the ground. Charlie stood over him, rubbing his knuckles and mourning.

"Damn it to hell—that's the finger I broke playing short-stop. I'm always hurting that finger."

"Get Pop into the cabin," Mac cut him short, "and strap him into his hammock."

"Aye aye, Skipper."

They dragged the ship by tractor out of the hangar, turned, and went out the desert plain to find elbow room for the take-off. They climbed in. McIntyre saw the deputy from his starboard conning port. He was staring disconsolately after them.

McIntyre fastened his safety belt, settled his corset, and spoke into the engineroom speaking tube. "All set, Charlie?"

"All set, Skipper. But you can't raise ship yet, Mac— *She ain't named!*"

"No time for your superstitions!"

Harriman's thin voice reached them. "Call her the *Lunatic*— It's the only appropriate name!"

McIntyre settled his head into the pads, punched two keys, then three more in rapid succession, and the *Lunatic* raised ground.

"How are you, Pop?"

Charlie searched the old man's face anxiously. Harriman licked his lips and managed to speak. "Doing fine, son. Couldn't be better."

"The acceleration is over; it won't be so bad from here on. I'll unstrap you so you can wiggle around a little. But I think you'd better stay in the hammock." He tugged at buckles. Harriman partially repressed a groan.

"What is it, Pop?"

"Nothing. Nothing at all. Just go easy on that side."

Charlie ran his fingers over the old man's side with the sure, delicate touch of a mechanic. "You ain't foolin' me none, Pop. But there isn't much I can do until we ground."

"Charlie—"

"Yes, Pop?"

"Can't I move to a port? I want to watch the Earth."

"Ain't nothin' to see yet; the ship hides it. As soon as we turn ship, I'll move you. Tell you what; I'll give you a sleepy pill, and then wake you when we do."

"No!"

"Huh?"

"I'll stay awake."

"Just as you say, Pop."

Charlie clambered monkey fashion to the nose of the ship, and anchored to the gymbals of the pilot's chair. McIntyre questioned him with his eyes.

"Yeah, he's alive all right," Charlie told him, "but he's in bad shape."

"How bad?"

"Couple of cracked ribs anyhow. I don't know what else. I don't know whether he'll last out the trip, Mac. His heart was pounding something awful."

"He'll last, Charlie. He's tough."

"Tough? He's delicate as a canary."

"I don't mean that. He's tough way down inside—where it counts."

"Just the same you'd better set her down awful easy if you want to ground with a full complement aboard."

"I will. I'll make one full swing around the Moon and ease her in on an involute approach curve. We've got enough fuel, I think."

They were now in a free orbit; after McIntyre turned ship, Charlie went back, unslung the hammock, and moved Harriman, hammock and all, to a side port. McIntyre steadied the ship about a transverse axis so that the tail pointed toward the sun, then gave a short blast on two tangential jets opposed in couple to cause the ship to spin slowly about her longitudinal axis, and thereby create a slight artificial gravity. The initial weightlessness when coasting commenced had knotted the old man with the characteristic nausea of free flight, and the pilot wished to save his passenger as much discomfort as possible.

But Harriman was not concerned with the condition of his stomach.

There it was, all as he had imagined it so many times. The Moon swung majestically past the view port, wider than he had ever seen it before, all of her familiar features cameo clear. She gave way to the Earth as the ship continued its slow swing, the Earth itself as he had envisioned her, appearing like a noble moon, many times as wide as the Moon appears to the Earthbound, and more luscious, more sensuously beautiful than the silver Moon could be. It was sunset near the Atlantic seaboard—the line of shadow cut down the coast line of North America, slashed through Cuba, and obscured all but the west coast of South America. He savored the mellow blue of the Pacific Ocean, felt the texture of the soft green and brown of the continents, admired the blue-white cold of the polar caps. Canada and the northern states were obscured by cloud, a vast low pressure area that spread across the continent. It shone with an even more satisfactory dazzling white than the polar caps.

As the ship swung slowly around, Earth would pass from view, and the stars would march across the port—the same stars he had always known, but steady, brighter, and unwinking against a screen of perfect, live black. Then the Moon would swim into view again to claim his thoughts.

He was serenely happy in a fashion not given to most men,

even in a long lifetime. He felt as if he were every man who has ever lived, looked up at the stars, and longed.

As the long hours came and went he watched and dozed and dreamed. At least once he must have fallen into deep sleep, or possibly delirium, for he came to with a start, thinking that his wife, Charlotte, was calling to him. "Delos!" the voice had said. "Delos! Come in from there! You'll catch your death of cold in that night air."

Poor Charlotte! She had been a good wife to him, a good wife. He was quite sure that her only regret in dying had been her fear that he could not take proper care of himself. It had not been her fault that she had not shared his dream, and his need.

Charlie rigged the hammock in such a fashion that Harriman could watch from the starboard port when they swung around the far face of the Moon. He picked out the landmarks made familiar to him by a thousand photographs with nostalgic pleasure, as if he were returning to his own country. McIntyre brought her slowly down as they came back around to the Earthward face, and prepared to land east of Mare Fecunditatis, about ten miles from Luna City.

It was not a bad landing, all things considered. He had to land without coaching from the ground, and he had no second pilot to watch the radar for him. In his anxiety to make it gentle he missed his destination by some thirty miles, but he did his cold-sober best. But at that it was bumpy.

As they grounded and the pumice dust settled around them, Charlie came up to the control station.

"How's our passenger?" Mac demanded.

"I'll see, but I wouldn't make any bets. That landing stunk, Mac."

"Damn it, I did my best."

"I know you did, Skipper. Forget it."

But the passenger was alive and conscious although bleeding from the nose and with a pink foam on his lips. He was feebly trying to get himself out of his cocoon. They helped him, working together.

"Where are the vacuum suits?" was his first remark.

"Steady, Mr. Harriman. You can't go out there yet. We've got to give you some first aid."

"Get me that suit! First aid can wait."

Silently they did as he ordered. His left leg was practically useless, and they had to help him through the lock, one on each side. But with his inconsiderable mass having a lunar weight of only twenty pounds, he was no burden. They found a place some fifty yards from the ship where they could prop him up and let him look, a chunk of scoria supporting his head.

McIntyre put his helmet against the old man's and spoke. "We'll leave you here to enjoy the view while we get ready for the trek into town. It's a forty-miler, pretty near, and we'll have to break out spare air bottles and rations and stuff. We'll be back soon."

Harriman nodded without answering, and squeezed their gauntlets with a grip that was surprisingly strong.

He sat very quietly, rubbing his hands against the soil of the Moon and sensing the curiously light pressure of his body against the ground. At long last there was peace in his heart. His hurts had ceased to pain him. He *was* where he had longed to be—he had followed his need. Over the western horizon hung the Earth at last quarter, a green-blue giant moon. Overhead the Sun shone down from a black and starry sky. And underneath the Moon, the soil of the Moon itself. He was on the Moon!

He lay back still while a bath of content flowed over him like a tide at flood, and soaked to his very marrow.

His attention strayed momentarily, and he thought once again that his name was called. Silly, he thought, I'm getting old—my mind wanders.

Back in the cabin Charlie and Mac were rigging shoulder yokes on a stretcher. "There. That will do," Mac commented. "We'd better stir Pop out; we ought to be going."

"I'll get him," Charlie replied. "I'll just pick him up and carry him. He don't weigh nothing."

Charlie was gone longer than McIntyre had expected him to be. He returned alone. Mac waited for him to close the lock, and swing back his helmet. "Trouble?"

"Never mind the stretcher, Skipper. We won't be needin' it.

"Yeah, I mean it," he continued. "Pop's done for. I did what was necessary."

McIntyre bent down without a word and picked up the wide skis necessary to negotiate the powdery ash. Charlie followed his example. Then they swung the spare air bottles over their shoulders, and passed out through the lock.

They didn't bother to close the outer door of the lock behind them.

The Long Watch

"Nine ships blasted off from Moon Base. Once in space, eight of them formed a globe around the smallest. They held this formation all the way to Earth.

"The small ship displayed the insignia of an admiral—yet there was no living thing of any sort in her. She was not even a passenger ship, but a drone, a robot ship intended for radio-active cargo. This trip she carried nothing but a lead coffin— and a Geiger counter that was never quiet."

—from the editorial *After Ten Years*, film 38, 17 June 2009, Archives of the *N. Y. Times*

JOHNNY DAHLQUIST blew smoke at the Geiger counter. He grinned wryly and tried it again. His whole body was radioactive by now. Even his breath, the smoke from his cigarette, could make the Geiger counter scream.

How long had he been here? Time doesn't mean much on the Moon. Two days? Three? A week? He let his mind run back: the last clearly marked time in his mind was when the Executive Officer had sent for him, right after breakfast—

"Lieutenant Dahlquist, reporting to the Executive Officer."

Colonel Towers looked up. "Ah, John Ezra. Sit down, Johnny. Cigarette?"

Johnny sat down, mystified but flattered. He admired Colonel Towers, for his brilliance, his ability to dominate, and for his battle record. Johnny had no battle record; he had been commissioned on completing his doctor's degree in nuclear physics and was now junior bomb officer of Moon Base.

The Colonel wanted to talk politics; Johnny was puzzled. Finally Towers had come to the point; it was not safe (so he said) to leave control of the world in political hands; power must be held by a scientifically selected group. In short—the Patrol.

Johnny was startled rather than shocked. As an abstract

idea, Towers' notion sounded plausible. The League of Nations had folded up; what would keep the United Nations from breaking up, too, and thus lead to another World War. "And you know how bad such a war would be, Johnny."

Johnny agreed. Towers said he was glad that Johnny got the point. The senior bomb officer could handle the work, but it was better to have both specialists.

Johnny sat up with a jerk. "You are going to *do* something about it?" He had thought the Exec was just talking.

Towers smiled. "We're not politicians; we don't just talk. We act."

Johnny whistled. "When does this start?"

Towers flipped a switch. Johnny was startled to hear his own voice, then identified the recorded conversation as having taken place in the junior officers' messroom. A political argument he remembered, which he had walked out on . . . a good thing, too! But being spied on annoyed him.

Towers switched it off. "We *have* acted," he said. "We know who is safe and who isn't. Take Kelly—" He waved at the loudspeaker. "Kelly is politically unreliable. You noticed he wasn't at breakfast?"

"Huh? I thought he was on watch."

"Kelly's watch-standing days are over. Oh, relax; he isn't hurt."

Johnny thought this over. "Which list am I on?" he asked. "Safe or unsafe?"

"Your name has a question mark after it. But I have said all along that you could be depended on." He grinned engagingly. "You won't make a liar of me, Johnny?"

Dahlquist didn't answer; Towers said sharply, "Come now —what do you think of it? Speak up."

"Well, if you ask me, you've bitten off more than you can chew. While it's true that Moon Base controls the Earth, Moon Base itself is a sitting duck for a ship. One bomb— *blooie!*"

Towers picked up a message form and handed it over; it read: I HAVE YOUR CLEAN LAUNDRY—ZACK. "That means every bomb in the *Trygve Lie* has been put out of commission. I have reports from every ship we need worry about." He stood up. "Think it over and see me after lunch. Major Morgan needs your help right away to change control frequencies on the bombs."

"The control frequencies?"

"Naturally. We don't want the bombs jammed before they reach their targets."

"What? You said the idea was to *prevent* war."

Towers brushed it aside. "There won't be a war—just a psychological demonstration, an unimportant town or two. A little bloodletting to save an all-out war. Simple arithmetic."

He put a hand on Johnny's shoulder. "You aren't squeamish, or you wouldn't be a bomb officer. Think of it as a surgical operation. And think of your family."

Johnny Dahlquist had been thinking of his family. "Please, sir, I want to see the Commanding Officer."

Towers frowned. "The Commodore is not available. As you know, I speak for him. See me again—after lunch."

The Commodore was decidedly not available; the Commodore was dead. But Johnny did not know that.

Dahlquist walked back to the messroom, bought cigarettes, sat down and had a smoke. He got up, crushed out the butt, and headed for the Base's west airlock. There he got into his space suit and went to the lockmaster. "Open her up, Smitty."

The marine looked surprised. "Can't let anyone out on the surface without word from Colonel Towers, sir. Hadn't you heard?"

"Oh, yes! Give me your order book." Dahlquist took it, wrote a pass for himself, and signed it "by direction of Colonel Towers." He added, "Better call the Executive Officer and check it."

The lockmaster read it and stuck the book in his pocket. "Oh, no, Lieutenant. Your word's good."

"Hate to disturb the Executive Officer, eh? Don't blame you." He stepped in, closed the inner door, and waited for the air to be sucked out.

Out on the Moon's surface he blinked at the light and hurried to the track-rocket terminus; a car was waiting. He squeezed in, pulled down the hood, and punched the starting button. The rocket car flung itself at the hills, dived through and came out on a plain studded with projectile rockets, like candles on a cake. Quickly it dived into a second tunnel through more hills. There was a stomach-wrenching deceleration and the car stopped at the underground atom-bomb armory.

As Dahlquist climbed out he switched on his walkie-talkie. The space-suited guard at the entrance came to port-arms.

Dahlquist said, "Morning, Lopez," and walked by him to the airlock. He pulled it open.

The guard motioned him back. "Hey! Nobody goes in without the Executive Officer's say-so." He shifted his gun, fumbled in his pouch and got out a paper. "Read it, Lieutenant."

Dahlquist waved it away. "I drafted that order myself. *You* read it; you've misinterpreted it."

"I don't see how, Lieutenant."

Dahlquist snatched the paper, glanced at it, then pointed to a line. "See? '—except persons specifically designated by the Executive Officer.' That's the bomb officers, Major Morgan and me."

The guard looked worried. Dahlquist said, "Damn it, look up 'specifically designated'—it's under '*Bomb Room, Security, Procedure for,*' in your standing orders. Don't tell me you left them in the barracks!"

"Oh, no, sir! I've got 'em." The guard reached into his pouch. Dahlquist gave him back the sheet; the guard took it, hesitated, then leaned his weapon against his hip, shifted the paper to his left hand, and dug into his pouch with his right.

Dahlquist grabbed the gun, shoved it between the guard's legs, and jerked. He threw the weapon away and ducked into the airlock. As he slammed the door he saw the guard struggling to his feet and reaching for his side arm. He dogged the outer door shut and felt a tingle in his fingers as a slug struck the door.

He flung himself at the inner door, jerked the spill lever, rushed back to the outer door and hung his weight on the handle. At once he could feel it stir. The guard was lifting up; the lieutenant was pulling down, with only his low Moon weight to anchor him. Slowly the handle raised before his eyes.

Air from the bomb room rushed into the lock through the spill valve. Dahlquist felt his space suit settle on his body as the pressure in the lock began to equal the pressure in the suit. He quit straining and let the guard raise the handle. It did not matter; thirteen tons of air pressure now held the door closed.

He latched open the inner door to the bomb room, so that it could not swing shut. As long as it was open, the airlock could not operate; no one could enter.

Before him in the room, one for each projectile rocket, were the atom bombs, spaced in rows far enough apart to defeat any faint possibility of spontaneous chain reaction. They were the deadliest things in the known universe, but they were his babies. He had placed himself between them and anyone who would misuse them.

But, now that he was here, he had no plan to use his temporary advantage.

The speaker on the wall sputtered into life. "Hey! Lieutenant! What goes on here? You gone crazy?" Dahlquist did not answer. Let Lopez stay confused—it would take him that much longer to make up his mind what to do. And Johnny Dahlquist needed as many minutes as he could squeeze. Lopez went on protesting. Finally he shut up.

Johnny had followed a blind urge not to let the bombs—*his* bombs!—be used for "demonstrations on unimportant towns." But what to do next? Well, Towers couldn't get through the lock. Johnny would sit tight until hell froze over.

Don't kid yourself, John Ezra! Towers could get in. Some high explosive against the outer door—then the air would whoosh out, our boy Johnny would drown in blood from his burst lungs—and the bombs would be sitting there, unhurt. They were built to stand the jump from Moon to Earth; vacuum would not hurt them at all.

He decided to stay in his space suit; explosive decompression didn't appeal to him. Come to think about it, death from old age was his choice.

Or they could drill a hole, let out the air, and open the door without wrecking the lock. Or Towers might even have a new airlock built outside the old. Not likely, Johnny thought; a *coup d'etat* depended on speed. Towers was almost sure to take the quickest way—blasting. And Lopez was probably calling the Base right now. Fifteen minutes for Towers to suit up and get here, maybe a short dicker—then *whoosh!* the party is over.

Fifteen minutes—

In fifteen minutes the bombs might fall back into the hands of the conspirators; in fifteen minutes he must make the bombs unusable.

An atom bomb is just two or more pieces of fissionable metal, such as plutonium. Separated, they are no more explosive than a pound of butter; slapped together, they explode. The complications lie in the gadgets and circuits and gun used to slap them together in the exact way and at the exact time and place required.

These circuits, the bomb's "brain," are easily destroyed—
but the bomb itself is hard to destroy because of its very simplicity. Johnny decided to smash the "brains"—and quickly!

The only tools at hand were simple ones used in handling
the bombs. Aside from a Geiger counter, the speaker on the
walkie-talkie circuit, a television rig to the base, and the
bombs themselves, the room was bare. A bomb to be worked
on was taken elsewhere—not through fear of explosion, but
to reduce radiation exposure for personnel. The radioactive
material in a bomb is buried in a "tamper"—in these bombs,
gold. Gold stops alpha, beta, and much of the deadly gamma
radiation—but not neutrons.

The slippery, poisonous neutrons which plutonium gives off
had to escape, or a chain reaction—explosion!—would result.
The room was bathed in an invisible, almost undetectable rain
of neutrons. The place was unhealthy; regulations called for
staying in it as short a time as possible.

The Geiger counter clicked off the "background" radiation,
cosmic rays, the trace of radioactivity in the Moon's crust,
and secondary radioactivity set up all through the room by
neutrons. Free neutrons have the nasty trait of infecting what
they strike, making it radioactive, whether it be concrete wall
or human body. In time the room would have to be abandoned.

Dahlquist twisted a knob on the Geiger counter; the instrument stopped clicking. He had used a suppressor circuit to cut
out noise of "background" radiation at the level then present.
It reminded him uncomfortably of the danger of staying here.
He took out the radiation exposure film all radiation personnel carry; it was a direct-response type and had been fresh
when he arrived. The most sensitive end was faintly darkened
already. Half way down the film a red line crossed it. Theoretically, if the wearer was exposed to enough radioactivity in
a week to darken the film to that line, he was, as Johnny reminded himself, a "dead duck".

Off came the cumbersome space suit; what he needed was
speed. Do the job and surrender—better to be a prisoner than
to linger in a place as "hot" as this.

He grabbed a ball hammer from the tool rack and got
busy, pausing only to switch off the television pick-up. The
first bomb bothered him. He started to smash the cover plate
of the "brain," then stopped, filled with reluctance. All his life
he had prized fine apparatus.

He nerved himself and swung; glass tinkled, metal creaked. His mood changed; he began to feel a shameful pleasure in destruction. He pushed on with enthusiasm, swinging, smashing, destroying!

So intent was he that he did not at first hear his name called. "Dahlquist! Answer me! Are you there?"

He wiped sweat and looked at the TV screen. Towers' perturbed features stared out.

Johnny was shocked to find that he had wrecked only six bombs. Was he going to be caught before he could finish? Oh, no! He *had* to finish. Stall, son, stall! "Yes, Colonel? You called me?"

"I certainly did! What's the meaning of this?"

"I'm sorry, Colonel."

Towers' expression relaxed a little. "Turn on your pick-up, Johnny, I can't see you. What was that noise?"

"The pick-up is on," Johnny lied. "It must be out of order. That noise—uh, to tell the truth, Colonel, I was fixing things so that nobody could get in here."

Towers hesitated, then said firmly, "I'm going to assume that you are sick and send you to the Medical Officer. But I want you to come out of there, right away. That's an order, Johnny."

Johnny answered slowly. "I can't just yet, Colonel. I came here to make up my mind and I haven't quite made it up. You said to see you after lunch."

"I meant you to stay in your quarters."

"Yes, sir. But I thought I ought to stand watch on the bombs, in case I decided you were wrong."

"It's not for you to decide, Johnny. I'm your superior officer. You are sworn to obey me."

"Yes, sir." This was wasting time; the old fox might have a squad on the way now. "But I swore to keep the peace, too. Could you come out here and talk it over with me? I don't want to do the wrong thing."

Towers smiled. "A good idea, Johnny. You wait there. I'm sure you'll see the light." He switched off.

"There," said Johnny. "I hope you're convinced that I'm a half-wit—you slimy mistake!" He picked up the hammer, ready to use the minutes gained.

He stopped almost at once; it dawned on him that wrecking the "brains" was not enough. There were no spare "brains," but there was a well-stocked electronics shop. Morgan could jury-rig control circuits for bombs. Why, he could himself—not a neat job, but one that would work. Damnation! He would have to wreck the bombs themselves—and in the next ten minutes.

But a bomb was solid chunks of metal, encased in a heavy tamper, all tied in with a big steel gun. It couldn't be done—not in ten minutes.

Damn!

Of course, there was one way. He knew the control circuits; he also knew how to beat them. Take this bomb: if he took out the safety bar, unhooked the proximity circuit, shorted the delay circuit, and cut in the arming circuit by hand—then unscrewed *that* and reached in *there*, he could, with just a long, stiff wire, set the bomb off.

Blowing the other bombs and the valley itself to Kingdom Come.

Also Johnny Dahlquist. That was the rub.

All this time he was doing what he had thought out, up to the step of actually setting off the bomb. Ready to go, the bomb seemed to threaten, as if crouching to spring. He stood up, sweating.

He wondered if he had the courage. He did not want to funk—and hoped that he would. He dug into his jacket and took out a picture of Edith and the baby. "Honeychile," he said, "if I get out of this, I'll never even try to beat a red light." He kissed the picture and put it back. There was nothing to do but wait.

What was keeping Towers? Johnny wanted to make sure that Towers was in blast range. What a joke on the jerk! Me—sitting here, ready to throw the switch on him. The idea tickled him; it led to a better: why blow himself up—alive?

There was another way to rig it—a "dead man" control. Jigger up some way so that the last step, the one that set off the bomb, would not happen as long as he kept his hand on a switch or a lever or something. Then, if they blew open the door, or shot him, or anything—up goes the balloon!

Better still, if he could hold them off with the threat of it, sooner or later help would come—Johnny was sure that most of the Patrol was not in this stinking conspiracy—and then: Johnny comes marching home! What a reunion! He'd resign and get a teaching job; he'd stood his watch.

All the while, he was working. Electrical? No, too little time. Make it a simple mechanical linkage. He had it doped out but had hardly begun to build it when the loudspeaker called him. "Johnny?"

"That you, Colonel?" His hands kept busy.

"Let me in."

"Well, now, Colonel, that wasn't in the agreement." Where in blue blazes was something to use as a long lever?

"I'll come in alone, Johnny, I give you my word. We'll talk face to face."

His word! "We can talk over the speaker, Colonel." Hey, that was it—a yardstick, hanging on the tool rack.

"Johnny, I'm warning you. Let me in, or I'll blow the door off."

A wire—he needed a wire, fairly long and stiff. He tore the antenna from his suit. "You wouldn't do that, Colonel. It would ruin the bombs."

"Vacuum won't hurt the bombs. Quit stalling."

"Better check with Major Morgan. Vacuum won't hurt them; explosive decompression would wreck every circuit." The Colonel was not a bomb specialist; he shut up for several minutes. Johnny went on working.

"Dahlquist," Towers resumed, "that was a clumsy lie. I checked with Morgan. You have sixty seconds to get into your suit, if you aren't already. I'm going to blast the door."

"No, you won't," said Johnny. "Ever hear of a 'dead man' switch?" Now for a counterweight—and a sling.

"Eh? What do you mean?"

"I've rigged number seventeen to set off by hand. But I put in a gimmick. It won't blow while I hang on to a strap I've got in my hand. But if anything happens to me—*up she goes!* You are about fifty feet from the blast center. Think it over."

There was a short silence. "I don't believe you."

"No? Ask Morgan. He'll believe me. He can inspect it, over the TV pickup." Johnny lashed the belt of his space suit to the end of the yardstick.

"You said the pick-up was out of order."

"So I lied. This time I'll prove it. Have Morgan call me."

Presently Major Morgan's face appeared. "Lieutenant Dahlquist?"

"Hi, Stinky. Wait a sec." With great care Dahlquist made one last connection while holding down the end of the yardstick. Still careful, he shifted his grip to the belt, sat down on the floor, stretched an arm and switched on the TV· pick-up. "Can you see me, Stinky?"

"I can see you," Morgan answered stiffly. "What is this nonsense?"

"A little surprise I whipped up." He explained it—what circuits he had cut out, what ones he had shorted, just how the jury-rigged mechanical sequence fitted in.

Morgan nodded. "But you're bluffing, Dahlquist. I feel sure that you haven't disconnected the 'K' circuit. You don't have the guts to blow yourself up."

Johnny chuckled. "I sure haven't. But that's the beauty of it. It can't go off, *so long as I am alive*. If your greasy boss, ex-Colonel Towers, blasts the door, then I'm dead and the bomb goes off. It won't matter to me, but it will to him. Better tell him." He switched off.

Towers came on over the speaker shortly. "Dahlquist?"

"I hear you."

"There's no need to throw away your life. Come out and you will be retired on full pay. You can go home to your family. That's a promise."

Johnny got mad. "You keep my family out of this!"

"Think of them, man."

"Shut up. Get back to your hole. I feel a need to scratch and this whole shebang might just explode in your lap."

2

JOHNNY SAT UP with a start. He had dozed, his hand hadn't let go the sling, but he had the shakes when he thought about it.

Maybe he should disarm the bomb and depend on their not daring to dig him out? But Towers' neck was already in hock for treason; Towers might risk it. If he did and the bomb were disarmed, Johnny would be dead and Towers would have the bombs. No, he had gone this far; he wouldn't let his baby girl grow up in a dictatorship just to catch some sleep.

He heard the Geiger counter clicking and remembered having used the suppressor circuit. The radioactivity in the room must be increasing, perhaps from scattering the "brain" circuits—the circuits were sure to be infected; they had lived too long too close to plutonium. He dug out his film.

The dark area was spreading toward the red line.

He put it back and said, "Pal, better break this deadlock or you are going to shine like a watch dial." It was a figure of speech; infected animal tissue does not glow—it simply dies, slowly.

The TV screen lit up; Towers' face appeared. "Dahlquist? I want to talk to you."

"Go fly a kite."

"Let's admit you have us inconvenienced."

"Inconvenienced, hell—I've got you stopped."

"For the moment. I'm arranging to get more bombs—"

"Liar."

"—but you are slowing us up. I have a proposition."

"Not interested."

"Wait. When this is over I will be chief of the world government. If you cooperate, even now, I will make you my administrative head."

Johnny told him what to do with it. Towers said, "Don't be stupid. What do you gain by dying?"

Johnny grunted. "Towers, what a prime stinker you are. You spoke of my family. I'd rather see them dead than living under a two-bit Napoleon like you. Now go away—I've got some thinking to do."

Towers switched off.

Johnny got out his film again. It seemed no darker but it reminded him forcibly that time was running out. He was hungry and thirsty—and he could not stay awake forever. It took four days to get a ship up from Earth; he could not expect rescue any sooner. And he wouldn't last four days—once the darkening spread past the red line he was a goner.

His only chance was to wreck the bombs beyond repair, and get out—before that film got much darker.

He thought about ways, then got busy. He hung a weight on the sling, tied a line to it. If Towers blasted the door, he hoped to jerk the rig loose before he died.

There was a simple, though arduous, way to wreck the bombs beyond any capacity of Moon Base to repair them. The heart of each was two hemispheres of plutonium, their flat surfaces polished smooth to permit perfect contact when slapped together. Anything less would prevent the chain reaction on which atomic explosion depended.

Johnny started taking apart one of the bombs.

He had to bash off four lugs, then break the glass envelope around the inner assembly. Aside from that the bomb came apart easily. At last he had in front of him two gleaming, mirror-perfect half globes.

A blow with the hammer—and one was no longer perfect. Another blow and the second cracked like glass; he had tapped its crystalline structure just right.

Hours later, dead tired, he went back to the armed bomb. Forcing himself to steady down, with extreme care he disarmed it. Shortly its silvery hemispheres too were useless. There was no longer a usable bomb in the room—but huge fortunes in the most valuable, most poisonous, and most deadly metal in the known world were spread around the floor.

Johnny looked at the deadly stuff. "Into your suit and out of here, son," he said aloud. "I wonder what Towers will say?"

He walked toward the rack, intending to hang up the hammer. As he passed, the Geiger counter chattered wildly.

Plutonium hardly affects a Geiger counter; secondary infection from plutonium does. Johnny looked at the hammer, then held it closer to the Geiger counter. The counter screamed.

Johnny tossed it hastily away and started back toward his suit.

As he passed the counter it chattered again. He stopped short.

He pushed one hand close to the counter. Its clicking picked up to a steady roar. Without moving he reached into his pocket and took out his exposure film.

It was dead black from end to end.

3

PLUTONIUM TAKEN INTO the body moves quickly to bone marrow. Nothing can be done; the victim is finished. Neutrons from it smash through the body, ionizing tissue, transmuting atoms into radioactive isotopes, destroying and killing. The fatal dose is unbelievably small; a mass a tenth the size of a grain of table salt is more than enough—a dose small enough to enter through the tiniest scratch. During the historic "Manhattan Project" immediate high amputation was considered the only possible first-aid measure.

Johnny knew all this but it no longer disturbed him. He sat on the floor, smoking a hoarded cigarette, and thinking. The events of his long watch were running through his mind.

He blew a puff of smoke at the Geiger counter and smiled without humor to hear it chatter more loudly. By now even his breath was "hot"—carbon-14, he supposed, exhaled from his blood stream as carbon dioxide. It did not matter.

There was no longer any point in surrendering, nor would he give Towers the satisfaction—he would finish out this watch right here. Besides, by keeping up the bluff that one bomb was ready to blow, he could stop them from capturing the raw material from which bombs were made. That might be important in the long run.

He accepted, without surprise, the fact that he was not unhappy. There was a sweetness about having no further worries of any sort. He did not hurt, he was not uncomfortable, he was no longer even hungry. Physically he still felt fine and his mind was at peace. He was dead—he knew that he was dead; yet for a time he was able to walk and breathe and see and feel.

He was not even lonesome. He was not alone; there were comrades with him—the boy with his finger in the dike, Colonel Bowie, too ill to move but insisting that he be carried across the line, the dying Captain of the *Chesapeake* still with deathless challenge on his lips, Rodger Young peering into the gloom. They gathered about him in the dusky bomb room.

And of course there was Edith. She was the only one he was aware of. Johnny wished that he could see her face more clearly. Was she angry? Or proud and happy?

Proud though unhappy—he could see her better now and even feel her hand. He held very still.

Presently his cigarette burned down to his fingers. He took a final puff, blew it at the Geiger counter, and put it out. It was his last. He gathered several butts and fashioned a roll-your-own with a bit of paper found in a pocket. He lit it carefully and settled back to wait for Edith to show up again. He was very happy.

He was still propped against the bomb case, the last of his salvaged cigarettes cold at his side, when the speaker called out again. "Johnny? Hey, Johnny! Can you hear me? This is

Kelly. It's all over. The *Lafayette* landed and Towers blew his brains out. Johnny? *Answer me.*"

When they opened the outer door, the first man in carried a Geiger counter in front of him on the end of a long pole. He stopped at the threshold and backed out hastily. "Hey, chief!" he called. "Better get some handling equipment—uh, and a lead coffin, too."

"Four days it took the little ship and her escort to reach Earth. Four days while all of Earth's people awaited her arrival. For ninety-eight hours all commercial programs were off television; instead there was an endless dirge—the Dead March *from* Saul, *the* Valhalla *theme,* Going Home, *the* Patrol's own *Landing Orbit.*

"The nine ships landed at Chicago Port. A drone tractor removed the casket from the small ship; the ship was then refueled and blasted off in an escape trajectory, thrown away into outer space, never again to be used for a lesser purpose.

"The tractor progressed to the Illinois town where Lieutenant Dahlquist had been born, while the dirge continued. There it placed the casket on a pedestal, inside a barrier marking the distance of safe approach. Space marines, arms reversed and heads bowed, stood guard around it; the crowds stayed outside this circle. And still the dirge continued.

"When enough time had passed, long, long after the heaped flowers had withered, the lead casket was enclosed in marble, just as you see it today."

Gentlemen, Be Seated

IT TAKES both agoraphobes and claustrophobes to colonize the Moon. Or make it agoraphiles and claustrophiles, for the men who go out into space had better not have phobias. If anything on a planet, in a planet, or in the empty reaches around the planets can frighten a man, he should stick to Mother Earth. A man who would make his living away from *terra firma* must be willing to be shut up in a cramped spaceship, knowing that it may become his coffin, and yet he must be undismayed by the wide-open spaces of space itself. Spacemen —men who *work* in space, pilots and jetmen and astrogators and such—are men who like a few million miles of elbow room.

On the other hand the Moon colonists need to be the sort who feel cozy burrowing around underground like so many pesky moles.

On my second trip to Luna City I went over to Richardson Observatory both to see the Big Eye and to pick up a story to pay for my vacation. I flashed my Journalists' Guild card, sweet-talked a bit, and ended with the paymaster showing me around. We went out the north tunnel, which was then being bored to the site of the projected coronascope.

It was a dull trip—climb on a scooter, ride down a completely featureless tunnel, climb off and go through an airlock, get on another scooter and do it all over again. Mr. Knowles filled in with sales talk. "This is temporary," he explained. "When we get the second tunnel dug, we'll cross-connect, take out the airlocks, put a northbound slidewalk in this one, a southbound slidewalk in the other one, and you'll make the trip in less than three minutes. Just like Luna City—or Manhattan."

"Why not take out the airlocks now?" I asked, as we entered another airlock—about the seventh. "So far, the pressure is the same on each side of each lock."

Knowles looked at me quizzically. "You wouldn't take ad-

277

vantage of a peculiarity of this planet just to work up a sensational feature story?"

I was irked. "Look here," I told him. "I'm as reliable as the next word-mechanic, but if something is not kosher about this project let's go back right now and forget it. I won't hold still for censorship."

"Take it easy, Jack," he said mildly—it was the first time he had used my first name; I noted it and discounted it. "Nobody's going to censor you. We're glad to cooperate with you fellows, but the Moon's had too much bad publicity now—publicity it didn't deserve."

I didn't say anything.

"Every engineering job has its own hazards," he insisted, "and its advantages, too. Our men don't get malaria and they don't have to watch out for rattlesnakes. I can show you figures that prove it's safer to be a sandhog in the Moon than it is to be a file clerk in Des Moines—all things considered. For example, we rarely have any broken bones in the Moon; the gravity is so low—while that Des Moines file clerk takes his life in his hands every time he steps in or out of his bathtub."

"Okay, okay," I interrupted, "so the place is safe. What's the catch?"

"It *is* safe. Not company figures, mind you, nor Luna City Chamber of Commerce, but Lloyd's of London."

"So you keep unnecessary airlocks. Why?"

He hesitated before he answered, "Quakes."

Quakes. Earthquakes—moonquakes, I mean. I glanced at the curving walls sliding past and I wished I were in Des Moines. Nobody wants to be buried alive, but to have it happen in the Moon—why, you wouldn't stand a chance. No matter how quick they got to you, your lungs would be ruptured. No air.

"They don't happen very often," Knowles went on, "but we have to be prepared. Remember, the Earth is eighty times the mass of the Moon, so the tidal stresses here are eighty times as great as the Moon's effect on Earth tides."

"Come again," I said. "There isn't any water on the Moon. How can there be tides?"

"You don't have to have water to have tidal stresses. Don't worry about it; just accept it. What you get is unbalanced stresses. They can cause quakes."

I nodded. "I see. Since everything in the Moon has to be

sealed airtight, you've got to watch out for quakes. These airlocks are to confine your losses." I started visualizing myself as one of the losses.

"Yes and no. The airlocks would limit an accident all right, if there was one—which there won't be—this place is *safe*. Primarily they let us work on a section of the tunnel at no pressure without disturbing the rest of it. But they are more than that; each one is a temporary expansion joint. You can tie a compact structure together and let it ride out a quake, but a thing as long as this tunnel has to give, or it will spring a leak. A flexible seal is hard to accomplish in the Moon."

"What's wrong with rubber?" I demanded. I was feeling jumpy enough to be argumentative. "I've got a ground-car back home with two hundred thousand miles on it, yet I've never touched the tires since they were sealed up in Detroit."

Knowles sighed. "I should have brought one of the engineers along, Jack. The volatiles that keep rubbers soft tend to boil away in vacuum and the stuff gets stiff. Same for the flexible plastics. When you expose them to low temperature as well they get brittle as eggshells."

The scooter stopped as Knowles was speaking and we got off just in time to meet half a dozen men coming out of the next airlock. They were wearing spacesuits, or, more properly, pressure suits, for they had hose connections instead of oxygen bottles, and no sun visors. Their helmets were thrown back and each man had his head pushed through the opened zipper in the front of his suit, giving him a curiously two-headed look. Knowles called out, "Hey, Konski!"

One of the men turned around. He must have been six feet two and fat for his size. I guessed him at three hundred pounds, earthside. "It's Mr. Knowles," he said happily. "Don't tell me I've gotten a raise."

"You're making too much money now, Fatso. Shake hands with Jack Arnold. Jack, this is Fatso Konski—the best sandhog in four planets."

"Only four?" inquired Konski. He slid his right arm out of his suit and stuck his bare hand into mine. I said I was glad to meet him and tried to get my hand back before he mangled it.

"Jack Arnold wants to see how you seal these tunnels," Knowles went on. "Come along with us."

Konski stared at the overhead. "Well, now that you mention it, Mr. Knowles, I've just finished my shift."

Knowles said, "Fatso, you're a money grubber and inhospitable as well. Okay—time-and-a-half." Konski turned and started unsealing the airlock.

The tunnel beyond looked much the same as the section we had left except that there were no scooter tracks and the lights were temporary, rigged on extensions. A couple of hundred feet away the tunnel was blocked by a bulkhead with a circular door in it. The fat man followed my glance. "That's the movable lock," he explained. "No air beyond it. We excavate just ahead of it."

"Can I see where you've been digging?"

"Not without we go back and get you a suit."

I shook my head. There were perhaps a dozen bladder-like objects in the tunnel, the size and shape of toy balloons. They seemed to displace exactly their own weight of air; they floated without displaying much tendency to rise or settle. Konski batted one out of his way and answered me before I could ask. "This piece of tunnel was pressurized today," he told me. "These tag-alongs search out stray leaks. They're sticky inside. They get sucked up against a leak, break, and the goo gets sucked in, freezes and seals the leak."

"Is that a permanent repair?" I wanted to know.

"Are you kidding? It just shows the follow-up man where to weld."

"Show him a flexible joint," Knowles directed.

"Coming up." We paused half-way down the tunnel and Konski pointed to a ring segment that ran completely around the tubular tunnel. "We put in a flex joint every hundred feet. It's glass cloth, gasketed onto the two steel sections it joins. Gives the tunnel a certain amount of springiness."

"Glass cloth? To make an airtight seal?" I objected.

"The cloth doesn't seal; it's for strength. You got ten layers of cloth, with a silicone grease spread between the layers. It gradually goes bad, from the outside in, but it'll hold five years or more before you have to put on another coat."

I asked Konski how he liked his job, thinking I might get some story. He shrugged. "It's all right. Nothing to it. Only one atmosphere of pressure. Now you take when I was working under the Hudson—"

"And getting paid a tenth of what you get here," put in Knowles.

"Mr. Knowles, you grieve me," Konski protested. "It ain't the money; it's the art of the matter. Take Venus. They pay as well on Venus and a man has to be on his toes. The muck is so loose you have to freeze it. It takes real caisson men to work there. Half of these punks here are just miners; a case of the bends would scare 'em silly."

"Tell him why you left Venus, Fatso."

Konski expressed dignity. "Shall we examine the movable shield, gentlemen?" he asked.

We puttered around a while longer and I was ready to go back. There wasn't much to see, and the more I saw of the place the less I liked it. Konski was undogging the door of the airlock leading back when something happened.

I was down on my hands and knees and the place was pitch dark. Maybe I screamed—I don't know. There was a ringing in my ears. I tried to get up and then stayed where I was. It was the darkest dark I ever saw, complete blackness. I thought I was blind.

A torchlight beam cut through it, picked me out, and then moved on. "What was it?" I shouted. "What happened? Was it a quake?"

"Stop yelling," Konski's voice answered me casually. "That was no quake, it was some sort of explosion. Mr. Knowles— you all right?"

"I guess so." He gasped for breath. "What happened?"

"Dunno. Let's look around a bit." Konski stood up and poked his beam around the tunnel, whistling softly. His light was the sort that has to be pumped; it flickered.

"Looks tight, but I hear— Oh, oh! Sister!" His beam was focused on a part of the flexible joint, near the floor.

The "tag-along" balloons were gathering at this spot. Three were already there; others were drifting in slowly. As we watched, one of them burst and collapsed in a sticky mass that marked the leak.

The hole sucked up the burst balloon and began to hiss. Another rolled onto the spot, joggled about a bit, then it, too, burst. It took a little longer this time for the leak to absorb and swallow the gummy mass.

Konski passed me the light. "Keep pumping it, kid." He shrugged his right arm out of the suit and placed his bare hand over the spot where, at that moment, a third bladder burst.

"How about it, Fats?" Mr. Knowles demanded.

"Couldn't say. Feels like a hole as big as my thumb. Sucks like the devil."

"How could you get a hole like that?"

"Search me. Poked through from the outside, maybe."

"You got the leak checked?"

"I think so. Go back and check the gage. Jack, give him the light."

Knowles trotted back to the airlock. Presently he sang out, "Pressure steady!"

"Can you read the vernier?" Konski called to him.

"Sure. Steady by the vernier."

"How much we lose?"

"Not more than a pound or two. What was the pressure before?"

"Earth-normal."

"Lost a pound four tenths, then."

"Not bad. Keep on going, Mr. Knowles. There's a tool kit just beyond the lock in the next section. Bring me back a number three patch, or bigger."

"Right." We heard the door open and clang shut, and we were again in total darkness. I must have made some sound for Konski told me to keep my chin up.

Presently we heard the door, and the blessed light shone out again. "Got it?" said Konski.

"No, Fatso. No . . ." Knowles' voice was shaking. "There's no air on the other side. The other door wouldn't open."

"Jammed, maybe?"

"No, I checked the manometer. There's no pressure in the next section."

Konski whistled again. "Looks like we'll wait till they come for us. In that case— Keep the light on me, Mr. Knowles. Jack, help me out of this suit."

"What are you planning to do?"

"If I can't get a patch, I got to make one, Mr. Knowles. This suit is the only thing around." I started to help him—a clumsy job since he had to keep his hand on the leak.

"You can stuff my shirt in the hole," Knowles suggested.

"I'd as soon bail water with a fork. It's got to be the suit; there's nothing else around that will hold the pressure." When he was free of the suit, he had me smooth out a portion of the back, then, as he snatched his hand away, I slapped the suit down over the leak. Konski promptly sat on it. "There," he said happily, "we've got it corked. Nothing to do but wait."

I started to ask him why he hadn't just sat down on the leak while wearing the suit; then I realized that the seat of the suit was corrugated with insulation—he needed a smooth piece to seal on to the sticky stuff left by the balloons.

"Let me see your hand," Knowles demanded.

"It's nothing much." But Knowles examined it anyway. I looked at it and got a little sick. He had a mark like a stigma on the palm, a bloody, oozing wound. Knowles made a compress of his handkerchief and then used mine to tie it in place.

"Thank you, gentlemen," Konski told us, then added, "we've got time to kill. How about a little pinochle?"

"With your cards?" asked Knowles.

"Why, Mr. Knowles! Well—never mind. It isn't right for paymasters to gamble anyhow. Speaking of paymasters, you realize this is pressure work now, Mr. Knowles?"

"For a pound and four tenths differential?"

"I'm sure the union would take that view—in the circumstances."

"Suppose *I* sit on the leak?"

"But the rate applies to helpers, too."

"Okay, miser—triple-time it is."

"That's more like your own sweet nature, Mr. Knowles. I hope it's a nice long wait."

"How long a wait do you think it will be, Fatso?"

"Well, it shouldn't take them more than an hour, even if they have to come all the way from Richardson."

"Hmm . . . what makes you think they will be looking for us?"

"Huh? Doesn't your office know where you are?"

"I'm afraid not. I told them I wouldn't be back today."

Konski thought about it. "I didn't drop my time card. They'll know I'm still inside."

"Sure they will—tomorrow, when your card doesn't show up at my office."

"There's that lunkhead on the gate. He'll know he's got three extra inside."

"Provided he remembers to tell his relief. And provided he wasn't caught in it, too."

"Yes, I guess so," Konski said thoughtfully. "Jack—better quit pumping that light. You just use up more oxygen."

We sat there in the darkness for quite a long time, speculating about what had happened. Konski was sure it was an explosion; Knowles said that it put him in mind of a time when he had seen a freight rocket crash on take off. When the talk started to die out, Konski told some stories. I tried to tell one, but I was so nervous—so *afraid*, I should say—that I couldn't remember the snapper. I wanted to scream.

After a long silence Konski said, "Jack, give us the light again. I got something figured out."

"What is it?" Knowles asked.

"If we had a patch, you could put on my suit and go for help."

"There's no oxygen for the suit."

"That's why I mentioned you. You're the smallest—there'll be enough air in the suit itself to take you through the next section."

"Well—okay. What are you going to use for a patch?"

"I'm sitting on it."

"Huh?"

"This big broad, round thing I'm sitting on. I'll take my pants off. If I push one of my hams against that hole, I'll guarantee you it'll be sealed tight."

"But—No, Fats, it won't do. Look what happened to your hand. You'd hemorrhage through your skin and bleed to death before I could get back."

"I'll give you two to one I wouldn't—for fifty, say."

"If I win, how do I collect?"

"You're a cute one, Mr. Knowles. But look—I've got two or three inches of fat padding me. I won't bleed much—a strawberry mark, no more."

Knowles shook his head. "It's not necessary. If we keep quiet, there's air enough here for several days."

"It's not the air, Mr. Knowles. Noticed it's getting chilly?"

I had noticed, but hadn't thought about it. In my misery and funk being cold didn't seem anything more than appropriate. Now I thought about it. When we lost the power line, we lost the heaters, too. It would keep getting colder and colder . . . and colder.

Mr. Knowles saw it, too. "Okay, Fats. Let's get on with it."

I sat on the suit while Konski got ready. After he got his pants off he snagged one of the tag-alongs, burst it, and smeared the sticky insides on his right buttock. Then he turned to me. "Okay, kid—up off the nest." We made the swap-over fast, without losing much air, though the leak hissed angrily. "Comfortable as an easy chair, folks." He grinned.

Knowles hurried into the suit and left, taking the light with him. We were in darkness again.

After a while, I heard Konski's voice. "There a game we can play in the dark, Jack. You play chess?"

"Why, yes—play at it, that is."

"A good game. Used to play it in the decompression chamber when I was working under the Hudson. What do you say to twenty on a side, just to make it fun?"

"Uh? Well, all right." He could have made it a thousand; I didn't care.

"Fine. King's pawn to king three."

"Uh—king's pawn to king's four."

"Conventional, aren't you? Puts me in mind of a girl I knew in Hoboken—" What he told about her had nothing to do with chess, although it did prove she was conventional, in a manner of speaking. "King's bishop to queen's bishop four. Remind me to tell you about her sister, too. Seems she hadn't always been a redhead, but she wanted people to think so. So she—sorry. Go ahead with your move."

I tried to think but my head was spinning. "Queen's pawn to queen three."

"Queen to king's bishop three. Anyhow, she—" He went on in great detail. It wasn't new and I doubt if it ever happened to him, but it cheered me up. I actually smiled, there in the dark. "It's your move," he added.

"Oh." I couldn't remember the board. I decided to get ready to castle, always fairly safe in the early game. "Queen's knight to queen's bishop three."

"Queen advances to capture your king's bishop's pawn—checkmate. You owe me twenty, Jack."

"Huh? Why that can't be!"

"Want to run over the moves?" He checked them off.

I managed to visualize them, then said, "Why, I'll be a dirty name! You hooked me with a fool's mate!"

He chuckled. "You should have kept your eye on my queen instead of on the redhead."

I laughed out loud. "Know any more stories?"

"Sure." He told another. But when I urged him to go on, he said, "I think I'll just rest a little while, Jack."

I got up. "You all right, Fats?" He didn't answer; I felt my way over to him in the dark. His face was cold and he didn't speak when I touched him. I could hear his heart faintly when I pressed an ear to his chest, but his hands and feet were like ice.

I had to pull him loose; he was frozen to the spot. I could feel the ice, though I knew it must be blood. I started to try to revive him by rubbing him, but the hissing of the leak brought me up short. I tore off my own trousers, had a panicky time before I found the exact spot in the dark, and sat down on it, with my right buttock pressed firmly against the opening.

It grabbed me like a suction cup, icy cold. Then it was fire spreading through my flesh. After a time I couldn't feel anything at all, except a dull ache and coldness.

There was a light someplace. It flickered on, then went out again. I heard a door clang. I started to shout.

"Knowles!" I screamed. "Mr. Knowles!"

The light flickered on again. "Coming, Jack—"

I started to blubber. "Oh, you made it! You made it."

"I didn't make it, Jack. I couldn't reach the next section. When I got back to the lock I passed out." He stopped to wheeze. "There's a crater—" The light flickered off and fell clanging to the floor. "Help me, Jack," he said querulously. "Can't you see I need help? I tried to—"

I heard him stumble and fall. I called to him, but he didn't answer.

I tried to get up, but I was stuck fast, a cork in a bottle . . .

I came to, lying face down—with a clean sheet under me. "Feeling better?" someone asked. It was Knowles, standing by my bed, dressed in a bathrobe.

"You're dead," I told him.

"Not a bit." He grinned. "They got to us in time."

"What happened?" I stared at him, still not believing my eyes.

"Just like we thought—a crashed rocket. An unmanned mail rocket got out of control and hit the tunnel."

"Where's Fats?"

"Hi!"

I twisted my head around; it was Konski, face down like myself.

"You owe me twenty," he said cheerfully.

"I owe you—" I found I was dripping tears for no good reason. "Okay, I owe you twenty. But you'll have to come to Des Moines to collect it."

The Black Pits of Luna

THE MORNING after we got to the Moon we went over to Rutherford. Dad and Mr. Latham—Mr. Latham is the man from the Harriman Trust that Dad came to Luna City to see —Dad and Mr. Latham had to go anyhow, on business. I got Dad to promise I could go along because it looked like just about my only chance to get out on the surface of the Moon. Luna City is all right, I guess, but I defy you to tell a corridor in Luna City from the sublevels in New York—except that you're light on your feet, of course.

When Dad came into our hotel suite to say we were ready to leave, I was down on the floor, playing mumblety-peg with my kid brother. Mother was lying down and had asked me to keep the runt quiet. She had been dropsick all the way out from Earth and I guess she didn't feel very good. The runt had been fiddling with the lights, switching them from "dusk" to "desert suntan" and back again. I collared him and sat him down on the floor.

Of course, I don't play mumblety-peg any more, but, on the Moon, it's a right good game. The knife practically floats and you can do all kinds of things with it. We made up a lot of new rules.

Dad said, "Switch in plans, my dear. We're leaving for Rutherford right away. Let's pull ourselves together."

Mother said, "Oh, mercy me—I don't think I'm up to it. You and Dickie run along. Baby Darling and I will just spend a quiet day right here."

Baby Darling is the runt.

I could have told her it was the wrong approach. He nearly put my eye out with the knife and said, "Who? What? I'm going too. Let's go!"

Mother said, "Oh, now, Baby Darling—don't cause Mother Dear any trouble. We'll go to the movies, just you and I."

The runt is seven years younger than I am, but don't call him "Baby Darling" if you want to get anything out of him. He started to bawl. "You said I could go!" he yelled.

"No, Baby Darling. I haven't mentioned it to you. I—"

"Daddy said I could go!"

"Richard, did you tell Baby he could go?"

"Why, no, my dear, not that I recall. Perhaps I—"

The kid cut in fast. "You said I could go anywhere Dickie went. You promised me you promised me you promised me." Sometimes you have to hand it to the runt; he had them jawing about who told him what in nothing flat. Anyhow, that is how twenty minutes later, the four of us were up at the rocket port with Mr. Latham and climbing into the shuttle for Rutherford.

The trip only takes about ten minutes and you don't see much, just a glimpse of the Earth while the rocket is still near Luna City and then not even that, since the atom plants where we were going are all on the back side of the Moon, of course. There were maybe a dozen tourists along and most of them were dropsick as soon as we went into free flight. So was Mother. Some people never will get used to rockets.

But Mother was all right as soon as we grounded and were inside again. Rutherford isn't like Luna City; instead of extending a tube out to the ship, they send a pressurized car out to latch on to the airlock of the rocket, then you jeep back about a mile to the entrance to underground. I liked that and so did the runt. Dad had to go off on business with Mr. Latham, leaving Mother and me and the runt to join up with the party of tourists for the trip through the laboratories.

It was all right but nothing to get excited about. So far as I can see, one atomics plant looks about like another; Rutherford could just as well have been the main plant outside Chicago. I mean to say everything that is anything is out of sight, covered up, shielded. All you get to see are some dials and instrument boards and people watching them. Remote control stuff, like Oak Ridge. The guide tells you about the experiments going on and they show you some movies—that's all.

I liked our guide. He looked like Tom Jeremy in *The Space Troopers*. I asked him if he was a spaceman and he looked at me kind of funny and said, no, that he was just a Colonial Services ranger. Then he asked me where I went to school and if I belonged to the Scouts. He said he was scoutmaster of Troop One, Rutherford City, Moonbat Patrol.

I found out there was just the one patrol—not many scouts on the Moon, I suppose.

Dad and Mr. Latham joined us just as we finished the tour

while Mr. Perrin—that's our guide—was announcing the trip outside. "The conducted tour of Rutherford," he said, talking as if it were a transcription, "includes a trip by spaceshuit out on the surface of the Moon, without extra charge, to see the Devil's Graveyard and the site of the Great Disaster of 1984. The trip is optional. There is nothing particularly dangerous about it and we've never had any one hurt, but the Commission requires that you sign a separate release for your own safety if you choose to make this trip. The trip takes about one hour. Those preferring to remain behind will find movies and refreshments in the coffee shop."

Dad was rubbing his hands together. "This is for me," he announced. "Mr. Latham, I'm glad we got back in time. I wouldn't have missed this for the world."

"You'll enjoy it," Mr. Latham agreed, "and so will you, Mrs. Logan. I'm tempted to come along myself."

"Why don't you?" Dad asked.

"No, I want to have the papers ready for you and the Director to sign when you get back and before you leave for Luna City."

"Why knock yourself out?" Dad urged him. "If a man's word is no good, his signed contract is no better. You can mail the stuff to me at New York."

Mr. Latham shook his head. "No, really—I've been out on the surface dozens of times. But I'll come along and help you into your spacesuits."

Mother said, "Oh dear," she didn't think she'd better go; she wasn't sure she could stand the thought of being shut up in a spacesuit and besides glaring sunlight always gave her a headache.

Dad said, "Don't be silly, my dear; it's the chance of a lifetime," and Mr. Latham told her that the filters on the helmets kept the light from being glaring. Mother always objects and then gives in. I suppose women just don't have any force of character. Like the night before—earth-night, I mean, Luna City time—she had bought a fancy moonsuit to wear to dinner in the Earth-View room at the hotel, then she got cold feet. She complained to Dad that she was too plump to dare to dress like that.

Well, she did show an awful lot of skin. Dad said, "Nonsense, my dear. You look ravishing." So she wore it and had a swell time, especially when a pilot tried to pick her up.

It was like that this time. She came along. We went into

the outfitting room and I looked around while Mr. Perrin was getting them all herded in and having the releases signed. There was the door to the airlock to the surface at the far end, with a bull's-eye window in it and another one like it in the door beyond. You could peek through and see the surface of the Moon beyond, looking hot and bright and sort of improbable, in spite of the amber glass in the windows. And there was a double row of spacesuits hanging up, looking like empty men. I snooped around until Mr. Perrin got around to our party.

"We can arrange to leave the youngster in the care of the hostess in the coffee shop," he was telling Mother. He reached down and tousled the runt's hair. The runt tried to bite him and he snatched his hand away in a hurry.

"Thank you, Mr. Perkins," Mother said, "I suppose that's best—though perhaps I had better stay behind with him."

" 'Perrin' is the name," Mr. Perrin said mildly. "It won't be necessary. The hostess will take good care of him."

Why do adults talk in front of kids as if they couldn't understand English? They should have just shoved him into the coffee shop. By now the runt knew he was being railroaded. He looked around belligerently. "I go, too," he said loudly. "You promised me."

"Now Baby Darling," Mother tried to stop him. "Mother Dear didn't tell you—" But she was just whistling to herself; the runt turned on the sound effects.

"You said I could go where Dickie went; you promised me when I was sick. You promised me you promised me—" and on and on, his voice getting higher and louder all the time.

Mr. Perrin looked embarrassed. Mother said, "Richard, you'll just have to deal with your child. After all, you were the one who promised him."

"Me, dear?" Dad looked surprised. "Anyway, I don't see anything so complicated about it. Suppose we did promise him that he could do what Dickie does—we'll simply take him along; that's all."

Mr. Perrin cleared his throat. "I'm afraid not. I can outfit your older son with a woman's suit; he's tall for his age. But we just don't make any provision for small children."

Well, we were all tangled up in a mess in no time at all. The runt can always get Mother to running in circles. Mother has the same effect on Dad. He gets red in the face and starts laying down the law to me. It's sort of a chain reaction, with me on the end and nobody to pass it along to. They came out with a very simple solution—I was to stay behind and take care of Baby Darling brat!

"But, Dad, you said—" I started in.

"Never mind!" he cut in. "I won't have this family disrupted in a public squabble. You heard what your mother said."

I was desperate. "Look, Dad," I said, keeping my voice low, "if I go back to Earth without once having put on a spacesuit and set foot on the surface, you'll just have to find another school to send me to. I won't go back to Lawrenceville; I'd be the joke of the whole place."

"We'll settle that when we get home."

"But, Dad, you promised me specifically—"

"That'll be enough out of you, young man. The matter is closed."

Mr. Latham had been standing near by, taking it in but keeping his mouth shut. At this point he cocked an eyebrow at Dad and said very quietly, "Well, R.J.—I thought your word was your bond?"

I wasn't supposed to hear it and nobody else did—a good thing, too, for it doesn't do to let Dad know that you know that he's wrong; it just makes him worse. I changed the subject in a hurry. "Look, Dad, maybe we all can go out. How about that suit over there?" I pointed at a rack that was inside a railing with a locked gate on it. The rack had a couple of dozen suits on it and at the far end, almost out of sight, was a small suit—the boots on it hardly came down to the waist of the suit next to it.

"Huh?" Dad brightened up. "Why, just the thing! Mr. Perrin! Oh, Mr. Perrin—here a minute! I thought you didn't have any small suits, but here's one that I think will fit."

Dad was fiddling at the latch of the railing gate. Mr. Perrin stopped him. "We can't use that suit, sir."

"Uh? Why not?"

"All the suits inside the railing are private property, not for rent."

"What? Nonsense—Rutherford is a public enterprise. I want that suit for my child."

"Well, you can't have it."

"I'll speak to the Director."

"I'm afraid you'll have to. That suit was specially built for his daughter."

And that's just what they did. Mr. Latham got the Director on the line, Dad talked to him, then the Director talked to Mr. Perrin, then he talked to Dad again. The Director didn't mind lending the suit, not to Dad, anyway, but he wouldn't order Mr. Perrin to take a below-age child outside.

Mr. Perrin was feeling stubborn and I don't blame him, but Dad soothed his feathers down and presently we were all climbing into our suits and getting pressure checks and checking our oxygen supply and switching on our walkie-talkies. Mr. Perrin was calling the roll by radio and reminding us that we were all on the same circuit, so we had better let him do most of the talking and not to make casual remarks or none of us would be able to hear. Then we were in the airlock and he was warning us to stick close together and not try to see how fast we could run or how high we could jump. My heart was knocking around in my chest.

The outer door of the lock opened and we filed out on the face of the Moon. It was just as wonderful as I dreamed it would be, I guess, but I was so excited that I hardly knew it at the time. The glare of the sun was the brightest thing I ever saw and the shadows so inky black you could hardly see into them. You couldn't hear anything but voices over your radio and you could reach down and switch off that.

The pumice was soft and kicked up around our feet like smoke, settling slowly, falling in slow motion. Nothing else moved. It was the *deadest* place you can imagine.

We stayed on a path, keeping close together for company, except twice when I had to take out after the runt when he found out he could jump twenty feet. I wanted to smack him, but did you ever try to smack anybody wearing a spacesuit? It's no use.

Mr. Perrin told us to halt presently and started his talk. "You are now in the Devil's Graveyard. The twin spires behind you are five thousand feet above the floor of the plain and have never been scaled. The spires, or monuments, have been named for apocryphal or mythological characters because of the fancied resemblance of this fantastic scene to a giant cemetery. Beelzebub, Thor, Siva, Cain, Set—" He pointed around us. "Lunologists are not agreed as to the origin of the strange shapes. Some claim to see indications of the action of air and water as well as volcanic action. If so, these spires must have been standing for an unthinkably long period, for today, as you see, the Moon——" It was the same sort of stuff you can read any month in *Spaceways Magazine*, only we were seeing it and that makes a difference, let me tell you.

The spires reminded me a bit of the rocks below the lodge in the Garden of the Gods in Colorado Springs when we went there last summer, only these spires were lots bigger and, instead of blue sky, there was just blackness and hard, sharp stars overhead. Spooky.

Another ranger had come with us, with a camera. Mr. Perrin tried to say something else, but the runt had started yapping away and I had to switch off his radio before anybody could hear anything. I kept it switched off until Mr. Perrin finished talking.

He wanted us to line up for a picture with the spires and the black sky behind us for a background. "Push your faces forward in your helmets so that your features will show. Everybody look pretty. There!" he added as the other guy snapped the shot. "Prints will be ready when you return, at ten dollars a copy."

I thought it over. I certainly needed one for my room at school and I wanted one to give to—anyhow, I needed another one. I had eighteen bucks left from my birthday money; I could sweet-talk Mother for the balance. So I ordered two of them.

We climbed a long rise and suddenly we were staring out across the crater, the disaster crater, all that was left of the first laboratory. It stretched away from us, twenty miles across, with the floor covered with shiny, bubbly green glass instead of pumice. There was a monument. I read it:

HERE ABOUT YOU
ARE THE MORTAL REMAINS
OF
Kurt Schaeffer
Maurice Feinstein
Thomas Dooley
Hazel Hayakawa
G. Washington Slappey
Sam Houston Adams
WHO DIED FOR THE TRUTH
THAT MAKES MEN FREE
On the Eleventh Day of August 1984

I felt sort of funny and backed away and went to listen to Mr. Perrin. Dad and some of the other men were asking him questions. "They don't know exactly," he was saying. "Nothing was left. Now we telemeter all the data back to Luna City, as it comes off the instruments, but that was before the line-of-sight relays were set up."

"What would have happened," some man asked, "if this blast had gone off on Earth?"

"I'd hate to try to tell you—but that's why they put the lab here, back of the Moon." He glanced at his watch. "Time to leave, everybody." They were milling around, heading back down toward the path, when Mother screamed.

"Baby! Where's Baby Darling?"

I was startled but I wasn't scared, not yet. The runt is always running around, first here and then there, but he doesn't go far away, because he always wants to have somebody to yap to.

My father had one arm around Mother; he signalled to me with the other. "Dick," he snapped, his voice sharp in my earphones, "what have you done with your brother?"

"Me?" I said. "Don't look at me—the last I saw Mother had him by the hand, walking up the hill here."

"Don't stall around, Dick. Mother sat down to rest when we got here and sent him to you."

"Well, if she did, he never showed up." At that, Mother started to scream in earnest. Everybody had been listening, of course—they had to; there was just the one radio circuit. Mr. Perrin stepped up and switched off Mother's talkie, making a sudden silence.

"Take care of your wife, Mr. Logan," he ordered, then added, "When did you see your child last?"

Dad couldn't help him any; when they tried switching Mother back into the hook-up, they switched her right off again. She couldn't help and she deafened us. Mr. Perrin addressed the rest of us. "Has anyone seen the small child we had with us? Don't answer unless you have something to contribute. Did anyone see him wander away?"

Nobody had. I figured he probably ducked out when everybody was looking at the crater and had their backs to him. I told Mr. Perrin so. "Seems likely," he agreed. "Attention, everybody! I'm going to search for the child. Stay right where you are. Don't move away from this spot. I won't be gone more than ten minutes."

"Why don't we all go?" somebody wanted to know.

"Because," said Mr. Perrin, "right now I've only got one lost. I don't want to make it a dozen." Then he left, taking big easy lopes that covered fifty feet at a step.

Dad started to take out after him, then thought better of it, for Mother suddenly keeled over, collapsing at the knees and floating gently to the ground. Everybody started talking at once. Some idiot wanted to take her helmet off, but Dad isn't crazy. I switched off my radio so I could hear myself think and started looking around, not leaving the crowd but standing up on the lip of the crater and trying to see as much as I could.

I was looking back the way we had come; there was no sense in looking at the crater—if he had been in there he would have shown up like a fly on a plate.

Outside the crater was different; you could have hidden a regiment within a block of us, rocks standing up every which way, boulders big as houses with blow holes all through them, spires, gulleys—it was a mess. I could see Mr. Perrin every now and then, casting around like a dog after a rabbit, and making plenty of time. He was practically flying. When he came to a big boulder he would jump right over it, leveling off face down at the top of his jump, so he could see better.

Then he was heading back toward us and I switched my radio back on. There was still a lot of talk. Somebody was saying, "We've got to find him before sundown," and somebody else answered, "Don't be silly; the sun won't be down for a week. It's his air supply, I tell you. These suits are only good for four hours." The first voice said, "Oh!" then added softly, "like a fish out of water—" It was then I got scared.

A woman's voice, sounding kind of choked, said, "The poor, poor darling! We've got to find him before he suffocates," and my father's voice cut in sharply, "Shut up talking that way!" I could hear somebody sobbing. It might have been Mother.

Mr. Perrin was almost up to us and he cut in, "Silence, everybody! I've got to call the base," and he added urgently, "Perrin, calling airlock control; Perrin, calling airlock control!"

A woman's voice answered, "Come in, Perrin." He told her what was wrong and added, "Send out Smythe to take this party back in; I'm staying. I want every ranger who's around and get me volunteers from among any of the experienced

Moon hands. Send out a radio direction-finder by the first ones to leave."

We didn't wait long, for they came swarming toward us like grasshoppers. They must have been running forty or fifty miles an hour. It would have been something to see, if I hadn't been so sick at my stomach.

Dad put up an argument about going back, but Mr. Perrin shut him up. "If you hadn't been so confounded set on having your own way, we wouldn't be in a mess. If you had kept track of your kid, he wouldn't be lost. I've got kids of my own; I don't let 'em go out on the face of the Moon when they're too young to take care of themselves. You go on back —I can't be burdened by taking care of you, too."

I think Dad might even have gotten in a fight with him if Mother hadn't gotten faint again. We went on back with the party.

The next couple of hours were pretty awful. They let us sit just outside the control room where we could hear Mr. Perrin directing the search, over the loudspeaker. I thought at first that they would snag the runt as soon as they started using the radio direction-finder—pick up his power hum, maybe, even if he didn't say anything—but no such luck; they didn't get anything with it. And the searchers didn't find anything either.

A thing that made it worse was that Mother and Dad didn't even try to blame me. Mother was crying quietly and Dad was consoling her, when he looked over at me with an odd expression. I guess he didn't really see me at all, but I thought he was thinking that if I hadn't insisted on going out on the surface this wouldn't have happened. I said, "Don't go looking at me, Dad. Nobody told me to keep an eye on him. I thought he was with Mother."

Dad just shook his head without answering. He was looking tired and sort of shrunk up. But Mother, instead of laying in to me and yelling, stopped her crying and managed to smile. "Come here, Dickie," she said, and put her other arm around me. "Nobody blames you, Dickie. Whatever happens, you weren't at fault. Remember that, Dickie."

So I let her kiss me and then sat with them for a while, but I felt worse than before. I kept thinking about the runt, somewhere out there, and his oxygen running out. Maybe it wasn't my fault, but I could have prevented it and I knew it. I shouldn't have depended on Mother to look out for him; she's no good at that sort of thing. She's the kind of person that would mislay her head if it wasn't knotted on tight—the ornamental sort. Mother's *good,* you understand, but she's not practical.

She would take it pretty hard if the runt didn't come back. And so would Dad—and so would I. The runt is an awful nuisance, but it was going to seem strange not to have him around underfoot. I got to thinking about that remark, "Like a fish out of water." I accidentally busted an aquarium once; I remember yet how they looked. Not pretty. If the runt was going to die like that—

I shut myself up and decided I just had to figure out some way to help find him.

After a while I had myself convinced that I *could* find him if they would just let me help look. But they wouldn't of course.

Dr. Evans the Director showed up again—he'd met us when we first came in—and asked if there was anything he could do for us and how was Mrs. Logan feeling? "You know I wouldn't have had this happen for the world," he added. "We're doing all we can. I'm having some ore-detectors shot over from Luna City. We might be able to spot the child by the metal in his suit."

Mother asked how about bloodhounds and Dr. Evans didn't even laugh at her. Dad suggested helicopters, then corrected himself and made it rockets. Dr. Evans pointed out that it was impossible to examine the ground closely from a rocket.

I got him aside presently and braced him to let me join the hunt. He was polite but unimpressed, so I insisted. "What makes you think you can find him?" he asked me. "We've got the most experienced Moon men available out there now. I'm afraid, son, that you would get yourself lost or hurt if you tried to keep up with them. In this country, if you once lose sight of landmarks, you can get hopelessly lost."

"But look, Doctor," I told him, "I know the runt—I mean my kid brother, better than anyone else in the world. I won't get lost—I mean I will get lost but just the way he did. You can send somebody to follow me."

He thought about it. "It's worth trying," he said suddenly. "I'll go with you. Let's suit up."

We made a fast trip out, taking thirty-foot strides—the best I could manage even with Dr. Evans hanging on to my belt to keep me from stumbling. Mr. Perrin was expecting us. He seemed dubious about my scheme. "Maybe the old 'lost mule' dodge will work," he admitted, "but I'll keep the regular search going just the same. Here, Shorty, take this flashlight. You'll need it in the shadows."

I stood on the edge of the crater and tried to imagine I was the runt, feeling bored and maybe a little bit griped at the lack of attention. What would I do next?

I went skipping down the slope, not going anywhere in particular, the way the runt would have done. Then I stopped and looked back, to see if Mother and Daddy and Dickie had noticed me. I was being followed all right; Dr. Evans and Mr. Perrin were close behind me. I pretended that no one was looking and went on. I was pretty close to the first rock outcroppings by now and I ducked behind the first one I came to. It wasn't high enough to hide me but it would have covered the runt. It felt like what he would do; he loved to play hide-and-go-seek—it made him the center of attention.

I thought about it. When the runt played that game, his notion of hiding was always to crawl *under* something, a bed, or a sofa, or an automobile, or even under the sink. I looked around. There were a lot of good places; the rocks were filled with blow holes and overhangs. I started working them over. It seemed hopeless; there must have been a hundred such places right around close.

Mr. Perrin came up to me as I was crawling out of the fourth tight spot. "The men have shined flashlights around in every one of these places," he told me. "I don't think it's much use, Shorty."

"Okay," I said, but I kept at it. I knew I could get at spots a grown man couldn't reach; I just hoped the runt hadn't picked a spot I couldn't reach.

It went on and on and I was getting cold and stiff and terribly tired. The direct sunlight is hot on the Moon, but the second you get in the shade, it's cold. Down inside those rocks it never got warm at all. The suits they gave us tourists are well enough insulated, but the extra insulation is in the gloves and the boots and the seats of the pants—and I had been spending most of my time down on my stomach, wiggling into tight places.

I was so numb I could hardly move and my whole front felt icy. Besides, it gave me one more thing to worry about—how about the runt? Was he cold, too?

If it hadn't been for thinking how those fish looked and how, maybe, the runt would be frozen stiff before I could get to him, I would have quit. I was about beat. Besides, it's rather scarey down inside those holes—you don't know what you'll come to next.

Dr. Evans took me by the arm as I came out of one of them, and touched his helmet to mine, so that I got his voice directly. "Might as well give up, son. You're knocking yourself out and you haven't covered an acre." I pulled away from him.

The next place was a little overhang, not a foot off the ground. I flashed a light into it. It was empty and didn't seem to go anywhere. Then I saw there was a turn in it. I got down flat and wiggled in. The turn opened out a little and dropped off. I didn't think it was worthwhile to go any deeper as the runt wouldn't have crawled very far in the dark, but I scrunched ahead a little farther and flashed the light down.

I saw a boot sticking out.

That's about all there is to it. I nearly bashed in my helmet getting out of there, but I was dragging the runt after me. He was limp as a cat and his face was funny. Mr. Perrin and Dr. Evans were all over me as I came out, pounding me on the back and shouting. "Is he *dead*, Mr. Perrin?" I asked, when I could get my breath. "He looks awful bad."

Mr. Perrin looked him over. "No . . . I can see a pulse in his throat. Shock and exposure, but this suit was specially built—we'll get him back fast." He picked the runt up in his arms and I took out after him.

Ten minutes later the runt was wrapped in blankets and drinking hot cocoa. I had some, too. Everybody was talking at once and Mother was crying again, but she looked normal and Dad had filled out.

He tried to write out a check for Mr. Perrin, but he brushed it off. "I don't need any reward; your boy found him. You can do me just one favor—"

"Yes?" Dad was all honey.

"Stay off the Moon. You don't belong here; you're not the pioneer type."

Dad took it. "I've already promised my wife that," he said without batting an eye. "You needn't worry."

I followed Mr. Perrin as he left and said to him privately, "Mr. Perrin—I just wanted to tell you that I'll be back, if you don't mind."

He shook hands with me and said, "I know you will, Shorty."

"It's Great to Be Back!"

"HURRY UP, ALLAN!" Home—back to Earth again! Her heart was pounding.

"Just a second." She fidgeted while her husband checked over a bare apartment. Earth-Moon freight rates made it silly to ship their belongings; except for the bag he carried, they had converted everything to cash. Satisfied, he joined her at the lift; they went on up to the administration level and there to a door marked: LUNA CITY COMMUNITY ASSOCIATION—*Anna Stone, Service Manager.*

Miss Stone accepted their apartment keys grimly. "Mr. and Mrs. MacRae. So you're actually leaving us?"

Josephine bristled. "Think we'd change our minds?"

The manager shrugged. "No. I knew nearly three years ago that you would go back—from your complaints."

"From my comp— Miss Stone, I've been as patient about the incredible inconveniences of this, this pressurized rabbit warren as anyone. I don't blame you personally, but—"

"Take it easy, Jo!" her husband cautioned her.

Josephine flushed. "Sorry, Miss Stone."

"Never mind. We just see things differently. I was here when Luna City was three air-sealed Quonset huts connected by tunnels you crawled through, on your knees." She stuck out a square hand. "I hope you enjoy being groundhogs again, I honestly do. Hot jets, good luck, and a safe landing."

Back in the lift, Josephine sputtered. " 'Groundhogs' indeed! Just because we prefer our native planet, where a person can draw a breath of fresh air—"

"You use the term," Allan pointed out.

"But I use it about people who've never been off Terra."

"We've both said more than once that we wished we had had sense enough never to have left Earth. We're groundhogs at heart, Jo."

"Yes, but— Oh, Allan, you're being obnoxious. This is the happiest day of my life. Aren't you glad to be going home? Aren't you?"

301

"Of course I am. It'll be great to be back. Horseback riding. Skiing."

"And opera. Real, live grand opera. Allan, we've simply got to have a week or two in Manhattan before we go to the country."

"I thought you wanted to feel rain on your face."

"I want that, too. I want it all at once and I can't wait. Oh, darling, it's like getting out of jail." She clung to him.

He unwound her as the lift stopped. "Don't blubber."

"Allan, you're a beast," she said dreamily. "I'm so happy."

They stopped again, in bankers' row. The clerk in the National City Bank office had their transfer of account ready. "Going home, eh? Just sign there, and your print. I envy you. Hunting, fishing."

"Surf bathing is more my style. And sailing."

"I," said Jo, "simply want to see green trees and blue sky."

The clerk nodded. "I know what you mean. It's long ago and far away. Well, have fun. Are you taking three months or six?"

"We're not coming back," Allan stated flatly. "Three years of living like a fish in an aquarium is enough."

"So?" The clerk shoved the papers toward him and added without expression, "Well—hot jets."

"Thanks." They went on up to the subsurface level and took the crosstown slidewalk out to the rocket port. The slidewalk tunnel broke the surface at one point, becoming a pressurized shed; a view window on the west looked out on the surface of the Moon—and, beyond the hills, the Earth.

The sight of it, great and green and bountiful, against the black lunar sky and harsh, unwinking stars, brought quick tears to Jo's eyes. Home—that lovely planet was hers! Allan looked at it more casually, noting the Greenwich. The sunrise line had just touched South America—must be about eight-twenty; better hurry.

They stepped off the slidewalk into the arms of some of their friends, waiting to see them off. "Hey—where have you lugs been? The *Gremlin* blasts off in seven minutes."

"But we aren't going in it," MacRae answered. "No, siree."

"What? Not going? Did you change your minds?"

Josephine laughed. "Pay no attention to him, Jack. We're going in the express instead; we swapped reservations. So we've got twenty minutes yet."

"Well! A couple of rich tourists, eh?"

"Oh, the extra fare isn't so much and I didn't want to make two changes and spend a week in space when we could be home in two days." She rubbed her bare middle significantly.

"She can't take free flight, Jack," her husband explained.

"Well, neither can I—I was sick the whole trip out. Still, I don't think you'll be sick, Jo; you're used to Moon weight now."

"Maybe," she agreed, "but there is a lot of difference between one-sixth gravity and no gravity."

Jack Crail's wife cut in. "Josephine MacRae, are you going to risk your life in an atomic-powered ship?"

"Why not, darling? You work in an atomics laboratory."

"Hummph! In the laboratory we take precautions. The Commerce Commission should never have licensed the expresses. I may be old-fashioned, but I'll go back the way I came, via Terminal and Supra-New York, in good old reliable fuel-rockets."

"Don't try to scare her, Emma," Crail objected. "They've worked the bugs out of those ships."

"Not to my satisfaction. I—"

"Never mind," Allan interrupted her. "The matter is settled, and we've still got to get over to the express launching site. Good-by, everybody! Thanks for the send-off. It's been grand knowing you. If you come back to God's country, look us up."

"Good-by, kids!" "Good-by, Jo—good-by, Allan." "Give my regards to Broadway!" "So long—be sure to write." "Good-by." "Aloha—hot jets!" They showed their tickets, entered the air lock, and climbed into the pressurized shuttle between Leyport proper and the express launching site. "Hang on, folks," the shuttle operator called back over his shoulder; Jo and Allan hurriedly settled into the cushions. The lock opened; the tunnel ahead was airless. Five minutes later they were climbing out twenty miles away, beyond the hills that shielded the lid of Luna City from the radioactive splash of the express ships.

In the *Sparrowhawk* they shared a compartment with a missionary family. The Reverend Doctor Simmons felt obliged to explain why he was traveling in luxury. "It's for the child," he told them, as his wife strapped the baby girl into a small acceleration couch rigged stretcher-fashion between her parents' couches. "Since she's never been in space, we daren't take a chance of her being sick for days on end." They all strapped down at the warning siren. Jo felt her heart begin to pound. At last . . . at long last!

The jets took hold, mashing them into the cushions. Jo had not known she could feel so heavy. This was worse, much worse, than the trip out. The baby cried as long as acceleration lasted, in wordless terror and discomfort.

After an interminable time they were suddenly weightless, as the ship went into free flight. When the terrible binding weight was free of her chest, Jo's heart felt as light as her body. Allan threw off his upper strap and sat up. "How do you feel, kid?"

"Oh, I feel fine!" Jo unstrapped and faced him. Then she hiccoughed. "That is, I think I do."

Five minutes later she was not in doubt; she merely wished to die. Allan swam out of the compartment and located the ship's surgeon, who gave her an injection. Allan waited until she had succumbed to the drug, then left for the lounge to try his own cure for spacesickness—Mothersill's Seasick Remedy washed down with champagne. Presently he had to admit that these two sovereign remedies did not work for him—or perhaps he should not have mixed them.

Little Gloria Simmons was not spacesick. She thought being weightless was fun, and went bouncing off floorplate, overhead, and bulkhead like a dimpled balloon. Jo feebly considered strangling the child, if she floated within reach—but it was too much effort.

Deceleration, logy as it made them feel, was welcome relief after nausea—except to little Gloria. She cried again, in fear and hurt, while her mother tried to explain. Her father prayed.

After a long, long time came a slight jar and the sound of the siren. Jo managed to raise her head. "What's the matter? Is there an accident?"

"I don't think so. I think we've landed."

"We can't have! We're still braking—I'm heavy as lead."

Allan grinned feebly. "So am I. Earth gravity—remember?"

The baby continued to cry.

They said good-by to the missionary family, as Mrs. Simmons decided to wait for a stewardess from the skyport. The MacRaes staggered out of the ship, supporting each other. "It can't be just the gravity," Jo protested, her feet caught in invisible quicksand. "I've taken Earth-normal acceleration in the centrifuge at the 'Y', back home—I mean back in Luna City. We're weak from spacesickness."

Allan steadied himself. "That's it. We haven't eaten anything for two days."

"Allan—didn't you eat anything either?"

"No. Not *permanently*, so to speak. Are you hungry?"

"Starving."

"How about dinner at Kean's Chophouse?"

"Wonderful. Oh, Allan, we're back!" Her tears started again.

They glimpsed the Simmonses once more, after chuting down the Hudson Valley and into Grand Central Station. While they were waiting at the tube dock for their bag, Jo saw the Reverend Doctor climb heavily out of the next tube capsule, carrying his daughter and followed by his wife. He set the child down carefully. Gloria stood for a moment, trembling on her pudgy legs, then collapsed to the dock. She lay there, crying thinly.

A spaceman—pilot, by his uniform—stopped and looked pityingly at the child. "Born in the Moon?" he asked.

"Why yes, she was, sir." Simmons' courtesy transcended his troubles.

"Pick her up and carry her. She'll have to learn to walk all over again." The spaceman shook his head sadly and glided away. Simmons looked still more troubled, then sat down on the dock beside his child, careless of the dirt.

Jo felt too weak to help. She looked around for Allan, but he was busy; their bag had arrived. It was placed at his feet and he started to pick it up, and then felt suddenly silly. It seemed nailed to the dock. He knew what was in it, rolls of microfilm and colorfilm, a few souvenirs, toilet articles, various irreplaceables—fifty pounds of mass. It *couldn't* weigh what it seemed to.

But it did. He had forgotten what fifty pounds weigh on Earth.

"Porter, mister?" The speaker was grey-haired and thin, but he scooped up the bag quite casually. Allan called out, "Come along, Jo," and followed him, feeling foolish. The porter slowed to match Allan's labored steps.

"Just down from the Moon?" he asked.

"Why, yes."

"Got a reservation?"

"No."

"You stick with me. I've got a friend on the desk at the Commodore." He led them to the Concourse slidewalk and thence to the hotel.

They were too weary to dine out; Allan had dinner sent to their room. Afterward, Jo fell asleep in a hot tub and he had trouble getting her out—she liked the support the water gave her. But he persuaded her that a rubber-foam mattress was nearly as good. They got to sleep very early.

She woke up, struggling, about four in the morning. "Allan. Allan!"

"Huh? What's the matter?" His hand fumbled at the light switch.

"Uh . . . nothing I guess. I dreamed I was back in the ship. The jets had run away with her. Allan, what makes it so stuffy in here? I've got a splitting headache."

"Huh? It can't be stuffy. This joint is air-conditioned." He sniffed the air. "I've got a headache, too," he admitted.

"Well, do something. Open a window."

He stumbled out of bed, shivered when the outer air hit him, and hurried back under the covers. He was wondering whether he could get to sleep with the roar of the city pouring in through the window when his wife spoke again. "Allan?"

"Yes. What is it?"

"Honey, I'm *cold*. May I crawl in with you?"

"Sure."

The sunlight streamed in the window, warm and mellow. When it touched his eyes, he woke and found his wife awake beside him. She sighed and snuggled. "Oh, darling, look! Blue sky—we're *home*. I'd forgotten how lovely it is."

"It's great to be back, all right. How do you feel?"

"Much better. How are you?"

"Okay, I guess." He pushed off the covers.

Jo squealed and jerked them back. "Don't do that!"

"Huh?"

"Mama's great big boy is going to climb out and close that window while mamma stays here under the covers."

"Well—all right." He could walk more easily than the night before—but it was good to get back into bed. Once there, he faced the telephone and shouted at it, "Service!"

"Order, please," it answered in a sweet contralto.

"Orange juice and coffee for two—extra coffee—six eggs, scrambled medium, and whole-wheat toast. And send up a *Times*, and the *Saturday Evening Post*."

"Ten minutes."

"Thank you." The delivery cupboard buzzed while he was shaving. He answered it and served Jo breakfast in bed. Breakfast over, he laid down his newspaper and said, "Can you pull your nose out of that magazine?"

"Glad to. The darn thing is too big and heavy to hold."

"Why don't you have the stat edition mailed to you from Luna City? Wouldn't cost more than eight or nine times as much."

"Don't be silly. What's on your mind?"

"How about climbing out of that frowsty little nest and going with me to shop for clothes?"

"Unh-uh. No, I am not going outdoors in a moonsuit."

" 'Fraid of being stared at? Getting prudish in your old age?"

"No, me lord, I simply refuse to expose myself to the outer air in six ounces of nylon and a pair of sandals. I want some warm clothes first." She squirmed further down under the covers.

"The Perfect Pioneer Woman. Going to have fitters sent up?"

"We can't afford that. Look—you're going anyway. Buy me just any old rag so long as it's warm."

MacRae looked stubborn. "I've tried shopping for you before."

"Just this once—please. Run over to Saks and pick out a street dress in a blue wool jersey, size ten. And a pair of nylons."

"Well—all right."

"That's a lamb. I won't be loafing. I've a list as long as your arm of people I've promised to call up, look up, have lunch with."

He attended to his own shopping first; his sensible shorts and singlet seemed as warm as a straw hat in a snow storm. It was not really cold and was quite balmy in the sun, but it seemed cold to a man used to a never-failing seventy-two degrees. He tried to stay underground, or stuck to the roofed-over section of Fifth Avenue.

He suspected that the salesmen had outfitted him in clothes

that made him look like a yokel. But they were warm. They were also heavy; they added to the pain across his chest and made him walk even more unsteadily. He wondered how long it would be before he got his ground-legs.

A motherly saleswoman took care of Jo's order and sold him a warm cape for her as well. He headed back, stumbling under his packages, and trying futilely to flag a ground-taxi. Everyone seemed in such a hurry! Once he was nearly knocked down by a teen-aged boy who said, "Watch it, Gramps!" and rushed off, before he could answer.

He got back, aching all over and thinking about a hot bath. He did not get it; Jo had a visitor. "Mrs. Appleby, my husband—Allan, this is Emma Crail's mother."

"Oh, how do you do, Doctor—or should it be 'Professor'?"

"Mister—"

"—when I heard you were in town I just couldn't wait to hear all about my poor darling. How is she? Is she thin? Does she look well? These modern girls—I've told her time and again that she must get out of doors—I walk in the Park every day—and look at me. She sent me a picture—I have it here somewhere; at least I think I have—and she doesn't look a bit well, undernourished. Those synthetic foods—"

"She doesn't eat synthetic foods, Mrs. Appleby."

"—must be quite impossible, I'm sure, not to mention the taste. What were you saying?"

"Your daughter doesn't live on synthetic foods," Allan repeated. "Fresh fruits and vegetables are one thing we have almost too much of in Luna City. The air-conditioning plant, you know."

"That's just what I was saying. I confess I don't see just how you get food out of air-conditioning machinery on the Moon—"

"*In* the Moon, Mrs. Appleby."

"—but it can't be healthy. Our air-conditioner at home is always breaking down and making the most horrible smells—simply unbearable, my dears—you'd think they could build a simple little thing like an air-conditioner so that—though of course if you expect them to manufacture synthetic foods as well—"

"Mrs. Appleby—"

"Yes, Doctor? What were you saying? Don't let me—"

"Mrs. Appleby," MacRae said desperately, "the air-conditioning plant in Luna City is a hydroponic farm, tanks of growing plants, green things. The plants take the carbon dioxide out of the air and put oxygen back in."

"But— Are you quite sure, Doctor? I'm sure Emma said—"

"Quite sure."

"Well . . . I don't pretend to understand these things, I'm the artistic type. Poor Herbert often said—Herbert was Emma's father; simply wrapped up in his engineering though I always saw to it that he heard good music and saw the reviews of the best books. Emma takes after her father, I'm afraid—I do wish she would give up that silly work she is in. Hardly the sort of work for a woman, do you think, Mrs. MacRae? All those atoms and neuters and things floating around in the air. I read all about it in the *Science Made Simple* column in the—"

"She's quite good at it and she seems to like it."

"Well, yes, I suppose. That's the important thing, to be happy at what you are doing no matter how silly it is. But I worry about the child—buried away from civilization, no one of her own sort to talk to, no theaters, no cultural life, no society—"

"Luna City has stereo transcriptions of every successful Broadway play." Jo's voice had a slight edge.

"Oh! Really? But it's not just going to the theater, my dear; it's the society of gentlefolk. Now when I was a girl, my parents—"

Allan butted in, loudly. "One o'clock. Have you had lunch, my dear?"

Mrs. Appleby sat up with a jerk. "Oh, heavenly days! I simply must fly. My dress designer—such a tyrant, but a genius; I must give you her address. It's been charming, my dears, and I can't thank you too much for telling me all about my poor darling. I do wish she would be sensible like you two; she knows I'm always ready to make a home for her—and her husband, for that matter. Now do come and see me, often. I love to talk to people who've been on the Moon—"

"In the Moon."

"It makes me feel closer to my darling. Good-by, then."

With the door locked behind her, Jo said, "Allan, I need a drink."

"I'll join you."

Jo cut her shopping short; it was too tiring. By four o'clock they were driving in Central Park, enjoying fall scenery to the lazy clop-clop of horse's hoofs. The helicopters, the pigeons, the streak in the sky where the Antipodes rocket had passed, made a scene idyllic in beauty and serenity. Jo swallowed a lump in her throat and whispered, "Allan, isn't it beautiful?"

"Sure is. It's great to be back. Say, did you notice they've torn up 42nd Street again?"

Back in their room, Jo collapsed on her bed, while Allan took off his shoes. He sat, rubbing his feet, and remarked, "I'm going barefooted all evening. Golly, how my feet hurt!"

"So do mine. But we're going to your father's, my sweet."

"Huh? Oh, damn, I forgot. Jo, whatever possessed you? Call him up and postpone it. We're still half dead from the trip."

"But, Allan, he's invited a lot of your friends."

"Balls of fire and cold mush! I haven't any real friends in New York. Make it next week."

" 'Next week' . . . h'm'm . . . look, Allan, let's go out to the country right away." Jo's parents had left her a tiny place in Connecticut, a worn-out farm.

"I thought you wanted a couple of weeks of plays and music first. Why the sudden change?"

"I'll show you." She went to the window, open since noon. "Look at that window sill." She drew their initials in the grime. "Allan, this city is *filthy*."

"You can't expect ten million people not to kick up dust."

"But we're breathing that stuff into our lungs. What's happened to the smog-control laws?"

"That's not smog; that's normal city dirt."

"Luna City was never like this. I could wear a white outfit there till I got tired of it. One wouldn't last a day here."

"Manhattan doesn't have a roof—and precipitrons in every air duct."

"Well, it should have. I either freeze or suffocate."

"I thought you were anxious to feel rain on your face?"

"Don't be tiresome. I want it out in the clean, green country."

"Okay. I want to start my book anyhow. I'll call your real estate agent."

"I called him this morning. We can move in anytime; he started fixing up the place when he got my letter."

It was a stand-up supper at his father's home, though Jo sat down at once and let food be fetched. Allan wanted to sit down, but his status as guest of honor forced him to stay on his aching feet. His father buttonholed him at the buffet. "Here, son, try this goose liver. It ought to go well after a diet of green cheese."

Allan agreed that it was good.

"See here, son, you really ought to tell these folks about your trip."

"No speeches, Dad. Let 'em read the *National Geographic*."

"Nonsense!" He turned around. "Quiet, everybody! Allan is going to tell us how the Lunatics live."

Allan bit his lip. To be sure, the citizens of Luna City used the term to each other, but it did not sound the same here. "Well, really, I haven't anything to say. Go on and eat."

"You talk and we'll eat." "Tell us about Looney City." "Did you see the Man-in-the-Moon?" "Go on, Allan, what's it like to live on the Moon?"

"Not 'on the Moon'—*in* the Moon."

"What's the difference?"

"Why, none, I guess." He hesitated; there was really no way to explain why the Moon colonists emphasized that they lived under the surface of the satellite planet—but it irritated him the way "Frisco" irritates a San Franciscan. " 'In the Moon' is the way we say it. We don't spend much time on the surface, except for the staff at Richardson Observatory, and the prospectors, and so forth. The living quarters are underground, naturally."

"Why 'naturally'? Afraid of meteors?"

"No more than you are afraid of lightning. We go underground for insulation against heat and cold and as support for pressure sealing. Both are cheaper and easier underground. The soil is easy to work and the interstices act like vacuum in a thermos bottle. It is vacuum."

"But Mr. MacRae," a serious-looking lady inquired, "doesn't it hurt your ears to live under pressure?"

Allan fanned the air. "It's the same pressure here—fifteen pounds."

She looked puzzled, then said, "Yes, I suppose so, but it is a little hard to imagine. I think it would terrify me to be sealed up in a cave. Suppose you had a blow-out?"

"Holding fifteen pounds pressure is no problem; engineers work in thousands of pounds per square inch. Anyhow, Luna City is compartmented like a ship. It's safe enough. The Dutch live behind dikes; down in Mississippi they have levees. Subways, ocean liners, aircraft—they're all artificial ways of living. Luna City seems strange just because it's far away."

She shivered. "It scares me."

A pretentious little man pushed his way forward. "Mr. MacRae—granted that it is nice for science and all that, why should taxpayers' money be wasted on a colony on the Moon?"

"You seem to have answered yourself," Allan told him slowly.

"Then how do you justify it? Tell me that, sir."

"It isn't necessary to justify it; the Lunar colony has paid for itself several times over. The Lunar corporations are all paying propositions. Artemis Mines, Spaceways, Spaceways Provisioning Corporation, Diana Recreations, Electronics Research Company, Lunar Biological Labs, not to mention all of Rutherford—look 'em up. I'll admit the Cosmic Research Project nicks the taxpayer a little, since it's a joint enterprise of the Harriman Foundation and the government."

"Then you admit it. It's the principle of the thing."

Allan's feet were hurting him very badly indeed. "What principle? Historically, research has always paid off." He turned his back and looked for some more goose liver.

A man touched him on the arm; Allan recognized an old schoolmate. "Allan, old boy, congratulations on the way you ticked off old Beetle. He's been needing it—I think he's some sort of a radical."

Allan grinned. "I shouldn't have lost my temper."

"A good job you did. Say, Allan, I'm going to take a couple of out-of-town buyers around to the hot spots tomorrow night. Come along."

"Thanks a lot, but we're going out in the country."

"Oh, you can't afford to miss this party. After all, you've been buried on the Moon; you owe yourself some relaxation after that deadly monotony."

Allan felt his cheeks getting warm. "Thanks just the same, but—ever seen the Earth View Room in Hotel Moon Haven?"

"No. Plan to take the trip when I've made my pile, of course."

"Well, there's a night club for you. Ever see a dancer leap thirty feet into the air and do slow rolls on the way down? Ever try a lunacy cocktail? Ever see a juggler work in low gravity?" Jo caught his eye across the room. "Er . . . excuse me, old man. My wife wants me." He turned away, then flung back over his shoulder, "Moon Haven itself isn't just a space-man's dive, by the way—it's recommended by the Duncan Hines Association."

Jo was very pale. "Darling, you've got to get me out of here. I'm suffocating. I'm really ill."

"Suits." They made their excuses.

Jo woke up with a stuffy cold, so they took a cab directly to her country place. There were low-lying clouds under them, but the weather was fine above. The sunshine and the drowsy beat of the rotors regained for them the joy of home-coming.

Allan broke the lazy revery. "Here's a funny thing, Jo. You couldn't hire me to go back to the Moon—but last night I found myself defending the Loonies every time I opened my mouth."

She nodded. "I know. Honest to Heaven, Allan, some people act as if the Earth were flat. Some of them don't really believe in anything, and some of them are so matter-of-fact that you know they don't really understand—and I don't know which sort annoys me the more."

It was foggy when they landed, but the house was clean, the agent had laid a fire and had stocked the refrigerator. They were sipping hot punch and baking the weariness out of their bones within ten minutes after the copter grounded. "This," said Allan, stretching, "is all right. It really is great to be back."

"Uh-huh. All except the highway." A new express-and-freight superhighway now ran not fifty yards from the house. They could hear the big diesels growling as they struck the grade.

"Forget the highway. Turn your back and you stare straight into the woods."

They regained their ground-legs well enough to enjoy short walks in the woods; they were favored with a long, warm Indian summer; the cleaning woman was efficient and taciturn. Allan worked on the results of three years research prepara-tory to starting his book. Jo helped him with the statistical work, got reacquainted with the delights of cooking, dreamed, and rested.

It was the day of the first frost that the toilet stopped up.

The village plumber was persuaded to show up the next day. Meanwhile they resorted to a homely little building, left over from another era and still standing out beyond the wood pile. It was spider-infested and entirely too well ventilated.

The plumber was not encouraging. "New septic tank. New sile pipe. Pay you to get new fixtures at the same time. Fifteen, sixteen hundred dollars. Have to do some calculating."

"That's all right," Allan told him. "Can you start today?"

The man laughed. "I can see plainly, Mister, that you don't know what it is to get materials and labor these days. Next spring—soon as the frost is out of the ground."

"That's impossible, man. Never mind the cost. Get it done."

The native shrugged. "Sorry not to oblige you. Good day."

When he left, Jo exploded. "Allan, he doesn't want to help us."

"Well—maybe. I'll try to get someone from Norwalk, or even from the City. You can't trudge through the snow out to that Iron Maiden all winter."

"I hope not."

"You must not. You've already had one cold." He stared morosely at the fire. "I suppose I brought it on by my misplaced sense of humor."

"How?"

"Well, you know how we've been subjected to steady kidding ever since it got noised around that we were colonials. I haven't minded much, but some of it rankled. You remember I went into the village by myself last Saturday?"

"Yes. What happened?"

"They started in on me in the barbershop. I let it ride at first, then the worm turned. I started talking about the Moon, sheer double-talk—corny old stuff like the vacuum worms and the petrified air. It was some time before they realized I was ribbing them—and when they did, nobody laughed. Our friend the rustic sanitary engineer was one of the group. I'm sorry."

"Don't be." She kissed him. "If I have to tramp through the snow, it will cheer me that you gave them back some of their sass."

The plumber from Norwalk was more helpful, but rain, and then sleet, slowed down the work. They both caught colds. On the ninth miserable day Allan was working at his desk when he heard Jo come in the back door, returning from a shopping trip. He turned back to his work, then presently became aware that she had not come in to say "hello." He went to investigate.

He found her collapsed on a kitchen chair, crying quietly. "Darling," he said urgently, "honey baby, whatever is the matter?"

She looked up. "I didn't bead to led you doe."

"Blow your nose. Then wipe your eyes. What do you mean, 'you didn't mean to let me know'. What happened?"

She let it out, punctuated with her handkerchief. First, the grocer had said he had no cleansing tissues; then, when she pointed to them, had stated that they were "sold". Finally, he had mentioned "bringing outside labor into town and taking the bread out of the mouths of honest folk".

Jo had blown up and had rehashed the incident of Allan and the barbershop wits. The grocer had simply grown more stiff. " 'Lady,' he said to me, 'I don't know whether you and your husband have been to the Moon or not, and I don't care. I don't take much stock in such things. In any case, I don't need your trade.' Oh, Allan, I'm so unhappy."

"Not as unhappy as he's going to be! Where's my hat?"

"Allan! You're not leaving this house. I won't have you fighting."

"I won't have him bullying you."

"He won't again. Oh my dear, I've tried so hard, but I can't stay here any longer. It's not just the villagers; it's the cold and the cockroaches and always having a runny nose. I'm tired out and my feet hurt all the time." She started to cry again.

"There, there! We'll leave, honey. We'll go to Florida. I'll finish my book while you lie in the sun."

"Oh, I don't want to go to Florida. *I want to go home!*"

"Huh? You mean—back to Luna City?"

"Yes. Oh, dearest, I know you don't want to, but I can't stand it any longer. It's not just the dirt and the cold and the comic-strip plumbing—it's not being understood. It wasn't any better in New York. These groundhogs don't know *anything*."

He grinned at her. "Keep sending, kid; I'm on your frequency."

"Allan!"

He nodded. "I found out I was a Loony at heart quite a while ago—but I was afraid to tell you. My feet hurt, too—and I'm damn sick of being treated like a freak. I've tried to be tolerant, but I can't stand groundhogs. I miss the folks in dear old Luna. They're civilized."

She nodded. "I guess it's prejudice, but I feel the same way."

"It's *not* prejudice. Let's be honest. What does it take to get to Luna City?"

"A ticket."

"Smarty pants. I don't mean as a tourist; I mean to get a job there. You know the answer: Intelligence. It costs a lot to send a man to the Moon and more to keep him there. To pay off, he has to be worth a lot. High I.Q., good compatibility index, superior education—everything that makes a person pleasant and easy and interesting to have around. We've been spoiled; the ordinary human cussedness that groundhogs take for granted, we now find intolerable, because Loonies *are* different. The fact that Luna City is the most comfortable environment man ever built for himself is beside the point—it's the people who count. Let's go home."

He went to the telephone—an old-fashioned, speech-only rig—and called the Foundation's New York office. While he was waiting, truncheon-like "receiver" to his ear, she said, "Suppose they won't have us?"

"That's what worries me." They knew that the Lunar companies rarely rehired personnel who had once quit; the physical examination was reputed to be much harder the second time.

"Hello . . . hello. Foundation? May I speak to the recruiting office? . . . hello—I *can't* turn on my view plate; this instrument is a hangover from the dark ages. This is Allan MacRae, physical chemist, contract number 1340729. And my wife, Josephine MacRae, 1340730. We want to sign up again. I said we wanted to sign up again . . . okay, I'll wait."

"Pray, darling, pray!"

"I'm praying— How's that! My appointment's still vacant? Fine, fine! How about my wife?" He listened with a worried look; Jo held her breath. Then he cupped the speaker. "Hey,

Jo—your job's filled. They want to know if you'll take an interim job as a junior accountant?"

"Tell 'em 'yes!' "

"That'll be fine. When can we take our exams? That's fine, thanks. Good-by." He hung up and turned to his wife. "Physical and psycho as soon as we like; professional exams waived."

"What are we waiting for?"

"Nothing." He dialed the Norwalk Copter Service. "Can you run us into Manhattan? Well, good grief, don't you have radar? All right, all right, g'-by!" He snorted. "Cabs all grounded by the weather. I'll call New York and try to get a modern cab."

Ninety minutes later they landed on top of Harriman Tower.

The psychologist was very cordial. "Might as well get this over before you have your chests thumped. Sit down. Tell me about yourselves." He drew them out, nodding from time to time. "I see. Did you ever get the plumbing repaired?"

"Well, it was being fixed."

"I can sympathize with your foot trouble, Mrs. MacRae; my arches always bother me here. That's your real reason, isn't it?"

"Oh, no!"

"Now, Mrs. MacRae—"

"Really it's not—truly. I want people to talk to who know what I mean. All that's really wrong with me is that I'm homesick for my own sort. I want to go home—and I've got to have this job to get there. I'll steady down, I know I will."

The doctor looked grave. "How about you, Mr. MacRae?"

"Well—it's about the same story. I've been trying to write a book, but I can't work. I'm homesick. I want to go back."

Feldman suddenly smiled. "It won't be too difficult."

"You mean we're in? If we pass the physical?"

"Never mind the physical—your discharge examinations are recent enough. Of course you'll have to go out to Arizona for reconditioning and quarantine. You're probably wondering why it seems so easy when it is supposed to be so hard. It's really simple: We don't want people lured back by the high pay. We do want people who will be happy and as permanent as possible—in short, we want people who think of Luna City as 'home.' Now that you're 'Moonstruck,' we want you back." He stood up and shoved out his hand.

Back in the Commodore that night, Jo was struck by a thought. "Allan—do you suppose we could get our own apartment back?"

"Why, I don't know. We could send old lady Stone a radio."

"Call her up instead, Allan. We can afford it."

"All right! I will!"

It took about ten minutes to get the circuit through. Miss Stone's face looked a trifle less grim when she recognized them.

"Miss Stone, we're coming home!"

There was the usual three-second lag, then—"Yes, I know. It came over the tape about twenty minutes ago."

"Oh. Say, Miss Stone, is our old apartment vacant?" They waited.

"I've held it; I knew you'd come back—after a bit. Welcome home, Loonies."

When the screen cleared, Jo said, "What did she mean, Allan?"

"Looks like we're in, kid. Members of the Lodge."

"I guess so—oh, Allan, look!" She had stepped to the window; scudding clouds had just uncovered the Moon. It was three days old and *Mare Fecunditatis*—the roll of hair at the back of the Lady-in-the-Moon's head—was cleared by the Sunrise line. Near the right-hand edge of that great, dark "sea" was a tiny spot, visible only to their inner eyes—Luna City.

The crescent hung, serene and silvery, over the tall buildings. "Darling, isn't it beautiful?"

"Certainly is. It'll be great to be back. Don't get your nose all runny."

"—We Also Walk Dogs"

"GENERAL SERVICES—Miss Cormet speaking!" She addressed the view screen with just the right balance between warm hospitable friendliness and impersonal efficiency. The screen flickered momentarily, then built up a stereo-picture of a dowager, fat and fretful, overdressed and underexercised.

"Oh, my dear," said the image, "I'm *so* upset. I wonder if you *can* help me."

"I'm sure we can," Miss Cormet purred as she quickly estimated the cost of the woman's gown and jewels (if real—she made a mental reservation) and decided that here was a client that could be profitable. "Now tell me your trouble. Your name first, if you please." She touched a button on the horseshoe desk which enclosed her, a button marked CREDIT DEPARTMENT.

"But it's all so *involved*," the image insisted. "Peter *would* go and break his hip." Miss Cormet immediately pressed the button marked MEDICAL. "I've *told* him that polo is dangerous. You've no idea, my dear, how a mother suffers. And just at this time, too. It's *so* inconvenient—"

"You wish us to attend him? Where is he now?"

"Attend him? Why, how silly! The Memorial Hospital will do that. We've endowed them enough, I'm sure. It's my dinner party I'm worried about. The Principessa will be so annoyed."

The answer light from the Credit Department was blinking angrily. Miss Cormet headed her off. "Oh, I see. We'll arrange it for you. Now, your name, please, and your address and present location."

"But don't you *know* my name?"

"One might guess," Miss Cormet diplomatically evaded, "but General Services always respects the privacy of its clients."

"Oh, yes, of course. How considerate. I am Mrs. Peter van Hogbein Johnson." Miss Cormet controlled her reaction. No need to consult the Credit Department for this one. But its transparency flashed at once, rating AAA—unlimited. "But I

319

don't see what you can *do*," Mrs. Johnson continued. "I can't be two places at once."

"General Services likes difficult assignments," Miss Cormet assured her. "Now—if you will let me have the details . . ."

She wheedled and nudged the woman into giving a fairly coherent story. Her son, Peter III, a slightly shopworn Peter Pan, whose features were familiar to Grace Cormet through years of stereogravure, dressed in every conceivable costume affected by the richly idle in their pastimes, had been so thoughtless as to pick the afternoon before his mother's most important social function to bung himself up—seriously. Furthermore, he had been so thoughtless as to do so half a continent away from his mater.

Miss Cormet gathered that Mrs. Johnson's technique for keeping her son safely under thumb required that she rush to his bedside at once, and, incidentally, to select his nurses. But her dinner party that evening represented the culmination of months of careful maneuvering. What was she to *do*?

Miss Cormet reflected to herself that the prosperity of General Services and her own very substantial income was based largely on the stupidity, lack of resourcefulness, and laziness of persons like this silly parasite, as she explained that General Services would see that her party was a smooth, social success while arranging for a portable full-length stereo screen to be installed in her drawing room in order that she might greet her guests and make her explanations while hurrying to her son's side. Miss Cormet would see that a most adept social manager was placed in charge, one whose own position in society was irreproachable and whose connection with General Services was known to no one. With proper handling the disaster could be turned into a social triumph, enhancing Mrs. Johnson's reputation as a clever hostess and as a devoted mother.

"A sky car will be at your door in twenty minutes," she added, as she cut in the circuit marked TRANSPORTA-TION, "to take you to the rocket port. One of our young men will be with it to get additional details from you on the way to the port. A compartment for yourself and a berth for your maid will be reserved on the 16:45 rocket for Newark. You may rest easy now. General Services will do your worrying."

"Oh, thank you, my dear. You've been such a help. You've no idea of the *responsibilities* a person in my position has."

Miss Cormet cluck-clucked in professional sympathy while

deciding that this particular old girl was good for still more fees. "You *do* look exhausted, madame," she said anxiously. "Should I not have a masseuse accompany you on the trip? Is your health at all delicate? Perhaps a physician would be still better."

"How thoughtful you are!"

"I'll send both," Miss Cormet decided, and switched off, with a faint regret that she had not suggested a specially chartered rocket. Special service, not listed in the master price schedule, was supplied on a cost-plus basis. In cases like this "plus" meant all the traffic would bear.

She switched to EXECUTIVE; an alert-eyed young man filled the screen. "Stand by for transcript, Steve," she said. "Special service, triple-A. I've started the immediate service."

His eyebrows lifted. "Triple-A—bonuses?"

"Undoubtedly. Give this old battleaxe the works—smoothly. And look—the client's son is laid up in a hospital. Check on his nurses. If any one of them has even a shred of sex-appeal, fire her out and put a zombie in."

"Gotcha, kid. Start the transcript."

She cleared her screen again; the "available-for-service" light in her booth turned automatically to green, then almost at once turned red again and a new figure built up in her screen.

No stupid waster this. Grace Cormet saw a well-kempt man in his middle forties, flat-waisted, shrewd-eyed, hard but urbane. The cape of his formal morning clothes was thrown back with careful casualness. "General Services," she said. "Miss Cormet speaking."

"Ah, Miss Cormet," he began, "I wish to see your chief."

"Chief of switchboard?"

"No, I wish to see the President of General Services."

"Will you tell me what it is you wish? Perhaps I can help you."

"Sorry, but I can't make explanations. I must see him, at once."

"And General Services is sorry. Mr. Clare is a very busy man; it is impossible to see him without appointment and without explanation."

"Are you recording?"

"Certainly."

"Then please cease doing so."

Above the console, in sight of the client, she switched off

the recorder. Underneath the desk she switched it back on again. General Services was sometimes asked to perform illegal acts; its confidential employees took no chances. He fished something out from the folds of his chemise and held it out to her. The stereo effect made it appear as if he were reaching right out through the screen.

Trained features masked her surprise—it was the sigil of a planetary official, and the color of the badge was green.

"I will arrange it," she said.

"Very good. Can you meet me and conduct me in from the waiting room? In ten minutes?"

"I will be there, Mister . . . Mister—" But he had cut off.

Grace Cormet switched to the switchboard chief and called for relief. Then, with her board cut out of service, she removed the spool bearing the clandestine record of the interview, stared at it as if undecided, and after a moment, dipped it into an opening in the top of the desk where a strong magnetic field wiped the unfixed patterns from the soft metal.

A girl entered the booth from the rear. She was blond, decorative, and looked slow and a little dull. She was neither. "Okay, Grace," she said. "Anything to turn over?"

"No. Clear board."

" 'S matter? Sick?"

"No." With no further explanation Grace left the booth, went on out past the other booths housing operators who handled unlisted services and into the large hall where the hundreds of catalogue operators worked. These had no such complex equipment as the booth which Grace had quitted. One enormous volume, a copy of the current price list of all of General Services' regular price-marked functions, and an ordinary look-and-listen enabled a catalogue operator to provide for the public almost anything the ordinary customer could wish for. If a call was beyond the scope of the catalogue it was transferred to the aristocrats of resourcefulness, such as Grace.

She took a short cut through the master files room, walked down an alleyway between dozens of chattering punched-card machines, and entered the foyer of that level. A pneumatic lift bounced her up to the level of the President's office. The President's receptionist did not stop her, nor, apparently, announce her. But Grace noted that the girl's hands were busy at the keys of her voder.

Switchboard operators do not walk into the office of the

president of a billion-credit corporation. But General Services was not organized like any other business on the planet. It was a *sui generis* business in which special training was a commodity to be listed, bought, and sold, but general resourcefulness and a ready wit were all important. In its hierarchy Jay Clare, the president, came first, his handyman, Saunders Francis, stood second, and the couple of dozen operators, of which Grace was one, who took calls on the unlimited switchboard came immediately after. They, and the field operators who handled the most difficult unclassified commissions—one group in fact, for the unlimited switchboard operators and the unlimited field operators swapped places indiscriminately.

After them came the tens of thousands of other employees spread over the planet, from the chief accountant, the head of the legal department, the chief clerk of the master files on down through the local managers, the catalogue operators to the last classified part time employee—stenographers prepared to take dictation when and where ordered, gigolos ready to fill an empty place at a dinner, the man who rented both armadillos and trained fleas.

Grace Cormet walked into Mr. Clare's office. It was the only room in the building not cluttered up with electro-mechanical recording and communicating equipment. It contained nothing but his desk (bare), a couple of chairs, and a stereo screen, which, when not in use, seemed to be Krantz' famous painting "The Weeping Buddha". The original was in fact in the sub-basement, a thousand feet below.

"Hello, Grace," he greeted her, and shoved a piece of paper at her. "Tell me what you think of that. Sance says it's lousy." Saunders Francis turned his mild pop eyes from his chief to Grace Cormet, but neither confirmed nor denied the statement.

Miss Cormet read:

CAN YOU AFFORD IT?
Can You Afford GENERAL SERVICES?
Can You Afford NOT to have General Services ? ? ? ? ?
In this jet-speed age can you afford to go on wasting time doing your own shopping, paying bills yourself, taking care of your living compartment?
We'll spank the baby and feed the cat.
We'll rent you a house and buy your shoes.

We'll write to your mother-in-law and add up your
check stubs.
No job too large; No job too small—
and all amazingly Cheap!
GENERAL SERVICES
Dial H-U-R-R-Y—U-P
P.S. *WE ALSO WALK DOGS*

"Well?" said Clare.

"Sance is right. It smells."

"Why?"

"Too logical. Too verbose. No drive."

"What's your idea of an ad to catch the marginal market?"
She thought a moment, then borrowed his stylus and wrote:

DO YOU WANT SOMEBODY MURDERED?
(Then *don't* call GENERAL SERVICES)
But for *any* other job dial HURRY-UP—*It pays!*
P.S. We also walk dogs.

"Mmmm . . . well, maybe," Mr. Clare said cautiously.
"We'll try it. Sance, give this a type B coverage, two weeks,
North America, and let me know how it takes." Francis put it
away in his kit, still with no change in his mild expression.
"Now as I was saying—"

"Chief," broke in Grace Cormet. "I made an appointment
for you in—" She glanced at her watchfinger. "—exactly two
minutes and forty seconds. Government man."

"Make him happy and send him away. I'm busy."

"Green Badge."

He looked up sharply. Even Francis looked interested.
"So?" Clare remarked. "Got the interview transcript with
you?"

"I wiped it."

"You did? Well, perhaps you know best. I like your
hunches. Bring him in."

She nodded thoughtfully and left.

She found her man just entering the public reception room
and escorted him past half a dozen gates whose guardians
would otherwise have demanded his identity and the nature of
his business. When he was seated in Clare's office, he looked
around. "May I speak with you in private, Mr. Clare?"

"Mr. Francis is my right leg. You've already spoken to
Miss Cormet."

"Very well." He produced the green sigil again and held it out. "No names are necessary just yet. I am sure of your discretion."

The President of General Services sat up impatiently. "Let's get down to business. You are Pierre Beaumont, Chief of Protocol. Does the administration want a job done?"

Beaumont was unperturbed by the change in pace. "You know me. Very well. We'll get down to business. The government may want a job done. In any case our discussion must not be permitted to leak out—"

"All of General Services relations are confidential."

"This is not confidential; this is secret." He paused.

"I understand you," agreed Clare. "Go on."

"You have an interesting organization here, Mr. Clare. I believe it is your boast that you will undertake any commission whatsoever—for a price."

"If it is legal."

"Ah, yes, of course. But legal is a word capable of interpretation. I admired the way your company handled the outfitting of the Second Plutonian Expedition. Some of your methods were, ah, ingenious."

"If you have any criticism of our actions in that case they are best made to our legal department through the usual channels."

Beaumont pushed a palm in his direction. "Oh, no, Mr. Clare—please! You misunderstand me. I was not criticising; I was admiring. Such resource! What a diplomat you would have made!"

"Let's quit fencing. What do you want?"

Mr. Beaumont pursed his lips. "Let us suppose that you had to entertain a dozen representatives of each intelligent race in this planetary system and you wanted to make each one of them completely comfortable and happy. Could you do it?"

Clare thought aloud. "Air pressure, humidity, radiation densities, atmosphere, chemistry, temperatures, cultural conditions—those things are all simple. But how about acceleration? We could use a centrifuge for the Jovians, but Martians and Titans—that's another matter. There is no way to reduce earth-normal gravity. No, you would have to entertain them out in space, or on Luna. That makes it not our pigeon; we never give service beyond the stratosphere."

Beaumont shook his head. "It won't be beyond the stratosphere. You may take it as an absolute condition that you are to accomplish your results on the surface of the Earth."

"Why?"

"Is it the custom of General Services to inquire why a client wants a particular type of service?"

"No. Sorry."

"Quite all right. But you do need more information in order to understand what must be accomplished and why it must be secret. There will be a conference, held on this planet, in the near future—ninety days at the outside. Until the conference is called no suspicion that it is to be held must be allowed to leak out. If the plans for it were to be antici- pated in certain quarters, it would be useless to hold the con- ference at all. I suggest that you think of this conference as a roundtable of leading, ah, scientists of the system, about of the same size and makeup as the session of the Academy held on Mars last spring. You are to make all preparations for the entertainments of the delegates, but you are to conceal these preparations in the ramifications of your organization until needed. As for the details—"

But Clare interrupted him. "You appear to have assumed that we will take on this commission. As you have explained it, it would involve us in a ridiculous failure. General Services does not like failures. You know and I know that low-gravity people cannot spend more than a few hours in high gravity without seriously endangering their health. Interplanetary get-togethers are always held on a low-gravity planet and al- ways will be."

"Yes," answered Beaumont patiently, "they always have been. Do you realize the tremendous diplomatic handicap which Earth and Venus labor under in consequence?"

"I don't get it."

"It isn't necessary that you should. Political psychology is not your concern. Take it for granted that it does and that the Administration is determined that *this* conference shall take place on Earth."

"Why not Luna?"

Beaumont shook his head. "Not the same thing at all. Even though we administer it, Luna City is a treaty port. Not the same thing, psychologically."

Clare shook his head. "Mr. Beaumont, I don't believe that you understand the nature of General Services, even as I fail to appreciate the subtle requirements of diplomacy. We don't work miracles and we don't promise to. We are just the handy-man of the last century, gone speed-lined and corporate. We are the latter day equivalent of the old servant class, but we are not Aladdin's genie. We don't even maintain research lab-oratories in the scientific sense. We simply make the best pos-sible use of modern advances in communication and organiza-tion to do what already *can* be done." He waved a hand at the far wall, on which there was cut in intaglio the time-honored trademark of the business—a Scottie dog, pull-ing against a leash and sniffing at a post. "*There* is the spirit of the sort of work we do. We walk dogs for people who are too busy to walk 'em themselves. My grandfather worked his way through college walking dogs. I'm still walking them. I don't promise miracles, nor monkey with politics."

Beaumont fitted his fingertips carefully together. "You walk dogs for a fee. But of course you do—you walk my pair. Five minim-credits seems rather cheap."

"It is. But a hundred thousand dogs, twice a day, soon runs up the gross take."

"The 'take' for walking this 'dog' would be considerable."

"How much?" asked Francis. It was his first sign of interest.

Beaumont turned his eyes on him. "My dear sir, the out-come of this, ah, roundtable should make a difference of liter-ally hundreds of billions of credits to this planet. We will not bind the mouth of the kine that tread the corn, if you pardon the figure of speech."

"How much?"

"Would thirty percent over cost be reasonable?"

Francis shook his head. "Might not come to much."

"Well, I certainly won't haggle. Suppose we leave it up to you gentlemen—your pardon, Miss Cormet!—to decide what the service is worth. I think I can rely on your planetary and racial patriotism to make it reasonable and proper."

Francis sat back, said nothing, but looked pleased.

"Wait a minute," protested Clare. "We haven't taken this job."

"We have discussed the fee," observed Beaumont.

Clare looked from Francis to Grace Cormet, then exam-ined his fingernails. "Give me twenty-four hours to find out whether or not it is possible," he said finally, "and I'll tell you whether or not we will walk your dog."

"I feel sure," answered Beaumont, "that you will." He gathered his cape about him.

"Okay, masterminds," said Clare bitterly, "you've bought it."

"I've been wanting to get back to field work," said Grace.

"Put a crew on everything but the gravity problem," suggested Francis. "It's the only catch. The rest is routine."

"Certainly," agreed Clare, "but you had better deliver on that. If you can't, we are out some mighty expensive preparations that we will never be paid for. Who do you want? Grace?"

"I suppose so," answered Francis. "She can count up to ten."

Grace Cormet looked at him coldly. "There are times, Sance Francis, when I regret having married you."

"Keep your domestic affairs out of the office," warned Clare. "Where do you start?"

"Let's find out who knows most about gravitation," decided Francis. "Grace, better get Doctor Krathwohl on the screen."

"Right," she acknowledged, as she stepped to the stereo controls. "That's the beauty about this business. You don't have to know anything; you just have to know where to find out."

Dr. Krathwohl was a part of the permanent staff of General Services. He had no assigned duties. The company found it worthwhile to support him in comfort while providing him with an unlimited drawing account for scientific journals and for attendance at the meetings which the learned hold from time to time. Dr. Krathwohl lacked the single-minded drive of the research scientist; he was a dilettante by nature.

Occasionally they asked him a question. It paid.

"Oh, hello, my dear!" Doctor Krathwohl's gentle face smiled out at her from the screen. "Look—I've just come across the most amusing fact in the latest issue of *Nature*. It throws a most interesting sidelight on Brownlee's theory of—"

"Just a second, Doc," she interrupted. "I'm kinda in a hurry."

"Yes, my dear?"

"Who knows the most about gravitation?"

"In what way do you mean that? Do you want an astrophysicist, or do you want to deal with the subject from a standpoint of theoretical mechanics? Farquarson would be the man in the first instance, I suppose."

"I want to know what makes it tick."

"Field theory, eh? In that case you don't want Farquarson. He is a descriptive ballistician, primarily. Dr. Julian's work in that subject is authoritative, possibly definitive."

"Where can we get hold of him?"

"Oh, but you can't. He died last year, poor fellow. A great loss."

Grace refrained from telling him how great a loss and asked, "Who stepped into his shoes?"

"Who what? Oh, you were jesting! I see. You want the name of the present top man in field theory. I would say O'Neil."

"Where is he?"

"I'll have to find out. I know him slightly—a difficult man."

"Do, please. In the meantime who could coach us a bit on what it's all about?"

"Why don't you try young Carson, in our engineering department? He was interested in such things before he took a job with us. Intelligent chap—I've had many an interesting talk with him."

"I'll do that. Thanks, Doc. Call the Chief's office as soon as you have located O'Neil. Speed." She cut off.

Carson agreed with Krathwohl's opinion, but looked dubious. "O'Neil is arrogant and non-cooperative. I've worked under him. But he undoubtedly knows more about field theory and space structure than any other living man."

Carson had been taken into the inner circle, the problem explained to him. He had admitted that he saw no solution. "Maybe we are making something hard out of this," Clare suggested. "I've got some ideas. Check me if I'm wrong, Carson."

"Go ahead, Chief."

"Well, the acceleration of gravity is produced by the proximity of a mass—right? Earth-normal gravity being produced by the proximity of the Earth. Well, what would be the effect of placing a large mass just over a particular point on the Earth's surface. Would not that serve to counteract the pull of the Earth?"

"Theoretically, yes. But it would have to be a damn big mass."

"No matter."

"You don't understand, Chief. To offset fully the pull of the Earth at a given point would require another planet the size of the Earth in contact with the Earth at that point. Of course since you don't want to cancel the pull completely, but simply to reduce it, you gain a certain advantage through using a smaller mass which would have its center of gravity closer to the point in question than would be the center of gravity of the Earth. Not enough, though. While the attraction builds up inversely as the square of the distance—in this case the half-diameter—the mass and the consequent attraction drops off directly as the *cube* of the diameter."

"What does that give us?"

Carson produced a sliderule and figured for a few moments. He looked up. "I'm almost afraid to answer. You would need a good-sized asteroid, of lead, to get anywhere at all."

"Asteroids have been moved before this."

"Yes, but what is to *hold it up?* No, Chief, there is no conceivable source of power, or means of applying it, that would enable you to hang a big planetoid over a particular spot on the Earth's surface and keep it there."

"Well, it was a good idea while it lasted," Clare said pensively.

Grace's smooth brow had been wrinkled as she followed the discussion. Now she put in, "I gathered that you could use an extremely heavy small mass more effectively. I seem to have read somewhere about some stuff that weighs *tons* per cubic inch."

"The core of dwarf stars," agreed Carson. "All we would need for that would be a ship capable of going light-years in a few days, some way to mine the interior of a star, and a new space-time theory."

"Oh, well, skip it."

"Wait a minute," Francis observed. "Magnetism is a lot like gravity, isn't it?"

"Well—yes."

"Could there be some way to *magnetize* these gazebos from the little planets? Maybe something odd about their body chemistry?"

"Nice idea," agreed Carson, "but while their internal economy is odd, it's not that odd. They are still organic."

"I suppose not. If pigs had wings they'd be pigeons."

The stereo annunciator blinked. Doctor Krathwohl announced that O'Neil could be found at his summer home in Portage, Wisconsin. He had not screened him and would prefer not to do so, unless the Chief insisted.

Clare thanked him and turned back to the others. "We are wasting time," he announced. "After years in this business we should know better than to try to decide technical questions. I'm not a physicist and I don't give a damn how gravitation works. That's O'Neil's business. And Carson's. Carson, shoot up to Wisconsin and get O'Neil on the job."

"Me?"

"You. You're an operator for this job—with pay to match. Bounce over to the port—there will be a rocket and a credit facsimile waiting for you. You ought to be able to raise ground in seven or eight minutes."

Carson blinked. "How about my job here?"

"The engineering department will be told, likewise the accounting Get going."

Without replying Carson headed for the door. By the time he reached it he was hurrying.

Carson's departure left them with nothing to do until he reported back—nothing to do, that is, but to start action on the manifold details of reproducing the physical and cultural details of three other planets and four major satellites, exclusive of their characteristic surface-normal gravitational accelerations. The assignment, although new, presented no real difficulties—to General Services. Somewhere there were persons who knew all the answers to these matters. The vast loose organization called General Services was geared to find them, hire them, put them to work. Any of the unlimited operators and a considerable percent of the catalogue operators could take such an assignment and handle it without excitement nor hurry.

Francis called in one unlimited operator. He did not even bother to select him, but took the first available on the ready panel—they were all "Can do!" people. He explained in detail the assignment, then promptly forgot about it. It would be done, and on time. The punched-card machines would chatter a bit louder, stereo screens would flash, and bright young people in all parts of the Earth would drop what they were doing and dig out the specialists who would do the actual work.

He turned back to Clare, who said, "I wish I knew what Beaumont is up to. Conference of scientists—phooey!"

"I thought you weren't interested in politics, Jay."

"I'm not. I don't give a hoot in hell about politics, inter-planetary or otherwise, except as it affects this business. But if I knew what was being planned, we might be able to squeeze a bigger cut out of it."

"Well," put in Grace, "I think you can take it for granted that the real heavy-weights from all the planets are about to meet and divide Gaul into three parts."

"Yes, but who gets cut out?"

"Mars, I suppose."

"Seems likely. With a bone tossed to the Venerians. In that case we might speculate a little in Pan-Jovian Trading Corp."

"Easy, son, easy," Francis warned. "Do that, and you might get people interested. This is a hush-hush job."

"I guess you're right. Still, keep your eyes open. There ought to be some way to cut a slice of pie before this is over."

Grace Cormet's telephone buzzed. She took it out of her pocket and said, "Yes?"

"A Mrs. Hogbein Johnson wants to speak to you."

"You handle her. I'm off the board."

"She won't talk to anyone but you."

"All right. Put her on the Chief's stereo, but stay in parallel yourself. You'll handle it after I've talked to her."

The screen came to life, showing Mrs. Johnson's fleshy face alone, framed in the middle of the screen in flat picture. "Oh, Miss Cormet," she moaned, "some dreadful mistake has been made. There is no stereo on this ship."

"It will be installed in Cincinnati. That will be in about twenty minutes."

"You are *sure?*"

"Quite sure."

"Oh, thank you! It's such a relief to talk with you. Do you know, I'm *thinking* of making you my social secretary."

"Thank you," Grace replied evenly, "but I am under contract."

"But how stupidly tiresome! You can break it."

"No, I'm sorry Mrs. Johnson. Good-by." She switched off the screen and spoke again into her telephone. "Tell Accounting to double her fee. And I *won't* speak with her again." She cut off and shoved the little instrument savagely back into her pocket. "Social secretary!"

It was after dinner and Clare had retired to his living apartment before Carson called back. Francis took the call in his own office.

"Any luck?" he asked, when Carson's image had built up.

"Quite a bit. I've seen O'Neil."

"Well? Will he do it?"

"You mean can he do it, don't you?"

"Well—can he?"

"Now that is a funny thing—I didn't think it was theoretically possible. But after talking with him, I'm convinced that it is. O'Neil has a new outlook on field theory—stuff he's never published. The man is a genius."

"I don't care," said Francis, "whether he's a genius or a Mongolian idiot—can he build some sort of a gravity thinner-outer?"

"I believe he can. I really do believe he can."

"Fine. You hired him?"

"No. That's the hitch. That's why I called back. It's like this: I happened to catch him in a mellow mood, and because we had worked together once before and because I had not aroused his ire quite as frequently as his other assistants he invited me to stay for dinner. We talked about a lot of things (you can't hurry him) and I broached the proposition. It interested him mildly—the idea, I mean; not the proposition—and he discussed the theory with me, or, rather, at me. But he won't work on it."

"Why not? You didn't offer him enough money. I guess I'd better tackle him."

"No, Mr. Francis, no. You don't understand. He's not interested in money. He's independently wealthy and has more than he needs for his research, or anything else he wants. But just at present he is busy on wave mechanics theory and he just won't be bothered with anything else."

"Did you make him realize it was important?"

"Yes and no. Mostly no. I tried to, but there isn't anything important to him but what *he* wants. It's a sort of intellectual snobbishness. Other people simply don't count."

"All right," said Francis. "You've done well so far. Here's what you do: After I switch off, you call EXECUTIVE and make a transcript of everything you can remember of what he said about gravitational theory. We'll hire the next best men, feed it to them, and see if it gives them any ideas to work on. In the meantime I'll put a crew to work on the details of Dr. O'Neil's background. He'll have a weak point some-where; it's just a matter of finding it. Maybe he's keeping a woman somewhere—"

"He's long past that."

"—or maybe he has a by-blow stashed away somewhere. We'll see. I want you to stay there in Portage. Since you can't hire him, maybe you can persuade him to hire you. You're our pipeline, I want it kept open. We've got to find something he wants, or something he is afraid of."

"He's not afraid of *anything*. I'm positive of that."

"Then he wants something. If it's not money, or women, it's something else. It's a law of nature."

"I doubt it," Carson replied slowly. "Say! Did I tell you about his hobby?"

"No. What is it?"

"It's china. In particular, Ming china. He has the best col-lection in the world, I'd guess. But I know what he wants!"

"Well, spill it, man, spill it. Don't be dramatic."

"It's a little china dish, or bowl, about four inches across and two inches high. It's got a Chinese name that means 'Flower of Forgetfulness.' "

"Hmmm—doesn't seem significant. You think he wants it pretty bad?"

"I *know* he does. He has a solid colorgraph of it in his study, where he can look at it. But it hurts him to talk about it."

"Find out who owns it and where it is."

"I know. British Museum. That's why he can't buy it."

"So?" mused Francis. "Well, you can forget it. Carry on."

Clare came down to Francis' office and the three talked it over. "I guess we'll need Beaumont on this," was his comment when he had heard the report. "It will take the Government to get anything loose from the British Museum." Francis looked morose. "Well—what's eating you? What's wrong with that?"

"I know," offered Grace. "You remember the treaty under which Great Britain entered the planetary confederation?"

"I was never much good at history."

"It comes to this: I doubt if the planetary government can touch anything that belongs to the Museum without asking the British Parliament."

"Why not? Treaty or no treaty, the planetary government is sovereign. That was established in the Brazilian Incident."

"Yeah, sure. But it could cause questions to be asked in the House of Commons and that would lead to the one thing Beaumont wants to avoid at all costs—publicity."

"Okay. What do you pro se?"

"I'd say that Sance an had better slide over to England and find out just how tigh they have the 'Flower of Forgetfulness' nailed down—and who does the nailing and what his weaknesses are."

Clare's eyes travelled past her to Francis, who was looking blank in the fashion that indicated assent to his intimates. "Okay," agreed Clare, "it's your baby. Taking a special?"

"No, we've got time to get the midnight out of New York. By-by."

"By. Call me tomorrow."

When Grace screened the Chief the next day he took one look at her and exclaimed, "Good Grief, kid! What have you done to your hair?"

"We located the guy," she explained succinctly. "His weakness is blondes."

"You've had your skin bleached, too."

"Of course. How do you like it?"

"It's stupendous—though I preferred you the way you were. But what does Sance think of it?"

"He doesn't mind—it's business. But to get down to cases, Chief, there isn't much to report. This will have to be a lefthanded job. In the ordinary way, it would take an earthquake to get anything out of that tomb."

"Don't do anything that can't be fixed!"

"You know me, Chief. I won't get you in trouble. But it will be expensive."

"Of course."

"That's all for now. I'll screen tomorrow."

She was a brunette again the next day. "What is this?" asked Clare. "A masquerade?"

"I wasn't the blonde he was weak for," she explained, "but I found the one he was interested in."

"Did it work out?"

"I think it will. Sance is having a facsimile integrated now. With luck, we'll see you tomorrow."

They showed up the next day, apparently empty handed. "Well?" said Clare, "well?"

"Seal the place up, Jay," suggested Francis. "Then we'll talk."

Clare flipped a switch controlling an interference shield which rendered his office somewhat more private than a coffin. "How about it?" he demanded. "Did you get it?"

"Show it to him, Grace."

Grace turned her back, fumbled at her clothing for a moment, then turned around and placed it gently on the Chief's desk.

It was not that it was beautiful—it *was* beauty. Its subtle simple curve had no ornamentation, decoration would have sullied it. One spoke softly in its presence, for fear a sudden noise would shatter it.

Clare reached out to touch, then thought better of it and drew his hand back. But he bent his head over it and stared down into it. It was strangely hard to focus—to allocate—the bottom of the bowl. It seemed as if his sight sank deeper and ever deeper into it, as if he were drowning in a pool of light.

He jerked up his head and blinked. "God," he whispered, "God—I didn't know such things existed."

He looked at Grace and looked away to Francis. Francis had tears in his eyes, or perhaps his own were blurred.

"Look, Chief," said Francis. "Look—couldn't we just keep it and call the whole thing off?"

"There's no use talking about it any longer," said Francis wearily. "We can't keep it, Chief. I shouldn't have suggested it and you shouldn't have listened to me. Let's screen O'Neil."

"We might just wait another day before we do anything about it," Clare ventured. His eyes returned yet again to the "Flower of Forgetfulness."

Grace shook her head. "No good. It will just be harder to-morrow. I *know*." She walked decisively over to the stereo and manipulated the controls.

O'Neil was annoyed at being disturbed and twice annoyed that they had used the emergency signal to call him to his dis-connected screen.

"What is this?" he demanded. "What do you mean by dis-turbing a private citizen when he has disconnected? Speak up —and it had better be good, or, so help me, I'll sue you!"

"We want you to do a little job of work for us, Doctor," Clare began evenly.

"What!" O'Neil seemed almost too surprised to be angry. "Do you mean to stand there, sir, and tell me that you have invaded the privacy of my home to ask *me* to work for *you?*"

"The pay will be satisfactory to you."

O'Neil seemed to be counting up to ten before answering. "Sir," he said carefully, "there are men in the world who seem to think they can buy anything, or anybody. I grant you that they have much to go on in that belief. But I am not for sale. Since you seem to be one of those persons, I will do my best to make this interview expensive for you. You will hear from my attorneys. Good night!"

"Wait a moment," Clare said urgently. "I believe that you are interested in china—"

"What if I am?"

"Show it to him, Grace." Grace brought the "Flower of Forgetfulness" up near the screen, handling it carefully, reverently.

O'Neil said nothing. He leaned forward and stared. He seemed to be about to climb through the screen. "Where did you get it?" he said at last.

"That doesn't matter."

"I'll buy it from you—at your own price."

"It's not for sale. But you may have it—if we can reach an agreement."

O'Neil eyed him. "It's stolen property."

"You're mistaken. Nor will you find anyone to take an interest in such a charge. Now about this job—"

O'Neil pulled his eyes away from the bowl. "What is it you wish me to do?"

Clare explained the problem to him. When he had concluded O'Neil shook his head. "That's ridiculous," he said.

"We have reason to feel that it is theoretically possible."

"Oh, certainly! It's theoretically possible to live forever, too. But no one has ever managed it."

"We think you can do it."

"Thank you for nothing. Say!" O'Neil stabbed a finger at him out of the screen. "You set that young pup Carson on me!"

"He was acting under my orders."

"Then, sir, I do not like your manners."

"How about the job? And this?" Clare indicated the bowl.

O'Neil gazed at it and chewed his whiskers. "Suppose," he said, at last, "I make an honest attempt, to the full extent of my ability, to supply what you want—and I fail."

Clare shook his head. "We pay only for results. Oh, your salary, of course, but not *this*. This is a bonus in addition to your salary, *if* you are successful."

O'Neil seemed about to agree, then said suddenly, "You may be fooling me with a colorgraph. I can't tell through this damned screen."

Clare shrugged. "Come see for yourself."

"I shall. I will. Stay where you are. Where are you? Damn it, sir, what's your *name?*"

He came storming in two hours later. "You've tricked me! The 'Flower' is still in England. I've investigated. I'll . . . I'll *punish* you, sir, with my own two hands."

"See for yourself," answered Clare. He stepped aside, so that his body no longer obscured O'Neil's view of Clare's desk top.

They let him look. They respected his need for quiet and let him look. After a long time he turned to them, but did not speak.

"Well?" asked Clare.

"I'll build your damned gadget," he said huskily. "I figured out an approach on the way here."

Beaumont came in person to call the day before the first session of the conference. "Just a social call, Mr. Clare," he stated. "I simply wanted to express to you my personal appreciation for the work you have done. And to deliver this." "This" turned out to be a draft on the Bank Central for the agreed fee. Clare accepted it, glanced at it, nodded, and placed it on his desk.

"I take it, then," he remarked, "that the Government is satisfied with the service rendered."

"That is putting it conservatively," Beaumont assured him. "To be perfectly truthful, I did not think you could do so much. You seem to have thought of everything. The Callistan delegation is out now, riding around and seeing the sights in one of the little tanks you had prepared. They are delighted. Confidentially, I think we can depend on their vote in the coming sessions."

"Gravity shields working all right, eh?"

"Perfectly. I stepped into their sightseeing tank before we turned it over to them. I was as light as the proverbial feather. Too light—I was very nearly spacesick." He smiled in wry amusement. "I entered the Jovian apartments, too. That was quite another matter."

"Yes, it would be," Clare agreed. "Two and a half times normal weight is oppressive to say the least."

"It's a happy ending to a difficult task. I must be going. Oh, yes, one other little matter—I've discussed with Doctor O'Neil the possibility that the Administration may be interested in other uses for his new development. In order to simplify the matter it seems desirable that you provide me with a quit-claim to the O'Neil effect from General Services."

Clare gazed thoughtfully at the "Weeping Buddha" and chewed his thumb. "No," he said slowly, "no. I'm afraid that would be difficult."

"Why not?" asked Beaumont. "It avoids the necessity of adjudication and attendant waste of time. We are prepared to recognize your service and recompense you."

"Hmmm. I don't believe you fully understand the situation, Mr. Beaumont. There is a certain amount of open territory between our contract with Doctor O'Neil and your contract with us. You asked of us certain services and certain chattels with which to achieve that service. We provided them—for a fee. All done. But our contract with Doctor O'Neil made him a full-time employee for the period of his employment. His research results and the patents embodying them are the property of General Services."

"Really?" said Beaumont. "Doctor O'Neil has a different impression."

"Doctor O'Neil is mistaken. Seriously, Mr. Beaumont—you asked us to develop a siege gun, figuratively speaking, to shoot a gnat. Did you expect us, as businessmen, to throw away the siege gun after one shot?"

"No, I suppose not. What do you propose to do?"

"We expect to exploit the gravity modulator commercially. I fancy we could get quite a good price for certain adaptations of it on Mars."

"Yes. Yes, I suppose you could. But to be brutally frank, Mr. Clare, I am afraid that is impossible. It is a matter of imperative public policy that this development be limited to terrestrials. In fact, the administration would find it necessary to intervene and make it government monopoly."

"Have you considered how to keep O'Neil quiet?"

"In view of the change in circumstances, no. What is your thought?"

"A corporation, in which he would hold a block of stock and be president. One of our bright young men would be chairman of the board." Clare thought of Carson. "There would be stock enough to go around," he added, and watched Beaumont's face.

Beaumont ignored the bait. "I suppose that this corporation would be under contract to the Government—its sole customer?"

"That is the idea."

"Mmmm . . . yes, it seems feasible. Perhaps I had better speak with Doctor O'Neil."

"Help yourself."

Beaumont got O'Neil on the screen and talked with him in low tones. Or, more properly, Beaumont's tones were low. O'Neil displayed a tendency to blast the microphone. Clare sent for Francis and Grace and explained to them what had taken place.

Beaumont turned away from the screen. "The Doctor wishes to speak with you, Mr. Clare."

O'Neil looked at him frigidly. "What is this claptrap I've had to listen to, sir? What's this about the O'Neil effect being your property?"

"It was in your contract, Doctor. Don't you recall?"

"Contract! I never read the damned thing. But I can tell you this: I'll take you to court. I'll tie you in knots before I'll let you make a fool of me that way."

"Just a moment, Doctor, please!" Clare soothed. "We have no desire to take advantage of a mere legal technicality, and no one disputes your interest. Let me outline what I had in mind—" He ran rapidly over the plan. O'Neil listened, but his expression was still unmollified at the conclusion.

"I'm not interested," he said gruffly. "So far as I am concerned the Government can have the whole thing. And I'll see to it."

"I had not mentioned one other condition," added Clare.

"Don't bother."

"I must. This will be just a matter of agreement between gentlemen, but it is essential. You have custody of the 'Flower of Forgetfulness.'"

O'Neil was at once on guard. "What do you mean, 'custody.' I own it. Understand me—*own* it."

"'Own it,'" repeated Clare. "Nevertheless, in return for the concessions we are making you with respect to your contract, we want something in return."

"What?" asked O'Neil. The mention of the bowl had upset his confidence.

"You own it and you retain possession of it. But I want your word that I, or Mr. Francis, or Miss Cormet, may come look at it from time to time—frequently."

O'Neil looked unbelieving. "You mean that you simply want to come to *look* at it?"

"That's all."

"Simply to *enjoy* it?"

"That's right."

O'Neil looked at him with new respect. "I did not understand you before, Mr. Clare. I apologize. As for the corporation nonsense—do as you like. I don't care. You and Mr. Francis and Miss Cormet may come to see the 'Flower' whenever you like. You have my word."

"Thank you, Doctor O'Neil—for all of us." He switched off as quickly as could be managed gracefully.

Beaumont was looking at Clare with added respect, too. "I think," he said, "that the next time I shall not interfere with your handling of the details. I'll take my leave. Adieu, gentlemen—and Miss Cormet."

When the door had rolled down behind him Grace remarked, "That seems to polish it off."

"Yes," said Clare. "We've 'walked his dog' for him; O'Neil has what he wants; Beaumont got what he wanted, and more besides."

"Just what is he after?"

"I don't know, but I suspect that he would like to be first president of the Solar System Federation, if and when there is such a thing. With the aces we have dumped in his lap, he might make it. Do you realize the potentialities of the O'Neil effect?"

"Vaguely," said Francis.

"Have you thought about what it will do to space navigation? Or the possibilities it adds in the way of colonization? Or its recreational uses? There's a fortune in that alone."

"What do we get out of it?"

"What do we get out of it? Money, old son. Gobs and gobs of money. There's always money in giving people what they want." He glanced up at the Scottie dog trademark.

"Money," repeated Francis. "Yeah, I suppose so."

"Anyhow," added Grace, "we can always go look at the 'Flower.'"

Searchlight

"WILL SHE HEAR YOU?"

"If she's on this face of the Moon. If she was able to get out of the ship. If her suit radio wasn't damaged. If she has it turned on. If she is alive. Since the ship is silent and no radar beacon has been spotted, it is unlikely that she or the pilot lived through it."

"She's got to be found! Stand by, Space Station. Tycho Base, acknowledge."

Reply lagged about three seconds, Washington to Moon and back. "Lunar Base, Commanding General."

"General, put every man on the Moon out searching for Betsy!"

Speed-of-light lag made the answer sound grudging. "Sir, do you know how big the Moon is?"

"No matter! Betsy Barnes is there somewhere—so every man is to search until she is found. If she's dead, your precious pilot would be better off dead, too!"

"Sir, the Moon is almost fifteen million square miles. If I used every man I have, each would have over a thousand square miles to search. I gave Betsy my best pilot. I won't listen to threats against him when he can't answer back. Not from anyone, sir! I'm sick of being told what to do by people who don't know Lunar conditions. My advice—my official advice, sir—is to let Meridian Station try. Maybe they can work a miracle."

The answer rapped back, "Very well, General! I'll speak to you later. Meridian Station! Report your plans."

Elizabeth Barnes, "Blind Betsy," child genius of the piano, had been making a USO tour of the Moon. She "wowed 'em" at Tycho Base, then lifted by jeep rocket for Farside Hardbase, to entertain our lonely missilemen behind the Moon. She should have been there in an hour. Her pilot was a safety pilot; such ships shuttled unpiloted between Tycho and Farside daily.

After lift-off her ship departed from its programming, was lost by Tycho's radars. It was . . . somewhere.

Not in space, else it would be radioing for help and its radar beacon would be seen by other ships, space stations, surface bases. It had crashed—or made emergency landing— somewhere on the vastness of Luna.

"Meridian Space Station, Director speaking—" Lag was unnoticeable; radio bounce between Washington and the station only 22,300 miles up was only a quarter second. "We've patched Earthside stations to blanket the Moon with our call. Another broadcast blankets the far side from Station Newton at the three-body stable position. Ships from Tycho are orbiting the Moon's rim—that band around the edge which is in radio shadow from us and from the Newton. If we hear—"

"Yes, yes! How about radar search?"

"Sir, a rocket on the surface looks to radar like a million other features the same size. Our one chance is to get them to answer . . . if they can. Ultrahigh-resolution radar might spot them in months—but suits worn in those little rockets carry only six hours air. We are praying they will hear and answer."

"When they answer, you'll slap a radio direction finder on them. Eh?"

"No, sir."

"In God's name, why *not?*"

"Sir, a direction finder is useless for this job. It would tell us only that the signal came from the Moon—which doesn't help."

"Doctor, you're saying that you might *hear* Betsy—and not know where she is?"

"We're as blind as she is. We hope that she will be able to lead us to her . . . if she hears us."

"How?"

"With a Laser. An intense, very tight beam of light. She'll hear it—"

"*Hear* a beam of light?"

"Yes, sir. We are jury-rigging to scan like radar—that won't show anything. But we are modulating it to give a carrier wave in radio frequency, then modulating that into audio frequency—and controlling that by a piano. If she hears us, we'll tell her to listen while we scan the Moon and run the scale on the piano—"

"All this while a little girl is *dying?*"

"Mister President—*shut up!*"

"Who was THAT?"

"I'm Betsy's father. They've patched me from Omaha. *Please*, Mr. President, keep quiet and let them work. I want my daughter back."

The President answered tightly, "Yes, Mr. Barnes. Go ahead, Director. Order anything you need."

In Station Meridian the director wiped his face. "Getting anything?"

"No. Boss, can't something be done about that Rio station? It's sitting right on the frequency!"

"We'll drop a brick on them. Or a bomb. Joe, tell the President."

"I heard, Director. They'll be silenced!"

"Sh! Quiet! Betsy—do you hear me?" The operator looked intent, made an adjustment.

From a speaker came a girl's light, sweet voice: "—to hear somebody! Gee, I'm glad! Better come quick—the Major is hurt."

The Director jumped to the microphone. "Yes, Betsy, we'll hurry. You've got to help us. Do you know where you are?"

"Somewhere on the Moon, I guess. We bumped hard and I was going to kid him about it when the ship fell over. I got unstrapped and found Major Peters and he isn't moving. Not dead—I don't think so; his suit puffs out like mine and I hear something when I push my helmet against him. I just now managed to get the door open." She added, "This can't be Farside; it's supposed to be night there. I'm in sunshine, I'm sure. This suit is pretty hot."

"Betsy, you must stay outside. You've got to be where you can see us."

She chuckled. "That's a good one. I see with my ears."

"Yes. You'll see us, with your ears. Listen, Betsy. We're going to scan the Moon with a beam of light. You'll hear it as a piano note. We've got the Moon split into the eighty-eight piano notes. When you hear one, yell, *'Now!'* Then tell us what note you heard. Can you do that?"

"Of course," she said confidently, "if the piano is in tune."

"It is. All right, we're starting—"

"Now!"

"What note, Betsy?"

"E flat the first octave above middle C."

"This note, Betsy?"

"That's what I said."

The Director called out, "Where's that on the grid? In Mare Nubium? Tell the General!" He said to the microphone, "We're finding you, Betsy honey! Now we scan just that part you're on. We change setup. Want to talk to your Daddy meanwhile?"

"Gosh! Could I?"

"Yes indeed!"

Twenty minutes later he cut in and heard: "—of course not, Daddy. Oh, a teensy bit scared when the ship fell. But people take care of me, always have."

"Betsy?"

"Yes, sir?"

"Be ready to tell us again."

"Now!" She added, "That's a bullfrog G, three octaves down."

"This note?"

"That's right."

"Get that on the grid and tell the General to get his ships up! That cuts it to a square ten miles on a side! Now, Betsy— we know *almost* where you are. We are going to focus still closer. Want to go inside and cool off?"

"I'm not too hot. Just sweaty."

Forty minutes later the General's voice rang out: "They've spotted the ship! *They see her waving!*"

Ordeal in Space

MAYBE WE SHOULD never have ventured out into space. Our race has but two basic, innate fears; noise and the fear of falling. Those terrible heights— Why should any man in his right mind let himself be placed where he could fall . . . and fall . . . and fall— But all spacemen are crazy. Everybody knows that.

The medicos had been very kind, he supposed. "You're lucky. You want to remember that, old fellow. You're still young and your retired pay relieves you of all worry about your future. You've got both arms and legs and are in fine shape."

"Fine shape!" His voice was unintentionally contemptuous.

"No, I mean it," the chief psychiatrist had persisted gently. "The little quirk you have does you no harm at all—except that you can't go out into space again. I can't honestly call acrophobia a neurosis; fear of falling is normal and sane. You've just got it a little more strongly than most—but that is not abnormal, in view of what you have been through."

The reminder set him to shaking again. He closed his eyes and saw the stars wheeling below him again. He was falling . . . falling endlessly. The psychiatrist's voice came through to him and pulled him back. "Steady, old man! Look around you."

"Sorry."

"Not at all. Now tell me, what do you plan to do?"

"I don't know. Get a job, I suppose."

"The Company will give you a job, you know."

He shook his head. "I don't want to hang around a spaceport." Wear a little button in his shirt to show that he was once a man, be addressed by a courtesy title of captain, claim the privileges of the pilots' lounge on the basis of what he used to be, hear the shop talk die down whenever he approached a group, wonder what they were saying behind his back—no, thank you!

"I think you're wise. Best to make a clean break, for a while at least, until you are feeling better."

"You think I'll get over it?"

The psychiatrist pursed his lips. "Possible. It's functional, you know. No trauma."

"But you don't think so?"

"I didn't say that. I honestly don't know. We still know very little about what makes a man tick."

"I see. Well, I might as well be leaving."

The psychiatrist stood up and shoved out his hand. "Holler if you want anything. And come back to see us in any case."

"Thanks."

"You're going to be all right. I know it."

But the psychiatrist shook his head as his patient walked out. The man did not walk like a spaceman; the easy, animal self-confidence was gone.

Only a small part of Great New York was roofed over in those days; he stayed underground until he was in that section, then sought out a passageway lined with bachelor rooms. He stuck a coin in the slot of the first one which displayed a lighted "vacant" sign, chucked his jump bag inside, and left. The monitor at the intersection gave him the address of the nearest placement office. He went there, seated himself at an interview desk, stamped in his finger prints, and started filling out forms. It gave him a curious back-to-the-beginning feeling; he had not looked for a job since pre-cadet days.

He left filling in his name to the last and hesitated even then. He had had more than his bellyful of publicity; he did not want to be recognized; he certainly did not want to be throbbed over—and most of all he did not want anyone telling him he was a hero. Presently he printed in the name "William Saunders" and dropped the forms in the slot.

He was well into his third cigarette and getting ready to strike another when the screen in front of him at last lighted up. He found himself staring at a nice-looking brunette. "Mr. Saunders," the image said, "will you come inside, please? Door seventeen."

The brunette in person was there to offer him a seat and a cigarette. "Make yourself comfortable, Mr. Saunders. I'm Miss Joyce. I'd like to talk with you about your application."

He settled himself and waited, without speaking.

When she saw that he did not intend to speak, she added, "Now take this name 'William Saunders' which you have given us—we know who you are, of course, from your prints."

"I suppose so."

"Of course I know what everybody knows about you, but your action in calling yourself 'William Saunders', Mr.—"

"Saunders."

"—Mr. Saunders, caused me to query the files." She held up a microfilm spool, turned so that he might read his own name on it. "I know quite a lot about you now—more than the public knows and more than you saw fit to put into your application. It's a good record, Mr. Saunders."

"Thank you."

"But I can't use it in placing you in a job. I can't even refer to it if you insist on designating yourself as 'Saunders.' "

"The name is Saunders." His voice was flat, rather than emphatic.

"Don't be hasty, Mr. Saunders. There are many positions in which the factor of prestige can be used quite legitimately to obtain for a client a much higher beginning rate of pay than—"

"I'm not interested."

She looked at him and decided not to insist. "As you wish. If you will go to reception room B, you can start your classification and skill tests."

"Thank you."

"*If* you should change your mind later, Mr. Saunders, we will be glad to reopen the case. Through that door, please."

Three days later found him at work for a small firm specializing in custom-built communication systems. His job was calibrating electronic equipment. It was soothing work, demanding enough to occupy his mind, yet easy for a man of his training and experience. At the end of his three months probation he was promoted out of the helper category.

He was building himself a well-insulated rut, working, sleeping, eating, spending an occasional evening at the public library or working out at the YMCA—and never, under any circumstances, going out under the open sky nor up to any height, not even a theater balcony.

He tried to keep his past life shut out of his mind, but his memory of it was still fresh; he would find himself daydreaming—the star-sharp, frozen sky of Mars, or the roaring night life of Venusburg. He would see again the swollen, ruddy bulk of Jupiter hanging over the port on Ganymede, its oblate bloated shape impossibly huge and crowding the sky.

Or he might, for a time, feel again the sweet quiet of the long watches on the lonely reaches between the planets. But such reveries were dangerous; they cut close to the edge of his new peace of mind. It was easy to slide over and find himself clinging for life to his last handhold on the steel sides of the *Valkyrie*, fingers numb and failing, and nothing below him but the bottomless well of space.

Then he would come back to Earth, shaking uncontrollably and gripping his chair or the workbench.

The first time it had happened at work he had found one of his benchmates, Joe Tully, staring at him curiously. "What's the trouble, Bill?" he had asked. "Hangover?"

"Nothing," he had managed to say. "Just a chill."

"You better take a pill. Come on—let's go to lunch."

Tully led the way to the elevator; they crowded in. Most of the employes—even the women—preferred to go down via the drop chute, but Tully always used the elevator. "Saunders", of course, never used the drop chute; this had eased them into the habit of lunching together. He knew that the chute was safe, that, even if the power should fail, safety nets would snap across at each floor level—but he could not force himself to step off the edge.

Tully said publicly that a drop-chute landing hurt his arches, but he confided privately to Saunders that he did not trust automatic machinery. Saunders nodded understandingly but said nothing. It warmed him toward Tully. He began feeling friendly and not on the defensive with another human being for the first time since the start of his new life. He began to want to tell Tully the truth about himself. If he could be sure that Joe would not insist on treating him as a hero—not that he really objected to the role of hero. As a kid, hanging around spaceports, trying to wangle chances to go inside the ships, cutting classes to watch take-offs, he had dreamed of being a "hero" someday, a hero of the spaceways, returning in triumph from some incredible and dangerous piece of exploration. But he was troubled by the fact that he still had the same picture of what a hero should look like and how he should behave; it did not include shying away from open windows, being fearful of walking across an open square, and growing too upset to speak at the mere thought of boundless depths of space.

Tully invited him home for dinner. He wanted to go, but fended off the invitation while he inquired where Tully lived. The Shelton Homes, Tully told him, naming one of those great, boxlike warrens that used to disfigure the Jersey flats. "It's a long way to come back," Saunders said doubtfully, while turning over in his mind ways to get there without exposing himself to the things he feared.

"You won't have to come back," Tully assured him. "We've got a spare room. Come on. My old lady does her own cooking—that's why I keep her."

"Well, all right," he conceded. "Thanks, Joe." The La Guardia Tube would take him within a quarter of a mile; if he could not find a covered way he would take a ground cab and close the shades.

Tully met him in the hall and apologized in a whisper. "Meant to have a young lady for you, Bill. Instead we've got my brother-in-law. He's a louse. Sorry."

"Forget it, Joe. I'm glad to be here." He was indeed. The discovery that Bill's flat was on the thirty-fifth floor had dismayed him at first, but he was delighted to find that he had no feeling of height. The lights were on, the windows occulted, the floor under him was rock solid; he felt warm and safe. Mrs. Tully turned out in fact to be a good cook, to his surprise—he had the bachelor's usual distrust of amateur cooking. He let himself go to the pleasure of feeling at home and safe and wanted; he managed not even to hear most of the aggressive and opinionated remarks of Joe's in-law.

After dinner he relaxed in an easy chair, glass of beer in hand, and watched the video screen. It was a musical comedy; he laughed more heartily than he had in months. Presently the comedy gave way to a religious program, the National Cathedral Choir; he let it be, listening with one ear and giving some attention to the conversation with the other.

The choir was more than half way through *Prayer for Travelers* before he became fully aware of what they were singing:

> "—hear us when we pray to Thee
> For those in peril on the sea.
>
> "Almighty Ruler of the all
> Whose power extends to great and small,
> Who guides the stars with steadfast law,

Whose least creation fills with awe;
Oh, grant Thy mercy and Thy grace
To those who venture into space."

He wanted to switch it off, but he had to hear it out, he could not stop listening to it, though it hurt him in his heart with the unbearable homesickness of the hopelessly exiled. Even as a cadet this one hymn could fill his eyes with tears; now he kept his face turned away from the others to try to hide from them the drops wetting his cheeks.

When the choir's "amen" let him do so he switched quickly to some other—any other—program and remained bent over the instrument, pretending to fiddle with it, while he composed his features. Then he turned back to the company, outwardly serene, though it seemed to him that anyone could see the hard, aching knot in his middle.

The brother-in-law was still sounding off.

"We ought to annex 'em," he was saying. "That's what we ought to do. Three-Planets Treaty—what a lot of ruddy rot! What right have they got to tell us what we can and can't do on Mars?"

"Well, Ed," Tully said mildly, "it's their planet, isn't it? They were there first."

Ed brushed it aside. "Did we ask the Indians whether or not they wanted us in North America? Nobody has any right to hang on to something he doesn't know how to use. With proper exploitation—"

"You been speculating, Ed?"

"Huh? It wouldn't be speculation if the government wasn't made up of a bunch of weak-spined old women. 'Rights of Natives,' indeed. What rights do a bunch of degenerates have?"

Saunders found himself contrasting Ed Schultz with Knath Sooth, the only Martian he himself had ever known well. Gentle Knath, who had been old before Ed was born, and yet was rated as young among his own kind. Knath . . . why, Knath could sit for hours with a friend or trusted acquaintance, saying nothing, needing to say nothing. "Growing together" they called it—his entire race had so grown together that they had needed no government, until the Earthman came.

Saunders had once asked his friend why he exerted himself so little, was satisfied with so little. More than an hour passed and Saunders was beginning to regret his inquisitiveness when Knath replied, "My fathers have labored and I am weary."

Saunders sat up and faced the brother-in-law. "They are not degenerate."

"Huh? I suppose *you* are an expert!"

"The Martians aren't degenerate, they're just tired," Saunders persisted.

Tully grinned. His brother-in-law saw it and became surly. "What gives you the right to an opinion? Have you ever been to Mars?"

Saunders realized suddenly that he had let his censors down. "Have you?" he answered cautiously.

"That's beside the point. The best minds all agree—" Bill let him go on and did not contradict him again. It was a relief when Tully suggested that, since they all had to be up early, maybe it was about time to think about beginning to get ready to go to bed.

He said goodnight to Mrs. Tully and thanked her for a wonderful dinner, then followed Tully into the guest room. "Only way to get rid of that family curse we're saddled with, Bill," he apologized. "Stay up as long as you like." Tully stepped to the window and opened it. "You'll sleep well here. We're up high enough to get honest-to-goodness fresh air." He stuck his head out and took a couple of big breaths. "Nothing like the real article," he continued as he withdrew from the window. "I'm a country boy at heart. What's the matter, Bill?"

"Nothing. Nothing at all."

"I thought you looked a little pale. Well, sleep tight. I've already set your bed for seven; that'll give us plenty of time."

"Thanks, Joe. Goodnight." As soon as Tully was out of the room he braced himself, then went over and closed the window. Sweating, he turned away and switched the ventilation back on. That done, he sank down on the edge of the bed.

He sat there for a long time, striking one cigarette after another. He knew too well that the peace of mind he thought he had regained was unreal. There was nothing left to him but shame and a long, long hurt. To have reached the point where he had to knuckle under to a tenth-rate knothead like Ed Schultz—it would have been better if he had never come out of the *Valkyrie* business.

Presently he took five grains of "Fly-Rite" from his pouch, swallowed it, and went to bed. He got up almost at once, forced himself to open the window a trifle, then compromised by changing the setting of the bed so that it would not turn out the lights after he got to sleep.

He had been asleep and dreaming for an indefinitely long time. He was back in space again—indeed, he had never been away from it. He was happy, with the full happiness of a man who has awakened to find it was only a bad dream.

The crying disturbed his serenity. At first it made him only vaguely uneasy, then he began to feel in some way responsible —he must do something about it. The transition to falling had only dream logic behind it, but it was real to him. He was grasping, his hands were slipping, had slipped—and there was nothing under him but the black emptiness of space—

He was awake and gasping, on Joe Tully's guest-room bed; the lights burned bright around him.

But the crying persisted.

He shook his head, then listened. It was real all right. Now he had it identified—a cat, a kitten by the sound of it.

He sat up. Even if he had not had the spaceman's traditional fondness for cats, he would have investigated. However, he liked cats for themselves, quite aside from their neat shipboard habits, their ready adaptability to changing accelerations, and their usefulness in keeping the ship free of those other creatures that go wherever man goes. So he got up at once and looked for this one.

A quick look around showed him that the kitten was not in the room, and his ear led him to the correct spot; the sound came in through the slightly opened window. He shied off, stopped, and tried to collect his thoughts.

He told himself that it was unnecessary to do anything more; if the sound came in through his window, then it must be because it came out of some nearby window. But he knew that he was lying to himself; the sound was close by. In some impossible way the cat was just outside his window, thirty-five stories above the street.

He sat down and tried to strike a cigarette, but the tube broke in his fingers. He let the fragments fall to the floor, got up and took six nervous steps toward the window, as if he were being jerked along. He sank down to his knees, grasped the window and threw it wide open, then clung to the windowsill, his eyes tight shut.

After a time the sill seemed to steady a bit. He opened his eyes, gasped, and shut them again. Finally he opened them again, being very careful not to look out at the stars, not to look down at the street. He had half expected to find the cat on a balcony outside his room—it seemed the only reasonable explanation. But there was no balcony, no place at all where a cat could reasonably be.

However, the mewing was louder than ever. It seemed to come from directly under him. Slowly he forced his head out, still clinging to the sill, and made himself look down. Under him, about four feet lower than the edge of the window, a narrow ledge ran around the side of the building. Seated on it was a woe-begone ratty-looking kitten. It stared up at him and meowed again.

It was barely possible that, by clinging to the sill with one hand and making a long arm with the other, he could reach it without actually going out the window, he thought—if he could bring himself to do it. He considered calling Tully, then thought better of it. Tully was shorter than he was, had less reach. And the kitten had to be rescued now, before the fluff-brained idiot jumped or fell.

He tried for it. He shoved his shoulders out, clung with his left arm and reached down with his right. Then he opened his eyes and saw that he was a foot or ten inches away from the kitten still. It sniffed curiously in the direction of his hand.

He stretched till his bones cracked. The kitten promptly skittered away from his clutching fingers, stopping a good six feet down the ledge. There it settled down and commenced washing its face.

He inched back inside and collapsed, sobbing, on the floor underneath the window. "I can't do it," he whispered. "I can't do it. Not again—"

The Rocket Ship *Valkyrie* was two hundred and forty-nine days out from Earth-Luna Space Terminal and approaching Mars Terminal on Deimos, outer Martian satellite. William Cole, Chief Communications Officer and relief pilot, was sleeping sweetly when his assistant shook him. "Hey! Bill! Wake up—we're in a jam."

"Huh? Wazzat?" But he was already reaching for his socks. "What's the trouble, Tom?"

Fifteen minutes later he knew that his junior officer had not exaggerated; he was reporting the facts to the Old Man— the primary piloting radar was out of whack. Tom Sandburg had discovered it during a routine check, made as soon as

Mars was inside the maximum range of the radar pilot. The captain had shrugged. "Fix it, Mister—and be quick about it. We need it."

Bill Cole shook his head. "There's nothing wrong with it, Captain—inside. She acts as if the antenna were gone completely."

"That's impossible. We haven't even had a meteor alarm."

"Might be anything, Captain. Might be metal fatigue and it just fell off. But we've got to replace that antenna. Stop the spin on the ship and I'll go out and fix it. I can jury-rig a replacement while she loses her spin."

The *Valkyrie* was a luxury ship, of her day. She was assembled long before anyone had any idea of how to produce an artificial gravity field. Nevertheless she had pseudogravity for the comfort of her passengers. She spun endlessly around her main axis, like a shell from a rifled gun; the resulting angular acceleration—miscalled "centrifugal force"—kept her passengers firm in their beds, or steady on their feet. The spin was started as soon as her rockets stopped blasting at the beginning of a trip and was stopped only when it was necessary to maneuver into a landing. It was accomplished, not by magic, but by reaction against the contrary spin of a flywheel located on her centerline.

The captain looked annoyed. "I've started to take the spin off, but I can't wait that long. Jury-rig the astrogational radar for piloting."

Cole started to explain why the astrogational radar could not be adapted to short-range work, then decided not to try. "It can't be done, sir. It's a technical impossibility."

"When I was your age I could jury-rig anything! Well, find me an answer, Mister. I can't take this ship down blind. Not even for the Harriman Medal."

Bill Cole hesitated for a moment before replying, "I'll have to go out while she's still got spin on her, Captain, and make the replacement. There isn't any other way to do it."

The captain looked away from him, his jaw muscles flexed. "Get the replacement ready. Hurry up about it."

Cole found the captain already at the airlock when he arrived with the gear he needed for the repair. To his surprise the Old Man was suited up. "Explain to me what I'm to do," he ordered Bill.

"You're not going out, sir?" The captain simply nodded.

Bill took a look at his captain's waist line, or where his

waist line used to be. Why, the Old Man must be thirty-five if he were a day! "I'm afraid I can't explain too clearly. I had expected to make the repair myself."

"I've never asked a man to do a job I wouldn't do myself. Explain it to me."

"Excuse me, sir—but can you chin yourself with one hand?"

"What's that got to do with it?"

"Well, we've got forty-eight passengers, sir, and—"

"Shut up!"

Sandburg and he, both in space suits, helped the Old Man down the hole after the inner door of the lock was closed and the air exhausted. The space beyond the lock was a vast, star-flecked emptiness. With spin still on the ship, every direction outward was "down," down for millions of uncounted miles. They put a safety line on him, of course—nevertheless it gave him a sinking feeling to see the captain's head disappear in the bottomless, black hole.

The line paid out steadily for several feet, then stopped. When it had been stopped for several minutes, Bill leaned over and touched his helmet against Sandburg's. "Hang on to my feet. I'm going to take a look."

He hung head down out the lock and looked around. The captain was stopped, hanging by both hands, nowhere near the antenna fixture. He scrambled back up and reversed himself. "I'm going out."

It was no great trick, he found, to hang by his hands and swing himself along to where the captain was stalled. The *Valkyrie* was a space-to-space ship, not like the sleek-sided jobs we see around earthports; she was covered with handholds for the convenience of repairmen at the terminals. Once he reached him, it was possible, by grasping the same steel rung that the captain clung to, to aid him in swinging back to the last one he had quitted. Five minutes later Sandburg was pulling the Old Man up through the hole and Bill was scrambling after him.

He began at once to unbuckle the repair gear from the captain's suit and transfer it to his own. He lowered himself back down the hole and was on his way before the older man had recovered enough to object, if he still intended to.

Swinging out to where the antenna must be replaced was not too hard, though he had all eternity under his toes. The suit impeded him a little—the gloves were clumsy—but he was used to spacesuits. He was a little winded from helping the captain, but he could not stop to think about that. The increased spin bothered him somewhat; the airlock was nearer the axis of spin than was the antenna—he felt heavier as he moved out.

Getting the replacement antenna shipped was another matter. It was neither large nor heavy, but he found it impossible to fasten it into place. He needed one hand to cling by, one to hold the antenna, and one to handle the wrench. That left him shy one hand, no matter how he tried it.

Finally he jerked his safety line to signal Sandburg for more slack. Then he unshackled it from his waist, working with one hand, passed the end twice through a handhold and knotted it; he left about six feet of it hanging free. The shackle on the free end he fastened to another handhold. The result was a loop, a bight, an improvised bosun's chair, which would support his weight while he man-handled the antenna into place. The job went fairly quickly then.

He was almost through. There remained one bolt to fasten on the far side, away from where he swung. The antenna was already secured at two points and its circuit connection made. He decided he could manage it with one hand. He left his perch and swung over, monkey fashion.

The wrench slipped as he finished tightening the bolt; it slipped from his grasp, fell free. He watched it go, out and out and out, down and down and down, until it was so small he could no longer see it. It made him dizzy to watch it, bright in the sunlight against the deep black of space. He had been too busy to look down, up to now.

He shivered. "Good thing I was through with it," he said. "It would be a long walk to fetch it." He started to make his way back.

He found that he could not.

He had swung past the antenna to reach his present position, using a grip on his safety-line swing to give him a few inches more reach. Now the loop of line hung quietly, just out of reach. There was no way to reverse the process.

He hung by both hands and told himself not to get panicky —he must think his way out. Around the other side? No, the steel skin of the *Valkyrie* was smooth there—no handhold for more than six feet. Even if he were not tired—and he had to admit that he was, tired and getting a little cold—even if he were fresh, it was an impossible swing for anyone not a chimpanzee.

He looked down—and regretted it.

There was nothing below him but stars, down and down, endlessly. Stars, swinging past as the ship spun with him, emptiness of all time and blackness and cold.

He found himself trying to hoist himself bodily onto the single narrow rung he clung to, trying to reach it with his toes. It was a futile, strength-wasting excess. He quieted his panic sufficiently to stop it, then hung limp.

It was easier if he kept his eyes closed. But after a while he always had to open them and look. The Big Dipper would swing past and then, presently, Orion. He tried to compute the passing minutes in terms of the number of rotations the ship made, but his mind would not work clearly, and, after a while, he would have to shut his eyes.

His hands were becoming stiff—and cold. He tried to rest them by hanging by one hand at a time. He let go with his left hand, felt pins-and-needles course through it, and beat it against his side. Presently it seemed time to spell his right hand.

He could no longer reach up to the rung with his left hand. He did not have the power left in him to make the extra pull; he was fully extended and could not shorten himself enough to get his left hand up.

He could no longer feel his right hand at all.

He could see it slip. It was slipping—

The sudden release in tension let him know that he was falling . . . falling. The ship dropped away from him.

He came to with the captain bending over him. "Just keep quiet, Bill."

"Where—"

"Take it easy. The patrol from Deimos was already close by when you let go. They tracked you on the 'scope, matched orbits with you, and picked you up. First time in history, I guess. Now keep quiet. You're a sick man—you hung there more than two hours, Bill."

The meowing started up again, louder than ever. He got up on his knees and looked out over the windowsill. The kitten was still away to the left on the ledge. He thrust his head cautiously out a little further, remembering not to look at anything but the kitten and the ledge. "Here, kitty!" he called. "Here, kit-kit-kitty! Here, kitty, come kitty!"

The kitten stopped washing and managed to look puzzled.

"Come, kitty," he repeated softly. He let go the windowsill with his right hand and gestured toward it invitingly. The kitten approached about three inches, then sat down. "Here, kitty," he pleaded and stretched his arm as far as possible.

The fluff ball promptly backed away again.

He withdrew his arm and thought about it. This was getting nowhere, he decided. If he were to slide over the edge and stand on the ledge, he could hang on with one arm and be perfectly safe. He knew that, he knew it would be safe—he needn't look down!

He drew himself back inside, reversed himself, and, with great caution, gripping the sill with both arms, let his legs slide down the face of the building. He focused his eyes carefully on the corner of the bed.

The ledge seemed to have been moved. He could not find it, and was beginning to be sure that he had reached past it, when he touched it with one toe—then he had both feet firmly planted on it. It seemed about six inches wide. He took a deep breath.

Letting go with his right arm, he turned and faced the kitten. It seemed interested in the procedure but not disposed to investigate more closely. If he were to creep along the ledge, holding on with his left hand, he could just about reach it from the corner of the window—

He moved his feet one at a time, baby fashion, rather than pass one past the other. By bending his knees a trifle, and leaning, he could just manage to reach it. The kitten sniffed his groping fingers, then leaped backward. One tiny paw missed the edge; it scrambled and regained its footing. "You little idiot!" he said indignantly, "do you want to bash your brains out?

"If any," he added. The situation looked hopeless now; the baby cat was too far away to be reached from his anchorage at the window, no matter how he stretched. He called "Kitty, kitty" rather hopelessly, then stopped to consider the matter.

He could give it up.

He could prepare himself to wait all night in the hope that the kitten would decide to come closer. Or he could go get it.

The ledge was wide enough to take his weight. If he made

himself small, flat to the wall, no weight rested on his left arm. He moved slowly forward, retaining the grip on the window as long as possible, inching so gradually that he hardly seemed to move. When the window frame was finally out of reach, when his left hand was flat to smooth wall, he made the mistake of looking down, down, past the sheer wall at the glowing pavement far below.

He pulled his eyes back and fastened them on a spot on the wall, level with his eyes and only a few feet away. He was still there!

And so was the kitten. Slowly he separated his feet, moving his right foot forward, and bent his knees. He stretched his right hand along the wall, until it was over and a little beyond the kitten.

He brought it down in a sudden swipe, as if to swat a fly. He found himself with a handful of scratching, biting fur.

He held perfectly still then, and made no attempt to check the minor outrages the kitten was giving him. Arms still outstretched, body flat to the wall, he started his return. He could not see where he was going and could not turn his head without losing some little of his margin of balance. It seemed a long way back, longer than he had come, when at last the fingertips of his left hand slipped into the window opening.

He backed up the rest of the way in a matter of seconds, slid both arms over the sill, then got his right knee over. He rested himself on the sill and took a deep breath. "Man!" he said aloud. "That was a tight squeeze. You're a menace to traffic, little cat."

He glanced down at the pavement. It was certainly a long way down—looked hard, too.

He looked up at the stars. Mighty nice they looked and mighty bright. He braced himself in the window frame, back against one side, foot pushed against the other, and looked at them. The kitten settled down in the cradle of his stomach and began to buzz. He stroked it absent-mindedly and reached for a cigarette. He would go out to the port and take his physical and his psycho tomorrow, he decided. He scratched the kitten's ears. "Little fluffhead," he said, "how would you like to take a long, long ride with me?"

The Green Hills of Earth

THIS IS THE STORY of Rhysling, the Blind Singer of the Spaceways—but not the official version. You sang his words in school:

> *"I pray for one last landing*
> *On the globe that gave me birth;*
> *Let me rest my eyes on the fleecy skies*
> *And the cool, green hills of Earth."*

Or perhaps you sang in French, or German. Or it might have been Esperanto, while Terra's rainbow banner rippled over your head.

The language does not matter—it was certainly an *Earth* tongue. No one has ever translated *"Green Hills"* into the lisping Venerian speech; no Martian ever croaked and whispered it in the dry corridors. This is ours. We of Earth have exported everything from Hollywood crawlies to synthetic radioactives, but this belongs solely to Terra, and to her sons and daughters wherever they may be.

We have all heard many stories of Rhysling. You may even be one of the many who have sought degrees, or acclaim, by scholarly evaluations of his published works—*Songs of the Spaceways, The Grand Canal, and other Poems, High and Far,* and *"UP SHIP!"*

Nevertheless, although you have sung his songs and read his verses, in school and out your whole life, it is at least an even money bet—unless you are a spaceman yourself—that you have never even heard of most of Rhysling's unpublished songs, such items as *Since the Pusher Met My Cousin, That Red-Headed Venusburg Gal, Keep Your Pants On, Skipper,* or *A Space Suit Built for Two.*

Nor can we quote them in a family magazine.

Rhysling's reputation was protected by a careful literary executor and by the happy chance that he was never interviewed. *Songs of the Spaceways* appeared the week he died; when it became a best seller, the publicity stories about him were pieced together from what people remembered about him plus the highly colored handouts from his publishers.

The resulting traditional picture of Rhysling is about as authentic as George Washington's hatchet or King Alfred's cakes.

In truth you would not have wanted him in your parlor; he was not socially acceptable. He had a permanent case of sun itch, which he scratched continually, adding nothing to his negligible beauty.

Van der Voort's portrait of him for the Harriman Centennial edition of his works shows a figure of high tragedy, a solemn mouth, sightless eyes concealed by black silk bandage. He was never solemn! His mouth was always open, singing, grinning, drinking, or eating. The bandage was any rag, usually dirty. After he lost his sight he became less and less neat about his person.

"Noisy" Rhysling was a jetman, second class, with eyes as good as yours, when he signed on for a loop trip to the Jovian asteroids in the R.S. *Goshawk*. The crew signed releases for everything in those days; a Lloyd's associate would have laughed in your face at the notion of insuring a spaceman. The Space Precautionary Act had never been heard of, and the Company was responsible only for wages, if and when. Half the ships that went further than Luna City never came back. Spacemen did not care; by preference they signed for shares, and any one of them would have bet you that he could jump from the 200th floor of Harriman Tower and ground safely, if you offered him three to two and allowed him rubber heels for the landing.

Jetmen were the most carefree of the lot and the meanest. Compared with them the masters, the radarmen, and the astrogators (there were no supers nor stewards in those days) were gentle vegetarians. Jetmen knew too much. The others trusted the skill of the captain to get them down safely; jetmen knew that skill was useless against the blind and fitful devils chained inside their rocket motors.

The *Goshawk* was the first of Harriman's ships to be converted from chemical fuel to atomic power-piles—or rather the first that did not blow up. Rhysling knew her well; she was an old tub that had plied the Luna City run, Supra-New York space station to Leyport and back, before she was converted for deep space. He had worked the Luna run in her and had been along on the first deep space trip, Drywater on Mars—and back, to everyone's surprise.

He should have made chief engineer by the time he signed for the Jovian loop trip, but, after the Drywater pioneer trip, he had been fired, blacklisted, and grounded at Luna City for having spent his time writing a chorus and several verses at a time when he should have been watching his gauges. The song was the infamous *The Skipper is a Father to his Crew,* with the uproariously unprintable final couplet.

The blacklist did not bother him. He won an accordion from a Chinese barkeep in Luna City by cheating at one-thumb and thereafter kept going by singing to the miners for drinks and tips until the rapid attrition in spacemen caused the Company agent there to give him another chance. He kept his nose clean on the Luna run for a year or two, got back into deep space, helped give Venusburg its original ripe reputation, strolled the banks of the Grand Canal when a second colony was established at the ancient Martian capital, and froze his toes and ears on the second trip to Titan.

Things moved fast in those days. Once the power-pile drive was accepted the number of ships that put out from the Luna-Terra system was limited only by the availability of crews. Jetmen were scarce; the shielding was cut to a minimum to save weight and few married men cared to risk possible exposure to radioactivity. Rhysling did not want to be a father, so jobs were always open to him during the golden days of the claiming boom. He crossed and recrossed the system, singing the doggerel that boiled up in his head and chording it out on his accordion.

The master of the *Goshawk* knew him; Captain Hicks had been astrogator on Rhysling's first trip in her. "Welcome home, Noisy," Hicks had greeted him. "Are you sober, or shall I sign the book for you?"

"You can't get drunk on the bug juice they sell here, Skipper." He signed and went below, lugging his accordion.

Ten minutes later he was back. "Captain," he stated darkly, "that number two jet ain't fit. The cadmium dampers are warped."

"Why tell me? Tell the Chief."

"I did, but he says they will do. He's wrong."

The captain gestured at the book. "Scratch out your name and scram. We raise ship in thirty minutes."

Rhysling looked at him, shrugged, and went below again.

It is a long climb to the Jovian planetoids; a Hawk-class clunker had to blast for three watches before going into free flight. Rhysling had the second watch. Damping was done by hand then, with a multiplying vernier and a danger gauge. When the gauge showed red, he tried to correct it—no luck.

Jetmen don't wait; that's why they are jetmen. He slapped the emergency discover and fished at the hot stuff with the tongs. The lights went out, he went right ahead. A jetman has to know his power room the way your tongue knows the inside of your mouth.

He sneaked a quick look over the top of the lead baffle when the lights went out. The blue radioactive glow did not help him any; he jerked his head back and went on fishing by touch.

When he was done he called over the tube, "Number two jet out. And for crissake get me some light down here!"

There was light—the emergency circuit—but not for him. The blue radioactive glow was the last thing his optic nerve ever responded to.

2

"*As Time and Space come bending back to shape this star-specked scene,*
The tranquil tears of tragic joy still spread their silver sheen;
Along the Grand Canal still soar the fragile Towers of Truth;
Their fairy grace defends this place of Beauty, calm and couth.

"*Bone-tired the race that raised the Towers, forgotten are their lores;*
Long gone the gods who shed the tears that lap these crystal shores.
Slow beats the time-worn heart of Mars beneath this icy sky;
The thin air whispers voicelessly that all who live must die—

"*Yet still the lacy Spires of Truth sing Beauty's madrigal*
And she herself will ever dwell along the Grand Canal!"

—from *The Grand Canal*, by permission of
Lux Transcriptions, Ltd., London and Luna City

ON THE SWING BACK they set Rhysling down on Mars at Drywater; the boys passed the hat and the skipper kicked in a half month's pay. That was all—*finish*—just another space bum who had not had the good fortune to finish it off when his luck ran out. He holed up with the prospectors and archeologists at How-Far? for a month or so, and could probably have stayed forever in exchange for his songs and his accordion playing. But spacemen die if they stay in one place; he hooked a crawler over to Drywater again and thence to Marsopolis.

The capital was well into its boom; the processing plants lined the Grand Canal on both sides and roiled the ancient waters with the filth of the runoff. This was before the Tri-Planet Treaty forbade disturbing cultural relics for commerce; half the slender, fairylike towers had been torn down, and others were disfigured to adapt them as pressurized buildings for Earthmen.

Now Rhysling had never seen any of these changes and no one described them to him; when he "saw" Marsopolis again, he visualized it as it had been, before it was rationalized for trade. His memory was good. He stood on the riparian esplanade where the ancient great of Mars had taken their ease and saw its beauty spreading out before his blinded eyes—ice blue plain of water unmoved by tide, untouched by breeze, and reflecting serenely the sharp, bright stars of the Martian sky, and beyond the water the lacy buttresses and flying towers of an architecture too delicate for our rumbling, heavy planet.

The result was *Grand Canal*.

The subtle change in his orientation which enabled him to see beauty at Marsopolis where beauty was not now began to affect his whole life. All women became beautiful to him. He knew them by their voices and fitted their appearances to the sounds. It is a mean spirit indeed who will speak to a blind man other than in gentle friendliness; scolds who had given their husbands no peace sweetened their voices to Rhysling.

It populated his world with beautiful women and gracious men. *Dark Star Passing, Berenice's Hair, Death Song of a Wood's Colt,* and his other love songs of the wanderers, the womenless men of space, were the direct result of the fact that his conceptions were unsullied by tawdry truths. It mellowed his approach, changed his doggerel to verse, and sometimes even to poetry.

He had plenty of time to think now, time to get all the lovely words just so, and to worry a verse until it sang true in his head. The monotonous beat of *Jet Song*—

> *When the field is clear, the reports all seen,*
> *When the lock sighs shut, when the lights wink green,*
> *When the check-off's done, when it's time to pray,*
> *When the Captain nods, when she blasts away—*
>
>> *Hear the jets!*
>> *Hear them snarl at your back*
>> *When you're stretched on the rack;*
>> *Feel your ribs clamp your chest,*
>> *Feel your neck grind its rest.*
>> *Feel the pain in your ship,*
>> *Feel her strain in their grip.*
>> *Feel her rise! Feel her drive!*
>> *Straining steel, come alive,*
>> *On her jets!*

—came to him not while he himself was a jetman but later while he was hitch-hiking from Mars to Venus and sitting out a watch with an old shipmate.

At Venusburg he sang his new songs and some of the old, in the bars. Someone would start a hat around for him; it would come back with a minstrel's usual take doubled or tripled in recognition of the gallant spirit behind the bandaged eyes.

It was an easy life. Any space port was his home and any ship his private carriage. No skipper cared to refuse to lift the extra mass of blind Rhysling and his squeeze box; he shuttled from Venusburg to Leyport to Drywater to New Shanghai, or back again, as the whim took him.

He never went closer to Earth than Supra-New York Space Station. Even when signing the contract for *Songs of the Spaceways* he made his mark in a cabin-class liner somewhere between Luna City and Ganymede. Horowitz, the original publisher, was aboard for a second honeymoon and heard Rhysling sing at a ship's party. Horowitz knew a good thing for the publishing trade when he heard it; the entire contents of *Songs* were sung directly into the tape in the communications room of that ship before he let Rhysling out of his sight. The next three volumes were squeezed out of Rhysling at

Venusburg, where Horowitz had sent an agent to keep him liquored up until he had sung all he could remember.

UP SHIP! is not certainly authentic Rhysling throughout. Much of it is Rhysling's, no doubt, and *Jet Song* is unquestionably his, but most of the verses were collected after his death from people who had known him during his wanderings.

The Green Hills of Earth grew through twenty years. The earliest form we know about was composed before Rhysling was blinded, during a drinking bout with some of the indentured men on Věnus. The verses were concerned mostly with the things the labor clients intended to do back on Earth if and when they ever managed to pay their bounties and thereby be allowed to go home. Some of the stanzas were vulgar, some were not, but the chorus was recognizably that of *Green Hills*.

We know exactly where the final form of *Green Hills* came from, and when.

There was a ship in at Venus Ellis Isle which was scheduled for the direct jump from there to Great Lakes, Illinois. She was the old *Falcon*, youngest of the Hawk class and the first ship to apply the Harriman Trust's new policy of extra-fare express service between Earth cities and any colony with scheduled stops.

Rhysling decided to ride her back to Earth. Perhaps his own song had gotten under his skin—or perhaps he just hankered to see his native Ozarks one more time.

The Company no longer permitted deadheads; Rhysling knew this but it never occurred to him that the ruling might apply to him. He was getting old, for a spaceman, and just a little matter of fact about his privileges. Not senile—he simply knew that he was one of the landmarks in space, along with Halley's Comet, the Rings, and Brewster's Ridge. He walked in the crew's port, went below, and made himself at home in the first empty acceleration couch.

The Captain found him there while making a last minute tour of his ship. "What are you doing here?" he demanded.

"Dragging it back to Earth, Captain." Rhysling needed no eyes to see a skipper's four stripes.

"You can't drag in this ship; you know the rules. Shake a leg and get out of here. We raise ship at once." The Captain was young; he had come up after Rhysling's active time, but Rhysling knew the type—five years at Harriman Hall with only cadet practice trips instead of solid, deep space experience. The two men did not touch in background nor spirit; space was changing.

"Now, Captain, you wouldn't begrudge an old man a trip home."

The officer hesitated—several of the crew had stopped to listen. "I can't do it. 'Space Precautionary Act, Clause Six: No one shall enter space save as a licensed member of a crew of a chartered vessel, or as a paying passenger of such a vessel under such regulations as may be issued pursuant to this act.' Up you get and out you go."

Rhysling lolled back, his hands under his head. "If I've got to go, I'm damned if I'll walk. Carry me."

The Captain bit his lip and said, "Master-at-Arms! Have this man removed."

The ship's policeman fixed his eyes on the overhead struts. "Can't rightly do it, Captain. I've sprained my shoulder." The other crew members, present a moment before, had faded into the bulkhead paint.

"Well, get a working party!"

"Aye, aye, sir." He, too, went away.

Rhysling spoke again. "Now look, Skipper—let's not have any hard feelings about this. You've got an out to carry me if you want to—the 'Distressed Spaceman' clause."

" 'Distressed Spaceman', my eye! You're no distressed spaceman; you're a space-lawyer. I know who you are; you've been bumming around the system for years. Well, you won't do it in my ship. That clause was intended to succor men who had missed their ships, not to let a man drag free all over space."

"Well, now, Captain, can you properly say I haven't missed my ship? I've never been back home since my last trip as a signed-on crew member. The law says I can have a trip back."

"But that was years ago. You've used up your chance."

"Have I now? The clause doesn't say a word about how soon a man has to take his trip back; it just says he's got it coming to him. Go look it up, Skipper. If I'm wrong, I'll not only walk out on my two legs, I'll beg your humble pardon in front of your crew. Go on—look it up. Be a sport."

Rhysling could feel the man's glare, but he turned and stomped out of the compartment. Rhysling knew that he had used his blindness to place the Captain in an impossible position, but this did not embarrass Rhysling—he rather enjoyed it.

Ten minutes later the siren sounded, he heard the orders on the bull horn for Up-Stations. When the soft sighing of the locks and the slight pressure change in his ears let him know that take-off was imminent he got up and shuffled down to the power room, as he wanted to be near the jets when they blasted off. He needed no one to guide him in any ship of the Hawk class.

Trouble started during the first watch. Rhysling had been lounging in the inspector's chair, fiddling with the keys of his accordion and trying out a new version of *Green Hills*.

> *"Let me breathe unrationed air again*
> *Where there's no lack nor dearth"*

And "something, something, something 'Earth' "—it would not come out right. He tried again.

> *"Let the sweet fresh breezes heal me*
> *As they rove around the girth*
> *Of our lovely mother planet,*
> *Of the cool green hills of Earth."*

That was better, he thought. "How do you like that, Archie?" he asked over the muted roar.

"Pretty good. Give out with the whole thing." Archie Macdougal, Chief Jetman, was an old friend, both spaceside and in bars; he had been an apprentice under Rhysling many years and millions of miles back.

Rhysling obliged, then said, "You youngsters have got it soft. Everything automatic. When I was twisting her tail you had to stay awake."

"You still have to stay awake." They fell to talking shop and Macdougal showed him the direct response damping rig which had replaced the manual vernier control which Rhysling had used. Rhysling felt out the controls and asked questions until he was familiar with the new installation. It was his conceit that he was still a jetman and that his present occupation as a troubadour was simply an expedient during one of the fusses with the company that any man could get into.

"I see you still have the old hand damping plates installed," he remarked, his agile fingers flitting over the equipment.

"All except the links. I unshipped them because they obscure the dials."

"You ought to have them shipped. You might need them."

"Oh, I don't know. I think—" Rhysling never did find out what Macdougal thought for it was at that moment the trouble tore loose. Macdougal caught it square, a blast of radioactivity that burned him down where he stood.

Rhysling sensed what had happened. Automatic reflexes of old habit came out. He slapped the discover and rang the alarm to the control room simultaneously. Then he remembered the unshipped links. He had to grope until he found them, while trying to keep as low as he could to get maximum benefit from the baffles. Nothing but the links bothered him as to location. The place was as light to him as any place could be; he knew every spot, every control, the way he knew the keys of his accordion.

"Power room! Power room! What's the alarm?"

"Stay out!" Rhysling shouted. "The place is 'hot.'" He could feel it on his face and in his bones, like desert sunshine.

The links he got into place, after cursing someone, anyone, for having failed to rack the wrench he needed. Then he commenced trying to reduce the trouble by hand. It was a long job and ticklish. Presently he decided that the jet would have to be spilled, pile and all.

First he reported. "Control!"

"Control aye aye!"

"Spilling jet three—emergency."

"Is this Macdougal?"

"Macdougal is dead. This is Rhysling, on watch. Stand by to record."

There was no answer; dumbfounded the Skipper may have been, but he could not interfere in a power room emergency. He had the ship to consider, and the passengers and crew. The doors had to stay closed.

The Captain must have been still more surprised at what Rhysling sent for record. It was:

> *"We rot in the molds of Venus,*
> *We retch at her tainted breath.*
> *Foul are her flooded jungles,*
> *Crawling with unclean death."*

Rhysling went on cataloguing the Solar System as he worked, "—harsh bright soil of Luna—", "—Saturn's rainbow rings—", "—the frozen night of Titan—", all the while opening and spilling the jet and fishing it clean. He finished with an alternate chorus—

> *"We've tried each spinning space mote*
> *And reckoned its true worth:*
> *Take us back again to the homes of men*
> *On the cool, green hills of Earth."*

—then, almost absentmindedly remembered to tack on his revised first verse:

> *"The arching sky is calling*
> *Spacemen back to their trade.*
> *All hands! Stand by! Free falling!*
> *And the lights below us fade.*
> *Out ride the sons of Terra,*
> *Far drives the thundering jet,*
> *Up leaps the race of Earthmen,*
> *Out, far, and onward yet—"*

The ship was safe now and ready to limp home shy one jet. As for himself, Rhysling was not so sure. That "sunburn" seemed sharp, he thought. He was unable to see the bright, rosy fog in which he worked but he knew it was there. He went on with the business of flushing the air out through the outer valve, repeating it several times to permit the level of radioaction to drop to something a man might stand under suitable armor. While he did this he sent one more chorus, the last bit of authentic Rhysling that ever could be:

> *"We pray for one last landing*
> *On the globe that gave us birth;*
> *Let us rest our eyes on fleecy skies*
> *And the cool, green hills of Earth."*

Logic of Empire

"DON'T BE a sentimental fool, Sam!"

"Sentimental, or not," Jones persisted, "I know human slavery when I see it. That's what you've got on Venus."

Humphrey Wingate snorted. "That's utterly ridiculous. The company's labor clients are employees, working under legal contracts, freely entered into."

Jones' eyebrows raised slightly. "So? What kind of a contract is it that throws a man into jail if he quits his job?"

"That's not the case. Any client can quit his job on the usual two weeks notice—I ought to know; I—"

"Yes, I know," agreed Jones in a tired voice. "You're a lawyer. You know all about contracts. But the trouble with you, you dunderheaded fool, is that all you understand is legal phrases. Free contract—nuts! What I'm talking about is *facts,* not legalisms. I don't care what the contract says—those people are slaves!"

Wingate emptied his glass and set it down. "So I'm a dunderheaded fool, am I? Well, I'll tell you what you are, Sam Houston Jones—you are a half-baked parlor pink. You've never had to work for a living in your life and you think it's just too dreadful that anyone else should have to. No, wait a minute," he continued, as Jones opened his mouth, "listen to me. The company's clients on Venus are a damn sight better off than most people of their own class here on Earth. They are certain of a job, of food, and a place to sleep. If they get sick, they're certain of medical attention. The trouble with people of that class is that they don't want to work—"

"Who does?"

"Don't be funny. The trouble is, if they weren't under a fairly tight contract, they'd throw up a good job the minute they got bored with it and expect the company to give 'em a free ride back to Earth. Now it may not have occurred to your fine, free charitable mind, but the company has obligations to its stockholders—you, for instance!—and it can't afford to run an interplanetary ferry for the benefit of a class of people that feel that the world owes them a living."

"You got me that time, pal," Jones acknowledged with a wry face, "—that crack about me being a stockholder. I'm ashamed of it."

"Then why don't you sell?"

Jones looked disgusted. "What kind of a solution is that? Do you think I can avoid the responsibility of *knowing* about it just unloading my stock?"

"Oh, the devil with it," said Wingate. "Drink up."

"Righto," agreed Jones. It was his first night aground after a practice cruise as a reserve officer; he needed to catch up on his drinking. Too bad, thought Wingate, that the cruise should have touched at Venus—

"All out! All out! Up *aaaall* you idlers! Show a leg there! Show a leg and grab a sock!" The raucous voice sawed its way through Wingate's aching head. He opened his eyes, was blinded by raw white light, and shut them hastily. But the voice would not let him alone. "Ten minutes till breakfast," it rasped. "Come and get it, or we'll throw it out!"

He opened his eyes again, and with trembling willpower forced them to track. Legs moved past his eyes, denim clad legs mostly, though some were bare—repulsive hairy nakedness. A confusion of male voices, from which he could catch words but not sentences, was accompanied by an obbligato of metallic sounds, muffled but pervasive—shrrg, shrrg, thump! Shrrg, shrrg, thump! The thump with which the cycle was completed hurt his aching head but was not as nerve stretching as another noise, a toneless whirring sibilance which he could neither locate nor escape.

The air was full of the odor of human beings, too many of them in too small a space. There was nothing so distinct as to be fairly termed a stench, nor was the supply of oxygen inadequate. But the room was filled with the warm, slightly musky smell of bodies still heated by bedclothes, bodies not dirty but not freshly washed. It was oppressive and unappetizing—in his present state almost nauseating.

He began to have some appreciation of the nature of his surroundings; he was in a bunkroom of some sort. It was crowded with men, men getting up, shuffling about, pulling on clothes. He lay on the bottom-most of a tier of four narrow bunks. Through the interstices between the legs which crowded around him and moved past his face he could see other such tiers around the walls and away from the walls, stacked floor to ceiling and supported by stanchions.

Someone sat down on the foot of Wingate's bunk, crowding his broad fundament against Wingate's ankles while he drew on his socks. Wingate squirmed his feet away from the intrusion. The stranger turned his face toward him. "Did I crowd 'ja, bud? Sorry." Then he added, not unkindly, "Better rustle out of there. The Master-at-Arms'll be riding you to get them bunks up." He yawned hugely, and started to get up, quite evidently having dismissed Wingate and Wingate's affairs from his mind.

"Wait a minute!" Wingate demanded hastily.

"Huh?"

"Where am I? In jail?"

The stranger studied Wingate's bloodshot eyes and puffy, unwashed face with detached but unmalicious interest. "Boy, oh boy, you must 'a' done a good job of drinking up your bounty money."

"Bounty money? What the hell are you talking about?"

"Honest to God, don't you know where you are?"

"No."

"Well . . ." The other seemed reluctant to proclaim a truth made silly by its self-evidence until Wingate's expression convinced him that he really wanted to know. "Well, you're in the *Evening Star*, headed for Venus."

A couple of minutes later the stranger touched him on the arm. "Don't take it so hard, bud. There's nothing to get excited about."

Wingate took his hands from his face and pressed them against his temples. "It's not real," he said, speaking more to himself than to the other. "It can't be real—"

"Stow it. Come and get your breakfast."

"I couldn't eat anything."

"Nuts. Know how you feel . . . felt that way sometimes myself. Food is just the ticket." The Master-at-Arms settled the issue by coming up and prodding Wingate in the ribs with his truncheon.

"What d'yuh think this is—sickbay, or first class? Get those bunks hooked up."

"Easy, mate, easy," Wingate's new acquaintance conciliated, "our pal's not himself this morning." As he spoke he dragged Wingate to his feet with one massive hand, then with the other shoved the tier of bunks up and against the wall. Hooks clicked into their sockets, and the tier stayed up, flat to the wall.

"He'll be a damn sight less himself if he interferes with my routine," the petty officer predicted. But he moved on. Wingate stood barefooted on the floorplates, immobile and overcome by a feeling of helpless indecision which was re-inforced by the fact that he was dressed only in his underwear. His champion studied him.

"You forgot your pillow. Here—" He reached down into the pocket formed by the lowest bunk and the wall and hauled out a flat package covered with transparent plastic. He broke the seal and shook out the contents, a single coverall garment of heavy denim. Wingate put it on gratefully. "You can get the squeezer to issue you a pair of slippers after breakfast," his friend added. "Right now we gotta eat."

The last of the queue had left the galley window by the time they reached it and the window was closed. Wingate's companion pounded on it. "Open up in there!"

It slammed open. "No seconds," a face announced.

The stranger prevented the descent of the window with his hand. "We don't want seconds, shipmate, we want firsts."

"Why the devil can't you show up on time?" the galley functionary groused. But he slapped two ration cartons down on the broad sill of the issuing window. The big fellow handed one to Wingate, and sat down on the floor-plates, his back supported by the galley bulkhead.

"What's your name, bud?" he enquired, as he skinned the cover off his ration. "Mine's Hartley—'Satchel' Hartley."

"Mine is Humphrey Wingate."

"Okay, Hump. Pleased to meet 'cha. Now what's all this song and dance you been giving me?" He spooned up an impossible bite of baked eggs and sucked coffee from the end of his carton.

"Well," said Wingate, his face twisted with worry, "I guess I've been shanghaied." He tried to emulate Hartley's method of drinking, and got the brown liquid over his face.

"Here—that's no way to do," Hartley said hastily. "Put the nipple in your mouth, then don't squeeze any harder than you suck. Like this." He illustrated. "Your theory don't seem very sound to me. The company don't need crimps when there's plenty of guys standing in line for a chance to sign up. What happened? Can't you remember?"

Wingate tried. "The last thing I recall," he said, "is arguing with a gyro driver over his fare."

Hartley nodded. "They'll gyp you every time. D'you think he put the slug on you?"

"Well . . . no, I guess not. I seem to be all right, except for the damndest hangover you can imagine."

"You'll feel better. You ought to be glad the *Evening Star* is a high-gravity ship instead of a trajectory job. Then you'd really be sick, and no foolin'."

"How's that?"

"I mean that she accelerates or decelerates her whole run. Has to, because she carries cabin passengers. If we had been sent by a freighter, it'd be a different story. They gun 'em into the right trajectory, then go weightless for the rest of the trip. Man, how the new chums do suffer!" He chuckled.

Wingate was in no condition to dwell on the hardships of space sickness. "What I can't figure out," he said, "is how I landed here. Do you suppose they could have brought me aboard by mistake, thinking I was somebody else?"

"Can't say. Say, aren't you going to finish your breakfast?"

"I've had all I want." Hartley took his statement as an invitation and quickly finished off Wingate's ration. Then he stood up, crumpled the two cartons into a ball, stuffed them down a disposal chute, and said,

"What are you going to do about it?"

"What am I going to do about it?" A look of decision came over Wingate's face. "I'm going to march right straight up to the Captain and demand an explanation, that's what I'm going to do!"

"I'd take that by easy stages, Hump," Hartley commented doubtfully.

"Easy stages, hell!" He stood up quickly. "Ow! My head!"

The Master-at-Arms referred them to the Chief Master-at-Arms in order to get rid of them. Hartley waited with Wingate outside the stateroom of the Chief Master-at-Arms to keep him company. "Better sell 'em your bill of goods pretty pronto," he advised.

"Why?"

"We'll ground on the Moon in a few hours. The stop to refuel at Luna City for deep space will be your last chance to get out, unless you want to walk back."

"I hadn't thought of that," Wingate agreed delightedly. "I thought I'd have to make the round trip in any case."

"Shouldn't be surprised but what you could pick up the *Morning Star* in a week or two. If it's their mistake, they'll have to return you."

"I can beat that," said Wingate eagerly. "I'll go right straight to the bank at Luna City, have them arrange a letter of credit with my bank, and buy a ticket on the Earth-Moon shuttle."

Hartley's manner underwent a subtle change. He had never in his life "arranged a letter of credit." Perhaps such a man *could* walk up to the Captain and lay down the law.

The Chief Master-at-Arms listened to Wingate's story with obvious impatience, and interrupted him in the middle of it to consult his roster of emigrants. He thumbed through it to the Ws, and pointed to a line. Wingate read it with a sinking feeling. There was his own name, correctly spelled. "Now get out," ordered the official, "and quit wasting my time."

But Wingate stood up to him. "You have no authority in this matter—none whatsoever. I insist that you take me to the Captain."

"Why, you—" Wingate thought momentarily that the man was going to strike him. He interrupted.

"Be careful what you do. You are apparently the victim of an honest mistake—but your legal position will be very shaky indeed, if you disregard the requirements of spacewise law under which this vessel is licensed. I don't think your Captain would be pleased to have to explain such actions on your part in federal court."

That he had gotten the man angry was evident. But a man does not get to be chief police officer of a major transport by jeopardizing his superior officers. His jaw muscles twitched but he pressed a button, saying nothing. A junior master-at-arms appeared. "Take this man to the Purser." He turned his back in dismissal and dialed a number on the ship's intercommunication system.

Wingate was let in to see the Purser, ex-officio company business agent, after only a short wait. "What's this all about?" that officer demanded. "If you have a complaint, why can't you present it at the morning hearings in the regular order?"

Wingate explained his predicament as clearly, convincingly,

and persuasively as he knew how. "And so you see," he concluded, "I want to be put aground at Luna City. I've no desire to cause the company any embarrassment over what was undoubtedly an unintentional mishap—particularly as I am forced to admit that I had been celebrating rather freely and, perhaps, in some manner, contributed to the mistake."

The Purser, who had listened noncommittally to his recital, made no answer. He shuffled through a high stack of file folders which rested on one corner of his desk, selected one, and opened it. It contained a sheaf of legal-size papers clipped together at the top. These he studied leisurely for several minutes, while Wingate stood waiting.

The Purser breathed with an asthmatic noisiness while he read, and, from time to time, drummed on his bared teeth with his fingernails. Wingate had about decided, in his none too steady nervous condition, that if the man approached his hand to his mouth just once more that he, Wingate, would scream and start throwing things. At this point the Purser chucked the dossier across the desk toward Wingate. "Better have a look at these," he said.

Wingate did so. The main exhibit he found to be a contract, duly entered into, between Humphrey Wingate and the Venus Development Company for six years of indentured labor on the planet Venus.

"That your signature?" asked the Purser.

Wingate's professional caution stood him in good stead. He studied the signature closely in order to gain time while he tried to collect his wits. "Well," he said at last, "I will stipulate that it looks very much like my signature, but I will not concede that it is my signature—I'm not a handwriting expert."

The Purser brushed aside the objection with an air of annoyance. "I haven't time to quibble with you. Let's check the thumbprint. Here." He shoved an impression pad across his desk. For a moment Wingate considered standing on his legal rights by refusing, but no, that would prejudice his case. He had nothing to lose; it *couldn't* be his thumbprint on the contract. Unless—

But it was. Even his untrained eye could see that the two prints matched. He fought back a surge of panic. This was probably a nightmare, inspired by his argument last night with Jones. Or, if by some wild chance it were real, it was a frameup in which he must find the flaw. Men of his sort were not framed; the whole thing was ridiculous. He marshalled his words carefully.

"I won't dispute your position, my dear sir. In some fashion both you and I have been made the victims of a rather sorry joke. It seems hardly necessary to point out that a man who is unconscious, as I must have been last night, may have his thumbprint taken without his knowledge. Superficially this contract is valid and I assume naturally your good faith in the matter. But, in fact, the instrument lacks one necessary element of a contract."

"Which is?"

"The intention on the part of both parties to enter into a contractual relationship. Notwithstanding signature and thumbprint I had no intention of contracting which can easily be shown by other factors. I am a successful lawyer with a good practice, as my tax returns will show. It is not reasonable to believe—and no court *will* believe—that I voluntarily gave up my accustomed life for six years of indenture at a much lower income."

"So you're a lawyer, eh? Perhaps there has been chicanery —on your part. How does it happen that you represent yourself here as a radio technician?"

Wingate again had to steady himself at this unexpected flank attack. He was in truth a radio expert—it was his cherished hobby—but how had they known? Shut up, he told himself. Don't admit anything. "The whole thing is ridiculous," he protested. "I insist that I be taken to see the Captain—I can break that contract in ten minutes time."

The Purser waited before replying. "Are you through speaking your piece?"

"Yes."

"Very well. You've had your say, now I'll have mine. You listen to me, Mister Spacelawyer. That contract was drawn up by some of the shrewdest legal minds in two planets. They had specifically in mind that worthless bums would sign it, drink up their bounty money, and then decide that they didn't want to go to work after all. That contract has been subjected to every sort of attack possible and revised so that it can't be broken by the devil himself.

"You're not peddling your curbstone law to another stumble-bum in this case; you are talking to a man who knows just where he stands, legally. As for seeing the Captain

—if you think the commanding officer of a major vessel has nothing more to do than listen to the *rhira*-dreams of a self-appointed word artist, you've got another think coming! Return to your quarters!"

Wingate started to speak, thought better of it, and turned to go. This would require some thought. The Purser stopped him. "Wait. Here's your copy of the contract." He chucked it, the flimsy white sheets riffled to the deck. Wingate picked them up and left silently.

Hartley was waiting for him in the passageway. "How d'ja make out, Hump?"

"Not so well. No, I don't want to talk about it. I've got to think." They walked silently back the way they had come toward the ladder which gave access to the lower decks. A figure ascended from the ladder and came toward them. Wingate noted it without interest.

He looked again. Suddenly the whole preposterous chain of events fell into place; he shouted in relief. "Sam!" he called out. "Sam—you cockeyed old so-and-so. I should have spotted your handiwork." It was all clear now; Sam had framed him with a phony shanghai. Probably the skipper was a pal of Sam's—a reserve officer, maybe—and they had cooked it up between them. It was a rough sort of a joke, but he was too relieved to be angry. Just the same he would make Jones pay for his fun, somehow, on the jump back from Luna City.

It was then that he noticed that Jones was not laughing.

Furthermore he was dressed—most unreasonably—in the same blue denim that the contract laborers were. "Hump," he was saying, "are you still drunk?"

"Me? No. What's the i—"

"Don't you realize we're in a jam?"

"Oh hell, Sam, a joke's a joke, but don't keep it up any longer. I've caught on, I tell you. I don't mind—it was a good gag."

"Gag, eh?" said Jones bitterly. "I suppose it was just a gag when you talked me into signing up."

"*I* persuaded *you* to sign up?"

"You certainly did. You were so damn sure you knew what you were talking about. You claimed that we could sign up, spend a month or so, on Venus, and come home. You wanted to bet on it. So we went around to the docks and signed up. It seemed like a good idea then—the only way to settle the argument."

Wingate whistled softly. "Well, I'll be—Sam, I haven't the slightest recollection of it. I must have drawn a blank before I passed out."

"Yeah, I guess so. Too bad you didn't pass out sooner. Not that I'm blaming you; you didn't drag me. Anyhow, I'm on my way up to try to straighten it out."

"Better wait a minute till you hear what happened to me. Oh yes—Sam, this is, uh, Satchel Hartley. Good sort." Hartley had been waiting uncertainly near them; he stepped forward and shook hands.

Wingate brought Jones up to date, and added, "So you see your reception isn't likely to be too friendly. I guess I muffed it. But we are sure to break the contract as soon as we can get a hearing on time alone."

"How do you mean?"

"We were signed up less than twelve hours before ship lifting. That's contrary to the Space Precautionary Act."

"Yes—yes, I see what you mean. The Moon's in her last quarter; they would lift ship some time after midnight to take advantage of favorable earthswing. I wonder what time it was when we signed on?"

Wingate took out his contract copy. The notary's stamp showed a time of eleven thirty-two. "Great Day!" he shouted. "I knew there would be a flaw in it somewhere. This contract is invalid on its face. The ship's log will prove it."

Jones studied it. "Look again," he said. Wingate did so. The stamp showed eleven thirty-two, but A.M., not P.M.

"But that's impossible," he protested.

"Of course it is. But it's official. I think we will find that the story is that we were signed on in the morning, paid our bounty money, and had one last glorious luau before we were carried aboard. I seem to recollect some trouble in getting the recruiter to sign us up. Maybe we convinced him by kicking in our bounty money."

"But we *didn't* sign up in the morning. It's not true and I can prove it."

"Sure you can prove it—*but how can you prove it without going back to Earth first!*"

"So you see it's this way," Jones decided after some minutes of somewhat fruitless discussion, "there is no sense in trying to break our contracts here and now; they'll laugh at us. The thing to do is to make money talk, and talk loud. The only way I can see to get us off at Luna City is to post non-performance bonds with the company bank there—cash, and damn big ones, too."

"How big?"

"Twenty thousand credits, at least, I should guess."

"But that's not equitable—it's all out of proportion."

"Quit worrying about equity, will you? Can't you realize that they've got us where the hair is short? This won't be a bond set by a court ruling; it's got to be big enough to make a minor company official take a chance on doing something that's not in the book."

"I can't raise such a bond."

"Don't worry about that. I'll take care of it."

Wingate wanted to argue the point, but did not. There are times when it is very convenient to have a wealthy friend.

"I've got to get a radiogram off to my sister," Jones went on, "to get this done—"

"Why your sister? Why not your family firm?"

"Because we need fast action, that's why. The lawyers that handle our family finances would fiddle and fume around trying to confirm the message. They'd send a message back to the Captain, asking if Sam Houston Jones were really aboard, and he would answer 'No', as I'm signed up as Sam Jones. I had some silly idea of staying out of the news broadcasts, on account of the family."

"You can't blame them," protested Wingate, feeling an obscure clannish loyalty to his colleagues in law, "they're handling other people's money."

"I'm not blaming them. But I've got to have fast action and Sis'll do what I ask her. I'll phrase the message so she'll know it's me. The only hurdle now is to persuade the Purser to let me send a message on tick."

He was gone for a long time on this mission. Hartley waited with Wingate, both to keep him company and because of a strong human interest in unusual events. When Jones finally appeared he wore a look of tight-lipped annoyance. Wingate, seeing the expression, felt a sudden, chilling apprehension. "Couldn't you send it? Wouldn't he let you?"

"Oh, he let me—finally," Jones admitted, "but that Purser —man, is he tight!"

Even without the alarm gongs Wingate would have been

acutely aware of the grounding at Luna City. The sudden change from the high gravity deceleration of their approach to the weak surface gravity—one-sixth earth normal—of the Moon took immediate toll on his abused stomach. It was well that he had not eaten much. Both Hartley and Jones were deep-space men and regarded enough acceleration to permit normal swallowing as adequate for any purpose. There is a curious lack of sympathy between those who are subject to spacesickness and those who are immune to it. Why the spectacle of a man regurgitating, choked, eyes streaming with tears, stomach knotted with pain, should seem funny is difficult to see, but there it is. It divides the human race into two distinct and antipathetic groups—amused contempt on one side, helpless murderous hatred on the other.

Neither Hartley nor Jones had the inherent sadism which is too frequently evident on such occasions—for example the great wit who suggests salt pork as a remedy—but, feeling no discomfort themselves, they were simply unable to comprehend (having forgotten the soul-twisting intensity of their own experience as new chums) that Wingate was literally suffering "a fate worse than death"—much worse, for it was stretched into a sensible eternity by a distortion of the time sense known only to sufferers from spacesicknesses, seasicknesses, and (we are told) smokers of hashish.

As a matter of fact, the stop on the Moon was less than four hours long. Toward the end of the wait Wingate had quieted down sufficiently again to take an interest in the expected reply to Jones' message, particularly after Jones had assured him that he would be able to spend the expected lay-over under bond at Luna City in a hotel equipped with a centrifuge.

But the answer was delayed. Jones had expected to hear from his sister within an hour, perhaps before the *Evening Star* grounded at the Luna City docks. As the hours stretched out he managed to make himself very unpopular at the radio room by his repeated inquiries. An over-worked clerk had sent him brusquely about his business for the seventeenth time when he heard the alarm sound preparatory to raising ship; he went back and admitted to Wingate that his scheme had apparently failed.

"Of course, we've got ten minutes yet," he finished unhopefully, "if the message should arrive before they raise ship, the Captain could still put us aground at the last minute. We'll go back and haunt 'em some more right up to the last. But it looks like a thin chance."

"Ten minutes—" said Wingate, "couldn't we manage somehow to slip outside and run for it?"

Jones looked exasperated. "Have you ever tried running in a total vacuum?"

Wingate had very little time in which to fret on the passage from Luna City to Venus. He learned a great deal about the care and cleaning of washrooms, and spent ten hours a day perfecting his new skill. Masters-at-Arms have long memories.

The *Evening Star* passed beyond the limits of ship-to-Terra radio communication shortly after leaving Luna City; there was nothing to do but wait until arrival at Adonis, port of the north polar colony. The company radio there was strong enough to remain in communication at all times except for the sixty days bracketing superior conjunction and a shorter period of solar interference at inferior conjunction. "They will probably be waiting for us with a release order when we ground," Jones assured Wingate, "and we'll go back on the return trip of the *Evening Star*—first class, this time. Or, at the very worst, we'll have to wait over for the *Morning Star*. That wouldn't be so bad, once I get some credit transferred; we could spend it at Venusburg."

"I suppose you went there on your cruise," Wingate said, curiosity showing in his voice. He was no Sybarite, but the lurid reputation of the most infamous, or famous—depending on one's evaluations—pleasure city of three planets was enough to stir the imagination of the least hedonistic.

"No—worse luck!" Jones denied. "I was on a hull inspection board the whole time. Some of my messmates went, though . . . boy!" He whistled softly and shook his head.

But there was no one awaiting their arrival, nor was there any message. Again they stood around the communication office until told sharply and officially to get on back to their quarters and stand by to disembark, "—and be quick about it!"

"I'll see you in the receiving barracks, Hump," were Jones' last words before he hurried off to his own compartment.

The Master-at-Arms responsible for the compartment in which Hartley and Wingate were billeted lined his charges up in a rough column of two's and, when ordered to do so by the metallic bray of the ship's loudspeaker, conducted them through the central passageway and down four decks to the lower passenger port. It stood open; they shuffled through the lock and out of the ship—not into the free air of Venus, but into a sheetmetal tunnel which joined it, after some fifty yards, to a building.

The air within the tunnel was still acrid from the atomized antiseptic with which it had been flushed out, but to Wingate it was nevertheless fresh and stimulating after the stale flatness of the repeatedly reconditioned air of the transport. That, plus the surface gravity of Venus, five-sixths of earth-normal, strong enough to prevent nausea yet low enough to produce a feeling of lightness and strength—these things combined to give him an irrational optimism, an up-and-at-'em frame of mind.

The exit from the tunnel gave into a moderately large room, windowless but brilliantly and glarelessly lighted from concealed sources. It contained no furniture.

"Squaaad—HALT!" called out the Master-at-Arms, and handed papers to a slight, clerkish-appearing man who stood near an inner doorway. The man glanced at the papers, counted the detachment, then signed one sheet, which he handed back to the ship's petty officer who accepted it and returned through the tunnel.

The clerkish man turned to the immigrants. He was dressed, Wingate noted, in nothing but the briefest of shorts, hardly more than a strap, and his entire body, even his feet, was a smooth mellow tan. "Now men," he said in a mild voice, "strip off your clothes and put them in the hopper." He indicated a fixture set in one wall.

"Why?" asked Wingate. His manner was uncontentious but he made no move to comply.

"Come now," he was answered, still mildly but with a note of annoyance, "don't argue. It's for your own protection. We can't afford to import disease."

Wingate checked a reply and unzipped his coverall. Several who had paused to hear the outcome followed his example. Suits, shoes, underclothing, socks, they all went into the hopper. "Follow me," said their guide.

In the next room the naked herd were confronted by four "barbers" armed with electric clippers and rubber gloves who proceeded to clip them smooth. Again Wingate felt disposed to argue, but decided the issue was not worth it. But he wondered if the female labor clients were required to submit to such drastic quarantine precautions. It would be a shame, it seemed to him, to sacrifice a beautiful head of hair that had been twenty years in growing.

The succeeding room was a shower room. A curtain of warm spray completely blocked passage through the room. Wingate entered it unreluctantly, even eagerly, and fairly wallowed in the first decent bath he had been able to take since leaving Earth. They were plentifully supplied with liquid green soap, strong and smelly, but which lathered freely. Half a dozen attendants, dressed as skimpily as their guide, stood on the far side of the wall of water and saw to it that the squad remained under the shower a fixed time and scrubbed. In some cases they made highly personal suggestions to insure thoroughness. Each of them wore a red cross on a white field affixed to his belt which lent justification to their officiousness.

Blasts of warm air in the exit passageway dried them quickly and completely.

"Hold still." Wingate complied, the bored hospital orderly who had spoken dabbed at Wingate's upper arm with a swab which felt cold to touch, then scratched the spot. "That's all, move on." Wingate added himself to the queue at the next table. The experience was repeated on the other arm. By the time he had worked down to the far end of the room the outer sides of each arm were covered with little red scratches, more than twenty of them.

"What's this all about?" he asked the hospital clerk at the end of the line, who had counted his scratches and checked his name off a list.

"Skin tests . . . to check your resistances and immunities."

"Resistance to what?"

"Anything. Both terrestrial and Venerian diseases. Fungoids, the Venus ones are, mostly. Move on, you're holding up the line." He heard more about it later. It took from two to three weeks to recondition the ordinary terrestrial to Venus conditions. Until that reconditioning was complete and immunity was established to the new hazards of another planet it was literally death to an Earth man to expose his skin and particularly his mucous membranes to the ravenous invisible parasites of the surface of Venus.

The ceaseless fight of life against life which is the dominant characteristic of life anywhere proceeds with especial intensity, under conditions of high metabolism, in the steamy jungles of Venus. The general bacteriophage which has so nearly eliminated disease caused by pathogenic micro-organisms on Earth was found capable of a subtle modification which made it potent against the analogous but different diseases of Venus. The hungry fungi were another matter.

Imagine the worst of the fungoid-type skin diseases you have ever encountered—ringworm, dhobie itch, athlete's foot, Chinese rot, saltwater itch, seven year itch. Add to that your conception of mold, of damp rot, of scale, of toadstools feeding on decay. Then conceive them speeded up in their processes, visibly crawling as you watch—picture them attacking your eyeballs, your armpits, the soft wet tissues inside your mouth, working down into your lungs.

The first Venus expedition was lost entirely. The second had a surgeon with sufficient imagination to provide what seemed a liberal supply of salicylic acid and mercury salicylate as well as a small ultraviolet radiator. Three of them returned.

But permanent colonization depends on adaptation to environment, not insulating against it. Luna City might be cited as a case which denies this proposition but it is only superficially so. While it is true that the "lunatics" are absolutely dependent on their citywide hermetically-sealed air bubble, Luna City is not a self-sustaining colony; it is an outpost, useful as a mining station, as an observatory, as a refueling stop beyond the densest portion of Terra's gravitational field.

Venus is a colony. The colonists breathe the air of Venus, eat its food, and expose their skins to its climate and natural hazards. Only the cold polar regions—approximately equivalent in weather conditions to an Amazonian jungle on a hot day in the rainy season—are tenable by terrestrials, but here they slop barefooted on the marshy soil in a true ecological balance.

Wingate ate the meal that was offered him—satisfactory but roughly served and dull, except for Venus sweet-sour melon, the portion of which he ate would have fetched a price in a Chicago gourmets' restaurant equivalent to the food budget for a week of a middle-class family—and located his assigned sleeping billet. Thereafter he attempted to locate Sam Houston Jones. He could find no sign of him among the other labor clients, nor any one who remembered having seen him. He was advised by one of the permanent staff of the conditioning station to enquire of the factor's clerk. This he did, in the ingratiating manner he had learned it was wise to use in dealing with minor functionaries.

"Come back in the morning. The lists will be posted."

"Thank you, sir. Sorry to have bothered you, but I can't find him and I was afraid he might have taken sick or something. Could you tell me if he is on the sick list."

"Oh, well— Wait a minute." The clerk thumbed through his records. "Hmmm . . . you say he was in the *Evening Star*?"

"Yes, sir."

"Well, he's not . . . Mmmm, no— Oh, yes, here he is. He didn't disembark here."

"What did you say!?"

"He went on with the *Evening Star* to New Auckland, South Pole. He's stamped in as a machinist's helper. If you had told me that, I'd 'a' known. All the metal workers in this consignment were sent to work on the new South Power Station."

After a moment Wingate pulled himself together enough to murmur, "Thanks for your trouble."

" 'S all right. Don't mention it." The clerk turned away.

South Pole Colony! He muttered it to himself. South Pole Colony, his only friend twelve thousand miles away. At last Wingate felt alone, alone and trapped, abandoned. During the short interval between waking up aboard the transport and finding Jones also aboard he had not had time fully to appreciate his predicament, nor had he, then, lost his upper class arrogance, the innate conviction that it could not be serious— such things just don't happen to people, not to people one *knows!*

But in the meantime he had suffered such assaults to his human dignity (the Chief Master-at-Arms had seen to some of it) that he was no longer certain of his essential inviolability from unjust or arbitrary treatment. But now, shaved and bathed without his consent, stripped of his clothing and attired in a harnesslike breechclout, transported millions of miles from his social matrix, subject to the orders of persons indifferent to his feelings and who claimed legal control over his person and actions, and now, most bitterly, cut off from the one human contact which had given him support and courage and hope, he realized at last with chilling thoroughness that anything could happen to him, to *him*, Humphrey Belmont Wingate, successful attorney-at-law and member of all the right clubs.

"Wingate!"

"That's you, Jack. Go on in, don't keep them waiting." Wingate pushed through the doorway and found himself in a fairly crowded room. Thirty-odd men were seated around the sides of the room. Near the door a clerk sat at a desk, busy with papers. One brisk-mannered individual stood in the cleared space between the chairs near a low platform on which all the illumination of the room was concentrated. The clerk at the door looked up to say, "Step up where they can see you." He pointed a stylus at the platform.

Wingate moved forward and did as he was bade, blinking at the brilliant light. "Contract number 482-23-06," read the clerk, "client Humphrey Wingate, six years, radio technician non-certified, pay grade six-D, contract now available for assignment." Three weeks it had taken them to condition him, three weeks with no word from Jones. He had passed his exposure test without infection; he was about to enter the active period of his indenture. The brisk man spoke up close on the last words of the clerk:

"Now here, patrons, if you please—we have an exceptionally promising man. I hardly dare tell you the ratings he received on his intelligence, adaptability, and general information tests. In fact I won't, except to tell you that Administration has put in a protective offer of a thousand credits. But it would be a shame to use any such client for the routine work of administration when we need good men so badly to wrest wealth from the wilderness. I venture to predict that the lucky bidder who obtains the services of this client will be using him as a foreman within a month. But look him over for yourselves, talk to him, and see for yourselves."

The clerk whispered something to the speaker. He nodded and added, "I am required to notify you, gentlemen and patrons, that this client has given the usual legal notice of two weeks, subject of course to liens of record." He laughed jovially, and cocked one eyebrow as if there were some huge joke behind his remarks. No one paid attention to the announcement; to a limited extent Wingate appreciated wryly the nature of the jest. He had given notice the day after he found out that Jones had been sent to South Pole Colony, and had discovered that while he was free theoretically to quit, it was freedom to starve on Venus, unless he first worked out his bounty, and his passage both ways.

Several of the patrons gathered around the platform and looked him over, discussing him as they did so. "Not too well muscled." "I'm not over-eager to bid on these smart boys; they're trouble-makers." "No, but a stupid client isn't worth his keep." "What can he *do*? I'm going to have a look at his record." They drifted over to the clerk's desk and scrutinized the results of the many tests and examinations that Wingate had undergone during his period of quarantine. All but one beady-eyed individual who sidled up closer to Wingate, and, resting one foot on the platform so that he could bring his face nearer, spoke in confidential tones.

"I'm not interested in those phony puff-sheets, bub. Tell me about yourself."

"There's not much to tell."

"Loosen up. You'll like my place. Just like a home—I run a free crock to Venusburg for my boys. Had any experience handling niggers?"

"No."

"Well, the natives ain't niggers anyhow, except in a manner of speaking. You look like you could boss a gang. Had any experience?"

"Not much."

"Well . . . maybe you're modest. I like a man who keeps his mouth shut. And my boys like me. I never let my pusher take kickbacks."

"No," put in another patron who had returned to the side of the platform, "you save that for yourself, Rigsbee."

"You stay out o' this, Van Huysen!"

The newcomer, a heavy-set, middle-aged man, ignored the other and addressed Wingate himself. "You have given notice. Why?"

"The whole thing was a mistake. I was drunk."

"Will you do honest work in the meantime?"

Wingate considered this. "Yes," he said finally. The heavy-set man nodded and walked heavily back to his chair, settling his broad girth with care and giving his harness a hitch.

When the others were seated the spokesman announced cheerfully, "Now, gentlemen, if you are quite through— Let's hear an opening offer for this contract. I wish I could afford to bid him in as my assistant, by George, I do! Now . . . do I hear an offer?"

"Six hundred."

"Please, patrons! Did you not hear me mention a protection of one thousand?"

"I don't think you mean it. He's a sleeper."

The company agent raised his eyebrows. "I'm sorry. I'll have to ask the client to step down from the platform."

But before Wingate could do so another voice said, "One thousand."

"Now that's better!" exclaimed the agent. "I should have known that you gentlemen wouldn't let a real opportunity escape you. But a ship can't fly on one jet. Do I hear eleven hundred? Come, patrons, you can't make your fortunes without clients. Do I hear—"

"Eleven hundred."

"Eleven hundred from Patron Rigsbee! And a bargain it would be at that price. But I doubt if you will get it. Do I hear twelve?"

The heavy-set man flicked a thumb upward. "Twelve hundred from Patron van Huysen. I see I've made a mistake and am wasting your time; the intervals should be not less than two hundred. Do I hear fourteen? Do I hear fourteen? Going once for twelve . . . going twi—"

"Fourteen," Rigsbee said sullenly.

"Seventeen," Van Huysen added at once.

"Eighteen," snapped Rigsbee.

"Nooo," said the agent, "no interval of less than two, please."

"All right, dammit, nineteen!"

"Nineteen I hear. It's a hard number to write; who'll make it twenty-one?" Van Huysen's thumb flicked again. "Twenty-one it is. It takes money to make money. What do I hear? What do I hear?" He paused. "Going once for twenty-one . . . going twice for twenty-one. Are you giving up so easily, Patron Rigsbee?"

"Van Huysen is a—" The rest was muttered too indistinctly to hear.

"One more chance, gentlemen. Going, going, . . . GONE! —" He smacked his palms sharply together. "—and sold to Patron van Huysen for twenty-one hundred credits. My congratulations, sir, on a shrewd deal."

Wingate followed his new master out the far door. They were stopped in the passageway by Rigsbee. "All right, Van, you've had your fun. I'll cut your losses for two thousand."

"Out of my way."

"Don't be a fool. He's no bargain. You don't know how to sweat a man—I do." Van Huysen ignored him, pushing on past. Wingate followed him out into warm winter drizzle to the parking lot where steel crocodiles were drawn up in parallel rows. Van Huysen paused beside a thirty-foot Remington. "Get in."

The long boxlike body of the crock was stowed to its load line with supplies Van Huysen had purchased at the base. Sprawled on the tarpaulin which covered the cargo were half a dozen men. One of them stirred as Wingate climbed over the side. "Hump! Oh, Hump!"

It was Hartley. Wingate was surprised at his own surge of emotion. He gripped Hartley's hand and exchanged friendly insults. "Chums," said Hartley, "meet Hump Wingate. He's a right guy. Hump, meet the gang. That's Jimmie right behind you. He rassles this velocipede."

The man designated gave Wingate a bright nod and moved forward into the operator's seat. At a wave from Van Huysen, who had seated his bulk in the little sheltered cabin aft, he pulled back on both control levers and the crocodile crawled away, its caterpillar treads clanking and chunking through the mud.

Three of the six were old-timers, including Jimmie, the driver. They had come along to handle cargo, the ranch products which the patron had brought in to market and the supplies he had purchased to take back. Van Huysen had bought the contracts of two other clients in addition to Wingate and Satchel Hartley. Wingate recognized them as men he had known casually in the *Evening Star* and at the assignment and conditioning station. They looked a little woebegone, which Wingate could thoroughly understand, but the men from the ranch seemed to be enjoying themselves. They appeared to regard the opportunity to ride a load to and from town as an outing. They sprawled on the tarpaulin and passed the time gossiping and getting acquainted with the new chums.

But they asked no personal questions. No labor client on Venus ever asked anything about what he had been before he shipped with the company unless he first volunteered information. It "wasn't done."

Shortly after leaving the outskirts of Adonis the car slithered down a sloping piece of ground, teetered over a low bank, and splashed logily into water. Van Huysen threw up a window in the bulkhead which separated the cabin from the hold and shouted, "Dumkopf! How many times do I tell you to take those launchings slowly?"

"Sorry, Boss," Jimmie answered. "I missed it."

"You keep your eyes peeled, or I get me a new crocker!" He slammed the port. Jimmie glanced around and gave the other clients a sly wink. He had his hands full; the marsh they were traversing looked like solid ground, so heavily was it overgrown with rank vegetation. The crocodile now functioned as a boat, the broad flanges of the treads acting as paddle wheels. The wedge-shaped prow pushed shrubs and marsh grass aside, or struck and ground down small trees. Occasionally the lugs would bite into the mud of a shoal bottom, and, crawling over a bar, return temporarily to the status of a land vehicle. Jimmie's slender, nervous hands moved constantly over the controls, avoiding large trees and continually seeking the easiest, most nearly direct route, while he split his attention between the terrain and the craft's compass.

Presently the conversation lagged and one of the ranch hands started to sing. He had a passable tenor voice and was soon joined by others. Wingate found himself singing the choruses as fast as he learned them. They sang *Pay Book* and *Since the Pusher Met My Cousin* and a mournful thing called *They Found Him in the Bush*. But this was followed by a light number, *The Night the Rain Stopped*, which seemed to have an endless string of verses recounting various unlikely happenings which occurred on that occasion. ("The Squeezer bought a round-a-drinks—")

Jimmie drew applause and enthusiastic support in the choruses with a ditty entitled *That Redheaded Venusburg Gal*, but Wingate considered it inexcusably vulgar. He did not have time to dwell on the matter; it was followed by a song which drove it out of his mind.

The tenor started it, slowly and softly. The others sang the refrains while he rested—all but Wingate; he was silent and thoughtful throughout. In the triplet of the second verse the tenor dropped out and the others sang in his place.

> "Oh, you stamp your paper and you sign your name,
>   ("Come away! Come away!)
> "They pay your bounty and you drown your shame.
>   ("Rue the day! Rue the day!)

"They land you down at Ellis Isle and put you in a pen;
"There you see what happens to the Six-Year men—
"They haven't paid their bounty and they sign 'em up again!
        ("Here to stay! Here to stay!)
"But me I'll save my bounty and a ticket on the ship,
        ("So you say! So you say!)
"And then you'll see me leavin' on the very next trip.
        ("Come the day! Come the day!)
"Oh, we've heard that kinda story just a thousand times and
        one.
"Now we wouldn't say you're lyin' but we'd like to see it
        done.
"We'll see you next at Venusburg apayin' for your fun!
        [Spoken slowly] *"And you'll never meet your bounty on*
        this hitch!
        ("Come away!")

It left Wingate with a feeling of depression not entirely accounted for by the tepid drizzle, the unappetizing landscape, nor by the blanket of pale mist which is the invariable Venerian substitute for the open sky. He withdrew to one corner of the hold and kept to himself, until, much later, Jimmie shouted, "Lights ahead!"

Wingate leaned out and peered eagerly toward his new home.

Four weeks and no word from Sam Houston Jones. Venus had turned once on its axis, the fortnight long Venerian "winter" had given way to an equally short "summer"—indistinguishable from "winter" except that the rain was a trifle heavier and a little hotter—and now it was "winter" again. Van Huysen's ranch, being near the pole, was, like most of the tenable area of Venus, never in darkness. The miles-thick, everpresent layer of clouds tempered the light of the low-hanging sun during the long day, and, equally, held the heat and diffused the light from a sun just below the horizon to produce a continuing twilight during the two-week periods which were officially "night", or "winter".

Four weeks and no word. Four weeks and no sun, no moon, no stars, no dawn. No clean crisp breath of morning air, no life-quickening beat of noonday sun, no welcome evening shadows, nothing, nothing at all to distinguish one sultry,

sticky hour from the next but the treadmill routine of sleep
and work and food and sleep again—nothing but the gathering ache in his heart for the cool blue skies of Terra.

He had acceded to the invariable custom that new men
should provide a celebration for the other clients and had
signed the Squeezer's chits to obtain happywater—*rhira*—for
the purpose—to discover, when first he signed the pay book,
that his gesture of fellowship had cost him another four
months of delay before he could legally quit his "job." There-
upon he had resolved never again to sign a chit, had fore-
sworn the prospect of brief holidays at Venusburg, had
promised himself to save every possible credit against his
bounty and transportation liens.

Whereupon he discovered that the mild alcoholoid drink
was neither a vice nor a luxury, but a necessity, as necessary
to human life on Venus as the ultraviolet factor present in all
colonial illuminating systems. It produces, not drunkenness,
but lightness of heart, freedom from worry, and without it he
could not *get to sleep*. Three nights of self-recrimination and
fretting, three days of fatigue-drugged uselessness under the
unfriendly eye of the Pusher, and he had signed for his bottle
with the rest, even though dully aware that the price of the
bottle had washed out more than half of the day's microscopic progress toward freedom.

Nor had he been assigned to radio operation. Van Huysen
had an operator. Wingate, although listed on the books as
standby operator, went to the swamps with the rest. He discovered on rereading his contract a clause which permitted his
patron to do this, and he admitted with half his mind—the
detached judicial and legalistic half—that the clause was reasonable and proper, not inequitable.

He went to the swamps. He learned to wheedle and bully
the little, mild amphibian people into harvesting the bulbous
underwater growth of *Hyacinthus veneris johnsoni*—Venus
swamproot—and to bribe the co-operation of their ma-
triarchs with promises of bonuses in the form of "thigarek", a
term which meant not only cigarette, but tobacco in any
form, the staple medium in trade when dealing with the natives.

He took his turn in the chopping sheds and learned, clumsily and slowly, to cut and strip the spongy outer husk from
the pea-sized kernel which alone had commercial value and
which must be removed intact, without scratch or bruise. The

juice from the pods made his hands raw and the odor made him cough and stung his eyes, but he enjoyed it more than the work in the marshes, for it threw him into the company of the female labor clients. Women were quicker at the work than men and their smaller fingers more dextrous in removing the valuable, easily damaged capsule. Men were used for such work only when accumulated crops required extra help.

He learned his new trade from a motherly old person whom the other women addressed as Hazel. She talked as she worked, her gnarled old hands moving steadily and without apparent direction or skill. He could close his eyes and imagine that he was back on Earth and a boy again, hanging around his grandmother's kitchen while she shelled peas and rambled on. "Don't you fret yourself, boy," Hazel told him. "Do your work and shame the devil. There's a great day coming."

"What kind of a great day, Hazel?"

"The day when the Angels of the Lord will rise up and smite the powers of evil. The day when the Prince of Darkness will be cast down into the pit and the Prophet shall reign over the children of Heaven. So don't you worry; it doesn't matter whether you are here or back home when the great day comes; the only thing that matters is your state of grace."

"Are you sure we will live long enough to see the day?"

She glanced around, then leaned over confidentially. "The day is almost upon us. Even now the Prophet moves up and down the land gathering his forces. Out of the clean farm country of the Mississippi Valley there comes the Man, known in this world"—she lowered her voice still more—"as *Nehemiah Scudder!*"

Wingate hoped that his start of surprise and amusement did not show externally. He recalled the name. It was that of a pipsqueak, backwoods evangelist, an unimportant nuisance back on Earth, the butt of an occasional guying news story, but a man of no possible consequence.

The chopping shed Pusher moved up to their bench. "Keep your eyes on your work, you! You're way behind now." Wingate hastened to comply, but Hazel came to his aid.

"You leave him be, Joe Tompson. It takes time to learn chopping."

"Okay, Mom," answered the Pusher with a grin, "but keep him pluggin'. See?"

"I will. You worry about the rest of the shed. This bench'll

have its quota." Wingate had been docked two days running
for spoilage. Hazel was lending him poundage now and the
Pusher knew it, but everybody liked her, even pushers, who
are reputed to like no one, not even themselves.

Wingate stood just outside the gate of the bachelors' compound. There was yet fifteen minutes before lock-up roll call;
he had walked out in a subconscious attempt to rid himself of
the pervading feeling of claustrophobia which he had had
throughout his stay. The attempt was futile; there was no
"outdoorness" about the outdoors on Venus, the bush
crowded the clearing in on itself, the leaden misty sky pressed
down on his head, and the steamy heat sat on his bare chest.
Still, it was better than the bunkroom in spite of the dehydra-
tors.

He had not yet obtained his evening ration of *rhira* and
felt, consequently, nervous and despondent, yet residual self-
respect caused him to cherish a few minutes clear thinking before he gave in to the cheerful soporific. It's getting me, he
thought, in a few more months I'll be taking every chance to
get to Venusburg, or, worse yet, signing a chit for married
quarters and condemning myself and my kids to a life-
sentence. When he first arrived the women clients, with their
uniformly dull minds and usually commonplace faces, had
seemed entirely unattractive. Now, he realized with dismay,
he was no longer so fussy. Why, he was even beginning to
lisp, as the other clients did, in unconscious imitation of the
amphibians.

Early, he had observed that the clients could be divided
roughly into two categories, the child of nature and the
broken men. The first were those of little imagination and
simple standards. In all probability they had known nothing
better back on Earth; they saw in the colonial culture, not
slavery, but freedom from responsibility, security, and an occasional spree. The others were the broken men, the outcasts,
they who had once been somebody, but, through some defect
of character, or some accident, had lost their places in society. Perhaps the judge had said, "Sentence suspended if you
ship for the colonies."

He realized with sudden panic that his own status was crys-
tallizing; he was becoming one of the broken men. His background on Earth was becoming dim in his mind; he had put

off for the last three days the labor of writing another letter
to Jones; he had spent all the last shift rationalizing the
necessity for taking a couple of days holiday at Venusburg.
Face it, son, face it, he told himself. You're slipping, you're
letting your mind relax into slave psychology. You've unloaded the problem of getting out of this mess onto Jones—
how do you know he *can* help you? For all you know he may
be dead. Out of the dimness of his memory he recaptured a
phrase which he had read somewhere, some philosopher of
history: "No slave is ever freed, *save he free himself.*"

All right, all right—pull up your socks, old son. Take a
brace. No more *rhira*—no, that wasn't practical; a man had
to have sleep. Very well, then, no *rhira* until lights-out, keep
your mind clear in the evenings and *plan*. Keep your eyes
open, find out all you can, cultivate friendships, and watch for
a chance.

Through the gloom he saw a human figure approaching the
gate of the compound. As it approached he saw that it was a
woman and supposed it to be one of the female clients. She
came closer, he saw that he was mistaken. It was Annek van
Huysen, daughter of the patron.

She was a husky, overgrown blond girl with unhappy eyes.
He had seen her many times, watching the clients as they returned from their labor, or wandering alone around the ranch
clearing. She was neither unsightly, nor in anywise attractive; her heavy adolescent figure needed more to flatter it
than the harness which all colonists wore as the maximum tolerable garment.

She stopped before him, and, unzipping the pouch at her
waist which served in lieu of pockets, took out a package of
cigarettes. "I found this back there. Did you lose it?"

He knew that she lied; she had picked up nothing since she
had come into sight. And the brand was one smoked on Earth
and by patrons; no client could afford such. What was she up
to?

He noted the eagerness in her face and the rapidity of her
breathing, and realized, with confusion, that this girl was
trying indirectly to make him a present. Why?

Wingate was not particularly conceited about his own physical beauty, or charm, nor had he any reason to be. But what
he had not realized was that among the common run of the
clients he stood out like a cock pheasant in a barnyard. But

that Annek found him pleasing he was forced to admit; there could be no other explanation for her trumped-up story and her pathetic little present.

His first impulse was to snub her. He wanted nothing of her and resented the invasion of his privacy, and he was vaguely aware that the situation could be awkward, even dangerous to him, involving, as it did, violations of custom which jeopardized the whole social and economic structure. From the viewpoint of the patrons, labor clients were almost as much beyond the pale as the amphibians. A liaison between a labor client and one of the womenfolk of the patrons could easily wake up old Judge Lynch.

But he had not the heart to be brusque with her. He could see the dumb adoration in her eyes; it would have required cold heartlessness to have repulsed her. Besides, there was nothing coy or provocative in her attitude; her manner was naive, almost childlike in its unsophistication. He recalled his determination to make friends; here was friendship offered, a dangerous friendship, but one which might prove useful in winning free.

He felt a momentary wave of shame that he should be weighing the potential usefulness of this defenseless child, but he suppressed it by affirming to himself that he would do her no harm, and, anyhow, there was the old saw about the vindictiveness of a woman scorned.

"Why, perhaps I did lose it," he evaded, then added, "It's my favorite brand."

"Is it?" she said happily. "Then do take it, in any case."

"Thank you. Will you smoke one with me? No, I guess that wouldn't do; your father would not want you to stay here that long."

"Oh, he's busy with his accounts. I saw that before I came out," she answered, and seemed unaware that she had given away her pitiful little deception. "But go ahead, I— I hardly ever smoke."

"Perhaps you prefer a meerschaum pipe, like your father."

She laughed more than the poor witticism deserved. After that they talked aimlessly, both agreeing that the crop was coming in nicely, that the weather seemed a little cooler than last week, and that there was nothing like a little fresh air after supper.

"Do you ever walk for exercise after supper?" she asked.

He did not say that a long day in the swamps offered more than enough exercise, but agreed that he did.

"So do I," she blurted out. "Lots of times up near the water tower."

He looked at her. "Is that so? I'll remember that." The signal for roll call gave him a welcome excuse to get away; three more minutes, he thought, and I would have had to make a date with her.

Wingate found himself called for swamp work the next day, the rush in the chopping sheds having abated. The crock lumbered and splashed its way around the long, meandering circuit, leaving one or more Earthmen at each supervision station. The car was down to four occupants, Wingate, Satchel, the Pusher, and Jimmie the Crocker, when the Pusher signalled for another stop. The flat, bright-eyed heads of amphibian natives broke water on three sides as soon as they were halted. "All right, Satchel," ordered the Pusher, "this is your billet. Over the side."

Satchel looked around. "Where's my skiff?" The ranchers used small flat-bottomed duralumin skiffs in which to collect their day's harvest. There was not one left in the crock.

"You won't need one. You goin' to clean this field for planting."

"That's okay. Still—I don't see nobody around, and I don't see no solid ground." The skiffs had a double purpose; if a man were working out of contact with other Earthmen and at some distance from safe dry ground, the skiff became his life boat. If the crocodile which was supposed to collect him broke down, or if for any other reason he had need to sit down or lie down while on station, the skiff gave him a place to do so. The older clients told grim stories of men who had stood in eighteen inches of water for twenty-four, forty-eight, seventy-two hours, and then drowned horribly, out of their heads from sheer fatigue.

"There's dry ground right over there." The Pusher waved his hand in the general direction of a clump of trees which lay perhaps a quarter of a mile away.

"Maybe so," answered Satchel equably. "Let's go see." He glanced at Jimmie, who turned to the Pusher for instructions.

"Damnation! Don't argue with me! Get over the side!"

"Not," said Satchel, "until I've seen something better than two feet of slime to squat on in a pinch."

The little water people had been following the argument with acute interest. They clucked and lisped in their own language; those who knew some pidgin English appeared to be giving newsy and undoubtedly distorted explanations of the events to their less sophisticated brethren. Fuming as he was, this seemed to add to the Pusher's anger.

"For the last time—get out there!"

"Well," said Satchel, settling his gross frame more comfortably on the floorplates, "I'm glad we've finished with that subject."

Wingate was behind the Pusher. This circumstance probably saved Satchel Hartley at least a scalp wound, for he caught the arm of the Pusher as he struck. Hartley closed in at once; the three wrestled for a few seconds on the bottom of the craft.

Hartley sat on the Pusher's chest while Wingate pried a blackjack away from the clenched fingers of the Pusher's right fist. "Glad you saw him reach for that, Hump," Satchel acknowledged, "or I'd be needin' an aspirin about now."

"Yeah, I guess so," Wingate answered, and threw the weapon as far as he could out into the marshy waste. Several of the amphibians streaked after it and dived. "I guess you can let him up now."

The Pusher said nothing to them as he brushed himself off, but he turned to the Crocker who had remained quietly in his saddle at the controls the whole time. "Why the hell didn't you help me?"

"I supposed you could take care of yourself, Boss," Jimmie answered noncommittally.

Wingate and Hartley finished that work period as helpers to labor clients already stationed. The Pusher had completely ignored them except for curt orders necessary to station them. But while they were washing up for supper back at the compound they received word to report to the Big House.

When they were ushered into the Patron's office they found the Pusher already there with his employer and wearing a self-satisfied smirk while Van Huysen's expression was black indeed.

"What's this I hear about you two?" he burst out. "Refusing work. Jumping my foreman. By Joe, I show you a thing or two!"

"Just a moment, Patron van Huysen," began Wingate quietly, suddenly at home in the atmosphere of a trial court, "no one refused duty. Hartley simply protested doing dangerous work without reasonable safeguards. As for the fracas, your foreman attacked us; we acted simply in self-defense, and desisted as soon as we had disarmed him."

The Pusher leaned over Van Huysen and whispered in his ear. The Patron looked more angry than before. "You did this with natives watching. Natives! You know colonial law? I could send you to the mines for this."

"No," Wingate denied, "your foreman did it in the presence of natives. Our role was passive and defensive throughout—"

"You call jumping my foreman peaceful? Now you listen to me— Your job here is to work. My foreman's job is to tell you where and how to work. He's not such a dummy as to lose me my investment in a man. He judges what work is dangerous, not you." The Pusher whispered again to his chief. Van Huysen shook his head. The other persisted, but the Patron cut him off with a gesture, and turned back to the two labor clients.

"See here—I give every dog one bite, but not two. For you, no supper tonight and no *rhira*. Tomorrow we see how you behave."

"But Patron van Huys—"

"That's all. Get to your quarters."

At lights out Wingate found, on crawling into his bunk, that someone had hidden therein a foodbar. He munched it gratefully in the dark and wondered who his friend could be. The food stayed the complaints of his stomach but was not sufficient, in the absence of *rhira*, to permit him to go to sleep. He lay there, staring into the oppressive blackness of the bunkroom and listening to the assorted irritating noises that men can make while sleeping, and considered his position. It had been bad enough but barely tolerable before; now, he was logically certain, it would be as near hell as a vindictive overseer could make it. He was prepared to believe, from what he had seen and the tales he had heard, that it would be very near indeed!

He had been nursing his troubles for perhaps an hour when he felt a hand touch his side. "Hump! Hump!" came a whisper, "come outside. Something's up." It was Jimmie.

He felt his way cautiously through the stacks of bunks and slipped out the door after Jimmie. Satchel was already outside and with him a fourth figure.

It was Annek van Huysen. He wondered how she had been able to get into the locked compound. Her eyes were puffy, as if she had been crying.

Jimmie started to speak at once, in cautious, low tones. "The kid tells us that I am scheduled to haul you two lugs back into Adonis tomorrow."

"What for?"

"She doesn't know. But she's afraid it's to sell you South. That doesn't seem likely. The Old Man has never sold anyone South—but then nobody ever jumped his pusher before. I don't know."

They wasted some minutes in fruitless discussion, then, after a bemused silence, Wingate asked Jimmie, "Do you know where they keep the keys to the crock?"

"No. Why do y—"

"I could get them for you," offered Annek eagerly.

"You can't drive a crock."

"I've watched you for some weeks."

"Well, suppose you can," Jimmie continued to protest, "suppose you run for it in the crock. You'd be lost in ten miles. If you weren't caught, you'd starve."

Wingate shrugged. "I'm not going to be sold South."

"Nor am I," Hartley added.

"Wait a minute."

"Well, I don't see any bet—"

"Wait a minute," Jimmie reiterated snappishly. "Can't you see I'm trying to think?"

The other three kept silent for several long moments. At last Jimmie said, "Okay. Kid, you'd better run along and let us talk. The less you know about this the better for you." Annek looked hurt, but complied docilely to the extent of withdrawing out of earshot. The three men conferred for some minutes. At last Wingate motioned for her to rejoin them.

"That's all, Annek," he told her. "Thanks a lot for everything you've done. We've figured a way out." He stopped, and then said awkwardly, "Well, good night."

She looked up at him.

Wingate wondered what to do or say next. Finally he led her around the corner of the barracks and bade her good night again. He returned very quickly, looking shame-faced. They re-entered the barracks.

Patron van Huysen also was having trouble getting to sleep. He hated having to discipline his people. By damn, why couldn't they all be good boys and leave him in peace? Not but what there was precious little peace for a rancher these days. It cost more to make a crop than the crop fetched in Adonis—at least it did after the interest was paid.

He had turned his attention to his accounts after dinner that night to try to get the unpleasantness out of his mind, but he found it hard to concentrate on his figures. That man Wingate, now . . . he had bought him as much to keep him away from that slavedriver Rigsbee as to get another hand. He had too much money invested in hands as it was in spite of his foreman always complaining about being short of labor. He would either have to sell some, or ask the bank to refinance the mortgage again.

Hands weren't worth their keep any more. You didn't get the kind of men on Venus that used to come when he was a boy. He bent over his books again. If the market went up even a little, the bank should be willing to discount his paper for a little more than last season. Maybe that would do it.

He had been interrupted by a visit from his daughter. Annek he was always glad to see, but this time what she had to say, what she finally blurted out, had only served to make him angry. She, preoccupied with her own thoughts, could not know that she hurt her father's heart, with a pain that was actually physical.

But that had settled the matter insofar as Wingate was concerned. He would get rid of the trouble-maker. Van Huysen ordered his daughter to bed with a roughness he had never before used on her.

Of course it was all his own fault, he told himself after he had gone to bed. A ranch on Venus was no place to raise a motherless girl. His Annekchen was almost a woman grown now; how was she to find a husband here in these outlands? What would she do if he should die? She did not know it, but there would be nothing left, nothing, not even a ticket to Terra. No, she would not become a labor client's vrouw; no, not while there was a breath left in his old tired body.

Well, Wingate would have to go, and the one they called Satchel, too. But he would not sell them South. No, he had never done that to one of his people. He thought with distaste of the great, factorylike plantations a few hundred miles fur ther from the pole, where the temperature was always twenty to thirty degrees higher than it was in his marshes and mortality among labor clients was a standard item in cost accounting. No, he would take them in and trade them at the assignment station; what happened to them at auction there would be none of his business. But he would not sell them directly South.

That gave him an idea; he did a little computing in his head and estimated that he might be able to get enough credit on the two unexpired labor contracts to buy Annek a ticket to Earth. He was quite sure that his sister would take her in, reasonably sure anyway, even though she had quarreled with him over marrying Annek's mother. He could send her a little money from time to time. And perhaps she could learn to be a secretary, or one of those other fine jobs a girl could get on Earth.

But what would the ranch be like without Annekchen?

He was so immersed in his own troubles that he did not hear his daughter slip out of her room and go outside.

Wingate and Hartley tried to appear surprised when they were left behind at muster for work. Jimmie was told to report to the Big House; they saw him a few minutes later, backing the big Remington out of its shed. He picked them up, then trundled back to the Big House and waited for the Patron to appear. Van Huysen came out shortly and climbed into his cabin with neither word nor look for anyone.

The crocodile started toward Adonis, lumbering a steady ten miles an hour. Wingate and Satchel conversed in subdued voices, waited, and wondered. After an interminable time the crock stopped. The cabin window flew open. "What's the matter?" Van Huysen demanded. "Your engine acting up?"

Jimmie grinned at him. "No, I stopped it."

"For what?"

"Better come up here and find out."

"By damn, I do!" The window slammed; presently Van Huysen reappeared, warping his ponderous bulk around the side of the little cabin. "Now what this monkeyshines?"

"Better get out and walk, Patron. This is the end of the line."

Van Huysen seemed to have no remark suitable in answer, but his expression spoke for him.

"No, I mean it," Jimmie went on. "This is the end of the line for you. I've stuck to solid ground the whole way, so you could walk back. You'll be able to follow the trail I broke;

you ought to be able to make it in three or four hours, fat as you are."

The Patron looked from Jimmie to the others. Wingate and Satchel closed in slightly, eyes unfriendly. "Better get goin', Fatty," Satchel said softly, "before you get chucked out headfirst."

Van Huysen pressed back against the rail of the crock, his hands gripping it. "I won't get out of my own crock," he said tightly.

Satchel spat in the palm of one hand, then rubbed the two together. "Okay, Hump. He asked for it—"

"Just a second." Wingate addressed Van Huysen, "See here, Patron van Huysen—we don't want to rough you up unless we have to. But there are three of us and we are determined. Better climb out quietly."

The older man's face was dripping with sweat which was not entirely due to the muggy heat. His chest heaved, he seemed about to defy them. Then something went out inside him. His figure sagged, the defiant lines in his face gave way to a whipped expression which was not good to see.

A moment later he climbed quietly, listlessly, over the side into the ankle-deep mud and stood there, stooped, his legs slightly bent at the knees.

When they were out of sight of the place where they had dropped their patron Jimmie turned the crock off in a new direction. "Do you suppose he'll make it?" asked Wingate.

"Who?" asked Jimmie. "Van Huysen? Oh, sure, he'll make it—probably." He was very busy now with his driving; the crock crawled down a slope and lunged into navigable water. In a few minutes the marsh grass gave way to open water. Wingate saw that they were in a broad lake whose further shores were lost in the mist. Jimmie set a compass course.

The far shore was no more than a strand; it concealed an overgrown bayou. Jimmie followed it a short distance, stopped the crock, and said, "This must be just about the place," in an uncertain voice. He dug under the tarpaulin folded up in one corner of the empty hold and drew out a broad flat paddle. He took this to the rail, and, leaning out, he smacked the water loudly with the blade: Slap! . . . slap, slap. . . . Slap!

He waited.

The flat head of an amphibian broke water near the side; it

studied Jimmie with bright, merry eyes. "Hello," said Jimmie.

It answered in its own language. Jimmie replied in the same tongue, stretching his mouth to reproduce the uncouth clucking syllables. The native listened, then slid underwater again.

He—or, more probably, she—was back in a few minutes, another with her. "Thigarek?" the newcomer said hopefully.

"Thigarek when we get there, old girl," Jimmie temporized. "Here . . . climb aboard." He held out a hand, which the native accepted and wriggled gracefully inboard. It perched its unhuman, yet oddly pleasing, little figure on the rail near the driver's seat. Jimmie got the car underway.

How long they were guided by their little pilot Wingate did not know, as the timepiece on the control panel was out of order, but his stomach informed him that it was too long. He rummaged through the cabin and dug out an iron ration which he shared with Satchel and Jimmie. He offered some to the native, but she smelled at it and drew her head away.

Shortly after that there was a sharp hissing noise and a column of steam rose up ten yards ahead of them. Jimmie halted the crock at once. "Cease firing!" he called out. "It's just us chickens."

"Who are you?" came a disembodied voice.

"Fellow travelers."

"Climb out where we can see you."

"Okay."

The native poked Jimmie in the ribs. "Thigarek," she stated positively.

"Huh? Oh, sure." He parceled out trade tobacco until she acknowledged the total, then added one more package for good will. She withdrew a piece of string from her left cheek pouch, tied up her pay, and slid over the side. They saw her swimming away, her prize carried high out of the water.

"Hurry up and show yourself!"

"Coming!" They climbed out into waist-deep water and advanced holding their hands overhead. A squad of four broke cover and looked them over, their weapons lowered but ready. The leader searched their harness pouches and sent one of his men on to look over the crocodile.

"You keep a close watch," remarked Wingate.

The leader glanced at him. "Yes," he said, "and no. The little people told us you were coming. They're worth all the watch dogs that were ever littered."

They got underway again with one of the scouting party

driving. Their captors were not unfriendly but not disposed to talk. "Wait till you see the Governor," they said.

Their destination turned out to be a wide stretch of moderately high ground. Wingate was amazed at the number of buildings and the numerous population. "How in the world can they keep a place like this a secret?" he asked Jimmie.

"If the state of Texas were covered with fog and had only the population of Waukegan, Illinois, you could hide quite a lot of things."

"But wouldn't it show on a map?"

"How well mapped do you think Venus is? Don't be a dope."

On the basis of the few words he had had with Jimmie beforehand Wingate had expected no more than a camp where fugitive clients lurked in the bush while squeezing a precarious living from the country. What he found was a culture and a government. True, it was a rough frontier culture and a simple government with few laws and an unwritten constitution, but a framework of customs was in actual operation and its gross offenders were punished—with no higher degree of injustice than one finds anywhere.

It surprised Humphrey Wingate that fugitive slaves, the scum of Earth, were able to develop an integrated society. It had surprised his ancestors that the transported criminals of Botany Bay should develop a high civilization in Australia. Not that Wingate found the phenomenon of Botany Bay surprising—that was history, and history is never surprising—after it happens.

The success of the colony was more credible to Wingate when he came to know more of the character of the Governor, who was also generalissimo, and administrator of the low and middle justice. (High justice was voted on by the whole community, a procedure that Wingate considered outrageously sloppy, but which seemed to satisfy the community.) As magistrate the Governor handed out decisions with a casual contempt for rules of evidence and legal theory that reminded Wingate of stories he had heard of the apocryphal Old Judge Bean, "The Law West of Pecos," but again the people seemed to like it.

The great shortage of women in the community (men outnumbered them three to one) caused incidents which more than anything else required the decisions of the Governor. Here, Wingate was forced to admit, was a situation in which traditional custom would have been nothing but a source of trouble; he admired the shrewd common sense and understanding of human nature with which the Governor sorted out conflicting strong human passions and suggested *modus operandi* for getting along together. A man who could maintain a working degree of peace in such matters did not need a legal education.

The Governor held office by election and was advised by an elected council. It was Wingate's private opinion that the Governor would have risen to the top in any society. The man had boundless energy, great gusto for living, a ready thunderous laugh—and the courage and capacity for making decisions. He was a "natural."

The three runaways were given a couple of weeks in which to get their bearings and find some job in which they could make themselves useful and self-supporting. Jimmie stayed with his crock, now confiscated for the community, but which still required a driver. There were other crockers available who probably would have liked the job, but there was tacit consent that the man who brought it in should drive it, if he wished. Satchel found a billet in the fields, doing much the same work he had done for Van Huysen. He told Wingate that he was actually having to work harder; nevertheless he liked it better because the conditions were, as he put it, "looser."

Wingate detested the idea of going back to agricultural work. He had no rational excuse, it was simply that he hated it. His radio experience at last stood him in good stead. The community had a jury-rigged, low-power radio on which a constant listening watch was kept, but which was rarely used for transmission, because of the danger of detection. Earlier runaway slave camps had been wiped out by the company police through careless use of radio. Nowadays they hardly dared use it, except in extreme emergency.

But they needed radio. The grapevine telegraph maintained through the somewhat slap-happy help of the little people enabled them to keep some contact with the other fugitive communities with which they were loosely confederated, but it was not really fast, and any but the simplest of messages were distorted out of recognition.

Wingate was assigned to the community radio when it was discovered that he had appropriate technical knowledge. The previous operator had been lost in the bush. His opposite number was a pleasant old codger, known as Doc, who could listen for signals but who knew nothing of upkeep and repair.

Wingate threw himself into the job of overhauling the anti-quated installation. The problems presented by lack of equipment, the necessity for "making do," gave him a degree of happiness he had not known since he was a boy, but was not aware of it.

He was intrigued by the problem of safety in radio communication. An idea, derived from some account of the pioneer days in radio, gave him a lead. His installation, like all others, communicated by frequency modulation. Somewhere he had seen a diagram for a totally obsolete type of transmitter, an amplitude modulator. He did not have much to go on, but he worked out a circuit which he believed would oscillate in that fashion and which could be hooked up from the gear at hand.

He asked the Governor for permission to attempt to build it. "Why not? Why not?" the Governor roared at him. "I haven't the slightest idea what you are talking about, son, but if you think you can build a radio that the company can't detect, go right ahead. You don't have to ask me; it's your pigeon."

"I'll have to put the station out of commission for sending."

"Why not?"

The problem had more knots in it than he had thought. But he labored at it with the clumsy but willing assistance of Doc. His first hookup failed; his forty-third attempt five weeks later worked. Doc, stationed some miles out in the bush, reported himself able to hear the broadcast via a small receiver constructed for the purpose, whereas Wingate picked up nothing whatsoever on the conventional receiver located in the same room with the experimental transmitter.

In the meantime he worked on his book.

Why he was writing a book he could not have told you. Back on Earth it could have been termed a political pamphlet against the colonial system. Here there was no one to convince of his thesis, nor had he any expectation of ever being able to present it to a reading public. Venus was his home. He knew that there was no chance for him ever to return; the only way lay through Adonis, and there, waiting for him, were warrants for half the crimes in the calendar, contract-jumping, theft, kidnapping, criminal abandonment, conspiracy, subverting government. If the company police ever laid hands on him, they would jail him and lose the key.

No, the book arose, not from any expectation of publication, but from a half-subconscious need to arrange his thoughts. He had suffered a complete upsetting of all the evaluations by which he had lived; for his mental health it was necessary that he formulate new ones. It was natural to his orderly, if somewhat unimaginative, mind that he set his reasons and conclusions forth in writing.

Somewhat diffidently he offered the manuscript to Doc. He had learned that the nickname title had derived from the man's former occupation on Earth; he had been a professor of economics and philosophy in one of the smaller universities. Doc had even offered a partial explanation of his presence on Venus. "A little matter involving one of my women students," he confided. "My wife took an unsympathetic view of the matter and so did the board of regents. The board had long considered my opinions a little too radical."

"Were they?"

"Heavens, no! I was a rockbound conservative. But I had an unfortunate tendency to express conservative principles in realistic rather than allegorical language."

"I suppose you're a radical now."

Doc's eyebrows lifted slightly. "Not at all. Radical and conservative are terms for emotional attitudes, not sociological opinions."

Doc accepted the manuscript, read it through, and returned it without comment. But Wingate pressed him for an opinion. "Well, my boy, if you insist—"

"I do."

"—I would say that you have fallen into the commonest fallacy of all in dealing with social and economic subjects— the 'devil theory.' "

"Huh?"

"You have attributed conditions to villainy that simply result from stupidity. Colonial slavery is nothing new; it is the inevitable result of imperial expansion, the automatic result of an antiquated financial structure—"

"I pointed out the part the banks played in my book."

"No, no, no! You think bankers are scoundrels. They are not. Nor are company officials, nor patrons, nor the governing classes back on Earth. Men are constrained by necessity and build up rationalizations to account for their acts. It is not even cupidity. Slavery is economically unsound, nonproductive, but men drift into it whenever the circumstances compel it. A different financial system—but that's another story."

"I still think it's rooted in human cussedness," Wingate said stubbornly.

"Not cussedness—simply stupidity. I can't prove it to you, but you will learn."

The success of the "silent radio" caused the Governor to send Wingate on a long swing around the other camps of the free federation to help them rig new equipment and to teach them how to use it. He spent four hard-working and soul-satisfying weeks, and finished with the warm knowledge that he had done more to consolidate the position of the free men against their enemies than could be done by winning a pitched battle.

When he returned to his home community, he found Sam Houston Jones waiting there.

Wingate broke into a run. "Sam!" he shouted. "Sam! *Sam!*" He grabbed his hand, pounded him on the back, and yelled at him the affectionate insults that sentimental men use in attempting to cover up their weakness. "Sam, you old scoundrel! When did you get here? How did you escape? And how the devil did you manage to come all the way from South Pole? Were you transferred before you escaped?"

"Howdy, Hump," said Sam. "Now one at a time, and not so fast."

But Wingate bubbled on. "My, but it's good to see your ugly face, fellow. And am I glad you came here—this is a great place. We've got the most up-and-coming little state in the whole federation. You'll like it. They're a great bunch—"

"What are you?" Jones asked, eyeing him. "President of the local champer of commerce?"

Wingate looked at him, and then laughed. "I get it. But seriously, you will like it. Of course, it's a lot different from what you were used to back on Earth—but that's all past and done with. No use crying over spilt milk, eh?"

"Wait a minute. You are under a misapprehension, Hump. Listen. I'm not an escaped slave. *I'm here to take you back.*"

Wingate opened his mouth, closed it, then opened it again. "But Sam," he said, "that's impossible. You don't know."

"I think I do."

"But you don't. There's no going back for me. If I did, I'd

have to face trial, and they've got me dead to rights. Even if I threw myself on the mercy of the court and managed to get off with a light sentence, it would be twenty years before I'd be a free man. No, Sam, it's impossible. You don't know the things I'm charged with."

"I don't, eh? It's cost me a nice piece of change to clear them up."

"Huh?"

"I know how you escaped. I know you stole a crock and kidnapped your patron and got two other clients to run with you. It took my best blarney and plenty of folding money to fix it. So help me, Hump—why didn't you pull something mild, like murder, or rape, or robbing a post office?"

"Well, now, Sam—I didn't do any of those things to cause you trouble. I had counted you out of my calculations. I was on my own. I'm sorry about the money."

"Forget it. Money isn't an item with me. I'm filthy with the stuff. You know that. It comes from exercising care in the choice of parents. I was just pulling your leg and it came off in my hand."

"Okay. Sorry." Wingate's grin was a little forced. Nobody likes charity. "But tell me what happened. I'm still in the dark."

"Right." Jones had been as much surprised and distressed at being separated from Wingate on grounding as Wingate had been. But there had been nothing for him to do about it until he received assistance from Earth. He had spent long weeks as a metal worker at South Pole, waiting and wondering why his sister did not answer his call for help. He had written letters to her to supplement his first radiogram, that being the only type of communication he could afford, but the days crept past with no answer.

When a message did arrive from her the mystery was cleared up. She had not received his radio to Earth promptly, because she too, was aboard the *Evening Star*—in the first class cabin, traveling, as was her custom, in a stateroom listed under her maid's name. "It was the family habit of avoiding publicity that stymied us," Jones explained. "If I hadn't sent the radio to her rather than to the family lawyers, or if she had been known by name to the purser, we would have gotten together the first day."

The message had not been relayed to her on Venus because the bright planet had by that time crawled to superior opposition on the far side of the sun from the Earth. For a matter of sixty earth days there was no communication, Earth to Venus. The message had rested, recorded but still scrambled, in the hands of the family firm, until she could be reached.

When she received it, she started a small tornado. Jones had been released, the liens against his contract paid, and ample credit posted to his name on Venus, in less than twenty-four hours. "So that was that," concluded Jones, "except that I've got to explain to big sister when I get home just how I got into this mess. She'll burn my ears."

Jones had charted a rocket for North Pole and had gotten on Wingate's trail at once. "If you had held on one more day, I would have picked you up. We retrieved your ex-patron about a mile from his gates."

"So the old villain made it. I'm glad of that."

"And a good job, too. If he hadn't I might never have been able to square you. He was pretty well done in, and his heart was kicking up plenty. Do you know that abandonment is a capital offense on this planet—with a mandatory death sentence if the victim dies?"

Wingate nodded. "Yeah, I know. Not that I ever heard of a patron being gassed for it, if the corpse was a client. But that's beside the point. Go ahead."

"Well, he was plenty sore. I don't blame him, though I don't blame you, either. Nobody wants to be sold South, and I gather that was what you expected. Well, I paid him for his crock, and I paid him for your contract—take a look at me, I'm your new owner!—and I paid for the contracts of your two friends as well. Still he wasn't satisfied. I finally had to throw in a first-class passage for his daughter back to Earth, and promise to find her a job. She's a big dumb ox, but I guess the family can stand another retainer. Anyhow, old son, you're a free man. The only remaining question is whether or not the Governor will let us leave here. It seems it's not done."

"No, that's a point. Which reminds me—how did you locate the place?"

"A spot of detective work too long to go into now. That's what took me so long. Slaves don't like to talk. Anyhow, we've a date to talk to the Governor tomorrow."

Wingate took a long time to get to sleep. After his first burst of jubilation he began to wonder. Did he want to go back? To return to the law, to citing technicalities in the interest of whichever side employed him, to meaningless social engagements, to the empty, sterile, bunkum-fed life of the fat and prosperous class he had moved among and served—did he want that, he, who had fought and worked with *men?* It seemed to him that his anachronistic little "invention" in radio had been of more worth than all he had ever done on Earth.

Then he recalled his book.

Perhaps he could get it published. Perhaps he could expose this disgraceful, inhuman system which sold men into legal slavery. He was really wide awake now. *There* was a thing to do! That was his job—to go back to Earth and plead the cause of the colonists. Maybe there was destiny that shapes men's lives after all. He was just the man to do it, the right social background, the proper training. *He* could make himself heard.

He fell asleep, and dreamt of cool, dry breezes, of clear blue sky. Of moonlight. . . .

Satchel and Jimmie decided to stay, even though Jones had been able to fix it up with the Governor. "It's like this," said Satchel. "There's nothing for us back on Earth, or we wouldn't have shipped in the first place. And you can't undertake to support a couple of deadheads. And this isn't such a bad place. It's going to be something someday. We'll stay and grow up with it."

They handled the crock which carried Jones and Wingate to Adonis. There was no hazard in it, as Jones was now officially their patron. What the authorities did not know they could not act on. The crock returned to the refugee community loaded with a cargo which Jones insisted on calling their ransom. As a matter of fact, the opportunity to send an agent to obtain badly needed supplies—one who could do so safely and without arousing the suspicions of the company authorities—had been the determining factor in the Governor's unprecedented decision to risk compromising the secrets of his constituency. He had been frankly not interested in Wingate's plans to agitate for the abolishment of the slave trade.

Saying goodbye to Satchel and Jimmie was something Wingate found embarrassing and unexpectedly depressing.

For the first two weeks after grounding on Earth both Wingate and Jones were too busy to see much of each other. Win-

gate had gotten his manuscript in shape on the return trip and
had spent the time getting acquainted with the waiting rooms
of publishers. Only one had shown any interest beyond a form
letter of rejection.

"I'm sorry, old man," that one had told him. "I'd like to
publish your book, in spite of its controversial nature, if it
stood any chance at all of success. But it doesn't. Frankly, it
has no literary merit whatsoever. I would as soon read a
brief."

"I think I understand," Wingate answered sullenly. "A big
publishing house can't afford to print anything which might
offend the powers-that-be."

The publisher took his cigar from his mouth and looked at
the younger man before replying. "I suppose I should resent
that," he said quietly, "but I won't. That's a popular miscon-
ception. The powers-that-be, as you call them, do not resort
to suppression in this country. We publish what the public will
buy. We're in business for that purpose.

"I was about to suggest, if you will listen, a means of making your book saleable. You need a collaborator, somebody
that knows the writing game and can put some guts in it."

Jones called the day that Wingate got his revised manuscript back from his ghost writer. "Listen to this, Sam," he
pleaded. "Look, what the dirty so-and-so has done to my
book. Look. '—I heard again the crack of the overseer's
whip. The frail body of my mate shook under the lash. He
gave one cough and slid slowly under the waist-deep water,
dragged down by his chains.' Honest, Sam, did you ever see
such drivel? And look at the new title: '*I Was a Slave on
Venus.*' It sounds like a confession magazine."

Jones nodded without replying. "And listen to this," Wingate went on, " '—crowded like cattle in the enclosure, their
naked bodies gleaming with sweat, the women slaves shrank
from the—' Oh, hell, I can't go on!"

"Well, they did wear nothing but harnesses."

"Yes, yes—but that has nothing to do with the case. Venus
costume is a necessary concomitant of the weather. There's
no excuse to leer about it. He's turned my book into a
damned sex show. And he had the nerve to defend his actions. He claimed that social pamphleteering is dependent on
extravagant language."

"Well, maybe he's got something. *Gulliver's Travels* certainly has some racy passages, and the whipping scenes in

Uncle Tom's Cabin aren't anything to hand a kid to read. Not to mention *Grapes of Wrath*."

"Well, I'm damned if I'll resort to that kind of cheap sensationalism. I've got a perfectly straightforward case that any one can understand."

"Have you now?" Jones took his pipe out of his mouth. "I've been wondering how long it would take you to get your eyes opened. What is your case? It's nothing new; it happened in the Old South, it happened again in California, in Mexico, in Australia, in South Africa. Why? Because in any expanding free-enterprise economy which does not have a money system designed to fit its requirements the use of mother-country capital to develop the colony inevitably results in subsistence-level wages at home and slave labor in the colonies. The rich get richer and the poor get poorer, and all the good will in the world on the part of the so-called ruling classes won't change it, because the basic problem is one requiring scientific analysis and a mathematical mind. Do you think you can explain those issues to the general public?"

"I can try."

"How far did I get when I tried to explain them to you—before you had seen the results? And you are a smart hombre. No, Hump, these things are too difficult to explain to people and too abstract to interest them. You spoke before a women's club the other day, didn't you?"

"Yes."

"How did you make out?"

"Well . . . the chairwoman called me up beforehand and asked me to hold my talk down to ten minutes, as their national president was to be there and they would be crowded for time."

"Hmm . . . you see where your great social message rates in competition. But never mind. Ten minutes is long enough to explain the issue to a person if they have the capacity to understand it. Did you sell anybody?"

"Well . . . I'm not sure."

"You're darn tootin' you're not sure. Maybe they clapped for you but how many of them came up afterwards and wanted to sign checks? No, Hump, sweet reasonableness won't get you anywhere in this racket. To make yourself heard you have to be a demagogue, or a rabble-rousing political preacher like this fellow Nehemiah Scudder. We're going merrily to hell and it won't stop until it winds up in a crash."

"But— Oh, the devil! What can we *do* about it?"

"Nothing. Things are bound to get a whole lot worse before they can get any better. Let's have a drink."

The Menace from Earth

MY NAME is Holly Jones and I'm fifteen. I'm very intelligent but it doesn't show, because I look like an underdone angel. Insipid.

I was born right here in Luna City, which seems to surprise Earthside types. Actually, I'm third generation; my grandparents pioneered in Site One, where the Memorial is. I live with my parents in Artemis Apartments, the new co-op in Pressure Five, eight hundred feet down near City Hall. But I'm not there much; I'm too busy.

Mornings I attend Tech High and afternoons I study or go flying with Jeff Hardesty—he's my partner—or whenever a tourist ship is in I guide groundhogs. This day the *Gripsholm* grounded at noon so I went straight from school to American Express.

The first gaggle of tourists was trickling in from Quarantine but I didn't push forward as Mr. Dorcas, the manager, knows I'm the best. Guiding is just temporary (I'm really a spaceship designer), but if you're doing a job you ought to do it well.

Mr. Dorcas spotted me. "Holly! Here, please. Miss Brentwood, Holly Jones will be your guide."

" 'Holly,' " she repeated. "What a quaint name. Are you really a guide, dear?"

I'm tolerant of groundhogs—some of my best friends are from Earth. As Daddy says, being born on Luna is luck, not judgment, and most people Earthside are stuck there. After all, Jesus and Gautama Buddha and Dr. Einstein were all groundhogs.

But they can be irritating. If high school kids weren't guides, whom could they hire? "My license says so," I said briskly and looked her over the way she was looking me over.

Her face was sort of familiar and I thought perhaps I had seen her picture in those society things you see in Earthside magazines—one of the rich playgirls we get too many of. She was almost loathsomely lovely . . . nylon skin, soft, wavy, silver-blond hair, basic specs about 35-24-34 and enough this and that to make me feel like a matchstick drawing, a low in-

timate voice and everything necessary to make plainer females think about pacts with the Devil. But I did not feel apprehensive; she was a groundhog and groundhogs don't count.

"All city guides are girls," Mr. Dorcas explained. "Holly is
very competent."

"Oh, I'm sure," she answered quickly and went into tourist
routine number one: surprise that a guide was needed just to
find her hotel, amazement at no taxicabs, same for no por-
ters, and raised eyebrows at the prospect of two girls walking
alone through "an underground city."

Mr. Dorcas was patient, ending with: "Miss Brentwood,
Luna City is the only metropolis in the Solar System where a
woman is really safe—no dark alleys, no deserted neighbor-
hoods, no criminal element."

I didn't listen; I just held out my tariff card for Mr. Dorcas
to stamp and picked up her bags. Guides shouldn't carry bags
and most tourists are delighted to experience the fact that
their thirty-pound allowance weighs only five pounds. But I
wanted to get her moving.

We were in the tunnel outside and me with a foot on the
slidebelt when she stopped. "I forgot! I want a city map."

"None available."

"Really?"

"There's only one. That's why you need a guide."

"But why don't they supply them? Or would that throw you
guides out of work?"

See? "You think guiding is makework? Miss Brentwood,
labor is so scarce they'd hire monkeys if they could."

"Then why not print maps?"

"Because Luna City isn't flat like—" I almost said, "—
groundhog cities," but I caught myself.

"—like Earthside cities," I went on. "All you saw from
space was the meteor shield. Underneath it spreads out and
goes down for miles in a dozen pressure zones."

"Yes, I know, but why not a map for each level?"

Groundhogs always say, "Yes, I know, but—"

"I can show you the one city map. It's a stereo tank twenty
feet high and even so all you see clearly are big things like the
Hall of the Mountain King and hydroponics farms and the
Bats' Cave."

"'The Bats' Cave,'" she repeated. "That's where they fly,
isn't it?"

"Yes, that's where we fly."

"Oh, I want to see it!"

"OK. It first . . . or the city map?"

She decided to go to her hotel first. The regular route to the Zurich is to slide up and west through Gray's Tunnel past the Martian Embassy, get off at the Mormon Temple, and take a pressure lock down to Diana Boulevard. But I know all the shortcuts; we got off at Macy-Gimbel Upper to go down their personnel hoist. I thought she would enjoy it.

But when I told her to grab a hand grip as it dropped past her, she peered down the shaft and edged back. "You're joking."

I was about to take her back the regular way when a neighbor of ours came down the hoist. I said, "Hello, Mrs. Greenberg," and she called back, "Hi, Holly. How are your folks?"

Susie Greenberg is more than plump. She was hanging by one hand with young David tucked in her other arm and holding the *Daily Lunatic*, reading as she dropped. Miss Brentwood stared, bit her lip, and said, "How do I do it?"

I said, "Oh, use both hands; I'll take the bags." I tied the handles together with my hanky and went first.

She was shaking when we got to the bottom. "Goodness, Holly, how do you stand it? Don't you get homesick?"

Tourist question number six. . . . I said, "I've been to Earth," and let it drop. Two years ago Mother made me visit my aunt in Omaha and I was *miserable*—hot and cold and dirty and beset by creepy-crawlies. I weighed a ton and I ached and my aunt was always chivvying me to go outdoors and exercise when all I wanted was to crawl into a tub and be quietly wretched. And I had hay fever. Probably you've never heard of hay fever—you don't die but you wish you could.

I was supposed to go to a girls' boarding school but I phoned Daddy and told him I was desperate and he let me come home. What groundhogs can't understand is that *they* live in savagery. But groundhogs are groundhogs and loonies are loonies and never the twain shall meet.

Like all the best hotels the Zurich is in Pressure One on the west side so that it can have a view of Earth. I helped Miss Brentwood register with the roboclerk and found her room; it had its own port. She went straight to it, began staring at Earth and going *ooh!* and *ahh!*

I glanced past her and saw that it was a few minutes past thirteen; sunset sliced straight down the tip of India—early enough to snag another client. "Will that be all, Miss Brentwood?"

Instead of answering she said in an awed voice, "Holly, isn't that the most beautiful sight you ever saw?"

"It's nice," I agreed. The view on that side is monotonous except for Earth hanging in the sky—but Earth is what tourists always look at even though they've just left it. Still, Earth is pretty. The changing weather is interesting if you don't have to be in it. Did you ever endure a summer in Omaha?

"It's gorgeous," she whispered.

"Sure," I agreed. "Do you want to go somewhere? Or will you sign my card?"

"What? Excuse me, I was daydreaming. No, not right now —yes, I do! Holly, I want to go out *there!* I must! Is there time? How much longer will it be light?"

"Huh? It's two days to sunset."

She looked startled. "How quaint. Holly, can you get us space suits? I've got to go outside."

I didn't wince—I'm used to tourist talk. I suppose a pressure suit looked like a space suit to them. I simply said, "We girls aren't licensed outside. But I can phone a friend."

Jeff Hardesty is my partner in spaceship designing, so I throw business his way. Jeff is eighteen and already in Goddard Institute, but I'm pushing hard to catch up so that we can set up offices for our firm: "Jones & Hardesty, Spaceship Engineers." I'm very bright in mathematics, which is everything in space engineering, so I'll get my degree pretty fast. Meanwhile we design ships anyhow.

I didn't tell Miss Brentwood this, as tourists think that a girl my age can't possibly be a spaceship designer.

Jeff has arranged his class to let him guide on Tuesdays and Thursdays; he waits at West City Lock and studies between clients. I reached him on the lockmaster's phone. Jeff grinned and said, "Hi, Scale Model."

"Hi, Penalty Weight. Free to take a client?"

"Well, I was supposed to guide a family party, but they're late."

"Cancel them. Miss Brentwood . . . step into pickup, please. This is Mr. Hardesty."

Jeff's eyes widened and I felt uneasy. But it did not occur to me that Jeff could be attracted by a *groundhog* . . . even though it is conceded that men are robot slaves of their body chemistry in such matters. I knew she was exceptionally decorative, but it was unthinkable that Jeff could be captivated by any groundhog, no matter how well designed. They don't speak our language!

I am not romantic about Jeff; we are simply partners. But anything that affects Jones & Hardesty affects me.

When we joined him at West Lock he almost stepped on his tongue in a disgusting display of adolescent rut. I was ashamed of him and, for the first time, apprehensive. Why are males so childish?

Miss Brentwood didn't seem to mind his behavior. Jeff is a big hulk; suited up for outside he looks like a Frost Giant from *Das Rheingold;* she smiled up at him and thanked him for changing his schedule. He looked even sillier and told her it was a pleasure.

I keep my pressure suit at West Lock so that when I switch a client to Jeff he can invite me to come along for the walk. This time he hardly spoke to me after that platinum menace was in sight. But I helped her pick out a suit and took her into the dressing room and fitted it. Those rental suits take careful adjusting or they will pinch you in tender places once out in vacuum . . . besides there are things about them that one girl ought to explain to another.

When I came out with her, not wearing my own, Jeff didn't even ask why I hadn't suited up—he took her arm and started toward the lock. I had to butt in to get her to sign my tariff card.

The days that followed were the longest in my life. I saw Jeff only once . . . on the slidebelt in Diana Boulevard, going the other way. She was with him.

Though I saw him but once, I knew what was going on. He was cutting classes and three nights running he took her to the Earthview Room of the Duncan Hines. None of my business!—I hope she had more luck teaching him to dance than I had. Jeff is a free citizen and if he wanted to make an utter fool of himself neglecting school and losing sleep over an upholstered groundhog that was his business.

But he should not have neglected the firm's business!

Jones & Hardesty had a tremendous backlog because we were designing Starship *Prometheus.* This project we had been slaving over for a year, flying not more than twice a week in order to devote time to it—and that's a sacrifice.

Of course you can't build a starship today, because of the power plant. But Daddy thinks that there will soon be a technological break-through and mass-conversion power plants will be built—which means starships. Daddy ought to know—he's Luna Chief Engineer for Space Lanes and Fermi Lecturer at Goddard Institute. So Jeff and I are designing a self-supporting interstellar ship on that assumption: quarters, auxiliaries, surgery, labs—everything.

Daddy thinks it's just practice but Mother knows better—Mother is a mathematical chemist for General Synthetics of Luna and is nearly as smart as I am. She realizes that Jones & Hardesty plans to be ready with a finished proposal while other designers are still floundering.

Which was why I was furious with Jeff for wasting time over this creature. We had been working every possible chance. Jeff would show up after dinner, we would finish our homework, then get down to real work, the *Prometheus* . . . checking each other's computations, fighting bitterly over details, and having a wonderful time. But the very day I introduced him to Ariel Brentwood, he failed to appear. I had finished my lessons and was wondering whether to start or wait for him—we were making a radical change in power plant shielding—when his mother phoned me. "Jeff asked me to call you, dear. He's having dinner with a tourist client and can't come over."

Mrs. Hardesty was watching me so I looked puzzled and said, "Jeff thought I was expecting him? He has his dates mixed." I don't think she believed me; she agreed too quickly.

All that week I was slowly convinced against my will that Jones & Hardesty was being liquidated. Jeff didn't break any more dates—how can you break a date that hasn't been made?—but we always went flying Thursday afternoons unless one of us was guiding. He didn't call. Oh, I know where he was; he took her iceskating in Fingal's Cave.

I stayed home and worked on the *Prometheus*, recalculating masses and moment arms for hydroponics and stores on the basis of the shielding change. But I made mistakes and twice I had to look up logarithms instead of remembering . . . I was so used to wrangling with Jeff over everything that I just couldn't function.

Presently I looked at the name plate of the sheet I was revising. "Jones & Hardesty" it read, like all the rest. I said to myself, "Holly Jones, quit bluffing; this may be The End. You knew that someday Jeff would fall for somebody."

"Of course . . . but not a *groundhog*."

"But he *did*. What kind of an engineer are you if you can't face facts? She's beautiful and rich—she'll get her father to give him a job Earthside. You hear me? *Earthside!* So you look for another partner . . . or go into business on your own."

I erased "Jones & Hardesty" and lettered "Jones & Company" and stared at it. Then I started to erase that, too—but it smeared; I had dripped a tear on it. Which was ridiculous!

The following Tuesday both Daddy and Mother were home for lunch which was unusual as Daddy lunches at the spaceport. Now Daddy can't even see you unless you're a spaceship but that day he picked to notice that I had dialed only a salad and hadn't finished it. "That plate is about eight hundred calories short," he said, peering at it. "You can't boost without fuel—aren't you well?"

"Quite well, thank you," I answered with dignity.

"Mmm . . . now that I think back, you've been moping for several days. Maybe you need a checkup." He looked at Mother.

"I do not either need a checkup!" I had *not* been moping—doesn't a woman have a right not to chatter?

But I hate to have doctors poking at me so I added, "It happens I'm eating lightly because I'm going flying this afternoon. But if you insist, I'll order pot roast and potatoes and sleep instead!"

"Easy, punkin'," he answered gently. "I didn't mean to intrude. Get yourself a snack when you're through . . . and say hello to Jeff for me."

I simply answered, "OK," and asked to be excused; I was humiliated by the assumption that I couldn't fly without Mr. Jefferson Hardesty but did not wish to discuss it.

Daddy called after me, "Don't be late for dinner," and Mother said, "Now, Jacob—" and to me, "Fly until you're tired, dear; you haven't been getting much exercise. I'll leave your dinner in the warmer. Anything you'd like?"

"No, whatever you dial for yourself." I just wasn't interested in food, which isn't like me. As I headed for Bats' Cave I wondered if I had caught something. But my cheeks didn't feel warm and my stomach wasn't upset even if I wasn't hungry.

Then I had a horrible thought. Could it be that I was jealous? *Me?*

It was unthinkable. I am not romantic; I am a career

woman. Jeff had been my partner and pal, and under my
guidance he could have become a great spaceship designer,
but our relationship was straightforward . . . a mutual respect for each other's abilities, with never any of that
lovey-dovey stuff. A career woman can't afford such things—
why look at all the professional time Mother had lost over
having me!

No, I couldn't be jealous; I was simply worried sick because my partner had become involved with a groundhog. Jeff
isn't bright about women and, besides, he's never been to
Earth and has illusions about it. If she lured him Earthside,
Jones & Hardesty was finished.

And somehow, "Jones & Company" wasn't a substitute: the
Prometheus might never be built.

I was at Bats' Cave when I reached this dismal conclusion.
I didn't feel like flying but I went to the locker room and got
my wings anyhow.

Most of the stuff written about Bats' Cave gives a wrong
impression. It's the air storage tank for the city, just like all
the colonies have—the place where the scavenger pumps,
deep down, deliver the air until it's needed. We just happen to
be lucky enough to have one big enough to fly in. But it never
was built, or anything like that; it's just a big volcanic bubble,
two miles across, and if it had broken through, way back
when, it would have been a crater.

Tourists sometimes pity us loonies because we have no
chance to swim. Well, I tried it in Omaha and got water up
my nose and scared myself silly. Water is for drinking, not
playing in; I'll take flying. I've heard groundhogs say, oh yes,
they had "flown" many times. But that's not *flying*. I did what
they talk about, between White Sands and Omaha. I felt
awful and got sick. Those things aren't safe.

I left my shoes and skirt in the locker room and slipped my
tail surfaces on my feet, then zipped into my wings and got
someone to tighten the shoulder straps. My wings aren't
ready-made condors; they are Storer-Gulls, custom-made for
my weight distribution and dimensions. I've cost Daddy a
pretty penny in wings, outgrowing them so often, but these
latest I bought myself with guide fees.

They're lovely!—titanalloy struts as light and strong as bird
bones, tension-compensated wrist-pinion and shoulder joints,
natural action in the alula slots, and automatic flap action in
stalling. The wing skeleton is dressed in styrene feather-foils

with individual quilling of scapulars and primaries. They almost fly themselves.

I folded my wings and went into the lock. While it was cycling I opened my left wing and thumbed the alula control—I had noticed a tendency to sideslip the last time I was airborne. But the alula opened properly and I decided I must have been overcontrolling, easy to do with Storer-Gulls; they're extremely maneuverable. Then the door showed green and I folded the wing and hurried out, while glancing at the barometer. Seventeen pounds—two more than Earth sea-level and nearly twice what we use in the city; even an ostrich could fly in that. I perked up and felt sorry for all groundhogs, tied down by six times proper weight, who never, never, *never* could fly.

Not even I could, on Earth. My wing loading is less than a pound per square foot, as wings and all I weigh less than twenty pounds. Earthside that would be over a hundred pounds and I could flap forever and never get off the ground.

I felt so good that I forgot about Jeff and his weakness. I spread my wings, ran a few steps, warped for lift and grabbed air—lifted my feet and was airborne.

I sculled gently and let myself glide toward the air intake at the middle of the floor—the Baby's Ladder, we call it, because you can ride the updraft clear to the roof, half a mile above, and never move a wing. When I felt it I leaned right, spoiling with right primaries, corrected, and settled in a counterclockwise soaring glide and let it carry me toward the roof.

A couple of hundred feet up, I looked around. The cave was almost empty, not more than two hundred in the air and half that number perched or on the ground—room enough for didoes. So as soon as I was up five hundred feet I leaned out of the updraft and began to beat. Gliding is no effort but flying is as hard work as you care to make it. In gliding I support a mere ten pounds on each arm—shucks, on Earth you work harder than that lying in bed. The lift that keeps you in the air doesn't take any work; you get it free from the shape of your wings just as long as there is air pouring past them.

Even without an updraft all a level glide takes is gentle sculling with your finger tips to maintain air speed; a feeble old lady could do it. The lift comes from differential air pressures but you don't have to understand it; you just scull a little and the air supports you, as if you were lying in an utterly perfect bed. Sculling keeps you moving forward just like sculling a rowboat . . . or so I'm told; I've never been in a rowboat. I had a chance to in Nebraska but I'm not that foolhardy.

But when you're really flying, you scull with forearms as well as hands and add power with your shoulder muscles. Instead of only the outer quills of your primaries changing pitch (as in gliding), now your primaries and secondaries clear back to the joint warp sharply on each downbeat and recovery; they no longer lift, they force you forward—while your weight is carried by your scapulars, up under your armpits.

So you fly faster, or climb, or both, through controlling the angle of attack with your feet—with the tail surfaces you wear on your feet, I mean.

Oh dear, this sounds complicated and isn't—you just *do* it. You fly exactly as a bird flies. Baby birds can learn it and they aren't very bright. Anyhow, it's easy as breathing after you learn . . . and more fun than you can imagine!

I climbed to the roof with powerful beats, increasing my angle of attack and slotting my alulae for lift without burble—climbing at an angle that would stall most fliers. I'm little but it's all muscle and I've been flying since I was six. Once up there I glided and looked around. Down at the floor near the south wall tourists were trying glide wings—if you call those things "wings." Along the west wall the visitors' gallery was loaded with goggling tourists. I wondered if Jeff and his Circe character were there and decided to go down and find out.

So I went into a steep dive and swooped toward the gallery, leveled off and flew very fast along it. I didn't spot Jeff and his groundhoggess but I wasn't watching where I was going and overtook another flier, almost collided. I glimpsed him just in time to stall and drop under, and fell fifty feet before I got control. Neither of us was in danger as the gallery is two hundred feet up, but I looked silly and it was my own fault; I had violated a safety rule.

There aren't many rules but they are necessary; the first is that orange wings always have the right of way—they're beginners. This flier did not have orange wings but I was overtaking. The flier underneath—or being overtaken—or nearer the wall—or turning counterclockwise, in that order, has the right of way.

I felt foolish and wondered who had seen me, so I went all the way back up, made sure I had clear air, then stooped like a hawk toward the gallery, spilling wings, lifting tail, and letting myself fall like a rock.

I completed my stoop in front of the gallery, lowering and spreading my tail so hard I could feel leg muscles knot and grabbing air with both wings, alulae slotted. I pulled level in an extremely fast glide along the gallery. I could see their eyes pop and thought smugly, "There! That'll show 'em!"

When darn if somebody didn't stoop on *me!* The blast from a flier braking right over me almost knocked me out of control. I grabbed air and stopped a sideslip, used some shipyard words and looked around to see who had blitzed me. I knew the black-and-gold wing pattern—Mary Muhlenburg, my best girl friend. She swung toward me, pivoting on a wing tip. "Hi, Holly! Scared you, didn't I?"

"You did not! You better be careful; the flightmaster'll ground you for a month."

"Slim chance! He's down for coffee."

I flew away, still annoyed, and started to climb. Mary called after me, but I ignored her, thinking, "Mary my girl, I'm going to get over you and fly you right out of the air."

This was a foolish thought as Mary flies every day and has shoulders and pectoral muscles like Mrs. Hercules. By the time she caught up with me I had cooled off and we flew side by side, still climbing. "Perch?" she called out.

"Perch," I agreed. Mary has lovely gossip and I could use a breather. We turned toward our usual perch, a ceiling brace for flood lamps—it isn't supposed to be a perch but the flightmaster hardly ever comes up there.

Mary flew in ahead of me, braked and stalled dead to a perfect landing. I skidded a little but Mary stuck out a wing and steadied me. It isn't easy to come into a perch, especially when you have to approach level. Two years ago a boy who had just graduated from orange wings tried it . . . knocked off his left alula and primaries on a strut—went fluttering and spinning down two thousand feet and crashed. He could have saved himself—you can come in safely with a badly damaged wing if you spill air with the other and accept the steeper glide, then stall as you land. But this poor kid didn't know how; he broke his neck, dead as Icarus. I haven't used that perch since.

We folded our wings and Mary sidled over. "Jeff is looking for you," she said with a sly grin.

My insides jumped but I answered coolly, "So? I didn't know he was here."

"Sure. Down there," she added, pointing with her left wing. "Spot him?"

Jeff wears striped red and silver, but she was pointing at the tourist glide slope, a mile away. "No."

"He's there all right." She looked at me sidewise. "But I wouldn't look him up if I were you."

"Why not? Or for that matter, why should I?" Mary can be exasperating.

"Huh? You always run when he whistles. But he has that Earthside siren in tow again today; you might find it embarrassing."

"Mary, whatever are you talking about?"

"Huh? Don't kid me, Holly Jones; you know what I mean."

"I'm sure I don't," I answered with cold dignity.

"Humph! Then you're the only person in Luna City who doesn't. Everybody knows you're crazy about Jeff; everybody knows she's cut you out . . . and that you are simply simmering with jealousy."

Mary is my dearest friend but someday I'm going to skin her for a rug. "Mary, that's preposterously ridiculous! How can you even think such a thing?"

"Look, darling, you don't have to pretend. I'm for you." She patted my shoulders with her secondaries.

So I pushed her over backwards. She fell a hundred feet, straightened out, circled and climbed, and came in beside me, still grinning. It gave me time to decide what to say.

"Mary Muhlenburg, in the first place I am not crazy about anyone, least of all Jeff Hardesty. He and I are simply friends. So it's utterly nonsensical to talk about me being 'jealous.' In the second place Miss Brentwood is a lady and doesn't go around 'cutting out' anyone, least of all me. In the third place she is simply a tourist Jeff is guiding—business, nothing more."

"Sure, sure," Mary agreed placidly. "I was wrong. Still—" She shrugged her wings and shut up.

"'Still' what? Mary, don't be mealy-mouthed."

"Mmm . . . I was wondering how you knew I was talking about Ariel Brentwood—since there isn't anything to it."

"Why, you mentioned her name."

"I did not."

I thought frantically. "Uh, maybe not. But it's perfectly

simple. Miss Brentwood is a client I turned over to Jeff myself, so I assumed that she must be the tourist you meant."

"So? I don't recall even saying she was a tourist. But since
she is just a tourist you two are splitting, why aren't you doing
the inside guiding while Jeff sticks to outside work? I thought
you guides had an agreement?"

"Huh? If he has been guiding her inside the city, I'm not
aware of it—"

"You're the only one who isn't."

"—and I'm not interested; that's up to the grievance committee. But Jeff wouldn't take a fee for inside guiding in any
case."

"Oh, sure!—not one he could *bank*. Well, Holly, seeing I
was wrong, why don't you give him a hand with her? She
wants to learn to glide."

Butting in on that pair was farthest from my mind. "If Mr.
Hardesty wants my help, he will ask me. In the meantime I
shall mind my own business . . . a practice I recommend to
you!"

"Relax, shipmate," she answered, unruffled. "I was doing
you a favor."

"Thank you, I don't need one."

"So I'll be on my way—got to practice for the gymkhana."
She leaned forward and dropped off. But she didn't practice
aerobatics; she dived straight for the tourist slope.

I watched her out of sight, then sneaked my left hand out
the hand slit and got at my hanky—awkward when you are
wearing wings but the floodlights had made my eyes water. I
wiped them and blew my nose and put my hanky away and
wiggled my hand back into place, then checked everything,
thumbs, toes, and fingers, preparatory to dropping off.

But I didn't. I just sat there, wings drooping, and thought.
I had to admit that Mary was partly right; Jeff's head was
turned completely . . . over a *groundhog*. So sooner or later
he would go Earthside and Jones & Hardesty was finished.

Then I reminded myself that I had been planning to be a
spaceship designer like Daddy long before Jeff and I teamed
up. I wasn't dependent on anyone; I could stand alone, like
Joan of Arc, or Lise Meitner.

I felt better . . . a cold, stern pride, like Lucifer in *Paradise Lost*.

I recognized the red and silver of Jeff's wings while he was
far off and I thought about slipping quietly away. But Jeff can

overtake me if he tries, so I decided, "Holly, don't be a fool! You've no reason to run . . . just be coolly polite."

He landed by me but didn't sidle up. "Hi, Decimal Point."

"Hi, Zero. Uh, stolen much lately?"

"Just the City Bank but they made me put it back." He frowned and added, "Holly, are you mad at me?"

"Why, Jeff, whatever gave you such a silly notion?"

"Uh . . . something Mary the Mouth said."

"Her? Don't pay any attention to what *she* says. Half of it's always wrong and she doesn't mean the rest."

"Yeah, a short circuit between her ears. Then you aren't mad?"

"Of *course* not. Why should I be?"

"No reason I know of. I haven't been around to work on the ship for a few days . . . but I've been awfully busy."

"Think nothing of it. I've been terribly busy myself."

"Uh, that's fine. Look, Test Sample, do me a favor. Help me out with a friend—a client, that is—well, she's a friend, too. She wants to learn to use glide wings."

I pretended to consider it. "Anyone I know?"

"Oh, yes. Fact is, you introduced us. Ariel Brentwood."

"'Brentwood?' Jeff, there are so many tourists. Let me think. Tall girl? Blonde? Extremely pretty?"

He grinned like a goof and I almost pushed him off. "That's Ariel!"

"I recall her . . . she expected me to carry her bags. But you don't need help, Jeff. She seemed very clever. Good sense of balance."

"Oh, yes, sure, all of that. Well, the fact is, I want you two to know each other. She's . . . well, she's just wonderful, Holly. A real person all the way through. You'll love her when you know her better. Uh . . . this seemed like a good chance."

I felt dizzy. "Why, that's very thoughtful, Jeff, but I doubt if she wants to know me better. I'm just a servant she hired—you know groundhogs."

"But she's not at all like the ordinary groundhog. And she does want to know you better—she *told* me so!"

After you told her to think so! I muttered. But I had talked myself into a corner. If I had not been hampered by polite upbringing I would have said, "On your way, vacuum skull! I'm not interested in your groundhog girl friends"—but what

I did say was, "OK, Jeff," then gathered the fox to my bosom and dropped off into a glide.

So I taught Ariel Brentwood to "fly." Look, those so-called wings they let tourists wear have fifty square feet of lift surface, no controls except warp in the primaries, a built-in dihedral to make them stable as a table, and a few meaningless degress of hinging to let the wearer think that he is "flying" by waving his arms. The tail is rigid, and canted so that if you stall (almost impossible) you land on your feet. All a tourist does is run a few yards, lift up his feet (he can't avoid it) and slide down a blanket of air. Then he can tell his grandchildren how he flew, really *flew*, "just like a bird."

An ape could learn to "fly" that much.

I put myself to the humiliation of strapping on a set of the silly things and had Ariel watch while I swung into the Baby's Ladder and let it carry me up a hundred feet to show her that you really and truly could "fly" with them. Then I thankfully got rid of them, strapped her into a larger set, and put on my beautiful Storer-Gulls. I had chased Jeff away (two instructors is too many), but when he saw her wing up, he swooped down and landed by us.

I looked up. "You again."

"Hello, Ariel. Hi, Blip. Say, you've got her shoulder straps too tight."

"Tut, tut," I said. "One coach at a time, remember? If you want to help, shuck those gaudy fins and put on some gliders . . . then I'll use you to show how not to. Otherwise get above two hundred feet and stay there; we don't need any dining-lounge pilots."

Jeff pouted like a brat but Ariel backed me up. "Do what teacher says, Jeff. That's a good boy."

He wouldn't put on gliders but he didn't stay clear, either. He circled around us, watching, and got bawled out by the flightmaster for cluttering the tourist area.

I admit Ariel was a good pupil. She didn't even get sore when I suggested that she was rather mature across the hips to balance well; she just said that she had noticed that I had the slimmest behind around there and she envied me. So I quit trying to get her goat, and found myself almost liking her as long as I kept my mind firmly on teaching. She tried hard and learned fast—good reflexes and (despite my dirty crack) good balance. I remarked on it and she admitted diffidently that she had had ballet training.

About mid-afternoon she said, "Could I possibly try real wings?"

"Huh? Gee, Ariel, I don't think so."

"Why not?"

There she had me. She had already done all that could be done with those atrocious gliders. If she was to learn more, she had to have real wings. "Ariel, it's dangerous. It's not what you've been doing, believe me. You might get hurt, even killed."

"Would you be held responsible?"

"No. You signed a release when you came in."

"Then I'd like to try it."

I bit my lip. If she had cracked up without my help, I wouldn't have shed a tear—but to let her do something too dangerous while she was my pupil . . . well, it smacked of David and Uriah. "Ariel, I can't stop you . . . but I should put my wings away and not have anything to do with it."

It was her turn to bite her lip. "If you feel that way, I can't ask you to coach me. But I still want to. Perhaps Jeff will help me."

"He probably will," I blurted out, "if he is as big a fool as I think he is!"

Her company face slipped but she didn't say anything because just then Jeff stalled in beside us. "What's the discussion?"

We both tried to tell him and confused him for he got the idea I had suggested it, and started bawling me out. Was I crazy? Was I trying to get Ariel hurt? Didn't I have any sense?

"*Shut up!*" I yelled, then added quietly but firmly, "Jefferson Hardesty, you wanted me to teach your girl friend, so I agreed. But don't butt in and don't think you can get away with talking to me like that. Now beat it! Take wing. Grab air!"

He swelled up and said slowly, "I absolutely forbid it."

Silence for five long counts. Then Ariel said quietly, "Come, Holly. Let's get me some wings."

"Right, Ariel."

But they don't rent real wings. Fliers have their own; they have to. However, there are second-hand ones for sale because kids outgrow them, or people shift to custom-made ones, or something. I found Mr. Schultz who keeps the key, and said that Ariel was thinking of buying but I wouldn't let her without a tryout. After picking over forty-odd pairs I found a set which Johnny Queveras had outgrown but which I knew were all right. Nevertheless I inspected them carefully. I could hardly reach the finger controls but they fitted Ariel.

While I was helping her into the tail surfaces I said, "Ariel? This is still a bad idea."

"I know. But we can't let men think they own us."

"I suppose not."

"They do own us, of course. But we shouldn't let them know it." She was feeling out the tail controls. "The big toes spread them?"

"Yes. But don't do it. Just keep your feet together and toes pointed. Look, Ariel, you really aren't ready. Today all you will do is glide, just as you've been doing. Promise?"

She looked me in the eye. "I'll do exactly what you say . . . not even take wing unless you OK it."

"OK. Ready?"

"I'm ready."

"All right. Wups! I goofed. They aren't orange."

"Does it matter?"

"It sure does." There followed a weary argument because Mr. Schultz didn't want to spray them orange for a tryout. Ariel settled it by buying them, then we had to wait a bit while the solvent dried.

We went back to the tourist slope and I let her glide, cautioning her to hold both alulae open with her thumbs for more lift at slow speeds, while barely sculling with her fingers. She did fine, and stumbled in landing only once. Jeff stuck around, cutting figure eights above us, but we ignored him. Presently I taught her to turn in a wide, gentle bank—you can turn those awful glider things but it takes skill; they're only meant for straight glide.

Finally I landed by her and said, "Had enough?"

"I'll never have enough! But I'll unwing if you say."

"Tired?"

"No." She glanced over her wing at the Baby's Ladder; a dozen fliers were going up it, wings motionless, soaring lazily. "I wish I could do that just once. It must be heaven."

I chewed it over. "Actually, the higher you are, the safer you are."

"Then why not?"

"Mmm . . . safer *provided* you know what you're doing. Going up that draft is just gliding like you've been doing. You lie still and let it lift you half a mile high. Then you come down the same way, circling the wall in a gentle glide. But you're going to be tempted to do something you don't understand yet—flap your wings, or cut some caper."

She shook her head solemnly. "I won't do anything you haven't taught me."

I was still worried. "Look, it's only half a mile up but you cover five miles getting there and more getting down. Half an hour at least. Will your arms take it?"

"I'm sure they will."

"Well . . . you can start down anytime; you don't have to go all the way. Flex your arms a little now and then, so they won't cramp. Just don't flap your wings."

"I won't."

"OK." I spread my wings. "Follow me."

I led her into the updraft, leaned gently right, then back left to start the counterclockwise climb, all the while sculling very slowly so that she could keep up. Once we were in the groove I called out, "Steady as you are!" and cut out suddenly, climbed and took station thirty feet over and behind her. "Ariel?"

"Yes, Holly?"

"I'll stay over you. Don't crane your neck; you don't have to watch me, I have to watch you. You're doing fine."

"I feel fine!"

"Wiggle a little. Don't stiffen up. It's a long way to the roof. You can scull harder if you want to."

"Aye aye, Cap'n!"

"Not tired?"

"Heavens, no! Girl, I'm living!" She giggled. "And mama said I'd never be an angel!"

I didn't answer because red-and-silver wings came charging at me, braked suddenly and settled into the circle between me and Ariel. Jeff's face was almost as red as his wings. "What the devil do you think you are doing?"

"Orange wings!" I yelled. "Keep clear!"

"Get down out of here! Both of you!"

"Get out from between me and my pupil. You know the rules."

"Ariel!" Jeff shouted. "Lean out of the circle and glide down. I'll stay with you."

"Jeff Hardesty," I said savagely, "I give you three seconds

to get out from between us—then I'm going to report you for violation of Rule One. For the third time—*Orange Wings!*"

Jeff growled something, dipped his right wing and dropped out of formation. The idiot sideslipped within five feet of Ariel's wing tip. I should have reported him for that; all the room you can give a beginner is none too much.

I said, "OK, Ariel?"

"OK, Holly. I'm sorry Jeff is angry."

"He'll get over it. Tell me if you feel tired."

"I'm not. I want to go all the way up. How high are we?"

"Four hundred feet, maybe."

Jeff flew below us a while, then climbed and flew over us . . . probably for the same reason I did: to see better. It suited me to have two of us watching her as long as he didn't interfere; I was beginning to fret that Ariel might not realize that the way down was going to be as long and tiring as the way up. I was hoping she would cry uncle. I knew I could glide until forced down by starvation. But a beginner gets tense.

Jeff stayed generally over us, sweeping back and forth— he's too active to glide very long—while Ariel and I continued to soar, winding slowly up toward the roof. It finally occurred to me when we were about halfway up that I could cry uncle myself; I didn't have to wait for Ariel to weaken. So I called out, "Ariel? Tired now?"

"No."

"Well, I am. Could we go down, please?"

She didn't argue, she just said, "All right. What am I to do?"

"Lean right and get out of the circle." I intended to have her move out five or six hundred feet, get into the return down draft, and circle the cave down instead of up. I glanced up, looking for Jeff. I finally spotted him some distance away and much higher but coming toward us. I called out, "Jeff! See you on the ground." He might not have heard me but he would see if he didn't hear; I glanced back at Ariel.

I couldn't find her.

Then I saw her, a hundred feet below—flailing her wings and falling, out of control.

I didn't know how it happened. Maybe she leaned too far, went into a sideslip and started to struggle. But I didn't try to figure it out; I was simply filled with horror. I seemed to hang there frozen for an hour while I watched her.

But the fact appears to be that I screamed "*Jeff!*" and broke into a stoop.

But I didn't seem to fall, couldn't overtake her. I spilled my wings completely—but couldn't manage to fall; she was as far away as ever.

You do start slowly, of course; our low gravity is the only thing that makes human flying possible. Even a stone falls a scant three feet in the first second. But that first second seemed endless.

Then I knew I was falling. I could feel rushing air—but I still didn't seem to close on her. Her struggles must have slowed her somewhat, while I was in an intentional stoop, wings spilled and raised over my head, falling as fast as possible. I had a wild notion that if I could pull even with her, I could shout sense into her head, get her to dive, then straighten out in a glide. But I couldn't *reach* her.

This nightmare dragged on for hours.

Actually we didn't have room to fall for more than twenty seconds; that's all it takes to stoop a thousand feet. But twenty seconds can be horribly long . . . long enough to regret every foolish thing I had ever done or said, long enough to say a prayer for us both . . . and to say good-by to Jeff in my heart. Long enough to see the floor rushing toward us and know that we were both going to crash if I didn't overtake her mighty quick.

I glanced up and Jeff was stooping right over us but a long way up. I looked down at once . . . and I was overtaking her . . . I was passing her—*I was under her!*

Then I was braking with everything I had, almost pulling my wings off. I grabbed air, held it, and started to beat without ever going to level flight. I beat once, twice, three times . . . and hit her from below, jarring us both.

Then the floor hit us.

I felt feeble and dreamily contented. I was on my back in a dim room. I think Mother was with me and I know Daddy was. My nose itched and I tried to scratch it, but my arms wouldn't work. I fell asleep again.

I woke up hungry and wide awake. I was in a hospital bed and my arms still wouldn't work, which wasn't surprising as they were both in casts. A nurse came in with a tray. "Hungry?" she asked.

"Starved," I admitted.

"We'll fix that." She started feeding me like a baby.

I dodged the third spoonful and demanded, "What happened to my arms?"

"Hush," she said and gagged me with a spoon.

But a nice doctor came in later and answered my question. "Nothing much. Three simple fractures. At your age you'll heal in no time. But we like your company so I'm holding you for observation of possible internal injury."

"I'm not hurt inside," I told him. "At least, I don't hurt."

"I told you it was just an excuse."

"Uh, Doctor?"

"Well?"

"Will I be able to fly again?" I waited, scared.

"Certainly. I've seen men hurt worse get up and go three rounds."

"Oh. Well, thanks. Doctor? What happened to the other girl? Is she . . . did she . . . ?"

"Brentwood? She's here."

"She's right here," Ariel agreed from the door. "May I come in?"

My jaw dropped, then I said, "Yeah. Sure. Come in."

The doctor said, "Don't stay long," and left. I said, "Well, sit down."

"Thanks." She hopped instead of walked and I saw that one foot was bandaged. She got on the end of the bed.

"You hurt your foot."

She shrugged. "Nothing. A sprain and a torn ligament. Two cracked ribs. But I would have been dead. You know why I'm not?"

I didn't answer. She touched one of my casts. "That's why. You broke my fall and I landed on top of you. You saved my life and I broke both your arms."

"You don't have to thank me. I would have done it for anybody."

"I believe you and I wasn't thanking you. You can't thank a person for saving your life. I just wanted to make sure you knew that I knew it."

I didn't have an answer so I said, "Where's Jeff? Is he all right?"

"He'll be along soon. Jeff's not hurt . . . though I'm surprised he didn't break both ankles. He stalled in beside us so

hard that he should have. But Holly . . . Holly my very dear
. . . I slipped in so that you and I could talk about him before he got here."

I changed the subject quickly. Whatever they had given me
made me feel dreamy and good, but not beyond being embarrassed. "Ariel, what happened? You were getting along fine—
then suddenly you were in trouble."

She looked sheepish. "My own fault. You said we were
going down, so I looked down. Really looked, I mean. Before
that, all my thoughts had been about climbing clear to the
roof; I hadn't thought about how far down the floor was.
Then I looked down . . . and got dizzy and panicky and went
all to pieces." She shrugged. "You were right. I wasn't ready."

I thought about it and nodded. "I see. But don't worry—
when my arms are well, I'll take you up again."

She touched my foot. "Dear Holly. But I won't be flying
again; I'm going back where I belong."

"Earthside?"

"Yes. I'm taking the *Billy Mitchell* on Wednesday."

"Oh. I'm sorry."

She frowned slightly. "Are you? Holly, you don't like me,
do you?"

I was startled silly. What can you say? Especially when it's
true? "Well," I said slowly, "I don't dislike you. I just don't
know you very well."

She nodded. "And I don't know you very well . . . even
though I got to know you a lot better in a very few seconds.
But Holly . . . listen please and don't get angry. It's about
Jeff. He hasn't treated you very well the last few days—while
I've been here, I mean. But don't be angry with him. I'm
leaving and everything will be the same."

That ripped it open and I couldn't ignore it, because if I
did, she would assume all sorts of things that weren't so. So I
had to explain . . . about me being a career woman . . .
how, if I had seemed upset, it was simply distress at breaking
up the firm of Jones & Hardesty before it even finished its
first starship . . . how I was *not* in love with Jeff but simply
valued him as a friend and associate . . . but if Jones & Hardesty couldn't carry on, then Jones & Company would. "So
you see, Ariel, it isn't necessary for you to give up Jeff. If you
feel you owe me something, just forget it. It isn't necessary."

She blinked and I saw with amazement that she was holding back tears. "Holly, Holly . . . you don't understand at all."

"I understand all right. I'm not a child."

"No, you're a grown woman . . . but you haven't found it out." She held up a finger. "One—Jeff doesn't love me."

"I don't believe it."

"Two . . . I don't love him."

"I don't believe that, either."

"Three . . . you say you don't love him—but we'll take that up when we come to it. Holly, am I beautiful?"

Changing the subject is a female trait but I'll never learn to do it that fast. "Huh?"

"I said, 'Am I beautiful?' "

"You know darn well you are!"

"Yes. I can sing a bit and dance, but I would get few parts if I were not, because I'm no better than a third-rate actress. So I have to be beautiful. How old am I?"

I managed not to boggle. "Huh? Older than Jeff thinks you are. Twenty-one, at least. Maybe twenty-two."

She sighed. "Holly, I'm old enough to be your mother."

"Huh? I don't believe that, either."

"I'm glad it doesn't show. But that's why, though Jeff is a dear, there never was a chance that I could fall in love with him. But how I feel about him doesn't matter; the important thing is that *he* loves *you*."

"*What?* That's the silliest thing you've said yet! Oh, he *likes* me—or did. But that's all." I gulped. "And it's all I want. Why, you should hear the way he talks to me."

"I have. But boys that age can't say what they mean; they get embarrassed."

"But—"

"Wait, Holly. I saw something you didn't because you were knocked cold. When you and I bumped, do you know what happened?"

"Uh, no."

"Jeff arrived like an avenging angel, a split second behind us. He was ripping his wings off as he hit, getting his arms free. He didn't even look at me. He just stepped across me and picked you up and cradled you in his arms, all the while bawling his eyes out."

"He *did?*"

"He did."

I mulled it over. Maybe the big lunk did kind of like me, after all.

Ariel went on, "So you see, Holly, even if you don't love him, you must be very gentle with him, because he loves you and you can hurt him terribly."

I tried to think. Romance was still something that a career woman should shun . . . but if Jeff really did feel that way— well . . . would it be compromising my ideals to marry him just to keep him happy? To keep the firm together? Eventually, that is?

But if I did, it wouldn't be Jones & Hardesty; it would be Hardesty & Hardesty.

Ariel was still talking: "—you might even fall in love with him. It does happen, hon, and if it did, you'd be sorry if you had chased him away. Some other girl would grab him; he's awfully nice."

"But—" I shut up for I heard Jeff's step—I can always tell it. He stopped in the door and looked at us, frowning.

"Hi, Ariel."

"Hi, Jeff."

"Hi, Fraction." He looked me over. "My, but you're a mess."

"You aren't pretty yourself. I hear you have flat feet."

"Permanently. How do you brush your teeth with those things on your arms?"

"I don't."

Ariel slid off the bed, balanced on one foot. "Must run. See you later, kids."

"So long, Ariel."

"Good-by, Ariel. Uh . . . thanks."

Jeff closed the door after she hopped away, came to the bed and said gruffly, "Hold still."

Then he put his arms around me and kissed me.

Well, I couldn't stop him, could I? With both arms broken? Besides, it was consonant with the new policy for the firm. I was startled speechless because Jeff never kisses me, except birthday kisses, which don't count. But I tried to kiss back and show that I appreciated it.

I don't know what the stuff was they had been giving me but my ears began to ring and I felt dizzy again.

Then he was leaning over me. "Runt," he said mournfully, "you sure give me a lot of grief."

"You're no bargain yourself, flathead," I answered with dignity.

"I suppose not." He looked me over sadly. "What are you crying for?"

I didn't know that I had been. Then I remembered why. "Oh, Jeff—I busted my pretty wings!"

"We'll get you more. Uh, brace yourself. I'm going to do it again."

"All right." He did.

I suppose Hardesty & Hardesty has more rhythm than Jones & Hardesty.

It really sounds better.

"If This Goes On—"

IT WAS COLD on the rampart. I slapped my numbed hands together, then stopped hastily for fear of disturbing the Prophet. My post that night was just outside his personal apartments—a post that I had won by taking more than usual care to be neat and smart at guard mount . . . but I had no wish to call attention to myself now.

I was young then and not too bright—a legate fresh out of West Point, and a guardsman in the Angels of the Lord, the personal guard of the Prophet Incarnate. At birth my mother had consecrated me to the Church and at eighteen my Uncle Absolom, a senior lay censor, had prayed an appointment to the Military Academy for me from the Council of Elders.

West Point had suited me. Oh, I had joined in the usual griping among classmates, the almost ritualistic complaining common to all military life, but truthfully I enjoyed the monastic routine—up at five, two hours of prayers and meditation, then classes and lectures in the endless subjects of a military education, strategy and tactics, theology, mob psychology, basic miracles. In the afternoons we practiced with vortex guns and blasters, drilled with tanks, and hardened our bodies with exercise.

I did not stand very high on graduation and had not really expected to be assigned to the Angels of the Lord, even though I had put in for it. But I had always gotten top marks in piety and stood well enough in most of the practical subjects; I was chosen. It made me almost sinfully proud—the holiest regiment of the Prophet's hosts, even the privates of which were commissioned officers and whose Colonel-in-Chief was the Prophet's Sword Triumphant, marshal of all the hosts. The day I was invested in the shining buckler and spear worn only by the Angels I vowed to petition to study for the priesthood as soon as promotion to captain made me eligible.

But this night, months later, though my buckler was still shining bright, there was a spot of tarnish in my heart. Somehow, life at New Jerusalem was not as I had imagined it while at West Point. The Palace and Temple were shot through with intrigue and politics; priests and deacons, ministers of state, and Palace functionaries all seemed engaged in a scramble for power and favor at the hand of the Prophet. Even the officers of my own corps seemed corrupted by it. Our proud motto *"Non Sibi, Sed Dei"* now had a wry flavor in my mouth.

Not that I was without sin myself. While I had not joined in the struggle for worldly preference, I had done something which I knew in my heart to be worse: I had looked with longing on a consecrated female.

Please understand me better than I understood myself. I was a grown man in body, an infant in experience. My own mother was the only woman I had ever known well. As a kid in junior seminary before going to the Point I was almost afraid of girls; my interests were divided between my lessons, my mother, and our parish's troop of Cherubim, in which I was a patrol leader and an assiduous winner of merit badges in everything from woodcraft to memorizing scripture. If there had been a merit badge to be won in the subject of girls —but of course there was not.

At the Military Academy I simply saw no females, nor did I have much to confess in the way of evil thoughts. My human feelings were pretty much still in freeze, and my occasional uneasy dreams I regarded as temptations sent by Old Nick. But New Jerusalem is not West Point and the Angels were neither forbidden to marry nor were we forbidden proper and sedate association with women. True, most of my fellows did not ask permission to marry, as it would have meant transferring to one of the regular regiments and many of them cherished ambitions for the military priesthood—but it was not forbidden.

Nor were the lay deaconesses who kept house around the Temple and the Palace forbidden to marry. But most of them were dowdy old creatures who reminded me of my aunts, hardly subjects for romantic thoughts. I used to chat with them occasionally around the corridors, no harm in that. Nor was I attracted especially by any of the few younger sisters— until I met Sister Judith.

I had been on watch in this very spot more than a month earlier. It was the first time I had stood guard outside the Prophet's apartments and, while I was nervous when first posted, at that moment I had been no more than alert against the possibility of the warden-of-the-watch making his rounds.

That night a light had shone brightly far down the inner corridor opposite my post and I had heard a sound of people moving; I had glanced at my wrist chrono—yes, that would be the Virgins ministering to the Prophet . . . no business of mine. Each night at ten o'clock their watch changed—their "guard mount" I called it, though I had never seen the ceremony and never would. All that I actually knew about it was that those coming on duty for the next twenty-four hours drew lots at that time for the privilege of personal attendance in the sacred presence of the Prophet Incarnate.

I had listened briefly and had turned away. Perhaps a quarter of an hour later a slight form engulfed in a dark cloak had slipped past me to the parapet, there to stand and look at the stars. I had had my blaster out at once, then had returned it sheepishly, seeing that it was a deaconess.

I had assumed that she was a lay deaconess; I swear that it did not occur to me that she might be a holy deaconess. There was no rule in my order book telling me to forbid them to come outside, but I had never heard of one doing so.

I do not think that she had seen me before I spoke to her. "Peace be unto you, sister."

She had jumped and suppressed a squeal, then had gathered her dignity to answer, "And to you, *little* brother."

It was then that I had seen on her forehead the Seal of Solomon, the mark of the personal family of the Prophet. "Your pardon, Elder Sister. I did not see."

"I am not annoyed." It had seemed to me that she invited conversation. I knew that it was not proper for us to converse privately; her mortal being was dedicated to the Prophet just as her soul was the Lord's, but I was young and lonely—and she was young and very pretty.

"Do you attend the Holy One this night, Elder Sister?"

She had shaken her head at that. "No, the honor passed me by. My lot was not drawn."

"It must be a great and wonderful privilege to serve him directly."

"No doubt, though I cannot say of my own knowledge. My lot has never yet been drawn." She had added impulsively, "I'm a little nervous about it. You see, I haven't been here long."

Even though she was my senior in rank, her display of feminine weakness had touched me. "I am sure that you will deport yourself with credit."

"Thank you."

We had gone on chatting. She had been in New Jerusalem, it developed, even less time than had I. She had been reared on a farm in upper New York State and there she had been sealed to the Prophet at the Albany Seminary. In turn I had told her that I had been born in the middle west, not fifty miles from the Well of Truth, where the First Prophet was incarnated. I then told her that my name was John Lyle and she had answered that she was called Sister Judith.

I had forgotten all about the warden-of-the-watch and his pesky rounds and was ready to chat all night, when my chrono had chimed the quarter hour. "Oh, dear!" Sister Judith had exclaimed. "I should have gone straight back to my cell." She had started to hurry away, then had checked herself. "You wouldn't tell on me. . . . John Lyle?"

"Me? Oh, never!"

I had continued to think about her the rest of the watch. When the warden did make rounds I was a shade less than alert.

A mighty little on which to found a course of folly, eh? A single drink is a great amount to a teetotaler; I was not able to get Sister Judith out of my mind. In the month that followed I saw her half a dozen times. Once I passed her on an escalator; she was going down as I was going up. We did not even speak, but she had recognized me and smiled. I rode that escalator all night that night in my dreams, but I could never get off and speak to her. The other encounters were just as trivial. Another time I heard her voice call out to me quietly, "Hello, John Lyle," and I turned just in time to see a hooded figure go past my elbow through a door. Once I watched her feeding the swans in the moat; I did not dare approach her but I think that she saw me.

The *Temple Herald* printed the duty lists of both my service and hers. I was standing a watch in five; the Virgins drew lots once a week. So it was just over a month later that our watches again matched. I saw her name—and vowed that I would win the guard mount that evening and again be posted at the post of honor before the Prophet's own apartments. I had no reason to think that Judith would seek me out on the rampart—but I was sure in my heart that she would. Never at West Point had I ever expended more spit-and-polish; I could have used my buckler for a shaving mirror.

But here it was nearly half past ten and no sign of Judith,

although I had heard the Virgins gather down the corridor promptly at ten. All I had to show for my efforts was the poor privilege of standing watch at the coldest post in the Palace.

Probably, I thought glumly, she comes out to flirt with the guardsmen on watch everytime she has a chance. I recalled bitterly that all women were vessels of iniquity and had always been so since the Fall of Man. Who was I to think that she had singled me out for special friendship? She had probably considered the night too cold to bother.

I heard a footstep and my heart leaped with joy. But it was only the warden making his rounds. I brought my pistol to the ready and challenged him; his voice came back, "Watchman, what of the night?"

I answered mechanically, "Peace on Earth," and added, "It is cold, Elder Brother."

"Autumn in the air," he agreed. "Chilly even in the Temple." He passed on by with his pistol and his bandolier of paralysis bombs slapping his armor to his steps. He was a nice old duffer and usually stopped for a few friendly words; tonight he was probably eager to get back to the warmth of the guardroom. I went back to my sour thoughts.

"Good evening, John Lyle."

I almost jumped out of my boots. Standing in the darkness just inside the archway was Sister Judith. I managed to splutter, "Good evening, Sister Judith," as she moved toward me.

"Ssh!" she cautioned me. "Someone might hear us. John . . . John Lyle—it finally happened. My lot was drawn!"

I said, "Huh?" then added lamely, "Felicitations, Elder Sister. May God make his face to shine on your holy service."

"Yes, yes, thanks," she answered quickly, "but John . . . I had intended to steal a few moments to chat with you. Now I can't—I must be at the robing room for indoctrination and prayer almost at once. I must run."

"You'd better hurry," I agreed. I was disappointed that she could not stay, happy for her that she was honored, and exultant that she had not forgotten me. "God go with you."

"But I just had to tell you that I had been chosen." Her eyes were shining with what I took to be holy joy; her next words startled me. "I'm scared, John Lyle."

"Eh? Frightened?" I suddenly recalled how I had felt, how my voice had cracked, the first time I ever drilled a platoon. "Do not be. You will be sustained."

"Oh, I hope so! Pray for me, John." And she was gone, lost in the dark corridor.

I did pray for her and I tried to imagine where she was, what she was doing. But since I knew as little about what went on inside the Prophet's private chambers as a cow knows about courts-martial, I soon gave it up and simply thought about Judith. Later, an hour or more, my revery was broken by a high scream inside the Palace, followed by a commotion, and running footsteps. I dashed down the inner corridor and found a knot of women gathered around the portal to the Prophet's apartments. Two or three others were carrying someone out the portal; they stopped when they reached the corridor and eased their burden to the floor.

"What's the trouble?" I demanded and drew my side arm clear.

An elderly Sister stepped in front of me. "It is nothing. Return to your post, legate."

"I heard a scream."

"No business of yours. One of the Sisters fainted when the Holy One required service of her."

"Who was it?"

"You are rather nosy, little brother." She shrugged. "Sister Judith, if it matters."

I did not stop to think but snapped, "Let me help her!" and started forward. She barred my way.

"Are you out of your mind? Her sisters will return her to her cell. Since when do the Angels minister to nervous Virgins?"

I could easily have pushed her aside with one finger, but she was right. I backed down and went unwillingly back to my post.

For the next few days I could not get Sister Judith out of my mind. Off watch, I prowled the parts of the Palace I was free to visit, hoping to catch sight of her. She might be ill, or she might be confined to her cell for what must certainly have been a major breach of discipline. But I never saw her.

My roommate, Zebadiah Jones, noticed my moodiness and tried to rouse me out of it. Zeb was three classes senior to me and I had been one of his plebes at the Point; now he was my closest friend and my only confidant. "Johnnie old son, you look like a corpse at your own wake. What's eating on you?"

"Huh? Nothing at all. Touch of indigestion, maybe."

"So? Come on, let's go for a walk. The air will do you good."

I let him herd me outside. He said nothing but banalities until we were on the broad terrace surrounding the south turret and free of the danger of eye and ear devices. When we were well away from anyone else he said softly, "Come on. Spill it."

"Shucks, Zeb, I can't burden anybody else with it."

"Why not? What's a friend for?"

"Uh, you'd be shocked."

"I doubt it. The last time I was shocked was when I drew four of a kind to an ace kicker. It restored my faith in miracles and I've been relatively immune ever since. Come on—we'll call this a privileged communication—elder adviser and all that sort of rot."

I let him persuade me. To my surprise Zeb was not shocked to find that I let myself become interested in a holy deaconess. So I told him the whole story and added to it my doubts and troubles, the misgivings that had been growing in me since the day I reported for duty at New Jerusalem.

He nodded casually. "I can see how it would affect you that way, knowing you. See here, you haven't admitted any of this at confession, have you?"

"No," I admitted with embarrassment.

"Then don't. Nurse your own fox. Major Bagby is broad-minded, you wouldn't shock him—but he might find it necessary to pass it on to his superiors. You wouldn't want to face Inquisition even if you were alabaster innocent. In fact, especially since you are innocent—and you *are*, you know; everybody has impious thoughts at times. But the Inquisitor expects to find sin; if he doesn't find it, he keeps on digging."

At the suggestion that I might be put to the Question my stomach almost turned over. I tried not to show it for Zeb went on calmly, "Johnnie my lad, I admire your piety and your innocence, but I don't envy it. Sometimes too much piety is more of a handicap than too little. You find yourself shocked at the idea that it takes politics as well as psalm singing to run a big country. Now take me; I noticed the same things when I was new here, but I hadn't expected anything different and wasn't shocked."

"But—" I shut up. His remarks sounded painfully like heresy; I changed the subject. "Zeb, what do you suppose it could have been that upset Judith so and caused her to faint the night she served the Prophet?"

"Eh? How should I know?" He glanced at me and looked away.

"Well, I just thought you might. You generally have all the gossip around the Palace."

"Well . . . oh, forget it, old son. It's really not important."

"Then you *do* know?"

"I didn't say that. Maybe I could make a close guess, but you don't want guesses. So forget it."

I stopped strolling, stepped in front of him and faced him. "Zeb, anything you know about it—or can guess—I want to hear. It's important to me."

"Easy now! You were afraid of shocking me; it could be that I don't want to shock you."

"What do you mean? Tell me!"

"Easy, I said. We're out strolling, remember, without a care in the world, talking about our butterfly collections and wondering if we'll have stewed beef again for dinner tonight."

Still fuming, I let him take me along with him. He went on more quietly, "John, you obviously aren't the type to learn things just by keeping your ear to the ground—and you've not yet studied any of the Inner Mysteries, now have you?"

"You know I haven't. The psych classification officer hasn't cleared me for the course. I don't know why."

"I should have let you read some of the installments while I was boning it. No, that was before you graduated. Too bad, for they explain things in much more delicate language than I know how to use—and justify every bit of it thoroughly, if you care for the dialectics of religious theory. John, what is your notion of the duties of the Virgins?"

"Why, they wait on him, and cook his food, and so forth."

"They surely do. And so forth. This Sister Judith—an innocent little country girl the way you describe her. Pretty devout, do you think?"

I answered somewhat stiffly that her devoutness had first attracted me to her. Perhaps I believed it.

"Well, it could be that she simply became shocked at overhearing a rather worldly and cynical discussion between the Holy One and, oh, say the High Bursar—taxes and tithes and the best way to squeeze them out of the peasants. It might be something like that, although the scribe for such a conference would hardly be a grass-green Virgin on her first service. No, it was almost certainly the 'And so forth.'"

"Huh? I don't follow you."

Zeb sighed. "You really are one of God's innocents, aren't you? Holy Name, I thought you knew and were just too stubbornly straight-laced to admit it. Why, even the Angels carry on with the Virgins at times, after the Prophet is through with them. Not to mention the priests and the deacons. I remember a time when—" He broke off suddenly, catching sight of my face. "Wipe that look off your face! Do you want somebody to notice us?"

I tried to do so, with terrible thoughts jangling around inside my head. Zeb went on quietly, "It's my guess, if it matters that much to you, that your friend Judith still merits the title 'Virgin' in the purely physical sense as well as the spiritual. She might even stay that way, if the Holy One is as angry with her as he probably was. She is probably as dense as you are and failed to understand the symbolic explanations given her—then blew her top when it came to the point where she couldn't fail to understand, so he kicked her out. Small wonder!"

I stopped again, muttering to myself biblical expressions I hardly thought I knew. Zeb stopped, too, and stood looking at me with a smile of cynical tolerance. "Zeb," I said, almost pleading with him, "these are terrible things. Terrible! Don't tell me that you approve?"

"Approve? Man, it's all part of the Plan. I'm sorry you haven't been cleared for higher study. See here, I'll give you a rough briefing. God wastes not. Right?"

"That's sound doctrine."

"God requires nothing of man beyond his strength. Right?"

"Yes, but—"

"Shut up. God commands man to be fruitful. The Prophet Incarnate, being especially holy, is required to be especially fruitful. That's the gist of it; you can pick up the fine points when you study it. In the meantime, if the Prophet can humble himself to the flesh in order to do his plain duty, who are you to raise a ruction? Answer me that."

I could not answer, of course, and we continued our walk in silence. I had to admit the logic of what he had said and that the conclusions were built up from the revealed doctrines. The trouble was that I wanted to eject the conclusions, throw them up as if they had been something poisonous I had swallowed.

Presently I was consoling myself with the thought that Zeb felt sure that Judith had not been harmed. I began to feel better, telling myself that Zeb was right, that it was not my place, most decidedly not my place, to sit in moral judgment on the Holy Prophet Incarnate.

My mind was just getting around to worrying the thought that my relief over Judith arose solely from the fact that I had looked on her sinfully, that there could not possibly be one rule for one holy deaconess, another rule for all the rest, and I was beginning to be unhappy again—when Zeb stopped suddenly. "What was that?"

We hurried to the parapet of the terrace and looked down the wall. The south wall lies close to the city proper. A crowd of fifty or sixty people was charging up the slope that led to the Palace walls. Ahead of them, running with head averted, was a man dressed in a long gabardine. He was headed for the Sanctuary gate.

Zebadiah looked down and answered himself. "That's what the racket is—some of the rabble stoning a pariah. He probably was careless enough to be caught outside the ghetto after five." He stared down and shook his head. "I don't think he is going to make it."

Zeb's prediction was realized at once; a large rock caught the man between the shoulder blades, he stumbled and went down. They were on him at once. He struggled to his knees, was struck by a dozen stones, went down in a heap. He gave a broken high-pitched wail, then drew a fold of the gabardine across his dark eyes and strong Roman nose.

A moment later there was nothing to be seen but a pile of rocks and a protruding slippered foot. It jerked and was still.

I turned away, nauseated. Zebadiah caught my expression.

"Why," I said defensively, "do these pariahs persist in their heresy? They seem such harmless fellows otherwise."

He cocked a brow at me. "Perhaps it's not heresy to them. Didn't you see that fellow resign himself to his God?"

"But that is not the true God."

"He must have thought otherwise."

"But they all know better; we've told them often enough."

He smiled in so irritating a fashion that I blurted out, "I don't understand you, Zeb—blessed if I do! Ten minutes ago you were introducing me in correct doctrine; now you seem to be defending heresy. Reconcile that."

He shrugged. "Oh, I can play the Devil's advocate. I made the debate team at the Point, remember? I'll be a famous theologian someday—if the Grand Inquisitor doesn't get me first."

"Well . . . Look—you *do* think it's right to stone the ungodly? Don't you?"

He changed the subject abruptly. "Did you notice who cast the first stone?" I hadn't and told him so; all I remembered was that it was a man in country clothes, rather than a woman or a child.

"It was Snotty Fassett." Zeb's lip curled.

I recalled Fassett too well; he was two classes senior to me and had made my plebe year something I want to forget. "So that's how it was," I answered slowly. "Zeb, I don't think I could stomach intelligence work."

"Certainly not as an *agent provocateur*," he agreed. "Still, I suppose the Council needs these incidents occasionally. These rumors about the Cabal and all. . . ."

I caught up this last remark. "Zeb, do you really think there is anything to this Cabal? I can't believe that there is any organized disloyalty to the Prophet."

"Well—there has certainly been some trouble out on the West Coast. Oh, forget it; our job is to keep the watch here."

2

BUT WE WERE NOT ALLOWED to forget it; two days later the inner guard was doubled. I did not see how there could be any real danger, as the Palace was as strong a fortress as ever was built, with its lower recesses immune even to fission bombs. Besides that, a person entering the Palace, even from the Temple grounds, would be challenged and identified a dozen times before he reached the Angel on guard outside the Prophet's own quarters. Nevertheless people in high places were getting jumpy; there must be something to it.

But I was delighted to find that I had been assigned as Zebadiah's partner. Standing twice as many hours of guard was

almost offset by having him to talk with—for me at least. As
for poor Zeb, I banged his ear endlessly through the long
night watches, talking about Judith and how unhappy I was
with the way things were at New Jerusalem. Finally he turned
on me.

"See here, Mr. Dumbjohn," he snapped, reverting to my
plebe year designation, "are you in love with her?"

I tried to hedge. I had not yet admitted to myself that my
interest was more than in her welfare. He cut me short.

"You do or you don't. Make up your mind. If you do, we'll
talk practical matters. If you don't, then shut up about her."

I took a deep breath and took the plunge. "I guess I do,
Zeb. It seems impossible and I know it's a sin, but there it is."

"All of that and folly, too. But there is no talking sense to
you. Okay, so you are in love with her. What next?"

"Eh?"

"What do you want to do? Marry her?"

I thought about it with such distress that I covered my face
with my hands. "Of course I do," I admitted. "But how can
I?"

"Precisely. You can't. You can't marry without transferring
away from here; her service can't marry at all. Nor is there
any way for her to break her vows, since she is already
sealed. But if you can face up to bare facts without blushing,
there is plenty you can do. You two could be very cozy—if
you could get over being such an infernal bluenose."

A week earlier I would not have understood what he was
driving at. But now I knew. I could not even really be angry
with him at making such a dishonorable and sinful suggestion;
he meant well—and some of the tarnish was now in my own
soul. I shook my head. "You shouldn't have said that, Zeb.
Judith is not that sort of a woman."

"Okay. Then forget it. And her. And shut up about her."

I sighed wearily. "Don't be rough on me, Zeb. This is more
than I know how to manage." I glanced up and down, then
took a chance and sat down on the parapet. We were not on
watch near the Holy One's quarters but at the east wall; our
warden, Captain Peter van Eyck, was too fat to get that far
oftener than once a watch, so I took a chance. I was bone
tired from not having slept much lately.

"Sorry."

"Don't be angry, Zeb. That sort of thing isn't for me and it
certainly isn't for Judith—for Sister Judith." I knew what I

wanted for us: a little farm, about a hundred and sixty acres, like the one I had been born on. Pigs and chickens and bare-footed kids with happy dirty faces and Judith to have her face light up when I came in from the fields and then wipe the perspiration from her face with her apron so that I could kiss her . . . no more connection with the Church and the Prophet than Sunday meeting and tithes.

But it could not be, it could never be. I put it out of my mind. "Zeb," I went on, "just as a matter of curiosity— You have intimated that these things go on all the time. How? We live in a goldfish bowl here. It doesn't seem possible."

He grinned at me so cynically that I wanted to slap him, but his voice had no leer in it. "Well, just for example, take your own case—"

"Out of the question!"

"Just for example, I said. Sister Judith isn't available right now; she is confined to her cell. But—"

"Huh? She's been *arrested?*" I thought wildly of the Question and what Zeb had said about the inquisitors.

"No, no, no! She isn't even locked in. She's been told to stay there, that's all, with prayer and bread-and-water as company. They are purifying her heart and instructing her in her spiritual duties. When she sees things in their true light, her lot will be drawn again—and this time she won't faint and make an adolescent fool of herself."

I pushed back my first reaction and tried to think about it calmly. "No," I said. "Judith will never do it. Not if she stays in her cell forever."

"So? I wouldn't be too sure. They can be very persuasive. How would you like to be prayed over in relays? But assume that she does see the light, just so that I can finish my story."

"Zeb, how do you know about this?"

"Sheol, man! I've been here going on three years. Do you think I wouldn't be hooked into the grapevine? You were worried about her—and making yourself a tiresome nuisance if I may say so. So I asked the birdies. But to continue. She sees the light, her lot is drawn, she performs her holy service to the Prophet. After that she is called once a week like the rest and her lot is drawn maybe once a month or less. Inside of a year—unless the Prophet finds some very exceptional beauty in her soul—they stop putting her name among the lots entirely. But it isn't necessary to wait that long, although it is more discreet."

"The whole thing is shameful!"

"Really? I imagine King Solomon had to use some such system; he had even more women on his neck than the Holy One has. Thereafter, if you can come to some mutual understanding with the Virgin involved, it is just a case of following well known customs. There is a present to be made to the Eldest Sister, and to be renewed as circumstances dictate. There are some palms to be brushed—I can tell you which ones. And this great pile of masonry has lots of dark back stairs in it. With all customs duly observed, there is no reason why, almost any night I have the watch and you don't, you should not find something warm and cuddly in your bed."

I was about to explode at the calloused way he put it when my mind went off at a tangent. "Zeb—now I know you are telling an untruth. You were just pulling my leg, admit it. There is an eye and an ear somewhere in our room. Why, even if I tried to find them and cut them out, I'd simply have the security watch banging on the door in three minutes."

"So what? There is an eye and an ear in every room in the place. You ignore them."

I simply let my mouth sag open.

"Ignore them," he went on. "Look, John, a little casual fornication is no threat to the Church—treason and heresy are. It will simply be entered in your dossier and nothing will be said about it—unless they catch you in something really important later, in which case they might use it to hang you instead of preferring the real charges. Old son, they *like* to have such peccadilloes in the files; it increases security. They are probably uneasy about you; you are too perfect; such men are dangerous. Which is probably why you've never been cleared for higher study."

I tried to straighten out in my mind the implied cross purposes, the wheels within wheels, and gave up. "I just don't get it. Look, Zeb, all this doesn't have anything to do with me . . . or with Judith. But I know what I've *got* to do. Somehow I've got to get her out of here."

"Hmm . . . a mighty strait gate, old son."

"I've got to."

"Well . . . I'd like to help you. I suppose I could get a message to her," he added doubtfully.

I caught his arm. "Would you, Zeb?"

He sighed. "I wish you would wait. No, that wouldn't help, seeing the romantic notions in your mind. But it is risky now. Plenty risky, seeing that she is under discipline by order of the Prophet. You'd look funny staring down the table of a court-martial board, looking at your own spear."

"I'll risk even that. Or even the Question."

He did not remind me that he himself was taking even more of a risk than I was; he simply said, "Very well, what is the message?"

I thought for a moment. It would have to be short. "Tell her that the legate she talked to the night her lot was drawn is worried about her."

"Anything else?"

"Yes! Tell her that I am hers to command!"

It seems flamboyant in recollection. No doubt it was—but it was exactly the way I felt.

At luncheon the next day I found a scrap of paper folded into my napkin. I hurried through the meal and slipped out to read it.

I need your help, it read, *and am so very grateful. Will you meet me tonight?* It was unsigned and had been typed in the script of a common voicewriter, used anywhere in the Palace, or out. When Zeb returned to our room, I showed it to him; he glanced at it and remarked in idle tones:

"Let's get some air. I ate too much, I'm about to fall asleep."

Once we hit the open terrace and were free of the hazard of eye and ear he cursed me out in low, dispassionate tones. "You'll never make a conspirator. Half the mess must know that you found something in your napkin. Why in God's name did you gulp your food and rush off? Then to top it off you handed it to me upstairs. For all you know the eye read it and photostated it for evidence. Where in the world were you when they were passing out brains?"

I protested but he cut me off. "Forget it! I know you didn't mean to put both of our necks in a bight—but good intentions are no good when the trial judge-advocate reads the charges. Now get this through your head: the first principle of intrigue is never to be seen doing anything unusual, no matter how harmless it may seem. You wouldn't believe how small a deviation from pattern looks significant to a trained analyst. You should have stayed in the refectory the usual time, hung around and gossiped as usual afterwards, then waited until you were safe to read it. Now where is it?"

"In the pocket of my corselet," I answered humbly. "Don't worry, I'll chew it up and swallow it."

"Not so fast. Wait here." Zeb left and was back in a few minutes. "I have a piece of paper the same size and shape; I'll pass it to you quietly. Swap the two, and then you can eat the real note—but don't be seen making the swap or chewing up the real one."

"All right. But what is the second sheet of paper?"

"Some notes on a system for winning at dice."

"Huh? But that's non-reg, too!"

"Of course, you hammer head. If they catch you with evidence of gambling, they won't suspect you of a much more serious sin. At worst, the skipper will eat you out and fine you a few days pay and a few hours contrition. Get this, John: if you are ever suspected of something, try to make the evidence point to a lesser offense. Never try to prove lily-white innocence. Human nature being what it is, your chances are better."

I guess Zeb was right; my pockets must have been searched and the evidence photographed right after I changed uniforms for parade, for half an hour afterwards I was called into the Executive Officer's office. He asked me to keep my eyes open for indications of gambling among the junior officers. It was a sin, he said, that he hated to have his younger officers fall into. He clapped me on the shoulder as I was leaving. "You're a good boy, John Lyle. A word to the wise, eh?"

Zeb and I had the midwatch at the south Palace portal that night. Half the watch passed with no sign of Judith and I was as nervous as a cat in a strange house, though Zeb tried to keep me calmed down by keeping me strictly to routine. At long last there were soft footfalls in the inner corridor and a shape appeared in the doorway. Zebadiah motioned me to remain on tour and went to check. He returned almost at once and motioned me to join him, while putting a finger to his lips. Trembling, I went in. It was not Judith but some woman strange to me who waited there in the darkness. I started to speak but Zeb put his hand over my mouth.

The woman took my arm and urged me down the corridor. I glanced back and saw Zeb silhouetted in the portal, covering our rear. My guide paused and pushed me into an almost pitchblack alcove, then she took from the folds of her robes a small object which I took to be a pocket ferretscope, from the small dial that glowed faintly on its side. She ran it up and down and around, snapped it off and returned it to her person. "Now you can talk," she said softly. "It's safe." She slipped away.

I felt a gentle touch at my sleeve. "Judith?" I whispered.

"Yes," she answered, so softly that I could hardly hear her.

Then my arms were around her. She gave a little startled cry, then her own arms went around my neck and I could feel her breath against my face. We kissed clumsily but with almost frantic eagerness.

It is no one's business what we talked about then, nor could I give a coherent account if I tried. Call our behavior romantic nonsense, call it delayed puppy love touched off by ignorance and unnatural lives—do puppies hurt less than grown dogs? Call it what you like and laugh at us, but at that moment we were engulfed in that dear madness more precious than rubies and fine gold, more to be desired than sanity. If you have never experienced it and do not know what I am talking about, I am sorry for you.

Presently we quieted down somewhat and talked more reasonably. When she tried to tell me about the night her lot had been drawn she began to cry. I shook her and said, "Stop it, my darling. You don't have to tell me about it. I know."

She gulped and said, "But you don't know. You can't know. I . . . he . . ."

I shook her again. "Stop it. Stop it at once. No more tears. I do know, exactly. And I know what you are in for still—unless we get you out of here. So there is no time for tears or nerves; we have to make plans."

She was dead silent for a long moment, then she said slowly, "You mean for me to . . . desert? I've thought of that. Merciful God, how I've thought about it! But how can I?"

"I don't know—yet. But we will figure out a way. We've *got* to." We discussed possibilities. Canada was a bare three hundred miles away and she knew the upstate New York country; in fact it was the only area she did know. But the border there was more tightly closed than it was anywhere else, patrol boats and radar walls by water, barbed wire and sentries by land . . . and sentry dogs. I had trained with such dogs; I wouldn't urge my worst enemy to go up against them. But Mexico was simply impossibly far away. If she headed south she would probably be arrested in twenty-four hours. No one would knowingly give shelter to an unveiled Virgin; under the inexorable rule of associative guilt any such good Samaritan would be as guilty as she of the same personal treason against the Prophet and would die the same death. Going north would be shorter at least, though it meant the same business of traveling by night, hiding by day, stealing food or going hungry. Near Albany lived an aunt of Judith's; she felt sure that her aunt would risk hiding her until some way could be worked out to cross the border. "She'll keep us safe. I know it."

"Us?" I must have sounded stupid. Until she spoke I had had my nose so close to the single problem of how she was to escape that it had not yet occurred to me that she would expect both of us to go.

"Did you mean to send me *alone?*"

"Why . . . I guess I hadn't thought about it any other way."

"No!"

"But—look, Judith, the urgent thing, the thing that must be done at once, is to get you out of here. Two people trying to travel and hide are many times more likely to be spotted than one. It just doesn't make sense to—"

"No! I won't go."

I thought about it, hurriedly. I still hadn't realized that "A" implies "B" and that I myself in urging her to desert her service was as much a deserter in my heart as she was. I said, "We'll get you out first, that's the important thing. You tell me where your aunt lives—then wait for me."

"Not without you."

"But you *must*. The Prophet—"

"Better that than to lose you now!"

I did not then understand women—and I still don't. Two minutes before she had been quietly planning to risk death by ordeal rather than submit her body to the Holy One. Now she was almost casually willing to accept it rather than put up with even a temporary separation. I don't understand women; I sometimes think there is no logic in them at all.

I said, "Look, my dear one, we have not yet even figured out how we are to get you out of the Palace. It's likely to be utterly impossible for us both to escape the same instant. You see that, don't you?"

She answered stubbornly, "Maybe. But I don't like it. Well, how do I get out? And when?"

I had to admit again that I did not know. I intended to consult Zeb as soon as possible, but I had no other notion.

But Judith had a suggestion. "John, you know the Virgin who guided you here? No? Sister Magdalene. I know it is safe to tell her and she *might* be willing to help us. She's very clever."

I started to comment doubtfully but we were interrupted by Sister Magdalene herself. "Quick!" she snapped at me as she slipped in beside us. "Back to the rampart!"

I rushed out and was barely in time to avoid being caught by the warden, making his rounds. He exchanged challenges with Zeb and myself—and then the old fool wanted to chat. He settled himself down on the steps of the portal and started recalling boastfully a picayune fencing victory of the week before. I tried dismally to help Zeb with chit-chat in a fashion normal for a man bored by a night watch.

At last he got to his feet. "I'm past forty and getting a little heavier, maybe. I'll admit frankly it warms me to know that I still have a wrist and eye as fast as you young blades." He straightened his scabbard and added, "I suppose I had better take a turn through the Palace. Can't take too many precautions these days. They do say the Cabal has been active again." He took out his torch light and flashed it down the corridor.

I froze solid. If he inspected that corridor, it was beyond hope that he would miss two women crouching in an alcove.

But Zebadiah spoke up calmly, casually. "Just a moment, Elder Brother. Would you show me that time riposte you used to win that last match? It was too fast for me to follow it."

He took the bait. "Why, glad to, son!" He moved off the steps, came out to where there was room. "Draw your sword. En garde! Cross blades in line of sixte. Disengage and attack me. There! Hold the lunge and I'll demonstrate it slowly. As your point approaches my chest—" (Chest indeed! Captain van Eyck was as pot-bellied as a kangaroo!) "—I catch it with the forte of my blade and force it over yours in riposte seconde. Just like the book, so far. But I do not complete the riposte. Strong as it is, you might parry or counter. Instead, as my point comes down, I beat your blade out of line—" He illustrated and the steel sang. "—and attack you anywhere, from chin to ankle. Come now, try it on me."

Zeb did so and they ran through the phrase; the warden retreated a step. Zeb asked to do it again to get it down pat. They ran through it repeatedly, faster each time, with the warden retreating each time to avoid by a hair Zeb's unbated point. It was strictly against regulations to fence with real swords and without mask and plastron, but the warden really was good . . . a swordsman so precise that he was confident of his own skill not to blind one of Zeb's eyes, not to let Zeb hurt him. In spite of my own galloping jitters I watched it closely; it was a beautiful demonstration of a once-useful military art. Zeb pressed him hard.

They finished up fifty yards away from the portal and that much closer to the guardroom. I could hear the warden puffing from the exercise. "That was fine, Jones," he gasped. "You caught on handsomely." He puffed again and added, "Lucky for me a real bout does not go on as long. I think I'll let you inspect the corridor." He turned away toward the guardroom, adding cheerfully, "God keep you."

"God go with you, sir," Zeb responded properly and brought his hilt to his chin in salute.

As soon as the warden turned the corner Zeb stood by again and I hurried back to the alcove. The women were still there, making themselves small against the back wall. "He's gone," I reassured them. "Nothing to fear for a while."

Judith had told Sister Magdalene of our dilemma and we discussed it in whispers. She advised us strongly not to try to reach any decisions just then. "I'm in charge of Judith's purification; I can stretch it out for another week, perhaps, before she has to draw lots again."

I said, "We've got to act before then!"

Judith seemed over her fears, now that she had laid her troubles in Sister Magdalene's lap. "Don't worry, John," she said softly, "the chances are my lot won't be drawn soon again in any case. We must do what she advises."

Sister Magdalene sniffed contemptuously. "You're wrong about that, Judy, when you are returned to duty, your lot will be drawn, you can be sure ahead of time. Not," she added, "but what you could live through it—the rest of us have. If it seems safer to—" She stopped suddenly and listened. "Sssh! Quiet as death." She slipped silently out of our circle.

A thin pencil of light flashed out and splashed on a figure

crouching outside the alcove. I dived and was on him before he could get to his feet. Fast as I had been, Sister Magdalene was just as fast; she landed on his shoulders as he went down. He jerked and was still.

Zebadiah came running in, checked himself at our sides. "John! Maggie!" came his tense whisper. "What is it?"

"We've caught a spy, Zeb," I answered hurriedly. "What'll we do with him?"

Zeb flashed his light. "You've knocked him out?"

"He won't come to," answered Magdalene's calm voice out of the darkness. "I slipped a vibroblade in his ribs."

"Sheol!"

"Zeb, I had to do it. Be glad I didn't use steel and mess up the floor with blood. But what do we do now?"

Zeb cursed her softly, she took it. "Turn him over, John. Let's take a look." I did so and his light flashed again. "Hey, Johnnie—it's Snotty Fassett." He paused and I could almost hear him think. "Well, we'll waste no tears on *him*. John!"

"Yeah, Zeb?"

"Keep the watch outside. If anyone comes, I am inspecting the corridor. I've got to dump this carcass somewhere."

Judith broke the silence. "There's an incinerator chute on the floor above. I'll help you."

"Stout girl. Get going, John."

I wanted to object that it was no work for a woman, but I shut up and turned away. Zeb took his shoulders, the women a leg apiece and managed well enough. They were back in minutes, though it seemed endless to me. No doubt Snotty's body was reduced to atoms before they were back—we might get away with it. It did not seem like murder to me then, and still does not; we did what we had to do, rushed along by events.

Zeb was curt. "This tears it. Our reliefs will be along in ten minutes; we've got to figure this out in less time than that. Well?"

Our suggestions were all impractical to the point of being ridiculous, but Zeb let us make them—then spoke straight to the point. "Listen to me, it's no longer just a case of trying to help Judith and you out of your predicament. As soon as Snotty is missed, we—all four of us—are in mortal danger of the Question. Right?"

"Right," I agreed unwillingly.

"But nobody has a plan?"

None of us answered. Zeb went on, "Then we've got to have help . . . and there is only one place we can get it. The Cabal."

3

"THE CABAL?" I repeated stupidly. Judith gave a horrified gasp.

"Why . . . why, that would mean our immortal souls! They worship Satan!"

Zeb turned to her. "I don't believe so."

She stared at him. "Are *you* a Cabalist?"

"No."

"Then how do you know?"

"And how," I insisted, "can *you* ask them for help?"

Magdalene answered. "I am a member—as Zebadiah knows."

Judith shrank away from her, but Magdalene pressed her with words. "Listen to me, Judith. I know how you feel—and once I was as horrified as you are at the idea of anyone opposing the Church. Then I learned—as you are learning—what really lies behind this sham we were brought up to believe in." She put an arm around the younger girl. "We aren't devil worshipers, dear, nor do we fight against God. We fight only against this self-styled Prophet who pretends to be the voice of God. Come with us, help us fight him—and we will help you. Otherwise we can't risk it."

Judith searched her face by the faint light from the portal. "You swear that this is true? The Cabal fights only against the Prophet and not against the Lord Himself?"

"I swear, Judith."

Judith took a deep shuddering breath. "God guide me," she whispered. "I go with the Cabal."

Magdalene kissed her quickly, then faced us men. "Well?"

I answered at once, "I'm in it if Judith is," then whispered to myself, "Dear Lord, forgive me my oath—I must!"

Magdalene was staring at Zeb. He shifted uneasily and said angrily, "I suggested it, didn't I? But we are all damned fools and the Inquisitor will break our bones."

There was no more chance to talk until the next day. I woke from bad dreams of the Question and worse, and heard Zeb's shaver buzzing merrily in the bath. He came in and pulled the covers off me, all the while running off at the mouth with cheerful nonsense. I hate having bed clothes dragged off me even when feeling well and I can't stand cheerfulness before breakfast; I dragged them back and tried to ignore him, but he grabbed my wrist. "Up you come, old son! God's sunshine is wasting. It's a beautiful day. How about two fast laps around the Palace and in for a cold shower?"

I tried to shake his hand loose and called him something that would lower my mark in piety if the ear picked it up. He still hung on and his forefinger was twitching against my wrist in a nervous fashion; I began to wonder if Zeb were cracking under the strain. Then I realized that he was tapping out code.

"B-E—N-A-T-U-R-A-L," the dots and dashes said, "S-H-O-W — N-O — S-U-R-P-R-I-S-E — W-E — W-I-L-L — B-E — C-A-L-L-E-D — F-O-R — E-X-A-M-I-N-A-T-I-O-N — D-U-R-I-N-G — T-H-E — R-E-C-R-E-A-T-I-O-N — P-E-R-I-O-D—T-H-I-S—A-F-T-E-R-N-O-O-N"

I hope I showed no surprise. I made surly answers to the stream of silly chatter he had kept up all through it, and got up and went about the mournful tasks of putting the body back in shape for another day. After a bit I found excuse to lay a hand on his shoulder and twitched out an answer: "O-K —I —U-N-D-E-R-S-T-A-N-D"

The day was a misery of nervous monotony. I made a mistake at dress parade, a thing I haven't done since beast barracks. When the day's duty was finally over I went back to our room and found Zeb there with his feet on the air conditioner, working an acrostic in the New York *Times*. "Johnnie my lamb," he asked, looking up, "what is a six-letter word meaning 'Pure in Heart'?"

"You'll never need to know," I grunted and sat down to remove my armor.

"Why, John, don't you think I will reach the Heavenly City?"

"Maybe—after ten thousand years penance."

There came a brisk knock at our door, it was shoved open, and Timothy Klyce, senior legate in the mess and brevet captain, stuck his head in. He sniffed and said in nasal Cape Cod accents, "Hello, you chaps want to take a walk?"

It seemed to me that he could not have picked a worse time. Tim was a hard man to shake and the most punctiliously devout man in the corps. I was still trying to think of an excuse when Zeb spoke up. "Don't mind if we do, provided we walk toward town. I've got some shopping to do."

I was confused by Zeb's answer and still tried to hang back, pleading paper work to do, but Zeb cut me short. "Pfui with paper work. I'll help you with it tonight. Come on." So I went, wondering if he had gotten cold feet about going through with it.

We went out through the lower tunnels. I walked along silently, wondering if possibly Zeb meant to try to shake Klyce in town and then hurry back. We had just entered a little jog in the passageway when Tim raised his hand in a gesture to emphasize some point in what he was saying to Zeb. His hand passed near my face, I felt a slight spray on my eyes—and I was blind.

Before I could cry out, even as I suppressed the impulse to do so, he grasped my upper arm hard, while continuing his sentence without a break. His grip on my arm guided me to the left, whereas my memory of the jog convinced me that the turn should have been to the right. But we did not bump into the wall and after a few moments the blindness wore off. We seemed to be walking in the same tunnel with Tim in the middle and holding each of us by an arm. He did not say anything and neither did we; presently he stopped us in front of a door. Klyce knocked once, then listened.

I could not make out an answer but he replied. "Two pilgrims, duly guided."

The door opened. He led us in, it closed silently behind us, and we were facing a masked and armored guard, with his blast pistol leveled on us. Reaching behind him, he rapped once on an inner door; immediately another man, armed and masked like the first, came out and faced us. He asked Zeb and myself separately:

"Do you seriously declare, upon your honor, that, unbiased by friends and uninfluenced by mercenary motives, you freely and voluntarily offer yourself to the service of this order?"

We each answered, "I do."

"Hoodwink and prepare them."

Leather helmets that covered everything but our mouths

and noses were slipped over our heads and fastened under our chins. Then we were ordered to strip off all our clothing. I did so while the goose bumps popped out on me. I was losing my enthusiasm rapidly—there is nothing that makes a man feel as helpless as taking his pants away from him. Then I felt the sharp prick of a hypodermic in my forearm and shortly, though I was awake, things got dreamy and I was no longer jittery. Something cold was pressed against my ribs on the left side of my back and I realized that it was almost certainly the hilt of a vibroblade, needing only the touch of the stud to make me as dead as Snotty Fassett—but it did not alarm me. Then there were questions, many questions, which I answered automatically, unable to lie or hedge if I had wanted to. I remember them in snatches:

"—of your own free will and accord?" "—conform to the ancient established usages—" "—a man, free born, of good repute, and well recommended."

Then, for a long time I stood shivering on the cold tile floor while a spirited discussion went on around me; it had to do with my motives in seeking admission. I could hear it all and I knew that my life hung on it, with only a word needed to cause a blade of cold energy to spring into my heart. And I knew that the argument was going against me.

Then a contralto voice joined the debate. I recognized Sister Magdalene and knew that she was vouching for me, but doped as I was I did not care; I simply welcomed her voice as a friendly sound. But presently the hilt relaxed from my ribs and I again felt the prick of a hypodermic. It brought me quickly out of my dazed state and I heard a strong bass voice intoning a prayer:

"Vouchsafe thine aid, Almighty Father of the Universe. . . . love, relief, and truth to the honor of Thy Holy Name. Amen."

And the answering chorus, "So mote it be!"

Then I was conducted around the room, still hoodwinked, while questions were again put to me. They were symbolic in nature and were answered for me by my guide. Then I was stopped and was asked if I were willing to take a solemn oath pertaining to this degree, being assured that it would in no material way interfere with duty that I owed to God, myself, family, country, or neighbor.

I answered, "I am."

I was then required to kneel on my left knee, with my left

hand supporting the Book, my right hand steadying certain instruments thereon.

The oath and charge was enough to freeze the blood of anyone foolish enough to take it under false pretenses. Then I was asked what, in my present condition, I most desired. I answered as I had been coached to answer: "Light!"

And the hoodwink was stripped from my head.

It is not necessary and not proper to record the rest of my instruction as a newly entered brother. It was long and of solemn beauty and there was nowhere in it any trace of the blasphemy or devil worship that common gossip attributed to us; quite the contrary it was filled with reverence for God, brotherly love, and uprightness, and it included instruction in the principles of an ancient and honorable profession and the symbolic meaning of the working tools thereof.

But I must mention one detail that surprised me almost out of the shoes I was not wearing. When they took the hoodwink off me, the first man I saw, standing in front of me dressed in the symbols of his office and wearing an expression of almost inhuman dignity, was Captain Peter van Eyck, the fat ubiquitous warden of my watch—*Master* of this lodge!

The ritual was long and time was short. When the lodge was closed we gathered in a council of war. I was told that the senior brethren had already decided not to admit Judith to the sister order of our lodge at this time even though the lodge would reach out to protect her. She was to be spirited away to Mexico and it was better, that being the case, for her not to know any secrets she did not need to know. But Zeb and I, being of the Palace guard, could be of real use; therefore we were admitted.

Judith had already been given hypnotic instructions which —it was hoped—would enable her to keep from telling what little she already knew if she should be put to the Question. I was told to wait and not to worry; the senior brothers would arrange to get Judith out of danger before she next was required to draw lots. I had to be satisfied with that.

For three days running Zebadiah and I reported during the afternoon recreation period for instruction, each time being taken by a different route and with different precautions. It was clear that the architect who had designed the Palace had been one of us; the enormous building had hidden in it traps and passages and doors which certainly did not appear in the official plans.

At the end of the third day we were fully accredited senior brethren, qualified with a speed possible only in time of crisis. The effort almost sprained my brain; I had to bone harder than I ever had needed to in school. Utter letter-perfection was required and there was an amazing lot to memorize—which was perhaps just as well, for it helped to keep me from worrying. We had not heard so much as a rumor of a kickback from the disappearance of Snotty Fassett, a fact much more ominous than would have been a formal investigation.

A security officer can't just drop out of sight without his passing being noticed. It was remotely possible that Snotty had been on a roving assignment and was not expected to check in daily with his boss, but it was much more likely that he had been where we had found him and killed him because some one of us was suspected and he had been ordered to shadow. If that was the case, the calm silence could only mean that the chief security officer was letting us have more rope, while his psychotechnicians analyzed our behavior—in which case the absence of Zeb and myself from any known location during our free time for several days running was almost certainly a datum entered on a chart. If the entire regiment started out equally suspect, then our personal indices each gained a fractional point each of those days.

I never boned savvy in such matters and would undoubtedly have simply felt relieved as the days passed with no overt trouble had it not been that the matter was discussed and worried over in the lodge room. I did not even know the name of the Guardian of Morals, nor even the location of his security office—we weren't supposed to know. I knew that he existed and that he reported to the Grand Inquisitor and perhaps to the Prophet himself but that was all. I discovered that my lodge brothers, despite the almost incredible penetration of the Cabal throughout the Temple and Palace, knew hardly more than I did—for the reason that we had no brothers, not one, in the staff of the Guardian of Morals. The reason was simple; the Cabal was every bit as careful in evaluating the character, *persona*, and psychological potentialities of a prospective brother as the service was in measuring a prospective intelligence officer—and the two types were as unlike as geese and goats. The Guardian would never accept the type of personality who would be attracted by the ideals of the Cabal; my brothers would never pass a—well, a man like Fassett.

I understand that, in the days before psychological measurement had become a mathematical science, an espionage apparatus could break down through a change in heart on the part of a key man—well, the Guardian of Morals had no such worry; his men *never* suffered a change in heart. I understand, too, that our own fraternity, in the early days when it was being purged and tempered for the ordeal to come, many times had blood on the floors of lodge rooms—I don't know; such records were destroyed.

On the fourth day we were not scheduled to go to the lodge room, having been told to show our faces where they would be noticed to offset our unwonted absences. I was spending my free time in the lounge off the mess room, leafing through magazines, when Timothy Klyce came in. He glanced at me, nodded, then started thumbing through a stack of magazines himself. Presently he said, "These antiques belong in a dentist's office. Have any of you chaps seen this week's *Time?*"

His complaint was addressed to the room as a whole; no one answered. But he turned to me. "Jack, I think you are sitting on it. Raise up a minute."

I grunted and did so. As he reached for the magazine his head came close to mine and he whispered, "Report to the Master."

I had learned a little at least so I went on reading. After a bit I put my magazine aside, stretched and yawned, then got up and ambled out toward the washroom. But I walked on past and a few minutes later entered the lodge room. I found that Zeb was already there, as were several other brothers; they were gathered around Master Peter and Magdalene. I could feel the tension in the room.

I said, "You sent for me, Worshipful Master?"

He glanced at me, looked back at Magdalene. She said slowly, "Judith has been arrested."

I felt my knees go soft and I had trouble standing. I am not unusually timid and physical bravery is certainly commonplace, but if you hit a man through his family or his loved ones you almost always get him where he is unprotected. "The Inquisition?" I managed to gasp.

Her eyes were soft with pity. "We think so. They took her away this morning and she has been incommunicado ever since."

"Has any charge been filed?" asked Zeb.

"Not publicly."

"Hm-m-m— That looks bad."

"And good as well," Master Peter disagreed. "If it is the matter we think it is—Fassett, I mean—and had they had any evidence pointing to the rest of you, all four of you would have been arrested at once. At least, that is in accordance with their methods."

"But what can we *do?*" I demanded.

Van Eyck did not answer. Magdalene said soothingly, "There is nothing for you to do, John. You couldn't get within several guarded doors of her."

"But we can't just do nothing!"

The lodge Master said, "Easy, son. Maggie is the only one of us with access to that part of the inner Palace. We must leave it in her hands."

I turned again to her; she sighed and said, "Yes, but there is probably little I can do." Then she left.

We waited. Zeb suggested that he and I should leave the lodge room and continue with being seen in our usual haunts; to my relief van Eyck vetoed it. "No. We can't be sure that Sister Judith's hypnotic protection is enough to see her through the ordeal. Fortunately you two and Sister Magdalene are the only ones she can jeopardize—but I want you here, safe, until Magdalene finds out what she can. Or fails to return," he added thoughtfully.

I blurted out, "Oh, Judith will never betray us!"

He shook his head sadly. "Son, *anyone* will betray *anything* under the Question—unless adequately guarded by hypno compulsion. We'll see."

I had paid no attention to Zeb, being busy with my own very self-centered thoughts. He now surprised me by saying angrily, "Master, you are keeping us here like pet hens—but you have just sent Maggie back to stick her head in a trap. Suppose Judith *has* cracked? They'll grab Maggie at once."

Van Eyck nodded. "Of course. That is the chance we must take since she is the only spy we have. But don't you worry about her. They'll never arrest her—she'll suicide first."

The statement did not shock me; I was too numbed by the danger to Judith. But Zeb burst out with, "The swine! Master, you shouldn't have sent her."

Van Eyck answered mildly, "Discipline, son. Control yourself. This is war and she is a soldier." He turned away.

So we waited . . . and waited . . . and waited. It is hard to tell anyone who has not lived in the shadow of the Inquisition how we felt about it. We knew no details but we sometimes saw those unlucky enough to live through it. Even if the inquisitors did not require the auto da fé, the mind of the victim was usually damaged, often shattered.

Presently Master Peter mercifully ordered the Junior Warden to examine both of us as to our progress in memorizing ritual. Zeb and I sullenly did as we were told and were forced with relentless kindness to concentrate on the intricate rhetoric. Somehow nearly two hours passed.

At last came three raps at the door and the Tyler admitted Magdalene. I jumped out of my chair and rushed to her. "Well?" I demanded. "Well?"

"Peace, John," she answered wearily. "I've seen her."

"How is she? Is she all right?"

"Better than we have any right to expect. Her mind is still intact and she hasn't betrayed us, apparently. As for the rest, she may keep a scar or two—but she's young and healthy; she'll recover."

I started to demand more facts but the Master cut me off. "Then they've already put her to the Question. In that case, how did you get in to see her?"

"Oh, that!" Magdalene shrugged it off as something hardly worth mentioning. "The inquisitor prosecuting her case proved to be an old acquaintance of mine; we arranged an exchange of favors."

Zeb started to interrupt; the Master snapped, "Quiet!" then added sharply, "The Grand Inquisitor isn't handling it himself? In that case I take it they don't suspect that it could be a Cabal matter?"

Maggie frowned. "I don't know. Apparently Judith fainted rather early in the proceedings; they may not have had time to dig into that possibility. In any case I begged a respite for her until tomorrow. The excuse is to let her recover strength for more questioning, of course. They will start in on her again early tomorrow morning."

Van Eyck pounded a fist into a palm. "They must not start again—we can't risk it! Senior Warden, attend me! The rest of you get out! Except you, Maggie."

I left with something unsaid. I had wanted to tell Maggie that she could have my hide for a door mat any time she lifted her finger.

Dinner that night was a trial. After the chaplain droned through his blessing I tried to eat and join in the chatter but there seemed to be a hard ring in my throat that kept me

from swallowing. Seated next to me was Grace-of-God Bear-
paw, half Scottish, half Cherokee. Grace was a classmate but
no friend of mine; we hardly ever talked and tonight he was
as taciturn as ever.

During the meal he rested his boot on mine; I impatiently
moved my foot away. But shortly his foot was touching mine
again and he started to tap against my boot:

"—hold still, you idiot—" he spelled out. "You have been
chosen—it will be on your watch tonight—details later—eat
and start talking—take a strip of adhesive tape on watch with
you—six inches by a foot—repeat message back."

I managed somehow to tap out my confirmation while continuing to pretend to eat.

4

WE RELIEVED the watch at midnight. As soon as the watch section had marched away from our post I told Zeb what Grace
had passed on to me at chow and asked him if he had the rest
of my instructions. He had not. I wanted to talk but he cut
me short; he seemed even more edgy than I was.

So I walked my post and tried to look alert. We were
posted that night at the north end of the west rampart; our
tour covered one of the Palace entrances. About an hour had
passed when I heard a hiss from the dark doorway. I approached cautiously and made out a female form. She was
too short to be Magdalene and I never knew who she was, for
she shoved a piece of paper in my hand and faded back into
the dark corridor.

I rejoined Zeb. "What shall I do? Read it with my flash?
That seems risky."

"Open it up."

I did and found that it was covered with fine script that
glowed in the darkness. I could read it but it was too dim to
be picked up by any electronic eye. I read it:

*At the middle of the watch exactly on the bell you will
enter the Palace by the door where you received this. Forty
paces inside, take the stair on your left; climb two flights.
Proceed north fifty paces. The lighted doorway on your right*

leads to the Virgins' quarters; there will be a guard at this door. He will not resist you but you must use a paralysis bomb on him to give him an alibi. The cell you seek is at the far end of the central east & west corridor of the quarters. There will be a light over the door and a Virgin on guard. She is not one of us. You must disable her completely but you are forbidden to injure or kill her. Use the adhesive tape as gag and blindfold and tie her up with her clothes. Take her keys, enter the cell, and remove Sister Judith. She will probably be unconscious. Bring her to your post and hand her over to the warden of your watch.

You must make all haste from the time you paralyze the guard, as an eye may see you when you pass the lighted doorway and the alarm may sound at once.

Do not swallow this note; the ink is poisonous. Drop it in the incinerator chute at the head of the stairs.

Go with God.

Zeb read it over my shoulder. "All you need," he said grimly, "is the ability to pass miracles at will. Scared?"

"Yes."

"Want me to go along?"

"No. I guess we had better carry out the orders as given."

"Yes, we had—if I know the Lodge Master. Besides, it just might happen that I might need to kill somebody rather suddenly while you are gone. I'll be covering your rear."

"I suppose so."

"Now let's shut up and bone military." We went back to walking our post.

At the two muted strokes of the middle of the watch I propped my spear against the wall, took off my sword and corselet and helmet and the rest of the ceremonial junk we were required to carry but which would hamper me on this job. Zeb shoved a gauntleted hand in mine and squeezed. Then I was off.

Two—four—six—forty paces. I groped in the dark along the left wall and found the opening, felt around with my foot. Ah, there were the steps! I was already in a part of the Palace I had never been in; I moved by dead reckoning in the dark and hoped the person who had written my orders understood that. One flight, two flights—I almost fell on my face when I stepped on a 'top' step that wasn't there.

Where was the refuse chute? It should be at hand level and the instructions said "head of the stairs." I was debating frantically whether to show a light or chance keeping it when my left hand touched its latch; with a sigh of relief I chucked away the evidence that could have incriminated so many others. I started to turn away, then was immediately filled with panic. Was that really an incinerator chute? Could it have been the panel for a delivery lift instead? I groped for it in the dark again, opened it and shoved my hand in.

My hand was scorched even through my gauntlet; I jerked it back with relief and decided to trust my instructions, have no more doubts. But forty paces north the passageway jogged and that was not mentioned in my orders; I stopped and reconnoitered very cautiously, peering around the jog at floor level.

Twenty-five feet away was the guard and the doorway. He was supposed to be one of us but I took no chances. I slipped a bomb from my belt, set it by touch to minimum intensity, pulled the primer and counted off five seconds to allow for point blank range. Then I threw it and ducked back into the jog to protect myself from the rays.

I waited another five seconds and stuck my head around. The guard was slumped down on the floor, with his forehead bleeding slightly where it had struck a fragment of the bomb case. I hurried out and stepped over him, trying to run and keep quiet at the same time. The central passage of the Virgins' quarters was dim, with only blue night lights burning, but I could see and I reached the end of the passage quickly —then jammed on the brakes. The female guard at the cell there, instead of walking a post, was seated on the floor with her back to the door.

Probably she was dozing, for she did not look up at once. Then she did so, saw me, and I had no time to make plans; I dove for her. My left hand muffled her scream; with the edge of my left hand I chopped the side of her neck—not a killing stroke but I had no time to be gentle; she went limp.

Half the tape across her mouth first, then the other half across her eyes, then tear clothing from her to bind her—and hurry, hurry, hurry all the way, for a security man might already have monitored the eye that was certainly at the main doorway and have seen the unconscious guard. I found her keys on a chain around her waist and straightened up with a silent apology for what I had done to her. Her little body was almost childlike; she seemed even more helpless than Judith.

But I had no time for soft misgivings; I found the right

key, got the door open—and then my darling was in my
arms.

She was deep in a troubled sleep and probably drugged.
She moaned as I picked her up but did not wake. But her
gown slipped and I saw some of what they had done to her—
I made a life vow, even as I ran, to pay it back seven times, if
the man who did it could live that long.

The guard was still where I had left him. I thought I had
gotten away with it without being monitored or waking anyone and was just stepping over him, when I heard a gasp
from the corridor behind me. Why are women restless at
night? If this woman hadn't gotten out of bed, no doubt to attend to something she should have taken care of before
retiring, I might never have been seen at all.

It was too late to silence her, I simply ran. Once around
the jog I was in welcome darkness but I overran the stair
head, had to come back, and feel for it—then had to grope
my way down step by step. I could hear shouts and high-
pitched voices somewhere behind me.

Just as I reached ground level, turned and saw the portal
outlined against the night sky before me, all the lights came
on and the alarms began to clang. I ran the last few paces
headlong and almost fell into the arms of Captain van Eyck.
He scooped her out of my arms without a word and trotted
away toward the corner of the building.

I stood staring after them half-wittedly when Zeb brought
me to my senses by picking up my corselet and shoving it out
for me to put in my arms. "Snap out of it, man!" he hissed.
"That general alarm is for *us*. You're supposed to be on guard
duty."

He strapped on my sword as I buckled the corselet, then
slapped my helmet on my head and shoved my spear into my
left hand. Then we stood back to back in front of the portal,
pistols drawn, safeties off, in drill-manual full alert. Pending
further orders, we were not expected nor permitted to do
anything else, since the alarm had not taken place on our
post.

We stood like statues for several minutes. We could hear
sounds of running feet and of challenges. The Officer of the
Day ran past us into the Palace, buckling his corselet over his
night clothes as he ran. I almost blasted him out of existence
before he answered my challenge. Then the relief watch sec-

tion swung past at double time with the relief warden at its head.

Gradually the excitement died away; the lights remained on but someone thought to shut off the alarm. Zeb ventured a whisper. "What in Sheol happened? Did you muff it?"

"Yes and no." I told him about the restless Sister.

"Hmmph! Well, son, this ought to teach you not to fool around with women when you are on duty."

"Confound it, I wasn't fooling with her. She just popped out of her cell."

"I didn't mean tonight," he said bleakly.

I shut up.

About half an hour later, long before the end of the watch, the relief section tramped back. Their warden halted them, our two reliefs fell out and we fell in the empty places. We marched back to the guardroom, stopping twice more on the way to drop reliefs and pick up men from our own section.

5

WE WERE HALTED in the inner parade facing the guardroom door and left at attention. There we stood for fifty mortal minutes while the Officer of the Day strolled around and looked us over. Once a man in the rear rank shifted his weight. It would have gone unnoticed at dress parade, even in the presence of the Prophet, but tonight the Officer of the Day bawled him out at once and Captain van Eyck noted down his name.

Master Peter looked just as angry as his superior undoubtedly was. He passed out several more gigs, even stopped in front of me and told the guardroom orderly to put me down for "boots not properly shined"—which was a libel, unless I had scuffed them in my efforts. I dared not look down to see but stared him in the eye and said nothing, while he stared back coldly.

But his manner recalled to me Zeb's lecture about intrigue. Van Eyck's manner was perfectly that of a subordinate officer let down and shamed by his own men; how should I feel if I were in fact new-born innocent?

Angry, I decided—angry and self-righteous. Interested and stimulated by the excitement at first, then angry at being kept standing at attention like a plebe. They were trying to soften us up by the strained wait; how would I have felt about it, say two months ago? Smugly sure of my own virtue, it would have offended me and humiliated me—to be kept standing like a pariah waiting to whine for the privilege of a ration card—to be placed on the report like a cadet with soup on his jacket.

By the time the Commander of the Guard arrived almost an hour later I was white-lipped with anger. The process was synthetic but the emotion was real. I had never really liked our Commander anyway. He was a short, supercilious little man with a cold eye and a way of looking through his junior officers instead of at them. Now he stood in front of us with his priest's robes thrown back over his shoulders and his thumbs caught in his sword belt.

He glared at us. "Heaven help me, Angels of the Lord indeed," he said softly into the dead silence—then barked, "Well?"

No one answered.

"Speak up!" he shouted. "Some one of you knows about this. Answer me! Or would you all rather face the Question?"

A murmur ran down our ranks—but no one spoke.

He ran his eyes over us again. His eye caught mine and I stared back truculently. "Lyle!"

"Yes, reverend sir?"

"What do you know of this?"

"I know that I would like to sit down, reverend sir!"

He scowled at me, then his eye got a gleam of cold amusement. "Better to stand before me, my son, than to sit before the Inquisitor." But he passed on and heckled the man next to me.

He badgered us endlessly, but Zeb and I seemed to receive neither more nor less attention than the others. At last he seemed to give up and directed the Officer of the Day to dismiss us. I was not fooled; it was a certainty that every word spoken had been recorded, every expression cinemographed, and that analysts were plotting the data against each of our past behavior patterns before we reached our quarters.

But Zeb is a wonder. He was gossiping about the night's events, speculating innocently about what could have caused the hurrah, even before we reached our room. I tried to answer in what I had decided was my own "proper" reaction and groused about the way we had been treated. "We're officers and gentlemen," I complained. "If he thinks we are guilty of something, he should prefer formal charges."

I went to bed still griping, then lay awake and worried. I tried to tell myself that Judith must have reached a safe place, or else the brass would not be in the dark about it. But I dropped off to sleep still fretting.

I felt someone touch me and I woke instantly. Then I relaxed when I realized that my hand was being gripped in the recognition grip of the lodge. "Quiet," a voice I did not recognize whispered in my ear. "I must give you certain treatment to protect you." I felt the bite of a hypodermic in my arm; in a few seconds I was relaxed and dreamy. The voice whispered, "You saw nothing unusual on watch tonight. Until the alarm was sounded your watch was quite without incident—" I don't know how long the voice droned on.

I was awakened a second time by someone shaking me roughly. I burrowed into my pillow and said, "Go 'way! I'm going to skip breakfast."

Somebody struck me between my shoulder blades; I turned and sat up, blinking. There were four armed men in the room, blasters drawn and pointed at me. "Come along!" ordered the one nearest to me.

They were wearing the uniform of Angels but without unit insignia. Each head was covered by a black mask that exposed only the eyes—and by these masks I knew them: proctors of the Grand Inquisitor.

I hadn't really believed it could happen to me. Not to *me* . . . not to Johnnie Lyle who had always behaved himself, been a credit to his parish and a pride to his mother. No! The Inquisition was a bogieman, but a bogieman for sinners—not for John Lyle.

But I knew with sick horror when I saw those masks that I was already a dead man, that my time had come and here at last was the nightmare that I could not wake up from.

But I was not dead yet. From somewhere I got the courage to pretend anger. "What are *you* doing here?"

"Come along," the faceless voice repeated.

"Show me your order. You can't just drag an officer out of his bed any time you feel—"

The leader gestured with his pistol; two of them grabbed my arms and hustled me toward the door, while the fourth fell in behind. But I am fairly strong; I made it hard for them while protesting, "You've got to let me get dressed, at least. You've no right to haul me away half naked, no matter what the emergency is. I've a right to appear in the uniform of my rank."

Surprisingly the appeal worked. The leader stopped. "Okay. But snap into it!"

I stalled as much as I dared while going through the motions of hurrying—jamming a zipper on my boot, fumbling clumsily with all my dressing. How could I leave some sort of a message for Zeb? Any sort of a sign that would show the brethren what had happened to me?

At last I got a notion, not a good one but the best I could manage. I dragged clothing out of my wardrobe, some that I would need, some that I did not, and with the bunch a sweater. In the course of picking out what I must wear I managed to arrange the sleeves of the sweater in the position taken by a lodge brother in giving the Grand Hailing Sign of Distress. Then I picked up loose clothing and started to put some of it back in the wardrobe; the leader immediately shoved his blaster in my ribs and said, "Never mind that. You're dressed."

I gave in, dropping the meaningless clothing on the floor. The sweater remained spread out as a symbol to him who could read it. As they led me away I prayed that our room servant would not arrive and "tidy" it out of meaning before Zeb spotted it.

They blindfolded me as soon as we reached the inner Palace. We went down six flights, four below ground level as I figured it, and reached a compartment filled with the breathless silence of a vault. The hoodwink was stripped from my eyes. I blinked.

"Sit down, my boy, sit down and make yourself comfortable." I found myself looking into the face of the Grand Inquisitor himself, saw his warm friendly smile and his collie-dog eyes.

His gentle voice continued, "I'm sorry to get you so rudely out of a warm bed, but there is certain information needed by our Holy Church. Tell me, my son, do you fear the Lord? Oh, of course you do; your piety is well known. So you won't mind helping me with this little matter even though it makes you late for breakfast. It's to the greater glory of God." He turned to his masked and black-robed assistant questioner, hovering behind him. "Make him ready—and pray be gentle."

I was handled quickly and roughly, but not painfully. They touched me as if they regarded me as so much lifeless matter to be manipulated as impersonally as machinery. They stripped me to the waist and fastened things to me, a rubber bandage tight around my right arm, electrodes in my fists which they taped closed, another pair of electrodes to my wrists, a third pair at my temples, a tiny mirror to the pulse in my throat. At a control board on the left wall one of them made some adjustments, then threw a switch and on the opposite wall a shadow show of my inner workings sprang into being.

A little light danced to my heart beat, a wiggly line on an iconoscope display showed my blood pressure's rise and fall, another like it moved with my breathing, and there were several others that I did not understand. I turned my head away and concentrated on remembering the natural logarithms from one to ten.

"You see our methods, son. Efficiency and kindness, those are our watch words. Now tell me— *Where did you put her?*"

I broke off with the logarithm of eight. "Put who?"

"Why did you do it?"

"I am sorry, Most Reverend Sir. I don't know what it is I am supposed to have done."

Someone slapped me hard, from behind. The lights on the wall jiggled and the Inquisitor studied them thoughtfully, then spoke to an assistant. "Inject him."

Again my skin was pricked by a hypodermic. They let me rest while the drug took hold; I spent the time continuing with the effort of recalling logarithms. But that soon became too difficult; I grew drowsy and lackadaisical, nothing seemed to matter. I felt a mild and childish curiosity about my surroundings but no fear. Then the soft voice of the Inquisitor broke into my reverie with a question. I can't remember what it was but I am sure I answered with the first thing that came into my head.

I have no way of telling how long this went on. In time they brought me back to sharp reality with another injection. The Inquisitor was examining a slight bruise and a little purple dot on my right forearm. He glanced up. "What caused this, my boy?"

"I don't know, Most Reverend Sir." At the instant it was truth.

He shook his head regretfully. "Don't be naive, my son—and don't assume that I am. Let me explain something to you. What you sinners never realize is that the Lord always prevails. Always. Our methods are based in loving-kindness but they proceed with the absolute certainty of a falling stone, and with the result equally preordained.

"First we ask the sinner to surrender himself to the Lord and answer from the goodness that remains in his heart. When that loving appeal fails—as it did with you—then we use the skills God has given us to open the unconscious mind. That is usually as far as the Question need go—unless some agent of Satan has been there before us and has tampered with the sacred tabernacle of the mind.

"Now, my son, I have just returned from a walk through your mind. I found much there that was commendable, but I found also, in murky darkness, a wall that had been erected by some other sinner, and what I want—what the Church needs—is behind that wall."

Perhaps I showed a trace of satisfaction or perhaps the lights gave me away, for he smiled sadly and added, "No wall of Satan can stop the Lord. When we find such an obstacle, there are two things to do: given time enough I could remove that wall gently, delicately, stone by stone, without any damage to your mind. I wish I had time to, I really do, for you are a good boy at heart, John Lyle, and you do not belong with the sinners.

"But while eternity is long, time is short; there is the second way. We can disregard the false barrier in the unconscious mind and make a straightforward assault on the conscious mind, with the Lord's banners leading us." He glanced away from me. "Prepare him."

His faceless crew strapped a metal helmet on my head, some other arrangements were made at the control board. "Now look here, John Lyle." He pointed to a diagram on the wall. "No doubt you know that the human nervous system is partly electrical in nature. There is a schematic representation of a brain, that lower part is the thalamus; covering it is the cortex. Each of the sensory centers is marked as you can see. Your own electrodynamic characteristics have been analyzed; I am sorry to say that it will now be necessary to heterodyne your normal senses."

He started to turn away, turned back. "By the way, John Lyle, I have taken the trouble to minister to you myself because, at this stage, my assistants through less experience in the Lord's work than my humble self sometimes mistake zeal for skill and transport the sinner unexpectedly to his reward. I don't want that to happen to you. You are merely a strayed lamb and I purpose saving you."

I said, "Thank you, Most Reverend Sir."

"Don't thank me, thank the Lord I serve. However," he went on, frowning slightly, "this frontal assault on the mind, while necessary, is unavoidably painful. You will forgive me?"

I hesitated only an instant. "I forgive you, holy sir."

He glanced at the lights and said wryly, "A falsehood. But you are forgiven that falsehood; it was well intended." He nodded at his silent helpers. "Commence."

A light blinded me, an explosion crashed in my ears. My right leg jerked with pain, then knotted in an endless cramp. My throat contracted; I choked and tried to throw up. Something struck me in the solar plexus; I doubled up and could not catch my breath. "Where did you put her?" A noise started low and soft, climbed higher and higher, increasing in pitch and decibels, until it was a thousand dull saws, a million squeaking slate pencils, then wavered in a screeching ululation that tore at the thin wall of reason. "Who helped you?" Agonizing heat was at my crotch; I could not get away from it. "Why did you do it?" I itched all over, intolerably, and tried to tear at my skin—but my arms would not work. The itching was worse than pain; I would have welcomed pain in lieu of scratching. "Where is she?"

Light . . . sound . . . pain . . . heat . . . convulsions . . . cold . . . falling . . . light and pain . . . cold and falling . . . nausea and sound. "Do you love the Lord?" Searing heat and shocking cold . . . pain and a pounding in my head that made me scream—"Where did you take her? Who else was in it? Give up and save your immortal soul." Pain and an endless nakedness to the outer darkness.

I suppose I fainted.

Some one was slapping me across the mouth. "Wake up, John Lyle, and confess! Zebadiah Jones has given you away."

I blinked and said nothing. It was not necessary to simulate a dazed condition, nor could I have managed it. But the words had been a tremendous shock and my brain was racing, trying to get into gear. Zeb? Old Zeb? Poor old Zeb! Hadn't they had time to give him hypnotic treatment, too? It did not occur to me even then to suspect that Zeb had broken under torture alone; I simply assumed that they had been able to tap his unconscious mind. I wondered if he were already dead and remembered that I had gotten him into this, against his good sense. I prayed for his soul and prayed that he would forgive me.

My head jerked to another roundhouse slap. "Wake up! You can hear me—Jones has revealed your sins."

"Revealed what?" I mumbled.

The Grand Inquisitor motioned his assistants aside and leaned over me, his kindly face full of concern. "Please, my son, do this for the Lord—and for me. You have been brave in trying to protect your fellow sinners from the fruits of their folly, but they failed you and your stiff-necked courage no longer means anything. But don't go to judgment with this on your soul. Confess, and let death come with your sins forgiven."

"So you mean to kill me?"

He looked faintly annoyed. "I did not say that. I know that you do not fear death. What you should fear is to meet your Maker with your sins still on your soul. Open your heart and confess."

"Most Reverend Sir, I have nothing to confess."

He turned away from me and gave orders in low, gentle tones. "Continue. The mechanicals this time; I don't wish to burn out his brain."

There is no point in describing what he meant by "the mechanicals" and no sense in making this account needlessly grisly. His methods differed in no important way from torture techniques used in the Middle Ages and even more recently— except that his knowledge of the human nervous system was incomparably greater and his knowledge of behavior psychology made his operations more adoit. In addition, he and his assistants behaved as if they were completely free of any sadistic pleasure in their work; it made them coolly efficient.

But let's skip the details.

I have no notion of how long it took. I must have passed out repeatedly, for my clearest memory is of catching a bucket of ice water in the face not once but over and over again, like a repeating nightmare—each time followed by the inevitable hypo. I don't think I told them anything of any importance while I was awake and the hypno instructions to my unconscious may have protected me while I was out of my head. I seem to remember trying to make up a lie about sins I had never committed; I don't remember what came of it.

I recall vaguely coming semi-awake once and hearing a voice say, "He can take more. His heart is strong."

I was pleasantly dead for a long time, but finally woke up as if from a long sleep. I was stiff and when I tried to shift in bed my side hurt me. I opened my eyes and looked around; I was in bed in a small, windowless but cheerful room. A sweet-faced young woman in a nurse's uniform came quickly to my side and felt my pulse.

"Hello."

"Hello," she answered. "How are we now? Better?"

"What happened?" I asked. "Is it over? Or is this just a rest?"

"Quiet," she admonished. "You are still too weak to talk. But it's over—you are safe among the brethren."

"I was rescued?"

"Yes. Now be quiet." She held up my head and gave me something to drink. I went back to sleep.

It took me days to convalesce and catch up with events. The infirmary in which I woke up was part of a series of sub-basements under the basement proper of a department store in New Jerusalem; there was some sort of underground connection between it and the lodge room under the Palace—just where and how I could not say; I was never in it. While conscious, I mean.

Zeb came to see me as soon as I was allowed to have visitors. I tried to raise up in bed. "Zeb! Zeb boy—I thought you were dead!"

"Who? Me?" He came over and shook my left hand. "What made you think that?"

I told him about the dodge the Inquisitor had tried to pull on me. He shook his head. "I wasn't even arrested. Thanks to you, pal. Johnnie, I'll never call you stupid again. If you hadn't had that flash of genius to rig your sweater so that I could read the sign in it, they might have pulled us both in and neither one of us have gotten out of it alive. As it was, I went straight to Captain van Eyck. He told me to lie doggo in the lodge room and then planned your rescue."

I wanted to ask how that had been pulled off but my mind jumped to a more important subject. "Zeb, where is Judith?

Can't you find her and bring her to see me? My nurse just smiles and tells me to rest."

He looked surprised. "Didn't they tell you?"

"Tell me what? No, I haven't seen anybody but the nurse and the doctor and they treat me like an idiot. Don't keep me in suspense, Zeb. Did anything go wrong? She's all right—*isn't she?*"

"Oh, sure! But she's in Mexico by now—we got a report by sensitive circuit two days ago."

In my physical weakness I almost wept. "Gone! Why, what a dirty, scabby trick! Why couldn't they have waited until I was well enough to tell her good-by?"

Zeb said quickly, "Hey, look, stupid—no, forget that 'stupid'; you aren't. Look, old man, your calendar is mixed up. She was on her way before you were rescued, before we were even sure you could be rescued. You don't think the brethren could bring her back just to let you two bill and coo, do you?"

I thought about it and calmed down. It made sense, even though I was bitterly disappointed. He changed the subject. "How do you feel?"

"Oh, pretty good."

"They tell me you get that cast off your leg tomorrow."

"So? They haven't told me." I twisted, trying to get comfortable. "I'm almost more anxious to get shut of this corset, but the doc says I'll have to wear it for several weeks yet."

"How about your hand? Can you bend your fingers?"

I tried it. "Fairly well. I may have to write left-handed for a while."

"All in all, it looks like you're too mean to die, old son. By the way, if it's any consolation to you, the laddy boy who worked on Judith got slightly dead in the raid in which you were rescued."

"He was? Well, I'm sorry. I had planned to save him for myself."

"No doubt, but you would have had to take your place in line, if he had lived. Lots of people wanted him. Me, for example."

"But I had thought of something special for him—I was going to make him bite hit nails."

"Bite his nails?" Zeb looked puzzled.

"Until he reached his elbows. Follow me?"

"Oh." Zeb grinned sourly. "Not nearly imaginative enough, boy. But he's dead, we can't touch him."

"He's infernally lucky. Zeb, why didn't you arrange to get him yourself? Or did you, and things were just too hurried to let you do a proper job?"

"Me? Why, I wasn't on the rescue raid. I haven't been back in the Palace at all."

"Huh?"

"You didn't think I was still on duty, did you?"

"I haven't had time to think about it."

"Well, naturally I couldn't go back after I ducked out to avoid arrest; I was through. No, my fine fellow, you and I are both deserters from the United States Army—with every cop and every postmaster in the country anxious to earn a deserter's reward by turning us in."

I whistled softly and let the implications of his remark sink in.

6

I HAD JOINED the Cabal on impulse. Certainly, under the stress of falling in love with Judith and in the excitement of the events that had come rushing over me as a result of meeting her, I had no time for calm consideration. I had not broken with the Church as a result of philosophical decision.

Of course I had known logically that to join the Cabal was to break with all my past ties, but it had not yet hit me emotionally. What was it going to be like never again to wear the uniform of an officer and a gentleman? I had been proud to walk down the street, to enter a public place, aware that all eyes were on me.

I put it out of my mind. The share was in the furrow, my hand was on the plow; there could be no turning back. I was in this until we won or until we were burned for treason.

I found Zeb looking at me quizzically. "Cold feet, Johnnie?"

"No. But I'm still getting adjusted. Things have moved fast."

"I know. Well, we can forget about retired pay, and our class numbers at the Point no longer matter." He took off his Academy ring, chucked it in the air, caught it and shoved it into his pocket. "But there is work to be done, old lad, and you will find that this is a military outfit, too—a real one. Personally, I've had my fill of spit-and-polish and I don't care if I never again hear that 'Sound off' and 'Officers, center!' and 'Watchman, what of the night?' manure again. The brethren will make full use of our best talents—and the fight really matters."

Master Peter van Eyck came to see me a couple of days later. He sat on the edge of my bed and folded his hands over his paunch and looked at me. "Feeling better, son?"

"I could get up if the doctor would let me."

"Good. We're shorthanded; the less time a trained officer spends on the sick list the better." He paused and chewed his lip. "But, son, I don't know just what to do with you."

"Eh? Sir?"

"Frankly, you should never have been admitted to the Order in the first place—a military command should not mess around with affairs of the heart. It confuses motivations, causes false decisions. Twice, because we took you in, we have had to show our strength in sorties that—from a strictly military standpoint—should never have happened."

I did not answer, there was no answer—he was right. My face was hot with embarrassment.

"Don't blush about it," he added kindly. "Contrariwise, it is good for the morale of the brethren to strike back occasionally. The point is, what to do with you? You are a stout fellow, you stood up well—but do you really understand the ideals of freedom and human dignity we are fighting for?"

I barely hesitated. "Master—I may not be much of a brain, and the Lord knows it's true that I've never thought much about politics. But I know which side I'm on!"

He nodded. "That's enough. We can't expect each man to be his own Tom Paine."

"His own what?"

"Thomas Paine. But then you've never heard of him, of course. Look him up in our library when you get a chance. Very inspiring stuff. Now about your assignment. It would be easy enough to put you on a desk job here—your friend Zebadiah has been working sixteen hours a day trying to straighten out our filing system. But I can't waste you two on clerical jobs. What is your savvy subject, your specialty?"

"Why, I haven't had any P.G. work yet, sir."

"I know. But what did you stand high in? How were you in applied miracles, and mob psychology?"

"I was fairly good in miracles, but I guess I'm too wooden for psychodynamics. Ballistics was my best subject."

"Well, we can't have everything. I could use a technician in morale and propaganda, but if you can't, you can't."

"Zeb stood one in his class in mob psychology, Master. The Commandant urged him to aim for the priesthood."

"I know and we'll use him, but not here. He is too much interested in Sister Magdalene; I don't believe in letting couples work together. It might distort their judgments in a pinch. Now about you. I wonder if you wouldn't make a good assassin?"

He asked the question seriously but almost casually; I had trouble believing it. I had been taught—I had always taken it for granted that assassination was one of the unspeakable sins, like incest, or blasphemy. I blurted out, "The brethren use *assassination?*"

"Eh? Why not?" Van Eyck studied my face. "I keep forgetting. John, would you kill the Grand Inquisitor if you got a chance?"

"Well—yes, of course. But I'd want to do it in a fair fight."

"Do you think you will ever be given that chance? Now let's suppose we are back at the day Sister Judith was arrested by him. Suppose you could stop him by killing him—but only by poisoning him, or knifing him in the back. What would you do?"

I answered savagely, "I would have killed him!"

"Would you have felt any shame, any guilt?"

"None!"

"So. But he is only one of many in this foulness. The man who eats meat cannot sneer at the butcher—and every bishop, every minister of state, every man who benefits from this tyranny, right up to the Prophet himself, is an accomplice before the fact in every murder committed by the inquisitors. The man who condones a sin because he enjoys the result of the sin is equally guilty of the sin. Do you see that?"

Oddly enough, I did see it, for it was orthodox doctrine as I had learned it. I had choked over its new application. But

Master Peter was still talking: "But we don't indulge in vengeance—vengeance still belongs to the Lord. I would never send *you* against the Inquisitor because you might be tempted to exult in it personally. We don't tempt a man with sin as a bait. What we do do, what we are doing, is engaging in a calculated military operation in a war already commenced. One key man is often worth a regiment; we pick out that key man and kill him. The bishop in one diocese may be such a man; the bishop in the next state may be just a bungler, propped up by the system. We kill the first, let the second stay where he is. Gradually we are eliminating their best brains. Now—" He leaned toward me. "—do you want a job picking off those key men? It's very important work."

It seemed to me that, in this business, someone was continually making me face up to facts, instead of letting me dodge unpleasant facts the way most people manage to do throughout their lives. Could I stomach such an assignment? Could I refuse it—since Master Peter had implied at least that assassins were volunteers—refuse it and try to ignore in my heart that it was going on and that I was condoning it?

Master Peter was right; the man who buys the meat is brother to the butcher. It was squeamishness, not morals . . . like the man who favors capital punishment but is himself too "good" to fit the noose or swing the axe. Like the person who regards war as inevitable and in some circumstances moral, but who avoids military service because he doesn't like the thought of killing.

Emotional infants, ethical morons—the left hand *must* know what the right hand doeth, and the heart is responsible for both. I answered almost at once, "Master Peter, I am ready to serve . . . that way or whatever the brethren decide I can do best."

"Good man!" He relaxed a bit and went on, "Between ourselves, it's the job I offer to every new recruit when I'm not sure that he understands that this is not a ball game, but a cause to which he must commit himself without any reservation—his life, his fortune, his sacred honor. We have no place for the man who wants to give orders but who won't clean the privy."

I felt relieved. "Then you weren't seriously picking me out for assassination work?"

"Eh? Usually I am not; few men are fitted for it. But in your case I am quite serious, because we already know that you have an indispensable and not very common qualification."

I tried to think what was so special about me and could not. "Sir?"

"Well you'll get caught eventually, of course. Three point seven accomplished missions per assassin is what we are running now—a good score, but we ought to do better as suitable men are so scarce. But with you we know already that when they do catch you and put you to the Question, you won't crack."

My face must have shown my feelings. The Question? Again? I was still half dead from the first time. Master Peter said kindly, "Of course you won't have to go up against it again to the fullest. We always protect assassins; we fix it so that they can suicide easily. You don't need to worry."

Believe me, having once suffered the Question, his assurance to me did not seem calloused; it was a real comfort. "How, sir?"

"Eh? A dozen different ways. Our surgeons can booby-trap you so that you can die at will in the tightest bonds anyone can put on you. There is the old hollow tooth, of course, with cyanide or such—but the proctors are getting wise to that; sometimes they gag a man's mouth open. But there are many ways. For example—" He stretched his arms wide and bent them back, but not far. "—if I were to cramp my arms backward in a position a man never assumes without very considerable conscious effort, a little capsule between my shoulder blades would rupture and I would make my last report. Yet you could pound me on the back all day and never break it."

"Uh . . . were you an assassin, sir?"

"Me? How could I be, in my job? But all of our people in positions of maximum exposure are loaded—it's the least we can do for them. Besides that, I've got a bomb in my belly—" He patted his paunch. "—that will take a roomful of people with me if it seems desirable."

"I could have used one of those last week," I said emphatically.

"You're here, aren't you? Don't despise your luck. If you need one, you'll have one." He stood up and prepared to leave. "In the meantime, don't give any special thought to being selected as an executioner. The psychological evaluation group will still have to pass on you and they are hard men to convince."

Despite his words, I did think about it, of course, though it ceased to worry me. I was put on light duty shortly thereafter and spent several days reading proof on the *Iconoclast*, a smug, mildly critical, little reform-from-within paper which the Cabal used to pave the way for its field missionaries. It was a "Yes, but—" paper, overtly loyal to the Prophet but just the sort of thing to arouse doubt in the minds of the stiff-necked and intolerant. Its acid lay in how a thing was said, not what was said. I had even seen copies of it around the Palace.

I also got acquainted with some of the ramifications of the amazing underground headquarters at New Jerusalem. The department store above us was owned by a Past Grand Master and was an extremely important means of liaison with the outside world. The shelves of the store fed us and clothed us; through taps into the visiphone circuits serving the store commercially we had connection with the outside and could even put in transcontinental calls if the message could be phrased or coded to allow for the likelihood that it would be monitored. The owner's delivery trucks could be used to spirit fugitives to or from our clandestine quarters—I learned that Judith started her flight that way, with a bill of lading that described her as gum boots. The store's manifold commercial operations were a complete and plausible blind for our extensive operations.

Successful revolution is Big Business—make no mistake about that. In a modern, complex, and highly industrialized state, revolution is not accomplished by a handful of conspirators whispering around a guttering candle in a deserted ruin. It requires countless personnel, supplies, modern machinery and modern weapons. And to handle these factors successfully there must be loyalty, secrecy, and superlative staff organization.

I was kept busy but my work was fill-in work, since I was awaiting assignment. I had time to dig into the library and I looked up Tom Paine, which led me to Patrick Henry and Thomas Jefferson and others—a whole new world was opened up to me. I had trouble at first in admitting the possibility of what I read; I think perhaps of all the things a police state can do to its citizens, distorting history is possibly the most pernicious. For example, I learned for the first time that the United States had not been ruled by a bloodthirsty emissary of Satan before the First Prophet arose in his wrath and cast him out—but had been a community of free men, deciding their own affairs by peaceful consent. I don't mean that the first republic had been a scriptural paradise, but it hadn't been anything like what I had learned in school.

For the first time in my life I was reading things which had not been approved by the Prophet's censors, and the impact on my mind was devastating. Sometimes I would glance over my shoulder to see who was watching me, frightened in spite of myself. I began to sense faintly that secrecy is the keystone of all tyranny. Not force, but secrecy . . . censorship. When any government, or any church for that matter, undertakes to say to its subjects, "This you may not read, this you must not see, this you are forbidden to know," the end result is tyranny and oppression, no matter how holy the motives. Mighty little force is needed to control a man whose mind has been hoodwinked; contrariwise, no amount of force can control a free man, a man whose mind is free. No, not the rack, not fission bombs, not anything—you can't conquer a free man; the most you can do is kill him.

My thoughts did not then fall into syllogisms; my head was filled with an inchoate spate of new ideas, each more exciting than the last. I discovered that travel between the planets, almost a myth in my world, had not stopped because the First Prophet had forbidden it as a sin against the omnipotence of God; it had ceased because it had gone into the red financially and the Prophet's government would not subsidize it. There was even an implied statement that the "infidels" (I still used that word in my mind) still sent out an occasional research ship and that there were human beings even now on Mars and Venus.

I grew so excited at that notion that I almost forgot the plight we were all in. If I had not been chosen for the Angels of the Lord, I would probably have gone into rocketry. I was good at anything of that sort, the things that called for quick reflexes combined with knowledge of the mathematical and mechanical arts. Maybe someday the United States would have space ships again. Perhaps I . . .

But the thought was crowded out by a dozen new ones. Foreign newspapers—why, I had not even been sure the infidels could read and write. The London *Times* made unbelievable and exciting reading. I gradually got it through my head that the Britishers apparently did not now eat human flesh, if indeed they ever had. They seemed remarkably like us, except that they were shockingly prone to do as they pleased—there were even letters in the *Times* criticizing the government. And there was another letter signed by a bishop of their infidel church, criticizing the people for not attending services. I don't know which one puzzled me the more; both of them seemed to indicate a situation of open anarchy.

Master Peter informed me that the psych board had turned me down for assassination duty. I found myself both relieved and indignant. What was wrong with me that they would not trust me with the job? It seemed like a slur on my character —by then.

"Take it easy," Van Eyck advised dryly. "They made a dummy run based on your personality profile and it figured almost an even chance that you would be caught your first time out. We don't like to expend men that fast."

"But—"

"Peace, lad. I'm sending you out to General Headquarters for assignment."

"General Headquarters? Where is that?"

"You'll know when you get there. Report to the staff metamorphist."

Dr. Mueller was the staff face-changer; I asked him what he had in mind for me. "How do I know until I find out what you are?" He had me measured and photographed, recorded my voice, analyzed my walk, and had a punched card made up of my physical characteristics. "Now we'll find your twin brother." I watched the card sorter go through several thousand cards and I was beginning to think I was a unique individual, resembling no one else sufficiently to permit me to be disguised successfully, when two cards popped out almost together. Before the machine whirred to a stop there were five cards in the basket.

"A nice assortment," Dr. Mueller mused as he looked them over, "one synthetic, two live ones, a deader, and one female. We can't use the woman for this job, but we'll keep it in mind; it might come in very handy someday to know that there is a female citizen you could impersonate successfully."

"What's a synthetic?" I enquired.

"Eh? Oh, it's a composite personality, very carefully built from faked records and faked backgrounds. A risky business —it involves tampering with the national archives. I don't like to use a synthetic, for there really isn't any way to fill in completely the background of a man who doesn't exist. I'd much rather patch into the real background of a real person."

"Then why use synthetics at all?"

"Sometimes we have to. When we have to move a refugee in a hurry, for example, and there is no real person we can match him with. So we try to keep a fairly broad assortment of synthetics built up. Now let me see," he added, shuffling the cards, "we have two to choose from—"

"Just a second, Doctor," I interrupted, "why do you keep dead men in the file?"

"Oh, they aren't legally dead. When one of the brethren dies and it is possible to conceal the fact, we maintain his public personality for possible future use. Now then," he continued, "can you sing?"

"Not very well."

"This one is out, then. He's a concert baritone. I can make a lot of changes in you, but I can't make a trained singer of you. It's Hobson's choice. How would you like to be Adam Reeves, commercial traveler in textiles?" He held up a card.

"Do you think I could get away with it?"

"Certainly—when I get through with you."

A fortnight later my own mother wouldn't have known me. Nor, I believe, could Reeves' mother have told me from her son. The second week Reeves himself was available to work with me. I grew to like him very much while I was studying him. He was a mild, quiet man with a retiring disposition, which always made me think of him as small although he was, of course, my height, weight, and bony structure. We resembled each other only superficially in the face.

At first, that is. A simple operation made my ears stand out a little more than nature intended; at the same time they trimmed my ear lobes. Reeves' nose was slightly aquiline; a little wax under the skin at the bridge caused mine to match. It was necessary to cap several of my teeth to make mine match his dental repair work; that was the only part I really minded. My complexion had to be bleached a shade or two; Reeves' work did not take him out into the sun much.

But the most difficult part of the physical match was artificial fingerprints. An opaque, flesh-colored flexible plastic was painted on my finger pads, then my fingers were sealed into molds made from Reeves' fingertips. It was touchy work; one finger was done over seven times before Dr. Mueller would pass it.

That was only the beginning; now I had to learn to act like Reeves—his walk, his gestures. the way he laughed, his table manners. I doubt if I could ever make a living as an actor— my coach certainly agreed and said so.

"Confound it, Lyle, won't you ever get it? Your life will depend on it. You've *got* to learn!"

"But I thought I was acting just like Reeves," I objected feebly.

"Acting! That's just the trouble—you were *acting* like Reeves. And it was as phony as a false leg. You've got to *be* Reeves. Try it. Worry about your sales record, think about your last trip, think about commissions and discounts and quotas. Go on. Try it."

Every spare minute I studied the current details of Reeves' business affairs, for I would actually have to sell textiles in his place. I had to learn a whole trade and I discovered that there was more to it than carrying around samples and letting a retailer make his choice—and I didn't know a denier from a continuous fibre. Before I finished I acquired a new respect for business men. I had always thought that buying and selling was simple; I was wrong again. I had to use the old phonographic tutor stunt and wear earphones to bed. I never sleep well that way and would wake up each morning with a splitting head and with my ears, still tender from the operations, sore as two boils.

But it worked, all of it. In two short weeks I *was* Adam Reeves, commercial traveler, right down to my thoughts.

7

"LYLE," Master Peter van Eyck said to me, "Reeves is due to catch the *Comet* for Cincinnati this afternoon. Are you ready?"

"Yes, sir."

"Good. Repeat your orders."

"Sir, I am to carry out my—I mean his—selling schedule from here to the coast. I check in at the San Francisco office of United Textiles, then proceed on his vacation. In Phoenix, Arizona, I am to attend church services at the South Side

Tabernacle. I am to hang around afterwards and thank the priest for the inspiration of his sermon; in the course of which I am to reveal myself to him by means of the accustomed usages of our order. He will enable me to reach General Headquarters."

"All correct. In addition to transferring you for duty, I am going to make use of you as a messenger. Report to the psychodynamics laboratory at once. The chief technician will instruct you."

"Very well, sir."

The lodge Master got up and came around his desk to me. "Good-by, John. Watch yourself, and may the Great Architect help you."

"Thank you, sir. Uh, is this message I am to carry important?"

"Quite important."

He let it go at that and I was a bit irked; it seemed silly to be mysterious about it when I would find out just what it was in a few minutes. But I was mistaken. At the laboratory I was told to sit down, relax, and prepare myself for hypnosis.

I came out of it with the pleasant glow that usually follows hypnosis. "That's all," I was told. "Carry out your orders."

"But how about the message I was to carry?"

"You have it."

"Hypnotically? But if I'm arrested, I'll be at the mercy of any psychoinvestigator who examines me!"

"No, you won't. It's keyed to a pair of signal words; you can't possibly remember until they are spoken to you. The chance that an examiner would hit on both words and in the right order is negligible. You can't give the message away, awake or asleep."

I had rather expected to be "loaded" for suicide, if I was to carry an important message—though I hadn't seen how they could do it at the last minute, other than supplying me with a pill, I mean, a method almost useless if the policeman knows his business. But if I couldn't give away the message I carried, then I preferred to take my chances; I didn't ask for poison. I'm not the suiciding type anyhow—when Satan comes for me, he'll have to drag me . . .

The rocket port serving New Jerusalem is easier to get to than is the case at most of the older cities. There was a tube station right across from the department store that hid our headquarters. I simply walked out of the store, took the bridge across the street, found the tube stall marked "Rocket Port," waited for an empty cartridge, and strapped myself and my luggage in. The attendant sealed me and almost at once I was at the port.

I bought my ticket and took my place at the end of the queue outside the port police station. I'll admit I was nervous; while I didn't anticipate having any trouble getting my travel pass validated, the police officers who must handle it were no doubt on the lookout for John Lyle, renegade army officer. But they were always looking for someone and I hoped the list of wanted faces was too long to make the search for me anything other than routine.

The line moved slowly and that looked like a bad sign—especially so when I noticed that several people had been thumbed out of line and sent to wait behind the station railing. I got downright jittery. But the wait itself gave me time to get myself in hand. I shoved my papers at the sergeant, glanced at my chrono, up at the station clock, and back at my wrist.

The sergeant had been going through my papers in a leisurely, thorough manner. He looked up. "Don't worry about catching your ship," he said not unkindly. "They can't leave until we clear their passenger list." He pushed a pad across the counter. "Your fingerprints, please."

I gave them without comment. He compared them with the prints on my travel pass and then with the prints Reeves had left there on his arrival a week earlier. "That's all, Mr. Reeves. A pleasant trip."

I thanked him and left.

The *Comet* was not too crowded. I picked a seat by a window, well forward, and had just settled down and was unfolding a late-afternoon copy of the *Holy City*, when I felt a touch on my arm.

It was a policeman.

"Will you step outside, please?"

I was herded outside with four other male passengers. The sergeant was quite decent about it. "I'm afraid I'll have to ask you four to return to the station for further identification. I'll order your baggage removed and have the passenger list changed. Your tickets will be honored on the next flight."

I let out a yelp. "But I've got to be in Cincinnati tonight!"

"I'm sorry." He turned to me. "You're Reeves, aren't you? Hmm . . . you are the right size and build. Still . . . let me see your pass again. Didn't you arrive in town just last week?"

"That's right."

He went through my papers again. "Uh, yes, I remember now; you came in Tuesday morning on the *Pilgrim*. Well, you can't be in two places at once, so I guess that clears you." He handed my papers back to me. "Go aboard again. Sorry we bothered you. The rest of you come along."

I returned to my seat and picked up my newspaper. A few minutes later the first heavy surge of the rockets threw us to the west. I continued reading the paper to cover up my agitation and relief, but soon got interested. I had been reading a Toronto paper only that morning, underground; the contrast was startling. I was back in a world for which the outside world hardly existed; the "foreign affairs" news, if you could call it that, consisted of glowing reports of our foreign missions and some accounts of atrocities among the infidels. I began to wonder where all that money went that was contributed each year for missionary work; the rest of the world, if you could believe *their* newspapers, didn't seem much aware that our missions existed.

Then I began going through the paper, picking out items that I knew to be false. By the time I was through we were down out of the ionosphere and gliding into Cincy. We had overtaken the sun and had sunset all over again.

There must be a peddler's pack in my family tree. I not only covered Reeves' territory in Cincinnati, but bettered his quota. I found that I got as much pleasure out of persuading some hard-boiled retailer that he should increase his line of yard goods as I ever had from military work. I stopped worrying about my disguise and thought only about textiles. Selling isn't just a way to eat; it's a game, it's fun.

I left for Kansas City on schedule and had no trouble with the police in getting a visa for my travel pass. I decided that New Jerusalem had been the only ticklish check point; from here west nobody would expect to pick up John Lyle, formerly officer and gentleman; he would be one of thousands of wanted men, lost in the files.

The rocket to K.C. was well filled; I had to sit beside another passenger, a well-built chap in his middle thirties. We looked each other over as I sat down, then each busied himself with his own affairs. I called for a lap table and started straightening out the order blanks and other papers I had accumulated during busy, useful days in Cincinnati. He lounged back and watched the news broadcast in the TV tank at the forward end of the car.

I felt a nudge about ten minutes later and looked around. My seatmate flicked a thumb toward the television tank; in it there was displayed a large public square filled with a mob. It was surging toward the steps of a massive temple, over which floated the Prophet's gold-and-crimson banner and the pennant of a bishopric. As I watched, the first wave of the crowd broke against the temple steps.

A squad of temple guards trotted out a side door near the giant front doors and set up their tripods on the terrace at the head of the wide stairs. The scene cut to another viewpoint; we were looking down right into the faces of the mob hurrying toward us—apparently from a telephoto pick-up somewhere on the temple roof.

What followed made me ashamed of the uniform I had once worn. Instead of killing them quickly, the guards aimed low and burned off their legs. One instant the first wave was running toward me up the steps—then they fell, the cauterized stumps of their legs jerking convulsively. I had been watching a youngish couple right in the center of the pick-up; they had been running hand in hand. As the beam swept across them they went down together.

She stayed down. He managed to lift himself on what had been his knees, took two awkward dying steps toward her and fell across her. He pulled her head to his, then the scene cut away from them to the wide view of the square.

I snatched the earphones hanging on the back of the seat in front of me and listened: "—apolis, Minnesota. The situation is well in hand and no additional troops will be needed. Bishop Jennings has declared martial law while the agents of Satan are rounded up and order restored. A period of prayer and fasting will commence at once.

"The Minnesota ghettos have been closed and all local pariahs will be relocated in the reservations in Wyoming and Montana in order to prevent future outbreaks. Let this be a warning to the ungodly everywhere who might presume to dispute the divine rule of the Prophet Incarnate.

"This on-the-spot cast by the No-Sparrow-Shall-Fall News Service is coming to you under the sponsorship of the Associated Merchants of the Kingdom, dealers in the finest of household aids toward grace. Be the first in your parish to possess a statuette of the Prophet that miraculously *glows in the dark!* Send one dollar, care of this station—"

I switched off the phones and hung them up. Why blame the pariahs? That mob wasn't made up of pariahs.

But I kept my lip zipped and let my companion speak first —which he did, with vehemence. "Serves them right, the bloody fools! Imagine charging against a fortified position with your bare hands." He kept his voice down and spoke almost in my ear.

"I wonder why they rioted?" was all that I answered.

"Eh? No accounting for the actions of an heretic. They aren't sane."

"You can sing that in church," I agreed firmly. "Besides, even a sane heretic—if there could be such a thing, I mean— could see that the government is doing a good job of running the country. Business is good." I patted my brief case happily. "For me, at least, praise the Lord."

We talked business conditions and the like for some time. As we talked I looked him over. He seemed to be the usual leading-citizen type, conventional and conservative, yet something about him made me uneasy. Was it just my guilty nerves? Or some sixth sense of the hunted?

My eyes came back to his hands and I had a vague feeling that I should be noticing something. But there was nothing unusual about them. Then I finally noticed a very minor thing, a calloused ridge on the bottom joint of the third finger of his left hand, the sort of a mark left by wearing a heavy ring for years and just the sort I carried myself from wearing my West Point class ring. It meant nothing, of course, since lots of men wear heavy seal rings on that finger. I was wearing one myself—not my West Point ring naturally, but one belonging to Reeves.

But why would this conventional-minded oaf wear such a ring habitually, then stop? A trifling thing, but it worried me; a hunted animal lives by noticing trifles. At the Point I had never been considered bright in psychology; I had missed cadet chevrons on that issue alone. But now seemed a good time to use what little I had learned . . . so I ran over in my mind all I had noticed about him.

The first thing he had noticed, the one thing he had commented on, was the foolhardiness of charging into a fortified position. That smacked of military orientation in his thinking.

But that did not prove he was a Pointer. On the contrary, an Academy man wears his ring at all times, even into his grave, even on leave and wearing mufti . . . unless for some good reason he does not wish to be recognized.

We were still chatting sociably and I was worrying over how to evaluate insufficient data when the stewardess served tea. The ship was just beginning to bite air as we came down out of the fringes of space and entered the long glide into Kansas City; it was somewhat bumpy and she slopped a little hot tea on his thigh. He yelped and uttered an expletive under his breath. I doubt if she caught what he said.

But I did catch it—and I thought about it furiously while I dabbed at him with a handkerchief. "B. J. idiot!" was the term he used and it was strictly West Point slang.

Ergo, the ring callus was no coincidence; he was a West Pointer, an army officer, pretending to be a civilian. Corollary: he was almost certainly on a secret service assignment. Was I his assignment?

Oh, come now, John! His ring might be at a jeweller's, being repaired; he might be going home on thirty days. But in the course of a long talk he had let me think that he was a business man. No, he was an undercover agent.

But even if he was not after *me*, he had made two bad breaks in my presence. But even the clumsiest tyro (like myself, say) does not make two such slips in maintaining an assumed identity—and the army secret service was not clumsy; it was run by some of the most subtle brains in the country. Very well, then—they were not accidental slips but calculated acts; I was intended to notice them and *think* that they were accidents. Why?

It could not be simply that he was not sure I was the man he wanted. In such case, under the old and tested principle that a man was sinful until proved innocent, he would simply have arrested me and I would have been put to the Question.

Then *why?*

It could only be that they wanted me to run free for a while yet—but to be scared out of my wits and run for cover . . . and thereby lead them to my fellow conspirators. It was a far-fetched hypothesis, but the only one that seemed to cover all the facts.

When I first concluded that my companion must be an agent on my trail I was filled with that cold, stomach-twisting fear that can be compared only with seasickness. But when I thought I had figured out their motives I calmed down. What would Zebadiah do? "The first principle of intrigue is not to be stampeded into any unusual act—". Sit tight and play dumb. If this cop wanted to follow me, I'd lead him into every department store in K.C.—and let him watch while I peddled yard goods.

Nevertheless my stomach felt tight as we got off the ship in Kansas City. I expected that gentle touch on the shoulder which is more frightening than a fist in the face. But nothing happened. He tossed me a perfunctory God-keep-you, pushed ahead of me, and headed for the lift to the taxicab platform while I was still getting my pass stamped. It did not reassure me, as he could have pointed me out half a dozen ways to a relief. But I went on over to the New Muehlbach by tube as casually as I could manage.

I had a fair week in K.C., met my quota and picked up one new account of pretty good size. I tried to spot any shadow that might have been placed on me, but I don't know to this day whether or not I was being trailed. If I was, somebody spent an awfully dull week. But, although I had about concluded that the incident had been nothing but imagination and my jumpy nerves, I was happy at last to be aboard the ship for Denver and to note that my companion of the week before was not a passenger.

We landed at the new field just east of Aurora, many miles from downtown Denver. The police checked my papers and fingerprinted me in the routine fashion and I was about to shove my wallet back into my pocket when the desk sergeant said, "Bare your left arm, please, Mr. Reeves."

I rolled up my sleeve while trying to show the right amount of fretful annoyance. A white-coated orderly took a blood sample. "Just a normal precaution," the sergeant explained. "The Department of Public Health is trying to stamp out spotted fever."

It was a thin excuse, as I knew from my own training in P.H.—but Reeves, textiles salesman, might not realize it. But the excuse got thinner yet when I was asked to wait in a side room of the station while my blood sample was run. I sat there fretting, trying to figure out what harm they could do me with ten c.c. of my blood—and what I could do about it even if I did know.

I had plenty of time to think. The situation looked anything but bright. My time was probably running out as I sat there—

yet the excuse on which they were holding me was just plausible enough that I didn't dare cut and run; that might be what they wanted. So I sat tight and sweated.

The building was a temporary structure and the wall between me and the sergeant's office was a thin laminate; I could hear voices through it without being able to make out the words. I did not dare press my ear to it for fear of being caught doing so. On the other hand I felt that I just had to do it. So I moved my chair over to the wall, sat down again, leaned back on two legs of the chair so that my shoulders and the back of my neck were against the wall. Then I held a newspaper I had found there up in front of my face and pressed my ear against the wall.

I could hear every word then. The sergeant told a story to his clerk which would have fetched him a month's penance if a morals proctor had been listening—still, I had heard the same story, only slightly cleaned up, right in the Palace, so I wasn't really shocked, nor was I in any mood to worry about other people's morals. I listened to several routine reports and an inquiry from some semi-moron who couldn't find the men's washroom, but not a word about myself. I got a crick in my neck from the position.

Just opposite me was an open window looking out over the rocket field. A small ship appeared in the sky, braked with nose units, and came in to a beautiful landing about a quarter of a mile away. The pilot taxied toward the administration building and parked outside the window, not twenty-five yards away.

It was the courier version of the *Sparrow Hawk*, ram jet with rocket take-off and booster, as sweet a little ship as was ever built. I knew her well; I had pushed one just like her, playing number-two position for Army in sky polo—that was the year we had licked both Navy and Princeton.

The pilot got out and walked away. I eyed the distance to the ship. If the ignition were not locked—Sheol! what if it was? Maybe I could short around it, I looked at the open window. It might be equipped with vibrobolts; if so, I would never know what hit me. But I could not spot any power leads or trigger connections and the flimsy construction of the building would make it hard to hide them. Probably there was nothing but contact alarms; there might not be so much as a selenium circuit.

While I was thinking about it I again heard voices next door; I flattened my ear and strained to listen.

"What's the blood type?"

"Type one, sergeant."

"Does it check?"

"No, Reeves is type three."

"Oho! Phone the main lab. We'll take him into town for a retinal."

I was caught cold and knew it. They knew positively that I wasn't Reeves. Once they photographed the pattern of blood vessels in the retina of either eye they would know just as certainly who I really was, in no longer time than it took to radio the picture to the Bureau of Morals & Investigation— less, if copies had been sent out to Denver and elsewhere with the tab on me.

I dove out the window.

I lit on my hands, rolled over in a ball, was flung to my feet as I unwound. If I set off an alarm I was too busy to hear it. The ship's door was open and the ignition was not locked— there was help indeed for the Son of a Widow! I didn't bother to taxi clear, but blasted at once, not caring if my rocket flame scorched my pursuers. We bounced along the ground, the little darling and I, then I lifted her nose by gyro and scooted away to the west.

8

I LET HER REACH for the sky, seeking altitude and speed where the ram jets would work properly. I felt exulted to have a good ship under me and those cops far behind. But I snapped out of that silly optimism as I leveled off for jet flight.

If a cat escapes up a tree, he must stay there until the dog goes away. That was the fix I was in and in my case the dog would not go away, nor could I stay up indefinitely. The alarm would be out by now; behind me, on all sides of me, police pilots would be raising ship in a matter of minutes, even seconds. I was being tracked, that was sure, and the blip of my craft on several screens was being fed as data into a computer that would vector them in on me no matter where

I turned. After that—well, it was land on command or be
shot down.

The miracle of my escape began to seem a little less miraculous. Or *too* miraculous, perhaps? Since when were the police so sloppy that they would leave a prisoner in a room with
an unguarded window? Wasn't it just a little too much of a
coincidence that a ship I knew how to herd should come to
that window and be left there—with the ignition unlocked—
just as the sergeant said loudly the one thing that would be
sure to make me try for it?

Maybe this was a second, and successful, attempt to panic
me. Maybe somebody else knew my liking for the *Sparrow
Hawk* courier, knew it because he had my dossier spread out
in front of him and was as familiar with my sky polo record
as I was. In which case they might not shoot me down just
yet; they might be counting on me to lead them straight to
my comrades.

Or perhaps, just possibly, it was a real escape—if I could
exploit it. Either way, I was neither ready to be caught again,
nor to lead them to my brethren—nor to die. I had an important message (I told myself); I was too busy to oblige them by
dying just now.

I flipped the ship's commer to the police & traffic frequency
and listened. There was some argument going on between the
Denver port and a transport in the air but no one as yet was
shouting for me to ground or get my pants shot off. Later
perhaps—I left it switched on and thought.

The dead-reckoner showed me some seventy-five miles
from Denver and headed north of west; I was surprised to see
that I had been in the air less than ten minutes . . . so
hopped up with adrenalin, no doubt, that my time sense was
distorted. The ram-jet tanks were nearly full; I had nearly ten
hours and six thousand miles at economy cruising—but of
course at that speed they could almost throw rocks at me.

A plan, silly and perhaps impossible and certainly born of
desperation but even so better than no plan at all, was beginning to form in my brain. I consulted the great circle
indicator and set a course for the Republic of Hawaii; my
baby nosed herself slightly south of west. Then I turned to
the fuel-speed-distance gnomograph and roughed a problem—
3100 miles about, at around 800 mph, ending with dry tanks
and depending on rocket juice and the nose units to cushion a
cold-jet landing. Risky.

Not that I cared. Somewhere below me, shortly after I set the autopilot on the indicated course and speed, analyzers in the cybernetwork would be telling their human operators that I was attempting to escape to the Free State of Hawaii, on such a course, such an altitude, and at max speed for that range . . . and that I would pass over the Pacific coast between San Francisco and Monterey in sixty-odd minutes unless intercepted. But interception was certain. Even if they were still playing with me, cat and mouse, ground-to-air snarlers would rise up from the Sacramento Valley. If they missed (most unlikely!), manned ships as fast or faster than my baby, with full tanks and no need to conserve radius, would be waiting at altitude at the coast. I had no hope of running that gauntlet.

Nor did I intend to. I *wanted* them to destroy the little honey I was pushing, destroy her completely and in the air—because I had no intention of being aboard when it happened.

Operation Chucklehead, phase two: how to get out of the durn thing! Leaving a jet plane in powered flight has all been figured out by careful engineers; you slap the jetison lever and pray; the rest is done for you. The survival capsule closes down on you and seals, then the capsule with you in it is shot clear of the ship. In due course, at proper pressure and terminal air speed, the drogue is fired; it pulls your chute open, and there you are, floating comfortably toward God's good earth, with your emergency oxygen bottle for company.

There is only one hitch: both the capsule and the abandoned ship start sending out radio signals, dots for the capsule, dashes for the ship, and, for good measure, the capsule has a built-in radar-beacon.

The whole thing is about as inconspicuous as a cow in church.

I sat there chewing my thumb and staring out ahead. It seemed to me that the yonder was looking even wilder and bluer than usual—my own mood, no doubt, for I knew that thirteen ground miles were slipping out from under me each minute and that it was high time for me to find my hat and go home. Of course, there was a door right alongside me; I could strap on a chute and leave. But you can't open a door in a ram-jet plane in powered flight; nor do you jettison it—to do so will cause the plane to behave like a kicked pup. Nor is an eight-hundred-mile-an-hour breeze to be ignored even at 60,000 feet; I'd be sliced like butter on the door frame.

The answer depended on how good an autopilot this buggy had. The better robopilots could do everything but sing hymns; some of the cheaper ones could hold course, speed, and altitude but there their talents ended. In particular I wanted to know whether or not this autopilot had an emergency circuit to deal with a case of "fire out," for I intended to stop the ship, step out, and let the ship continue on in the direction of Hawaii by itself—if it could.

A ram jet won't operate at all except at high speed; that's why ram ships have rocket power as well, else they could never take off. If you drop below the critical speed of your jet engines your fire goes out, then you must start it again, either by rocket power or by diving to gain speed. It is a touchy business and a number of ram-jet pilots have been gathered to their heavenly reward through an unexpected case of "fire out."

My earlier experience with the courier *Sparrow Hawk* told me nothing, as you don't use autopilots in sky polo. Believe me, you don't. So I looked for the instruction manual in the glove compartment, failed to find it, then looked over the pilot itself. The data plate failed to say. No doubt, with a screw driver and plenty of time, I could have opened it, worried out the circuits and determined the fact—say in about a day and a half; those autopilots are a mass of transistors and spaghetti.

So I pulled the personal chute out of its breakaway clips and started shrugging my way into it while sighing, "Pal, I *hope* you have the necessary gimmick built into your circuits." The autopilot didn't answer, though I wouldn't have been much surprised if it had. Then I squeezed back into place and proceeded to override the autopilot manually. I didn't have too much time; I was already over the Deseret basin and I could see the setting sun glinting on the waters of the Great Salt Lake ahead and to the right.

First I took her down some, because 60,000 feet is thin and chilly—too little partial pressure of oxygen for the human lung. Then I started up in a gentle curving climb that would neither tear her wings off nor gee me into a blackout. I had to take her fairly high, because I intended to cut out the rocket motors entirely and force my best girl to light her stovepipes by diving for speed, it being my intention to go into a vertical stall, which would create "fire out"—and get off in a hurry at that point. For obvious reasons I did not want the rocket motors to cut loose just as I was trying to say good-by.

I kept curving her up until I was lying on my back with the earth behind me and sky ahead. I nursed it along, throttling her down, with the intention of stalling with the fire dead at thirty thousand feet—still thin but within jumping distance of breathable air and still high enough to give my lady a chance to go into her dive without cracking up on the Utah plateau. At about 28,000 I got that silly, helpless feeling you get when the controls go mushy and won't bite. Suddenly a light flashed red on the instrument board and both fires were out. It was time to leave.

I almost forgot the seat bottle. I was still stuffing the mouthpiece between my teeth and snapping the nosepiece over my nose while I was trying with the other hand to get the door open—all of this greatly impeded by the fact that the ship and I together were effectively in free fall; the slight air drag at the top of the stall trajectory made me weigh a few ounces, no more.

The door would not open. I finally remembered to slap the spill valve, then it came open and I was almost snatched outside. I hung there for a second or two, while the ground spun crazily overhead, then the door slammed shut and latched—and I shoved myself away from the plane. I didn't jump—we were falling together, I shoved.

I may have banged my head against a wing. In any case there is a short blank in my memory before I found myself sitting on space about twenty-five yards from the ship. She was spinning slowly and earth and sky were revolving lazily around me. There was a thin cold wind as I fell but I was not yet aware of the cold. We stayed pretty well together for a few moments—or hours; time had stopped—then the ship straightened out into a dive and pulled away from me.

I tried to follow her down by eye and became aware of the icy wind of my fall. My eyes hurt and I remembered something I had read about frozen eyeballs; I covered them with both hands. It helped a lot.

Suddenly I became frightened, panicky at the thought that I had delayed the jump too long and was about to smash into the desert floor. I uncovered my eyes and sneaked a look.

No, the ground was still a long way off, two or three miles perhaps. My guess was not worth much as it was already dark down there. I tried to catch sight of the ship, could not see it, then suddenly spotted it as her fires came on. I risked frozen eyes and watched, exultation in my heart. The autopilot did indeed have built into it the emergency circuit for "fire out" and everything was proceeding according to plan. The little sweetheart leveled off, headed west on course, and began to climb for the altitude she had been told to use. I sent a prayer after her that she would win through and end up in the clean Pacific, rather than be shot down.

I watched her glowing tailpipes out of sight while I continued to fall.

The triumph of my little ship had made me forget to be scared. I had known when I bailed out that it would have to be a delayed jump. My own body, in leaving the ship, would make a secondary blip on the screen of anything tracking the ship; my only hope of convincing the trackers that what they had witnessed was a real emergency—"fire out"—lay in getting away from the ship quickly and then in not being spotted on the way down. That meant that I must fall rapidly right out of the picture and not pull the rip cord until I was close to the ground, in visual darkness and in ground radar shadow.

But I had never made a delayed jump before; in fact I had jumped only twice, the two easy practice jumps under a jumpmaster which are required of every cadet in order to graduate. I wasn't especially uncomfortable as long as I kept my eyes closed, but I began to get a truly overpowering urge to pull that rip cord. My hand went to the handle and gripped it. I told myself to let go but I couldn't make myself do it. I was still much too high, dead sure to be spotted if I broke out that great conspicuous bumbershoot and floated down the rest of the way.

I had intended to rip the chute out somewhere between one thousand and five hundred feet above ground, but my nerve played out and I couldn't wait that long. There was a large town almost under me—Provo, Utah, by what I remembered of the situation from higher up. I convinced myself that I had to pull the rip cord to keep from landing right in the city.

I remembered just in time to remove the oxygen face piece, thereby avoiding a mouthful of broken teeth most likely, for I had never gotten around to strapping the bottle to me; I had been holding it in my left hand all the way down. I suppose I could have taken time even then to secure it, but what I did was to throw it in the general direction of a farm, hoping that it would land on plowed ground rather than on some honest citizen's skull. Then I pulled the handle.

For the horrible split second I thought that I had a faultily-packed chute. Then it opened and knocked me out—or I fainted with fright. I came to, hanging in the harness with the ground swinging and turning slowly beneath me. I was still too high up and I seemed to be floating toward the lights of Provo. So I took a deep breath—real air tasted good after the canned stuff—gathered a double handful of shrouds and spilled some wind.

I came down fast then and managed to let go just in time to get full support for the landing. I couldn't see the ground well in the evening darkness but I knew it was close; I gathered up my knees just as it says in the manual, then took it rather unexpectedly, stumbling, falling, and getting tangled in the chute. It is supposed to be equal to a fourteen-foot free jump; all I can say is it seems like more.

Then I was sitting on my tail in a field of sugar beets, and rubbing my left ankle.

Spies always bury their parachutes so I suppose I should have buried mine. But I didn't feel up to it and I didn't have any tools; I stuffed it into a culvert I found running under the road that edged the field, then started slogging that road toward the lights of Provo. My nose and right ear had been bleeding and the blood was dry on my face; I was covered with dirt, I had split my trousers, my hat was the Lord knows where—Denver, maybe, or over Nevada—, my left ankle seemed slightly sprained, my right hand was badly skinned, and I had had a childish accident. I felt swell.

I could hardly keep from whistling as I walked, I felt so good. Sure, I was still hunted, but the Prophet's proctors thought I was still high in the sky and headed for Hawaii. At least I hoped they believed that and, in any case, I was still free, alive, and reasonably intact. If one has to be hunted, Utah was a better place for it than most; it had been a center of heresy and schism ever since the suppression of the Mormon church, back in the days of the First Prophet. If I could keep out of the direct sight of the Prophet's police, it was unlikely that any of the natives would turn me in.

Nevertheless I lay flat in the ditch every time a truck or a ground car came along and I left the road and took to the fields again before it entered the city proper. I swung wide and entered by a dimly lighted side street. It lacked two hours of curfew; I needed to carry out the first part of my plan before the night patrol took to the streets.

I wandered around dark residential streets and avoided any direct encounters with people for most of an hour before finding what I wanted—some sort of a flier I could steal. It turned out to be a Ford family skycar, parked in a vacant lot. The house next to it was dark.

I sneaked up to it, keeping to the shadows, and broke my penknife jimmying the door—but I got it open. The ignition was locked, but I had not expected that sort of luck twice. I had had an extremely practical education at taxpayers' expense which included detailed knowledge of I.C. engines, and this time there was no hurry; it took me twenty minutes, working in the dark, to short around the lock.

After a quick reconnoitre of the street I got in and started the electric auxiliary and glided quietly into the street, then rounded a corner before turning on the car's lights. Then I drove away as openly as a farmer returning from prayer meeting in town. Nevertheless I was afraid of running into a police check point at the city limits, so as soon as the houses thinned out I ran the car into the first open field and went on well away from the road—then unexpectedly dropped a front wheel into an irrigation ditch. That determined my take-off point.

The main engine coughed and took hold; the rotor unfolded its airfoils with a loud creak. She was sloppy on the take-off, being canted over into the ditch, but she made it. The ground dropped away.

9

THE CAR I had stolen was a jalopy, old, not properly kept up, a bad valve knock in the engine, and a vibration in the rotor that I didn't like at all. But she would run and she had better than half a tank of fuel, enough to get me to Phoenix. I couldn't complain.

Worst was a complete lack of any navigating equipment other than an old-style uncompensated Sperry robot and a bundle of last year's strip maps of the sort the major oil companies give away. There was radio, but it was out of order.

Well, Columbus got by with less. Phoenix was almost due south and almost five hundred miles away. I estimated my drift by crossing my eyes and praying, set the robot on course and set her to hold real altitude of five hundred feet. Any more might get me into the cybernetwork; any less might get some local constable annoyed with me. I decided that running lights were safer than no running lights, this being no time to pick up a ticket, so I switched them on to "dim." After that I took a look around.

No sign of pursuit to the north—apparently my latest theft had not been noticed as yet. As for my first—well, the sweet darling was either shot down by now or far out over the Pacific. It occurred to me that I was hanging up quite a record for a mother's boy—accessory before and after the fact in murder, perjury before the Grand Inquisitor, treason, impersonation, grand larceny twice. There was still arson, and barratry, whatever that was, and rape. I decided I could avoid rape, but barratry I might manage, if I could find out what it meant. I still felt swell even though my nose was bleeding again.

It occurred to me that marrying a holy deaconess might be considered statutory rape under the law and that made me feel better; by then I didn't want to miss anything.

I stayed at the controls, overriding the pilot and avoiding towns, until we were better than a hundred miles south of Provo. From there south, past the Grand Canyon and almost to the ruins of the old "66" roadcity, people are awfully scarce; I decided that I could risk some sleep. So I set the pilot on eight hundred feet, ground altitude, told it firmly to watch out for trees and bluffs, went back to the after passenger bench and went at once to sleep.

I dreamt that the Grand Inquisitor was trying to break my nerve by eating juicy roast beef in my presence. "Confess!" he said, as he stabbed a bite and chewed. "Make it easy on yourself. Will you have some rare, or the slice off the end?" I was about to confess, too, when I woke up.

It was bright moonlight and we were just approaching the Grand Canyon. I went quickly to the controls and overrode the order about altitude—I was afraid that the simple little robot might have a nervous breakdown and start shedding capacitances in lieu of tears if it tried to hold the ship just eight hundred feet away from that Gargantuan series of ups and downs and pinnacles.

In the meantime I was enjoying the view so much that I forgot that I was starving. If a person hasn't seen the Canyon, there is no point in describing it—but I strongly recommend seeing it by moonlight from the air.

We sliced across it in about twenty minutes and I turned the ship back to automatic and started to forage, rummaging through the instrument panel compartment and the lockers. I turned up a chocolate almond bar and a few peanuts, which was a feast as I was ready for raw skunk. . . . I had eaten last in Kansas City. I polished them off and went back to sleep.

I don't recall setting the pilot alarm but must have done so for it woke me up just before dawn. Dawn over the desert was another high-priced tourist item but I had navigating to do and could not spare it more than a glance. I turned the crate at right angles for a few minutes to check drift and speed made good over ground to south, then figured a bit on the edge of a strip map. With luck and assuming that my guesses about wind were about right, Phoenix should show up in about half an hour.

My luck held. I passed over some mighty rough country, then suddenly, spread out to the right, was a wide flat desert valley, green with irrigated crops and with a large city in it— the Valley of the Sun and Phoenix. I made a poor landing in a boxed-in, little dry arroyo leading into the Salt River Canyon; I tore off one wheel and smashed the rotor but I didn't care—the important thing was that it wasn't likely to be found there very soon, it and my fingerprints . . . Reeves' prints, I mean. Half an hour later, after picking my way around enormous cacti and still bigger red boulders, I came out on the highway that leads down the canyon and into Phoenix.

It was going to be a long walk into Phoenix, especially with one sore ankle, but I decided not to risk hitching a ride. Traffic was light and I managed to get off the road and hide each time for the first hour. Then I was caught on a straight up-and-down piece by a freighter; there was nothing to do but give the driver a casual wave as I flattened myself to the rock wall and pretend to be nonchalant. He brought his heavy vehicle to a quick, smooth stop. "Want a lift, bud?"

I made up my mind in a hurry. "Yes, thanks!"

He swung a dural ladder down over the wide tread and I climbed into the cab. He looked me over. "Brother!" he said admiringly. "Was it a mountain lion, or a bear?"

I had forgotten how I looked. I glanced down at myself. "Both," I answered solemnly. "Strangled one in each hand."

"I believe it."

"Fact is," I added, "I was riding a unicycle and bounced it off the road. On the high side, luckily, but I wrecked it."

"A unicycle? On *this* road? Not all the way from Globe?"

"Well, I had to get off and push at times. It was the down grade that got me, though."

He shook his head. "Let's go back to the lion-and-bear theory. I like it better." He didn't question me further, which suited me. I was beginning to realize that off-hand fictions led to unsuspected ramifications; I had never been over the road from Globe.

Nor had I ever been inside a big freighter before and I was interested to see how much it resembled, inside, the control room of an Army surface cruiser—the same port and starboard universal oleo speed gears controlling the traction treads, much the same instrument board giving engine speed, port and starboard motor speeds, torque ratios, and so forth. I could have herded it myself.

Instead I played dumb and encouraged him to talk. "I've never been in one of these big babies before. Tell me how it works, will you?"

That set him off and I listened with half an ear while thinking about how I should tackle Phoenix. He demonstrated how he applied both power and steering to the treads simply by tilting the two speed bars, one in each fist, and then discussed the economy of letting the diesel run at constant speed while he fed power as needed to the two sides. I let him talk—my first need was a bath and a shave and a change of clothes, that was sure; else I'd be picked up on sight for suspected vagrancy.

Presently I realized he had asked a question. "I think I see," I answered. "The Waterburies drive the treads."

"Yes and no," he went on. "It's a diesel-electric hook up. The Waterburies just act like a gear system, although there aren't any gears in them; they're hydraulic. Follow me?"

I said I thought so (I could have sketched them)—and filed away in my mind the idea that, if the Cabal should ever need cruiser pilots in a hurry, freighter jacks could be trained for the job in short order.

We were going downhill slightly even after we left the canyon; the miles flowed past. My host pulled off the road and ground to a stop by a roadside restaurant and oil station. "All out," he grunted. "Breakfast for us and go-juice for the go-buggy."

"Sounds good." We each consumed a tall stack with eggs and bacon and big, sweet Arizona grapefruit. He wouldn't let me pay for his and tried to pay for mine. As we went back to the freighter he stopped at the ladder and looked me over.

"The police gate is about three-quarters of a mile on in," he said softly. "I suppose that's as good a spot to check in as any." He looked at me and glanced away.

"Mmm . . ." I said. "I think I could stand to walk the rest of the way, to settle my breakfast. Thanks a lot for the lift."

"Don't mention it. Uh, there's a side road about two hundred yards back. It swings south and then west again, into town. Better for walking. Less traffic."

"Uh, thanks."

I walked back to the side road, wondering if my criminal career was that plain to everyone. One thing sure, I *had* to improve my appearance before tackling the city. The side road led through ranches and I passed several ranch houses without having the nerve to stop. But I came presently to a little house occupied by a Spanish-Indian family with the usual assortment of children and dogs. I took a chance; many of these people were clandestine Catholics, I knew, and probably hated the proctors as much as I did.

The Senora was home. She was fat and kindly and mostly Indian by her appearance. We couldn't talk much as my Spanish is strictly classroom quality, but I could ask for *agua,* and *agua* I got, both to drink and to wash myself. She sewed up the rip in my trousers while I stood foolishly in my shorts with the children making comments; she brushed me off and she even let me use her husband's razor. She protested over letting me pay her but I was firm about it. I left there looking passable.

The road swung back into town as the freighter jack had said—and without benefit of police. Eventually I found a neighborhood shopping center and in it a little tailor shop. There I waited while the rest of my transformation back to respectability was completed. With my clothes freshly pressed, the spots removed, a brand-new shirt and hat I was then able to walk down the street and exchange a blessing with any proctor I might meet while looking him calmly in the eye. A phone book gave me the address of the South Side

Tabernacle; a map on the wall of the tailor shop got me oriented without asking questions. It was within walking distance.

I hurried down the street and reached the church just as eleven o'clock services were starting. Sighing with relief I slipped into a back pew and actually enjoyed the services, just as I had as a boy, before I had learned what was back of them. I felt peaceful and secure; in spite of everything I had made it safely. I let the familiar music soak into my soul while I looked forward to revealing myself to the priest afterwards and then let him do the worrying for a while.

To tell the truth I went to sleep during the sermon. But I woke up in time and I doubt if anyone noticed. Afterwards I hung around, waited for a chance to speak to the priest, and told him how much I had enjoyed his sermon. He shook hands and I gave him the recognition grip of the brethren.

But he did not return it. I was so upset by that that I almost missed what he was saying. "Thank you, my boy. It's always good news to a new pastor to hear that his ministrations are appreciated."

I guess my face gave me away. He added, "Something wrong?"

I stammered, "Oh, no, reverend sir. You see, I'm a stranger myself. Then you aren't the Reverend Baird?" I was in cold panic. Baird was my only contact with the brethren short of New Jerusalem; without someone to hide me I would be picked up in a matter of hours. Even as I answered I was making wild plans to steal another ship that night and then try to run the border patrol into Mexico.

His voice cut into my thoughts as if from a great distance. "No, I'm afraid not, my son. Did you wish to see the Reverend Baird?"

"Well, it wasn't terribly important, sir. He is an old friend of my uncle. I was to look him up while I was here and pay my respects." Maybe that nice Indian woman would hide me until dark?

"That won't be difficult. He's here in town. I'm just supplying his pulpit while he is laid up."

My heart made a full turn at about twelve gee; I tried to keep it out of my face. "Perhaps if he is sick I had better not disturb him."

"Oh, not at all. A broken bone in his foot—he'll enjoy a bit of company. Here." The priest fumbled under his robes, found a piece of paper and a pencil and wrote out the address. "Two streets over and half a block down. You can't miss it."

Of course I did miss it, but I doubled back and found it, an old vine-grown house with a suggestion of New England about it. It was set well back in a large, untidy garden—eucalyptus, palms, shrubs, and flowers, all in pleasant confusion. I pressed the announcer and heard the whine of an old-style scanner; a speaker inquired: "Yes?"

"A visitor to see the Reverend Baird, if he so pleases."

There was a short silence while he looked me over, then: "You'll have to let yourself in. My housekeeper has gone to the market. Straight through and out into the back garden." The door clicked and swung itself open.

I blinked at the darkness, then went down a central hallway and out through the back door. An old man was lying in a swing there, with one foot propped up on pillows. He lowered his book and peered at me over his glasses.

"What do you want of me, son?"

"Light."

An hour later I was washing down the last of some superb enchiladas with cold, sweet milk. As I reached for a cluster of muscatel grapes Father Baird concluded his instructions to me. "Nothing to do until dark, then. Any questions?"

"I don't think so, sir. Sanchez takes me out of town and delivers me to certain others of the brethren who will see to it that I get to General Headquarters. My end of it is simple enough."

"True. You won't be comfortable however."

I left Phoenix concealed in a false bottom of a little vegetable truck. I was stowed like cargo, with my nose pressed against the floor boards. We were stopped at a police gate at the edge of town; I could hear brusque voices with that note of authority, and Sanchez' impassioned Spanish in reply. Someone rummaged around over my head and the cracks in the false bottom gleamed with light.

Finally a voice said, "It's okay, Ezra. That's Father Baird's handyman. Makes a trip out to the Father's ranch every night or so."

"Well, why didn't he say so?"

"He gets excited and loses his English. Okay. Get going, chico. Vaya usted con Dios!"

"Gracias, senores. Buenas noches."

At the Reverend Baird's ranch I was transferred to a helicopter, no rickety heap this time, but a new job, silent and well equipped. She was manned by a crew of two, who exchanged pass grips with me but said nothing other than to tell me to get into the passenger compartment and stay there. We took off at once.

The windows of the passenger space had been covered; I don't know which way we went, nor how far. It was a rough ride, as the pilot seemed dead set on clipping daisies the whole way. It was a reasonable precaution to avoid being spotted in a scope, but I hoped he knew what he was doing—I wouldn't want to herd a heli that way in broad daylight. He must have scared a lot of coyotes—I know he frightened me.

At last I heard the squeal of a landing beam. We slid along it, hovered, and bumped gently to a stop. When I got out I found myself staring into the maw of a tripod-mounted blaster backed up by two alert and suspicious men.

But my escort gave the password, each of the guards questioned me separately, and we exchanged recognition signals. I got the impression that they were a little disappointed that they couldn't let me have it; they seemed awfully eager. When they were satisfied, a hoodwink was slipped over my head and I was led away. We went through a door, walked maybe fifty yards, and crowded into a compartment. The floor dropped away.

My stomach caught up with me and I groused to myself because I hadn't been warned that it was an elevator, but I kept my mouth shut. We left the lift, walked a way, and I was nudged onto a platform of some sort, told to sit down and hang on—whereupon we lurched away at breakneck speed. It felt like a rollercoaster—not a good thing to ride blindfolded. Up to then I hadn't really been scared. I began to think that the hazing was intentional, for they could have warned me.

We made another elevator descent, walked several hundred paces, and my hoodwink was removed. I caught my first sight of General Headquarters.

I didn't recognize it as such; I simply let out a gasp. One of my guards smiled. "They all do that," he said dryly.

It was a limestone cavern so big that one felt outdoors rather than underground and so magnificently lavish in its formations as to make one think of fairyland, or the Gnome King's palace. I had assumed that we were underground from the descents we had made, but nothing had prepared me for what I saw.

I have seen photographs of what the Carlsbad Caverns used to be, before the earthquake of '96 destroyed them; General Headquarters was something like that, although I can't believe that the Carlsbad Caverns were as big or half as magnificent. I could not at first grasp the immensity of the room I was in; underground there is nothing to judge size by and the built-in range-finder of a human's two-eyed vision is worthless beyond about fifty feet without something in the distance to give him scale—a house, a man, a tree, even the horizon itself. Since a natural cave contains nothing at all that is well known, customary, the human eye can't size it.

So, while I realized that the room I stood in was big, I could not guess just how big; my brain scaled it down to fit my prejudices. We were standing higher than the main floor and at one end of the room; the whole thing was softly flood-lighted. I got through craning my neck and *oh*ing and *ah*ing, looked down and saw a toy village some distance away below us. The little buildings seemed to be about a foot high.

Then I saw tiny people walking around among the build-ings—and the whole thing suddenly snapped into scale. The toy village was at least a quarter of a mile away; the whole room was not less than a mile long and many hundreds of feet high. Instead of the fear of being shut in that people nor-mally experience in caves I was suddenly hit by the other fear, the fear of open spaces, agoraphobia. I wanted to slink along close to the walls, like a timid mouse.

The guide who had spoken touched my arm. "You'll have plenty of time for rubbernecking later. Let's get going." They led me down a path which meandered between stalagmites, from baby-finger size to Egyptian pyramids, around black pools of water with lilypads of living stone growing on them, past dark wet domes that were old when man was new, under creamy translucent curtains of onyx and sharp rosy-red and dark green stalactites. My capacity to wonder began to be overloaded and presently I quit trying.

We came out on a fairly level floor of bat droppings and made good time to the village. The buildings, I saw as I got closer, were not buildings in the outdoors sense, but were mere partitions of that honeycomb plastic used for sound-deadening—space separators for efficiency and convenience. Most of them were not roofed. We stopped in front of the largest of these pens; the sign over its door read ADMINIS-TRATION. We entered and I was taken into the personnel office. This room almost made me homesick, so matter of fact, so professionally military was it in its ugly, efficient appointments. There was even the elderly staff clerk with the nervous sniff who seems to be general issue for such an office since the time of Caesar. The sign on his desk described him as Warrant Officer R. E. Giles and he had quite evidently come back to his office after working hours to check me in.

"Pleased to meet you, Mr. Lyle," he said, shaking hands and exchanging recognition. Then he scratched his nose and sniffed. "You're a week or so early and your quarters aren't ready. Suppose we billet you tonight with a blanket roll in the lounge of B.O.Q. and get you squared away in the morning?"

I said that would be perfectly satisfactory and he seemed relieved.

10

I GUESS I had been expecting to be treated as some sort of a conquering hero on my arrival—you know, my new comrades hanging breathlessly on every word of my modest account of my adventures and hairbreadth escapes and giving thanks to the Great Architect that I had been allowed to win through with my all-important message.

I was wrong. The personnel adjutant sent for me before I had properly finished breakfast, but I didn't even see him; I saw Mr. Giles. I was a trifle miffed and interrupted him to ask how soon it would be convenient for me to pay my formal call on the commanding officer.

He sniffed. "Oh, yes. Well, Mr. Lyle, the C.G. sends his compliments to you and asks you to consider that courtesy calls have been made, not only on him but on department heads. We're rather pushed for time right now. He'll send for you the first spare moment he has."

I knew quite well that the general had not sent me any such message and that the personnel clerk was simply following a previously established doctrine. It didn't make me feel better.

But there was nothing I could do about it; the system took

me in hand. By noon I had been permanently billeted, had had my chest thumped and so forth, and had made my reports. Yes, I got a chance to tell my story—to a recording machine. Flesh-and-blood men did receive the message I carried, but I got no fun out of that; I was under hypnosis at the time, just as I had been when it was given to me.

This was too much for me; I asked the psychotechnician who operated me what the message was I carried. He answered stiffly, "We aren't permitted to tell couriers what they carry." His manner suggested that my question was highly improper.

I lost my temper a bit. I didn't know whether he was senior to me or not as he was not in uniform, but I didn't care. "For pity's sake! What is this? Don't the brethren *trust* me? Here I risk my neck—"

He cut in on me in a much more conciliatory manner. "No, no, it's not that at all. It's for your protection."

"Huh?"

"Doctrine. The less you know that you don't need to know the less you can spill if you are ever captured—and the safer it is for you and for everybody. For example, do you know where you are now? Could you point it out on a map?"

"No."

"Neither do I. We don't need to know so we weren't told. However," he went on, "I don't mind telling you, in a general way, what you were carrying—just routine reports, confirming stuff we already had by sensitive circuits mostly. You were coming this way, so they dumped a lot of such stuff into you. I took three spools from you."

"Just routine stuff? Why, the Lodge Master told me I was carrying a message of vital importance. That fat old joker!"

The technician grudged a smile. "I'm afraid he was pulling — Oh!"

"Eh?"

"I know what he meant. You were carrying a message of vital importance—to you. You carried your own credentials hypnotically. If you had not been, you would never have been allowed to wake up."

I had nothing to say. I left quietly.

My rounds of the medical office, psych office, quartermaster, and so forth had begun to give me a notion of the size of the place. The "toy village" I had first seen was merely the administrative group. The power plant, a packaged pile, was in a separate cavern with many yards of rock wall as secondary shielding. Married couples were quartered where they pleased—about a third of us were female—and usually chose to set up their houses (or pens) well away from the central grouping. The armory and ammo dump were located in a side passage, a safe distance from offices and quarters.

There was fresh water in abundance, though quite hard, and the same passages that carried the underground streams appeared to supply ventilation—at least the air was never stale. It stayed at a temperature of 69.6 Fahrenheit and a relative humidity of 32%, winter and summer, night and day.

By lunchtime I was hooked into the organization, and found myself already hard at work at a temporary job immediately after lunch—in the armory, repairing and adjusting blasters, pistols, squad guns, and assault guns. I could have been annoyed at being asked, or ordered, to do what was really gunnery sergeant work, but the whole place seemed to be run with a minimum of protocol—we cleared our own dishes away at mess, for example. And truthfully it felt good to sit at a bench in the armory, safe and snug, and handle calipers and feather gauges and drifts again—good, useful work.

Just before dinner that first day I wandered into the B.O.Q. lounge and looked around for an unoccupied chair. I heard a familiar baritone voice behind me: "Johnnie! John Lyle!" I whirled around and there, hurrying toward me, was Zebadiah Jones—good old Zeb, large as life and his ugly face split with a grin.

We pounded each other on the back and swapped insults. "When did you get here?" I finally asked him.

"Oh, about two weeks ago."

"You did? You were still at New Jerusalem when I left. How did you do it?"

"Nothing to it. I was shipped as a corpse—in a deep trance. Sealed up in a coffin and marked 'contagious'."

I told him about my own mixed-up trip and Zeb seemed impressed, which helped my morale. Then I asked him what he was doing.

"I'm in the Psych & Propaganda Bureau," he told me, "under Colonel Novak. Just now I'm writing a series of oh-so-respectful articles about the private life of the Prophet and his acolytes and attending priests, how many servants they have, how much it costs to run the Palace, all about the fancy ceremonies and rituals, and such junk. All of it perfectly true, of course, and told with unctuous approval. But I lay it on a shade too thick. The emphasis is on the jewels and the solid gold trappings and how much it all costs, and I keep telling the yokels what a privilege it is for them to be permitted to pay for such frippery and how flattered they should feel that God's representative on earth lets them take care of him."

"I guess I don't get it," I said, frowning. "People like that circusy stuff. Look at the way the tourists to New Jerusalem scramble for tickets to a Temple ceremony."

"Sure, sure—but we don't peddle this stuff to people on a holiday to New Jerusalem; we syndicate it to little local papers in poor farming communities in the Mississippi Valley, and in the Deep South, and in the back country of New England. That is to say, we spread it among some of the poorest and most puritanical elements of the population, people who are emotionally convinced that poverty and virtue are the same thing. It grates on their nerves; in time it should soften them up and make doubters of them."

"Do you seriously expect to start a rebellion with picayune stuff like that?"

"It's not picayune stuff, because it acts directly on their emotions, below the logical level. You can sway a thousand men by appealing to their prejudices quicker than you can convince one man by logic. It doesn't have to be a prejudice about an important matter either. Johnnie, you savvy how to use connotation indices, don't you?"

"Well, yes and no. I know what they are; they are supposed to measure the emotional effects of words."

"That's true, as far as it goes. But the index of a word isn't fixed like the twelve inches in a foot; it is a complex variable function depending on context, age and sex and occupation of the listener, the locale and a dozen other things. An index is a particular solution of the variable that tells you whether a particular word used in a particular fashion to a particular reader or type of reader will affect that person favorably, unfavorably, or simply leave him cold. Given proper measurements of the group addressed it can be as mathematically exact as any branch of engineering. We never have all the data we need so it remains an art—but a very precise art, especially as we employ 'feedback' through field sampling. Each article I do is a little more annoying than the last—and the reader never knows why."

"It sounds good, but I don't see quite how it's done."

"I'll give you a gross case. Which would you rather have? A nice, thick, juicy, tender steak—or a segment of muscle tissue from the corpse of an immature castrated bull?"

I grinned at him. "You can't upset me. I'll take it by either name . . . not too well done. I wished they would announce chow around here; I'm starved."

"You think you aren't affected because you were braced for it. But how long would a restaurant stay in business if it used that sort of terminology? Take another gross case, the Anglo-Saxon monosyllables that naughty little boys write on fences. You can't use them in polite company without offending, yet there are circumlocutions or synonyms for every one of them which may be used in any company."

I nodded agreement. "I suppose so. I certainly see how it could work on other people. But personally, I guess I'm immune to it. Those taboo words don't mean a thing to me—except that I'm reasonably careful not to offend other people. I'm an educated man, Zeb—'Sticks and stones may break my bones, et cetera.' But I see how you could work on the ignorant."

Now I should know better than to drop my guard with Zeb. The good Lord knows he's tripped me up enough times. He smiled at me quietly and made a short statement involving some of those taboo words.

"You leave my mother out of this!"

I was the one doing the shouting and I came up out of my chair like a dog charging into battle. Zeb must have anticipated me exactly and shifted his weight before he spoke, for, instead of hanging one on his chin, I found my wrist seized in his fist and his other arm around me, holding me in a clinch that stopped the fight before it started. "Easy, Johnnie," he breathed in my ear. "I apologize. I most humbly apologize and ask your forgiveness. Believe me, I wasn't insulting you."

"So you say!"

"So I say, most humbly. Forgive me?"

As I simmered down I realized that my outbreak had been very conspicuous. Although we had picked a quiet corner to talk, there were already a dozen or more others in the lounge, waiting for dinner to be announced. I could feel the dead silence and sense the question in the minds of others as to whether or not it was going to be necessary to intervene. I started to turn red with embarrassment rather than anger. "Okay. Let me go."

He did so and we sat down again. I was still sore and not at all inclined to forget Zeb's unpardonable breach of good manners, but the crisis was past. But he spoke quietly, "Johnnie, believe me, I was not insulting you nor any member of your family. That was a scientific demonstration of the dynamics of connotational indices, and that is all it was."

"Well—you didn't have to make it so personal."

"Ah, but I did have to. We were speaking of the psychodynamics of emotion . . . and emotions are personal, subjective things which must be experienced to be understood. You were of the belief that you, as an educated man, were immune to this form of attack—so I ran a lab test to show you that no one is immune. Now just what did I say to you?"

"You said— Never mind. Okay, so it was a test. But I don't care to repeat it. You've made your point: I don't like it."

"But what did I say? All I said, in fact, was that you were the legitimate offspring of a legal marriage. Right? What is insulting about that?"

"But—" I stopped and ran over in my mind the infuriating, insulting, and degrading things he had said—and, do you know, that is absolutely all they added up to. I grinned sheepishly. "It was the *way* you said it."

"Exactly, exactly! To put it technically, I selected terms with high negative indices, for this situation and for this listener. Which is precisely what we do with this propaganda, except that the emotional indices are lesser quantitatively to avoid arousing suspicion and to evade the censors—slow poison, rather than a kick in the belly. The stuff we write is all about the Prophet, lauding him to the skies . . . so the irritation produced in the reader is transferred to him. The method cuts below the reader's conscious thought and acts on the taboos and fetishes that infest his subconscious."

I remembered sourly my own unreasoned anger. "I'm convinced. It sounds like heap big medicine."

"It is, chum, it is. There is magic in words, black magic—if you know how to invoke it."

After dinner Zeb and I went to his cubicle and continued to bat the breeze. I felt warm and comfortable and very, very contented. The fact that we were part of a revolutionary plot, a project most unlikely to succeed and which would most probably end with us both dead in battle or burned for treason, affected me not at all. Good old Zeb! What if he did get under my guard and hit me where it hurt? He was my "family"—all the family that I had. To be with him now made me feel the way I used to feel when my mother would sit me down in the kitchen and feed me cookies and milk.

We talked about this and that, in the course of which I learned more about the organization and discovered—was very surprised to discover—that not all of our comrades were brethren. Lodge Brothers, I mean. "But isn't that dangerous?"

"What isn't? And what did you expect, old son? Some of our most valuable comrades can't join the Lodge; their own religious faith forbids it. But we don't have any monopoly on hating tyranny and loving freedom and we need all the help we can get. Anybody going our direction is a fellow traveler. Anybody."

I thought it over. The idea was logical, though somehow vaguely distasteful. I decided to gulp it down quickly. "I suppose so. I imagine even the pariahs will be of some use to us, when it comes to the fighting, even if they aren't eligible for membership."

Zeb gave me a look I knew too well. "Oh, for Pete's sake, John! When are you going to give up wearing diapers?"

"Huh?"

"Haven't you gotten it through your head yet that the whole 'pariah' notion is this tyranny's scapegoat mechanism that every tyranny requires?"

"Yes, but—"

"Shut up. Take sex away from people. Make it forbidden, evil, limit it to ritualistic breeding. Force it to back up into suppressed sadism. Then hand the people a scapegoat to hate. Let them kill a scapegoat occasionally for cathartic release. The mechanism is ages old. Tyrants used it centuries before the word 'psychology' was ever invented. It works, too. Look at yourself."

"Look, Zeb, I don't have anything against the pariahs."

"You had better not have. You'll find a few dozen of them in the Grand Lodge here. And by the way, forget that word 'pariah.' It has, shall we say, a very high negative index."

He shut up and so did I; again I needed time to get my thoughts straight. Please understand me—it is easy to be free when you have been brought up in freedom; it is *not* easy otherwise. A zoo tiger, escaped, will often slink back into the peace and security of his bars. If he can't get back, they tell me he will pace back and forth within the limits of bars that are no longer there. I suppose I was still pacing in my conditioned pattern.

The human mind is a tremendously complex thing; it has compartments in it that its owner himself does not suspect. I had thought that I had given my mind a thorough housecleaning already and had rid it of all the dirty superstitions I had been brought up to believe. I was learning that the "housecleaning" had been no more than a matter of sweeping the dirt under the rugs—it would be years before the cleansing would be complete, before the clean air of reason blew through every room.

All right, I told myself, if I meet one of these par— no, "comrades," I'll exchange recognition with him and be polite —as long as he is polite to me! At the time I saw nothing hypocritical in the mental reservation.

Zeb lay back, smoking, and let me stew. I knew that he smoked and he knew that I disapproved. But it was a minor sin and, when we were rooming together in the Palace barracks, I would never have thought of reporting him. I even knew which room servant was his bootlegger. "Who is sneaking your smokes in now?" I asked, wishing to change the subject.

"Eh? Why, you buy them at the P.X., of course." He held the dirty thing out and looked at it. "These Mexican cigarettes are stronger than I like. I suspect that they use real tobacco in them, instead of the bridge sweepings I'm used to. Want one?"

"Huh? Oh, no, thanks!"

He grinned wryly. "Go ahead, give me your usual lecture. It'll make you feel better."

"Now look here, Zeb, I wasn't criticizing. I suppose it's just one of the many things I've been wrong about."

"Oh, no. It's a dirty, filthy habit that ruins my wind and stains my teeth and may eventually kill me off with lung cancer." He took a deep inhalation, let the smoke trickle out of the corners of his mouth, and looked profoundly contented. "But it just happens that I *like* dirty, filthy habits."

He took another puff. "But it's not a sin and my punishment for it is here and now, in the way my mouth tastes each morning. The Great Architect doesn't give a shout in Sheol about it. Catch on, old son? He isn't even watching."

"There is no need to be sacrilegious."

"I wasn't being so."

"You weren't, eh? You were scoffing at one of the most fundamental—perhaps the one fundamental—proposition in religion: the certainty that God is watching!"

"*Who* told *you?*"

For a moment all I could do was to sputter. "Why, it isn't necessary. It's an axiomatic certainty. It's—"

"I repeat, *who* told *you?* See here, I retract what I said. Perhaps the Almighty is watching me smoke. Perhaps it is a mortal sin and I will burn for it for eons. Perhaps. But who told *you?* Johnnie, you've reached the point where you are willing to kick the Prophet out and hang him to a tall, tall tree. Yet you are willing to assert your own religious convictions and to use them as a touchstone to judge my conduct. So I repeat: who told you? What hill were you standing on when the lightning came down from Heaven and illuminated you? Which archangel carried the message?"

I did not answer at once. I could not. When I did it was with a feeling of shock and cold loneliness. "Zeb . . . I think I understand you at last. You are an—atheist. Aren't you?"

Zeb looked at me bleakly. "Don't call me an atheist," he said slowly, "unless you are really looking for trouble."

"Then you aren't one?" I felt a wave of relief, although I still didn't understand him.

"No, I am not. Not that it is any of your business. My religious faith is a private matter between me and my God. What my inner beliefs are you will have to judge by my actions . . . for you are not invited to question me about them. I decline to explain them nor to justify them to you. Nor to anyone . . . not the Lodge Master . . . nor to the Grand Inquisitor, if it comes to that."

"But you do believe in God?"

"I told you so, didn't I? Not that you had any business asking me."

"Then you must believe in other things?"

"Of course I do! I believe that a man has an obligation to be merciful to the weak . . . patient with the stupid . . . generous with the poor. I think he is obliged to lay down his life for his brothers, should it be required of him. But I don't propose to prove any of those things; they are beyond proof. And I don't demand that you believe as I do."

I let out my breath. "I'm satisfied, Zeb."

Instead of looking pleased he answered, "That's mighty kind of you, brother, mighty kind! Sorry—I shouldn't be sarcastic. But I had no intention of asking for your approval. You goaded me—accidentally, I'm sure—into discussing matters that I never intend to discuss." He stopped to light up another of those stinking cigarettes and went on more quietly. "John, I suppose that I am, in my own cantankerous way, a very narrow man myself. I believe very strongly in freedom of religion—but I think that that freedom is best expressed as freedom to keep quiet. From my point of view, a great deal of openly expressed piety is insufferable conceit."

"Huh?"

"Not every case—I've known the good and the humble and the devout. But how about the man who claims to know what the Great Architect is thinking? The man who claims to be privy to His Inner Plans? It strikes me as sacrilegious conceit of the worst sort—this character probably has never been any closer to His Trestle Board than you or I. But it makes him feel good to claim to be on chummy terms with the Almighty, it builds his ego, and lets him lay down the law to you and me. Pfui! Along comes a knothead with a loud voice, an I.Q. around 90, hair in his ears, dirty underwear, and a lot of ambition. He's too lazy to be a farmer, too stupid to be an engineer, too unreliable to be a banker—but, brother, can he pray! After a while he has gathered around him other knotheads who don't have his vivid imagination and self-assurance but like the idea of having a direct line to Omnipotence. Then this character is no longer Nehemiah Scudder but the First Prophet."

I was going along with him, feeling shocked but rather pleasantly so, until he named the First Prophet. Perhaps my own spiritual state at that time could have been described as that of a "primitive" follower of the First Prophet—that is to say, I had decided that the Prophet Incarnate was the devil himself and that all of his works were bad, but that belief did not affect the basics of the faith I had learned from my mother. The thing to do was to purge and reform the Church, not to destroy it. I mention this because my own case paralleled a very serious military problem that was to develop later.

I found that Zeb was studying my face. "Did I get you on the raw again, old fellow? I didn't mean to."

"Not at all," I answered stiffly, and went on to explain that, in my opinion, the sinfulness of the present gang of devils that had taken over the Church in no way invalidated the true faith. "After all, no matter what you think nor how much you may like to show off your cynicism, the doctrines are a matter of logical necessity. The Prophet Incarnate and his cohorts can pervert them, but they can't destroy them—and it doesn't matter whether the real Prophet had dirty underwear or not."

Zeb sighed as if he were very tired. "Johnnie, I certainly did not intend to get into an argument about religion with you. I'm not the aggressive type—you know that. I had to be pushed into the Cabal." He paused. "You say the doctrines are a matter of logic?"

"You've explained the logic to me yourself. It's a perfect, consistent structure."

"So it is. Johnnie, the nice thing about citing God as an authority is that you can prove anything you set out to prove. It's just a matter of selecting the proper postulates, then insisting that your postulates are 'inspired.' Then no one can possibly prove that you are wrong."

"You are asserting that the First Prophet was *not* inspired?"

"I am asserting nothing. For all you know, *I* am the First Prophet, come back to kick out the defilers of my temple."

"Don't be—" I was all wound up to kick it around further when there came a knock at Zeb's door. I stopped and he called out, "Come in!"

It was Sister Magdalene.

She nodded at Zeb, smiled sweetly at my open-mouthed surprise and said, "Hello, John Lyle. Welcome." It was the first time I had ever seen her other than in the robes of a holy deaconess. She seemed awfully pretty and much younger.

"Sister Magdalene!"

"No. Staff Sergeant Andrews. 'Maggie,' to my friends."

"But what happened? Why are you here?"

"Right at the moment I'm here because I heard at dinner that you had arrived. When I didn't find you in your own quarters I concluded that you would be with Zeb. As for the rest, I couldn't go back, any more than you or Zeb—and our hideout back in New Jerusalem was getting overcrowded, so they transferred me."

"Well, it's good to see you!"

"It's good to see you, John." She patted me on the cheek and smiled again. Then she climbed on Zeb's bed and squatted tailor-fashion, showing a rather immodest amount of limb in the process. Zeb lit another cigarette and handed it to her; she accepted it, drew smoke deep into her lungs, and let it go as if she had been smoking all her life.

I had never seen a woman smoke—never. I could see Zeb watching me, confound him!—and I most carefully ignored it. Instead I grinned and said, "This is a *wonderful* reunion! If only—"

"I know," agreed Maggie. "If only Judith were here. Have you heard from her yet, John?"

"Heard from her? How could I?"

"That's right, you couldn't—not yet. But you can write to her now."

"Huh? How?"

"I don't know the code number off hand, but you can drop it at my desk—I'm in G-2. Don't bother to seal it; all personal mail has to be censored and paraphrased. I wrote to her last week but I haven't had an answer yet."

I thought about excusing myself at once and writing a letter, but I didn't. It was wonderful to be with both of them and I didn't want to cut the evening short. I decided to write before I went to bed—while realizing, with surprise, that I had been so much on the go that, so far as I could remember, I hadn't even had time to think about Judith since . . . well, since Denver, at least.

But I did not get to write to her even later that night. It was past eleven o'clock and Maggie was saying something about reveille coming early when an orderly showed up: "The Commanding General's compliments and will Legate Lyle see him at once, sir."

I gave my hair a quick brush with Zeb's gear and hurried away, while wishing mightily that I had something fit to report in, rather than a civilian suit much the worse for wear.

The inner sanctum was deserted and dark except for a light that I could see in the far inner office—even Mr. Giles was not at his desk. I found my way in, knocked on the door frame, stepped inside, clicked my heels and saluted. "Legate Lyle reports to the Commanding General as ordered, sir."

An elderly man seated at a big desk with his back to me turned and looked up, and I got another surprise. "Ah, yes, John Lyle," he said gently. He got up and came toward me, with his hand out. "It's been a long time, hasn't it?"

It was Colonel Huxley, head of the Department of Applied Miracles when I was a cadet—and almost my only friend among the officers at that time. Many was the Sunday afternoon that I had relaxed in his quarters, my stock unhooked, free for the moment from the pressure of discipline.

I took his hand. "Colonel—I mean 'General,' sir. . . . I thought you were dead!"

"Dead colonel into live general, eh! No, Lyle, though I was listed as dead when I went underground. They usually do that when an officer disappears; it looks better. You're dead, too —did you know?"

"Uh, no, I didn't, sir. Not that it matters. This is wonderful, sir!"

"Good."

"But— I mean, how did you ever—well—" I shut up.

"How did I land here and in charge at that? I've been a Brother since I was your age, Lyle. But I didn't go underground until I had to—none of us do. In my case the pressure for me to join the priesthood became a bit too strong; the Superintendent was quite restless about having a lay officer know too much about the more abstruse branches of physics and chemistry. So I took a short leave and died. Very sad." He smiled. "But sit down. I've been meaning to send for you all day, but it's been a busy day. They all are. It wasn't until now that I've had time to listen to the record of your report."

We sat down and chatted, and I felt that my cup runneth over. Huxley I respected more than any officer I had ever served under. His very presence resolved any residual doubts I might have—if the Cabal was right for him, it was right for me, and never mind the subtleties of doctrine.

At last he said, "I didn't call you in at this late hour just to chat, Lyle. I've a job for you."

"Yes, sir?"

"No doubt you've already noticed what a raw militia we have here. This is between ourselves and I'm not criticizing our comrades—every one of them has pledged his life to our cause, a harder thing for them to do than for you and me, and they have all placed themselves under military discipline, a thing still harder. But I haven't enough trained soldiers to handle things properly. They mean well but I am tremendously handicapped in trying to turn the organization into an efficient fighting machine. I'm swamped with administrative details. Will you help me?"

I stood up. "I shall be honored to serve with the General to the best of my ability."

"Fine! We'll call you my personal aide for the time being. That's all for tonight, Captain. I'll see you in the morning."

I was halfway out the door before his parting designation sunk in—then I decided that it was a slip of the tongue.

But it was not. I found my own office the next morning by the fact that a sign had been placed on it reading: "CAPTAIN LYLE." From the standpoint of a professional military man there is one good thing about revolutions: the opportunities for swift promotion are excellent . . . even if the pay is inclined to be irregular.

My office adjoined General Huxley's and from then on I almost lived in it—eventually I had a cot installed back of my desk. The very first day I was still fighting my way down a stack of papers in my incoming basket at ten at night. I had promised myself that I would find the bottom, then write a long letter to Judith. But it turned out to be a very short note, as there was a memorandum addressed to me personally, rather than to the General, at the bottom.

It was addressed to "Legate J. Lyle," then someone had scratched out "Legate" and written "Captain." It went on:

MEMORANDUM FOR ALL PERSONNEL NEWLY
    REPORTED
SUBJECT: Personal Conversion Report.
1. You are requested and directed to write out, as fully as possible, all of the events, thoughts, considerations, and incidents which led up to your decision to join our fight for freedom. This account should be as detailed as possible and as subjective as possible. A report written hastily, too briefly, or too superficially will be returned to be expanded and corrected and may be supplemented by hypno examination.
2. This report will be treated as confidential as a whole and any portion of it may be classified secret by the writer. You may substitute letters or numbers for proper names if this will help you to speak freely, but the report must be complete.
3. No time off from regular duties is allotted for this purpose, but this report must be treated as extra-duty of highest priority. A draft of your report will be expected by (*here some one had written in a date and hour less than forty-eight hours away; I used some profane expressions under my breath.*)
BY ORDER OF THE COMMANDING GENERAL
(s) M. NOVAK, Col., F.U.S.A.
Chief of Psychology

I was considerably annoyed by this demand and decided to write to Judith first anyway. The note didn't go very well— how can one write a love letter when you know that one or more strangers will read it and that one of them will rephrase your tenderest words? Besides that, while writing to Judith, my thoughts kept coming back to that night on the rampart of the Palace when I had first met her. It seemed to me that my own personal conversion, as the nosy Colonel Novak called it, started then . . . although I had begun to have doubts before then. Finally I finished the note, decided not to go to bed at once but to tackle that blasted report.

After a while I noticed that it was one o'clock in the morning and I still hadn't carried my account up to the point where I was admitted to the Brotherhood. I stopped writing rather reluctantly (I found that I had grown interested) and locked it in my desk.

At breakfast the next morning I got Zebadiah aside, showed him the memorandum, and asked him about it. "What's the big idea?" I asked. "You work for this particular brass. Are they still suspicious of us, even after letting us in here?"

Zeb barely glanced at it. "Oh, that— Shucks, no. Although I might add that a spy, supposing one could get this far, would be bound to be caught when his personal story went through semantic analysis. Nobody can tell a lie that long and that complicated."

"But what's it for?"

"What do you care? Write it out—and be sure you do a thorough job. Then turn it in."

I felt myself grow warm. "I don't know as I will. I rather think I'll ask the General about it first."

"Do so, if you want to make a ruddy fool of yourself. But look, John, the psychomathematicians who will read that mess of bilge you will write, won't have the slightest interest in you as an individual. They don't even want to know who you are—a girl goes through your report and deletes all personal names, including your own, if you haven't done so yourself, and substitutes numbers . . . all this before an analyst sees it. You're just data, that's all; the Chief has some heap big project on the fire—I don't know what it is myself—and he is trying to gather together a large enough statistical universe to be significant."

I was mollified. "Well, why don't they say so, then? This memo is just a bald order—irritating."

Zeb shrugged. "That is because it was prepared by the semantics division. If the propaganda division had written it, you would have gotten up early and finished the job before breakfast." He added, "By the way, I hear you've been promoted. Congratulations."

"Thanks." I grinned at him slyly. "How does it feel to be junior to me, Zeb?"

"Huh? Did they bump you that far? I thought you were a captain."

"I am."

"Well, excuse me for breathing—but I'm a major."

"Oh. Congratulations."

"Think nothing of it. You have to be at least a colonel around here, or you make your own bed."

I was too busy to make my bed very often. More than half the time I slept on the couch in my office and once I went a week without bathing. It was evident at once that the Cabal was bigger and had more complicated ramifications to it than I had ever dreamed and furthermore that it was building to a crescendo. I was too close to the trees to see the woods, even though everything but the utter top-secret, burn-after-reading items passed across my desk.

I simply endeavored to keep General Huxley from being smothered in pieces of paper—and found myself smothered instead. The idea was to figure out what he would do, if he had time, and then do it for him. A person who has been trained in the principles of staff or doctrinal command can do this; the trick is to make your mind work like your boss's mind in all routine matters, and to be able to recognize what is routine and what he must pass on himself. I made my share of mistakes, but apparently not too many for he didn't fire me, and three months later I was a major with the fancy title of assistant chief of staff. Chalk most of it up to the West Point ring, of course—a professional has a great advantage.

I should add that Zeb was a short-tailed colonel by then and acting chief of propaganda, his section chief having been transferred to a regional headquarters I knew only by the code name JERICHO.

But I am getting ahead of my story. I heard from Judith about two weeks later—a pleasant-enough note but with the juice pressed out of it through rephrasing. I meant to answer her at once but actually delayed a week—it was so pesky hard to know what to say. I could not possibly tell her any news except that I was well and busy. If I had told her I loved her three times in one letter some idiot in cryptography would have examined it for "pattern" and rejected it completely when he failed to find one.

The mail went to Mexico through a long tunnel, partly artificial but mostly natural, which led right under the international border. A little electric railroad of the sort used in mines ran through this tunnel and carried not only my daily headaches in the way of official mail but also a great deal of freight to supply our fair-sized town. There were a dozen other entrances to GHQ on the Arizona side of the border, but I never knew where any of them were—it was not my pidgin. The whole area overlay a deep layer of paleozoic limestone and it may well be honeycombed from California to Texas. The area known as GHQ had been in use for more than twenty years as a hideout for refugee brethren. Nobody knew the extent of the caverns we were in; we simply lighted and used what we needed. It was a favorite sport of us troglodytes —permanent residents were "trogs"; transients were "bats" because they flew by night—we trogs liked to go on "spelling bees," picnics which included a little amateur speleology in the unexplored parts.

It was permitted by regulations, but just barely and subject to stringent safety precautions, for you could break a leg awfully easily in those holes. But the General permitted it because it was necessary; we had only such recreations as we could make ourselves and some of us had not seen daylight in years.

Zeb and Maggie and I went on a number of such outings when I could get away. Maggie always brought another woman along. I protested at first but she pointed out to me that it was necessary in order to avoid gossip . . . mutual chaperonage. She assured me that she was certain that Judith would not mind, under the circumstances. It was a different girl each time and it seemed to work out that Zeb always paid a lot of attention to the other girl while I talked with Maggie. I had thought once that Maggie and Zeb would marry, but now I began to wonder. They seemed to suit each other like ham and eggs, but Maggie did not seem jealous and I can only describe Zeb, in honesty, as shameless—that is, if he thought Maggie would care.

One Saturday morning Zeb stuck his head in my sweat box and said, "Spelling bee. Two o'clock. Bring a towel."

I looked up from a mound of papers. "I doubt if I can make it," I answered. "And why a towel?"

But he was gone. Maggie came through my office later to take the weekly consolidated intelligence report in to the Old Man, but I did not attempt to question her, as Maggie was all business during working hours—the perfect office sergeant. I had lunch at my desk, hoping to finish up, but knowing it was impossible. About a quarter of two I went in to get General Huxley's signature on an item that was to go out that night by hypnoed courier and therefore had to go at once to psycho in order that the courier might be operated. He glanced at it and signed it, then said, "Sergeant Andy tells me you have a date."

"Sergeant Andrews is mistaken," I said stiffly. "There are still the weekly reports from Jericho, Nod, and Egypt to be gone over."

"Place them on my desk and get out. That's an order. I can't have you going stale from overwork."

I did not tell him that he had not even been to lodge himself in more than a month; I got out.

I dropped the message with Colonel Novak and hurried to where we always met near the women's mess. Maggie was there with the other girl—a blonde named Miriam Booth who was a clerk in Quartermaster's stores. I knew her by sight but had never spoken to her. They had our picnic lunch and Zeb arrived while I was being introduced. He was carrying, as usual, the portable flood we would use when we picked out a spot and a blanket to sit on and use as a table. "Where's your towel?" he demanded.

"Were you serious? I forgot it."

"Run get it. We'll start off along Appian Way. You can catch up. Come on, kids."

They started off, which left me with nothing but to do as I was told. After grabbing a towel from my room I dogtrotted until I had them in sight, then slowed to a walk, puffing. Desk work had ruined my wind. They heard me and waited.

We were all dressed alike, with the women in trousers and each with a safety line wrapped around the waist and torch clipped to the belt. I had gotten used to women in men's clothes, much as I disliked it—and, after all, it is impractical and quite immodest to climb around in caves wearing skirts.

We left the lighted area by taking a turn that appeared to lead into a blind wall; instead it led into a completely concealed but easily negotiated tunnel. Zeb tied our labyrinth string and started paying it out as soon as we left permanent and marked paths, as required by the standing order; Zeb was always careful about things that mattered.

For perhaps a thousand paces we could see blazes and other indications that others had been this way before, such as a place where someone had worked a narrow squeeze wider with a sledge. Then we left the obvious path and turned into a blind wall. Zeb put down the flood and turned it on. "Sling your torches. We climb this one."

"Where are we going?"

"A place Miriam knows about. Give me a leg up, Johnnie."

The climb wasn't much. I got Zeb up all right and the girls could have helped each other up, but we took them up roped, for safety's sake. We picked up our gear and Miriam led us away, each of us using his torch.

We went down the other side and there was another passage so well hidden that it could have been missed for ten thousand years. We stopped once while Zeb tied on another ball of string. Shortly Miriam said, "Slow up, everybody. I think we're there."

Zeb flashed his torch around, then set up the portable flood and switched it on. He whistled. "Whew! This is all right!"

Maggie said softly, "It's lovely." Miriam just grinned triumphantly.

I agreed with them all. It was a perfect small domed cavern, perhaps eighty feet wide and much longer. How long, I could not tell, as it curved gently away in a gloom-filled turn. But the feature of the place was a quiet, inky-black pool that filled most of the floor. In front of us was a tiny beach of real sand that might have been laid down a million years ago for all I know.

Our voices echoed pleasantly and a little bit spookily in the chamber, being broken up and distorted by stalactites and curtains hanging from the roof. Zeb walked down to the water's edge, squatted and tested it with his hand. "Not too cold," he announced. "Well, the last one in is a proctor's nark."

I recognized the old swimming hole call, even though the last time I had heard it, as a boy, it had been "last one in is a dirty pariah." But here I could not believe it.

Zeb was already unbuttoning his shirt. I stepped up to him

quickly and said privately, "Zeb! Mixed bathing? You must be joking?"

"Not a bit of it." He searched my face. "Why not? What's the matter with you, boy? Afraid someone will make you do penance? They won't, you know. That's all over with."

"But—"

"But what?"

I could not answer. The only way I could make the words come out would have been in the terms we had been taught in the Church, and I knew that Zeb would laugh at me—in front of the women. Probably they would laugh, too, since they had known and I hadn't. "But Zeb," I insisted, "I *can't*. You didn't tell me . . . and I don't even have a bathing outfit."

"Neither do I. Didn't you ever go in raw as a kid—and get paddled for it?" He turned away without waiting for me to answer this enormity and said, "Are you frail vessels waiting on something?"

"Just for you two to finish your debate," Maggie answered, coming closer. "Zeb, I think Mimi and I will use the other side of that boulder. All right?"

"Okay. But wait a second. No diving, you both understand. And a safety man on the bank at all times—John and I will take turns."

"Pooh!" said Miriam. "I dove the last time I was here."

"You weren't with me, that's sure. No diving—or I'll warm your pants where they are tightest."

She shrugged. "All right, Colonel Crosspatch. Come on, Mag." They went on past us and around a boulder half as big as a house. Miriam stopped, looked right at me, and waggled a finger. "No peeking, now!" I blushed to my ears.

They disappeared and we heard no more of them, except for giggles. I said hurriedly, "Look. You do as you please— and on your own head be it. But I'm not going in. I'll sit here on the bank and be safety man."

"Suit yourself. I was going to match you for first duty, but nobody is twisting your arm. Pay out a line, though, and have it ready for heaving. Not that we'll need it; both the girls are strong swimmers."

I said desperately, "Zeb, I'm sure the General would forbid swimming in these underground pools."

"That's why we didn't mention it. 'Never worry the C.O.

unnecessarily'—standing orders in Joshua's Army, circa 1400 B.C." He went right on peeling off his clothes.

I don't know why Miriam warned me not to peek—not that I would!—for when she was undressed she came straight out from behind that boulder, not toward us but toward the water. But the flood light was full on her and she even turned toward us for an instant, then shouted, "Come on, Maggie! Zeb is going to be last if you hurry."

I did not want to look and I could not take my eyes off her. I had never seen anything remotely resembling the sight she was in my life—and only once a picture, one in the possession of a boy in my parish school and on that occasion I had gotten only a glimpse and then had promptly reported him.

But I could not stop looking, burning with shame as I was. Zeb beat Maggie into the water—I don't think she cared. He went into the water quickly, almost breaking his own injunction against diving. Sort of a surface dive I would call it, running into the water and then breaking into a racing start. His powerful crawl was soon overtaking Miriam, who had started to swim toward the far end.

Then Maggie came out from behind the boulder and went into the water. She did not make a major evolution of it, the way Miriam had, but simply walked quickly and with quiet grace into the water. When she was waist deep, she let herself sink forward and struck out in a strong breast stroke, then shifted to a crawl and followed the others, whom I could hear but hardly see in the distance.

Again I could not take my eyes away if my eternal soul had depended on it. What is it about the body of a human woman that makes it the most terribly beautiful sight on earth? Is it, as some claim, simply a necessary instinct to make sure that we comply with God's will and replenish the earth? Or is it some stranger, more wonderful thing?

I found myself quoting: "How fair and how pleasant art thou, O love, for delights!

"This thy stature is like to a palm tree, and thy breasts to clusters of grapes."

Then I broke off, ashamed, remembering that the Song of Songs which is Solomon's was a chaste and holy allegory having nothing to do with such things.

I sat down on the sand and tried to compose my soul. After a while I felt better and my heart stopped pounding so hard. When they all came swimming back with Zeb in the lead, racing Miriam, I even managed to throw them a smile. It no longer seemed quite so terrible and as long as they stayed in the water the women were not shockingly exposed. Perhaps evil was truly in the eye of the beholder—in which case the idea was to keep it out of mine.

Zeb called out, "Ready to be relieved?"

I answered firmly, "No. Go ahead and have your fun."

"Okay." He turned like a dolphin and started back the other way. Miriam followed him. Maggie came in to where it was shallow, rested her finger tips on the bottom, and held facing me, with just her head and her ivory shoulders out of the inky water, while her waist-length mane of hair floated around her.

"Poor John," she said softly. "I'll come out and spell you."

"Oh, no, really!"

"Are you sure?"

"Quite sure."

"All right." She turned, flipped herself over, and started after the others. For one ghostly, magic instant she was partly out of the water.

Maggie came back to my end of the cavern about ten minutes later. "I'm cold," she said briefly, climbed out and strode quickly to the protection of the boulder. Somehow she was not naked, but merely unclothed, like Mother Eve. There is a difference—Miriam had been naked.

With Maggie out of the water and neither one of us speaking I noticed for the first time that there was no other sound. Now there is nothing so quiet as a cave; anywhere else at all there is noise, but the complete zero decibel which obtains underground if one holds still and says nothing is very different.

The point is that I should have been able to hear Zeb and Miriam swimming. Swimming need not be noisy but it can't be as quiet as a cave. I sat up suddenly and started forward—then stopped with equal suddenness as I did not want to invade Maggie's dressing room, which another dozen steps would have accomplished.

But I was really worried and did not know what to do. Throw a line? Where? Peel down and search for them? If necessary. I called out softly, "Maggie!"

"What is it, John?"

"Maggie, I'm worried."

She came at once from behind the rock. She had already pulled on her trousers, but held her towel so that it covered her from the waist up; I had the impression she had been drying her hair. "Why, John?"

"Keep very quiet and listen."

She did so. "I don't hear anything."

"That's just it. We should. I could hear you all swimming even when you were down at the far end, out of my sight. Now there isn't a sound, not a splash. Do you suppose they possibly could both have hit their heads on the bottom at the same time?"

"Oh. Stop worrying, John. They're all right."

"But I *am* worried."

"They're just resting, I'm sure. There is another little beach down there, about half as big as this. That's where they are. I climbed up on it with them, then I came back. I was cold."

I made up my mind, realizing that I had let my modesty hold me back from my plain duty. "Turn your back. No, go behind the boulder—I want to undress."

"What? I tell you it's not necessary." She did not budge.

I opened my mouth to shout. Before I got it out Maggie had a hand over my mouth, which caused her towel to be disarranged and flustered us both. "Oh, heavens!" she said sharply. "Keep your big mouth shut." She turned suddenly and flipped the towel; when she turned back she had it about her like a stole, covering her front well enough, I suppose, without the need to hold it.

"John Lyle, come here and sit down. Sit down by me." She sat on the sand and patted the place by her—and such was the firmness with which she spoke that I did as I was told.

"By me," she insisted. "Come closer. I don't want to shout." I inched gingerly closer until my sleeve brushed her bare arm. "That's better," she agreed, keeping her voice low so that it did not resound around the cavern. "Now listen to me. There are two people down there, of their own free will. They are entirely safe—I saw them. And they are both excellent swimmers. The thing for you to do, John Lyle, is to mind your own business and restrain that nasty itch to interfere."

"I'm afraid I don't understand you." Truthfully, I was afraid I did.

"Oh, goodness me! See here, does Miriam mean anything to you?"

"Why, no, not especially."

"I should think not, since you haven't addressed six words to her since we started out. Very well, then—since you have no cause to be jealous, if two people choose to be alone, why should you stick your nose in? Understand me now?"

"Uh, I guess so."

"Then just be quiet."

I was quiet. She didn't move. I was acutely aware of her nakedness—for now she was naked, though covered—and I hoped that she was not aware that I was aware. Besides that I was acutely aware of being almost a participant in—well, I don't know what. I told myself angrily that I had no right to assume the worst, like a morals proctor.

Presently I said, "Maggie . . ."

"Yes, John?"

"I don't understand you."

"Why not, John? Not that it is really needful."

"Uh, you don't seem to give a hoot that Zeb is down there, with Miriam—alone."

"Should I give a hoot?"

Confound the woman! She was deliberately misunderstanding me. "Well . . . look, somehow I had gotten the impression that you and Zeb—I mean . . . well, I suppose I sort of expected that you two meant to get married, when you could."

She laughed a low chuckle that had little mirth in it. "I suppose you could have gotten that impression. But, believe me, the matter is all settled and for the best."

"Huh?"

"Don't misunderstand me. I am very fond of Zebadiah and I know he is equally fond of me. But we are both dominant types psychologically—you should see my profile chart; it looks like the Rocky Mountains! Two such people should not marry. Such marriages are *not* made in Heaven, believe me! Fortunately we found it out in time."

"Oh."

"Oh, indeed."

Now I don't know just how the next thing happened. I was thinking that she seemed rather forlorn—and the next thing I knew I was kissing her. She lay back in my arms and returned the kiss with a fervor I would not have believed possible. As for me, my head was buzzing and my eyeballs were knocking together and I couldn't have told you whether I was a thousand feet underground or on dress parade.

Then it was over. She looked up for a bare moment into my eyes and whispered, "Dear John . . ." Then she got suddenly to her feet, leaned over me, careless of the towel, and patted my cheek. "Judith is a very lucky girl. I wonder if she knows it."

"Maggie!" I said.

She turned away and said, without looking back, "I really must finish dressing. I'm cold."

She had not felt cold to me.

She came out shortly, fully dressed and towelling her hair vigorously. I got my dry towel and helped her. I don't believe I suggested it; the idea just took care of itself. Her hair was thick and lovely and I enjoyed doing it. It sent goose pimples over me.

Zeb and Miriam came back while I was doing so, not racing but swimming slowly; we could hear them laughing long before they were in sight. Miriam climbed out of the water as shamelessly as any harlot of Gomorrah, but I hardly noticed her. Zeb looked me in the eye and said aggressively, "Ready for your swim, chum?"

I started to say that I did not believe that I would bother and was going to make some excuse about my towel already being wet—when I noticed Maggie watching me . . . not saying anything but watching. I answered, "Why, surely! You two took long enough." I called out, "Miriam! Get out from behind that rock! I want to use it."

She squealed and giggled and came out, still arranging her clothes. I went behind it with quiet dignity.

I hope I still had quiet dignity when I came out. In any case I set my teeth, walked out and straight into the water. It was bitingly cold at first, but only for a moment. I was never varsity but I swam on my class team and I've even been in the Hudson on New Year's Day. I liked that black pool, once I was in.

I just had to swim down to the other end. Sure enough, there was a little shelf beach there. I did not go up on it.

On the way back I tried to swim down to the bottom. I could not find it, but it must have been over twenty feet down. I liked it down there—black and utterly still. Had I the breath for it, or gills, it seemed to me that it would have been a good place to stay, away from Prophets, away from Cabals, and paperwork, and worries, and problems too subtle for me.

I came up gasping, then struck out hard for our picnic beach. The girls already had the food laid out and Zeb shouted for me to hurry. Zeb and Maggie did not look up as I got out of the water, but I caught Miriam eyeing me. I don't think I blushed. I never did like blondes anyhow. I think Lilith must have been a blonde.

11

THE SUPREME COUNCIL, consisting of heads of departments, General Huxley, and a few others, met weekly or oftener to advise the General, exchange views, and consider the field reports. About a month after our rather silly escapade in the underground pool they were in session and I was with them, not as a member but as a recorder. My own girl was ill and I had borrowed Maggie from G-2 to operate the voicewriter, since she was cleared for top secret. We were always terribly shorthanded of competent personnel. My nominal boss, for example, was Wing General Penoyer, who carried the title of Chief of Staff. But I hardly ever saw him, as he was also Chief of Ordnance. Huxley was his own chief of staff and I was sort of a glorified aide—"midshipmite, and bosun tite, and crew of the captain's gig." I even tried to see to it that Huxley took his stomach medicine regularly.

This meeting was bigger than usual. The regional commanders of Gath, Canaan, Jericho, Babylon, and Egypt were present in person; Nod and Damascus were represented by deputies—every Cabal district of the United States except Eden and we were holding a sensitive hook-up to Louisville for that command, using idea code that the sensitives themselves would not understand. I could feel the pressure of something big coming up, although Huxley had not taken me into his confidence. The place was tyled so that a mouse couldn't have got in.

We droned through the usual routine reports. It was duly recorded that we now had eighty-seven hundred and nine accepted members, either lodge brethren or tested and bound members of the parallel military organization. There were listed as recruited and instructed more than ten times that number of fellow travelers who could be counted on to rise against the Prophet, but who had not been intrusted with knowledge of the actual conspiracy.

The figures themselves were not encouraging. We were always in the jaws of a dilemma; a hundred thousand men was a handful to conquer a continent-wide country whereas the less than nine thousand party to the conspiracy itself were 'way too many to keep a secret. We necessarily relied on the ancient cell system wherein no man knew more than he had to know and could not give away too much no matter what an inquisitor did to him—no, not even if he had been a spy. But we had our weekly losses even at this passive stage.

One entire lodge had been surprised in session and arrested in Seattle four days earlier; it was a serious loss but only three of the chairs had possessed critical knowledge and all three had suicided successfully. Prayers would be said for all of them at a grand session that night, but here it was a routine report. We had lost four hatchet men that week but twenty-three assassinations had been accomplished—one of them the Elder Inquisitor for the entire lower Mississippi Valley.

The Chief of Communications reported that the brethren were prepared to disable 91% (figured on population coverage) of the radio & TV stations in the country, and that with the aid of assault groups we could reasonably hope to account for the rest—with the exception of the Voice of God station at New Jerusalem, which was a special problem.

The Chief of Combat Engineering reported readiness to sabotage the power supply of the forty-six largest cities, again with the exception of New Jerusalem, the supply of which was self-contained with the pile located under the Temple. Even there major interruption could be accomplished at distribution stations if the operation warranted the expenditure of sufficient men. Major surface transportation and freight routes could be sabotaged sufficiently with present plans and personnel to reduce traffic to 12% of normal.

The reports went on and on—newspapers, student action groups, rocket field seizure or sabotage, miracles, rumor propagation, water supply, incident incitement, counter-espionage, long-range weather prediction, weapons distribution. War is a simple matter compared with revolution. War is an applied science, with well-defined principles tested in history; analogous solutions may be found from ballista to H-bomb. But every revolution is a freak, a mutant, a monstrosity, its conditions never to be repeated and its operations carried out by amateurs and individualists.

While Maggie recorded the data I was arranging it and

transmitting it to the calculator room for analysis. I was much too busy even to attempt a horse-back evaluation in my head. There was a short wait while the analysts finished programming and let the "brain" have it—then the remote-printer in front of me chattered briefly and stopped. Huxley leaned across me and tore off the tape before I could reach it.

He glanced at it, then cleared his throat and waited for dead silence. "Brethren," he began, "comrades—we agreed long ago on our doctrine of procedure. When every predictable factor, calculated, discounted for probable error, weighted and correlated with all other significant factors, gave a calculated risk of two to one in our favor, we would strike. Today's solution of the probability equation, substituting this week's data for the variables, gives an answer of two point one three. I propose to set the hour of execution. How say you?"

It was a delayed shock; no one said anything. Hope delayed too long makes reality hard to believe—and all of these men had waited for years, some for most of a lifetime. Then they were on their feet, shouting, sobbing, cursing, pounding each others' backs.

Huxley sat still until they quieted, an odd little smile on his face. Then he stood up and said quietly, "I don't think we need poll the sentiment. I will set the hour after I have—"

"General! If you please! I do not agree." It was Zeb's boss, Sector General Novak, Chief of Psych. Huxley stopped speaking and the silence fairly ached. I was as stunned as the rest.

Then Huxley said quietly, "This council usually acts by unanimous consent. We have long since arrived at the method for setting the date . . . but I know that you would not disagree without good reason. We will listen now to Brother Novak."

Novak came slowly forward and faced them. "Brethren," he began, running his eyes over bewildered and hostile faces, "you know me, and you know I want this thing as much as you do. I have devoted the last seventeen years to it—it has cost me my family and my home. But I can't let you go ahead without warning you, when I am sure that the time is not yet. I think—no, I *know* with mathematical certainty that we are not ready for revolution." He had to wait and hold up both hands for silence; they did not want to hear him. "Hear me out! I concede that all military plans are ready. I admit that if we strike now we have a strong probability of being able to seize the country. Nevertheless we are not ready—"

"Why not?"

"—because a majority of the people still believe in the established religion, they believe in the Divine authority of the Prophet. We can seize power but we can't hold it."

"The Devil we won't!"

"*Listen* to me! No people was ever held in subjection long except through their own consent. For three generations the American people have been conditioned from cradle to grave by the cleverest and most thorough psychotechnicians in the world. They *believe!* If you turn them loose now, without adequate psychological preparation, they will go back to their chains . . . like a horse returning to a burning barn. We can win the revolution but it will be followed by a long and bloody civil war—which we will lose!"

He stopped, ran a trembling hand across his eyes, then said to Huxley, "That's all."

Several were on their feet at once. Huxley pounded for order, then recognized Wing General Penoyer.

Penoyer said, "I'd like to ask Brother Novak a few questions."

"Go ahead."

"Can his department tell us what percentage of the population is sincerely devout?"

Zebadiah, present to assist his chief, looked up; Novak nodded and he answered, "Sixty-two per cent, plus-or-minus three per cent."

"And the percentage who secretly oppose the government whether we have enlisted them or not?"

"Twenty-one per cent plus, proportional error. The balance can be classed as conformists, not devout but reasonably contented."

"By what means were the data obtained?"

"Surprise hypnosis of representative types."

"Can you state the trend?"

"Yes, sir. The government lost ground rapidly during the first years of the present depression, then the curve flattened out. The new tithing law and to some extent the vagrancy decrees were unpopular and the government again lost ground before the curve again flattened at a lower level. About that time business picked up a little but we simultaneously started our present intensified propaganda campaign; the government has been losing ground slowly but steadily the past fifteen months."

"And what does the first derivative show?"

Zeb hesitated and Novak took over. "You have to figure the second derivative," he answered in a strained voice; "the rate is accelerating."

"Well?"

The Psych Chief answered firmly but reluctantly, "On extrapolation, it will be three years and eight months before we can risk striking."

Penoyer turned back to Huxley. "I have my answer, sir. With deep respect to General Novak and his careful scientific work, I say—win while we can! We may never have another chance."

He had the crowd with him. "Penoyer is right! If we wait, we'll be betrayed."—"You can't hold a thing like this together forever."—"I've been underground ten years; I don't want to be buried here."—"Win . . . and worry about making converts when we control communications."—"Strike now! Strike now!"

Huxley let them carry on, his own face expressionless, until they had it out of their systems. I kept quiet myself, since I was too junior to be entitled to a voice here, but I went along with Penoyer; I couldn't see waiting nearly four years.

I saw Zeb talking earnestly with Novak. They seemed to be arguing about something and were paying no attention to the racket. But when Huxley at last held up a hand for silence Novak left his place and hurried up to Huxley's elbow. The General listened for a moment, seemed almost annoyed, then undecided. Novak crooked a finger at Zeb, who came running up. The three whispered together for several moments while the council waited.

Finally Huxley faced them again. "General Novak has proposed a scheme which may change the whole situation. The Council is recessed until tomorrow."

Novak's plan (or Zeb's, though he never admitted authorship) required a delay of nearly two months, to the date of the annual Miracle of the Incarnation. For what was contemplated was no less than tampering with the Miracle itself. In hindsight it was an obvious and probably essential stratagem; the psych boss was right. In essence, a dictator's strength depends not upon guns but on the faith his people place in him. This had been true of Caesar, of Napoleon, of

Hitler, of Stalin. It was necessary to strike first at the foundation of the Prophet's power: the popular belief that he ruled by direct authority of God.

Future generations will undoubtedly find it impossible to believe the importance, the extreme importance both to religious faith and political power, of the Miracle of Incarnation. To comprehend it even intellectually it is necessary to realize that the people literally believed that the First Prophet actually and physically returned from Heaven once each year to judge the stewardship of his Divinely appointed successor and to confirm him in his office. The people *believed* this—the minority of doubters dared not open their faces to dispute it for fear of being torn limb from limb . . . and I am speaking of a rending that leaves blood on the pavement, not some figure of speech. Spitting on the Flag would have been much safer.

I had believed it myself, all my life; it would never have occurred to me to doubt such a basic article of faith—and I was what is called an educated man, one who had been let into the secrets of and trained in the production of lesser miracles. I believed it.

The ensuing two months had all the endless time-stretching tension of the waiting period while coming into range and before "Commence firing!"—yet we were so busy that each day and each hour was too short. In addition to preparing the still-more-miraculous intervention in the Miracle we used the time to whet our usual weapons to greater fineness. Zeb and his boss, Sector General Novak, were detached almost at once. Novak's orders read "—proceed to BEULAHLAND and take charge of OPERATION BEDROCK." I cut the orders myself, not trusting them to a clerk, but no one told me where Beulahland might be found on a map.

Huxley himself left when they did and was gone for more than a week, leaving Penoyer as acting C.-in-C. He did not tell me why he was leaving, of course, nor where he was going, but I could fill in. Operation Bedrock was a psychological maneuver but the means must be physical—and my boss had once been head of the Department of Applied Miracles at the Point. He may have been the best physicist in the entire Cabal; in any case I could guess with certainty that he intended at the very least to see for himself that the means were adequate and the techniques foolproof. For all I know he may actually have used soldering iron and screwdriver and electronic micrometer himself that week—the General did not mind getting his hands dirty.

I missed Huxley personally. Penoyer was inclined to reverse my decisions on minor matters and waste my time and his on details a top C.O. can't and should not cope with. But he was gone part of the time, too. There was much coming and going and more than once I had to chase down the senior department head present, tell him that he was acting, and get him to sign where I had initialed. I took to scrawling "I. M. Dumbjohn, Wing General F.U.S.A., Acting" as indecipherably as possible on all routine internal papers—I don't think anybody ever noticed.

Before Zeb left another thing happened which really has nothing to do with the people of the United States and the struggle to regain their freedoms—but my own personal affairs are so tied into this account that I mention it. Perhaps the personal angle really is important; certainly the order under which this journal was started called for it to be "personal" and "subjective"—however I had retained a copy and added to it because I found it helped me to get my own confused thoughts straight while going through a metamorphosis as drastic as that from caterpillar into moth. I am typical, perhaps, of the vast majority, the sort of person who has to have his nose rubbed in a thing before he recognizes it, while Zeb and Maggie and General Huxley were of the elite minority of naturally free souls . . . the original thinkers, the leaders.

I was at my desk, trying to cope with the usual spate of papers, when I received a call to see Zeb's boss at my earliest convenience. Since he already had his orders, I left word with Huxley's orderly and hurried over.

He cut short the formalities. "Major, I have a letter for you which Communications sent over for analysis to determine whether it should be rephrased or simply destroyed. However, on the urgent recommendation of one of my division heads I am taking the responsibility of letting you read it without paraphrasing. You will have to read it here."

I said, "Yes, sir," feeling quite puzzled.

He handed it to me. It was fairly long and I suppose it could have held half a dozen coded messages, even idea codes that could come through paraphrasing. I don't remember much of it—just the impact it had on me. It was from Judith.

"My dear John. . . . I shall always think of you fondly

and I shall never forget what you have done for me. . . . never meant for each other . . . Mr. Mendoza has been most considerate . . . I know you will forgive me. . . . he needs me; it must have been fate that brought us together. . . . if you ever visit Mexico City, you must think of our home as yours. . . . I will always think of you as my strong and wise older brother and I will always be a sister—" There was more, lots more, all of the same sort—I think the process is known as "breaking it gently."

Novak reached out and took the letter from me. "I didn't intend for you to have time to memorize it," he said dryly, then dropped it at once into his desk incinerator. He glanced back at me. "Maybe you had better sit down, Major. Do you smoke?"

I did not sit down, but I was spinning so fast that I accepted the cigarette and let him light it for me. Then I choked on tobacco smoke and the sheer physical discomfort helped to bring me back to reality. I thanked him and got out —went straight to my room, called my office and left word where I could be found if the General really wanted me. But I told my secretary that I was suddenly quite ill and not to disturb me if it could possibly be helped.

I may have been there about an hour—I wouldn't know— lying face down and doing nothing, not even thinking. There came a gentle tap at the door, then it was pushed open; it was Zeb. "How do you feel?" he said.

"Numb," I answered. It did not occur to me to wonder how he knew and at the time I had forgotten the "division head" who had prevailed upon Novak to let me see it in the clear.

He came on in, sprawled in a chair, and looked at me. I rolled over and sat on the edge of the bed. "Don't let it throw you, Johnnie," he said quietly. " 'Men have died and worms have eaten them—but not for love.' "

"You don't know!"

"No, I don't," he agreed. "Each man is his own prisoner, in solitary confinement for life. Nevertheless on this particular point the statistics are fairly reliable. Try something for me. Visualize Judith in your mind. See her features. Listen to her voice."

"Huh?"

"Do it."

I tried, I really tried—and, do you know, I couldn't. I had never had a picture of her; her face now eluded me.

Zeb was watching me. "You'll get well," he said firmly. "Now look here, Johnnie. . . . I could have told you. Judith is a very female sort of woman, all gonads and no brain. And she's quite attractive. Turned loose, she was bound to find a man, as sure as nascent oxygen will recombine. But there is no use in talking to a man in love."

He stood up. "Johnnie, I've got to go. I hate like the mischief to walk out and leave you in the shape you are in, but I've already checked out and Grandfather Novak is ready to leave. He'll eat me out as it is, for holding him up this long. But one more word of advice before I go—"

I waited. "I suggest," he continued, "that you see a lot of Maggie while I'm away. She's good medicine."

He started to leave; I said sharply, "Zeb—what happened to you and Maggie? Something like this?"

He looked back at me sharply. "Huh? No. Not at all the same thing. It wasn't . . . well, it wasn't similar."

"I don't understand you—I guess I just don't understand people. You're urging me to see a lot of Maggie—and I thought she was your girl. Uh, wouldn't you be jealous?"

He stared at me, laughed, and clapped me on the shoulder. "She's a free citizen, Johnnie, believe me. If you ever did anything to hurt Maggie, I'd tear off your head and beat you to death with it. Not that you ever would. But jealous of her? No. It doesn't enter the picture. I think she's the greatest gal that ever trod shoe leather—but I would rather marry a mountain lioness."

He left on that, leaving me again with my mouth open. But I took his advice, or Maggie took it for me. Maggie knew all about it—Judith, I mean—and I assumed that Zeb had told her. He hadn't; it seemed that Judith had written to her first. In any case I didn't have to look her up; she looked me up right after dinner that night. I talked with her a while and felt much better, so much so that I went back to my office and made up for time lost that afternoon.

Maggie and I made a habit thereafter of taking a walk together after dinner. We went on no more spelling bees; not only was there no time for such during those last days but also neither one of us felt like trying to work up another foursome with Zeb away. Sometimes I could spare only twenty minutes or even less before I would have to be back at my desk—but it was the high point of the day; I looked forward to it.

Even without leaving the floodlighted main cavern, without leaving the marked paths, there were plenty of wonderfully beautiful walks to take. If I could afford to be away as much as an hour, there was one place in particular we liked to go—north in the big room, a good half mile from the buildings. The path meandered among frozen limestone mushrooms, great columns, domes, and fantastic shapes that have no names and looked equally like souls in torment or great exotic flowers, depending on the mood one was in. At a spot nearly a hundred feet higher than the main floor we had found a place only a few feet off the authorized path where nature had contrived a natural stone bench. We could sit there and stare down at the toy village, talk, and Maggie would smoke. I had taken to lighting her cigarettes for her, as I had seen Zeb do. It was a little attention she liked and I had learned to avoid getting smoke caught in my throat.

About six weeks after Zeb had left and only days before M-Hour we were doing this and were talking about what it would be like after the revolution and what we would do with ourselves. I said that I supposed I would stay in the regular army, assuming that there was such and that I was eligible for it. "What will you do, Maggie?"

She exhaled smoke slowly. "I haven't thought that far, John. I haven't any profession—that is to say, we are trying our best to make the one I did have obsolete." She smiled wryly. "I'm not educated in anything useful. I can cook and I can sew and I can keep house; I suppose I should try to find a job as a housekeeper—competent servants are always scarce, they say."

The idea of the courageous and resourceful Sister Magdalene, so quick with a vibroblade when the need arose, tramping from one employment bureau to another in search of menial work to keep her body fed was an idea at once distasteful to me—"General Housework & Cooking, live in, Thur. eve. & alternate Sundays off; references required." Maggie? Maggie who had saved my own probably worthless life at least twice and never hesitated nor counted the cost. Not Maggie!

I blurted out, "Look, you don't have to do *that*."

"It's what I know."

"Yes, but—well, why don't you cook and keep house for

me? I'll be drawing enough to support both of us, even if I have to go back to my permanent rank. Maybe it isn't much but—shucks! you're welcome to it."

She looked up. "Why, John, how very generous!" She crushed out the cigarette and threw it aside. "I do appreciate it—but it wouldn't work. I imagine there will be just as many gossips after we have won as before. Your colonel would not like it."

I blushed red and almost shouted, "That wasn't what I meant at all!"

"What? Then what did you mean?"

I had not really known until the words came out. Now I knew but not how to express it. "I meant— Look, Maggie, you seem to like me well enough . . . and we get along well together. That is, why don't we—" I halted, hung up.

She stood up and faced me. "John, are you proposing marriage—to *me?*"

I said gruffly, "Uh, that was the general idea." It bothered me to have her standing in front of me, so I stood up, too.

She looked at me gravely, searching my face, then said humbly, "I'm honored . . . and grateful . . . and I am deeply touched. But—*oh, no, John!*" The tears started out of her eyes and she started to bawl. She stopped as quickly, wiping her face with her sleeve, and said brokenly, "Now you've made me cry. I haven't cried in years."

I started to put my arms around her; she pushed me back. "No, John! Listen to me first. I'll accept that job as your housekeeper, but I won't marry you."

"Why not?"

" 'Why not?' Oh, my dear, my very dear— Because I am an old, tired woman, that's why."

"Old? You can't be more than a year or two older than I am—three, at the outside. It doesn't matter."

"I'm a thousand years older than you are. Think who I am —where I've been—what I've known. First I was 'bride,' if you care to call it that, to the Prophet."

"Not your fault!"

"Perhaps. Then I was mistress to your friend Zebadiah. You knew that?"

"Well . . . I was pretty sure of it."

"That isn't all. There were other men. Some because it was needful and a woman has few bribes to offer. Some from loneliness, or even boredom. After the Prophet has tired of her, a woman doesn't seem very valuable, even to herself."

"I don't care. I don't care! It doesn't matter!"

"You say that now. Later it would matter to you, dreadfully. I think I know you, my dear."

"Then you don't know me. We'll start fresh."

She sighed deeply. "You think that you love me, John?"

"Uh? Yes, I guess that's it."

"You loved Judith. Now you are hurt—so you think you love me."

"But— Oh, I don't know what love is! I know I want you to marry me and live with me."

"Neither do I know," she said so softly that I almost missed it. Then she moved into my arms as easily and naturally as if she had always lived there.

When we had finished kissing each other I said, "You will marry me, then?"

She threw her head back and stared as if she were frightened. "Oh, no!"

"Huh? But I thought—"

"No, dear, no! I'll keep your house and cook your food and make your bed—and sleep in it, if you want me to. But you don't need to marry me."

"But—Sheol! Maggie, I won't have it that way."

"You won't? We'll see." She was out of my arms although I had not let go. "I'll see you tonight. About one—after everyone is asleep. Leave your door unlatched."

"Maggie!" I shouted.

She was headed down the path, running as if she were flying. I tried to catch up, tripped on a stalagmite and fell. When I picked myself up she was out of sight.

Here is an odd thing—I had always thought of Maggie as quite tall, stately, almost as tall as I was. But when I held her in my arms, she was short. I had to lean way over to kiss her.

12

ON THE NIGHT of the Miracle all that were left of us gathered in the main communications room—my boss and myself, the chief of communications and his technical crew, a few staff officers. A handful of men and a few dozen women, too many to crowd into the comm shack, were in the main mess-hall where a relay screen had been rigged for them. Our underground city was a ghost town now, with only a skeleton crew to maintain communications for the commanding general; all the rest had gone to battle stations. We few who were left had no combat stations in this phase. Strategy had been settled; the hour of execution was set for us by the Miracle. Tactical decisions for a continent could not be made from headquarters and Huxley was too good a general to try. His troops had been disposed and his subordinate commanders were now on their own; all he could do was wait and pray.

All that we could do, too—I didn't have any fingernails left to bite.

The main screen in front of us showed, in brilliant color and perfect perspective, the interior of the Temple. The services had been going on all day—processional, hymns, prayers and more prayers, sacrifice, genuflexion, chanting, endless monotony of colorful ritual. My old regiment was drawn up in two frozen ranks, helmets shining, spears aligned like the teeth of a comb. I made out Peter van Eyck, Master of my home lodge, his belly corseted up, motionless before his platoon.

I knew, from having handled the despatch, that Master Peter had stolen a print of the film we had to have. His presence in the ceremonies was reassuring; had his theft even been suspected our plans could not possibly succeed. But there he was.

Around the other three walls of the comm room were a dozen smaller screens, scenes from as many major cities—crowds in Rittenhouse Square, the Hollywood Bowl jam-packed, throngs in local temples. In each case the eyes of all were riveted on a giant television screen showing the same scene in the Great Temple that we were watching. Throughout all America it would be the same—every mortal soul who could possibly manage it was watching some television screen somewhere—waiting, waiting, waiting for the Miracle of the Incarnation.

Behind us a psychoperator bent over a sensitive who worked under hypnosis. The sensitive, a girl about nineteen, stirred and muttered; the operator bent closer.

Then he turned to Huxley and the communications chief. "The Voice of God Station has been secured, sir."

Huxley merely nodded; I felt like turning handsprings, if my knees had not been so weak. This was the key tactic and one that could not possibly be executed until minutes before the Miracle. Since television moves only on line-of-sight or in its own special cable the only possible way to tamper with this nationwide broadcast was at the station of origin. I felt a wild burst of exultation at their success—followed by an equally sudden burst of sorrow, knowing that not one of them could hope to live out the night.

Never mind—if they could hold out for a few more minutes their lives would have counted. I commended their souls to the Great Architect. We had men for such jobs where needed, mostly brethren whose wives had faced an inquisitor.

The comm chief touched Huxley's sleeve. "It's coming, sir." The scene panned slowly up to the far end of the Temple, passed over the altar, and settled in close-up on an ivory archway above and behind the altar—the entrance to the Sanctum Sanctorum. It was closed with heavy cloth-of-gold drapes.

The pick-up camera held steady with the curtained entranceway exactly filling the screen. "They can take over any time now, sir."

Huxley turned his head to the psychoperator. "Is that ours yet? See if you can get a report from the Voice of God."

"Nothing, sir. I'll let you know."

I could not take my eyes off the screen. After an interminable wait, the curtains stirred and slowly parted, drawn up and out on each side—and there, standing before us almost life size and so real that I felt he could step out of the screen, was the Prophet Incarnate!

He turned his head, letting his gaze rove from side to side, then looked right at me, his eyes staring right into mine. I wanted to hide. I gasped and said involuntarily, "You mean we can duplicate *that?*"

The comm chief nodded. "To the millimeter, or I'll eat the difference. Our best impersonator, prepared by our best plastic surgeons. That may be our film already."

"But it's real."

Huxley glanced at me. "A little less talk, please, Lyle." It was the nearest he had ever come to bawling me out; I shut up and studied the screen. That powerful, totally unscrupulous face, that burning gaze—an actor? No! I knew that face; I had seen it too many times in too many ceremonies. Something had gone wrong and this was the Prophet Incarnate himself. I began to sweat that stinking sweat of fear. I very much believe that had he called me by name out of that screen I would have confessed my treasons and thrown myself on his mercy.

Huxley said crossly, "Can't you raise New Jerusalem?"

The psychoperator answered, "No, sir. I'm sorry, sir."

The Prophet started his invocation.

His compelling, organlike voice rolled through magnificent periods. Then he asked the blessings of Eternal God for the people this coming year. He paused, looked at me again, then rolled his eyes up to Heaven, lifted his hands and commenced his petition to the First Prophet, asking him to confer on his people the priceless bounty of seeing and hearing him in the flesh, and offering for that purpose the flesh of the present prophet as an instrument. He waited.

The transformation started—and my hackles stood up. I knew now that we had lost; something had gone wrong . . . and God alone knew how many men had died through the error.

The features of the Prophet began to change; he stretched an inch or two in height; his rich robes darkened—and there standing in his place, dressed in a frock coat of a bygone era, was the Reverend Nehemiah Scudder, First Prophet and founder of the New Crusade. I felt my stomach tighten with fear and dread and I was a little boy again, watching it for the first time in my parish church.

He spoke to us first with his usual yearly greeting of love and concern for his people. Gradually he worked himself up, his face sweating and his hands clutching in the style that had called down the Spirit in a thousand Mississippi Valley camp meetings; my heart began to beat faster. He was preaching against sin in all its forms—the harlot whose mouth is like honey, the sins of the flesh, the sins of the spirit, the money changers.

At the height of his passion he led into a new subject in a fashion that caught me by surprise: "But I did not return to you this day to speak to you of the little sins of little people. No! I come to tell you of a truly hellish thing and to bid you to gird on your armor and fight. Armageddon is upon you! Rise up, mine hosts, and fight you the Battle of the Lord! For

Satan is upon you! He is here! Here among you! Here tonight in the flesh! With the guile of the serpent he has come among you, taking on the form of the Vicar of the Lord! Yea! He has disguised himself falsely, taken on the shape of the *Prophet Incarnate!*

"Smite him! Smite his hirelings! In the Name of God destroy them all!"

13

"BRUEHLER FROM VOICE OF GOD," the psychoperator said quietly. "The station is now off the air and demolition will take place in approximately thirty seconds. An attempt will be made to beat a retreat before the building goes up. Good luck. Message ends."

Huxley muttered something and left the now-dark big screen. The smaller screens, monitoring scenes around the country, were confusing but heartening. There was fighting and rioting everywhere. I watched it, still stunned, and tried to figure out which was friend and which was foe. In the Hollywood Bowl the crowd boiled up over the stage and by sheer numbers overran and trampled the officials and clergy seated there. There were plenty of guards stationed around the edges of the bowl and it should not have happened that way. But instead of the murderous enfilading fire one would have expected, there was one short blast from a tripod mounted on the hillside northeast of the stage, then the guard was shot— apparently by another of the guards.

Apparently the chancy tour de force against the Prophet himself was succeeding beyond all expectations. If government forces were everywhere as disorganized as they were at the Hollywood Bowl, the job would not be one of fighting but of consolidating an accomplished fact.

The monitor from Hollywood went dead and I shifted to another screen, Portland, Oregon. More fighting. I could see men with white armbands, the only uniform we had allowed ourselves for M-Hour—but not all the violence came from our brethren in the armbands. I saw an armed proctor go down before bare fists and not get up.

Testing messages and early reports were beginning to come in, now that it was feasible to use our own radio—now that we had at long, long last shown our hand. I stopped looking and went back to help my boss keep track of them. I was still dazed and could still see in my mind the incredible face of the Prophet—both Prophets. If I had been emotionally battered by it, what did the people think? The devout, the believers?

The first clear-cut report other than contact messages was from Lucas in New Orleans:

HAVE TAKEN CONTROL OF CITY CENTER, POWER AND COMM STATIONS. MOP-UP SQUADS SEIZING WARD POLICE STATIONS. FEDERAL GUARDS HERE DEMORALIZED BY STEREOCAST. SPORADIC FIGHTING BROKE OUT AMONG GUARDS THEMSELVES. LITTLE ORGANIZED RESISTANCE. ESTABLISHING ORDER UNDER MARTIAL LAW. SO MOTE IT BE!—LUCAS.

Then reports started pouring in: Kansas City, Detroit, Philadelphia, Denver, Boston, Minneapolis—all the major cities. They varied but told the same story; our synthetic Prophet's call to arms, followed at once by a cutting of all regular methods of communication, had made of the government forces a body without a head, flopping around and fighting itself. The power of the Prophet was founded on superstition and fraud; we had turned superstition back on him to destroy him.

Lodge that night was the grandest I have ever attended. We tyled the communications room itself, with the comm chief sitting as secretary and passing incoming messages to General Huxley, sitting as Master in the east, as fast as they came in. I was called on to take a chair myself, Junior Warden, an honor I had never had before. The General had to borrow a hat and it was ridiculously too small for him, but it didn't matter—I have never seen ritual so grand, before or since. We all spake the ancient words from our hearts, as if we were saying them for the first time. If the stately progress was interrupted to hear that Louisville was ours, what better interruption? We were building anew; after an endless time of building in speculation we were at last building operatively.

14

TEMPORARY CAPITAL was set up at St. Louis, for its central location. I piloted Huxley there myself. We took over the Prophet's proctor base there, restoring to it its old name of Jefferson Barracks. We took over the buildings of the University, too, and handed back to it the name of Washington. If the people no longer recalled the true significance of those names, they soon would and here was a good place to start. (I learned for the first time that Washington had been one of us.)

However, one of Huxley's first acts as military governor—he would not let himself be called even "Provisional President"—was to divorce all official connection between the Lodge and the Free United States Army. The Brotherhood had served its purpose, had kept alive the hopes of free men; now it was time to go back to its ancient ways and let public affairs be handled publicly. The order was not made public, since the public had no real knowledge of us, always a secret society and for three generations a completely clandestine one. But it was read and recorded in all lodges and, so far as I know, honored.

There was one necessary exception: my home lodge at New Jerusalem and the cooperating sister order there of which Maggie had been a member. For we did not yet hold New Jerusalem although the country as a whole was ours.

This was more serious than it sounds. While we had the country under military control, with all communication centers in our hands, with the Federal Forces demoralized, routed, and largely dispersed or disarmed and captured, we did not hold the country's heart in our hands. More than half of the population were not with us; they were simply stunned, confused, and unorganized. As long as the Prophet was still alive, as long as the Temple was still a rallying point, it was still conceivably possible for him to snatch back the victory from us.

A fraud, such as we had used, has only a temporary effect; people revert to their old thinking habits. The Prophet and his cohorts were not fools; they included some of the shrewdest applied psychologists this tired planet has ever seen. Our own counterespionage became disturbingly aware that they were rapidly perfecting their own underground, using the still devout and that numerous minority, devout or not, who had waxed fat under the old regime and saw themselves growing leaner under the new. We could not stop this counterrevolution—Sheol! the Prophet had not been able to stop *us* and we had worked under much greater handicaps. The Prophet's spies could work almost openly in the smaller towns and the country; we had barely enough men to guard the television stations—we could not possibly put a snooper under every table.

Soon it was an open secret that we had faked the call to Armageddon. One would think that this fact in itself would show to anyone who knew it that *all* of the Miracles of Incarnation had been frauds—trick television and nothing more. I mentioned this to Zebadiah and got laughed at for being naive. People believe what they want to believe and logic has no bearing on it, he assured me. In this case they wanted to believe in their old time religion as they learned it at their mothers' knees; it restored security to their hearts. I could sympathize with that, I understood it.

In any case, New Jerusalem must fall—and time was against us.

While we were worrying over this, a provisional constitutional convention was being held in the great auditorium of the university. Huxley opened it, refused again the title, offered by acclamation, of president—then told them bluntly that all laws since the inauguration of President Nehemiah Scudder were of no force, void, and that the old constitution and bill of rights were effective as of now, subject to the exigencies of temporary military control. Their single purpose, he said, was to work out orderly methods of restoring the old free democratic processes; any permanent changes in the constitution, if needed, would have to wait until after free elections.

Then he turned the gavel over to Novak and left.

I did not have time for politics, but I hid out from work and caught most of one afternoon session because Zebadiah had tipped me off that significant fireworks were coming up. I slipped into a back seat and listened. One of Novak's bright young men was presenting a film. I saw the tail end of it only, but it seemed to be more or less a standard instruction film, reviewing the history of the United States, discussing civil liberty, explaining the duties of a citizen in a free democracy— not the sort of thing ever seen in the Prophet's schools but making use of the same techniques which had long been used in every school in the country. The film ended and the bright young man—I could never remember his name, perhaps because I disliked him. Stokes? Call him Stokes, anyway. Stokes began to speak.

"This reorientation film," he began, "is of course utterly useless in recanalizing an adult. His habits of thought are much too set to be affected by anything as simple as this."

"Then why waste our time with it?" someone called out.

"Please! Nevertheless this film was prepared for adults— provided the adult has been placed in a receptive frame of mind. Here is the prologue—" the screen lighted up again. It was a simple and beautiful pastoral scene with very restful music. I could not figure what he was getting at, but it was soothing; I remembered that I had not had much sleep the past four nights—come to think about it, I couldn't remember when I had had a good night's sleep. I slouched back and relaxed.

I didn't notice the change from scenery to abstract patterns. I think the music continued but it was joined by a voice, warm, soothing, monotonous. The patterns were going round and around and I was beginning to bore . . . right . . . into . . . the . . . screen.

Then Novak had left his chair and switched off the projector with a curse. I jerked awake with that horrid shocked feeling that makes one almost ready to cry. Novak was speaking sharply but quietly to Stokes—then Novak faced the rest of us. "Up on your feet!" he ordered. "Seventh inning stretch. Take a deep breath. Shake hands with the man next to you. Slap him on the back, hard!"

We did so and I felt foolish. Also irritated. I had felt so good just a moment before and now I was reminded of the mountain of work I must move if I were to have ten minutes with Maggie that evening. I thought about leaving but the b. y. m. had started talking again.

"As Dr. Novak has pointed out," he went on, not sounding quite so sure of himself, "it is not necessary to use the prologue on this audience, since you don't need reorientation. But this film, used with the preparatory technique and possibly in some cases with a light dose of one of the hypnotic drugs, can be depended on to produce an optimum political temperament in 83% of the populace. This has been demonstrated on a satisfactory test group. The film itself represents several years of work analyzing the personal conversion reports of almost everyone—surely everyone in this audience!—who joined our organization while it was still underground. The irrelevant has been eliminated; the essential has been abstracted. What remains will convert a devout follower of the Prophet to free manhood—provided he is in a state receptive to suggestion when he is exposed to it."

So *that* was why we had each been required to bare our souls. It seemed logical to me. God knew that we were sitting on a time bomb, and we couldn't wait for every lunk to fall in love with a holy deaconess and thereby be shocked out of his groove; there wasn't time. But an elderly man whom I did not know was on his feet on the other side of the hall—he looked like the pictures of Mark Twain, an angry Mark Twain. "Mr. Chairman!"

"Yes, comrade? State your name and district."

"You know what my name is, Novak—Winters, from Vermont. Did you okay this scheme?"

"No." It was a simple declarative.

"He's one of your boys."

"He's a free citizen. I supervised the preparation of the film itself and the research which preceded it. The use of null-vol suggestion techniques came from the research group he headed. I disapproved the proposal, but agreed to schedule time to present it. I repeat, he is a free citizen, free to speak, just as you are."

"May I speak now?"

"You have the floor."

The old man drew himself up and seemed to swell up. "I shall! Gentlemen . . . ladies . . . comrades! I have been in this for more than forty years—more years than that young pup has been alive. I have a brother, as good a man as I am, but we haven't spoken in many years—because he is honestly devout in the established faith and he suspects me of heresy. Now this cub, with his bulging forehead and his whirling lights, would 'condition' my brother to make him 'politically reliable.' "

He stopped to gasp asthmatically and went on. "Free men aren't 'conditioned!' Free men are free because they are ornery and cussed and prefer to arrive at their own prejudices in their own way—not have them spoonfed by a self-appointed mind tinkerer! We haven't fought, our brethren haven't bled and died, just to change bosses, no matter how sweet their motives. I tell you, we got into the mess we are in through the efforts of those same mind tinkerers. They've studied for years how to saddle a man and ride him. They started with advertising and propaganda and things like that, and they perfected it to the point where what used to be simple, honest swindling such as any salesman might use became a mathematical science that left the ordinary man helpless." He pointed his finger at Stokes. "I tell you that the American citizen needs no protection from anything—except the likes of him."

"This is ridiculous," Stokes snapped, his voice rather high. "You wouldn't turn high explosives over to children. That is what the franchise would be now."

"The American people are not children."

"They might as well be!—most of them."

Winters turned his eyes around the hall. "You see what I mean, friends? He's as ready to play God as the Prophet was. I say give 'em their freedom, give 'em their clear rights as men and free men and children under God. If they mess it up again, that's their doing—but we have no right to operate on their minds." He stopped and labored again to catch his breath; Stokes looked contemptuous. "We *can't* make the world safe for children, nor for men either—and God didn't appoint us to do it."

Novak said gently, "Are you through, Mr. Winters?"

"I'm through."

"And you've had *your* say, too, Stokes. Sit down."

Then I had to leave, so I slipped out—and missed what must have been a really dramatic event if you care for that sort of thing; I don't. Old Mr. Winters dropped dead about the time I must have been reaching the outer steps.

Novak did not let them recess on that account. They passed two resolutions; that no citizen should be subjected to hypnosis or other psychomanipulative technique without his written consent, and that no religious or political test should be used for franchise in the first elections.

I don't know who was right. It certainly would have made life easier in the next few weeks if we had known that the people were solidly behind us. Temporarily rulers we might be, but we hardly dared go down a street in uniform at night in groups of less than six.

Oh yes, we had uniforms now—almost enough for one for each of us, of the cheapest materials possible and in the standard army sizes, either too large or too small. Mine was too tight. They had been stockpiled across the Canadian border and we got our own people into uniform as quickly as possible. A handkerchief tied around the arm is not enough.

Besides our own simple powder-blue dungarees there were several other uniforms around, volunteer brigades from outside the country and some native American outfits. The Mormon Battalions had their own togs and they were all growing beards as well—they went into action singing the long-forbidden "Come, Come, Ye Saints!" Utah was one state we didn't have to worry about, now that the Saints had their beloved temple back. The Catholic Legion had its distinctive uniform, which was just as well since hardly any of them spoke English. The Onward Christian Soldiers dressed differently from us because they were a rival underground and rather resented our coup d'état—we should have waited. Joshua's Army from the pariah reservations in the northwest (plus volunteers from all over the world) had a get-up that can only be described as outlandish.

Huxley was in tactical command of them all. But it wasn't an army; it was a rabble.

The only thing that was hopeful about it was that the Prophet's army had not been large, less than two hundred thousand, more of an internal police than an army, and of that number only a few had managed to make their way back to New Jerusalem to augment the Palace garrison. Besides that, since the United States had not had an external war for more than a century, the Prophet could not recruit veteran soldiers from the remaining devout.

Neither could we. Most of our effectives were fit only to guard communication stations and other key installations around the country and we were hard put to find enough of them to do that. Mounting an assault on New Jerusalem called for scraping the bottom of the barrel.

Which we did, while smothering under a load of paperwork that made the days in the old GHQ seem quiet and untroubled. I had thirty clerks under me now and I don't know what half of them did. I spend a lot of my time just keeping Very

Important Citizens who Wanted to Help from getting in to see Huxley.

I recall one incident which, while not important, was not exactly routine and was important to me. My chief secretary came in with a very odd look on her face. "Colonel," she said, "your twin brother is out there."

"Eh? I have no brothers."

"A Sergeant Reeves," she amplified.

He came in, we shook hands, and exchanged inanities. I really was glad to see him and told him about all the orders I had sold and then lost for him. I apologized, pled exigency of war and added, "I landed one new account in K.C.—Emery, Bird, Thayer. You might pick it up some day."

"I will. Thanks."

"I didn't know you were a soldier."

"I'm not, really. But I've been practicing at it ever since my travel permit, uh—got itself lost."

"I'm sorry about that."

"Don't be. I've learned to handle a blaster and I'm pretty good with a grenade now. I've been okayed for Operation Strikeout."

"Eh? That code word is supposed to be confo."

"It is? Better tell the boys; they don't seem to realize it. Anyhow, I'm in. Are you? Or shouldn't I ask that?"

I changed the subject. "How do you like soldiering? Planning to make a career of it?"

"Oh, it's all right—but not *that* all right. But what I came in to ask you, Colonel, are *you?*"

"Eh?"

"Are you staying in the army afterwards? I suppose you can make a good thing out of it, with your background—whereas they wouldn't let me shine brightwork, once the fun is over. But if by any chance you aren't, what do you think of the textile business?"

I was startled but I answered, "Well, to tell the truth I rather enjoyed it—the selling end, at least."

"Good. I'm out of a job where I was, of course—and I've been seriously considering going in on my own, a jobbing business and manufacturers' representative. I'll need a partner. Eh?"

I thought it over. "I don't know," I said slowly. "I haven't thought ahead any farther than Operation Strikeout. I might

stay in the army—though soldiering does not have the appeal
for me it once had . . . too many copies to make out and
certify. But I don't know. I think what I really want is simply
to sit under my own vine and my own fig tree."

" '—and none shall make you afraid,' " he finished. "A
good thought. But there is no reason why you shouldn't unroll
a few bolts of cloth while you are sitting there. The fig crop
might fail. Think it over."

"I will. I surely will."

15

MAGGIE AND I were married the day before the assault on
New Jerusalem. We had a twenty-minute honeymoon, holding
hands on the fire escape outside my office, then I flew Huxley
to the jump-off area. I was in the flagship during the attack. I
had asked permission to pilot a rocket-jet as my combat assignment but he had turned me down.

"What for, John?" he had asked. "This isn't going to be
won in the air; it will be settled on the ground."

He was right, as usual. We had few ships and still fewer pilots who could be trusted. Some of the Prophet's air force
had been sabotaged on the ground; a goodly number had escaped to Canada and elsewhere and been interned. With what
planes we had we had been bombing the Palace and Temple
regularly, just to make them keep their heads down.

But we could not hurt them seriously that way and both
sides knew it. The Palace, ornate as it was above ground, was
probably the strongest bomb-proof ever built. It had been designed to stand direct impact of a fission bomb without damage to personnel in its deepest tunnels—and that was where
the Prophet was spending his days, one could be sure. Even
the part above ground was relatively immune to ordinary HE
bombs such as we were using.

We weren't using atomic bombs for three reasons: we
didn't have any; the United States was not known to have had
any since the Johannesburg Treaty after World War III. We
could not get any. We might have negotiated a couple of
bombs from the Federation had we been conceded to be the

legal government of the United States, but, while Canada had recognized us, Great Britain had not and neither had the North African Confederacy. Brazil was teetering; she had sent a chargé d'affaires to St. Louis. But even if we had actually been admitted to the Federation, it is most unlikely that a mass weapon would have been granted for an internal disorder.

Lastly, we would not have used one if it had been laid in our laps. No, we weren't chicken hearted. But an atom bomb, laid directly on the Palace, would certainly have killed around a hundred thousand or more of our fellow citizens in the surrounding city—and almost as certainly would not have killed the Prophet.

It was going to be necessary to go in and dig him out, like a holed-up badger.

Rendezvous was made on the east shore of the Delaware River. At one minute after midnight we moved east, thirty-four land cruisers, thirteen of them modern battlewagons, the rest light cruisers and obsolescent craft—all that remained of the Prophet's mighty East Mississippi fleet; the rest had been blown up by their former commanders. The heavy ships would be used to breach the walls; the light craft were escort to ten armored transports carrying the shock troops—five thousand fighting men hand-picked from the whole country. Some of them had had some military training in addition to what we had been able to give them in the past few weeks; all of them had taken part in the street fighting.

We could hear the bombing at New Jerusalem as we started out, the dull *Crrump!*, the gooseflesh shiver of the concussion wave, the bass rumble of the ground sonic. The bombing had been continuous the last thirty-six hours; we hoped that no one in the Palace had had any sleep lately, whereas our troops had just finished twelve hours impressed sleep.

None of the battlewagons had been designed as a flagship, so we had improvised a flag plot just abaft the conning tower, tearing out the long-range televisor to make room for the battle tracker and concentration plot. I was sweating over my jury-rigged tracker, hoping to Heaven that the makeshift shock absorbers would be good enough when we opened up. Crowded in behind me was a psychoperator and his crew of sensitives, eight women and a neurotic fourteen-year-old boy. In a pinch, each would have to handle four circuits. I wondered if they could do it. One thin blonde girl had a dry, chronic cough and a big thyroid patch on her throat.

We lumbered along in approach zigzag. Huxley wandered from comm to plot and back again, calm as a snail, looking over my shoulder, reading despatches casually, watching the progress of the approach on my screens.

The pile of despatches at my elbow grew. The *Cherub* had fouled her starboard tread; she had dropped out of formation but would rejoin in thirty minutes. Penoyer reported his columns extended and ready to deploy. Because of the acute shortage of command talent, we were using broad-command organization; Penoyer commanded the left wing and his own battlewagon; Huxley was force commander, right wing commander, and skipper of his own flagship.

At 12:32 the televisors went out. The enemy had analyzed our frequency variation pattern, matched us and blown every tube in the circuits. It is theoretically impossible; they did it. At 12:37 radio went out.

Huxley seemed unperturbed. "Shift to light-phone circuits," was all he said.

The communications officer had anticipated him; our audio circuits were now on infra-red beams, ship to ship. Huxley hung over my shoulder most of the next hour, watching the position plot lines grow. Presently he said, "I think we will deploy now, John. Some of those pilots aren't any too steady; I think we will give them time to settle down in their positions before anything more happens."

I passed the order and cut my tracker out of circuit for fifteen minutes; it wasn't built for so many variables at such high speeds and there was no sense in overloading it. Nineteen minutes later the last transport had checked in by phone, I made a preliminary set up, threw the starting switch and let the correction data feed in. For a couple of minutes I was very busy balancing data, my hands moving among knobs and keys; then the machine was satisfied with its own predictions and I reported, "Tracking, sir."

Huxley leaned over my shoulder. The line was a little ragged but I was proud of them—some of those pilots had been freighter jacks not four weeks earlier.

At three A.M. we made the precautionary signal, "Coming on the range," and our own turret rumbled as they loaded it.

At 3:31 Huxley gave the command, "Concentration Plan III, open fire."

Our own big fellow let go. The first shot shook loose a lot of dust and made my eyes water. The craft rolled back on her treads to the recoil and I nearly fell out of my saddle. I had never ridden one of the big booster guns before and I hadn't expected the long recoil. Our big rifle had secondary firing chambers up the barrel, electronically synchronized with the progress of the shell; it maintained max pressure all the way up and gave a much higher muzzle velocity and striking power. It also gave a bone-shaking recoil. But the second time I was ready for it.

Huxley was at the periscope between shots, trying to observe the effects of our fire. New Jerusalem had answered our fire but did not yet have us ranged. We had the advantage of firing at a stationary target whose range we knew to the meter; on the other hand even a heavy land cruiser could not show the weight of armor that underlay the Palace's gingerbread.

Huxley turned from the scope and remarked, "Smoke, John."

I turned to the communications officer. "Stand by, sensitives; all craft!"

The order never got through. Even as I gave it the comm officer reported loss of contact. But the psychoperator was already busy and I knew the same thing was happening in all the ships; it was normal casualty routine.

Of our nine sensitives, three—the boy and two women—were wide-awakes; the other six were hypnos. The technician hooked the boy first to one in Penoyer's craft. The kid established rapport almost at once and Penoyer got through a report:

"BLANKETED BY SMOKE. HAVE SHIFTED LEFT WING TO PSYCHO. WHAT HOOK-UP?—PENOYER."

I answered, "Pass down the line." Doctrine permitted two types of telepathic hook-up: relay, in which a message would be passed along until it reached its destination; and command mesh, in which there was direct hookup from flag to each ship under that flag, plus ship-to-ship for adjacent units. In the first case each sensitive carries just one circuit, that is, is in rapport with just one other telepath; in the second they might have to handle as many as four circuits. I wanted to hold off overloading them as long as possible.

The technician tied the other two wide-awakes into our flanking craft in the battle line, then turned his attention to the hypnos. Four of them required hypodermics; the other two went under in response to suggestion. Shortly we were hooked up with the transports and second-line craft, as well as with the bombers and the rocket-jet spotting the fall of shot. The jet reported visibility zero and complained that he wasn't getting anything intelligible by radar. I told him to stand by; the morning breeze might clear the smoke away presently.

We weren't dependent on him anyway; we knew our positions almost to the inch. We had taken departure from a benchmark and our deadreckoning was checked for the whole battle line every time any skipper identified a map-shown landmark. In addition, the deadreckoners of a tread-driven cruiser are surprisingly accurate; the treads literally measure every yard of ground as they pass over it and a little differential gadget compares the treads and keeps just as careful track of direction. The smoke did not really bother us and we could keep on firing accurately even if radar failed. On the other hand, if the Palace commander kept us in smoke he himself was entirely dependent on radar.

His radar was apparently working; shot was falling all around us. We hadn't been hit yet but we could feel the concussions when shells struck near us and some of the reports were not cheerful. Penoyer reported the *Martyr* hit; the shell had ruptured her starboard engine room. The skipper had tried to cross connect and proceed at half speed, but the gear train was jammed; she was definitely out of action. The *Archangel* had overheated her gun. She was in formation but would be harmless until the turret captain got her straightened out.

Huxley ordered them to shift to Formation E, a plan which used changing speeds and apparently random courses—carefully planned to avoid collision between ships, however. It was intended to confuse the fire control of the enemy.

At 4:11 Huxley sent the bombers back to base. We were inside the city now and the walls of the Palace lay just beyond —too close to target for comfort; we didn't want to lose ships to our own bombs.

At 4:17 we were struck. The port upper tread casing was split, the barbette was damaged so that the gun would no longer train, and the conning tower was cracked along its after surface. The pilot was killed at his controls.

I helped the psychoperator get gas helmets over the heads

of the hypnos. Huxley picked himself up off the floor plates, put on his own helmet, and studied the set-up on my battle tracker, frozen at the instant the shell hit us.

"The *Benison* should pass by this point in three minutes, John. Tell them to proceed dead slow. come along starboard side, and pick us up. Tell Penoyer I am shifting my flag."

We made the transfer without mishap, Huxley, myself, the psychoperator, and his sensitives. One sensitive was dead, killed by a flying splinter. One went into a deep trance and we could not rouse her. We left her in the disabled battlewagon; she was as safe there as she could be.

I had torn the current plot from my tracker and brought it along. It had the time-predicted plots for Formation E. We would have to struggle along with those, as the tracker could not be moved and was probably beyond casual repair in any case. Huxley studied the chart.

"Shift to full communication mesh, John. I plan to assault shortly."

I helped the psychoperator get his circuits straightened out. By dropping the *Martyr* out entirely and by using "Pass down the line" on Penoyer's auxiliaries, we made up for the loss of two sensitives. All carried four circuits now, except the boy who had five, and the girl with the cough, who was managing six. The psychoperator was worried but there was nothing to do about it.

I turned back to General Huxley. He had seated himself and at first I thought he was in deep thought; then I saw that he was unconscious. It was not until I tried to rouse him and failed that I saw the blood seeping down the support column of his chair and wetting floor plates. I moved him gently and found, sticking out from between his ribs near his spine, a steel splinter.

I felt a touch at my elbow, it was the psychoperator. "Penoyer reports that he will be within assault radius in four minutes. Requests permission to change formation and asks time of execution."

Huxley was out. Dead or wounded, he would fight no more this battle. By all rules, command devolved on Penoyer, and I should tell him so at once. But time was pressing hard, it would involve a drastic change of set-up, and we had been forced to send Penoyer into battle with only three sensitives. It was a physical impossibility.

What should I do? Turn the flag over to the skipper of the

Benison? I knew the man, stolid, unimaginative, a gunner by disposition. He was not even in his conning tower but had been fighting his ship from the fire control station in the turret. If I called him down here, he would take many minutes to comprehend the situation—and then give the wrong orders.

With Huxley out I had not an ounce of real authority. I was a brevet short-tailed colonel, only days up from major and a legate by rights; I was what I was as Huxley's flunky. Should I turn command over to Penoyer—and lose the battle with proper military protocol? *What would Huxley have me do, if he could make the decision?*

It seemed to me that I worried that problem for an hour. The chronograph showed thirteen seconds between reception of Penoyer's despatch and my answer:

"Change formation at will. Stand by for execution signal in six minutes." The order given, I sent word to the forward dressing station to attend to the General.

I shifted the right wing to assault echelon, then called the transport *Sweet Chariot*: "Sub-plan D; leave formation and proceed on duty assigned." The psychoperator eyed me but transmitted my orders. Sub-plan D called for five hundred light infantry to enter the Palace through the basement of the department store that was connected with the lodge room. From the lodge room they would split into squads and proceed on assigned tasks. All of our shock troops had all the plans of the Palace graven into their brains; these five hundred had had additional drill as to just where they were to go, what they were to do.

Most of them would be killed, but they should be able to create confusion during the assault. Zeb had trained them and now commanded them.

We were ready. "All units, stand by to assault. Right wing, outer flank of right bastion; left wing, outer flank of left bastion. Zigzag emergency full speed until within assault distance. Deploy for full concentration fire, one salvo, and assault. Stand by to execute. Acknowledge."

The acknowledgments were coming in and I was watching my chronometer preparatory to giving the command of execution when the boy sensitive broke off in the middle of a report and shook himself. The technician grabbed the kid's wrist and felt for his pulse; the boy shook him off.

"Somebody new," he said. "I don't quite get it." Then he commenced in a sing-song, "To commanding general from

Lodge Master Peter van Eyck: assault center bastion with full
force. I will create a diversion."

"Why the center?" I asked.

"It is much more damaged."

If this were authentic, it was crucially important. But I was
suspicious. If Master Peter had been detected, it was a trap.
And I didn't see how he, in his position, had been able to set
up a sensitive circuit in the midst of battle.

"Give me the word," I said.

"Nay, you give me."

"Nay, I will not."

"I will spell it, or halve it."

"Spell it, then."

We did so. I was satisfied. "Cancel last signal. Heavy cruisers assault center bastion, left wing to left flank, right wing
to right flank. Odd numbered auxiliaries make diversion assaults on right and left bastions. Even numbers remain with
transports. Acknowledge."

Nineteen seconds later I gave the command to execute,
then we were off. It was like riding a rocket plane with a
dirty, over-heated firing chamber. We crashed through walls
of masonry, lurched sickeningly on turns, almost overturned
when we crashed into the basement of some large demolished
building and lumbered out again. It was out of my hands
now, up to each skipper.

As we slewed into firing position, I saw the psychoperator
peeling back the boy's eyelids. "I'm afraid he's gone," he said
tonelessly. "I had to overload him too much on that last
hook-up." Two more of the women had collapsed.

Our big gun cut loose for the final salvo; we waited for an
interminable period—all of ten seconds. Then we were moving, gathering speed as we rolled. The *Benison* hit the Palace
wall with a blow that I thought would wreck her, but she did
not mount. But the pilot had his forward hydraulic jacks
down as soon as we hit; her bow reared slowly up. We
reached an angle so steep that it seemed she must turn turtle,
then the treads took hold, we ground forward and slid
through the breach in the wall.

Our gun spoke again, at point-blank range, right into the
inner Palace. A thought flashed through my head—this was
the exact spot where I had first laid eyes on Judith. I had
come full circle.

The *Benison* was rampaging around, destroying by her very

weight. I waited until the last cruiser had had time to enter, then gave the order, "Transports, assault." That done, I called Penoyer, informed him that Huxley was wounded and that he was now in command.

I was all through. I did not even have a job, a battle station. The battle surged around me, but I was not part of it—I, who two minutes ago had been in usurped full command.

I stopped to light a cigarette and wondered what to do with myself. I put it out after one soul-satisfying drag and scrambled up into the fire control tower of the turret and peered out the after slits. A breeze had come up and the smoke was clearing; the transport *Jacob's Ladder* I could see just pulling out of the breach. Her sides fell away and ranks of infantry sprang out, blasters ready. A sporadic fire met them; some fell but most returned the fire and charged the inner Palace. The *Jacob's Ladder* cleared the breach and the *Ark* took her place.

The troops commander in the *Ark* had orders to take the Prophet alive. I hurried down ladders from the turret, ran down the passageway between the engine rooms, and located the escape hatch in the floor plates, clear at the stern of the *Benison*. Somehow I got it unclamped, swung up the hatch cover, and stuck my head down. I could see men running, out beyond the treads. I drew my blaster, dropped to the ground, and tried to catch up with them, running out the stern between the big treads.

They were men from the *Ark*, right enough. I attached myself to a platoon and trotted along with them. We swarmed into the inner Palace.

But the battle was over; we encountered no organized resistance. We went on down and down and down and found the Prophet's bombproof. The door was open and he was there.

But we did not arrest him. The Virgins had gotten to him first; he no longer looked imperious. They had left him barely something to identify at an inquest.

Coventry

"HAVE YOU ANYTHING to say before sentence is pronounced on you?" The mild eyes of the Senior Judge studied the face of the accused. His question was answered by a sullen silence.

"Very well—the jury has determined that you have violated a basic custom agreed to under the Covenant, and that through this act did damage another free citizen. It is the opinion of the jury and of the court that you did so knowingly, and aware of the probability of damage to a free citizen. Therefore, you are sentenced to choose between the Two Alternatives."

A trained observer might have detected a trace of dismay breaking through the mask of indifference with which the young man had faced his trial. Dismay was unreasonable; in view of his offence, the sentence was inevitable—but reasonable men do not receive the sentence.

After waiting a decent interval, the judge turned to the bailiff. "Take him away."

The prisoner stood up suddenly, knocking over his chair. He glared wildly around at the company assembled and burst into speech.

"Hold on!" he yelled. "I've got something to say first!" In spite of his rough manner there was about him the noble dignity of a wild animal at bay. He stared at those around him, breathing heavily, as if they were dogs waiting to drag him down.

"Well?" he demanded, "Well? Do I get to talk, or don't I? It 'ud be the best joke of this whole comedy, if a condemned man couldn't speak his mind at the last!"

"You may speak," the Senior Judge told him, in the same unhurried tones with which he had pronounced sentence, "David MacKinnon, as long as you like, and in any manner that you like. There is no limit to that freedom, even for those who have broken the Covenant. Please speak into the recorder."

MacKinnon glanced with distaste at the microphone near his face. The knowledge that any word he spoke would be recorded and analyzed inhibited him. "I don't ask for records," he snapped.

"But we must have them," the judge replied patiently, "in order that others may determine whether, or not, we have dealt with you fairly, and according to the Covenant. Oblige us, please."

"Oh—very well!" He ungraciously conceded the requirement and directed his voice toward the instrument. "There's no sense in me talking at all—but, just the same, I'm going to talk and you're going to listen. . . . You talk about your precious 'Covenant' as if it were something holy. I don't agree to it and I don't accept it. You act as if it had been sent down from Heaven in a burst of light. My grandfathers fought in the Second Revolution—but they fought to abolish superstition . . . not to let sheep-minded fools set up new ones.

"There were men in those days!" He looked contemptuously around him. "What is there left today? Cautious, compromising 'safe' weaklings with water in their veins. You've planned your whole world so carefully that you've planned the fun and zest right out of it. Nobody is ever hungry, nobody ever gets hurt. Your ships can't crack up and your crops can't fail. You even have the weather tamed so it rains politely—after midnight. Why wait till midnight, I don't know . . . you all go to bed at nine o'clock!

"If one of you safe little people *should* have an unpleasant emotion—perish the thought!—you'd trot right over to the nearest psychodynamics clinic and get your soft little minds readjusted. Thank God I never succumbed to that dope habit. I'll keep my own feelings, thanks, no matter how bad they taste.

"You won't even make love without consulting a psychotechnician— Is her mind as flat and insipid as mine? Is there any emotional instability in her family? It's enough to make a man gag. As for fighting over a woman—if any one had the guts to do that, he'd find a proctor at his elbow in two minutes, looking for the most convenient place to paralyze him, and inquiring with sickening humility, 'May I do you a service, sir?' "

The bailiff edged closer to MacKinnon. He turned on him. "Stand back, you. I'm not through yet." He turned and added, "You've told me to choose between the Two Alternatives. Well, it's no hard choice for me. Before I'd submit to treatment, before I'd enter one of your neat little, safe little, pleasant little reorientation homes and let my mind be pried into by a lot of soft-fingered doctors—before I did anything like that, I'd choose a nice, clean death. Oh, no—there is just one choice for me, not two. I take the choice of going to Coventry—and glad of it, too . . . I hope I never hear of the United States again!

"But there is just one thing I want to ask you before I go—Why do you bother to live anyhow? I would think that anyone of you would welcome an end to your silly, futile lives just from sheer boredom. That's all." He turned back to the bailiff. "Come on, you."

"One moment, David MacKinnon." The Senior Judge held up a restraining hand. "We have listened to you. Although custom does not compel it, I am minded to answer some of your statements. Will you listen?"

Unwilling, but less willing to appear loutish in the face of a request so obviously reasonable, the younger man consented.

The judge commenced to speak in gentle, scholarly words appropriate to a lecture room. "David MacKinnon, you have spoken in a fashion that doubtless seems wise to you. Nevertheless, your words were wild, and spoken in haste. I am moved to correct your obvious misstatements of fact. The Covenant is not a superstition, but a simple temporal contract entered into by those same revolutionists for pragmatic reasons. They wished to insure the maximum possible liberty for every person.

"You yourself have enjoyed that liberty. No possible act, nor mode of conduct, was forbidden to you, as long as your action did not damage another. Even an act specifically prohibited by law could not be held against you, unless the state was able to prove that your particular act damaged, or caused evident danger of damage, to a particular individual.

"Even if one should willfully and knowingly damage another—as you have done—the state does not attempt to sit in moral judgment, nor to punish. We have not the wisdom to do that, and the chain of injustices that have always followed such moralistic coercion endanger the liberty of all. Instead, the convicted is given the choice of submitting to psychological readjustment to correct his tendency to wish to damage others, or of having the state withdraw itself from him—of sending him to Coventry.

"You complain that our way of living is dull and unromantic, and imply that we have deprived you of excitement to which you feel entitled. You are free to hold and express your esthetic opinion of our way of living, but you must not expect us to live to suit your tastes. You are free to seek danger and adventure if you wish—there is danger still in experimental laboratories; there is hardship in the mountains of the Moon, and death in the jungles of Venus—but you are not free to expose us to the violence of your nature."

"Why make so much of it?" MacKinnon protested contemptuously. "You talk as if I had committed a murder—I simply punched a man in the nose for offending me outrageously!"

"I agree with your esthetic judgment of that individual," the judge continued calmly, "and am personally rather gratified that you took a punch at him—but your psychometrical tests show that you believe yourself capable of judging morally your fellow citizens and feel justified in personally correcting and punishing their lapses. You are a dangerous individual, David MacKinnon, a danger to all of us, for we can not predict what damage you may do next. From a social standpoint, your delusion makes you as mad as the March Hare.

"You refuse treatment—therefore we withdraw our society from you, we cast you out, we divorce you. To Coventry with you." He turned to the bailiff. "Take him away."

MacKinnon peered out of a forward port of the big transport helicopter with repressed excitement in his heart. There! That must be it—that black band in the distance. The helicopter drew closer, and he became certain that he was seeing the Barrier—the mysterious, impenetrable wall that divided the United States from the reservation known as Coventry.

His guard looked up from the magazine he was reading and followed his gaze. "Nearly there, I see," he said pleasantly. "Well, it won't be long now."

"It can't be any too soon for me!"

The guard looked at him quizzically, but with tolerance. "Pretty anxious to get on with it, eh?"

MacKinnon held his head high. "You've never brought a man to the Gateway who was more anxious to pass through!"

"Mmm—maybe. They all say that, you know. Nobody goes through the Gate against his own will."

"I mean it!"

"They all do. Some of them come back, just the same."

"Say—maybe you can give me some dope as to conditions inside?"

"Sorry," the guard said, shaking his head, "but that is no concern of the United States, nor of any of its employees. You'll know soon enough."

MacKinnon frowned a little. "It seems strange—I tried inquiring, but found no one who would admit that they had any notion about the inside. And yet you say that some come out. Surely some of them must talk. . . ."

"That's simple," smiled the guard, "part of their reorientation is a subconscious compulsion not to discuss their experiences."

"That's a pretty scabby trick. Why should the government deliberately conspire to prevent me, and people like me, from knowing what we are going up against?"

"Listen, buddy," the guard answered, with mild exasperation, "you've told the rest of us to go to the devil. You've told us that you could get along without us. You are being given plenty of living room in some of the best land on this continent, and you are being allowed to take with you everything that you own, or your credit could buy. What the deuce else do you expect?"

MacKinnon's face settled in obstinate lines. "What assurance have I that there will be any land left for me?"

"That's your problem. The government sees to it that there is plenty of land for the population. The divvy-up is something you rugged individualists have to settle among yourselves. You've turned down our type of social cooperation; why should you expect the safeguards of our organization?" The guard turned back to his reading and ignored him.

They landed on a small field which lay close under the blank black wall. No gate was apparent, but a guardhouse was located at the side of the field. MacKinnon was the only passenger. While his escort went over to the guardhouse, he descended from the passenger compartment and went around to the freight hold. Two members of the crew were letting down a ramp from the cargo port. When he appeared, one of them eyed him, and said, "Okay, there's your stuff. Help yourself."

He sized up the job, and said, "It's quite a lot, isn't it? I'll need some help. Will you give me a hand with it?"

The crew member addressed paused to light a cigarette before replying, "It's your stuff. If you want it, get it out. We take off in ten minutes." The two walked around him and re-entered the ship.

"Why, you—" MacKinnon shut up and kept the rest of his anger to himself. The surly louts! Gone was the faintest trace of regret at leaving civilization. He'd show them! He could get along without them.

But it was twenty minutes and more before he stood beside his heaped up belongings and watched the ship rise. Fortunately the skipper had not been adamant about the time limit. He turned and commenced loading his steel tortoise. Under the romantic influence of the classic literature of a bygone day he had considered using a string of burros, but had been unable to find a zoo that would sell them to him. It was just as well—he was completely ignorant of the limits, foibles, habits, vices, illnesses, and care of those useful little beasts, and unaware of his own ignorance. Master and servant would have vied in making each other unhappy.

The vehicle he had chosen was not an unreasonable substitute for burros. It was extremely rugged, easy to operate, and almost fool-proof. It drew its power from six square yards of sunpower screens on its low curved roof. These drove a constant-load motor, or, when halted, replenished the storage battery against cloudy weather, or night travel. The bearings were "everlasting," and every moving part, other than the caterpillar treads and the controls, were sealed up, secure from inexpert tinkering.

It could maintain a steady six miles per hour on smooth, level pavement. When confronted by hills, or rough terrain, it did not stop, but simply slowed until the task demanded equalled its steady power output.

The steel tortoise gave MacKinnon a feeling of Crusoe-like independence. It did not occur to him his chattel was the end product of the cumulative effort and intelligent co-operation of hundreds of thousands of men, living and dead. He had been used all his life to the unfailing service of much more intricate machinery, and honestly regarded the tortoise as a piece of equipment of the same primitive level as a woodsman's axe, or a hunting knife. His talents had been devoted in the past to literary criticism rather than engineering, but that did not prevent him from believing that his native intelligence and the aid of a few reference books would be all that he would really need to duplicate the tortoise, if necessary.

Metal ores were necessary, he knew, but saw no obstacle in that, his knowledge of the difficulties of prospecting, mining, and metallurgy being as sketchy as his knowledge of burros.

His goods filled every compartment of the compact little freighter. He checked the last item from his inventory and ran a satisfied eye down the list. Any explorer or adventurer of the past might well be pleased with such equipment, he thought. He could imagine showing Jack London his knockdown cabin. See, Jack, he would say, it's proof against any kind of weather—perfectly insulated walls and floor—and can't rust. It's so light that you can set it up in five minutes by yourself, yet it's so strong that you can sleep sound with the biggest grizzly in the world snuffling right outside your door.

And London would scratch his head, and say, Dave, you're a wonder. If I'd had that in the Yukon, it would have been a cinch!

He checked over the list again. Enough concentrated and desiccated food and vitamin concentrates to last six months. That would give him time enough to build hothouses for hydroponics, and get his seeds started. Medical supplies—he did not expect to need those, but foresight was always best. Reference books of all sorts. A light sporting rifle—vintage: last century. His face clouded a little at this. The War Department had positively refused to sell him a portable blaster. When he had claimed the right of common social heritage, they had grudgingly provided him with the plans and specifications, and told him to build his own. Well, he would, the first spare time he got.

Everything else was in order. MacKinnon climbed into the cockpit, grasped the two hand controls, and swung the nose of the tortoise toward the guardhouse. He had been ignored since the ship had landed; he wanted to have the gate opened and to leave.

Several soldiers were gathered around the guardhouse. He picked out a legate by the silver stripe down the side of his kilt and spoke to him. "I'm ready to leave. Will you kindly open the Gate?"

"Okay," the officer answered him, and turned to a soldier who wore the plain grey kilt of a private's field uniform. "Jenkins, tell the power house to dilate—about a number three opening, tell them," he added, sizing up the dimensions of the tortoise.

He turned to MacKinnon. "It is my duty to tell you that you may return to civilization, even now, by agreeing to be hospitalized for your neurosis."

"I have no neurosis!"

"Very well. If you change your mind at any future time, return to the place where you entered. There is an alarm there with which you may signal to the guard that you wish the gate opened."

"I can't imagine needing to know that."

The legate shrugged. "Perhaps not—but we send refugees to quarantine all the time. If I were making the rules, it might be harder to get out again." He was cut off by the ringing of an alarm. The soldiers near them moved smartly away, drawing their blasters from their belts as they ran. The ugly snout of a fixed blaster poked out over the top of the guardhouse and pointed toward the Barrier.

The legate answered the question on MacKinnon's face. "The power house is ready to open up." He waved smartly toward that building, then turned back. "Drive straight through the center of the opening. It takes a lot of power to suspend the stasis; if you touch the edge, we'll have to pick up the pieces."

A tiny, bright dot appeared in the foot of the barrier opposite where they waited. It spread into a half circle across the lampblack nothingness. Now it was large enough for MacKinnon to see the countryside beyond through the arch it had formed. He peered eagerly.

The opening grew until it was twenty feet wide, then stopped. It framed a scene of rugged, barren hills. He took this in, and turned angrily on the legate. "I've been tricked!" he exclaimed. "That's not fit land to support a man."

"Don't be hasty," he told MacKinnon. "There's good land beyond. Besides—you don't have to enter. But if you are going, go!"

MacKinnon flushed, and pulled back on both hand controls. The treads bit in and the tortoise lumbered away, straight for the Gateway to Coventry.

When he was several yards beyond the Gate, he glanced back. The Barrier loomed behind him, with nothing to show where the opening had been. There was a little sheetmetal shed adjacent to the point where he had passed through. He supposed that it contained the alarm the legate had mentioned, but he was not interested and turned his eyes back to his driving.

Stretching before him, twisting between rocky hills, was a road of sorts. It was not paved and the surface had not been repaired recently, but the grade averaged downhill and the tortoise was able to maintain a respectable speed. He continued down it, not because he fancied it, but because it was the only road which led out of surroundings obviously unsuited to his needs.

The road was untravelled. This suited him; he had no wish to encounter other human beings until he had located desirable land to settle on, and had staked out his claim. But the hills were not devoid of life; several times he caught glimpses of little dark shapes scurrying among the rocks, and occasionally bright, beady eyes stared back into his.

It did not occur to him at first that these timid little animals, streaking for cover at his coming, could replenish his larder—he was simply amused and warmed by their presence. When he did happen to consider that they might be used as food, the thought was at first repugnant to him—the custom of killing for "sport" had ceased to be customary long before his time; and inasmuch as the development of cheap synthetic proteins in the latter half of the preceding century had spelled the economic ruin of the business of breeding animals for slaughter, it is doubtful if he had ever tasted animal tissue in his life.

But once considered, it was logical to act. He expected to live off the country; although he had plenty of food on hand for the immediate future, it would be wise to conserve it by using what the country offered. He suppressed his esthetic distaste and ethical misgivings, and determined to shoot one of the little animals at the first opportunity.

Accordingly, he dug out the rifle, loaded it, and placed it handy. With the usual perversity of the world-as-it-is, no game was evident for the next half hour. He was passing a little shoulder of rocky outcropping when he saw his prey. It peeked at him from behind a small boulder, its sober eyes wary but unperturbed. He stopped the tortoise and took careful aim, resting and steadying the rifle on the side of the cockpit. His quarry accommodated him by hopping out into full view.

He pulled the trigger, involuntarily tensing his muscles and squinting his eyes as he did so. Naturally, the shot went high and to the right.

But he was much too busy just then to be aware of it. It seemed that the whole world had exploded. His right shoulder was numb, his mouth stung as if he had been kicked there, and his ears rang in a strange and unpleasant fashion. He was surprised to find the gun still intact in his hands and apparently none the worse for the incident.

He put it down, clambered out of the car, and rushed up to where the small creature had been. There was no sign of it anywhere. He searched the immediate neighborhood, but did not find it. Mystified, he returned to his conveyance, having decided that the rifle was in some way defective, and that he should inspect it carefully before attempting to fire it again.

His recent target watched his actions cautiously from a vantage point yards away, to which it had stampeded at the sound of the shot. It was equally mystified by the startling events, being no more used to firearms than was MacKinnon.

Before he started the tortoise again, MacKinnon had to see to his upper lip, which was swollen and tender and bleeding from a deep scratch. This increased his conviction that the gun was defective. Nowhere in the romantic literature of the nineteenth and twentieth centuries, to which he was addicted, had there been a warning that, when firing a gun heavy enough to drop a man in his tracks, it is well not to hold the right hand in such a manner that the recoil will cause the right thumb and thumb nail to strike the mouth.

He applied an antiseptic and a dressing of sorts, and went on his way, somewhat subdued. The arroyo by which he had entered the hills had widened out, and the hills were greener. He passed around one sharp turn in the road, and found a broad fertile valley spread out before him. It stretched away until it was lost in the warm day's haze.

Much of the valley was cultivated, and he could make out human habitations. He continued toward it with mixed feelings. People meant fewer hardships, but it did not look as if staking out a claim would be as simple as he had hoped. However—Coventry was a big place.

He had reached the point where the road gave onto the floor of the valley, when two men stepped out into his path. They were carrying weapons of some sort at the ready. One of them called out to him:

"Halt!"

MacKinnon did so, and answered him as they came abreast. "What do you want?"

"Customs inspection. Pull over there by the office." He indicated a small building set back a few feet from the road, which MacKinnon had not previously noticed. He looked from it back to the spokesman, and felt a slow, unreasoning heat spread up from his viscera. It rendered his none too stable judgment still more unsound.

"What the deuce are you talking about?" he snapped. "Stand aside and let me pass."

The one who had remained silent raised his weapon and aimed it at MacKinnon's chest. The other grabbed his arm and pulled the weapon out of line. "Don't shoot the dumb fool, Joe," he said testily. "You're always too anxious." Then to MacKinnon, "You're resisting the law. Come on—be quick about it!"

"The law?" MacKinnon gave a bitter laugh and snatched his rifle up from the seat. It never reached his shoulder—the man who had done all the talking fired casually, without apparently taking time to aim. MacKinnon's rifle was smacked from his grasp and flew into the air, landing in the roadside ditch behind the tortoise.

The man who had remained silent followed the flight of the gun with detached interest, and remarked, "Nice shot, Blackie. Never touched him."

"Oh, just luck," the other demurred, but grinned his pleasure at the compliment. "Glad I didn't nick him, though—saves writing out a report." He reassumed an official manner, spoke again to MacKinnon, who had been sitting dumbfounded, rubbing his smarting hands. "Well, tough guy? Do you behave, or do we come up there and get you?"

MacKinnon gave in. He drove the tortoise to the designated spot, and waited sullenly for orders. "Get out and start unloading," he was told.

He obeyed, under compulsion. As he piled his precious possessions on the ground, the one addressed as Blackie separated the things into two piles, while Joe listed them on a printed form. He noticed presently that Joe listed only the items that went into the first pile. He understood this when Blackie told him to reload the tortoise with the items from that pile, and commenced himself to carry goods from the other pile into the building. He started to protest—

Joe punched him in the mouth, coolly and without rancor.

MacKinnon went down, but got up again, fighting. He was in such a blind rage that he would have tackled a charging rhino. Joe timed his rush, and clipped him again. This time he could not get up at once.

Blackie stepped over to a washstand in one corner of the office. He came back with a wet towel and chucked it at MacKinnon. "Wipe your face on that, bud, and get back in the buggy. We got to get going."

MacKinnon had time to do a lot of serious thinking as he drove Blackie into town Beyond a terse answer of "Prize court" to MacKinnon's inquiry as to their destination, Blackie did not converse, nor did MacKinnon press him, anxious as he was to have information His mouth pained him from repeated punishment, his head ached, and he was no longer tempted to precipitate action by hasty speech.

Evidently Coventry was not quite the frontier anarchy he had expected it to be. There was a government of sorts, apparently, but it resembled nothing that he had ever been used to. He had visualized a land of noble, independent spirits who gave each other wide berth and practised mutual respect. There would be villains, of course, but they would be treated to summary, and probably lethal, justice as quickly as they demonstrated their ugly natures. He had a strong, though subconscious, assumption that virtue is necessarily triumphant.

But having found government, he expected it to follow the general pattern that he had been used to all his life—honest, conscientious, reasonably efficient, and invariably careful of a citizen's rights and liberties. He was aware that government had not always been like that, but he had never experienced it —the idea was as remote and implausible as cannibalism, or chattel slavery.

Had he stopped to think about it, he might have realized that public servants in Coventry would never have been examined psychologically to determine their temperamental fitness for their duties, and, since every inhabitant of Coventry was there—as he was—for violating a basic custom and refusing treatment thereafter, it was a foregone conclusion that most of them would be erratic and arbitrary.

He pinned his hope on the knowledge that they were going to court. All he asked was a chance to tell his story to the judge.

His dependence on judicial procedure may appear inconsistent in view of how recently he had renounced all reliance on organized government, but while he could renounce government verbally, but he could not do away with a lifetime of environmental conditioning. He could curse the court that had humiliated him by condemning him to the Two Alternatives, but he expected courts to dispense justice. He could assert his own rugged independence, but he expected persons he encountered to behave as if they were bound by the Covenant—he had met no other sort. He was no more able to discard his past history than he would have been to discard his accustomed body.

But he did not know it yet.

MacKinnon failed to stand up when the judge entered the court room. Court attendants quickly set him right, but not before he had provoked a glare from the bench. The judge's appearance and manner were not reassuring. He was a well-fed man, of ruddy complexion, whose sadistic temper was evident in face and mien. They waited while he dealt drastically with several petty offenders. It seemed to MacKinnon, as he listened, that almost everything was against the law.

Nevertheless, he was relieved when his name was called. He stepped up and undertook at once to tell his story. The judge's gavel cut him short.

"What is this case?" the judge demanded, his face set in grim lines. "Drunk and disorderly, apparently. I shall put a stop to this slackness among the young if it takes the last ounce of strength in my body!" He turned to the clerk. "Any previous offences?"

The clerk whispered in his ear. The judge threw MacKinnon a look of mixed annoyance and suspicion, then told the customs' guard to come forward. Blackie told a clear, straightforward tale with the ease of a man used to giving testimony. MacKinnon's condition was attributed to resisting an officer in the execution of his duty. He submitted the inventory his colleague had prepared, but failed to mention the large quantity of goods which had been abstracted before the inventory was made.

The judge turned to MacKinnon. "Do you have anything to say for yourself?"

"I certainly have, Doctor," he began eagerly. "There isn't a word of—"

Bang! The gavel cut him short. A court attendant hurried to MacKinnon's side and attempted to explain to him the proper form to use in addressing the court. The explanation confused him. In his experience, "judge" naturally implied a medical man—a psychiatrist skilled in social problems. Nor had he heard of any special speech forms appropriate to a courtroom. But he amended his language as instructed.

"May it please the Honorable Court, this man is lying. He and his companion assaulted and robbed me. I was simply—"

"Smugglers generally think they are being robbed when customs officials catch them," the judge sneered. "Do you deny that you attempted to resist inspection?"

"No, Your Honor, but—"

"That will do. Penalty of fifty per cent is added to the established scale of duty. Pay the clerk."

"But, Your Honor, I can't—"

"Can't you pay it?"

"I haven't any money. I have only my possessions."

"So?" He turned to the clerk. "Condemnation proceedings. Impound his goods. Ten days for vagrancy. The community can't have these immigrant paupers roaming at large, and preying on law-abiding citizens. Next case!"

They hustled him away. It took the sound of a key grating in a barred door behind him to make him realize his predicament.

"Hi, pal, how's the weather outside?" The detention cell had a prior inmate, a small, well-knit man who looked up from a game of solitaire to address MacKinnon. He sat astraddle a bench on which he had spread his cards, and studied the newcomer with unworried. bright, beady eyes.

"Clear enough outside—but stormy in the courtroom," MacKinnon answered, trying to adopt the same bantering tone and not succeeding very well. His mouth hurt him and spoiled his grin.

The other swung a leg over the bench and approached him with a light, silent step. "Say, pal, you must 'a' caught that in a gear box," he commented, inspecting MacKinnon's mouth. "Does it hurt?"

"Like the devil," MacKinnon admitted.

"We'll have to do something about that." He went to the cell door and rattled it. "Hey! Lefty! The house is on fire! Come arunnin'!"

The guard sauntered down and stood opposite their cell door. "Wha' d'yuh want, Fader?" he said noncommittally.

"My old school chum has been slapped in the face with a wrench, and the pain is inordinate. Here's a chance for you to get right with Heaven by oozing down to the dispensary, snagging a dressing and about five grains of neoanodyne."

The guard's expression was not encouraging. The prisoner looked grieved. "Why, Lefty," he said, "I thought you would jump at a chance to do a little pure charity like that." He waited for a moment, then added, "Tell you what—you do it, and I'll show you how to work that puzzle about 'How old is Ann?' Is it a go?"

"Show me first."

"It would take too long. I'll write it out and give it to you."

When the guard returned, MacKinnon's cellmate dressed his wounds with gentle deftness, talking the while. "They call me Fader Magee. What's your name, pal?"

"David MacKinnon. I'm sorry, but I didn't quite catch your first name."

"Fader. It isn't," he explained with a grin, "the name my mother gave me. It's more a professional tribute to my shy and unobtrusive nature."

MacKinnon looked puzzled. "Professional tribute? What is your profession?"

Magee looked pained. "Why, Dave," he said, "I didn't ask *you* that. However," he went on, "it's probably the same as yours—self-preservation."

Magee was a sympathetic listener, and MacKinnon welcomed the chance to tell someone about his troubles. He related the story of how he had decided to enter Coventry rather than submit to the sentence of the court, and how he had hardly arrived when he was hijacked and hauled into court. Magee nodded. "I'm not surprised," he observed. "A man has to have larceny in his heart, or he wouldn't be a customs guard."

"But what happens to my belongings?"

"They auction them off to pay the duty."

"I wonder how much there will be left for me?"

Magee stared at him. "Left over? There won't be anything left over. You'll probably have to pay a deficiency judgment."

"Huh? What's that?"

"It's a device whereby the condemned pays for the execution," Magee explained succinctly, if somewhat obscurely. "What it means to you is that when your ten days is up, you'll still be in debt to the court. Then it's the chain gang for you, my lad—you'll work it off at a dollar a day."

"Fader—you're kidding me."

"Wait and see. You've got a lot to learn, Dave."

Coventry was an even more complex place than MacKinnon had gathered up to this time. Magee explained to him that there were actually three sovereign, independent jurisdictions. The jail where they were prisoners lay in the so-called New America. It had the forms of democratic government, but the treatment he had already received was a fair sample of the fashion in which it was administered.

"This place is heaven itself compared with the Free State," Magee maintained. "I've been there—" The Free State was an absolute dictatorship; the head man of the ruling clique was designated the "Liberator." Their watchwords were Duty and Obedience; an arbitrary discipline was enforced with a severity that left no room for any freedom of opinion. Governmental theory was vaguely derived from the old functionalist doctrines. The state was thought of as a single organism with a single head, a single brain, and a single purpose. Anything not compulsory was forbidden. "Honest so help me," claimed Magee, "you can't go to bed in that place without finding one of their damned secret police between the sheets."

"But at that," he continued, "it's an easier place to live than with the Angels."

"The Angels?"

"Sure. We still got 'em. Must have been two or three thousand die-hards that chose to go to Coventry after the Revolution—you know that. There's still a colony up in the hills to the north, complete with Prophet Incarnate and the works. They aren't bad hombres, but they'll pray you into heaven even if it kills you."

All three states had one curious characteristic in common —each one claimed to be the only legal government of the entire United States, and each looked forward to some future day when they would reclaim the "unredeemed" portion; i.e., outside Coventry. To the Angels, this was an event which would occur when the First Prophet returned to earth to lead them again. In New America it was hardly more than a convenient campaign plank, to be forgotten after each election. But in the Free State it was a fixed policy.

Pursuant to this purpose there had been a whole series of wars between the Free State and New America. The Liberator held, quite logically, that New America was an unredeemed section, and that it was necessary to bring it under the rule of the Free State before the advantages of their culture could be extended to the outside.

Magee's words demolished MacKinnon's dream of finding an anarchistic utopia within the barrier, but he could not let his fond illusion die without a protest. "But see here, Fader," he persisted, "isn't there some place where a man can live quietly by himself without all this insufferable interference?"

"No—" considered Fader, "no . . . not unless you took to the hills and hid. Then you 'ud be all right, as long as you steered clear of the Angels. But it would be pretty slim pickin's, living off the country. Ever tried it?"

"No . . . not exactly—but I've read all the classics: Zane Grey, and Emerson Hough, and so forth."

"Well . . . maybe you could do it. But if you really want to go off and be a hermit, you 'ud do better to try it on the Outside, where there aren't so many objections to it."

"No"—MacKinnon's backbone stiffened at once—"no, I'll never do that. I'll never submit to psychological reorientation just to have a chance to be let alone. If I could go back to where I was before a couple of months ago, before I was arrested, it might be all right to go off to the Rockies, or look up an abandoned farm somewhere . . . But with that diagnosis staring me in the face . . . after being told I wasn't fit for human society until I had had my emotions re-tailored to fit a cautious little pattern, I couldn't face it. Not if it meant going to a sanatarium—"

"I see," agreed Fader, nodding, "you want to go to Coventry, but you don't want the Barrier to shut you off from the rest of the world."

"No, that's not quite fair . . . Well, maybe, in a way. Say, you don't think I'm not fit to associate with, do you?"

"You look all right to me," Magee reassured him, with a grin, "but I'm in Coventry too, remember. Maybe I'm no judge."

"You don't talk as if you liked it much. Why are you here?"

Magee held up a gently admonishing finger. "Tut! Tut! That is the one question you must never ask a man here. You must assume that he came here because he knew how swell everything is here."

"Still . . . you don't seem to like it."

"I didn't say I didn't like it. I do like it; it has flavor. Its little incongruities are a source of innocent merriment. And anytime they turn on the heat I can always go back through the Gate and rest up for a while in a nice quiet hospital, until things quiet down."

MacKinnon was puzzled again. "Turn on the heat? Do they supply too hot weather here?"

"Huh? Oh, I didn't mean weather control—there isn't any of that here, except what leaks over from outside. I was just using an old figure of speech."

"What does it mean?"

Magee smiled to himself. "You'll find out."

After supper—bread, stew in a metal dish, a small apple—Magee introduced MacKinnon to the mysteries of cribbage. Fortunately, MacKinnon had no cash to lose. Presently Magee put the cards down without shuffling them. "Dave," he said, "are you enjoying the hospitality offered by this institution?"

"Hardly— Why?"

"I suggest that we check out."

"A good idea, but how?"

"That's what I've been thinking about. Do you suppose you could take another poke on that battered phiz of yours, in a good cause?"

MacKinnon cautiously fingered his face. "I suppose so—if necessary. It can't do me much more harm, anyhow."

"That's mother's little man! Now listen—this guard, Lefty, in addition to being kind o' unbright, is sensitive about his appearance. When they turn out the lights, you—"

"Let me out of here! Let me out of here!" MacKinnon beat on the bars and screamed. No answer came. He renewed the racket, his voice an hysterical falsetto. Lefty arrived to investigate, grumbling.

"What the hell's eating on you?" he demanded, peering through the bars.

MacKinnon changed to tearful petition. "Oh, Lefty, please let me out of here. Please! I can't stand the dark. It's dark in here—please don't leave me alone." He flung himself, sobbing, on the bars.

The guard cursed to himself. "Another slugnutty. Listen, you—shut up, and go to sleep, or I'll come in there, and give you something to yelp for!" He started to leave.

MacKinnon changed instantly to the vindictive, unpredictable anger of the irresponsible. "You big ugly baboon! You rat-faced idiot! Where'd you get that nose?"

Lefty turned back, fury in his face. He started to speak. MacKinnon cut him short. "Yah! Yah! Yah!" he gloated, like a nasty little boy, "Lefty's mother was scared by a wart-hog—"

The guard swung at the spot where MacKinnon's face was pressed between the bars of the door. MacKinnon ducked and grabbed simultaneously. Off balance at meeting no resistance, the guard rocked forward, thrusting his forearm between the bars. MacKinnon's fingers slid along his arm, and got a firm purchase on Lefty's wrist.

He threw himself backwards, dragging the guard with him, until Lefty was jammed up against the outside of the barred door, with one arm inside, to the wrist of which MacKinnon clung as if welded.

The yell which formed in Lefty's throat miscarried; Magee had already acted. Out of the darkness, silent as death, his slim hands had snaked between the bars and imbedded themselves in the guard's fleshy neck. Lefty heaved, and almost broke free, but MacKinnon threw his weight to the right and twisted the arm he gripped in an agonizing, bone-breaking leverage.

It seemed to MacKinnon that they remained thus, like some grotesque game of statues, for an endless period. His pulse pounded in his ears until he feared that it must be heard by others, and bring rescue to Lefty. Magee spoke at last:

"That's enough," he whispered. "Go through his pockets."

He made an awkward job of it, for his hands were numb and trembling from the strain, and it was anything but convenient to work between the bars. But the keys were there, in the last pocket he tried. He passed them to Magee, who let the guard slip to the floor, and accepted them.

Magee made a quick job of it. The door swung open with a distressing creak. Dave stepped over Lefty's body, but Magee kneeled down, unhooked a truncheon from the guard's belt, and cracked him behind the ear with it. MacKinnon paused.

"Did you kill him?" he asked.

"Cripes, no," Magee answered softly, "Lefty is a friend of mine. Let's go."

They hurried down the dimly lighted passageway between cells toward the door leading to the administrative offices—their only outlet. Lefty had carelessly left it ajar, and light shone through the crack, but as they silently approached it, they heard ponderous footsteps from the far side. Dave looked hurriedly for cover, but the best he could manage was to slink back into the corner formed by the cell block and the wall. He glanced around for Magee, but he had disappeared.

The door swung open; a man stepped through, paused, and looked around. MacKinnon saw that he was carrying a black-light, and wearing its complement—rectifying spectacles. He realized then that the darkness gave him no cover. The black-light swung his way; he tensed to spring—

He heard a dull *"clunk!"* The guard sighed, swayed gently, then collapsed into a loose pile. Magee stood over him, poised on the balls of his feet, and surveyed his work, while caressing the business end of the truncheon with the cupped fingers of his left hand.

"That will do," he decided. "Shall we go, Dave?"

He eased through the door without waiting for an answer; MacKinnon was close behind him. The lighted corridor led away to the right and ended in a large double door to the street. On the left wall, near the street door, a smaller office door stood open.

Magee drew MacKinnon to him. "It's a cinch," he whispered. "There'll be nobody in there now but the desk sergeant. We get past him, then out that door, and into the ozone—" He motioned Dave to keep behind him, and crept silently up to the office door. After drawing a small mirror from a pocket in his belt, he lay down on the floor, placed his head near the door frame, and cautiously extended the tiny mirror an inch or two past the edge.

Apparently he was satisfied with the reconnaissance the im-provised periscope afforded, for he drew himself back onto his knees and turned his head so that MacKinnon could see the words shaped by his silent lips. "It's all right," he breathed, "there is only—"

Two hundred pounds of uniformed nemesis landed on his shoulders. A clanging alarm sounded through the corridor. Magee went down fighting, but he was outclassed and caught off guard. He jerked his head free and shouted, "Run for it, kid!"

MacKinnon could hear running feet somewhere, but could see nothing but the struggling figures before him. He shook his head and shoulders like a dazed animal, then kicked the larger of the two contestants in the face. The man screamed and let go his hold. MacKinnon grasped his small companion by the scruff of the neck and hauled him roughly to his feet.

Magee's eyes were still merry. "Well played, my lad," he commended in clipped syllables, as they burst out the street door, "—if hardly cricket! Where did you learn *La Savate*?"

MacKinnon had not time to answer, being fully occupied in keeping up with Magee's weaving, deceptively rapid progress. They ducked across the street, down an alley, and between two buildings.

The succeeding minutes, or hours, were confusion to MacKinnon. He remembered afterwards crawling along a roof top and letting himself down to crouch in the blackness of an interior court, but he could not remember how they had gotten on the roof. He also recalled spending an interminable period alone, compressed inside a most unsavory refuse bin, and his terror when footsteps approached the bin and a light flashed through a crack.

A crash and the sound of footsteps in flight immediately thereafter led him to guess that Fader had drawn the pursuit away from him. But when Fader did return, and open the top of the bin, MacKinnon almost throttled him before identification was established.

When the active pursuit had been shaken off, Magee guided him across town, showing a sophisticated knowledge of back ways and shortcuts, and a genius for taking full advantage of cover. They reached the outskirts of the town in a dilapidated quarter, far from the civic center. Magee stopped. "I guess this is the end of the line, kid," he told Dave. "If you follow this street, you'll come to open country shortly. That's what you wanted, wasn't it?"

"I suppose so," MacKinnon replied uneasily, and peered down the street. Then he turned back to speak again to Magee.

But Magee was gone. He had faded away into the shadows. There was neither sight nor sound of him.

MacKinnon started in the suggested direction with a heavy heart. There was no possible reason to expect Magee to stay with him; the service Dave had done him with a lucky kick had been repaid with interest—yet he had lost the only friendly companionship he had found in a strange place. He felt lonely and depressed.

He continued along, keeping to the shadows, and watching carefully for shapes that might be patrolmen. He had gone a few hundred yards, and was beginning to worry about how

far it might be to open countryside, when he was startled into
gooseflesh by a hiss from a dark doorway.

He did his best to repress the panic that beset him, and was
telling himself that policemen never hiss, when a shadow detached itself from the blackness and touched him on the arm.

"Dave," it said softly.

MacKinnon felt a childlike sense of relief and wellbeing.
"Fader!"

"I changed my mind, Dave. The gendarmes would have
you in tow before morning. You don't know the ropes. . . .
so I came back."

Dave was both pleased and crestfallen. "Hell's bells,
Fader," he protested, "you shouldn't worry about me. I'll get
along."

Magee shook him roughly by the arm. "Don't be a chump.
Green as you are, you'd start to holler about your civil rights,
or something, and get clipped in the mouth again.

"Now see here," he went on, "I'm going to take you to
some friends of mine who will hide you until you're smart-
ened up to the tricks around here. But they're on the wrong
side of the law, see? You'll have to be all three of the three
sacred monkeys—see no evil, hear no evil, tell no evil. Think
you can do it?"

"Yes, but—"

"No 'buts' about it. Come along!"

The entrance was in the rear of an old warehouse. Steps
led down into a little sunken pit. From this open areaway—
foul with accumulated refuse—a door let into the back wall
of the building. Magee tapped lightly but systematically,
waited and listened. Presently he whispered, "Pssst! It's the
Fader."

The door opened quickly, and Magee was encircled by two
great, fat arms. He was lifted off his feet, while the owner of
those arms planted a resounding buss on his cheek. "Fader!"
she exclaimed, "are you all right, lad? We've missed you."

"Now that's a proper welcome, Mother," he answered,
when he was back on his own feet, "but I want you to meet a
friend of mine. Mother Johnston, this is David MacKinnon."

"May I do you a service?" David acknowledged, with automatic formality, but Mother Johnston's eyes tightened with
instant suspicion.

"Is he stooled?" she snapped.

"No, Mother, he's a new immigrant—but I vouch for him. He's on the dodge, and I've brought him here to cool."

She softened a little under his sweetly persuasive tones. "Well—"

Magee pinched her cheek. "That's a good girl! When are you going to marry me?"

She slapped his hand away. "Even if I were forty years younger, I'd not marry such a scamp as you! Come along then," she continued to MacKinnon, "as long as you're a friend of the Fader—though it's no credit to you!" She waddled quickly ahead of them, down a flight of stairs, while calling out for someone to open the door at its foot.

The room was poorly lighted and was furnished principally with a long table and some chairs, at which an odd dozen people were seated, drinking and talking. It reminded MacKinnon of prints he had seen of old English pubs in the days before the Collapse.

Magee was greeted with a babble of boisterous welcome. "Fader!"—"It's the kid himself!"—"How d'ja do it this time, Fader? Crawl down the drains?"—"Set 'em up, Mother—the Fader's back!"

He accepted the ovation with a wave of his hand and a shout of inclusive greeting, then turned to MacKinnon. "Folks," he said, his voice cutting through the confusion, "I want you to know Dave—the best pal that ever kicked a jailer at the right moment. If it hadn't been for Dave, I wouldn't be here."

Dave found himself seated between two others at the table and a stein of beer thrust into his hand by a not uncomely young woman. He started to thank her, but she had hurried off to help Mother Johnston take care of the sudden influx of orders. Seated opposite him was a rather surly young man who had taken little part in the greeting to Magee. He looked MacKinnon over with a face expressionless except for a recurrent tic which caused his right eye to wink spasmodically every few seconds.

"What's your line?" he demanded.

"Leave him alone, Alec," Magee cut in swiftly, but in a friendly tone. "He's just arrived inside; I told you that. But he's all right," he continued, raising his voice to include the others present, "he's been here less than twenty-four hours, but he's broken jail, beat up two customs busies, and sassed old

Judge Fleishacker right to his face. How's that for a busy day?"

Dave was the center of approving interest, but the party with the tic persisted. "That's all very well, but I asked him a fair question: What's his line? If it's the same as mine, I won't stand for it—it's too crowded now."

"That cheap racket you're in is always crowded, but he's not in it. Forget about his line."

"Why don't he answer for himself," Alec countered suspiciously. He half stood up. "I don't believe he's stooled—"

It appeared that Magee was cleaning his nails with the point of a slender knife. "Put your nose back in your glass, Alec," he remarked in a conversational tone, without looking up, "—or must I cut it off and put it there?"

The other fingered something nervously in his hand. Magee seemed not to notice it, but nevertheless told him, "If you think you can use a vibrator on me faster than I use steel, go ahead—it will be an interesting experiment."

The man facing him stood uncertainly for a moment longer, his tic working incessantly. Mother Johnston came up behind him and pushed him down by the shoulders, saying, "Boys! Boys! Is that any way to behave?—and in front of a guest, too! Fader, put that toadsticker away—I'm ashamed of you."

The knife was gone from his hands. "You're right as always, Mother," he grinned. "Ask Molly to fill up my glass again."

An old chap sitting on MacKinnon's right had followed these events with alcoholic uncertainty, but he seemed to have gathered something of the gist of it, for now he fixed Dave with serum-filled eye, and enquired, "Boy, are you stooled to the rogue?" His sweetly sour breath reached MacKinnon as the old man leaned toward him and emphasized his question with a trembling, joint-swollen finger.

Dave looked to Magee for advice and enlightenment. Magee answered for him. "No, he's not—Mother Johnston knew that when she let him in. He's here for sanctuary—as our customs provide!"

An uneasy stir ran around the room. Molly paused in her serving and listened openly. But the old man seemed satisfied. "True . . . true enough," he agreed, and took another pull at his drink, "sanctuary may be given when needed, if—" His words were lost in a mumble.

The nervous tension slackened. Most of those present were subconsciously glad to follow the lead of the old man, and excuse the intrusion on the score of necessity. Magee turned back to Dave. "I thought that what you didn't know couldn't hurt you—or us—but the matter has been opened."

"But what did he mean?"

"Gramps asked you if you had been stooled to the rogue—whether or not you were a member of the ancient and honorable fraternity of thieves, cutthroats, and pickpockets!"

Magee stared into Dave's face with a look of sardonic amusement. Dave looked uncertainly from Magee to the others, saw them exchange glances, and wondered what answer was expected of him. Alec broke the pause. "Well," he sneered, "what are you waiting for? Go ahead and put the question to him—or are the great Fader's friends free to use this club without so much as a by-your-leave?"

"I thought I told you to quiet down, Alec," the Fader replied evenly. "Besides—you're skipping a requirement. All the comrades present must first decide whether or not to put the question at all."

A quiet little man with a chronic worried look in his eyes answered him. "I don't think that quite applies, Fader. If he had come himself, or fallen into our hands—in that case, yes. But you brought him here. I think I speak for all when I say he should answer the question. Unless someone objects, I will ask him myself." He allowed an interval to pass. No one spoke up. "Very well then . . . Dave, you have seen too much and heard too much. Will you leave us now—or will you stay and take the oath of our guild? I must warn you that once stooled you are stooled for life—and there is but one punishment for betraying the rogue."

He drew his thumb across his throat in an age-old deadly gesture. Gramps made an appropriate sound effect by sucking air wetly through his teeth, and chuckled.

Dave looked around. Magee's face gave him no help. "What is it that I have to swear to?" he temporized.

The parley was brought to an abrupt ending by the sound of pounding outside. There was a shout, muffled by two closed doors and a stairway, of "Open up down there!" Magee got lightly to his feet and beckoned to Dave.

"That's for us, kid," he said. "Come along."

He stepped over to a ponderous, old-fashioned radio-phonograph which stood against the wall, reached under it, fiddled for a moment, then swung out one side panel of it. Dave saw that the mechanism had been cunningly rearranged in such a fashion that a man could squeeze inside it. Magee urged him into it, slammed the panel closed, and left him.

His face was pressed up close to the slotted grill which was intended to cover the sound box. Molly had cleared off the two extra glasses from the table, and was dumping one drink so that it spread along the table top and erased the rings their glasses had made.

MacKinnon saw the Fader slide under the table, and reached up. Then he was gone. Apparently he had, in some fashion, attached himself to the underside of the table.

Mother Johnston made a great-to-do of opening up. The lower door she opened at once, with much noise. Then she clumped slowly up the steps, pausing, wheezing, and complaining aloud. He heard her unlock the outer door.

"A fine time to be waking honest people up!" she protested. "It's hard enough to get the work done and make both ends meet, without dropping what I'm doing every five minutes, and—"

"Enough of that, old girl," a man's voice answered, "just get along downstairs. We have business with you."

"What sort of business?" she demanded.

"It might be selling liquor without a license, but it's not— this time."

"I don't—this is a private club. The members own the liquor; I simply serve it to them."

"That's as may be. It's those members I want to talk to. Get out of the way now, and be spry about it."

They came pushing into the room with Mother Johnston, still voluble, carried along in by the van. The speaker was a sergeant of police; he was accompanied by a patrolman. Following them were two other uniformed men, but they were soldiers. MacKinnon judged by the markings on their kilts that they were corporal and private—provided the insignia in New America were similar to those used by the United States Army.

The sergeant paid no attention to Mother Johnston. "All right, you men," he called out, "line up!"

They did so, ungraciously but promptly. Molly and Mother Johnston watched them, and moved closer to each other. The police sergeant called out, "All right, corporal—take charge!"

The boy who washed up in the kitchen had been staring

round-eyed. He dropped a glass. It bounced around on the hard floor, giving out bell-like sounds in the silence.

The man who had questioned Dave spoke up. "What's all this?"

The sergeant answered with a pleased grin. "Conscription —that's what it is. You are all enlisted in the army for the duration."

"Press gang!" It was an involuntary gasp that came from no particular source.

The corporal stepped briskly forward. "Form a column of twos," he directed. But the little man with the worried eyes was not done.

"I don't understand this," he objected. "We signed an armistice with the Free State three weeks ago."

"That's not your worry," countered the sergeant, "nor mine. We are picking up every able-bodied man not in essential industry. Come along."

"Then you can't take me."

"Why not?"

He held up the stump of a missing hand. The sergeant glanced from it to the corporal, who nodded grudgingly, and said, "Okay—but report to the office in the morning, and register."

He started to march them out when Alec broke ranks and backed up to the wall, screaming, "You can't do this to me! I won't go!" His deadly little vibrator was exposed in his hand, and the right side of his face was drawn up in a spastic wink that left his teeth bare.

"Get him, Steeves," ordered the corporal. The private stepped forward, but stopped when Alec brandished the vibrator at him. He had no desire to have a vibroblade between his ribs, and there was no doubt as to the uncontrolled dangerousness of his hysterical opponent.

The corporal, looking phlegmatic, almost bored, levelled a small tube at a spot on the wall over Alec's head. Dave heard a soft *pop!*, and a thin tinkle. Alec stood motionless for a few seconds, his face even more strained, as if he were exerting the limit of his will against some unseen force, then slid quietly to the floor. The tonic spasm in his face relaxed, and his features smoothed into those of a tired and petulant, and very bewildered, little boy.

"Two of you birds carry him," directed the corporal. "Let's get going."

The sergeant was the last to leave. He turned at the door and spoke to Mother Johnston. "Have you seen the Fader lately?"

"The Fader?" She seemed puzzled. "Why, he's in jail."

"Ah, yes . . . so he is." He went out.

Magee refused the drink that Mother Johnston offered him. Dave was surprised to see that he appeared worried for the first time. "I don't understand it," Magee muttered, half to himself, then addressed the one-handed man. "Ed—bring me up to date."

"Not much news since they tagged you, Fader. The armistice was before that. I thought from the papers that things were going to be straightened out for once."

"So did I. But the government must expect war if they are going in for general conscription." He stood up. "I've got to have more data. Al!" The kitchen boy stuck his head into the room.

"What 'cha want, Fader?"

"Go out and make palaver with five or six of the beggars. Look up their 'king.' You know where he makes his pitch?"

"Sure—over by the auditorium."

"Find out what's stirring, but don't let them know I sent you."

"Right, Fader. It's in the bag." The boy swaggered out.

"Molly."

"Yes, Fader?"

"Will you go out, and do the same thing with some of the business girls? I want to know what they hear from their customers." She nodded agreement. He went on, "Better look up that little redhead that has her beat up on Union Square. She can get secrets out of a dead man. Here—" He pulled a wad of bills out of his pocket and handed her several. "You better take this grease . . . You might have to pay off a cop to get back out of the district."

Magee was not disposed to talk, and insisted that Dave get some sleep. He was easily persuaded, not having slept since he entered Coventry. That seemed like a lifetime past; he was exhausted. Mother Johnson fixed him a shakedown in a dark, stuffy room on the same underground level. It had none of the hygienic comforts to which he was accustomed—air-conditioning, restful music, hydraulic mattress, nor soundproofing—and he missed his usual relaxing soak and auto-massage, but he was too tired to care. He slept in clothing and under covers for the first time in his life.

He woke up with a headache, a taste in his mouth like tired sin, and a sense of impending disaster. At first he could not remember where he was—he thought he was still in detention Outside. His surroundings were inexplicably sordid; he was about to ring for the attendant and complain, when his memory pieced in the events of the day before. Then he got up and discovered that his bones and muscles were painfully sore, and—which was worse—that he was, by his standards, filthy dirty. He itched.

He entered the common room, and found Magee sitting at the table. He greeted Dave. "Hi, kid. I was about to wake you. You've slept almost all day. We've got a lot to talk about."

"Okay—shortly. Where's the 'fresher?"

"Over there."

It was not Dave's idea of a refreshing chamber, but he managed to take a sketchy shower in spite of the slimy floor. Then he discovered that there was no air blast installed, and he was forced to dry himself unsatisfactorily with his handkerchief. He had no choice in clothes. He must put back on the ones he had taken off, or go naked. He recalled that he had seen no nudity anywhere in Coventry, even at sports—a difference in customs, no doubt.

He put his clothes back on, though his skin crawled at the touch of the once-used linen.

But Mother Johnston had thrown together an appetizing breakfast for him. He let coffee restore his courage as Magee talked. It was, according to Fader, a serious situation. New America and the Free State had compromised their differences and had formed an alliance. They quite seriously proposed to break out of Coventry and attack the United States.

MacKinnon looked up at this. "That's ridiculous, isn't it? They would be outnumbered enormously. Besides, how about the Barrier?"

"I don't know—yet. But they have some reason to think that they can break through the Barrier. . . . and there are rumors that whatever it is can be used as a weapon, too, so that a small army might be able to whip the whole United States."

MacKinnon looked puzzled. "Well," he observed, "I haven't any opinion of a weapon I know nothing about, but as to the Barrier. . . . I'm not a mathematical physicist, but I was always told that it was theoretically impossible to break the Barrier—that it was just a nothingness that there was no way to touch. Of course, you can fly over it, but even that is supposed to be deadly to life."

"Suppose they had found some way to shield from the effects of the Barrier's field?" suggested Magee. "Anyhow, that's not the point, for us. The point is: they've made this combine; the Free State supplies the techniques and most of the officers; and New America, with its bigger population, supplies most of the men. And that means to us that we don't dare show our faces any place, or we are in the army before you can blink.

"Which brings me to what I was going to suggest. I'm going to duck out of here as soon as it gets dark, and light out for the Gateway, before they send somebody after me who is bright enough to look under a table. I thought maybe you might want to come along."

"Back to the psychologists?" MacKinnon was honestly aghast.

"Sure—why not? What have you got to lose? This whole damn place is going to be just like the Free State in a couple of days—and a Joe of your temperament would be in hot water all the time. What's so bad about a nice, quiet hospital room as a place to hide out until things quiet down? You don't have to pay any attention to the psych boys—just make animal noises at 'em every time one sticks his nose into your room, until they get discouraged."

Dave shook his head. "No," he said slowly, "I can't do that."

"Then what will you do?"

"I don't know yet. Take to the hills I guess. Go live with the Angels if it comes to a showdown. I wouldn't mind them praying for my soul as long as they left my mind alone."

They were each silent for a while. Magee was mildly annoyed at MacKinnon's bullheaded stubbornness in the face of what seemed to him a reasonable offer. Dave continued busily to stow away grilled ham, while considering his position. He cut off another bite. "My, but this is good," he remarked, to break the awkward silence, "I don't know when I've had anything taste so good—Say!"

"What?" inquired Magee, looking up, and seeing the concern written on MacKinnon's face.

"This ham—is it synthetic, or is it *real meat?*"

"Why, it's real. What about it?"

Dave did not answer. He managed to reach the refreshing room before that which he had eaten departed from him.

Before he left, Magee gave Dave some money with which he could have purchased for him things that he would need in order to take to the hills. MacKinnon protested, but the Fader cut him short. "Quit being a damn fool, Dave. I can't use New American money on the Outside, and you can't stay alive in the hills without proper equipment. You lie doggo here for a few days while Al, or Molly, picks up what you need, and you'll stand a chance—unless you'll change your mind and come with me?"

Dave shook his head at this, and accepted the money.

It was lonely after Magee left. Mother Johnston and Dave were alone in the club, and the empty chairs reminded him depressingly of the men who had been impressed. He wished that Gramps or the one-handed man would show up. Even Alec, with his nasty temper, would have been company—he wondered if Alec had been punished for resisting the draft.

Mother Johnston inveigled him into playing checkers in an attempt to relieve his evident low spirits. He felt obligated to agree to her gentle conspiracy, but his mind wandered. It was all very well for the Senior Judge to tell him to seek adventure in interplanetary exploration, but only engineers and technicians were eligible for such billets. Perhaps he should have gone in for science, or engineering, instead of literature; then he might now be on Venus, contending against the forces of nature in high adventure, instead of hiding from uniformed bullies. It wasn't fair. No—he must not kid himself; there was no room for an expert in literary history in the raw frontier of the planets; that was not human injustice, that was a hard fact of nature, and he might as well face it.

He thought bitterly of the man whose nose he had broken, and thereby landed himself in Coventry. Maybe he was an "upholstered parasite" after all—but the recollection of the phrase brought back the same unreasoning anger that had gotten him into trouble. He was *glad* that he had socked that so-and-so! What right had he to go around sneering and calling people things like that?

He found himself thinking in the same vindictive spirit of his father, although he would have been at a loss to explain the connection. The connection was not superficially evident, for his father would never have stooped to name-calling. Instead, he would have offered the sweetest of smiles, and quoted something nauseating in the way of sweetness-and-light. Dave's father was one of the nastiest little tyrants that ever dominated a household under the guise of loving-kindness. He was of the more-in-sorrow-than-in-anger, this-hurts-me-more-than-it-does-you school, and all his life had invariably been able to find an altruistic rationalization for always having his own way. Convinced of his own infallible righteousness, he had never valued his son's point of view on anything, but had dominated him in everything—always from the highest moralistic motives.

He had had two main bad effects on his son: the boy's natural independence, crushed at home, rebelled blindly at every sort of discipline, authority, or criticism which he encountered elsewhere and subconsciously identified with the not-to-be-criticized paternal authority. Secondly, through years of association Dave imitated his father's most dangerous social vice —that of passing unself-critical moral judgments on the actions of others.

When Dave was arrested for breaking a basic custom; to wit, atavistic violence; his father washed his hands of him with the statement that he had tried his best to "make a man of him," and could not be blamed for his son's failure to profit by his instruction.

A faint knock caused them to put away the checker board in a hurry. Mother Johnston paused before answering. "That's not our knock," she considered, "but it's not loud enough to be the noises. Be ready to hide."

MacKinnon waited by the fox hole where he had hidden the night before, while Mother Johnston went to investigate. He heard her unbar and unlock the upper door, then she called out to him in a low but urgent voice, "Dave! Come here, Dave—hurry!"

It was Fader, unconscious, with his own bloody trail behind him.

Mother Johnston was attempting to pick up the limp form. MacKinnon crowded in, and between the two of them they managed to get him downstairs and to lay him on the long table. He came to for a moment as they straightened his limbs. "Hi, Dave," he whispered, managing to achieve the ghost of his debonair grin. "Somebody trumped my ace."

"You keep quiet!" Mother Johnston snapped at him, then

in a lower voice to Dave, "Oh, the poor darling—Dave, we must get him to the Doctor."

"Can't . . . do . . . that," muttered the Fader. "Got . . . to get to the . . . Gate—" His voice trailed off. Mother Johnston's fingers had been busy all the while, as if activated by some separate intelligence. A small pair of scissors, drawn from some hiding place about her large person, clipped away at his clothing, exposing the superficial extent of the damage. She examined the trauma critically.

"This is no job for me," she decided, "and he must sleep while we move him. Dave, get that hypodermic kit out of the medicine chest in the 'fresher."

"No, Mother!" It was Magee, his voice strong and vibrant.

"Get me a pepper pill," he went on. "There's—"

"But Fader—"

He cut her short. "I've got to get to the Doctor all right, but how the devil will I get there if I don't walk?"

"We would carry you."

"Thanks, Mother," he told her, his voice softened, "I know you would—but the police would be curious. Get me that pill."

Dave followed her into the 'fresher, and questioned her while she rummaged through the medicine chest. "Why don't we just send for a doctor?"

"There is only one doctor we can trust, and that's *the* Doctor. Besides, none of the others are worth the powder to blast them."

Magee was out again when they came back into the room. Mother Johnston slapped his face until he came around, blinking and cursing. Then she fed him the pill.

The powerful stimulant, improbable offspring of common coal tar, took hold almost at once. To all surface appearance Magee was a well man. He sat up and tried his own pulse, searching it out in his left wrist with steady, sensitive fingers. "Regular as a metronome," he announced, "the old ticker can stand that dosage all right."

He waited while Mother Johnston applied sterile packs to his wounds, then said goodbye. MacKinnon looked at Mother Johnston. She nodded.

"I'm going with you," he told the Fader.

"What for? It will just double the risk."

"You're in no fit shape to travel alone—stimulant, or no stimulant."

"Nuts. *I'd* have to look after *you*."

"I'm going with you."

Magee shrugged his shoulders and capitulated.

Mother Johnston wiped her perspiring face, kissed both of them.

Until they were well out of town their progress reminded MacKinnon of their nightmare flight of the previous evening. Thereafter they continued to the north-northwest by a highway which ran toward the foothills, and they left the highway only when necessary to avoid the sparse traffic. Once they were almost surprised by a police patrol car, equipped with blacklight and almost invisible, but the Fader sensed it in time and they crouched behind a low wall which separated the adjacent field from the road.

Dave inquired how he had known the patrol was near. Magee chuckled. "Damned if I know," he said, "but I believe I could smell a cop staked out in a herd of goats."

The Fader talked less and less as the night progressed. His usually untroubled countenance became lined and old as the effect of the drug wore off. It seemed to Dave as if this unaccustomed expression gave him a clearer insight into the man's character—that the mask of pain was his true face rather than the unworried features Magee habitually showed the world. He wondered for the ninth time what the Fader had done to cause a court to adjudge him socially insane.

This question was uppermost in his mind with respect to every person he met in Coventry. The answer was obvious in most cases; their types of instability were gross and showed up at once. Mother Johnston had been an enigma until she had explained it herself. She had followed her husband into Coventry. Now that she was a widow, she preferred to remain with the friends she knew and the customs and conditions she was adjusted to, rather than change for another and possibly less pleasing environment.

Magee sat down beside the road. "It's no use, kid," he admitted, "I can't make it."

"The hell we can't. I'll carry you."

Magee grinned faintly. "No, I mean it." Dave persisted. "How much farther is it?"

"Matter of two or three miles, maybe."

"Climb aboard." He took Magee pickaback and started on. The first few hundred yards were not too difficult; Magee was forty pounds lighter than Dave. After that the strain of the additional load began to tell. His arms cramped from supporting Magee's knees; his arches complained at the weight and the unnatural load distribution; and his breathing was made difficult by the clasp of Magee's arms around his neck.

Two miles to go—maybe more. Let your weight fall forward, and your foot must follow it, else you fall to the ground. It's automatic—as automatic as pulling teeth. How long is a mile? Nothing in a rocket ship, thirty seconds in a pleasure car, a ten minute crawl in a steel snail, fifteen minutes to trained troops in good condition. How far is it with a man on your back, on a rough road, when you are tired to start with?

Five thousand, two hundred, and eighty feet—a meaningless figure. But every step takes twenty-four inches off the total. The remainder is still incomprehensible—an infinity. Count them. Count them till you go crazy—till the figures speak themselves outside your head, and the jar! . . . jar! . . . jar! . . . of your enormous, benumbed feet beats in your brain. Count them backwards, subtracting two each time —no, that's worse; each remainder is still an unattainable, inconceivable figure.

His world closed in, lost its history and held no future. There was nothing, nothing at all, but the torturing necessity of picking up his foot again and placing it forward. No feeling but the heartbreaking expenditure of will necessary to achieve that meaningless act.

He was brought suddenly to awareness when Magee's arms relaxed from around his neck. He leaned forward, and dropped to one knee to keep from spilling his burden, then eased it slowly to the ground. He thought for a moment that the Fader was dead—he could not locate his pulse, and the slack face and limp body were sufficiently corpse-like, but he pressed an ear to Magee's chest, and heard with relief the steady *flub-dub* of his heart.

He tied Magee's wrists together with his handkerchief, and forced his own head through the encircled arms. But he was unable, in his exhausted condition, to wrestle the slack weight into position on his back. Fader regained consciousness while MacKinnon was struggling. His first words were, "Take it easy, Dave. What's the trouble?"

Dave explained. "Better untie my wrists," advised the Fader, "I think I can walk for a while."

And walk he did, for nearly three hundred yards, before he

was forced to give up again. "Look, Dave," he said, after he had partially recovered, "did you bring along any more of those pepper pills?"

"Yes—but you can't take any more dosage. It would kill you."

"Yeah, I know—so they say. But that isn't the idea—yet. I was going to suggest that you might take one."

"Why, of course! Good grief, Fader, but I'm dumb."

Magee seemed no heavier than a light coat, the morning star shone brighter, and his strength seemed inexhaustible. Even when they left the highway and started up the cart trail that led to the Doctor's home in the foothills, the going was tolerable and the burden not too great. MacKinnon knew that the drugs burned the working tissue of his body long after his proper reserves were gone, and that it would take him days to recover from the reckless expenditure, but he did not mind. No price was too high to pay for the moment when he at last arrived at the gate of the Doctor's home—on his own two feet, his charge alive and conscious.

MacKinnon was not allowed to see Magee for four days. In the meantime, he was encouraged to keep the routine of a semi-invalid himself in order to recover the twenty-five pounds he had lost in two days and two nights, and to make up for the heavy strain on his heart during the last night. A high-caloric diet, sun baths, rest, and peaceful surroundings plus his natural good health caused him to regain weight and strength rapidly, but he "enjoyed ill health" exceedingly because of the companionship of the Doctor himself—and Persephone.

Persephone's calendar age was fifteen. Dave never knew whether to think of her as much older, or much younger. She had been born in Coventry, and had lived her short life in the house of the Doctor, her mother having died in childbirth in that same house. She was completely childlike in many respects, being without experience in the civilized world Outside, and having had very little contact with the inhabitants of Coventry, except when she saw them as patients of the Doctor. But she had been allowed to read unchecked from the library of a sophisticated and protean-minded man of science. MacKinnon was continually being surprised at the extent of her academic and scientific knowledge—much greater than his own. She made him feel as if he were conversing with some aged and omniscient matriarch, then she would come out with some naive concept of the outer world, and he would be brought up sharply with the realization that she was, in fact, an inexperienced child.

He was mildly romantic about her. Not seriously, of course, in view of her barely nubile age, but she was pleasant to see, and he was hungry for feminine companionship. He was quite young enough himself to feel continual interest in the delightful differences, mental and physical, between male and female.

Consequently, it was a blow to his pride as sharp as had been the sentence to Coventry to discover that she classed him with the other inhabitants of Coventry as a poor unfortunate who needed help and sympathy because he was not quite right in his head.

He was furious and for one whole day he sulked alone, but the human necessity for self-justification and approval forced him to seek her out and attempt to reason with her. He explained carefully and with emotional candor the circumstances leading up to his trial and conviction, and embellished the account with his own philosophy and evaluations, then confidently awaited her approval.

It was not forthcoming. "I don't understand your viewpoint," she said. "You broke his nose, yet he had done you no harm of any sort. You expect me to approve that?"

"But Persephone," he protested, "you ignore the fact that he called me a most insulting name."

"I don't see the connection," she said. "He made a noise with his mouth—a verbal label. If the label does not fit you, the noise is meaningless. If the label is true in your case—if you *are* the thing that the noise refers to, you are neither more, nor less, that thing by reason of some one uttering the verbal label. In short, he did not damage you.

"But what you did to him was another matter entirely. You broke his nose. That is damage. In self-protection the rest of society must seek you out, and determine whether or not you are so unstable as to be likely to damage some one else in the future. If you are, you must be quarantined for treatment, or leave society—whichever you prefer."

"You think I'm crazy, don't you?" he accused.

"Crazy? Not the way you mean it. You haven't paresis, or

a brain tumor, or any other lesion that the Doctor could find. But from the viewpoint of your semantic reactions you are as socially *unsane* as any fanatic witchburner."

"Come now—that's not just!"

"What is justice?" She picked up the kitten she had been playing with. "I'm going in—it's getting chilly." Off she went into the house, her bare feet noiseless in the grass.

Had the science of semantics developed as rapidly as psycho-dynamics and its implementing arts of propaganda and mob psychology, the United States might never have fallen into dictatorship, then been forced to undergo the Second Revolution. All of the scientific principles embodied in the Covenant which marked the end of the revolution were formulated as far back as the first quarter of the twentieth century.

But the work of the pioneer semanticists, C. K. Ogden, Alfred Korzybski, and others, were known to but a handful of students, whereas psycho-dynamics, under the impetus of repeated wars and the frenzy of high-pressure merchandising, progressed by leaps and bounds.

Semantics, "the meaning of meaning," gave a method for the first time of applying the scientific method to every act of everyday life. Because semantics dealt with spoken and written words as a determining aspect of human behavior it was at first mistakenly thought by many to be concerned *only* with words and of interest only to professional word manipulators, such as advertising copy writers and professors of etymology. A handful of unorthodox psychiatrists attempted to apply it to personal human problems, but their work was swept away by the epidemic mass psychoses that destroyed Europe and returned the United States to the Dark Ages.

The Covenant was the first scientific social document ever drawn up by man, and due credit must be given to its principal author, Dr. Micah Novak, the same Novak who served as staff psychologist in the revolution. The revolutionists wished to establish maximum personal liberty. How could they accomplish that to a degree of high mathematical probability?

First they junked the concept of "justice." Examined semantically "justice" has no referent—there is no observable phenomenon in the space-time-matter continuum to which one can point, and say, "This is justice." Science can deal only with that which can be observed and measured. Justice is not such a matter; therefore it can never have the same meaning to one as to another; any "noises" said about it will only add to confusion.

But damage, physical or economic, can be pointed to and measured. Citizens were forbidden by the Covenant to damage another. Any act not leading to damage, physical or economic, to some particular person, they declared to be lawful.

Since they had abandoned the concept of "justice," there could be no rational standards of punishment. Penology took its place with lycanthropy and other forgotten witchcrafts. Yet, since it was not practical to permit a source of danger to remain in the community, social offenders were examined and potential repeaters were given their choice of psychological readjustment, or of having society withdraw itself from them —Coventry.

Early drafts of the Covenant contained the assumption that the socially unsane would naturally be hospitalized and readjusted, particularly since current psychiatry was quite competent to cure all non-lesional psychoses and cure or alleviate lesional psychoses, but Novak set his face against this.

"*No!*" he protested. "The government must never again be permitted to tamper with the mind of any citizen without his consent, or else we set up a greater tyranny than we had before. Every man must be free to accept, or reject, the Covenant, even though we think him insane!"

The next time David MacKinnon looked up Persephone he found her in a state of extreme agitation. His own wounded pride was forgotten at once. "Why, my dear," he said, "whatever in the world is the matter?"

Gradually he gathered that she had been present at a conversation between Magee and the Doctor, and had heard for the first time, of the impending military operation against the United States. He patted her hand. "So that's all it is," he observed in a relieved voice. "I thought something was wrong with you yourself."

" 'That's all—' David MacKinnon, do you mean to stand there and tell me that you knew about this, and don't consider it worth worrying about?"

"Me? Why should I? And for that matter, what could *I* do?"

"What could you do? You could go outside and warn them —that's what you could do . . . As to why you should—

Dave, you're impossible!" She burst into tears and ran from the room.

He stared after her, mouth open, then borrowed from his remotest ancestor by observing to himself that women are hard to figure out.

Persephone did not appear at lunch. MacKinnon asked the Doctor where she was.

"Had her lunch," the Doctor told him, between mouthfuls. "Started for the Gateway."

"What! Why did you let her do that?"

"Free agent. Wouldn't have obeyed me anyway. She'll be all right."

Dave did not hear the last, being already out of the room and running out of the house. He found her just backing her little monocycle runabout out of its shed. "Persephone!"

"What do you want?" she asked with frozen dignity beyond her years.

"You mustn't do this! That's where the Fader got hurt!"

"I am going. Please stand aside."

"Then I'm going with you."

"Why should you?"

"To take care of you."

She sniffed. "As if anyone would dare to touch me."

There was a measure of truth in what she said. The Doctor, and every member of his household, enjoyed a personal immunity unlike that of anyone else in Coventry. As a natural consequence of the set-up, Coventry had almost no competent medical men. The number of physicians who committed social damage was small. The proportion of such who declined psychiatric treatment was negligible, and this negligible remainder were almost sure to be unreliable bunglers in their profession. The Doctor was a natural healer, in voluntary exile in order that he might enjoy the opportunity to practice his art in the richest available field. He cared nothing for dry research; what he wanted was patients, the sicker the better, that he might make them well again.

He was above custom and above law. In the Free State the Liberator depended on him for insulin to hold his own death from diabetes at arm's length. In New America his beneficiaries were equally powerful. Even among the Angels of the Lord the Prophet himself accepted the dicta of the Doctor without question.

But MacKinnon was not satisfied. Some ignorant fool, he was afraid, might do the child some harm without realizing her protected status. He got no further chance to protest; she started the little runabout suddenly, and forced him to jump out of its path. When he had recovered his balance, she was far down the lane. He could not catch her.

She was back in less than four hours. He had expected that; if a person as elusive as Fader had not been able to reach the Gate at night, it was not likely that a young girl could do so in daylight.

His first feeling was one of simple relief, then he eagerly awaited an opportunity to speak to her. During her absence he had been turning over the situation in his mind. It was a foregone conclusion that she would fail; he wished to rehabilitate himself in her eyes; therefore, he would help her in the project nearest her heart—he himself would carry the warning to the Outside!

Perhaps she would ask for such help. In fact, it seemed likely. By the time she returned he had convinced himself that she was certain to ask his help. He would agree—with simple dignity—and off he would go, perhaps to be wounded, or killed, but an heroic figure, even if he failed.

He pictured himself subconsciously as a blend of Sydney Carton, the White Knight, the man who carried the message to Garcia—and just a dash of d'Artagnan.

But she did not ask him—she would not even give him a chance to talk with her.

She did not appear at dinner. After dinner she was closeted with the Doctor in his study. When she reappeared she went directly to her room. He finally concluded that he might as well go to bed himself.

To bed, and then to sleep, and take it up again in the morning— But it's not as simple as that. The unfriendly walls stared back at him, and the other, critical half of his mind decided to make a night of it. Fool! She doesn't want your help. Why should she? What have you got that Fader hasn't got?— and better. To her, you are just one of the screwloose multitude you've seen all around you in this place.

But *I'm* not crazy!—just because I choose not to submit to the dictation of others doesn't make me *crazy*. Doesn't it, though? All the rest of them in here are lamebrains, what's so fancy about you? Not all of them—how about the Doctor, and— Don't kid yourself, chump, the Doctor and Mother Johnston are here for their own reasons; they weren't sentenced. And Persephone was born here.

How about Magee?—He was certainly rational—or seemed so. He found himself resenting, with illogical bitterness, Magee's apparent stability. Why should he be any different from the rest of us?

The rest of us? He had classed himself with the other inhabitants of Coventry. All right, all right, admit it, you fool— you're just like the rest of them; turned out because the decent people won't have you—and too damned stubborn to admit that you need treatment.

But the thought of treatment turned him cold, and made him think of his father again. Why should that be? He recalled something the Doctor had said to him a couple of days before: "What you need, son, is to stand up to your father and tell him off. Pity more children don't tell their parents to go to hell!"

He turned on the light and tried to read. But it was no use. Why should Persephone care what happened to the people Outside?—She didn't know them; she had no friends there. If *he* had no obligations to them, how could *she* possibly care? No obligations? You had a soft, easy life for many years—all they asked was that you behave yourself. For that matter, where would you be now, if the Doctor had stopped to ask whether or not he owed you anything?

He was still wearily chewing the bitter cud of self-examination when the first cold and colorless light of morning filtered in. He got up, threw a robe around him, and tiptoed down the hall to Magee's room. The door was ajar. He stuck his head in, and whispered, "Fader— Are you awake?"

"Come in, kid," Magee answered quietly. "What's the trouble? No can sleep?"

"No—"

"Neither can I. Sit down, and we'll carry the banner together."

"Fader, I'm going to make a break for it. I'm going Outside."

"Huh? When?"

"Right away."

"Risky business, kid. Wait a few days, and I'll try it with you."

"No, I can't wait for you to get well. I'm going out to warn the United States!"

Magee's eyes widened a little, but his voice was unchanged. "You haven't let that spindly kid sell you a bill of goods, Dave?"

"No. Not exactly. I'm doing this for myself—It's something I need to do. See here, Fader, what about this weapon? Have they really got something that could threaten the United States?"

"I'm afraid so," Magee admitted. "I don't know much about it, but it makes blasters look sick. More range— I don't know what they expect to do about the Barrier, but I saw 'em stringing heavy power lines before I got winged. Say, if you do get outside, here's a chap you might look up; in fact, be sure to. He's got influence." Magee scrawled something on a scrap of paper, folded the scrap, and handed it to MacKinnon, who pocketed it absent-mindedly and went on:

"How closely is the Gate guarded, Fader?"

"You can't get out the Gate; that's out of the question. Here's what you will have to do—" He tore off another piece of paper and commenced sketching and explaining.

Dave shook hands with Magee before he left. "You'll say goodbye for me, won't you? And thank the Doctor? I'd rather just slide out before anyone is up."

"Of course, kid," the Fader assured him.

MacKinnon crouched behind bushes and peered cautiously at the little band of Angels filing into the bleak, ugly church. He shivered, both from fear and from the icy morning air. But his need was greater than his fear. Those zealots had food —and he must have it.

The first two days after he left the house of the Doctor had been easy enough. True, he had caught cold from sleeping on the ground; it had settled in his lungs and slowed him down. But he did not mind that now if only he could refrain from sneezing or coughing until the little band of faithful were safe inside the temple. He watched them pass—dour-looking men, women in skirts that dragged the ground and whose work-lined faces were framed in shawls—sallow drudges with too many children. The light had gone out of their faces. Even the children were sober.

The last of them filed inside, leaving only the sexton in the churchyard, busy with some obscure duty. After an interminable time, during which MacKinnon pressed a finger against his upper lip in a frantic attempt to forestall a sneeze, the sexton entered the grim building and closed the doors.

MacKinnon crept out of his hiding place and hurried to the house he had previously selected, on the edge of the clearing, farthest from the church.

The dog was suspicious, but he quieted him. The house was locked, but the rear door could be forced. He was a little giddy at the sight of food when he found it—hard bread, and strong, unsalted butter made from goats' milk. A misstep two days before had landed him in a mountain stream. The mishap had not seemed important until he discovered that his food tablets were a pulpy mess. He had eaten them the rest of the day, then mold had taken them, and he had thrown the remainder away.

The bread lasted him through three more sleeps, but the butter melted and he was unable to carry it. He soaked as much of it as he could into the bread, then licked up the rest, after which he was very thirsty.

Some hours after the last of the bread was gone, he reached his first objective—the main river to which all other streams in Coventry were tributary. Some place, down stream, it dived under the black curtain of the Barrier, and continued seaward. With the gateway closed and guarded, its outlet constituted the only possible egress to a man unassisted.

In the meantime it was water, and thirst was upon him again, and his cold was worse. But he would have to wait until dark to drink; there were figures down there by the bank —some in uniform, he thought. One of them made fast a little skiff to a landing. He marked it for his own and watched it with jealous eyes. It was still there when the sun went down.

The early morning sun struck his nose and he sneezed. He came wide awake, raised his head, and looked around. The little skiff he had appropriated floated in midstream. There were no oars. He could not remember whether or not there had been any oars. The current was fairly strong; it seemed as if he should have drifted clear to the Barrier in the night. Perhaps he had passed under it—no, that was ridiculous.

Then he saw it, less than a mile away, black and ominous —but the most welcome sight he had seen in days. He was too weak and feverish to enjoy it, but it renewed the determination that kept him going.

The little boat scraped against bottom. He saw that the current at a bend had brought him to the bank. He hopped awkwardly out, his congealed joints complaining, and drew the bow of the skiff up onto the sand. Then he thought better of it, pushed it out once more, shoved as hard as he was able and watched it disappear around the meander. No need to advertise where he had landed.

He slept most of that day, rousing himself once to move out of the sun when it grew too hot. But the sun had cooked much of the cold out of his bones, and he felt much better by nightfall.

Although the Barrier was only a mile or so away, it took most of the night to reach it by following the river bank. He knew when he had reached it by the clouds of steam that rose from the water. When the sun came up, he considered the situation. The Barrier stretched across the water, but the juncture between it and the surface of the stream was hidden by billowing clouds. Someplace, down under the surface of the water—how far down he did not know—somewhere down there, the Barrier ceased, and its raw edge turned the water it touched to steam.

Slowly, reluctantly and most unheroically, he commenced to strip off his clothes. The time had come and he did not relish it. He came across the scrap of paper that Magee had handed him, and attempted to examine it. But it had been pulped by his involuntary dip in the mountain stream and was quite illegible. He chucked it away. It did not seem to matter.

He shivered as he stood hesitating on the bank, although the sun was warm. Then his mind was made up for him; he spied a patrol on the far bank.

Perhaps they had seen him, perhaps not. He dived.

Down, down, as far as his strength would take him. Down and try to touch bottom, to be sure of avoiding that searing, deadly base. He felt mud with his hands. Now to swim under it. Perhaps it was death to pass under it, as well as over it; he would soon know. But which way was it? There was no direction down here.

He stayed down until his congested lungs refused. Then he rose part way, and felt scalding water on his face. For a timeless interval of unutterable sorrow and loneliness he realized that he was trapped between heat and water—trapped under the Barrier.

Two private soldiers gossiped idly on a small dock which lay under the face of the Barrier. The river which poured out from beneath it held no interest for them, they had watched it for many dull tours of guard duty. An alarm clanged behind them and brought them to alertness. "What sector, Jack?"

"This bank. There he is now—see!"

They fished him out and had him spread out on the dock by the time the sergeant of the guard arrived. "Alive, or dead?" he enquired.

"Dead, I think," answered the one who was not busy giving artificial resuscitation.

The sergeant clucked in a manner incongruous to his battered face, and said, "Too bad. I've ordered the ambulance; send him up to the infirmary anyhow."

The nurse tried to keep him quiet, but MacKinnon made such an uproar that she was forced to get the ward surgeon. "Here! Here! What's all this nonsense?" the medico rebuked him, while reaching for his pulse. Dave managed to convince him that he would not quiet down, not accept a soporific until he had told his story. They struck a working agreement that MacKinnon was to be allowed to talk— "But keep it short, mind you!"—and the doctor would pass the word along to his next superior, and in return Dave would submit to a hypodermic.

The next morning two other men, unidentified, were brought to MacKinnon by the surgeon. They listened to his full story and questioned him in detail. He was transferred to corps area headquarters that afternoon by ambulance. There he was questioned again. He was regaining his strength rapidly, but he was growing quite tired of the whole rigamarole, and wanted assurance that his warning was being taken seriously. The latest of his interrogators reassured him. "Compose yourself," he told Dave, "you are to see the commanding officer this afternoon."

The corps area commander, a nice little chap with a quick, birdlike manner and a most unmilitary appearance, listened gravely while MacKinnon recited his story for what seemed to him the fiftieth time. He nodded agreement when David finished. "Rest assured, David MacKinnon, that all necessary steps are being taken."

"But how about their weapon?"

"That is taken care of—and as for the Barrier, it may not

be as easy to break as our neighbors think. But your efforts are appreciated. May I do you some service?"

"Well, no—not for myself, but there are two of my friends in there—" He asked that something be done to rescue Magee, and that Persephone be enabled to come out, if she wished.

"I know of that girl," the general remarked. "We will get in touch with her. If at any time she wishes to become a citizen, it can be arranged. As for Magee, that is another matter—" He touched the stud of his desk visiphone. "Send Captain Randall in."

A neat, trim figure in the uniform of a captain of the United States Army entered with a light step. MacKinnon glanced at him with casual, polite interest, then his expression went to pieces. "Fader!" he yelled.

Their mutual greeting was hardly sufficiently decorous for the private office of a commanding general, but the general did not seem to mind. When they had calmed down, MacKinnon had to ask the question uppermost in his mind. "But see here, Fader, all this doesn't make sense—" He paused, staring, then pointed a finger accusingly, "I know! You're in the secret service!"

The Fader grinned cheerfully. "Did you think," he observed, "that the United States Army would leave a plague spot like that unwatched?"

The general cleared his throat. "What do you plan to do now, David MacKinnon?"

"Eh? Me? Why, I don't have any plans—" He thought for a moment, then turned to his friend. "Do you know, Fader, I believe I'll turn in for psychological treatment after all. You're on the Outside—"

"I don't believe that will be necessary," interrupted the general gently.

"No? Why not, sir?"

"You have cured yourself. You may not be aware of it, but four psychotechnicians have interviewed you. Their reports agree. I am authorized to tell you that your status as a free citizen has been restored, if you wish it."

The general and Captain "the Fader" Randall managed tactfully between them to terminate the interview. Randall walked back to the infirmary with his friend. Dave wanted a thousand questions answered at once. "But Fader," he demanded, "you must have gotten out before I did."

"A day or two."

"Then my job was unnecessary!"

"I wouldn't say that," Randall contradicted. "I might not have gotten through. As a matter of fact, they had all the details even before I reported. There are others—Anyhow," he continued, to change the subject, "now that you are here, what will you do?"

"Me? It's too soon to say . . . It won't be classical literature, that's a cinch. If I wasn't such a dumbie in math, I might still try for interplanetary."

"Well, we can talk about it tonight," suggested Fader, glancing at his chrono. "I've got to run along, but I'll stop by later, and we'll go over to the mess for dinner."

He was out the door with speed reminiscent of the thieves' kitchen. Dave watched him, then said suddenly, "Hey! Fader! Why couldn't I get into the secret ser—"

But the Fader was gone—he must ask himself.

Misfit

"... for the purpose of conserving and improving our interplanetary resources, and providing useful, healthful occupations for the youth of this planet."

Excerpt from the enabling act, H.R. 7118, setting up the Cosmic Construction Corps.

"ATTENTION TO MUSTER!" The parade ground voice of a First Sergeant of Space Marines cut through the fog and drizzle of a nasty New Jersey morning. "As your names are called, answer 'Here', step forward with your baggage, and embark. Atkins!"

"Here!"

"Austin!"

"Hyar!"

"Ayres!"

"Here!"

One by one they fell out of ranks, shouldered the hundred and thirty pounds of personal possessions allowed them, and trudged up the gangway. They were young—none more than twenty-two—in some cases luggage outweighed the owner.

"Kaplan!"

"Here!"

"Keith!"

"Heah!"

"Libby!"

"Here!" A thin gangling blonde had detached himself from the line, hastily wiped his nose, and grabbed his belongings. He slung a fat canvas bag over his shoulder, steadied it, and lifted a suitcase with his free hand. He started for the companionway in an unsteady dog trot. As he stepped on the gangway his suitcase swung against his knees. He staggered against a short wiry form dressed in the powder-blue of the Space Navy. Strong fingers grasped his arm and checked his fall.

"Steady, son. Easy does it." Another hand readjusted the canvas bag.

"Oh, excuse me, uh"—the embarrassed youngster automatically counted the four bands of silver braid below the shooting star—"Captain. I didn't—"

"Bear a hand and get aboard, son."

"Yes, sir."

The passage into the bowels of the transport was gloomy. When the lad's eyes adjusted he saw a gunner's mate wearing the brassard of a Master-at-Arms, who hooked a thumb towards an open air-tight door.

"In there. Find your locker and wait by it." Libby hurried to obey. Inside he found a jumble of baggage and men in a wide low-ceilinged compartment. A line of glow-tubes ran around the junction of bulkhead and ceiling and trisected the overhead; the soft roar of blowers made a background to the voices of his shipmates. He picked his way through heaped luggage and located his locker, seven-ten, on the far wall outboard. He broke the seal on the combination lock, glanced at the combination, and opened it. The locker was very small, the middle of a tier of three. He considered what he should keep in it. A loudspeaker drowned out the surrounding voices and demanded his attention:

"Attention! Man all space details; first section. Raise ship in twelve minutes. Close air-tight doors. Stop blowers at minus two minutes. Special orders for passengers; place all gear on deck, and lie down on red signal light. Remain down until release is sounded. Masters-at-Arms check compliance."

The gunner's mate popped in, glanced around and immediately commenced supervising rearrangement of the baggage. Heavy items were lashed down. Locker doors were closed. By the time each boy had found a place on the deck and the Master-at-Arms had okayed the pad under his head, the glow-tubes turned red and the loudspeaker brayed out.

"All hands—Up Ship! Stand by for acceleration." The Master-at-Arms hastily reclined against two cruise bags, and watched the room. The blowers sighed to a stop. There followed two minutes of dead silence. Libby felt his heart commence to pound. The two minutes stretched interminably. Then the deck quivered and a roar like escaping high-pressure steam beat at his ear drums. He was suddenly very heavy and a weight lay across his chest and heart. An indefinite time later the glow-tubes flashed white, and the announcer bellowed:

"Secure all getting underway details; regular watch, first section." The blowers droned into life. The Master-at-Arms stood up, rubbed his buttocks and pounded his arms, then said:

"Okay, boys." He stepped over and undogged the airtight door to the passageway. Libby got up and blundered into a bulkhead, nearly falling. His legs and arms had gone to sleep, besides which he felt alarmingly light, as if he had sloughed off at least half of his inconsiderable mass.

For the next two hours he was too busy to think, or to be homesick. Suitcases, boxes, and bags had to be passed down into the lower hold and lashed against angular acceleration. He located and learned how to use a waterless water closet. He found his assigned bunk and learned that it was his only eight hours in twenty-four; two other boys had the use of it too. The three sections ate in three shifts, nine shifts in all—twenty-four youths and a master-at-arms at one long table which jam-filled a narrow compartment off the galley.

After lunch Libby restowed his locker. He was standing before it, gazing at a photograph which he intended to mount on the inside of the locker door, when a command filled the compartment:

"Attention!"

Standing inside the door was the Captain flanked by the Master-at-Arms. The Captain commenced to speak. "At rest, men. Sit down. McCoy, tell control to shift this compartment to smoke filter." The gunner's mate hurried to the communicator on the bulkhead and spoke into it in a low tone. Almost at once the hum of the blowers climbed a half-octave and stayed there. "Now light up if you like. I'm going to talk to you.

"You boys are headed out on the biggest thing so far in your lives. From now on you're men, with one of the hardest jobs ahead of you that men have ever tackled. What we have to do is part of a bigger scheme. You, and hundreds of thousands of others like you, are going out as pioneers to fix up the solar system so that human beings can make better use of it.

"Equally important, you are being given a chance to build yourselves into useful and happy citizens of the Federation.

For one reason or another you weren't happily adjusted back on Earth. Some of you saw the jobs you were trained for abolished by new inventions. Some of you got into trouble from not knowing what to do with the modern leisure. In any case you were misfits. Maybe you were called bad boys and had a lot of black marks chalked up against you.

"But everyone of you starts even today. The only record you have in this ship is your name at the top of a blank sheet of paper. It's up to you what goes on that page.

"Now about our job—We didn't get one of the easy repair-and-recondition jobs on the Moon, with week-ends at Luna City, and all the comforts of home. Nor did we draw a high-gravity planet where a man can eat a full meal and expect to keep it down. Instead we've got to go out to Asteroid HS-5388 and turn it into Space Station E-M3. She has no atmosphere at all, and only about two per cent Earth-surface gravity. We've got to play human fly on her for at least six months, no girls to date, no television, no recreation that you don't devise yourselves, and hard work every day. You'll get space sick, and so homesick you can taste it, and agoraphobia. If you aren't careful you'll get ray-burnt. Your stomach will act up, and you'll wish to God you'd never enrolled.

"But if you behave yourself, and listen to the advice of the old spacemen, you'll come out of it strong and healthy, with a little credit stored up in the bank, and a lot of knowledge and experience that you wouldn't get in forty years on Earth. You'll be men, and you'll know it.

"One last word. It will be pretty uncomfortable to those that aren't used to it. Just give the other fellow a little consideration, and you'll get along all right. If you have any complaint and can't get satisfaction any other way, come see me. Otherwise, that's all. Any questions?"

One of the boys put up his hand. "Captain?" he enquired timidly.

"Speak up, lad, and give your name."

"Rogers, sir. Will we be able to get letters from home?"

"Yes, but not very often. Maybe every month or so. The chaplain will carry mail, and any inspection and supply ships."

The ship's loudspeaker blatted out, "All hands! Free flight in ten minutes. Stand by to lose weight." The Master-at-Arms supervised the rigging of grab-lines. All loose gear was made fast, and little cellulose bags were issued to each man. Hardly was this done when Libby felt himself get light on his feet—a sensation exactly like that experienced when an express elevator makes a quick stop on an upward trip, except that the sensation continued and became more intense. At first it was a pleasant novelty, then it rapidly became distressing. The blood pounded in his ears, and his feet were clammy and cold. His saliva secreted at an abnormal rate. He tried to swallow, choked, and coughed. Then his stomach shuddered and contracted with a violent, painful, convulsive reflex and he was suddenly, disastrously nauseated. After the first excruciating spasm, he heard McCoy's voice shouting.

"Hey! Use your sick-kits like I told you. Don't let that stuff get in the blowers." Dimly Libby realized that the admonishment included him. He fumbled for his cellulose bag just as a second temblor shook him, but he managed to fit the bag over his mouth before the eruption occurred. When it subsided, he became aware that he was floating near the overhead and facing the door. The chief Master-at-Arms slithered in the door and spoke to McCoy.

"How are you making out?"

"Well enough. Some of the boys missed their kits."

"Okay. Mop it up. You can use the starboard lock." He swam out.

McCoy touched Libby's arm. "Here, Pinkie, start catching them butterflies." He handed him a handful of cotton waste, then took another handful himself and neatly dabbed up a globule of the slimy filth that floated about the compartment. "Be sure your sick-kit is on tight. When you get sick, just stop and wait until it's over." Libby imitated him as best as he could. In a few minutes the room was free of the worst of the sickening debris. McCoy looked it over, and spoke:

"Now peel off them dirty duds, and change your kits. Three or four of you bring everything along to the starboard lock."

At the starboard spacelock, the kits were put in first, the inner door closed, and the outer opened. When the inner door was opened again the kits were gone—blown out into space by the escaping air. Pinkie addressed McCoy,

"Do we have to throw away our dirty clothes too?"

"Huh uh, we'll just give them a dose of vacuum. Take 'em into the lock and stop 'em to those hooks on the bulkheads. Tie 'em tight."

This time the lock was left closed for about five minutes. When the lock was opened the garments were bone dry—all the moisture boiled out by the vacuum of space. All that remained of the unpleasant rejecta was a sterile powdery residue. McCoy viewed them with approval. "They'll do. Take them back to the compartment. Then brush them—hard—in front of the exhaust blowers."

The next few days were an eternity of misery. Homesickness was forgotten in the all-engrossing wretchedness of spacesickness. The Captain granted fifteen minutes of mild acceleration for each of the nine meal periods, but the respite accentuated the agony. Libby would go to a meal, weak and ravenously hungry. The meal would stay down until free flight was resumed, then the sickness would hit him all over again.

On the fourth day he was seated against a bulkhead, enjoying the luxury of a few remaining minutes of weight while the last shift ate, when McCoy walked in and sat down beside him. The gunner's mate fitted a smoke filter over his face and lit a cigarette. He inhaled deeply and started to chat.

"How's it going, bud?"

"All right, I guess. This spacesickness— Say, McCoy, how do you ever get used to it?"

"You get over it in time. Your body acquires new reflexes, so they tell me. Once you learn to swallow without choking, you'll be all right. You even get so you like it. It's restful and relaxing. Four hours sleep is as good as ten."

Libby shook his head dolefully. "I don't think I'll ever get used to it."

"Yes, you will. You'd better anyway. This here asteroid won't have any surface gravity to speak of; the Chief Quartermaster says it won't run over two per cent Earth normal. That ain't enough to cure spacesickness. And there won't be any way to accelerate for meals either."

Libby shivered and held his head between his hands.

Locating one asteroid among a couple of thousand is not as easy as finding Trafalgar Square in London—especially against the star-crowded backdrop of the galaxy. You take off from Terra with its orbital speed of about nineteen miles per second. You attempt to settle into a composite conoid curve that will not only intersect the orbit of the tiny fast-moving body, but also accomplish an exact rendezvous. Asteroid HS-5388, 'Eighty-eight,' lay about two and two-tenths astronomical units out from the sun, a little more than two hundred million miles; when the transport took off it lay beyond the sun better than three hundred million miles. Captain Doyle instructed the navigator to plot the basic ellipsoid to tack in free flight around the sun through an elapsed distance of some three hundred and forty million miles. The principle involved is the same as used by a hunter to wing a duck in flight by 'leading' the bird in flight. But suppose that you face directly into the sun as you shoot; suppose the bird can not be seen from where you stand, and you have nothing to aim by but some old reports as to how it was flying when last seen?

On the ninth day of the passage Captain Doyle betook himself to the chart room and commenced punching keys on the ponderous integral calculator. Then he sent his orderly to present his compliments to the navigator and to ask him to come to the chartroom. A few minutes later a tall heavyset form swam through the door, steadied himself with a grabline and greeted the captain.

"Good morning, Skipper."

"Hello, Blackie." The Old Man looked up from where he was strapped into the integrator's saddle. "I've been checking your corrections for the meal time accelerations."

"It's a nuisance to have a bunch of ground-lubbers on board, sir."

"Yes, it is, but we have to give those boys a chance to eat, or they couldn't work when we got there. Now I want to decelerate starting about ten o'clock, ship's time. What's our eight o'clock speed and co-ordinates?"

The Navigator slipped a notebook out of his tunic. "Three hundred fifty-eight miles per second; course is right ascension fifteen hours, eight minutes, twenty-seven seconds, declination minus seven degrees, three minutes; solar distance one hundred and ninety-two million four hundred eighty thousand miles. Our radial position is twelve degrees above course, and almost dead on course in R.A. Do you want Sol's co-ordinates?"

"No, not now." The captain bent over the calculator, frowned and chewed the tip of his tongue as he worked the controls. "I want you to kill the acceleration about one million miles inside Eighty-eight's orbit. I hate to waste the fuel, but the belt is full of junk and this damned rock is so small that we will probably have to run a search curve. Use twenty hours on deceleration and commence changing course to port after eight hours. Use normal asymptotic approach. You should have her in a circular trajectory abreast of Eighty-eight, and paralleling her orbit by six o'clock tomorrow morning. I shall want to be called at three."

"Aye aye, sir."

"Let me see your figures when you get 'em. I'll send up the order book later."

The transport accelerated on schedule. Shortly after three the Captain entered the control room and blinked his eyes at the darkness. The sun was still concealed by the hull of the transport and the midnight blackness was broken only by the dim blue glow of the instrument dials, and the crack of light from under the chart hood. The Navigator turned at the familiar tread.

"Good morning, Captain."

"Morning, Blackie. In sight yet?"

"Not yet. We've picked out half a dozen rocks, but none of them checked."

"Any of them close?"

"Not uncomfortably. We've overtaken a little sand from time to time."

"That can't hurt us—not on a stern chase like this. If pilots would only realize that the asteroids flow in fixed directions at computable speeds nobody would come to grief out here." He stopped to light a cigarette. "People talk about space being dangerous. Sure, it used to be; but I don't know of a case in the past twenty years that couldn't be charged up to some fool's recklessness."

"You're right, Skipper. By the way, there's coffee under the chart hood."

"Thanks; I had a cup down below." He walked over by the lookouts at stereoscopes and radar tanks and peered up at the star-flecked blackness. Three cigarettes later the lookout nearest him called out.

"Light ho!"

"Where away?"

His mate read the exterior dials of the stereoscope. "Plus point two, abaft one point three, slight drift astern." He shifted to radar and added, "Range seven nine oh four three."

"Does that check?"

"Could be, Captain. What is her disk?" came the Navigator's muffled voice from under the hood. The first lookout hurriedly twisted the knobs of his instrument, but the Captain nudged him aside.

"I'll do this, son." He fitted his face to the double eye

guards and surveyed a little silvery sphere, a tiny moon. Carefully he brought two illuminated cross-hairs up until they were exactly tangent to the upper and lower limbs of the disk. "Mark!"

The reading was noted and passed to the Navigator, who shortly ducked out from under the hood.

"That's our baby, Captain."

"Good."

"Shall I make a visual triangulation?"

"Let the watch officer do that. You go down and get some sleep. I'll ease her over until we get close enough to use the optical range finder."

"Thanks, I will."

Within a few minutes the word had spread around the ship that Eighty-eight had been sighted. Libby crowded into the starboard troop deck with a throng of excited mess mates and attempted to make out their future home from the view port. McCoy poured cold water on their excitement.

"By the time that rock shows up big enough to tell anything about it with your naked eye we'll all be at our grounding stations. She's only about a hundred miles thick, yuh know."

And so it was. Many hours later the ship's announcer shouted:

"All hands! Man your grounding stations. Close all air-tight doors. Stand by to cut blowers on signal."

McCoy forced them to lie down throughout the ensuing two hours. Short shocks of rocket blasts alternated with nauseating weightlessness. Then the blowers stopped and check valves clicked into their seats. The ship dropped free for a few moments—a final quick blast—five seconds of falling, and a short, light, grinding bump. A single bugle note came over the announcer, and the blowers took up their hum.

McCoy floated lightly to his feet and poised, swaying, on his toes. "All out, troops—this is the end of the line."

A short chunky lad, a little younger than most of them, awkwardly emulated him, and bounded toward the door, shouting as he went, "Come on, fellows! Let's go outside and explore!"

The Master-at-Arms squelched him. "Not so fast, kid. Aside from the fact that there is no air out there, go right ahead. You'll freeze to death, burn to death, and explode like a ripe tomato. Squad leader, detail six men to break out spacesuits. The rest of you stay here and stand by."

The working party returned shortly loaded down with a couple of dozen bulky packages. Libby let go the four he carried and watched them float gently to the deck. McCoy unzipped the envelope from one suit, and lectured them about it.

"This is a standard service type, general issue, Mark IV, Modification 2." He grasped the suit by the shoulders and shook it out so that it hung like a suit of long winter underwear with the helmet lolling helplessly between the shoulders of the garment. "It's self-sustaining for eight hours, having an oxygen supply for that period. It also has a nitrogen trim tank and a carbon-dioxide-water-vapor cartridge filter."

He droned on, repeating practically verbatim the description and instructions given in training regulations. McCoy knew these suits like his tongue knew the roof of his mouth; the knowledge had meant his life on more than one occasion.

"The suit is woven from glass fibre laminated with nonvolatile asbesto-cellutite. The resulting fabric is flexible, very durable; and will turn all rays normal to solar space outside the orbit of Mercury. It is worn over your regular clothing, but notice the wire-braced accordion pleats at the major joints. They are so designed as to keep the internal volume of the suit nearly constant when the arms or legs are bent. Otherwise the gas pressure inside would tend to keep the suit blown up in an erect position, and movement while wearing the suit would be very fatiguing.

"The helmet is moulded from a transparent silicone, leaded and polarized against too great ray penetration. It may be equipped with external visors of any needed type. Orders are to wear not less than a number-two amber on this body. In addition, a lead plate covers the cranium and extends on down the back of the suit, completely covering the spinal column.

"The suit is equipped with two-way telephony. If your radio quits, as these have a habit of doing, you can talk by putting your helmets in contact. Any questions?"

"How do you eat and drink during the eight hours?"

"You don't stay in 'em any eight hours. You can carry sugar balls in a gadget in the helmet, but you boys will always eat at the base. As for water, there's a nipple in the helmet near your mouth which you can reach by turning your head to the left. It's hooked to a built-in canteen. But don't drink any more water when you're wearing a suit than you have to. These suits ain't got any plumbing."

Suits were passed out to each lad, and McCoy illustrated how to don one. A suit was spread supine on the deck, the front zipper that stretched from neck to crotch was spread wide and one sat down inside this opening, whereupon the lower part was drawn on like long stockings. Then a wiggle into each sleeve and the heavy flexible gauntlets were smoothed and patted into place. Finally an awkward backward stretch of the neck with shoulders hunched enabled the helmet to be placed over the head.

Libby followed the motions of McCoy and stood up in his suit. He examined the zipper which controlled the suit's only opening. It was backed by two soft gaskets which would be pressed together by the zipper and sealed by internal air pressure. Inside the helmet a composition mouthpiece for exhalation led to the filter.

McCoy bustled around, inspecting them, tightening a belt here and there, instructing them in the use of the external controls. Satisfied, he reported to the conning room that his section had received basic instruction and was ready to disembark. Permission was received to take them out for thirty minutes acclimatization.

Six at a time, he escorted them through the air lock, and out on the surface of the planetoid. Libby blinked his eyes at the unaccustomed luster of sunshine on rock. Although the sun lay more than two hundred million miles away and bathed the little planet with radiation only one fifth as strong as that lavished on mother Earth, nevertheless the lack of atmosphere resulted in a glare that made him squint. He was glad to have the protection of his amber visor. Overhead the sun, shrunk to penny size, shone down from a dead black sky in which unwinking stars crowded each other and the very sun itself.

The voice of a mess mate sounded in Libby's earphones, "Jeepers! That horizon looks close. I'll bet it ain't more'n a mile away."

Libby looked out over the flat bare plain and subconsciously considered the matter. "It's less," he commented, "than a third of a mile away."

"What the hell do you know about it, Pinkie? And who asked you, anyhow?"

Libby answered defensively, "As a matter of fact, it's one thousand six hundred and seventy feet, figuring that my eyes are five feet three inches above ground level."

"Nuts. Pinkie, you are always trying to show off how much you think you know."

"Why, I am not," Libby protested. "If this body is a hundred miles thick and as round as it looks: why, naturally the horizon *has* to be just that far away."

"Says *who?*"

McCoy interrupted.

"Pipe down! Libby is a lot nearer right than you were."

"He is exactly right," put in a strange voice. "I had to look it up for the navigator before I left control."

"Is that so?"—McCoy's voice again—"If the Chief Quartermaster says you're right, Libby, you're right. How did you know?"

Libby flushed miserably. "I—I don't know. That's the only way it could be."

The gunner's mate and the quartermaster stared at him but dropped the subject.

By the end of the 'day' (ship's time, for Eighty-eight had a period of eight hours and thirteen minutes), work was well under way. The transport had grounded close by a low range of hills. The Captain selected a little bowl-shaped depression in the hills, some thousand feet long and half as broad, in which to establish a permanent camp. This was to be roofed over, sealed, and an atmosphere provided.

In the hill between the ship and the valley, quarters were to be excavated; dormitories, mess hall, officers' quarters, sick bay, recreation room, offices, store rooms, and so forth. A tunnel must be bored through the hill, connecting the sites of these rooms, and connecting with a ten foot airtight metal tube sealed to the ship's portside air-lock. Both the tube and tunnel were to be equipped with a continuous conveyor belt for passengers and freight.

Libby found himself assigned to the roofing detail. He helped a metalsmith struggle over the hill with a portable atomic heater, difficult to handle because of a mass of eight hundred pounds, but weighing here only sixteen pounds. The rest of the roofing detail were breaking out and preparing to move by hand the enormous translucent tent which was to be the 'sky' of the little valley.

The metalsmith located a landmark on the inner slope of the valley, set up his heater, and commenced cutting a deep horizontal groove or step in the rock. He kept it always at the same level by following a chalk mark drawn along the rock wall. Libby enquired how the job had been surveyed so quickly.

"Easy," he was answered, "two of the quartermasters went ahead with a transit, leveled it just fifty feet above the valley floor, and clamped a searchlight to it. Then one of 'em ran like hell around the rim, making chalk marks at the height at which the beam struck."

"Is this roof going to be just fifty feet high?"

"No, it will average maybe a hundred. It bellies up in the middle from the air pressure."

"Earth normal?"

"Half Earth normal."

Libby concentrated for an instant, then looked puzzled. "But look— This valley is a thousand feet long and better than five hundred wide. At half of fifteen pounds per square inch, and allowing for the arch of the roof, that's a load of one and an eighth billion pounds. What fabric can take that kind of a load?"

"Cobwebs."

"Cobwebs?"

"Yeah, cobwebs. Strongest stuff in the world, stronger than the best steel. Synthetic spider silk. This gauge we're using for the roof has a tensile strength of four thousand pounds a running inch."

Libby hesitated a second, then replied, "I see. With a rim about eighteen hundred thousand inches around, the maximum pull at the point of anchoring would be about six hundred and twenty-five pounds per inch. Plenty safe margin."

The metalsmith leaned on his tool and nodded. "Something like that. You're pretty quick at arithmetic, aren't you, bud?"

Libby looked startled. "I just like to get things straight."

They worked rapidly around the slope, cutting a clean smooth groove to which the 'cobweb' could be anchored and sealed. The white-hot lava spewed out of the discharge vent and ran slowly down the hillside. A brown vapor boiled off the surface of the molten rock, arose a few feet and sublimed almost at once in the vacuum to white powder which settled to the ground. The metalsmith pointed to the powder.

"That stuff 'ud cause silicosis if we let it stay there, and breathed it later."

"What do you do about it?"

"Just clean it out with the blowers of the air conditioning plant."

Libby took this opening to ask another question. "Mister—?"

"Johnson's my name. No mister necessary."

"Well, Johnson, where do we get the air for this whole valley, not to mention the tunnels? I figure we must need twenty-five million cubic feet or more. Do we manufacture it?"

"Naw, that's too much trouble. We brought it with us."

"On the transport?"

"Uh huh, at fifty atmospheres."

Libby considered this. "I see—that way it would go into a space eighty feet on a side."

"Matter of fact it's in three specially constructed holds—giant air bottles. This transport carried air to Ganymede. I was in her then—a recruit, but in the air gang even then."

In three weeks the permanent camp was ready for occupancy and the transport cleared of its cargo. The storerooms bulged with tools and supplies. Captain Doyle had moved his administrative offices underground, signed over his command to his first officer, and given him permission to proceed on 'duty assigned'—in this case; return to Terra with a skeleton crew.

Libby watched them take off from a vantage point on the hillside. An overpowering homesickness took possession of him. Would he ever go home? He honestly believed at the time that he would swap the rest of his life for thirty minutes each with his mother and with Betty.

He started down the hill toward the tunnel lock. At least the transport carried letters to them, and with any luck the chaplain would be by soon with letters from Earth. But tomorrow and the days after that would be no fun. He had enjoyed being in the air gang, but tomorrow he went back to his squad. He did not relish that—the boys in his squad were all right, he guessed, but he just could not seem to fit in.

This company of the C.C.C. started on its bigger job; to pock-mark Eighty-eight with rocket tubes so that Captain

Doyle could push this hundred-mile marble out of her orbit and herd her in to a new orbit between Earth and Mars, to be used as a space station—a refuge for ships in distress, a haven for life boats, a fueling stop, a naval outpost.

Libby was assigned to a heater in pit H-16. It was his business to carve out carefully calculated emplacements in which the blasting crew then set off the minute charges which accomplished the major part of the excavating. Two squads were assigned to H-16, under the general supervision of an elderly marine gunner. The gunner sat on the edge of the pit, handling the plans, and occasionally making calculations on a circular slide rule which hung from a lanyard around his neck.

Libby had just completed a tricky piece of cutting for a three-stage blast, and was waiting for the blasters, when his phones picked up the gunner's instructions concerning the size of the charge. He pressed his transmitter button.

"Mr. Larsen! You've made a mistake!"

"Who said that?"

"This is Libby. You've made a mistake in the charge. If you set off that charge, you'll blow this pit right out of the ground, and us with it."

Marine Gunner Larsen spun the dials on his slide rule before replying, "You're all het up over nothing, son. That charge is correct."

"No, I'm not, sir," Libby persisted, "you've multiplied where you should have divided."

"Have you had any experience at this sort of work?"

"No, sir."

Larsen addressed his next remark to the blasters. "Set the charge."

They started to comply. Libby gulped, and wiped his lips with his tongue. He knew what he had to do, but he was afraid. Two clumsy stiff-legged jumps placed him beside the blasters. He pushed between them and tore the electrodes from the detonator. A shadow passed over him as he worked, and Larsen floated down beside him. A hand grasped his arm.

"You shouldn't have done that, son. That's direct disobedience of orders. I'll have to report you." He commenced reconnecting the firing circuit.

Libby's ears burned with embarrassment, but he answered back with the courage of timidity at bay. "I had to do it, sir. You're still wrong."

Larsen paused and ran his eyes over the dogged face. "Well —it's a waste of time, but I don't like to make you stand by a charge you're afraid of. Let's go over the calculation together."

Captain Doyle sat at his ease in his quarters, his feet on his desk. He stared at a nearly empty glass tumbler.

"That's good beer, Blackie. Do you suppose we could brew some more when it's gone?"

"I don't know, Cap'n. Did we bring any yeast?"

"Find out, will you?" He turned to a massive man who occupied the third chair. "Well, Larsen, I'm glad it wasn't any worse than it was."

"What beats me, Captain, is how I could have made such a mistake. I worked it through twice. If it had been a nitro explosive, I'd have known off hand that I was wrong. If this kid hadn't had a hunch, I'd have set it off."

Captain Doyle clapped the old warrant officer on the shoulder. "Forget it, Larsen. You wouldn't have hurt anybody; that's why I require the pits to be evacuated even for small charges. These isotope explosives are tricky at best. Look what happened in pit A-9. Ten days' work shot with one charge, and the gunnery officer himself approved that one. But I want to see this boy. What did you say his name was?"

"Libby, A. J."

Doyle touched a button on his desk. A knock sounded at the door. A bellowed "Come in!" produced a stripling wearing the brassard of Corpsman Mate-of-the-Deck.

"Have Corpsman Libby report to me."

"Aye aye, sir."

Some few minutes later Libby was ushered into the Captain's cabin. He looked nervously around, and noted Larsen's presence, a fact that did not contribute to his peace of mind. He reported in a barely audible voice, "Corpsman Libby, sir."

The Captain looked him over. "Well, Libby, I hear that you and Mr. Larsen had a difference of opinion this morning. Tell me about it."

"I—I didn't mean any harm, sir."

"Of course not. You're not in any trouble; you did us all a good turn this morning. Tell me, how did you know that the calculation was wrong? Had any mining experience?"

"No, sir. I just saw that he had worked it out wrong."

"But how?"

Libby shuffled uneasily. "Well, sir, it just seemed wrong— It didn't fit."

"Just a second, Captain. May I ask this young man a couple of questions?" It was Commander "Blackie" Rhodes who spoke.

"Certainly. Go ahead."

"Are you the lad they call 'Pinkie'?"

Libby blushed. "Yes, sir."

"I've heard some rumors about this boy." Rhodes pushed his big frame out of his chair, went over to a bookshelf, and removed a thick volume. He thumbed through it, then with open book before him, started to question Libby.

"What's the square root of ninety-five?"

"Nine and seven hundred forty-seven thousandths."

"What's the cube root?"

"Four and five hundred sixty-three thousandths."

"What's its logarithm?"

"Its what, sir?"

"Good Lord, can a boy get through school today without knowing?"

The boy's discomfort became more intense. "I didn't get much schooling, sir. My folks didn't accept the Covenant until Pappy died, and we had to."

"I see. A logarithm is a name for a power to which you raise a given number, called the base, to get the number whose logarithm it is. Is that clear?"

Libby thought hard. "I don't quite get it, sir."

"I'll try again. If you raise ten to the second power— square it—it gives one hundred. Therefore the logarithm of a hundred to the base ten is two. In the same fashion the logarithm of a thousand to the base ten is three. Now what is the logarithm of ninety-five?"

Libby puzzled for a moment. "I can't make it come out even. It's a fraction."

"That's okay."

"Then it's one and nine hundred seventy-eight thousandths —just about."

Rhodes turned to the Captain. "I guess that about proves it, sir."

Doyle nodded thoughtfully. "Yes, the lad seems to have intuitive knowledge of arithmetical relationships. But let's see what else he has."

"I am afraid we'll have to send him back to Earth to find out properly."

Libby caught the gist of this last remark. "Please, sir, you aren't going to send me home? Maw 'ud be awful vexed with me."

"No, no, nothing of the sort. When your time is up, I want you to be checked over in the psychometrical laboratories. In the meantime I wouldn't part with you for a quarter's pay. I'd give up smoking first. But let's see what else you can do."

In the ensuing hour the Captain and the Navigator heard Libby: one, deduce the Pythagorean proposition; two, derive Newton's laws of motion and Kepler's laws of ballistics from a statement of the conditions in which they obtained; three, judge length, area, and volume by eye with no measurable error. He had jumped into the idea of relativity and non-rectilinear space-time continua, and was beginning to pour forth ideas faster than he could talk, when Doyle held up a hand.

"That's enough, son. You'll be getting a fever. You run along to bed now, and come see me in the morning. I'm taking you off field work."

"Yes, sir."

"By the way, what is your full name?"

"Andrew Jackson Libby, sir."

"No, your folks wouldn't have signed the Covenant. Good night."

"Good night, sir."

After he had gone, the two older men discussed their discovery.

"How do you size it up, Captain?"

"Well, he's a genius, of course—one of those wild talents that will show up once in a blue moon. I'll turn him loose among my books and see how he shapes up. Shouldn't wonder if he were a page-at-a-glance reader, too."

"It beats me what we turn up among these boys—and not a one of 'em any account back on Earth."

Doyle nodded. "That was the trouble with these kids. They didn't feel needed."

Eighty-eight swung some millions of miles further around the sun. The pock-marks on her face grew deeper, and were lined with durite, that strange close-packed laboratory product which (usually) would confine even atomic disintegration.

Then Eighty-eight received a series of gentle pats, always on the side headed along her course. In a few weeks' time the rocket blasts had their effect and Eighty-eight was plunging in an orbit toward the sun.

When she reached her station one and three-tenths the distance from the sun of Earth's orbit, she would have to be coaxed by another series of pats into a circular orbit. Thereafter she was to be known as E-M3, Earth-Mars Space Station Spot Three.

Hundreds of millions of miles away two other C.C.C. companies were inducing two other planetoids to quit their age-old grooves and slide between Earth and Mars to land in the same orbit as Eighty-eight. One was due to ride this orbit one hundred and twenty degrees ahead of Eighty-eight, the other one hundred and twenty degrees behind. When E-M1, E-M2, and E-M3 were all on station no hard-pushed traveler of the spaceways on the Earth-Mars passage would ever again find himself far from land—or rescue.

During the months that Eighty-eight fell free toward the sun, Captain Doyle reduced the working hours of his crew and turned them to the comparatively light labor of building a hotel and converting the little roofed-in valley into a garden spot. The rock was broken down into soil, fertilizers applied, and cultures of anaerobic bacteria planted. Then plants, conditioned by thirty-odd generations of low gravity at Luna City, were set out and tenderly cared for. Except for the low gravity, Eighty-eight began to feel like home.

But when Eighty-eight approached a tangent to the hypothetical future orbit of E-M3, the company went back to maneuvering routine, watch on and watch off, with the Captain living on black coffee and catching catnaps in the plotting room.

Libby was assigned to the ballistic calculator, three tons of thinking metal that dominated the plotting room. He loved the big machine. The Chief Fire Controlman let him help adjust it and care for it. Libby subconsciously thought of it as a person—his own kind of person.

On the last day of the approach, the shocks were more frequent. Libby sat in the right-hand saddle of the calculator and droned out the predictions for the next salvo, while gloating over the accuracy with which the machine tracked. Captain Doyle fussed around nervously, occasionally stopping to peer over the Navigator's shoulder. Of course the figures were right, but what if it didn't work? No one had ever moved so large a mass before. Suppose it plunged on and on—and on. Nonsense! It couldn't. Still he would be glad when they were past the critical speed.

A marine orderly touched his elbow. "Helio from the Flagship, sir."

"Read it."

"Flag to Eighty-eight; private message, Captain Doyle; am lying off to watch you bring her in.—Kearney."

Doyle smiled. Nice of the old geezer. Once they were on station, he would invite the Admiral to ground for dinner and show him the park.

Another salvo cut loose, heavier than any before. The room trembled violently. In a moment the reports of the surface observers commenced to trickle in. "Tube nine, clear!" "Tube ten, clear!"

But Libby's drone ceased.

Captain Doyle turned on him. "What's the matter, Libby? Asleep? Call the polar stations. I have to have a parallax."

"Captain—" The boy's voice was low and shaking.

"Speak up, man!"

"Captain—the machine isn't tracking."

"Spiers!" The grizzled head of the Chief Fire Controlman appeared from behind the calculator.

"I'm already on it, sir. Let you know in a moment."

He ducked back again. After a couple of long minutes he reappeared. "Gyros tumbled. It's a twelve hour calibration job, at least."

The Captain said nothing, but turned away, and walked to the far end of the room. The Navigator followed him with his eyes. He returned, glanced at the chronometer, and spoke to the Navigator.

"Well, Blackie, if I don't have that firing data in seven minutes, we're sunk. Any suggestions?"

Rhodes shook his head without speaking.

Libby timidly raised his voice. "Captain—"

Doyle jerked around. "Yes?"

"The firing data is tube thirteen, seven point six three; tube twelve, six point nine oh; tube fourteen, six point eight nine."

Doyle studied his face. "You sure about that, son?"

"It *has* to be that, Captain."

Doyle stood perfectly still. This time he did not look at

Rhodes but stared straight ahead. Then he took a long pull on his cigarette, glanced at the ash, and said in a steady voice,

"Apply the data. Fire on the bell."

Four hours later, Libby was still droning out firing data, his face grey, his eyes closed. Once he had fainted but when they revived him he was still muttering figures. From time to time the Captain and the Navigator relieved each other, but there was no relief for him.

The salvos grew closer together, but the shocks were lighter.

Following one faint salvo, Libby looked up, stared at the ceiling, and spoke.

"That's all, Captain."

"Call polar stations!"

The reports came back promptly, "Parallax constant, sidereal-solar rate constant."

The Captain relaxed into a chair. "Well, Blackie, we did it —thanks to Libby!" Then he noticed a worried, thoughtful look spread over Libby's face. "What's the matter, man? Have we slipped up?"

"Captain, you know you said the other day that you wished you had Earth-normal gravity in the park?"

"Yes. What of it?"

"If that book on gravitation you lent me is straight dope, I think I know a way to accomplish it."

The Captain inspected him as if seeing him for the first time. "Libby, you have ceased to amaze me. Could you stop doing that sort of thing long enough to dine with the Admiral?"

"Gee, Captain, that would be swell!"

The audio circuit from Communications cut in.

"Helio from Flagship: 'Well done, Eighty-eight.' "

Doyle smiled around at them all. "That's pleasant confirmation."

The audio brayed again.

"Helio from Flagship: 'Cancel last signal, stand by for correction.' "

A look of surprise and worry sprang into Doyle's face— then the audio continued:

"Helio from Flagship: 'Well done, E-M3.' "

Methuselah's Children

PART ONE

"MARY SPERLING, you're a fool not to marry him!"

Mary Sperling added up her losses and wrote a check before answering, "There's too much difference in age." She passed over her credit voucher. "I shouldn't gamble with you —sometimes I think you're a sensitive."

"Nonsense! You're just trying to change the subject. You must be nearly thirty . . . and you won't be pretty forever."

Mary smiled wryly. "Don't I know it!"

"Bork Vanning can't be much over forty and he's a plus citizen. You should jump at the chance."

"You jump at it. I must run now. Service, Ven."

"Service," Ven answered, then frowned at the door as it contracted after Mary Sperling. She itched to know why Mary would not marry a prime catch like the Honorable Bork Vanning and was almost as curious as to why and where Mary was going, but the custom of privacy stopped her.

Mary had no intention of letting anyone know where she was going. Outside her friend's apartment she dropped down a bounce tube to the basement, claimed her car from the robopark, guided it up the ramp and set the controls for North Shore. The car waited for a break in the traffic, then dived into the high-speed stream and hurried north. Mary settled back for a nap.

When its setting was about to run out, the car beeped for instructions; Mary woke up and glanced out. Lake Michigan was a darker band of darkness on her right. She signaled traffic control to let her enter the local traffic lane; it sorted out her car and placed her there, then let her resume manual control. She fumbled in the glove compartment.

The license number which traffic control automatically photographed as she left the controlways was not the number the car had been wearing.

She followed a side road uncontrolled for several miles, turned into a narrow dirt road which led down to the shore, and stopped. There she waited, lights out, and listened. South of her the lights of Chicago glowed; a few hundred yards inland the controlways whined, but here there was nothing but the little timid noises of night creatures. She reached into the glove compartment, snapped a switch; the instrument panel glowed, uncovering other dials behind it. She studied these while making adjustments. Satisfied that no radar watched her and that nothing was moving near her, she snapped off the instruments, sealed the window by her and started up again.

What appeared to be a standard Camden speedster rose quietly up, moved out over the lake, skimming it—dropped into the water and sank. Mary waited until she was a quarter mile off shore in fifty feet of water, then called a station. "Answer," said a voice.

" 'Life is short——' "

" '—but the years are long.' "

" 'Not,' " Mary responded, " 'while the evil days come not.' "

"I sometimes wonder," the voice answered conversationally. "Okay, Mary. I've checked you."

"Tommy?"

"No—Cecil Hedrick. Are your controls cast loose?"

"Yes. Take over."

Seventeen minutes later the car surfaced in a pool which occupied much of an artificial cave. When the car was beached, Mary got out, said hello to the guards and went on through a tunnel into a large underground room where fifty or sixty men and women were seated. She chatted until a clock announced midnight, then she mounted a rostrum and faced them.

"I am," she stated, "one hundred and eighty-three years old. Is there anyone here who is older?"

No one spoke. After a decent wait she went on, "Then in accordance with our customs I declare this meeting opened. Will you choose a moderator?"

Someone said, "Go ahead, Mary." When no one else spoke up, she said, "Very well." She seemed indifferent to the honor and the group seemed to share her casual attitude—an air of never any hurry, of freedom from the tension of modern life.

"We are met as usual," she announced, "to discuss our welfare and that of our sisters and brothers. Does any Family representative have a message from his family? Or does anyone care to speak for himself?"

A man caught her eye and spoke up. "Ira Weatheral, speaking for the Johnson Family. We've met nearly two months early. The trustees must have a reason. Let's hear it."

She nodded and turned to a prim little man in the first row. "Justin . . . if you will, please."

The prim little man stood up and bowed stiffly. Skinny legs stuck out below his badly-cut kilt. He looked and acted like an elderly, dusty civil servant, but his black hair and the firm, healthy tone of his skin said that he was a man in his prime. "Justin Foote," he said precisely, "reporting for the trustees. It has been eleven years since the Families decided on the experiment of letting the public know that there were, living among them, persons who possessed a probable life expectancy far in excess of that anticipated by the average man, as well as other persons who had proved the scientific truth of such expectation by having lived more than twice the normal life span of human beings."

Although he spoke without notes he sounded as if he were reading aloud a prepared report. What he was saying they all knew but no one hurried him; his audience had none of the febrile impatience so common elsewhere. "In deciding," he droned on, "to reverse the previous long-standing policy of silence and concealment as to the peculiar aspect in which we differ from the balance of the human race, the Families were moved by several considerations. The reason for the original adoption of the policy of concealment should be noted:

"The first offspring resulting from unions assisted by the Howard Foundation were born in 1875. They aroused no comment, for they were in no way remarkable. The Foundation was an openly-chartered non-profit corporation——"

On March 17, 1874, Ira Johnson, medical student, sat in the law offices of Deems, Wingate, Alden, & Deems and listened to an unusual proposition. At last he interrupted the senior partner. "Just a moment! Do I understand that you are trying to *hire* me to marry one of these women?"

The lawyer looked shocked. "Please, Mr. Johnson. Not at all."

"Well, it certainly sounded like it."

"No, no, such a contract would be void, against public policy. We are simply informing you, as administrators of a trust, that should it come about that you *do* marry one of the young ladies on this list it would then be our pleasant duty to endow each child of such a union according to the scale here set forth. But there would be no contract with us involved, nor is there any 'proposition' being made to you—and we certainly do not urge any course of action on you. We are simply informing you of certain facts."

Ira Johnson scowled and shuffled his feet. "What's it all about? Why?"

"That is the business of the Foundation. One might put it that we approve of your grandparents."

"Have you discussed me with them?" Johnson said sharply. He felt no affection for his grandparents. A tight-fisted foursome—if any one of them had had the grace to die at a reasonable age he would not now be worried about money enough to finish medical school.

"We have talked with them, yes. But not about you."

The lawyer shut off further discussion and young Jóhnson accepted gracelessly a list of young women, all strangers, with the intention of tearing it up the moment he was outside the office. Instead, that night he wrote seven drafts before he found the right words in which to start cooling off the relation between himself and his girl back home. He was glad that he had never actually popped the question to her—it would have been deucedly awkward.

When he did marry (from the list) it seemed a curious but not too remarkable coincidence that his wife as well as himself had four living, healthy, active grandparents.

"—an openly chartered non-profit corporation," Foote continued, "and its avowed purpose of encouraging births among persons of sound American stock was consonant with the customs of that century. By the simple expedient of being close-mouthed about the true purpose of the Foundation no unusual methods of concealment were necessary until late in that period during the World Wars sometimes loosely termed 'The Crazy Years——' "

Selected headlines April to June 1969:

BABY BILL BREAKS BANK
2-year toddler youngest winner $1,000,000 TV jackpot
White House phones congrats
COURT ORDERS STATEHOUSE SOLD
Colorado Supreme Bench Rules State Old Age Pension
Has First Lien All State Property

**N.Y. YOUTH MEET DEMANDS UPPER LIMIT
ON FRANCHISE**

"U.S. BIRTH RATE 'TOP SECRET' "—DEFENSE SEC

CAROLINA CONGRESSMAN COPS BEAUTY CROWN
**"Available for draft for President" she announces while
starting tour to show her qualifications**

IOWA RAISES VOTING AGE TO FORTY-ONE
Rioting on Des Moines Campus

**EARTH-EATING FAD MOVES WEST: CHICAGO
PARSON EATS CLAY SANDWICH IN PULPIT**
"Back to simple things," he advises flock.

**LOS ANGELES HI-SCHOOL MOB DEFIES
SCHOOL BOARD**
**"Higher Pay, Shorter Hours, no Homework—We Demand
Our Right to Elect Teachers, Coaches."**

SUICIDE RATE UP NINTH SUCCESSIVE YEAR
AEC Denies Fall-Out to Blame

" '—The Crazy Years.' The trustees of that date decided—correctly, we now believe—that any minority during that period of semantic disorientation and mass hysteria was a probable target for persecution, discriminatory legislation, and even of mob violence. Furthermore the disturbed financial condition of the country and in particular the forced exchange of trust securities for government warrants threatened the solvency of the trust.

"Two courses of action were adopted: the assets of the Foundation were converted into real wealth and distributed widely among members of the Families to be held by them as owners-of-record; and the so-called 'Masquerade' was adopted as a permanent policy. Means were found to simulate the death of any member of the Families who lived to a socially embarrassing age and to provide him with a new identity in another part of the country.

"The wisdom of this later policy, though irksome to some, became evident at once during the Interregnum of the Prophets. The Families at the beginning of the reign of the First Prophet had ninety-seven per cent of their members with publicly avowed ages of less than fifty years. The close public registration enforced by the secret police of the Prophets made changes of public identity difficult, although a few were accomplished with the aid of the revolutionary Cabal.

"Thus, a combination of luck and foresight saved our se-

FUTURE HISTORY

DATES	STORIES	CHARACTERS	TECHNICAL
A.D.			
	Life Line	Pinero	
		Martin	
		Douglas	
	The Roads Must Roll	Gaines	
	Blowups Happen	Blekinsop	
	The Man Who Sold the Moon	Harper / Erickson / King / Lentz / Harriman / McIntyre / Cummings	Douglas-Martin sun-power screens
	Delilah & the Space Rigger		
	Space Jockey		
	Requiem	Wingate	
	The Long Watch	Sam Jones	
	Gentlemen, Be Seated	Satchel	
	The Black Pits of Luna—	Rhysling	
	It's Great to Be Back		
	"—We Also Walk Dogs"	Nehemiah Scudder	
	Searchlight		
2000			Mechanized roads / Commercial rocket travel / Helicopters / Interplanetary travel
	Ordeal in Space		
	The Green Hills of Earth		Growth of submolar mechanics, atomic cont. artificial radioactives, Uranium 235
	Logic of Empire		
	The Menace from Earth		
		Novak	
		John Lyle / Zeb Jones	
		Master Peter- / Magedelene / MacKinnon / "Fader" Randall / Persephone / The "Doctor"	Lazarus Long
	"If This Goes On—"		
	Coventry		(Hiatus) / Developments in psychometrics and psychodynamics
2100			
	Misfit	Ford	Interplanetary travel resumed / Developments in psychometrics and psychodynamics / Limited use of telepathy
	Universe (prologue only)	Libby / McCoy / Rhodes / Doyle	
	Methuselah's Children		
	Universe		Static submolar engineering (parastatics)
	Commonsense		

DATA	SOCIOLOGICAL	REMARKS
Transatlantic rocket flight	THE "CRAZY YEARS" Strike of '76 The "FALSE DAWN" First rocket to the Moon	Considerable technical advance during this period, accompanied by a gradual deterioration of mores, orientation and social institutions, terminating in mass psychoses in the sixth decade, and the interregnum.
Antipodes rocket service		The interregnum was followed by a period of reconstruction in which the Voorhis financial proposals gave a temporary economic stability and chance for re-orientation. This was ended by the opening of new frontiers and a return to nineteenth-century economy.
	Luna City founded Space Precautionary Act Harriman's Lunar Corporations PERIOD OF IMPERIAL EXPLOITATION Revolution in Little America Interplanetary exploration and exploitation American-Australasian anschluss	
Bacteriophage The Travel Unit and the Fighting Unit		Three revolutions ended the short period of interplanetary imperialism: Antarctica, U.S., and Venus. Space travel ceased until 2072.
Commercial stereoptics	Rise of religious fanaticism The "New Crusade" Rebellion and independence of Venusian colonists Religious dictatorship in U.S.	Little research and only minor technical advances during this period. Extreme puritanism. Certain aspects of psychodynamics and psychometrics, mass psychology and social control developed by the priest class.
Booster guns Synthetic foods Weather control Wave mechanics The "Barrier"	THE FIRST HUMAN CIVILIZATION	Re-establishment of civil liberty. Renascence of scientific research. Resumption of space travel. Luna City refounded. Science of social relations, based on the negative basic statements of semantics. Rigor of epistemology. The Covenant.
Atomic "tailoring," Elements 98-416 Parastatic engineering		Beginning of the consolidation of the Solar System.
		First attempt at interstellar exploration.
Rigor of colloids Symbiotic research Longevity		Civil disorder, followed by the end of human adolescence, and beginning of first mature culture.

cret from public disclosure. This was well—we may be sure that things would have gone harshly at that time for any group possessing a prize beyond the power of the Prophet to confiscate.

"The Families took no part as such in the events leading up to the Second American Revolution, but many members participated and served with credit in the Cabal and in the fighting which preceded the fall of New Jerusalem. We took advantage of the period of disorganization which followed to readjust the ages of our kin who had grown conspicuously old. In this we were aided by certain members of the Families who, as members of the Cabal, held key posts in the Reconstruction.

"It was argued by many at the Families' meeting of 2075, the year of the Covenant, that we should reveal ourselves, since civil liberty was firmly reestablished. The majority did not agree at that time . . . perhaps through long habits of secrecy and caution. But the renascence of culture in the ensuing fifty years, the steady growth of tolerance and good manners, the semantically sound orientation of education, the increased respect for the custom of privacy and for the dignity of the individual—all of these things led us to believe that the time had at last come when it was becoming safe to reveal ourselves and to take our rightful place as an odd but nonetheless respected minority in society.

"There were compelling reasons to do so. Increasing numbers of us were finding the 'Masquerade' socially intolerable in a new and better society. Not only was it upsetting to pull up roots and seek a new background every few years but also it grated to have to live a lie in a society where frank honesty and fair dealing were habitual with most people. Besides that, the Families as a group had learned many things through our researches in the bio-sciences, things which could be of great benefit to our poor short-lived brethren. We needed freedom to help them.

"These and similar reasons were subject to argument. But the resumption of the custom of positive physical identification made the 'Masquerade' almost untenable. Under the new orientation a sane and peaceful citizen welcomes positive identification under appropriate circumstances even though jealous of his right of privacy at all other times—so we dared not object; it would have aroused curiosity, marked us as an eccentric group, set apart, and thereby have defeated the whole purpose of the 'Masquerade.'

"We necessarily submitted to personal identification. By the time of the meeting of 2125, eleven years ago, it had become extremely difficult to counterfeit new identities for the ever-increasing number of us holding public ages incompatible with personal appearance; we decided on the experiment of letting volunteers from this group up to ten per cent of the total membership of the Families reveal themselves for what they were and observe the consequences, while maintaining all other secrets of the Families' organization.

"The results were regrettably different from our expectations."

Justin Foote stopped talking. The silence had gone on for several moments when a solidly built man of medium height spoke up. His hair was slightly grizzled—unusual in that group—and his face looked space tanned. Mary Sperling had noticed him and had wondered who he was—his live face and gusty laugh had interested her. But any member was free to attend the conclaves of the Families' council; she had thought no more of it.

He said, "Speak up, Bud. What's your report?"

Foote made his answer to the chair. "Our senior psychometrician should give the balance of the report. My remarks were prefatory."

"For the love o'——" the grizzled stranger exclaimed. "Bud, do you mean to stand there and admit that all you had to say were things we already knew?"

"My remarks were a foundation . . . and my name is Justin Foote, not 'Bud.' "

Mary Sperling broke in firmly. "Brother," she said to the stranger, "since you are addressing the Families, will you please name yourself? I am sorry to say that I do not recognize you."

"Sorry, Sister. Lazarus Long, speaking for myself."

Mary shook her head. "I still don't place you."

"Sorry again—that's a 'Masquerade' name I took at the time of the First Prophet . . . it tickled me. My Family name is Smith . . . Woodrow Wilson Smith."

" 'Woodrow Wilson Sm——' *How old are you?*"

"Eh? Why, I haven't figured it lately. One hun . . . no, two hundred and—thirteen years. Yeah, that's right, two hundred and thirteen."

There was a sudden, complete silence. Then Mary said quietly, "Did you hear me inquire for anyone older than myself?"

"Yes. But shucks, Sister, you were doing all right. I ain't attended a meeting of the Families in over a century. Been some changes."

"I'll ask you to carry on from here." She started to leave the platform.

"Oh no!" he protested. But she paid no attention and found a seat. He looked around, shrugged and gave in. Sprawling one hip over a corner of the speaker's table he announced, "All right, let's get on with it. Who's next?"

Ralph Schultz of the Schultz Family looked more like a banker than a psychometrician. He was neither shy nor absent-minded and he had a flat, underemphasized way of talking that carried authority. "I was part of the group that proposed ending the 'Masquerade.' I was wrong. I believed that the great majority of our fellow citizens, reared under modern educational methods, could evaluate any data without excessive emotional disturbance. I anticipated that a few abnormal people would dislike us, even hate us; I even predicted that most people would envy us—everybody who enjoys life would like to live a long time. But I did not anticipate any serious trouble. Modern attitudes have done away with interracial friction; any who still h. or race prejudice are ashamed to voice it. I believed that our society was so tolerant that we could live peacefully and openly with the short-lived.

"I was wrong.

"The Negro hated and envied the white man as long as the white man enjoyed privileges forbidden the Negro by reason of color. This was a sane, normal reaction. When discrimination was removed, the problem solved itself and cultural assimilation took place. There is a similar tendency on the part of the short-lived to envy the long-lived. We assumed that this expected reaction would be of no social importance in most people once it was made clear that we owe our peculiarity to our genes—no fault nor virtue of our own, just good luck in our ancestry.

"This was mere wishful thinking. By hindsight it is easy to see that correct application of mathematical analysis to the data would have given a different answer, would have spotlighted the false analogy. I do not defend the misjudgment, no defense is possible. We were led astray by our hopes.

"What actually happened was this: we showed our short-lived cousins the greatest boon it is possible for a man to imagine . . . then we told them it could never be theirs. This faced them with an unsolvable dilemma. They have rejected the unbearable facts, they refuse to believe us. Their envy now turns to hate, with an emotional conviction that we are depriving them of their rights . . . deliberately, maliciously.

"That rising hate has now swelled into a flood which threatens the welfare and even the lines of all our revealed brethren . . . and which is potentially as dangerous to the rest of us. The danger is very great and very pressing." He sat down abruptly.

They took it calmly, with the unhurried habit of years. Presently a female delegate stood up. "Eve Barstow, for the Cooper Family. Ralph Schultz, I am a hundred and nineteen years old, older, I believe, than you are. I do not have your talent for mathematics ar human behavior but I have known a lot of people. Human beings are inherently good and gentle and kind. Oh, they have their weaknesses but most of them are decent enough if you give them half a chance. I cannot believe that they would hate me and destroy me simply because I have lived a long time. What have you to go on? You admit one mistake—why not two?"

Schultz looked at her soberly and smoothed his kilt. "You're right, Eve. I could easily be wrong again. That's the trouble with psychology; it is a subject so terribly complex, so many unknowns, such involved relationships, that our best efforts sometimes look silly in the bleak light of later facts." He stood up again, faced the others, and again spoke with flat authority. "But I am not making a long-range prediction this time; I am talking about facts, no guesses, not wishful think-ing—and with those facts a prediction so short-range that it is like predicting that an egg will break when you see it already on its way to the floor. But Eve is right . . . as far as she went. Individuals *are* kind and decent . . . as individuals and to other individuals. Eve is in no danger from her neighbors and friends, and I am in no danger from mine. But she is in danger from *my* neighbors and friends—and I from hers. Mass psychology is not simply a summation of individual psy-chologies; that is a prime theorem of social psychodynamics

—not just my opinion; no exception has ever been found to this theorem. It is the social mass-action rule, the mob-hysteria law, known and used by military, political, and religious leaders, by advertising men and prophets and propagandists, by rabble rousers and actors and gang leaders, for generations before it was formulated in mathematical symbols. It works. It is working now.

"My colleagues and I began to suspect that a mob-hysteria trend was building up against us several years ago. We did not bring our suspicions to the council for action because we could not prove anything. What we observed then could have been simply the mutterings of the crackpot minority present in even the healthiest society. The trend was at first so minor that we could not be sure it existed, for all social trends are intermixed with other social trends, snarled together like a plate of spaghetti—worse than that, for it takes an abstract topological space of many dimensions (ten or twelve are not uncommon and hardly adequate) to describe mathematically the interplay of social forces. I cannot overemphasize the complexity of the problem.

"So we waited and worried and tried statistical sampling, setting up our statistical universes with great care.

"By the time we were sure, it was almost too late. Sociopsychological trends grow or die by a 'yeast growth' law, a complex power law. We continued to hope that other favorable factors would reverse the trend—Nelson's work in symbiotics, our own contributions to geriatrics, the great public interest in the opening of the Jovian satellites to immigration. Any major break-through offering longer life and greater hope to the short-lived could end the smouldering resentment against us.

"Instead the smouldering has burst into flame, into an uncontrolled forest fire. As nearly as we can measure it, the rate has doubled in the past thirty-seven days and the rate itself is accelerated. I can't guess how far or how fast it will go—and that's why we asked for this emergency session. Because we can expect trouble at any moment." He sat down hard, looking tired.

Eve did not argue with him again and no one else argued with him at all; not only was Ralph Schultz considered expert in his own field but also every one of them, each from his own viewpoint, had seen the grosser aspects of the trend building up against their revealed kin. But, while the acceptance of the problem was unanimous, there were as many opinions about what to do about it as there were people present. Lazarus let the discussion muddle along for two hours before he held up a hand. "We aren't getting anywhere," he stated, "and it looks like we won't get anywhere tonight. Let's take an over-all look at it, hitting just the high spots:

"We can——" He started ticking plans off on his fingers— "do nothing, sit tight, and see what happens.

"We can junk the 'Masquerade' entirely, reveal our full numbers, and demand our rights politically.

"We can sit tight on the surface and use our organization and money to protect our revealed brethren, maybe haul 'em back into the 'Masquerade.'

"We can reveal ourselves and ask for a place to colonize where we can live by ourselves.

"Or we can do something else. I suggest that you sort yourselves out according to those four major points of view—say in the corners of the room, starting clockwise in that far right hand corner—each group hammer out a plan and get it ready to submit to the Families. And those of you who don't favor any of those four things gather in the middle of the room and start scrappin' over just what it is you do think. Now, if I hear no objection, I am going to declare this lodge recessed until midnight tomorrow night. How about it?"

No one spoke up. Lazarus Long's streamlined version of parliamentary procedure had them somewhat startled; they were used to long, leisurely discussions until it became evident that one point of view had become unanimous. Doing things in a hurry was slightly shocking.

But the man's personality was powerful, his years gave him prestige, and his slightly archaic way of speaking added to his patriarchal authority; nobody argued.

"Okay," Lazarus announced, clapping his hands once. "Church is out until tomorrow night." He stepped down from the platform.

Mary Sperling came up to him. "I would like to know you better," she said, looking him in the eyes.

"Sure, Sis. Why not?"

"Are you staying for discussion?"

"No."

"Could you come home with me?"

"Like to. I've no pressing business elsewhere."

"Come then." She led him through the tunnel to the underground pool connecting with Lake Michigan. He widened his eyes at the pseudo-Camden but said nothing until they were submerged.

"Nice little car you've got."

"Yes."

"Has some unusual features."

She smiled. "Yes. Among other things, it blows up—quite thoroughly—if anyone tries to investigate it."

"Good." He added, "You a designing engineer, Mary?"

"Me? Heavens, no! Not this past century, at least, and I no longer try to keep up with such things. But you can order a car modified the way this one is through the Families, if you want one. Talk to——"

"Never mind, I've no need for one. I just like gadgets that do what they were designed to do and do it quietly and efficiently. Some good skull sweat in this one."

"Yes." She was busy then, surfacing, making a radar check, and getting them back ashore without attracting notice.

When they reached her apartment she put tobacco and drink close to him, then went to her retiring room, threw off her street clothes and put on a soft loose robe that made her look even smaller and younger than she had looked before. When she rejoined Lazarus, he stood up, struck a cigarette for her, then paused as he handed it to her and gave a gallant and indelicate whistle.

She smiled briefly, took the cigarette, and sat down in a large chair, pulling her feet under her. "Lazarus, you reassure me."

"Don't you own a mirror, girl?"

"Not that," she said impatiently. "You yourself. You know that I have passed the reasonable life expectancy of our people—I've been expecting to die, been resigned to it, for the past ten years. Yet there you sit . . . years and *years* older than I am. You give me hope."

He sat up straight. "*You* expecting to die? Good grief, girl —you look good for another century."

She made a tired gesture. "Don't try to jolly me. You know that appearance has nothing to do with it. Lazarus, I don't *want* to die!"

Lazarus answered soberly, "I wasn't trying to kid you, Sis. You simply don't look like a candidate for corpse."

She shrugged gracefully. "A matter of biotechniques. I'm holding my appearance at the early thirties."

"Or less, I'd say. I guess I'm not up on the latest dodges, Mary. You heard me say that I had not attended a get-together for more than a century. As a matter of fact I've been completely out of touch with the Families the whole time."

"Really? May I ask why?"

"A long story and a dull one. What it amounts to is that I got bored with them. I used to be a delegate to the annual meetings. But they got stuffy and set in their ways—or so it seemed to me. So I wandered off. I spent the Interregnum on Venus, mostly. I came back for a while after the Covenant was signed but I don't suppose I've spent two years on Earth since then. I like to move around."

Her eyes lit up. "Oh, tell me about it! I've never been out in deep space. Just Luna City, once."

"Sure," he agreed. "Sometime. But I want to hear more about this matter of your appearance. Girl, you sure don't look your age."

"I suppose not. Or, rather, of course I don't. As to how it's done, I can't tell you much. Hormones and symbiotics and gland therapy and some psychotherapy—things like that. What it adds up to is that, for members of the Families, senility is postponed and that senescence can be arrested at least cosmetically." She brooded for a moment. "Once they thought they were on the track of the secret of immortality, the true Fountain of Youth. But it was a mistake. Senility is simply postponed . . . and shortened. About ninety days from the first clear warning—then death from old age." She shivered. "Of course, most of our cousins don't wait—a couple of weeks to make certain of the diagnosis, then euthanasia."

"The hell you say! Well, *I* won't go that way. When the Old Boy comes to get *me*, he'll have to drag me—and I'll be kicking and gouging eyes every step of the way!"

She smiled lopsidedly. "It does me good to hear you talk that way. Lazarus, I wouldn't let my guards down this way with anyone younger than myself. But your example gives me courage."

"We'll outlast the lot of 'em, Mary, never you fear. But about the meeting tonight: I haven't paid any attention to the news and I've only recently come earthside—does this chap Ralph Schultz know what he is talking about?"

"I think he must. His grandfather was a brilliant man and so is his father."

"I take it you know Ralph."

"Slightly. He is one of my grandchildren."

"That's amusing. He looks older than you do."

"Ralph found it suited him to arrest his appearance at about forty, that's all. His father was my twenty-seventh child. Ralph must be—let me see—oh, eighty or ninety years younger than I am, at least. At that, he is older than some of my children."

"You've done well by the Families, Mary."

"I suppose so. But they've done well by me, too. I've enjoyed having children and the trust benefits for my thirty-odd come to quite a lot. I have every luxury one could want." She shivered again. "I suppose that's why I'm in such a funk—I enjoy life."

"Stop it! I thought my sterling example and boyish grin had cured you of that nonsense."

"Well . . . you've helped."

"Mmm . . . look, Mary, why don't you marry again and have some more squally brats? Keep you too busy to fret."

"What? At my age? Now, really, Lazarus!"

"Nothing wrong with your age. You're younger than I am." She studied him for a moment. "Lazarus, are you proposing a contract? If so, I wish you would speak more plainly."

His mouth opened and he gulped. "Hey, wait a minute! Take it easy! I was speaking in general terms . . . I'm not the domestic type. Why, every time I've married my wife has grown sick of the sight of me inside of a few years. Not but what I—well, I mean you're a very pretty girl and a man ought to——"

She shut him off by leaning forward and putting a hand over his mouth, while grinning impishly. "I didn't mean to panic you, cousin. Or perhaps I did—men are so funny when they think they are about to be trapped."

"Well——" he said glumly.

"Forget it, dear. Tell me, what plan do you think they will settle on?"

"That bunch tonight?"

"Yes."

"None, of course. They won't get anywhere. Mary, a committee is the only known form of life with a hundred bellies and no brain. But presently somebody with a mind of his own will bulldoze them into accepting his plan. I don't know what it will be."

"Well . . . what course of action do *you* favor?"

"Me? Why, none. Mary, if there is any one thing I have learned in the past couple of centuries, it's this: These things *pass*. Wars and depressions and Prophets and Covenants—they pass. The trick is to stay alive through them."

She nodded thoughtfully. "I think you are right."

"Sure I'm right. It takes a hundred years or so to realize just how good life is." He stood up and stretched. "But right now this growing boy could use some sleep."

"Me, too."

Mary's flat was on the top floor, with a sky view. When she had come back to the lounge she had cut the inside lighting and let the ceiling shutters fold back; they had been sitting, save for an invisible sheet of plastic, under the stars. As Lazarus raised his head in stretching, his eye had rested on his favorite constellation. "Odd," he commented. "Orion seems to have added a fourth star to his belt."

She looked up. "That must be the big ship for the Second Centauri Expedition. See if you can see it move."

"Couldn't tell without instruments."

"I suppose not," she agreed. "Clever of them to build it out in space, isn't it?"

"No other way to do it. It's too big to assemble on Earth. I can doss down right here, Mary. Or do you have a spare room?"

"Your room is the second door on the right. Shout if you can't find everything you need." She put her face up and kissed him goodnight, a quick peck. " 'Night."

Lazarus followed her and went into his own room.

Mary Sperling woke at her usual hour the next day. She got up quietly to keep from waking Lazarus, ducked into her 'fresher, showered and massaged, swallowed a grain of sleep surrogate to make up for the short night, followed it almost as quickly with all the breakfast she permitted her waistline, then punched for the calls she had not bothered to take the night before. The phone played back several calls which she promptly forgot, then she recognized the voice of Bork Vanning. " 'Hello,' " the instrument said. " 'Mary, this is Bork, calling at twenty-one o'clock. I'll be by at ten o'clock tomorrow morning, for a dip in the lake and lunch somewhere. Unless I hear from you it's a date. 'Bye, my dear. Service.' "

"Service," she repeated automatically. Drat the man! Couldn't he take no for an answer? Mary Sperling, you're slipping!—a quarter your age and yet you can't seem to handle him.

Call him and leave word that—no, too late; he'd be here any minute. Bother!

2

WHEN LAZARUS went to bed he stepped out of his kilt and chucked it toward a wardrobe . . . which snagged it, shook it out, and hung it up neatly. "Nice catch," he commented, then glanced down at his hairy thighs and smiled wryly; the kilt had concealed a blaster strapped to one thigh, a knife to the other. He was aware of the present gentle custom against personal weapons, but he felt naked without them. Such customs were nonsense anyhow, foolishment from old women—there was no such thing as a "dangerous weapon," there were only dangerous men.

When he came out of the 'fresher, he put his weapons where he could reach them before sprawling in sleep.

He came instantly wide awake with a weapon in each hand . . . then remembered where he was, relaxed, and looked around to see what had wakened him.

It was a murmur of voices through the air duct. Poor soundproofing he decided, and Mary must be entertaining callers—in which case he should not be slug-a-bed. He got up, refreshed himself, strapped his best friends back on his thighs, and went looking for his hostess.

As the door to the lounge dilated noiselessly in front of him the sound of voices became loud and very interesting. The lounge was el-shaped and he was out of sight; he hung back and listened shamelessly. Eavesdropping had saved his skin on several occasions; it worried him not at all—he enjoyed it.

A man was saying, "Mary, you're completely unreasonable! You know you're fond of me, you admit that marriage to me would be to your advantage. So why *won't* you?"

"I told you, Bork. Age difference."

"That's foolish. What do you expect? Adolescent romance? Oh, I admit that I'm not as young as you are . . . but a woman needs an older man to look up to and keep her steady. I'm not too old for you; I'm just at my prime."

Lazarus decided that he already knew this chap well enough to dislike him. Sulky voice——

Mary did not answer. The man went on: "Anyhow, I have a surprise for you on that point. I wish I could tell you now, but . . . well, it's a state secret."

"Then don't tell me. It can't change my mind in any case, Bork."

"Oh, but it would! Mmm . . . I *will* tell you—I know *you* can be trusted."

"Now, Bork, you shouldn't assume that——"

"It doesn't matter; it will be public knowledge in a few days anyhow. Mary . . . *I'll never grow old on you!*"

"What do you mean?" Lazarus decided that her tone was suddenly suspicious.

"Just what I said. Mary, they've found the secret of eternal youth!"

"*What?* Who? How? When?"

"Oh, so now you're interested, eh? Well, I won't keep you waiting. You know these old Johnnies that call themselves the Howard Families?"

"Yes . . . I've heard of them, of course," she admitted slowly. "But what of it? They're fakes."

"Not at all. I *know*. The Administration has been quietly investigating their claims. Some of them are unquestionably more than a hundred years old—and *still young!*"

"That's very hard to believe."

"Nevertheless it's true."

"Well . . . how do they do it?"

"Ah! That's the point. They claim that it is a simple matter of heredity, that they live a long time because they come from long lived stock. But that's preposterous, scientifically incompatible with the established facts. The Administration checked most carefully and the answer is certain: they have the secret of staying young."

"You can't be sure of that."

"Oh, come, Mary! You're a dear girl but you're questioning the expert opinion of the best scientific brains in the world. Never mind. Here's the part that is confidential. We don't have their secret yet—but we will have it shortly. Without any excitement or public notice, they are to be picked up and questioned. We'll get the secret—and you and I will never grow old! What do you think of *that?* Eh?"

Mary answered very slowly, almost inaudibly, "It would be nice if everyone could live a long time."

"Huh? Yes, I suppose it would. But in any case you and I will receive the treatment, whatever it is. Think about *us,* dear. Year after year after year of happy, youthful marriage. Not less than a century. Maybe even——"

"Wait a moment, Bork. This 'secret.' It wouldn't be for everybody?"

"Well, now . . . that's a matter of high policy. Population pressure is a pretty unwieldy problem even now. In practice it might be necessary to restrict it to essential personnel—and their wives. But don't fret your lovely head about it; you and I will have it."

"You mean I'll have it *if* I marry you."

"Mmm . . . that's a nasty way to put it, Mary. I'd do anything in the world for you that I could—because I *love* you. But it would be utterly simple if you were married to me. So say you will."

"Let's let that be for the moment. How do you propose to get this 'secret' out of them?"

Lazarus could almost hear his wise nod. "Oh, they'll talk!"

"Do you mean to say you'd send them to Coventry if they didn't?"

"Coventry? Hm! You don't understand the situation at all, Mary; this isn't any minor social offense. This is *treason*— treason against the whole human race. We'll use means! Ways that the Prophets used . . . if they don't coöperate willingly."

"Do you mean that? Why, that's against the Covenant!"

"Covenant be damned! This is a matter of life and death— do you think we'd let a scrap of paper stand in our way? You can't bother with petty legalities in the fundamental things men live by—not something they will fight to the death for. And that is precisely what this is. These . . . these dog-in-the-manger scoundrels are trying to keep life itself from us. Do you think we'll bow to 'custom' in an emergency like this?"

Mary answered in a hushed and horrified voice: "Do you really think the Council will violate the Covenant?"

"*Think* so? The Action-in-Council was recorded last night. We authorized the Administrator to use 'full expediency.' "

Lazarus strained his ears through a long silence. At last Mary spoke. "Bork——"

"Yes, my dear?"

"You've got to do something about this. You must stop it."

"Stop it? You don't know what you're saying. I couldn't . . . and I would not if I could."

"But you *must*. You must convince the Council. They're making a mistake, a tragic mistake. There is nothing to be gained by trying to coerce those poor people. *There is no secret!*"

"What? You're getting excited, my dear. You're setting your judgment up against some of the best and wisest men on the planet. Believe me, we know what we are doing. We don't relish using harsh methods any more than you do, but it's for the general welfare. Look, I'm sorry I ever brought it up. Naturally you are soft and gentle and warmhearted and I love you for it. Why not marry me and not bother your head about matters of public policy?"

"Marry *you*? Never!"

"Aw, Mary—you're upset. Give me just one good reason why not?"

"I'll tell you why! Because *I* am one of those people you want to persecute!"

There was another pause. "Mary . . . you're not well."

"Not well, am I? I am as well as a person can be at my age. Listen to me, you fool! I have grandsons twice your age. I was here when the First Prophet took over the country. I was here when Harriman launched the first Moon rocket. You weren't even a squalling brat—your *grandparents* hadn't even met, when I was a woman grown and married. And you stand there and glibly propose to push around, even to torture, me and my kind. Marry *you*? I'd rather marry one of my own grandchildren!"

Lazarus shifted his weight and slid his right hand inside the flap of his kilt; he expected trouble at once. You can depend on a woman, he reflected, to blow her top at the wrong moment.

He waited. Bork's answer was cool; the tones of the experienced man of authority replaced those of thwarted passion. "Take it easy, Mary. Sit down, I'll look after you. First I want you to take a sedative. Then I'll get the best psychotherapist in the city—in the whole country. You'll be all right."

"Take your hands off me!"

"Now, Mary . . ."

Lazarus stepped out into the room and pointed at Vanning with his blaster. "This monkey giving you trouble, Sis?"

Vanning jerked his head around. "Who are you?" he demanded indignantly. "What are you doing here?"

Lazarus still addressed Mary. "Say the word, Sis, and I'll cut him into pieces small enough to hide."

"No, Lazarus," she answered with her voice now under control. "Thanks just the same. Please put your gun away. I wouldn't want anything like that to happen."

"Okay." Lazarus holstered the gun but let his hand rest on the grip.

"Who are you?" repeated Vanning. "What's the meaning of this intrusion?"

"I was just about to ask you that, Bud," Lazarus said mildly, "but we'll let it ride. I'm another one of those old Johnnies you're looking for . . . like Mary here."

Vanning looked at him keenly. "I wonder——" he said. He looked back at Mary. "It can't be, it's preposterous. Still . . . it won't hurt to investigate your story. I've plenty to detain you on, in any event, I've never seen a clearer case of antisocial atavism." He moved toward the videophone.

"Better get away from that phone, Bud," Lazarus said quickly, then added to Mary, "I won't touch my gun, Sis. I'll use my knife."

Vanning stopped. "Very well," he said in annoyed tones, "put away that vibroblade. I won't call from here."

"Look again, it ain't a vibroblade. It's steel. Messy."

Vanning turned to Mary Sperling. "I'm leaving. If you are wise, you'll come with me." She shook her head. He looked annoyed, shrugged, and faced Lazarus Long. "As for you, sir, your primitive manners have led you into serious trouble. You will be arrested shortly."

Lazarus glanced up at the ceiling shutters. "Reminds me of a patron in Venusburg who wanted to have me arrested."

"Well?"

"I've outlived him quite a piece."

Vanning opened his mouth to answer—then turned suddenly and left so quickly that the outer door barely had time to clear the end of his nose. As the door snapped closed Lazarus said musingly, "Hardest man to reason with I've met in years. I'll bet he never used an unsterilized spoon in his life."

Mary looked startled, then giggled. He turned toward her. "Glad to see you sounding perky, Mary. Kinda thought you were upset."

"I was. I hadn't known you were listening. I was forced to improvise as I went along."

"Did I queer it?"

"No. I'm glad you came in—thanks. But we'll have to hurry now."

"I suppose so. I think he meant it—there'll be a proctor looking for me soon. You, too, maybe."

"That's what I meant. So let's get out of here."

Mary was ready to leave in scant minutes but when they stepped out into the public hall they met a man whose brassard and hypo kit marked him as a proctor. "Service," he said. "I'm looking for a citizen in company with Citizen Mary Sperling. Could you direct me?"

"Sure," agreed Lazarus. "She lives right down there." He pointed at the far end of the corridor. As the peace officer looked in that direction, Lazarus tapped him carefully on the back of the head, a little to the left, with the butt of his blaster, and caught him as he slumped.

Mary helped Lazarus wrestle the awkward mass into her apartment. He knelt over the cop, pawed through his hypo kit, took a loaded injector and gave him a shot. "There," he said, "that'll keep him sleepy for a few hours." Then he blinked thoughtfully at the hypo kit, detached it from the proctor's belt. "This might come in handy again. Anyhow, it won't hurt to take it." As an afterthought he removed the proctor's peace brassard and placed it, too, in his pouch.

They left the apartment again and dropped to the parking level. Lazarus noticed as they rolled up the ramp that Mary had set the North Shore combination. "Where are we going?" he asked.

"The Families' Seat. No place else to go where we won't be checked on. But we'll have to hide somewhere in the country until dark."

Once the car was on beamed control headed north Mary asked to be excused and caught a few minutes sleep. Lazarus watched a few miles of scenery, then nodded himself.

They were awakened by the jangle of the emergency alarm and by the speedster slowing to a stop. Mary reached up and shut off the alarm. "All cars resume local control," intoned a voice. "Proceed at speed twenty to the nearest traffic control tower for inspection. All cars resume local control. Proceed at——"

She switched that off, too. "Well, that's us," Lazarus said cheerfully. "Got any ideas?"

Mary did not answer. She peered out and studied their surroundings. The steel fence separating the high-speed control way they were on from the uncontrolled local-traffic strip lay about fifty yards to their right but no changeover ramp broke the fence for at least a mile ahead—where it did, there would be, of course, the control tower where they were ordered to undergo inspection. She started the car again, operating it manually, and wove through stopped or slowly moving traffic while speeding up. As they got close to the barrier Lazarus felt himself shoved into the cushions; the car surged and lifted, clearing the barrier by inches. She set it down rolling on the far side.

A car was approaching from the north and they were slashing across his lane. The other car was moving no more than ninety but its driver was taken by surprise—he had no reason to expect another car to appear out of nowhere against him on a clear road. Mary was forced to duck left, then right, and left again; the car slewed and reared up on its hind wheel, writhing against the steel grip of its gyros. Mary fought it back into control to the accompaniment of a teeth-shivering grind of herculene against glass as the rear wheel fought for traction.

Lazarus let his jaw muscles relax and breathed out gustily. "*Whew!*" he sighed. "I hope we won't have to do *that* again."

Mary glanced at him, grinning. "Women drivers make you nervous?"

"Oh, no, no, not at all! I just wish you would warn me when something like that is about to happen."

"I didn't know myself," she admitted, then went on worriedly, "I don't know quite what to do now. I thought we could lie quiet out of town until dark . . . but I had to show my hand a little when I took that fence. By now somebody will be reporting it to the tower. Mmm. . . ."

"Why wait until dark?" he asked. "Why not just bounce over to the lake in this Dick Dare contraption of yours and let it swim us home?"

"I don't like to," she fretted. "I've attracted too much attention already. A trimobile faked up to look like a groundster is handy, but . . . well, if anyone sees us taking it under water and the proctors hear of it, somebody is going to guess the answer. Then they'll start fishing—everything from seismo to sonar and Heaven knows what else."

"But isn't the Seat shielded?"

"Of course. But anything that big they can find—if they know what they're looking for and keep looking."

"You're right, of course," Lazarus admitted slowly. "Well, we certainly don't want to lead any nosy proctors to the Families' Seat. Mary, I think we had better ditch your car and get lost." He frowned. "Anywhere but the Seat."

"No, it has to be the Seat," she answered sharply.

"Why? If you chase a fox, he——"

"Quiet a moment! I want to try something." Lazarus shut up; Mary drove with one hand while she fumbled in the glove compartment.

"Answer," a voice said.

"Life is short——" Mary replied.

They completed the formula. "Listen," Mary went on hurriedly, "I'm in trouble—get a fix on me."

"Okay."

"Is there a sub in the pool?"

"Yes."

"Good! Lock on me and home them in." She explained hurriedly the details of what she wanted, stopping once to ask Lazarus if he could swim. "That's all," she said at last, "but move! We're short on minutes."

"Hold it, Mary!" the voice protested. "You know I can't send a sub out in the daytime, certainly not on a calm day. It's too easy to——"

"Will you, or won't you!"

A third voice cut in. "I was listening, Mary—Ira Barstow. We'll pick you up."

"But——" objected the first voice.

"Stow it, Tommy. Just mind your burners and home me in. See you, Mary."

"Right, Ira!"

While she had been talking to the Seat, Mary had turned off from the local-traffic strip into the unpaved road she had followed the night before, without slowing and apparently without looking. Lazarus gritted his teeth and hung on. They passed a weathered sign reading CONTAMINATED AREA—PRO-

CEED AT YOUR OWN RISK and graced with the conventional purple trefoil. Lazarus blinked at it and shrugged—he could not see how, at the moment, his hazard could be increased by a neutron or so.

Mary slammed the car to a stop in a clump of stunted trees near the abandoned road. The lake lay at their feet, just beyond a low bluff. She unfastened her safety belt, struck a cigarette, and relaxed. "Now we wait. It'll take at least half an hour for them to reach us no matter how hard Ira herds it. Lazarus, do you think we were seen turning off into here?"

"To tell the truth, Mary, I was too busy to look."

"Well . . . nobody ever comes here, except a few reckless boys."

("—and girls," Lazarus added to himself.) Then he went on aloud, "I noted a 'hot' sign back there. How high is the count?"

"That? Oh, pooh. Nothing to worry about unless you decided to build a house here. We're the ones who are hot. If we didn't have to stay close to the communicator, we——"

The communicator spoke. "Okay, Mary. Right in front of you."

She looked startled. "Ira?"

"This is Ira speaking but I'm still at the Seat. Pete Hardy was available in the Evanston pen, so we homed him in on you. Quicker."

"Okay—thanks!" She was turning to speak to Lazarus when he touched her arm.

"Look behind us."

A helicopter was touching down less than a hundred yards from them. Three men burst out of it. They were dressed as proctors.

Mary jerked open the door of the car and threw off her gown in one unbroken motion. She turned and called, "Come on!" as she thrust a hand back inside and tore a stud loose from the instrument panel. She ran.

Lazarus unzipped the belt of his kilt and ran out of it as he followed her to the bluff. She went dancing down it; he came after with slightly more caution, swearing at sharp stones. The blast shook them as the car exploded, but the bluff saved them.

They hit the water together.

The lock in the little submarine was barely big enough for one at a time; Lazarus shoved Mary into it first and tried to slap her when she resisted, and discovered that slapping will not work under water. Then he spent an endless time, or so it seemed, wondering whether or not he could breathe water. "What's a fish got that I ain't got?" he was telling himself, when the outer latch moved under his hand and he was able to wiggle in.

Eleven dragging seconds to blow the lock clear of water and he had a chance to see what damage, if any, the water had done to his blaster.

Mary was speaking urgently to the skipper. "Listen, Pete— there are three proctors back up there with a whirly. My car blew up in their faces just as we hit the water. But if they aren't all dead or injured, there will be a smart boy who will figure out that there was only one place for us to go—under water. We've got to be away from here before they take to the air to look for us."

"It's a losing race," Pete Hardy complained, slapping his controls as he spoke. "Even if it's only a visual search, I'll have to get outside and stay outside the circle of total reflection faster than he can gain altitude—and I can't." But the little sub lunged forward reassuringly.

Mary worried about whether or not to call the Seat from the sub. She decided not to; it would just increase the hazard both to the sub and to the Seat itself. So she calmed herself and waited, huddled small in a passenger seat too cramped for two. Peter Hardy swung wide into deep water, hugging the bottom, picking up the Muskegon-Gary bottom beacons and conned himself in blind.

By the time they surfaced in the pool inside the Seat she had decided against any physical means of communication, even the carefully shielded equipment at the Seat. Instead she hoped to find a telepathic sensitive ready and available among the Families' dependents cared for there. Sensitives were as scarce among healthy members of the Howard Families as they were in the rest of the population, but the very inbreeding which had conserved and reinforced their abnormal longevity had also conserved and reinforced bad genes as well as good; they had an unusually high percentage of physical and mental defectives. Their board of genetic control plugged away at the problem of getting rid of bad strains while conserving the longevity strain, but for many generations they would continue to pay for their long lives with an excess of defectives.

But almost five per cent of these defectives were telepathically sensitive.

Mary went straight to the sanctuary in the Seat where some of these dependents were cared for, with Lazarus Long at her heels. She braced the matron. "Where's Little Stephen? I need him."

"Keep your voice down," the matron scolded. "Rest hour —you can't."

"Janice, I've got to see him," Mary insisted. "This won't wait. I've got to get a message out to all the Families—at once."

The matron planted her hands on her hips. "Take it to the communication office. You can't come here disturbing my children at all hours. I won't have it."

"Janice, please! I don't dare use anything but telepathy. You know I wouldn't do this unnecessarily. Now take me to Stephen."

"It wouldn't do you any good if I did. Little Stephen has had one of his bad spells today."

"Then take me to the strongest sensitive who can possibly work. Quickly, Janice! The safety of every member may depend on it."

"Did the trustees send you?"

"No, no! There wasn't time!"

The matron still looked doubtful. While Lazarus was trying to recall how long it had been since he had socked a lady, she gave in. "All right—you can see Billy, though I shouldn't let you. Mind you, don't tire him out." Still bristling, she led them along a corridor past a series of cheerful rooms and into one of them. Lazarus looked at the thing on the bed and looked away.

The matron went to a cupboard and returned with a hypodermic injector. "Does he work under a hypnotic?" Lazarus asked.

"No," the matron answered coldly, "he has to have a stimulant to be aware of us at all." She swabbed skin on the arm of the gross figure and made the injection. "Go ahead," she said to Mary and lapsed into grim-mouthed silence.

The figure on the bed stirred, its eyes rolled loosely, then seemed to track. It grinned. "Aunt Mary!" it said. "Oooh! Did you bring Billy Boy something?"

"No," she said gently. "Not this time, hon. Aunt Mary was

in too much of a hurry. Next time? A surprise? Will that do?"

"All right," it said docilely.

"That's a good boy." She reached out and tousled its hair; Lazarus looked away again. "Now will Billy Boy do something for Aunt Mary? A big, *big* favor?"

"Sure."

"Can you hear your friends?"

"Oh, sure."

"All of them?"

"Uh huh. Mostly they don't say anything," it added.

"Call to them."

There was a very short silence. "They heard me."

"Fine! Now listen carefully, Billy Boy: All the Families—urgent warning! Elder Mary Sperling speaking. Under an Action-in-Council the Administrator is about to arrest every revealed member. The Council directed him to use 'full expedience'—and it is my sober judgment that they are determined to use any means at all, regardless of the Covenant, to try to squeeze out of us the so-called secret of our long lives. They even intend to use the tortures developed by the inquisitors of the Prophets!" Her voice broke. She stopped and pulled herself together. "Now get busy! Find them, warn them, hide them! You may have only minutes left to save them!"

Lazarus touched her arm and whispered; she nodded and went on:

"If any cousin is arrested, rescue him *by any means at all!* Don't try to appeal to the Covenant, don't waste time arguing about justice . . . rescue him! Now *move!*"

She stopped and then spoke in a tired, gentle voice, "Did they hear us, Billy Boy?"

"Sure."

"Are they telling their folks?"

"Uh huh. All but Jimmie-the-Horse. He's mad at me," it added confidentially.

" 'Jimmie-the-Horse'? Where is he?"

"Oh, where he lives."

"In Montreal," put in the matron. "There are two other sensitives there—your message got through. Are you finished?"

"Yes . . ." Mary said doubtfully. "But perhaps we had better have some other Seat relay it back."

"No!"

"But, Janice——"

"I won't permit it. I suppose you had to send it but I want to give Billy the antidote now. So get out."

Lazarus took her arm. "Come on, kid. It either got through or it didn't; you've done your best. A good job, girl."

Mary went on to make a full report to the Resident Secretary; Lazarus left her on business of his own. He retraced his steps, looking for a man who was not too busy to help him; the guards at the pool entrance were the first he found. "Service——" he began.

"Service to you," one of them answered. "Looking for someone?" He glanced curiously at Long's almost complete nakedness, glanced away again—how anybody dressed, or did not dress, was a private matter.

"Sort of," admitted Lazarus. "Say, Bud, do you know of anyone around here who would lend me a kilt?"

"You're looking at one," the guard answered pleasantly. "Take over, Dick—back in a minute." He led Lazarus to bachelors' quarters, outfitted him, helped him to dry his pouch and contents, and made no comment about the arsenal strapped to his hairy thighs. How elders behaved was no business of his and many of them were even touchier about their privacy than most people. He had seen Aunt Mary Sperling arrive stripped for swimming but had not been surprised as he had heard Ira Barstow briefing Pete for the underwater pickup; that the elder with her chose to take a dip in the lake weighed down by the hardware did surprise him but not enough to make him forget his manners.

"Anything else you need?" he asked. "Do those shoes fit?"

"Well enough. Thanks a lot, Bud." Lazarus smoothed the borrowed kilt. It was a little too long for him but it comforted him. A loin strap was okay, he supposed—if you were on Venus. But he had never cared much for Venus customs. Damn it, a man liked to be *dressed*. "I feel better," he admitted. "Thanks again. By the way, what's your name?"

"Edmund Hardy, of the Foote Family."

"That so? What's your line?"

"Charles Hardy and Evelyn Foote. Edward Hardy-Alice Johnson and Terence Briggs-Eleanor Weatheral. Oliver——"

"That's enough. I sorta thought so. You're one of my great-great-grandsons."

"Why, that's interesting," commented Hardy agreeably.

"Gives us a sixteenth of kinship, doesn't it—not counting convergence. May I ask your name?"

"Lazarus Long."

Hardy shook his head. "Some mistake. Not in my line."

"Try Woodrow Wilson Smith instead. It was the one I started with."

"Oh, that one! Yes, surely. But I thought you were . . . uh——"

"Dead? Well, I ain't."

"Oh, I didn't mean that at all," Hardy protested, blushing at the blunt Anglo-Saxon monosyllable. He hastily added, "I'm glad to have run across you, Gran'ther. I've always wanted to hear the straight of the story about the Families' Meeting in 2012."

"That was before you were born, Ed," Lazarus said gruffly, "and don't call me 'Gran'ther.' "

"Sorry, sir—I mean 'Sorry, Lazarus.' Is there any other service I can do for you?"

"I shouldn't have gotten shirty. No—yes, there is, too. Where can I swipe a bite of breakfast? I was sort of rushed this morning."

"Certainly." Hardy took him to the bachelors' pantry, operated the autochef for him, drew coffee for his watch mate and himself, and left. Lazarus consumed his "bite of breakfast"—about three thousand calories of sizzling sausages, eggs, jam, hot breads, coffee with cream, and ancillary items, for he worked on the assumption of always topping off his reserve tanks because you never knew how far you might have to lift before you had another chance to refuel. In due time he sat back, belched, gathered up his dishes and shoved them in the incinerator, then went looking for a newsbox.

He found one in the bachelors' library, off their lounge. The room was empty save for one man who seemed to be about the same age as that suggested by Lazarus' appearance. There the resemblance stopped; the stranger was slender, mild in feature, and was topped off by finespun carroty hair quite unlike the grizzled wiry bush topping Lazarus. The stranger was bending over the news receiver with his eyes pressed to the microviewer.

Lazarus cleared his throat loudly and said, "Howdy."

The man jerked his head up and exclaimed, "Oh! Sorry—I was startled. Do y' a service?"

"I was looking for the newsbox. Mind if we throw it on the screen?"

"Not at all." The smaller man stood up, pressed the rewind button, and set the controls for projection. "Any particular subject?"

"I wanted to see," said Lazarus, "if there was any news about us—the Families."

"I've been watching for that myself. Perhaps we had better use the sound track and let it hunt."

"Okay," agreed Lazarus, stepping up and changing the setting to audio. "What's the code word?"

" 'Methuselah.' "

Lazarus punched in the setting; the machine chattered and whined as it scanned and rejected the track speeding through it, then it slowed with a triumphant click. "The DAILY DATA," it announced. "The only midwest news service subscribing to every major grid. Leased videochannel to Luna City. Tri-S correspondents throughout the System. First, Fast, and Most! Lincoln, Nebraska—Savant Denounces Oldsters! Dr. Witwell Oscarsen, President Emeritus of Bryan Lyceum, calls for official reconsideration of the status of the kin group styling themselves the 'Howard Families.' 'It is proved,' he says, 'that these people have solved the age-old problem of extending, perhaps indefinitely, the span of human life. For that they are to be commended; it is a worthy and potentially fruitful research. But their claim that their solution is no more than hereditary predisposition defies both science and common sense. Our modern knowledge of the established laws of genetics enables us to deduce with certainty that they are withholding from the public some secret technique or techniques whereby they accomplish their results.

" 'It is contrary to our customs to permit scientific knowledge to be held as a monopoly for the few. When concealing such knowledge strikes at life itself, the action becomes treason to the race. As a citizen, I call on the Administration to act forcefully in this matter and I remind them that the situation is not one which could possibly have been foreseen by the wise men who drew up the Covenant and codified our basic customs. Any custom is man-made and is therefore a finite attempt to describe an infinity of relationships. It follows as the night from day that any custom necessarily has its exceptions. To be bound by them in the face of new——' "

Lazarus pressed the *hold* button. "Had enough of that guy?"

"Yes, I had already heard it." The stranger sighed. "I have rarely heard such complete lack of semantic rigor. It surprises me—Dr. Oscarsen has done sound work in the past."

"Reached his dotage," Lazarus stated, as he told the machine to try again. "Wants what he wants when he wants it—and thinks that constitutes a natural law."

The machine hummed and clicked and again spoke up. "The DAILY DATA, the only midwest news——"

"Can't we scramble that commercial?" suggested Lazarus. His companion peered at the control panel. "Doesn't seem to be equipped for it."

"Ensenada, Baja California. Jeffers and Lucy Weatheral today asked for special proctor protection, alleging that a group of citizens had broken into their home, submitted them to personal indignity and committed other asocial acts. The Weatherals are, by their own admission, members of the notorious Howard Families and claim that the alleged incident could be traced to that supposed fact. The district provost points out that they have offered no proof and has taken the matter under advisement. A town mass meeting has been announced for tonight which will air——"

The other man turned toward Lazarus. "Cousin, did we hear what I thought we heard? That is the first case of asocial group violence in more than twenty years . . . yet they reported it like a breakdown in a weather integrator."

"Not quite," Lazarus answered grimly. "The connotations of the words used in describing us were loaded."

"Yes, true, but loaded cleverly. I doubt if there was a word in that dispatch with an emotional index, taken alone, higher than one point five. The newscasters are allowed two zero, you know."

"You a psychometrician?"

"Uh, no. I should have introduced myself. I'm Andrew Jackson Libby."

"Lazarus Long."

"I know. I was at the meeting last night."

" 'Libby . . . Libby,' " Lazarus mused. "Don't seem to place it in the Families. Seems familiar, though."

"My case is a little like yours——"

"Changed it during the Interregnum, eh?"

"Yes and no. I was born after the Second Revolution. But my people had been converted to the New Crusade and had broken with the Families and changed their name. I was a grown man before I knew I was a Member."

"The deuce you say! That's interesting—how did you come to be located . . . if you don't mind my asking?"

"Well, you see I was in the Navy and one of my superior officers——"

"Got it! Got it! I *thought* you were a spaceman. You're Slipstick Libby, the Calculator."

Libby grinned sheepishly. "I have been called that."

"Sure, sure. The last can I piloted was equipped with your paragravitic rectifier. And the control bank used your fractional differential on the steering jets. But I installed that myself—kinda borrowed your patent."

Libby seemed undisturbed by the theft. His face lit up. "You are interested in symbolic logic?"

"Only pragmatically. But look, I put a modification on your gadget that derives from the rejected alternatives in your thirteenth equation. It helps like this: suppose you are cruising in a field of density 'x' with an n-order gradient normal to your course and you want to set your optimum course for a projected point of rendezvous capital 'A' at matching-in vector 'rho' using automatic selection the entire jump, then if——"

They drifted entirely away from Basic English as used by earthbound laymen. The newsbox beside them continued to hunt; three times it spoke up, each time Libby touched the rejection button without consciously hearing it.

"I see your point," he said at last. "I had considered a somewhat similar modification but concluded that it was not commercially feasible, too expensive for anyone but enthusiasts such as yourself. But your solution is cheaper than mine."

"How do you figure that?"

"Why, it's obvious from the data. Your device contains sixty-two moving parts, which should require, if we assume standardized fabrication processes, a probable——" Libby hesitated momentarily as if he were programing the problem. "—a probable optimax of five thousand two hundred and eleven operation in manufacture assuming null-therblig automation, whereas mine——"

Lazarus butted in. "Andy," he inquired solicitously, "does your head ever ache?"

Libby looked sheepish again. "There's nothing abnormal

about my talent," he protested. "It is theoretically possible to develop it in any normal person."

"Sure," agreed Lazarus, "and you can teach a snake to tap dance once you get shoes on him. Never mind, I'm glad to have fallen in with you. I heard stories about you way back when you were a kid. You were in the Cosmic Construction Corps, weren't you?"

Libby nodded. "Earth-Mars Spot Three."

"Yeah, that was it—chap on Mars gimme the yarn. Trader at Drywater. I knew your maternal grandfather, too. Stiff-necked old coot."

"I suppose he was."

"He was, all right. I had quite a set-to with him at the Meeting in 2012. He had a powerful vocabulary." Lazarus frowned slightly. "Funny thing, Andy . . . I recall that vividly, I've always had a good memory—yet it seems to be getting harder for me to keep things straight. Especially this last century."

"Inescapable mathematical necessity," said Libby.

"Huh? Why?"

"Life experience is linearly additive, but the correlation of memory impressions is an unlimited expansion. If mankind lived as long as a thousand years, it would be necessary to invent some totally different method of memory association in order to be eclectively time-binding. A man would otherwise flounder helplessly in the wealth of his own knowledge, unable to evaluate. Insanity, or feeble-mindedness."

"That so?" Lazarus suddenly looked worried. "Then we'd better get busy on it."

"Oh, it's quite possible of solution."

"Let's work on it. Let's not get caught short."

The newsbox again demanded attention, this time with the buzzer and flashing light of a spot bulletin: "Hearken to the DATA. Flash! High Council Suspends Covenant! Under the Emergency Situation clause of the Covenant an unprecedented Action-in-Council was announced today directing the Administrator to detain and question all members of the so-called Howard Families—*by any means expedient!* The Administrator authorized that the following statement be released by all licensed news outlets: (I quote) 'The suspension of the Covenant's civil guarantees applies only to the group known as the Howard Families except that government agents are empowered to act as circumstances require to apprehend speedily the persons affected by the Action-in-Council. Citizens are urged to tolerate cheerfully any minor inconvenience this may cause them; your right of privacy will be respected in every way possible; your right of free movement may be interrupted temporarily, but full economic restitution will be made.'

"Now, Friends and Citizens, what does this mean?—to you and you and also you! The DAILY DATA brings you now your popular commentator, Albert Reifsnider:

"Reifsnider reporting: Service, Citizens! There is no cause for alarm. To the average free citizen this emergency will be somewhat less troublesome than a low-pressure minimum too big for the weather machines. Take it easy! Relax! Help the proctors when requested and tend to your private affairs. If inconvenienced, don't stand on custom—coöperate with Service!

"That's what it means today. What does it mean tomorrow and the day after that? Next year? It means that your public servants have taken a forthright step to obtain for you the boon of a longer and happier life! Don't get your hopes too high . . . but it looks like the dawn of a new day. Ah, indeed it does! The jealously guarded secret of a selfish few will soon——"

Long raised an eyebrow at Libby, then switched it off.

"I suppose that," Libby said bitterly, "is an example of 'factual detachment in news reporting.'"

Lazarus opened his pouch and struck a cigarette before replying. "Take it easy, Andy. There are bad times and good times. We're overdue for bad times. The people are on the march again . . . this time at us."

3

THE BURROW KNOWN as the Families' Seat became jammed as the day wore on. Members kept trickling in, arriving by tunnels from downstare and from Indiana. As soon as it was dark a traffic jam developed at the underground pool entrance—sporting subs, fake ground cars such as Mary's, ostensible surface cruisers modified to dive, each craft loaded with refugees some half suffocated from lying in hiding on deep bottom most of the day while waiting for a chance to sneak in.

The usual meeting room was much too small to handle the crowd; the resident staff cleared the largest room, the refectory, and removed partitions separating it from the main lounge. There at midnight Lazarus climbed onto a temporary rostrum. "Okay," he announced, "let's pipe it down. You down in front sit on the floor so the rest can see. I was born in 1912. Anybody older?"

He paused, then added, "Nominations for chairman . . . speak up."

Three were proposed; before a fourth could be offered the last man nominated got to his feet. "Axel Johnson, of the Johnson Family. I want my name withdrawn and I suggest that the others do likewise. Lazarus cut through the fog last night; let him handle it. This is no time for Family politics."

The other names were withdrawn; no more were offered. Lazarus said, "Okay if that's the way you want it. Before we get down to arguing, I want a report from the Chief Trustee. How about it, Zack? Any of our kinfolk get nabbed?"

Zaccur Barstow did not need to identify himself; he simply said, "Speaking for the Trustees: our report is not complete, but we do not as yet know that any Member has been arrested. Of the nine thousand two hundred and eighty-five revealed Members, nine thousand one hundred and six had been reported, when I left the communication office ten minutes ago, as having reached hiding, in other Family strongholds, or in the homes of unrevealed Members, or elsewhere. Mary Sperling's warning was amazingly successful in view of how short the time was from the alarm to the public execution of the Action-in-Council—but we still have one hundred and seventy-nine revealed cousins unreported. Probably most of these will trickle in during the next few days. Others are probably safe but unable to get in touch with us."

"Get to the point, Zack," Lazarus insisted. "Any reasonable chance that all of them will make it home safe?"

"Absolutely none."

"Why?"

"Because three of them are known to be in public conveyances between here and the Moon, traveling under their revealed identities. Others we don't know about are almost certainly caught in similar predicaments."

"Question!" A cocky little man near the front stood up and pointed his finger at the Chief Trustee. "Were all those Members now in jeopardy protected by hypnotic injunction?"

"No. There was no——"

"I demand to know why not!"

"Shut up!" bellowed Lazarus. "You're out of order. Nobody's on trial here and we've got no time to waste on spilled milk. Go ahead, Zack."

"Very well. But I will answer the question to this extent: everyone knows that a proposal to protect our secrets by hypnotic means was voted down at the Meeting which relaxed the 'Masquerade.' I seem to recall that the cousin now objecting helped then to vote it down."

"That is not true! And I insist that——"

"*PIPE DOWN!*" Lazarus glared at the heckler, then looked him over carefully. "Bud, you strike me as a clear proof that the Foundation should 'a' bred for brains instead of age." Lazarus looked around at the crowd. "Everybody will get his say, but in order as recognized by the chair. If he butts in again, I'm going to gag him with his own teeth—is my ruling sustained?"

There was a murmur of mixed shock and approval; no one objected. Zaccur Barstow went on, "On the advice of Ralph Schultz the trustees have been proceeding quietly for the past three months to persuade revealed Members to undergo hypnotic instruction. We were largely successful." He paused.

"Make it march, Zack," Lazarus urged. "Are we covered? Or not?"

"We are *not*. At least two of our cousins certain to be arrested are not so protected."

Lazarus shrugged. "That tears it. Kinfolk, the game's over. One shot in the arm of babble juice and the 'Masquerade' is over. It's a new situation—or will be in a few hours. What do you propose to do about it?"

In the control room of the Antipodes Rocket *Wallaby*, South Flight, the telecom hummed, went *spung!* and stuck out a tab like an impudent tongue. The copilot rocked forward in his gymbals, pulled out the message and tore it off.

He read it, then reread it. "Skipper, brace yourself."

"Trouble?"

"Read it."

The captain did so, and whistled. "Bloody! I've never arrested anybody. I don't believe I've even *seen* anybody arrested. How do we start?"

"I bow to your superior authority."

"That so?" the captain said in nettled tones. "Now that you're through bowing you can tool aft and make the arrest."

"Uh? That's not what I meant. You're the bloke with the authority. I'll relieve you at the conn."

"You didn't read me. I'm delegating the authority. Carry out your orders."

"Just a moment, Al, I didn't sign up for——"

"Carry out your orders!"

"Aye aye, sir!"

The copilot went aft. The ship had completed its reëntry, was in its long, flat, screaming approach-glide; he was able to walk—he wondered what an arrest in free-fall would be like? Snag him with a butterfly net? He located the passenger by seat check, touched his arm. "Service, sir. There's been a clerical error. May I see your ticket?"

"Why, certainly."

"Would you mind stepping back to the reserve stateroom? It's quieter there and we can both sit down."

"Not at all."

Once they were in the private compartment the chief officer asked the passenger to sit down, then looked annoyed. "Stupid of me!—I've left my lists in the control room." He turned and left. As the door slid to behind him, the passenger heard an unexpected click. Suddenly suspicious, he tried the door. It was locked.

Two proctors came for him at Melbourne. As they escorted him through the skyport he could hear remarks from a curious and surprisingly unfriendly crowd: "There's one of the laddies now!" "Him? My word, he doesn't look *old*." "What price ape glands?" "Don't stare, Herbert." "Why not? Not half bad enough for him."

They took him to the office of the Chief Provost, who invited him to sit down with formal civility. "Now then, sir," the Provost said with a slight local twang, "if you will help us by letting the orderly make a slight injection in your arm——"

"For what purpose?"

"You want to be socially coöperative, I'm sure. It won't hurt you."

"That's beside the point. I insist on an explanation. I am a citizen of the United States."

"So you are, but the Federation has concurrent jurisdiction in any member state—and I am acting under its authority. Now bare your arm, please."

"I refuse. I stand on my civil rights."

"Grab him, lads."

It took four men to do it. Even before the injector touched his skin, his jaw set and a look of sudden agony came into his face. He then sat quietly, listlessly, while the peace officers waited for the drug to take effect. Presently the Provost gently rolled back one of the prisoner's eyelids and said, "I think he's ready. He doesn't weigh over ten stone; it has hit him rather fast. Where's that list of questions?"

A deputy handed it to him; he began, "Horace Foote, do you hear me?"

The man's lips twitched, he seemed about to speak. His mouth opened and blood gushed down his chest.

The Provost bellowed and grabbed the prisoner's head, made quick examination. "*Surgeon!* He's bitten his tongue half out of his head!"

The captain of the Luna City Shuttle *Moonbeam* scowled at the message in his hand. "What child's play is this?" He glared at his third officer. "Tell me that, Mister."

The third officer studied the overhead. Fuming, the captain held the message at arm's length, peered at it and read aloud: "—imperative that subject persons be prevented from doing themselves injury. You are directed to render them unconscious without warning them." He shoved the flimsy away from him. "What do they think I'm running? Coventry? Who do they think they are?—telling *me* in *my* ship what I must do with *my* passengers! I won't—so help me, I won't! There's no rule requiring me to . . . is there, Mister?"

The third officer went on silently studying the ship's structure.

The captain stopped pacing. "Purser! *Purser!* Why is that man never around when I want him?"

"I'm here, Captain."

"About time!"

"I've been here all along, sir."

"Don't argue with me. Here—attend to this." He handed the despatch to the purser and left.

A shipfitter, supervised by the purser, the hull officer, and the medical officer, made a slight change in the air-conditioning ducts to one cabin; two worried passengers sloughed off their cares under the influence of a nonlethal dose of sleeping gas.

"Another report, sir."

"Leave it," the Administrator said in a tired voice.

"And Councilor Bork Vanning presents his compliments and requests an interview."

"Tell him that I regret that I am too busy."

"He insists on seeing you, sir."

Administrator Ford answered snappishly, "Then you may tell the Honorable Mr. Vanning that he does not give orders in this office!" The aide said nothing; Administrator Ford pressed his fingertips wearily against his forehead and went on slowly, "No, Gerry, don't tell him that. Be diplomatic . . . but don't let him in."

"Yes, sir."

When he was alone, the Administrator picked up the report. His eye skipped over official heading, date line, and file number: "Synopsis of Interview with Conditionally Proscribed Citizen Arthur Sperling, full transcript attached. Conditions of Interview: Subject received normal dosage of neosco., having previously received unmeasured dosage of gaseous hypnotal. Antidote———" How the devil could you cure subordinates of wordiness? Was there something in the soul of a career civil servant that cherished red tape? His eye skipped on down:

"—stated that his name was Arthur Sperling of the Foote Family and gave his age as one hundred thirty-seven years. (Subject's apparent age is forty-five plus-or-minus four: see bio report attached.) Subject admitted that he was a member of the Howard Families. He stated that the Families numbered slightly more than one hundred thousand members. He was asked to correct this and it was suggested to him that the correct number was nearer ten thousand. He persisted in his original statement."

The Administrator stopped and reread this part.

He skipped on down, looking for the key part: "—insisted that his long life was the result of his ancestry and had no other cause. Admitted that artificial means had been used to preserve his youthful appearance but maintained firmly that his life expectancy was inherent, not acquired. It was suggested to him that his elder relatives had subjected him without his knowledge to treatment in his early youth to increase his life span. Subject admitted possibility. On being pressed for names of persons who might have performed, or might be performing, such treatments he returned to his original statement that no such treatments exist.

"He gave the names (surprise association procedure) and in some cases the addresses of nearly two hundred members of his kin group not previously identified as such in our records. (List attached) His strength ebbed under this arduous technique and he sank into full apathy from which he could not be roused by any stimuli within the limits of his estimated tolerance (see Bio Report).

"Conclusions under Expedited Analysis, Kelly-Holmes Approximation Method: Subject does not possess and does not believe in the Search Object. Does not remember experiencing Search Object but is mistaken. Knowledge of Search Object is limited to a small group, of the order of twenty. A member of this star group will be located through not more than triple-concatenation elimination search. (Probability of unity, subject to assumptions: first, that topologic social space is continuous and is included in the physical space of the Western Federation and, second, that at least one concatenative path exists between apprehended subjects and star group. Neither assumption can be verified as of this writing, but the first assumption is strongly supported by statistical analysis of the list of names supplied by Subject of previously unsuspected members of Howard kin group, which analysis also supports Subject's estimate of total size of group, and second assumption when taken negatively postulates that star group holding Search Object has been able to apply it with no social-space of contact, an absurdity.)

"Estimated Time for Search: 71 hrs, plus-or-minus 20 hrs. Prediction but not time estimate vouched for by cognizant bureau. Time estimate will be re———"

Ford slapped the report on a stack cluttering his old-fashioned control desk. The dumb fools! Not to recognize a negative report when they saw one—yet they called themselves *psychographers!*

He buried his face in his hands in utter weariness and frustration.

Lazarus rapped on the table beside him, using the butt of his blaster as a gavel. "Don't interrupt the speaker," he boomed, then added, "Go ahead but cut it short."

Bertram Hardy nodded curtly. "I say again, these mayflies we see around us have no rights that we of the Families are bound to respect. We should deal with them with stealth, with cunning, with guile, and when we eventually consolidate our position . . . with *force!* We are no more obligated to respect their welfare than a hunter is obliged to shout a warning at his quarry. The——"

There was a catcall from the rear of the room. Lazarus again banged for order and tried to spot the source. Hardy ploughed steadily on. "The so-called human race has split in two; it is time we admitted it. On one side, *Homo vivens,* ourselves . . . on the other—*Homo moriturus!* With the great lizards, with the sabertooth tiger and the bison, their day is done. We would no more mix our living blood with theirs than we would attempt to breed with apes. I say temporize with them, tell them any tale, assure them that we will bathe them in the fountain of youth—gain time, so that when these two naturally antagonistic races join battle, *as they inevitably must,* the victory will be ours!"

There was no applause but Lazarus could see wavering uncertainty in many faces. Bertram Hardy's ideas ran counter to thought patterns of many years of gentle living yet his words seemed to ring with destiny. Lazarus did not believe in destiny; he believed in . . . well, never mind—but he wondered how Brother Bertram would look with both arms broken.

Eve Barstow got up. "If that is what Bertram means by the survival of the fittest," she said bitterly, "I'll go live with the asocials in Coventry. However, he has offered a plan; I'll have to offer another plan if I won't take his. I won't accept any plan which would have us live at the expense of our poor transient neighbors. Furthermore it is clear to me now that our mere presence, the simple fact of our rich heritage of life, is damaging to the spirit of our poor neighbor. Our longer years and richer opportunities make his best efforts seem futile to him—any effort save a hopeless struggle against an appointed death. Our mere presence saps his strength, ruins his judgment, fills him with panic fear of death.

"So I propose a plan. Let's disclose ourselves, tell *all* the truth, and ask for our share of the Earth, some little corner where we may live apart. If our poor friends wish to surround it with a great barrier like that around Coventry, so be it—it is better that we never meet face to face."

Some expressions of doubt changed to approval. Ralph Schultz stood up. "Without prejudice to Eve's basic plan, I must advise you that it is my professional opinion that the psychological insulation she proposes cannot be accomplished that easily. As long as we're on this planet they won't be able to put us out of their minds. Modern communications———"

"Then we must move to another planet!" she retorted.

"Where?" demanded Bertram Hardy. "Venus? I'd rather live in a steam bath. Mars? Worn-out and worthless."

"We will rebuild it," she insisted.

"Not in your lifetime nor mine. No, my dear Eve, your tenderheartedness sounds well but it doesn't make sense. There is only one planet in the System fit to live on—we're standing on it."

Something in Bertram Hardy's words set off a response in Lazarus Long's brain, then the thought escaped him. Something . . . something that he had heard of said just a day or two ago . . . or was it longer than? Somehow it seemed to be associated with his first trip out into space, too, well over a century ago. Thunderation! it was maddening to have his memory play tricks on him like that——

Then he had it—the starship! The interstellar ship they were putting the finishing touches on out there between Earth and Luna. "Folks," he drawled, "before we table this idea of moving to another planet, let's consider all the possibilities." He waited until he had their full attention. "Did you ever stop to think that not all the planets swing around this one Sun?"

Zaccur Barstow broke the silence. "Lazarus . . . are you making a serious suggestion?"

"Dead serious."

"It does not sound so. Perhaps you had better explain."

"I will." Lazarus faced the crowd. "There's a spaceship hanging out there in the sky, a roomy thing, built to make the long jumps between stars. Why don't we take it and go looking for our own piece of real estate?"

Bertram Hardy was first to recover. "I don't know whether our chairman is lightening the gloom with another of his wisecracks or not, but, assuming that he is serious, I'll answer. My objection to Mars applies to this wild scheme ten times over. I understand that the reckless fools who are actually intending to man that ship expect to make the jump in about a century —then maybe their grandchildren will find something, or maybe they won't. Either way, I'm not interested. I don't care to spend a century locked up in a steel tank, nor do I expect to live that long. I won't buy it."

"Hold it," Lazarus told him. "Where's Andy Libby?"

"Here," Libby answered, standing up.

"Come on down front. Slipstick, did you have anything to do with designing the new Centarus ship?"

"No. Neither this one nor the first one."

Lazarus spoke to the crowd. "That settles it. If that ship didn't have Slipstick's finger in the drive design, then she's not as fast as she could be, not by a good big coefficient. Slipstick, better get busy on the problem, son. We're likely to need a solution."

"But, Lazarus, you mustn't assume that——"

"Aren't there theoretical possibilities?"

"Well, you know there are, but——"

"Then get that carrot top of yours working on it."

"Well . . . all right." Libby blushed as pink as his hair.

"Just a moment, Lazarus." It was Zaccur Barstow. "I like this proposal and I think we should discuss it at length . . . not let ourselves be frightened off by Brother Bertram's distaste for it. Even if Brother Libby fails to find a better means of propulsion—and frankly, I don't think he will; I know a little something of field mechanics—even so, I shan't let a century frighten me. By using cold-rest and manning the ship in shifts, most of us should be able to complete one hop. There is——"

"What makes you think," demanded Bertram Hardy, "that they'll let *us* man the ship anyhow?"

"Bert," Lazarus said coldly, "address the chair when you want to sound off. You're not even a Family delegate. Last warning."

"As I was saying," Barstow continued, "there is an appropriateness in the long-lived exploring the stars. A mystic might call it our true vocation." He pondered. "As for the ship Lazarus suggested, perhaps they will not let us have that . . . but the Families are rich. If we need a starship—or ships —we can build them, we can pay for them. I think we had better hope that they will let us do this . . . for it may be that there is no way, not another way of any sort, out of our dilemma which does not include our own extermination."

Barstow spoke these last words softly and slowly, with great sadness. They bit into the company like damp chill. To most of them the problem was so new as not yet to be real; no one had voiced the possible consequence of failing to find a solution satisfactory to the short-lived majority. For their senior trustee to speak soberly of his fear that the Families might be exterminated—hunted down and killed—stirred up in each one the ghost they never mentioned.

"Well," Lazarus said briskly when the silence had grown painful, "before we work this idea over, let's hear what other plan anyone has to offer. Speak up."

A messenger hurried in and spoke to Zaccur Barstow. He looked startled and seemed to ask to have the message repeated. He then hurried across the rostrum to Lazarus, whispered to him. Lazarus looked startled. Barstow hurried out.

Lazarus looked back at the crowd. "We'll take a recess," he announced. "Give you time to think about other plans . . . and time for a stretch and a smoke." He reached for his pouch.

"What's up?" someone called out.

Lazarus struck a cigarette, took a long drag, let it drift out. "We'll have to wait and see," he said. "I don't know. But at least half a dozen of the plans put forward tonight we won't have to bother to vote on. The situation has changed again— how much, I couldn't say."

"What do you mean?"

"Well," Lazarus drawled, "it seems the Federation Administrator wanted to talk to Zack Barstow right away. He asked for him by name . . . *and he called over our secret Families' circuit.*"

"Huh? That's impossible!"

"Yep. So is a baby, son."

4

ZACCUR BARSTOW TRIED to quiet himself down as he hurried into the phone booth.

At the other end of the same videophone circuit the Honorable Slayton Ford was doing the same thing—trying to calm his nerves. He did not underrate himself. A long and brilliant public career crowned by years as Administrator for the Council and under the Covenant of the Western Administration had made Ford aware of his own superior ability and unmatched experience; no ordinary man could possibly make him feel at a disadvantage in negotiation.

But this was different.

What would a man be like who had lived more than two ordinary lifetimes? Worse than that—a man who had had four or five times the adult experience that Ford himself had had? Slayton Ford knew that his own opinions had changed and changed again since his own boyhood; he knew that the boy he had been, or even the able young man he had been, would be no match for the mature man he had become. So what would this Barstow be like? Presumably he was the most able, the most astute, of a group all of whom had had much more experience than Ford could possibly have—how could he guess such a man's evaluations, intentions, ways of thinking, his possible resources?

Ford was certain of only one thing: he did not intend to trade Manhattan Island for twenty-four dollars and a case of whisky, nor sell humanity's birthright for a mess of pottage.

He studied Barstow's face as the image appeared in his phone. A good face and strong . . . it would be useless to try to bully this man. And the man looked young—why, he looked younger than Ford himself! The subconscious image of the Administrator's own stern and implacable grandfather faded out of his mind and his tension eased off. He said quietly, "You are Citizen Zaccur Barstow?"

"Yes, Mister Administrator."

"You are chief executive of the Howard Families?"

"I am the current speaker trustee of our Families' Foundation. But I am responsible to my cousins rather than in authority over them."

Ford brushed it aside. "I assume that your position carries with it leadership. I can't negotiate with a hundred thousand people."

Barstow did not blink. He saw the power play in the sudden admission that the administration knew the true numbers of the Families and discounted it. He had already adjusted himself to the shock of learning that the Families' secret headquarters was no longer secret and the still more upsetting fact that the Administrator knew how to tap into their private communication system; it simply proved that one or more Members had been caught and forced to talk.

So it was now almost certain that the authorities already knew every important fact about the Families.

Therefore it was useless to try to bluff—just the same, don't volunteer any information; they might not have all the facts this soon.

Barstow answered without noticeable pause. "What is it you wish to discuss with me, sir?"

"The policy of the Administration toward your kin group. The welfare of yourself and your relatives."

Barstow shrugged. "What can we discuss? The Covenant has been tossed aside and you have been given power to do as you like with us—to squeeze a secret out of us that we don't have. What can we do but pray for mercy?"

"Please!" The Administrator gestured his annoyance. "Why fence with me? We have a problem, you and I. Let's discuss it openly and try to reach a solution. Yes?"

Barstow answered slowly, "I would like to . . . and I believe that you would like to, also. But the problem is based on a false assumption, that we, the Howard Families, know how to lengthen human life. We don't."

"Suppose I tell you that I know there is no such secret?"

"Mmm . . . I would like to believe you. But how can you reconcile that with the persecution of my people? You've been harrying us like rats."

Ford made a wry face. "There is an old, old story about a theologian who was asked to reconcile the doctrine of Divine mercy with the doctrine of infant damnation. 'The Almighty,' he explained, 'finds it necessary to do things in His official and public capacity which in His private and personal capacity He deplores.'"

Barstow smiled in spite of himself. "I see the analogy. Is it actually pertinent?"

"I think it is."

"So. You didn't call me simply to make a headsman's apology?"

"No. I hope not. You keep in touch with politics? I'm sure you must; your position would require it." Barstow nodded; Ford explained at length:

Ford's administration had been the longest since the signing of the Covenant; he had lasted through four Councils. Nevertheless his control was now so shaky that he could not risk forcing a vote of confidence—certainly not over the Howard Families. On that issue his nominal majority was already a minority. If he refused the present decision of the Council, forced it to a vote of confidence, Ford would be out of office and the present minority leader would take over as administrator. "You follow me? I can either stay in office and try to cope with this problem while restricted by a Council directive with which I do not agree . . . or I can drop out and let my successor handle it."

"Surely you're not asking my advice?"

"No, no! Not on that. I've made my decision. The Action-in-Council would have been carried out in any case, either by me or by Mr. Vanning—so I decided to do it. The question is: will I have your help, or will I not?"

Barstow hesitated, while rapidly reviewing Ford's political career in his mind. The earlier part of Ford's long administration had been almost a golden age of statesmanship. A wise and practical man, Ford had shaped into workable rules the principles of human freedom set forth by Novak in the language of the Covenant. It had been a period of good will, of prosperous expansion, of civilizing processes which seemed to be permanent, irreversible.

Nevertheless a setback had come and Barstow understood the reasons at least as well as Ford did. Whenever the citizens fix their attention on one issue to the exclusion of others, the situation is ripe for scalawags, demagogues, ambitious men on horseback. The Howard Families, in all innocence, had created the crisis in public morals from which they now suffered, through their own action, taken years earlier, in letting the short-lived learn of their existence. It mattered not at all that the "secret" did not exist; the corrupting effect did exist.

Ford at least understood the true situation——

"We'll help," Barstow answered suddenly.

"Good. What do you suggest?"

Barstow chewed his lip. "Isn't there some way you can stall off this drastic action, this violation of the Covenant itself?"

Ford shook his head. "It's too late."

"Even if you went before the public and told the citizens, face to face, that you knew that——"

Ford cut him short. "I wouldn't last in office long enough to make the speech. Nor would I be believed. Besides that—understand me clearly, Zaccur Barstow—no matter what sympathy I may have personally for you and your people, I would not do so if I could. This whole matter is a cancer eating into vitals of our society; it must be settled. I have had my hand forced, true . . . but there is no turning back. It must be pressed on to a solution."

In at least one respect Barstow was a wise man; he knew that another man could oppose him and not be a villain. Nevertheless he protested, "My people are being persecuted."

"Your people," Ford said forcefully, "are a fraction of a tenth of one per cent of all the people . . . and I must find a solution for all! I've called on you to find out if you have any suggestions toward a solution for everyone. Do you?"

"I'm not sure," Barstow answered slowly. "Suppose I concede that you must go ahead with this ugly business of arresting my people, of questioning them by unlawful means—I suppose I have no choice about that——"

"You have no choice. Neither have I." Ford frowned. "It will be carried out as humanely as I can manage it—I am not a free agent."

"Thank you. But, even though you tell me it would be useless for you yourself to go to the people, nevertheless you have enormous propaganda means at your disposal. Would it be possible, while we stall along, to build up a campaign to convince the people of the true facts? Prove to them that there *is* no secret?"

Ford answered, "Ask yourself: will it work?"

Barstow sighed. "Probably not."

"Nor would I consider it a solution even if it would! The people—even my trusted assistants—are clinging to their belief in a fountain of youth because the only alternative is too bitter to think about. Do you know what it would mean to them? For them to believe the bald truth?"

"Go on."

"Death has been tolerable to me only because Death has been the Great Democrat, treating all alike. But now Death plays favorites. Zaccur Barstow, can you understand the bitter, bitter jealousy of the ordinary man of—oh, say 'fifty'—who looks on one of your sort? Fifty years . . . twenty of them he is a child, he is well past thirty before he is skilled in his profession. He is forty before he is established and respected. For not more than the last ten years of his fifty he has really amounted to something."

Ford leaned forward in the screen and spoke with sober emphasis: "And now, when he has reached his goal, what is his prize? His eyes are failing him, his bright young strength is gone, his heart and wind are 'not what they used to be.' He is not senile yet . . . but he feels the chill of the first frost. He knows what is in store for him. He knows—he knows!

"But it was inevitable and each man learned to be resigned to it.

"Now *you* come along," Ford went on bitterly. "You shame him in his weakness, you humble him before his children. He dares not plan for the future; you blithely undertake plans that will not mature for fifty years—for a hundred. No matter what success he has achieved, what excellence he has attained, you will catch up with him, pass him—outlive him. In his weakness you are *kind* to him.

"Is it any wonder that he hates you?"

Barstow raised his head wearily. "Do *you* hate me, Slayton Ford?"

"No. No, I cannot afford to hate anyone. But I can tell you this," Ford added suddenly, "had there been a secret, I would have it out of you if I had to tear you to pieces!"

"Yes. I understand that." Barstow paused to think. "There is little that we of the Howard Families can do. We did not plan it this way; it was planned for us. But there is one thing we can offer."

"Yes?"

Barstow explained.

Ford shook his head. "Medically what you suggest is feasible and I have no doubt that a half interest in your heritage would lengthen the span of human life. But even if women were willing to accept the germ plasm of your men—I do not say that they would—it would be psychic death for all other men. There would be an outbreak of frustration and hatred that would split the human race to ruin. No, no matter what we wish, our customs are what they are. We can't breed men like animals; they won't stand for it."

"I know it," agreed Barstow, "but it is all we have to offer . . . a share in our fortune through artificial impregnation."

"Yes. I suppose I should thank you but I feel no thanks and I shan't. Now let's be practical. Individually you old ones are doubtless honorable, lovable men. But as a group you are as dangerous as carriers of plague. So you must be quarantined."

Barstow nodded. "My cousins and I had already reached that conclusion."

Ford looked relieved. "I'm glad you're being sensible about it."

"We can't help ourselves. Well? A segregated colony? Some remote place that would be a Coventry of our own? Madagascar, perhaps? Or we might take the British Isles, build them up again and spread from there into Europe as the radioactivity died down."

Ford shook his head. "Impossible. That would simply leave the problem for my grandchildren to solve. By that time you and yours would have grown in strength; you might defeat us. No, Zaccur Barstow, you and your kin must leave this planet entirely!"

Barstow looked bleak. "I knew it would come to that. Well, where shall we go?"

"Take your choice of the Solar System. Anywhere you like."

"But *where?* Venus is no prize, but even if we chose it, would they accept us? The Venerians won't take orders from Earth; that was settled in 2020. Yes, they now accept screened immigrants under the Four Planets Convention . . . but would they accept a hundred thousand whom Earth found too dangerous to keep? I doubt it."

"So do I. Better pick another planet."

"What planet? In the whole system there is not another body that will support human life as it is. It would take almost superhuman effort, even with unlimited money and the best of modern engineering, to make the most promising of them fit for habitation."

"Make the effort. We will be generous with help."

"I am sure you would. But is that any better solution in the long run than giving us a reservation on Earth? Are you going to put a stop to space travel?"

Ford sat up suddenly. "Oh! I see your thought. I had not followed it through, but let's face it. Why not? Would it not be better to give up space travel than to let this situation degenerate into open war? It was given up once before."

"Yes, when the Venerians threw off their absentee landlords. But it started up again and Luna City is rebuilt and ten times more tonnage moves through the sky than ever did before. Can you stop it? If you can, will it stay stopped?"

Ford turned it over and over in his mind. He could not stop space travel, no administration could. But could an interdict be placed on whatever planet these oldsters were shipped to?

And would it help? One generation, two, three . . . what difference would it make? Ancient Japan had tried some solution like that; the foreign devils had come sailing in anyhow. Cultures could not be kept apart forever, and when they did come in contact, the hardier displaced the weaker; that was a natural law.

A permanent and effective quarantine was impossible. That left only one answer—an ugly one. But Ford was tough-minded; he could accept what was necessary. He started making plans, Barstow's presence in the screen forgotten. Once he gave the Chief Provost the location of the Howard Families headquarters it should be reduced in an hour, two at the most . . . unless they had extraordinary defenses—but anywise it was just a matter of time. From those who would be arrested at their headquarters it should be possible to locate and arrest every other member of their group. With luck he would have them all in twenty-four to forty-eight hours.

The only point left undecided in his mind was whether to liquidate them all, or simply to sterilize them. Either would be a final solution and there was no third solution. But which was the more humane?

Ford knew that this would end his career. He would leave office in disgrace, perhaps be sent to Coventry, but he gave it no thought; he was so constituted as to be unable to weigh his own welfare against his concept of his public duty.

Barstow could not read Ford's mind but he did sense that Ford had reached a decision and he surmised correctly how bad that decision must be for himself and his kin. Now was the time, he decided, to risk his one lone trump.

"Mister Administrator——"

"Eh? Oh, sorry! I was preoccupied." That was a vast understatement; he was shockingly embarrassed to find himself still facing a man he had just condemned to death. He gathered formality about him like a robe. "Thank you, Zaccur Barstow, for talking with me. I am sorry that——"

"Mister Administrator!"

"Yes?"

"I propose that you move us entirely out of the Solar System."

"*What?*" Ford blinked. "Are you speaking seriously?"

Barstow spoke rapidly, persuasively, explaining Lazarus Long's half-conceived scheme, improvising details as he went along, skipping over obstacles and emphasizing advantages.

"It might work," Ford at last said slowly. "There are difficulties you have not mentioned, political difficulties and a terrible hazard of time. Still, it might." He stood up. "Go back to your people. Don't spring this on them yet. I'll talk with you later."

Barstow walked back slowly while wondering what he could tell the Members. They would demand a full report; technically he had no right to refuse. But he was strongly inclined to coöperate with the Administrator as long as there was any chance of a favorable outcome. Suddenly making up his mind, he turned, went to his office, and sent for Lazarus.

"Howdy, Zack," Long said as he came in. "How'd the palaver go?"

"Good and bad," Barstow replied. "Listen——" He gave him a brief, accurate résumé. "Can you go back in there and tell them something that will hold them?"

"Mmm . . . reckon so."

"Then do it and hurry back here."

They did not like the stall Lazarus gave them. They did not want to keep quiet and they did not want to adjourn the meeting. "Where is Zaccur?"—"We demand a report!"—"Why all the mystification?"

Lazarus shut them up with a roar. "Listen to me, you damned idiots! Zack'll talk when he's ready—don't joggle his elbow. He knows what he's doing."

A man near the back stood up. "I'm going home!"

"Do that," Lazarus urged sweetly. "Give my love to the proctors."

The man looked startled and sat down.

"Anybody else want to go home?" demanded Lazarus. "Don't let me stop you. But it's time you bird-brained dopes realized that you have been outlawed. The only thing that stands between you and the proctors is Zack Barstow's ability to talk sweet to the Administrator. So do as you like . . . the meeting's adjourned."

"Look, Zack," said Lazarus a few minutes later, "let's get this straight. Ford is going to use his extraordinary powers to help us glom onto the big ship and make a getaway. Is that right?"

"He's practically committed to it."

"Hmmm—— He'll have to do this while pretending to the Council that everything he does is just a necessary step in squeezing the 'secret' out of us—he's going to double-cross 'em. That right?"

"I hadn't thought that far ahead. I——"

"But that's true, isn't it?"

"Well . . . yes, it must be true."

"Okay. Now, is our boy Ford bright enough to realize what he is letting himself in for and tough enough to go through with it?"

Barstow reviewed what he knew of Ford and added his impressions from the interview. "Yes," he decided, "he knows and he's strong enough to face it."

"All right. Now how about you, pal? Are *you* up to it, too?" Lazarus' voice was accusing.

"Me? What do you mean?"

"You're planning on double-crossing *your* crowd, too, aren't you? Have you got the guts to go through with it when the going gets tough?"

"I don't understand you, Lazarus," Barstow answered worriedly. "I'm not planning to deceive anyone—at least, no member of the Families."

"Better look at your cards again," Lazarus went on remorselessly. "Your part of the deal is to see to it that every man, woman and child takes part in this exodus. Do you expect to sell the idea to each one of them separately and get a hundred thousand people to agree? *Unanimously?* Shucks, you couldn't get that many to whistle 'Yankee Doodle' unanimously."

"But they will *have* to agree," protested Barstow. "They have no choice. We either emigrate, or they hunt us down and kill us. I'm certain that is what Ford intends to do. And he will."

"Then why didn't you walk into the meeting and tell 'em that? Why did you send me in to give 'em a stall?"

Barstow rubbed a hand across his eyes. "I don't know."

"I'll tell you why," continued Lazarus. "You think better with your hunches than most men do with the tops of their minds. You sent me in there to tell 'em a tale because you knew damn' well the truth wouldn't serve. If you told 'em it was get out or get killed, some would get panicky and some would get stubborn. And some old-woman-in-kilts would decide to go home and stand on his Covenant rights. Then he'd spill the scheme before it ever dawned on him that the government was playing for keeps. That's right, isn't it?"

Barstow shrugged and laughed unhappily. "You're right. I didn't have it figured out but you're absolutely right."

"But you did have it figured out," Lazarus assured him. "You had the right answers. Zack, I like your hunches; that's why I'm stringing along. All right, you and Ford are planning to pull a whizzer on every man jack on this globe—I'm asking you again: *have you got the guts to see it through?*"

5

THE MEMBERS STOOD AROUND in groups, fretfully. "I can't understand it," the Resident Archivist was saying to a worried circle around her. "The Senior Trustee never interfered in my work before. But he came bursting into my office with that Lazarus Long behind him and ordered me out."

"What did he say?" asked one of her listeners.

"Well, *I* said, 'May I do you a service, Zaccur Barstow?' and he said, 'Yes, you may. Get out and take your girls with you.' Not a word of ordinary courtesy!"

"A lot you've got to complain about," another voice added gloomily. It was Cecil Hedrick, of the Johnson Family, chief communications engineer. "Lazarus Long paid a call on me, and he was a damned sight less polite."

"What did he do?"

"He walks into the communication cell and tells me he is going to take over my board—Zaccur's orders. I told him that nobody could touch my burners but me and my operators, and anyhow, where was his authority? You know what he did? You won't believe it but he pulled a blaster on me."

"You don't mean it!"

"I certainly do. I tell you, that man is dangerous. He ought to go for psycho adjustment. He's an atavism if I ever saw one."

Lazarus Long's face stared out of the screen into that of the Administrator. "Got it all canned?" he demanded.

Ford cut the switch on the facsimulator on his desk. "Got it all," he confirmed.

"Okay," the image of Lazarus replied. "I'm clearing." As the screen went blank Ford spoke into his interoffice circuit. "Have the High Chief Provost report to me at once—in corpus."

The public safety boss showed up as ordered with an expression on his lined face in which annoyance struggled with discipline. He was having the busiest night of his career, yet the Old Man had sent orders to report in the flesh. What the devil were viewphones for, anyway, he thought angrily—and asked himself why he had ever taken up police work. He rebuked his boss by being coldly formal and saluting unnecessarily. "You sent for me, sir."

Ford ignored it. "Yes, thank you. Here." He pressed a stud; a film spool popped out of the facsimulator. "This is a complete list of the Howard Families. Arrest them."

"Yes, sir." The Federation police chief stared at the spool and debated whether or not to ask how it had been obtained —it certainly hadn't come through *his* office . . . did the Old Man have an intelligence service he didn't even know about?

"It's alphabetical, but keyed geographically," the Administrator was saying. "After you put it through sorters, send the —no, *bring* the original back to me. You can stop the psycho interviews, too," he added. "Just bring them in and hold them. I'll give you more instructions later."

The High Chief Provost decided that this was not a good time to show curiosity. "Yes, sir." He saluted stiffly and left.

Ford turned back to his desk controls and sent word that he wanted to see the chiefs of the bureaus of land resources and of transportation control. On afterthought he added the chief of the bureau of consumption logistics.

Back in the Families' Seat a rump session of the trustees was meeting; Barstow was absent. "I don't like it," Andrew Weatherall was saying. "I could understand Zaccur deciding to delay reporting to the Members but I had supposed that he simply wanted to talk to us first. I certainly did expect him to consult us. What do you make of it, Philip?"

Philip Hardy chewed his lip. "I don't know. Zaccur's got a head on his shoulders . . . but it certainly seems to me that he should have called us together and advised with us. Has he spoken with you, Justin?"

"No, he has not," Justin Foote answered frigidly.

"Well, what should we do? We can't very well call him in

and demand an accounting unless we are prepared to oust him from office and if he refuses. I, for one, am reluctant to do that."

They were still discussing it when the proctors arrived.

Lazarus heard the commotion and correctly interpreted it —no feat, since he had information that his brethren lacked. He was aware that he should submit peacefully and conspicuously to arrest—set a good example. But old habits die hard; he postponed the inevitable by ducking into the nearest men's 'fresher.

It was a dead end. He glanced at the air duct—no, too small. While thinking he fumbled in his pouch for a cigarette; his hand found a strange object, he pulled it out. It was the brassard he had "borrowed" from the proctor in Chicago.

When the proctor working point of the mop-squad covering that wing of the Seat stuck his head into that 'fresher, he found another "proctor" already there. "Nobody in here," announced Lazarus. "I've checked it."

"How the devil did you get ahead of me?"

"Around your flank. Stoney Island Tunnel and through their air vents." Lazarus trusted that the real cop would be unaware that there was no Stoney Island Tunnel. "Got a cigarette on you?"

"Huh? This is no time to catch a smoke."

"Shucks," said Lazarus, "my legate is a good mile away."

"Maybe so," the proctor replied, "but mine is right behind us."

"So? Well, skip it—I've got something to tell him anyhow." Lazarus started to move past but the proctor did not get out of his way. He was glancing curiously at Lazarus' kilt. Lazarus had turned it inside out and its blue lining made a fair imitation of a proctor's service uniform—if not inspected closely.

"What station did you say you were from?" inquired the proctor.

"This one," answered Lazarus and planted a short jab under the man's breastbone. Lazarus' coach in rough-and-tumble had explained to him that a solar plexus blow was harder to dodge than one to the jaw; the coach had been dead since the roads strike of 1966, his skill lived on.

Lazarus felt more like a cop with a proper uniform kilt and a bandolier of paralysis bombs slung under his left arm. Besides, the proctor's kilt was a better fit. To the right the passage outside led to the Sanctuary and a dead end; he went to the left by Hobson's choice although he knew he would run into his unconscious benefactor's legate. The passage gave into a hall which was crowded with Members herded into a group of proctors. Lazarus ignored his kin and sought out the harassed officer in charge. "Sir," he reported, saluting smartly, "There's sort of a hospital back there. You'll need fifty or sixty stretchers."

"Don't bother me, tell your legate. We've got our hands full."

Lazarus almost did not answer; he had caught Mary Sperling's eye in the crowd—she stared at him and looked away. He caught himself and answered, "Can't tell him, sir. Not available."

"Well, go on outside and tell the first-aid squad."

"Yes, sir." He moved away, swaggering a little, his thumbs hooked in the band of his kilt. He was far down the passage leading to the transbelt tunnel serving the Waukegan outlet when he heard shouts behind him. Two proctors were running to overtake him.

Lazarus stopped in the archway giving into the transbelt tunnel and waited for them. "What's the trouble?" he asked easily as they came up.

"The legate——" began one. He got no further; a paralysis bomb tinkled and popped at his feet. He looked surprised as the radiations wiped all expression from his face; his mate fell across him.

Lazarus waited behind a shoulder of the arch, counted seconds up to fifteen: "Number one jet fire! Number two jet fire! Number three jet fire!"—added a couple to be sure the paralyzing effect had died away. He had cut it finer than he liked. He had not ducked quite fast enough and his left foot tingled from exposure.

He then checked. The two were unconscious, no one else was in sight. He mounted the transbelt. Perhaps they had not been looking for him in his proper person, perhaps no one had given him away. But he did not hang around to find out. One thing he was damn' well certain of, he told himself, if anybody had squealed on him, it wasn't Mary Sperling.

It took two more parabombs and a couple of hundred words of pure fiction to get him out into the open air. Once he was there and out of immediate observation the brassard

and the remaining bombs went into his pouch and the bandolier ended up behind some bushes; he then looked up a clothing store in Waukegan.

He sat down in a sales booth and dialed the code for kilts.
He let cloth designs flicker past in the screen while he ignored
the persuasive voice of the catalogue until a pattern showed
up which was distinctly unmilitary and not blue, whereupon
he stopped the display and punched an order for his size. He
noted the price, tore an open-credit voucher from his wallet,
stuck it into the machine and pushed the switch. Then he enjoyed a smoke while the tailoring was done.

Ten minutes later he stuffed the proctor's kilt into the refuse hopper of the sales booth and left, nattily and loudly attired. He had not been in Waukegan the past century but he
found a middle-priced autel without drawing attention by
asking questions, dialed its registration board for a standard
suite and settled down for seven hours of sound sleep.

He breakfasted in his suite, listening with half an ear to the
news box; he was interested, in a mild way, in hearing what
might be reported concerning the raid on the Families. But it
was a detached interest; he had already detached himself
from it in his own mind. It had been a mistake, he now realized, to get back in touch with the Families—a darn good
thing he was clear of it all with his present public identity
totally free of any connection with the whing-ding.

A phrase caught his attention: "—including Zaccur Barstow, alleged to be their tribal chief.

"The prisoners are being shipped to a reservation in
Oklahoma, near the ruins of the Okla-Orleans road city about
twenty-five miles east of Harriman Memorial Park. The Chief
Provost describes it as a 'Little Coventry,' and has ordered all
aircraft to avoid it by ten miles laterally. The Administrator
could not be reached for a statement but a usually reliable
source inside the administration informs us that the mass arrest was accomplished in order to speed up the investigations
whereby the administration expects to obtain the 'Secret of
the Howard Families'—their techniques for indefinitely pro-
longing life. This forthright action in arresting and transporting
every member of the outlaw group is expected to have a salu-
tary effect in breaking down the resistance of their leaders to
the legitimate demands of society. It will bring home forcibly
to them that the civil rights enjoyed by decent citizens must

not be used as a cloak behind which to damage society as a whole.

"The chattels and holdings of the members of this criminal conspiracy have been declared subject to the Conservator General and will be administered by his agents during the imprisonment of——"

Lazarus switched it off. "Damnation!" he thought. "Don't fret about things you can't help." Of course, he had expected to be arrested himself . . . but he had escaped. That was that. It wouldn't do the Families any good for him to turn himself in—and besides, he owed the Families nothing, not a tarnation thing.

Anyhow, they were better off all arrested at once and quickly placed under guard. If they had been smelled out one at a time, anything could have happened—lynchings, even pogroms. Lazarus knew from hard experience how close under the skin lay lynch law and mob violence in the most sweetly civilized; that was why he had advised Zack to rig it—that and the fact that Zack and the Administrator had to have the Families in one compact group to stand a chance of carrying out their scheme. They were well off . . . and no skin off his nose.

But he wondered how Zack was getting along, and what he would think of Lazarus' disappearance. And what Mary Sperling thought—it must have been a shock to her when he turned up making a noise like a proctor. He wished he could straighten that out with her.

Not that it mattered what any of them thought. They would all either be light-years away very soon . . . or dead. A closed book.

He turned to the phone and called the post office. "Captain Aaron Sheffield," he announced, and gave his postal number. "Last registered with Goddard Field post office. Will you please have my mail sent to——" He leaned closer and read the code number from the suite's mail receptacle.

"Service," assented the voice of the clerk. "Right away, Captain."

"Thank you."

It would take a couple of hours, he reflected, for his mail to catch up with him—a half hour in trajectory, three times that in fiddle-faddle. Might as well wait here . . . no doubt the search for him had lost itself in the distance but there was nothing in Waukegan he wanted. Once the mail showed up he would hire a U-push-it and scoot down to——

To where? What was he going to do now?

He turned several possibilities over in his mind and came at last to the blank realization that there was nothing, from one end of the Solar System to the other, that he really wanted to do.

It scared him a little. He had once heard, and was inclined to credit, that a loss of interest in living marked the true turning point in the battle between anabolism and catabolism—old age. He suddenly envied normal short-lived people—at least they could go make nuisances of themselves to their children. Filial affection was not customary among Members of the Families; it was not a feasible relationship to maintain for a century or more. And friendship, except between Members, was bound to be regarded as a passing and shallow matter. There was no one whom Lazarus wanted to see.

Wait a minute . . . who was that planter on Venus? The one who knew so many folk songs and who was so funny when he was drunk? He'd go look him up. It would make a nice hop and it would be fun, much as he disliked Venus.

Then he recalled with cold shock that he had not seen the man for—how long? In any case, he was certainly dead by now.

Libby had been right, he mused glumly, when he spoke of the necessity for a new type of memory association for the long-lived. He hoped the lad would push ahead with the necessary research and come up with an answer before Lazarus was reduced to counting on his fingers. He dwelt on the notion for a minute or two before recalling that he was most unlikely ever to see Libby again.

The mail arrived and contained nothing of importance. He was not surprised; he expected no personal letters. The spools of advertising went into the refuse chute; he read only one item, a letter from Pan-Terra Docking Corp. telling him that his convertible cruiser *I Spy* had finished her overhaul and had been moved to a parking dock, rental to start forthwith. As instructed, they had not touched the ship's astrogational controls—was that still the Captain's pleasure?

He decided to pick her up later in the day and head out into space. Anything was better than sitting Earthbound and admitting that he was bored.

Paying his score and finding a jet for hire occupied less

than twenty minutes. He took off and headed for Goddard Field, using the low local-traffic level to avoid entering the control pattern with a flight plan. He was not consciously avoiding the police because he had no reason to think that they could be looking for "Captain Sheffield"; it was simply habit, and it would get him to Goddard Field soon enough.

But long before he reached there, while over eastern Kansas, he decided to land and did so.

He picked the field of a town so small as to be unlikely to rate a full-time proctor and there he sought out a phone booth away from the field. Inside it, he hesitated. How did you go about calling up the head man of the entire Federation—and get him? If he simply called Novak Tower and asked for Administrator Ford, he not only would not be put through to him but his call would be switched to the Department of Public Safety for some unwelcome inquiries, sure as taxes.

Well, there was only one way to beat that, and that was to call the Department of Safety himself and, somehow, get the Chief Provost on the screen—after that he would play by ear.

"Department of Civil Safety," a voice answered. "What service, citizen?"

"Service to you," he began in his best control-bridge voice. "I am Captain Sheffield. Give me the Chief." He was not overbearing; his manner simply assumed obedience.

Short silence—— "What is it about, please?"

"I said I was *Captain Sheffield*." This time Lazarus' voice showed restrained annoyance.

Another short pause—— "I'll connect you with the Chief Deputy's office," the voice said doubtfully.

This time the screen came to life. "Yes?" asked the Chief Deputy, looking him over.

"Get me the Chief—hurry."

"What's it about?"

"Good Lord, man—get me the Chief! I'm *Captain Sheffield!*"

The Chief Deputy must be excused for connecting him; he had had no sleep and more confusing things had happened in the last twenty-four hours than he had been able to assimilate. When the High Chief Provost appeared in the screen, Lazarus spoke first. "Oh, there you are! I've had the damnedest time cutting through your red tape. Get me the Old Man and *move!* Use your closed circuit."

"What the devil do you mean? Who are you?"

"Listen, brother," said Lazarus in tones of slow exasperation, "I would not have routed through your damned hidebound department if I hadn't been in a jam. Cut me in to the Old Man. *This is about the Howard Families.*"

The police chief was instantly alert. "Make your report."

"Look," said Lazarus in tired tones, "I know you would like to look over the Old Man's shoulder, but this isn't a good time to try. If you obstruct me and force me to waste two hours by reporting in corpus, I will. But the Old Man will want to know why and you can bet your pretty parade kit, I'll tell him."

The Chief Provost decided to take a chance—cut this character in on a three-way; then, if the Old Man didn't burn this joker off the screen in about three seconds, he'd know he had played safe and guessed lucky. If he did—well, you could always blame it on a cross-up in communications. He set the combo.

Administrator Ford looked flabbergasted when he recognized Lazarus in the screen. "You?" he exclaimed. "How on Earth——Did Zaccur Barstow——"

"Seal your circuit!" Lazarus cut in.

The Chief Provost blinked as his screen went dead and silent. So the Old Man *did* have secret agents outside the department . . . interesting—and not to be forgotten.

Lazarus gave Ford a quick and fairly honest account of how he happened to be at large, then added, "So you see, I could have gone to cover and escaped entirely. In fact I still can. But I want to know this: is the deal with Zaccur Barstow to let us emigrate still on?"

"Yes, it is."

"Have you figured out how you are going to get a hundred thousand people inboard the *New Frontiers* without tipping your hand? You can't trust your own people, you know that."

"I know. The present situation is a temporary expedient while we work it out."

"And I'm the man for the job. I've got to be, I'm the only agent on the loose that either one of you can afford to trust. Now listen——"

Eight minutes later Ford was nodding his head slowly and saying, "It might work. It might. Anyway, you start your preparations. I'll have a letter of credit waiting for you at Goddard."

"Can you cover your tracks on that? I can't flash a letter of credit from the Administrator; people would wonder."

"Credit me with some intelligence. By the time it reaches you it will appear to be a routine banking transaction."

"Sorry. Now how can I get through to you when I need to?"

"Oh, yes—note this code combination." Ford recited it slowly. "That puts you through to my desk without relay. No, don't write it down; memorize it."

"And how can I talk to Zack Barstow?"

"Call me and I'll hook you in. You can't call him directly unless you can arrange a sensitive circuit."

"Even if I could, I can't cart a sensitive around with me. Well, cheerio—I'm clearing."

"Good luck!"

Lazarus left the phone booth with restrained haste and hurried back to reclaim his hired ship. He did not know enough about current police practice to guess whether or not the High Chief Provost had traced the call to the Administrator; he simply took it for granted because he himself would have done so in the Provost's shoes. Therefore the nearest available proctor was probably stepping on his heels—time to move, time to mess up the trail a little.

He took off again and headed west, staying in the local, uncontrolled low level until he reached a cloud bank that walled the western horizon. He then swung back and cut air for Kansas City, staying carefully under the speed limit and flying as low as local traffic regulations permitted. At Kansas City he turned his ship in to the local U-push-it agency and flagged a ground taxi, which carried him down the controlway to Joplin. There he boarded a local jet bus from St. Louis without buying a ticket first, thereby insuring that his flight would not be recorded until the bus's trip records were turned in on the west coast.

Instead of worrying he spent the time making plans.

One hundred thousand people with an average mass of a hundred and fifty—no, make it a hundred and sixty pounds, Lazarus reconsidered—a hundred and sixty each made a load of sixteen million pounds, eight thousand tons. The *I Spy* could boost such a load against one gravity but she would be as logy as baked beans. It was out of the question anyhow; people did not stow like cargo; the *I Spy* could lift that dead weight—but "dead" was the word, for that was what they would be.

He needed a transport.

Buying a passenger ship big enough to ferry the Families from Earth up to where the *New Frontiers* hung in her construction orbit was not difficult; Four Planets Passenger Service would gladly unload such a ship at a fair price. Passenger trade competition being what it was, they were anxious to cut their losses on older ships no longer popular with tourists. But a passenger ship would not do; not only would there be unhealthy curiosity in what he intended to do with such a ship, but—and this settled it—he could not pilot it single-handed. Under the Revised Space Precautionary Act, passenger ships were required to be built for human control throughout on the theory that no automatic safety device could replace human judgment in an emergency.

It would have to be a freighter.

Lazarus knew the best place to find one. Despite efforts to make the Moon colony ecologically self-sufficient, Luna City still imported vastly more tonnage than she exported. On Earth this would have resulted in "empties coming back"; in space transport it was sometimes cheaper to let empties accumulate, especially on Luna where an empty freighter was worth more as metal than it had cost originally as a ship back Earthside.

He left the bus when it landed at Goddard City, went to the space field, paid his bills, and took possession of the *I Spy*, filed a request for earliest available departure for Luna. The slot he was assigned was two days from then, but Lazarus did not let it worry him; he simply went back to the docking company and indicated that he was willing to pay liberally for a swap in departure time. In twenty minutes he had oral assurance that he could boost for Luna that evening.

He spent the remaining several hours in the maddening red tape of interplanetary clearance. He first picked up the letter of credit Ford had promised him and converted it into cash. Lazarus would have been quite willing to use a chunk of the cash to speed up his processing just as he had paid (quite legally) for a swap in slot with another ship. But he found himself unable to do so. Two centuries of survival had taught him that a bribe must be offered as gently and as indirectly as a gallant suggestion is made to a proud lady; in a very few minutes he came to the glum conclusion that civic virtue and public honesty could be run into the ground—the functionaries at Goddard Field seemed utterly innocent of the very notion of cumshaw, squeeze, or the lubricating effect of money in routine transactions. He admired their incorruptibility; he did not have to like it—most especially when filling out useless forms cost him the time he had intended to devote to a gourmet's feast in the Skygate Room.

He even let himself be vaccinated again rather than go back to the *I Spy* and dig out the piece of paper that showed he had been vaccinated on arrival Earthside a few weeks earlier.

Nevertheless, twenty minutes before his revised slot time, he lay at the controls of the *I Spy*, his pouch bulging with stamped papers and his stomach not bulging with the sandwich he had managed to grab. He had worked out the "Hohmann's-S" trajectory he would use; the results had been fed into the autopilot. All the lights on his board were green save the one which would blink green when field control started his count down. He waited in the warm happiness that always filled him when about to boost.

A thought hit him and he raised up against his straps. Then he loosened the chest strap and sat up, reached for his copy of the current *Terra Pilot and Traffic Hazards Supplement.* Mmm . . .

New Frontiers hung in a circular orbit of exactly twenty-four hours, keeping always over meridian 106° west at declination zero at a distance from Earth center of approximately twenty-six thousand miles.

Why not pay her a call, scout out the lay of the land?

The *I Spy*, with tanks topped off and cargo spaces empty, had many mile-seconds of reserve boost. To be sure, the field had cleared him for Luna City, not for the intersteller ship . . . but, with the Moon in its present phase, the deviation from his approved flight pattern would hardly show on a screen, probably would not be noticed until the film record was analyzed at some later time—at which time Lazarus would receive a traffic citation, perhaps even have his license suspended. But traffic tickets had never worried him . . . and it was certainly worthwhile to reconnoitre.

He was already setting up the problem in his ballistic calculator. Aside from checking the orbit elements of the *New Frontiers* in the *Terra Pilot* Lazarus could have done it in his sleep; satellite-matching maneuvers were old hat for any pilot and a doubly-tangent trajectory for a twenty-four hour orbit was one any student pilot knew by heart.

He fed the answers into his autopilot during the count down, finished with three minutes to spare, strapped himself down again and relaxed as the acceleration hit him. When the ship went into free fall, he checked his position and vector via the field's transponder. Satisfied, he locked his board, set the alarm for rendezvous, and went to sleep.

6

ABOUT FOUR HOURS LATER the alarm woke him. He switched it off; it continued to ring—a glance at his screen showed him why. The Gargantuan cylindrical body of the *New Frontiers* lay close aboard. He switched off the radar alarm circuit as well and completed matching with her by the seat of his pants, not bothering with the ballistic calculator. Before he had completed the maneuver the communications alarm started beeping. He slapped a switch; the rig hunted frequencies and the vision screen came to life. A man looked at him. "*New Frontiers* calling: what ship are you?"

"Private vessel *I Spy*, Captain Sheffield. My compliments to your commanding officer. May I come inboard to pay a call?"

They were pleased to have visitors. The ship was completed save for inspection, trials, and acceptance; the enormous gang which had constructed her had gone to Earth and there was no one aboard but the representatives of the Jordan Foundation and a half dozen engineers employed by the corporation which had been formed to build the ship for the foundation. These few were bored with inactivity, bored with each other, anxious to quit marking time and get back to the pleasures of Earth; a visitor was a welcome diversion.

When the *I Spy*'s airlock had been sealed to that of the big ship, Lazarus was met by the engineer in charge—technically "captain" since the *New Frontiers* was a ship under way even though not under power. He introduced himself and took Lazarus on a tour of the ship. They floated through miles of corridors, visited laboratories, storerooms, libraries containing hundreds of thousands of spools, acres of hydroponic tanks for growing food and replenishing oxygen, and comfortable, spacious, even luxurious quarters for a crew colony of ten thousand people. "We believe that the *Vanguard* expedition was somewhat undermanned," the skipper-engineer explained. "The socio-dynamicists calculate that this colony will be able to maintain the basics of our present level of culture."

"Doesn't sound like enough," Lazarus commented. "Aren't there more than ten thousand types of specialization?"

"Oh, certainly! But the idea is to provide experts in all basic arts and indispensable branches of knowledge. Then, as the colony expands, additional specializations can be added through the aid of the reference libraries—anything from tap-dancing to tapestry weaving. That's the general idea though it's out of my line. Interesting subject, no doubt, for those who like it."

"Are you anxious to get started?" asked Lazarus.

The man looked almost shocked. "Me? D'you mean to suggest that *I* would go in this thing? My dear sir, I'm an engineer, not a damn' fool."

"Sorry."

"Oh, I don't mind a reasonable amount of spacing when there's a reason for it—I've been to Luna City more times than I can count and I've even been to Venus. But you don't think the man who built the *Mayflower* sailed in her, do you? For my money the only thing that will keep these people who signed up for it from going crazy before they get there is that it's a dead cinch they're all crazy before they start."

Lazarus changed the subject. They did not dally in the main drive space, nor in the armored cell housing the giant atomic converter, once Lazarus learned that they were unmanned, fully-automatic types. The total absence of moving parts in each of these divisions, made possible by recent developments in parastatics, made their inner workings of intellectual interest only, which could wait. What Lazarus did want to see was the control room, and there he lingered, asking endless questions until his host was plainly bored and remaining only out of politeness.

Lazarus finally shut up, not because he minded imposing on his host but because he was confident that he had learned enough about the controls to be willing to chance conning the ship.

He picked up two other important data before he left the ship: in nine Earth days the skeleton crew was planning a weekend on Earth, following which the acceptance trials would be held. But for three days the big ship would be empty, save possibly for a communications operator—Lazarus was too wary to be inquisitive on this point. But there would be no guard left in her because no need for a guard could be imagined. One might as well guard the Mississippi River.

The other thing he learned was how to enter the ship from the outside without help from the inside; he picked that datum up through watching the mail rocket arrive just as he was about to leave the ship.

At Luna City, Joseph McFee, factor for Diana Terminal Corp., subsidiary of Diana Freight Lines, welcomed Lazarus warmly. "Well! Come in, Cap'n, and pull up a chair. What'll you drink?" He was already pouring as he talked—tax-free paint-remover from his own amateur vacuum still. "Haven't seen you in . . . well, too long. Where d'you raise from last and what's the gossip there? Heard any new ones?"

"From Goddard," Lazarus answered and told him what the skipper had said to the V.I.P. McFee answered with the one about the old maid in free fall, which Lazarus pretended not to have heard. Stories led to politics, and McFee expounded his notion of the "only possible solution" to the European questions, a solution predicated on a complicated theory of McFee's as to why the Covenant could not be extended to any culture below a certain level of industrialization. Lazarus did not give a hoot either way but he knew better than to hurry McFee; he nodded at the right places, accepted more of the condemned rocket juice when offered, and waited for the right moment to come to the point.

"Any company ships for sale now, Joe?"

"Are there? I should hope to shout. I've got more steel sitting out on that plain and cluttering my inventory that I've had in ten years. Looking for some? I can make you a sweet price."

"Maybe. Maybe not. Depends on whether you've got what I want."

"You name it, I've got it. Never saw such a dull market. Some days you can't turn an honest credit." McFee frowned. "You know what the trouble is? Well, I'll tell you—it's this Howard Families commotion. Nobody wants to risk any money until he knows where he stands. How can a man make plans when he doesn't know whether to plan for ten years or a hundred? You mark my words: if the administration manages to sweat the secret loose from those babies, you'll see the biggest boom in long-term investments ever. But if not . . . well, long-term holdings won't be worth a peso a dozen and there will be an eat-drink-and-be-merry craze that will make the Reconstruction look like a tea party."

He frowned again. "What kind of metal you looking for?"

"I don't want metal, I want a ship."

McFee's frown disappeared, his eyebrows shot up. "So? What sort?"

"Can't say exactly. Got time to look 'em over with me?"

They suited up and left the dome by North Tunnel, then strolled around grounded ships in the long, easy strides of low gravity. Lazarus soon saw that just two ships had both the lift and the air space needed. One was a tanker and the better buy, but a mental calculation showed him that it lacked deck space, even including the floor plates of the tanks, to accommodate eight thousand tons of passengers. The other was an older ship with cranky piston-type injection meters, but she was fitted for general merchandise and had enough deck space. Her pay load was higher than necessary for the job, since passengers weigh little for the cubage they clutter—but that would make her lively, which might be critically important.

As for the injectors, he could baby them—he had herded worse junk than this.

Lazarus haggled with McFee over terms, not because he wanted to save money but because failure to do so would have been out of character. They finally reached a complicated three-cornered deal in which McFee bought the *I Spy* for himself, Lazarus delivered clear title to it unmortgaged and accepted McFee's unsecured note in payment, then purchased the freighter by endorsing McFee's note back to him and adding cash. McFree in turn would be able to mortgage the *I Spy* at the Commerce Clearance Bank in Luna City, use the proceeds plus cash or credit of his own to redeem his own paper—presumably before his accounts were audited, though Lazarus did not mention that.

It was not quite a bribe. Lazarus merely made use of the fact that McFee had long wanted a ship of his own and regarded the *I Spy* as the ideal bachelor's go-buggy for business or pleasure; Lazarus simply held the price down to where

McFee could swing the deal. But the arrangements made certain that McFee would not gossip about the deal, at least until he had had time to redeem his note. Lazarus further confused the issue by asking McFee to keep his eyes open for a good buy in trade tobacco . . . which made McFee sure that Captain Sheffield's mysterious new venture involved Venus, that being the only major market for such goods.

Lazarus got the freighter ready for space in only four days through lavish bonuses and overtime payments. At last he dropped Luna City behind him, owner and master of the *City of Chillicothe*. He shortened the name in his mind to *Chili* in honor of a favorite dish he had not tasted in a long time—fat red beans, plenty of chili powder, chunks of meat . . . real meat, not the synthetic pap these youngsters called "meat." He thought about it and his mouth watered.

He had not a care in the world.

As he approached Earth, he called traffic control and asked for a parking orbit, as he did not wish to put the Chili down; it would waste fuel and attract attention. He had no scruples about orbiting without permission but there was a chance that the *Chili* might be spotted, charted, and investigated as a derelict during his absence; it was safer to be legal.

They gave him an orbit; he matched in and steadied down, then set the *Chili*'s identification beacon to his own combination, made sure that the radar of the ship's gig could trip it, and took the gig down to the auxiliary small-craft field at Goddard. He was careful to have all necessary papers with him this time; by letting the gig be sealed in bond he avoided customs and was cleared through the space port quickly. He had no destination in mind other than to find a public phone and check in with Zack and Ford—then, if there was time, try to find some real chili. He had not called the Administrator from space because ship-to-ground required relay, and the custom of privacy certainly would not protect them if the mixer who handled the call overheard a mention of the Howard Families.

The Administrator answered his call at once, although it was late at night in the longitude of Novak Tower. From the puffy circles under Ford's eyes Lazarus judged that he had been living at his desk. "Hi," said Lazarus, "better get Zack Barstow on a three-way. I've got things to report."

"So it's you," Ford said grimly. "I thought you had run out on us. Where have you been?"

"Buying a ship," Lazarus answered. "As you knew. Let's get Barstow."

Ford frowned, but turned to his desk. By split screen, Barstow joined them. He seemed surprised to see Lazarus and not altogether relieved. Lazarus spoke quickly:

"What's the matter, pal? Didn't·Ford tell you what I was up to?"

"Yes, he did," admitted Barstow, "but we didn't know where you were or what you were doing. Time dragged on and you didn't check in . . . so we decided we had seen the last of you."

"Shucks," complained Lazarus, "you know I wouldn't ever do anything like *that*. Anyhow, here I am and here's what I've done so far——" He told them of the *Chili* and of his reconnaissance of the *New Frontiers*. "Now here's how I see it: sometime this weekend, while the *New Frontiers* is sitting out there with nobody inboard her, I set the *Chili* down in the prison reservation, we load up in a hurry, rush out to the *New Frontiers*, grab her, and scoot. Mr. Administrator, that calls for a lot of help from you. Your proctors will have to look the other way while I land and load. Then we need to sort of slide past the traffic patrol. After that it would be a whole lot better if no naval craft was in a position to do anything drastic about the *New Frontiers*—if there is a communication watch left in her, they may be able to holler for help before we can silence them."

"Give me credit for some foresight," Ford answered sourly. "I know you will have to have a diversion to stand any chance of getting away with it. The scheme is fantastic at the best."

"Not too fantastic," Lazarus disagreed, "if you are willing to use your emergency powers to the limit at the last minute."

"Possibly. But we can't wait four days."

"Why not?"

"The situation won't hold together that long."

"Neither will mine," put in Barstow.

Lazarus looked from one to the other. "Huh? What's the trouble? What's up?"

They explained:

Ford and Barstow were engaged in a preposterously improbable task, that of putting over a complex and subtle fraud, a triple fraud with a different face for the Families, for the public, and for the Federation Council. Each aspect presented unique and apparently insurmountable difficulties.

Ford had no one whom he dared take into his confidence, for even his most trusted personal staff member might be infected with the mania of the delusional Fountain of Youth . . . or might not be, but there was no way to know without compromising the conspiracy. Despite this, he had to convince the Council that the measures he was taking were the best for achieving the Council's purpose.

Besides that, he had to hand out daily news releases to convince the citizens that their government was just about to gain for them the "secret" of living forever. Each day the statements had to be more detailed, the lies more tricky. The people were getting restless at the delay; they were sloughing off the coat of civilization, becoming mob.

The Council was feeling the pressure of the people. Twice Ford had been forced to a vote of confidence; the second he had won by only two votes. "I won't win another one—we've got to *move*."

Barstow's troubles were different but just as sticky. He had to have confederates, because his job was to prepare all the hundred thousand members for the exodus. They had to know, before the time came to embark, if they were to leave quietly and quickly. Nevertheless he did not dare tell them the truth too soon because among so many people there were bound to be some who were stupid and stubborn . . . and it required just one fool to wreck the scheme by spilling it to the proctors guarding them.

Instead he was forced to try to find leaders whom he could trust, convince them, and depend on them to convince others. He needed almost a thousand dependable "herdsmen" to be sure of getting his people to follow him when the time came. Yet the very number of confederates he needed was so great as to make certain that somebody would prove weak.

Worse than that, he needed other confederates for a still touchier purpose. Ford and he had agreed on a scheme, weak at best, for gaining time. They were doling out the techniques used by the Families in delaying the symptoms of senility under the pretense that the sum total of these techniques was the "secret." To put over this fraud Barstow had to have the help of the biochemists, gland therapists, specialists in symbiotics and in metabolism, and other experts among the Fami-

lies, and these in turn had to be prepared for police interrogation by the Families' most skilled psychotechnicians . . . because they had to be able to put over the fraud even under the
influence of babble drugs. The hypnotic false indoctrination
required for this was enormously more complex than that
necessary for a simple block against talking. Thus far the
swindle had worked . . . fairly well. But the discrepancies
became more hard to explain each day.

Barstow could not keep these matters juggled much longer.
The great mass of the Families, necessarily kept in ignorance,
were getting out of hand even faster than the public outside.
They were rightfully angry at what had been done to them;
they expected anyone in authority to do something about it—
and do it now!

Barstow's influence over his kin was melting away as fast as
that of Ford over the Council.

"It can't be four days," repeated Ford. "More like twelve
hours . . . twenty-four at the outside. The Council meets
again tomorrow afternoon."

Barstow looked worried. "I'm not sure I can prepare them
in so short a time. I may have trouble getting them aboard."

"Don't worry about it," Ford snapped.

"Why not?"

"Because," Ford said bluntly, "any who stay behind will be
dead—if they're lucky."

Barstow said nothing and looked away. It was the first time
that either one of them had admitted explicitly that this was
no relatively harmless piece of political chicanery but a desperate and nearly hopeless attempt to avoid a massa-
cre . . . and that Ford himself was on both sides of the
fence.

"Well," Lazarus broke in briskly, "now that you boys have
settled that, let's get on with it. I can ground the *Chili* in——"
He stopped and estimated quickly where she would be in
orbit, how long it would take him to rendezvous. "—well, by
twenty-two Greenwich. Add an hour to play safe. How about
seventeen o'clock Oklahoma time tomorrow afternoon?
That's today, actually."

The other two seemed relieved. "Good enough," agreed
Barstow. "I'll have them in the best shape I can manage."

"All right," agreed Ford, "if that's the fastest it can be
done." He thought for a moment. "Barstow, I'll withdraw at

once all proctors and government personnel now inside the reservation barrier and shut you off. Once the gate contracts, you can tell them all.'

"Right. I'll do my best."

"Anything else before we clear?" asked Lazarus. "Oh, yes —Zack, we'd better pick a place for me to land, or I may shorten a lot of lives with my blast."

"Uh, yes. Make your approach from the west. I'll rig a standard berth marker. Okay?"

"Okay."

"Not okay," denied Ford. "We'll have to give him a pilot beam to come in on."

"Nonsense," objected Lazarus. "I could set her down on top of the Washington Monument."

"Not this time, you couldn't. Don't be surprised at the weather."

As Lazarus approached his rendezvous with the *Chili* he signalled from the gig; the *Chili's* transponder echoed, to his relief—he had little faith in gear he had not personally over- hauled and a long search for the *Chili* at this point would have been disastrous.

He figured the relative vector, gunned the gig, flipped, and gunned to brake—homed-in three minutes off estimate, feel- ing smug. He cradled the gig, hurried inside, and took her down.

Entering the stratosphere and circling two-thirds of the globe took no longer than he had estimated. He used part of the hour's leeway he had allowed himself by being very stingy in his maneuvers in order to spare the worn, obsolescent in- jection meters. Then he was down in the troposphere and making his approach, with skin temperatures high but not dangerously so. Presently he realized what Ford had meant about the weather. Oklahoma and half of Texas were covered with deep, thick clouds. Lazarus was amazed and somehow pleased; it reminded him of other days, when weather was something experienced rather than controlled. Life had lost some flavor, in his opinion, when the weather engineers had learned how to harness the elements. He hoped that their planet—if they found one!—would have some nice, lively weather.

Then he was down in it and too busy to meditate. In spite of her size the freighter bucked and complained. Whew! Ford must have ordered this little charivari the minute the time was set—and, at that, the integrators must have had a big low-pressure area close at hand to build on.

Somewhere a pattern controlman was shouting at him; he switched it off and gave all his attention to his approach radar and the ghostly images in the infra-red rectifier while comparing what they told him with his inertial tracker. The ship passed over a miles-wide scar on the landscape—the ruins of the Okla-Orleans Road City. When Lazarus had last seen it, it had been noisy with life. Of all the mechanical monstrosities the human race had saddled themselves with, he mused, those dinosaurs easily took first prize.

Then the thought was cut short by a squeal from his board; the ship had picked up the pilot beam.

He wheeled her in, cut his last jet as she scraped, and slapped a series of switches; the great cargo ports rumbled open and rain beat in.

Eleanor Johnson huddled into herself, half crouching against the storm, and tried to draw her cloak more tightly about the baby in the crook of her left arm. When the storm had first hit, the child had cried endlessly, stretching her nerves taut. Now it was quiet, but that seemed only new cause for alarm.

She herself had wept, although she had tried not to show it. In all her twenty-seven years she had never been exposed to weather like this; it seemed symbolic of the storm that had overturned her life, swept her away from her cherished first home of her own with its homey old-fashioned fireplace, its shiny service cell, its thermostat which she could set to the temperature she liked without consulting others—a tempest which had swept her away between two grim proctors, arrested like some poor psychotic, and landed her after terrifying indignities here in the cold sticky red clay of this Oklahoma field.

Was it true? Could it possibly be true? Or had she not yet borne her baby at all and this was another of the strange dreams she had while carrying it?

But the rain was too wetly cold, the thunder too loud; she could never have slept through such a dream. Then what the Senior Trustee had told them must be true, too—it had to be true; she had seen the ship ground with her own eyes, its blast bright against the black of the storm. She could no longer see it but the crowd around her moved slowly forward; it must be in front of her. She was close to the outskirts of the crowd; she would be one of the last to get aboard.

It was very necessary to board the ship—Elder Zaccur Barstow had told them with deep solemnness what lay in store for them if they failed to board. She had believed his earnestness; nevertheless she wondered how it could possibly be true—could anyone be so wicked, so deeply and terribly wicked as to want to kill anyone as harmless and helpless as herself and her baby?

She was struck by panic terror—suppose there was no room left by the time she got up to the ship? She clutched her baby more tightly; the child cried again at the pressure.

A woman in the crowd moved closer and spoke to her. "You must be tired. May I carry the baby for a while?"

"No. No, thank you. I'm all right." A flash of lightning showed the woman's face; Eleanor Johnson recognized her— Elder Mary Sperling.

But the kindness of the offer steadied her. She knew now what she must do. If they were filled up and could take no more, she must pass her baby forward, hand to hand over the heads of the crowd. They could not refuse space to anything as little as her baby.

Something brushed her in the dark. The crowd was moving forward again.

When Barstow could see that loading would be finished in a few more minutes he left his post at one of the cargo doors and ran as fast as he could through the splashing sticky mud to the communications shack. Ford had warned him to give notice just before they raised ship; it was necessary to Ford's plan for diversion. Barstow fumbled with an awkward unpowered door, swung it open and rushed in. He set the private combination which should connect him directly to Ford's control desk and pushed the key.

He was answered at once but it was not Ford's face on the screen. Barstow burst out with, "Where is the Administrator? I want to talk with him," before he recognized the face in front of him.

It was a face well known to all the public—Bork Vanning, Leader of the Minority in the Council. "You're talking to the Administrator," Vanning said and grinned coldly. "The new

Administrator. Now who the devil are you and why are you calling?"

Barstow thanked all gods, past and present, that recognition was onesided. He cut the connection with one unaimed blow and plunged out of the building.

Two cargo ports were already closed; stragglers were moving through the other two. Barstow hurried the last of them inside with curses and followed them, slammed pell-mell to the control room. "Raise ship!" he shouted to Lazarus. "Fast!"

"What's all the shootin' fer?" asked Lazarus, but he was already closing and sealing the ports. He tripped the acceleration screamer, waited a scant ten seconds . . . and gave her power.

"Well," he said conversationally six minutes later, "I hope everybody was lying down. If not, we've got some broken bones on our hands. What's that you were saying?"

Barstow told him about his attempt to report to Ford.

Lazarus blinked and whistled a few bars of *Turkey in the Straw*. "It looks like we've run out of minutes. It does look like it." He shut up and gave his attention to his instruments, one eye on his ballistic track, one on radar-aft.

7

LAZARUS HAD his hands full to jockey the *Chili* into just the right position against the side of the *New Frontiers*; the overstrained meters made the smaller craft skittish as a young horse. But he did it. The magnetic anchors clanged home; the gas-tight seals slapped into place; and their ears popped as the pressure in the *Chili* adjusted to that in the giant ship. Lazarus dived for the drop hole in the deck of the control room, pulled himself rapidly hand over hand to the port of contact, and reached the passenger lock of the *New Frontiers* to find himself facing the skipper-engineer.

The man looked at him and snorted. "You again, eh? Why the deuce didn't you answer our challenge? You can't lock onto us without permission; this is private property. What do you mean by it?"

"It means," said Lazarus, "that you and your boys are going back to Earth a few days early—in this ship."

"Why, that's ridiculous!"

"Brother," Lazarus said gently, his blaster suddenly growing out his left fist, "I'd sure hate to hurt you after you were so nice to me . . . but I sure will, unless you knuckle under awful quick."

The official simply stared unbelievingly. Several of his juniors had gathered behind him; one of them sunfished in the air, started to leave. Lazarus winged him in the leg, at low power; he jerked and clutched at nothing. "Now you'll have to take care of him," Lazarus observed.

That settled it. The skipper called together his men from the announcing system microphone at the passenger lock; Lazarus counted them as they arrived—twenty-nine, a figure he had been careful to learn on his first visit. He assigned two men to hold each of them. Then he took a look at the man he had shot.

"You aren't really hurt, bub," he decided shortly and turned to the skipper-engineer. "Soon as we transfer you, get some radiation salve on that burn. The Red Cross kit's on the after bulkhead of the control room."

"This is piracy! You can't get away with this."

"Probably not," Lazarus agreed thoughtfully. "But I sort of hope we do." He turned his attention back to his job. "Shake it up there! Don't take all day."

The *Chili* was slowly being emptied. Only the one exit could be used but the pressure of the half hysterical mob behind them forced along those in the bottleneck of the trunk joining the two ships; they came boiling out like bees from a disturbed hive.

Most of them had never been in free fall before this trip; they burst out into the larger space of the giant ship and drifted helplessly, completely disoriented. Lazarus tried to bring order into it by grabbing anyone he could see who seemed to be able to handle himself in zero gravity, ordered him to speed things up by shoving along the helpless ones—shove them anywhere, on back into the big ship, get them out of the way, make room for the thousands more yet to come. When he had conscripted a dozen or so such herdsmen he spotted Barstow in the emerging throng, grabbed him and put him in charge. "Keep 'em moving, just anyhow. I've got to get for'ard to the control room. If you spot Andy Libby, send him after me."

A man broke loose from the stream and approached Barstow. "There's a ship trying to lock onto ours. I saw it through a port."

"Where?" demanded Lazarus.

The man was handicapped by slight knowledge of ships and shipboard terms, but he managed to make himself understood. "I'll be back," Lazarus told Barstow. "Keep 'em moving—and don't let any of those babies get away—our guests there." He holstered his blaster and fought his way back through the swirling mob in the bottleneck.

Number three port seemed to be the one the man had meant. Yes, there was something there. The port had an armor-glass bull's-eye in it, but instead of stars beyond Lazarus saw a lighted space. A ship of some sort had locked against it.

Its occupants either had not tried to open the *Chili's* port or just possibly did not know how. The port was not locked from the inside; there had been no reason to bother. It should have opened easily from either side once pressure was balanced . . . which the tell-tale, shining green by the latch, showed to be the case.

Lazarus was mystified.

Whether it was a traffic control vessel, a Naval craft, or something else, its presence was bad news. But why didn't they simply open the door and walk in? He was tempted to lock the port from the inside, hurry and lock all the others, finish loading and try to run for it.

But his monkey ancestry got the better of him; he could not leave alone something he did not understand. So he compromised by kicking the blind latch into place that would keep them from opening the port from outside, then slithered cautiously alongside the bull's-eye and sneaked a peep with one eye.

He found himself staring at Slayton Ford.

He pulled himself to one side, kicked the blind latch open, pressed the switch to open the port. He waited there, a toe caught in a handihold, blaster in one hand, knife in the other.

One figure emerged. Lazarus saw that it was Ford, pressed the switch again to close the port, kicked the blind latch into place, while never taking his blaster off his visitor. "Now what the hell?" he demanded. "What are you doing here? And who else is here? Patrol?"

"I'm alone."

"Huh?"

"I want to go with you . . . if you'll have me."

Lazarus looked at him and did not answer. Then he went back to the bull's-eye and inspected all that he could see. Ford appeared to be telling the truth, for no one else was in sight. But that was not what held Lazarus' eye.

Why, the ship wasn't a proper deep-space craft at all. It did not have an airlock but merely a seal to let it fasten to a larger ship; Lazarus was staring right into the body of the craft. It looked like—yes, it was a "Joy-boat Junior," a little private strato-yacht, suitable only for point-to-point trajectory, or at the most for rendezvous with a satellite provided the satellite could refuel it for the return leg.

There was no fuel for it here. A lightning pilot possibly could land that tin toy without power and still walk away from it . . . provided he had the skill to play Skip-to-M'Lou in and out of the atmosphere while nursing his skin temperatures—but Lazarus wouldn't want to try it. No, sir! He turned to Ford. "Suppose we turned you down. How did you figure on getting back?"

"I didn't figure on it," Ford answered simply.

"Mmm—— Tell me about it, but make it march; we're minus on minutes."

Ford had burned all bridges. Turned out of office only hours earlier, he had known that, once all the facts came out, life-long imprisonment in Coventry was the best he could hope for—if he managed to avoid mob violence or mind-shattering interrogation.

Arranging the diversion was the thing that finally lost him his thin margin of control. His explanations for his actions were not convincing to the Council. He had excused the storm and the withdrawing of proctors from the reservation as a drastic attempt to break the morale of the Families—a possible excuse but not too plausible. His orders to Naval craft, intended to keep them away from the *New Frontiers*, had apparently not been associated in anyone's mind with the Howard Families affair; nevertheless the apparent lack of sound reason behind them had been seized on by the opposition as another weapon to bring him down. They were watching for anything to catch him out—one question asked in

Council concerned certain monies from the Administrator's discretionary fund which had been paid indirectly to one Captain Aaron Sheffield; were these monies in fact expended in the public interest?

Lazarus' eyes widened. "You mean they were onto me?"

"Not quite. Or you wouldn't be here. But they were close behind you. I think they must have had help from a lot of my people at the last."

"Probably. But we made it, so let's not fret. Come on. The minute everybody is out of this ship and into the big girl, we've got to boost." Lazarus turned to leave.

"You're going to let me go along?"

Lazarus checked his progress, twisted to face Ford. "How else?" He had intended at first to send Ford down in the *Chili*. It was not gratitude that changed his mind, but respect. Once he had lost office Ford had gone straight to Huxley Field north of Novak Tower, cleared for the vacation satellite *Monte Carlo*, and had jumped for the *New Frontiers* instead. Lazarus liked that. "Go for broke" took courage and character that most people didn't have. Don't grab a toothbrush, don't wind the cat—just do it! "Of course you're coming along," he said easily. "You're my kind of boy, Slayton."

The *Chili* was more than half emptied now but the spaces near the interchange were still jammed with frantic mobs. Lazarus cuffed and shoved his way through, trying not to bruise women and children unnecessarily but not letting the possibility slow him up. He scrambled through the connecting trunk with Ford hanging onto his belt, pulled aside once they were through and paused in front of Barstow.

Barstow stared past him. "Yeah, it's him," Lazarus confirmed. "Don't stare—it's rude. He's going with us. Have you seen Libby?"

"Here I am, Lazarus." Libby separated himself from the throng and approached with the ease of a veteran long used to free fall. He had a small satchel strapped to one wrist.

"Good. Stick around. Zack, how long till you're all loaded?"

"God knows. I can't count them. An hour, maybe."

"Make it less. If you put some husky boys on each side of the hole, they can snatch them through faster than they are coming. We've got to shove out of here a little sooner than is humanly possible. I'm going to the control room. Phone me there the instant you have everybody in, our guests here out, and the *Chili* broken loose. Andy! Slayton! Let's go."

"Lazarus——"

"Later, Andy. We'll talk when we get there."

Lazarus took Slayton Ford with him because he did not know what else to do with him and felt it would be better to keep him out of sight until some plausible excuse could be dreamed up for having him along. So far no one seemed to have looked at him twice, but once they quieted down, Ford's well-known face would demand explanation.

The control room was about a half mile forward of where they had entered the ship. Lazarus knew that there was a passenger belt leading to it but he didn't have time to look for it; he simply took the first passageway leading forward. As soon as they got away from the crowd they made good time even though Ford was not as skilled in the fishlike maneuvers of free fall as were the other two.

Once there, Lazarus spent the enforced wait in explaining to Libby the extremely ingenious but unorthodox controls of the star ship. Libby was fascinated and soon was putting himself through dummy runs. Lazarus turned to Ford. "How about you, Slayton? Wouldn't hurt to have a second relief pilot."

Ford shook his head. "I've been listening but I could never learn it. I'm not a pilot."

"*Huh?* How did you get here?"

"Oh. I do have a license, but I haven't had time to keep in practice. My chauffeur always pilots me. I haven't figured a trajectory in many years."

Lazarus looked him over. "And yet you plotted an orbit rendezvous? With no reserve fuel?"

"Oh, that. I had to."

"I see. The way the cat learned to swim. Well, that's one way." He turned back to speak to Libby, was interrupted by Barstow's voice over the announcing system:

"Five minutes, Lazarus! Acknowledge."

Lazarus found the microphone, covered the light under it with his hand and answered, "Okay, Zack! Five minutes." Then he said, "Cripes, I haven't even picked a course. What do you think, Andy? Straight out from Earth to shake the busies off our tail? Then pick a destination? How about it, Slayton? Does that fit with what you ordered Navy craft to do?"

"No, Lazarus, no!" protested Libby.

"Huh? Why not?"

"You should head right straight down for the Sun."

"For the Sun? For Pete's sake, why?"

"I tried to tell you when I first saw you. It's because of the space drive you asked me to develop."

"But, Andy, we haven't got it."

"Yes, we have. Here." Libby shoved the satchel he had been carrying toward Lazarus.

Lazarus opened it.

Assembled from odd bits of other equipment, looking more like the product of a boy's workshop than the output of a scientist's laboratory, the gadget which Libby referred to as a "space drive" underwent Lazarus' critical examination. Against the polished sophisticated perfection of the control room it looked uncouth, pathetic, ridiculously inadequate.

Lazarus poked at it tentatively. "What is it?" he asked. "Your model?"

"No, no. That's *it*. That's the space drive."

Lazarus looked at the younger man not unsympathetically. "Son," he asked slowly, "have you come unzipped?"

"No, no, no!" Libby sputtered. "I'm as sane as you are. This is a radically new notion. That's why I want you to take us down near the Sun. If it works at all, it will work best where light pressure is strongest."

"And if it doesn't work," inquired Lazarus, "what does that make us? Sunspots?"

"Not straight down into the Sun. But head for it now and as soon as I can work out the data, I'll give you corrections to warp you into your proper trajectory. I want to pass the Sun in a very flat hyperbola, well inside the orbit of Mercury, as close to the photosphere as this ship can stand. I don't know how close that is, so I couldn't work it out ahead of time. But the data will be here in the ship and there will be time to correlate them as we go."

Lazarus looked again at the giddy little cat's cradle of apparatus. "Andy . . . if you are sure that the gears in your head are still meshed, I'll take a chance. Strap down, both of you." He belted himself into the pilot's couch and called Barstow. "How about it, Zack?"

"Right now!"

"Hang on tight!" With one hand Lazarus covered a light in his leftside control panel; acceleration warning shrieked throughout the ship. With the other he covered another; the hemisphere in front of them was suddenly spangled with the starry firmament, and Ford gasped.

Lazarus studied it. A full twenty degrees of it was blanked out by the dark circle of the nightside of Earth. "Got to duck around a corner, Andy. We'll use a little Tennessee windage." He started easily with a quarter gravity, just enough to shake up his passengers and make them cautious, while he started a slow operation of precessing the enormous ship to the direction he needed to shove her in order to get out of Earth's shadow. He raised acceleration to a half gee, then to a gee.

Earth changed suddenly from a black silhouette to a slender silver crescent as the half-degree white disc of the Sun came out from behind her. "I want to clip her about a thousand miles out, Slipstick," Lazarus said tensely, "at two gees. Gimme a temporary vector."

Libby hesitated only momentarily and gave it to him. Lazarus again sounded acceleration warning and boosted to twice Earth-normal gravity. Lazarus was tempted to raise the boost to emergency-full but he dared not do so with a shipload of groundlubbers; even two gees sustained for a long period might be too much of a strain for some of them. Any Naval pursuit craft ordered to intercept them could boost at much higher gee and their selected crews could stand it. But it was just a chance they would have to take . . . and anyhow, he reminded himself, a Navy ship could not maintain a high boost for long; her mile-seconds were strictly limited by her reaction-mass tanks.

The *New Frontiers* had no such old-fashioned limits, no tanks; her converter accepted any mass at all, turned it into pure radiant energy. Anything would serve—meteors, cosmic dust, stray atoms gathered in by her sweep field, or anything from the ship herself, such as garbage, dead bodies, deck sweepings, anything at all. Mass was energy. In dying, each tortured gram gave up nine hundred million trillion ergs of thrust.

The crescent of Earth waxed and swelled and slid off toward the left edge of the hemispherical screen while the Sun remained dead ahead. A little more than twenty minutes later, when they were at closest approach and the crescent, now at half phase, was sliding out of the bowl screen, the ship-to-ship circuit came to life. *"New Frontiers!"* a forceful voice sounded. "Maneuver to orbit and lay to! This is an official traffic control order."

Lazarus shut it off. "Anyhow," he said cheerfully, "if they try to catch us, they won't like chasing us down into the Sun! Andy, it's a clear road now and time we corrected, maybe. You want to compute it? Or will you feed me the data?"

"I'll compute it," Libby answered. He had already discovered that the ship's characteristics pertinent to astrogation, including her "black body" behavior, were available at both piloting stations. Armed with this and with the running data from instruments he set out to calculate the hyperboloid by which he intended to pass the Sun. He made a half-hearted attempt to use the ship's ballistic calculator but it baffled him; it was a design he was not used to, having no moving parts of any sort, even in the exterior controls. So he gave it up as a waste of time and fell back on the strange talent for figures lodged in his brain. His brain had no moving parts, either, but he was used to it.

Lazarus decided to check on their popularity rating. He switched on the ship-to-ship again, found that it was still angrily squawking, although a little more faintly. They knew his own name now—one of his names—which caused him to decide that the boys in the *Chili* must have called traffic control almost at once. He tut-tutted sadly when he learned that "Captain Sheffield's" license to pilot had been suspended. He shut it off and tried the Naval frequencies . . . then shut them off also when he was able to raise nothing but code and scramble, except that the words "New Frontiers" came through once in clear.

He said something about "Sticks and stones may break my bones——" and tried another line of investigation. Both by long-range radar and by paragravitic detector he could tell that there were ships in their neighborhood but this alone told him very little; there were bound to be ships this close to Earth and he had no easy way to distinguish, from these data alone, an unarmed liner or freighter about her lawful occasions from a Naval cruiser in angry pursuit.

But the *New Frontiers* had more resources for analyzing what was around her than had an ordinary ship; she had been specially equipped to cope unassisted with any imaginable strange conditions. The hemispherical control room in which they lay was an enormous multi-screened television receiver which could duplicate the starry heavens either in view-aft or view-forward at the selection of the pilot. But it also had other circuits, much more subtle; simultaneously or separately it could act as an enormous radar screen as well, displaying on it the blips of any body within radar range.

But that was just a starter. Its inhuman senses could apply differential analysis to doppler data and display the result in a visual analog. Lazarus studied his lefthand control bank, tried to remember everything he had been told about it, made a change in the set up.

The simulated stars and even the Sun faded to dimness; about a dozen lights shined brightly.

He ordered the board to check them for angular rate; the bright lights turned cherry red, became little comets trailing off to pink tails—all but one, which remained white and grew no tail. He studied the others for a moment, decided that their vectors were such that they would remain forever strangers, and ordered the board to check the line-of-sight doppler on the one with a steady bearing.

It faded to violet, ran halfway through the spectrum and held steady at blue-green. Lazarus thought a moment, subtracted from the inquiry their own two gees of boost; it turned white again. Satisfied he tried the same tests with view-aft.

"Lazarus——"

"Yeah, Lib?"

"Will it interfere with what you are doing if I give you the corrections now?"

"Not at all. I was just taking a look-see. If this magic lantern knows what it's talking about, they didn't manage to get a pursuit job on our tail in time."

"Good. Well, here are the figures . . ."

"Feed 'em in yourself, will you? Take the conn for a while. I want to see about some coffee and sandwiches. How about you? Feel like some breakfast?"

Libby nodded absent-mindedly, already starting to revise the ship's trajectory. Ford spoke up eagerly, the first word he had uttered in a long time. "Let me get it. I'd be glad to." He seemed pathetically anxious to be useful.

"Mmm . . . you might get into some kind of trouble, Slayton. No matter what sort of a selling job Zack did, your name is probably 'Mud' with most of the members. I'll phone aft and raise somebody."

"Probably nobody would recognize me under these circumstances," Ford argued. "Anyway, it's a legitimate errand—I can explain that."

Lazarus saw from his face that it was necessary to the man's morale. "Okay . . . if you can handle yourself under two gees."

Ford struggled heavily up out of the acceleration couch he was in. "I've got space legs. What kind of sandwiches?"

"I'd say corned beef, but it would probably be some damned substitute. Make mine cheese, with rye if they've got it, and use plenty of mustard. And a gallon of coffee. What are you having, Andy?"

"Me? Oh, anything that is convenient."

Ford started to leave, bracing himself heavily against double weight, then he added, "Oh—it might save time if you could tell me where to go."

"Brother," said Lazarus, "if this ship isn't pretty well crammed with food, we've all made a terrible mistake. Scout around. You'll find some."

Down, down, down toward the Sun, with speed increasing by sixty-four feet per second for every second elapsed. Down and still down for fifteen endless hours of double weight. During this time they traveled seventeen million miles and reached the inconceivable speed of six hundred and forty miles per second. The figures mean little—think instead of New York to Chicago, a half hour's journey even by stratomail, done in a single heartbeat.

Barstow had a rough time during heavy weight. For all of the others it was a time to lie down, try hopelessly to sleep, breathe painfully and seek new positions in which to rest from the burdens of their own bodies. But Zaccur Barstow was driven by his sense of responsibility; he kept going though the Old Man of the Sea sat on his neck and raised his weight to three hundred and fifty pounds.

Not that he could do anything for them, except crawl wearily from one compartment to another and ask about their welfare. Nothing could be done, no organization to relieve their misery was possible, while high boost continued. They lay where they could, men, women, and children crowded together like cattle being shipped, without even room to stretch out, in spaces never intended for such extreme overcrowding.

The only good thing about it, Barstow reflected wearily,

was that they were all too miserable to worry about anything but the dragging minutes. They were too beaten down to make trouble. Later on there would be doubts raised, he was sure, about the wisdom of fleeing; there would be embarrassing questions asked about Ford's presence in the ship, about Lazarus' peculiar and sometimes shady actions, about his own contradictory role. But not yet.

He really must, he decided reluctantly, organize a propaganda campaign before trouble could grow. If it did—and it surely would if he didn't move to offset it, and . . . well, that would be the last straw. It would be.

He eyed a ladder in front of him, set his teeth, and struggled up to the next deck. Picking his way through the bodies there he almost stepped on a woman who was clutching a baby too tightly to her. Barstow noticed that the infant was wet and soiled and he thought of ordering its mother to take care of the matter, since she seemed to be awake. But he let it go—so far as he knew there was not a clean diaper in millions of miles. Or there might be ten thousand of them on the deck above . . . which seemed almost as far away.

He plodded on without speaking to her. Eleanor Johnson had not been aware of his concern. After the first great relief at realizing that she and her baby were safe inside the ship she had consigned all her worries to her elders and now felt nothing but the apathy of emotional reaction and of inescapable weight. Baby had cried when that awful weight had hit them, then had become quiet, too quiet. She had roused herself enough to listen for its heartbeat; then, sure that he was alive, she had sunk back into stupor.

Fifteen hours out, with the orbit of Venus only four hours away, Libby cut the boost. The ship plunged on, in free fall, her terrific speed still mounting under the steadily increasing pull of the Sun. Lazarus was awakened by no weight. He glanced at the copilot's couch and said, "On the curve?"

"As plotted."

Lazarus looked him over. "Okay, I've got it. Now get out of here and get some sleep. Boy, you look like a used towel."

"I'll just stay here and rest."

"You will like hell. You haven't slept even when I had the conn; if you stay here, you'll be watching instruments and figuring. So beat it! Slayton, chuck him out."

Libby smiled shyly and left. He found the spaces abaft the control room swarming with floating bodies but he managed to find an unused corner, passed his kilt belt through a handi-hold, and slept at once.

Free fall should have been as great a relief to everyone else; it was not, except to the fraction of one per cent who were salted spacemen. Free-fall nausea, like seasickness, is a joke only to those not affected; it would take a Dante to describe a hundred thousand cases of it. There were anti-nausea drugs aboard, but they were not found at once; there were medical men among the Families, but they were sick, too. The misery went on.

Barstow, himself long since used to free flight, floated forward to the control room to pray relief for the less fortunate. "They're in bad shape," he told Lazarus. "Can't you put spin on the ship and give them some let-up? It would help a lot."

"And it would make maneuvering difficult, too. Sorry. Look, Zack, a lively ship will be more important to them in a pinch than just keeping their suppers down. Nobody dies from seasickness anyhow . . . they just wish they could."

The ship plunged on down, still gaining speed as it fell toward the Sun. The few who felt able continued slowly to assist the enormous majority who were ill.

Libby continued to sleep, the luxurious return-to-the-womb sleep of those who have learned to enjoy free fall. He had had almost no sleep since the day the Families had been arrested; his overly active mind had spent all its time worrying the problem of a new space drive.

The big ship precessed around him; he stirred gently and did not awake. It steadied in a new attitude and the acceleration warning brought him instantly awake. He oriented himself, placed himself flat against the after bulkhead, and waited; weight hit him almost at once—three gees this time and he knew that something was badly wrong. He had gone almost a quarter mile aft before he found a hide-away; nevertheless he struggled to his feet and started the unlikely task of trying to climb that quarter mile—now straight up—at three times his proper weight, while blaming himself for having let Lazarus talk him into leaving the control room.

He managed only a portion of the trip . . . but an heroic portion, one about equal to climbing the stairs of a ten-story building while carrying a man on each shoulder . . . when resumption of free fall relieved him. He zipped the rest of the way like a salmon returning home and was in the control room quickly. "What happened?"

Lazarus said regretfully, "Had to vector, Andy." Slayton Ford said nothing but looked worried.

"Yes, I know. But why?" Libby was already strapping himself against the copilot's couch while studying the astrogational situation.

"Red lights on the screen." Lazarus described the display, giving coördinates and relative vectors.

Libby nodded thoughtfully. "Naval craft. No commercial vessels would be in such trajectories. A minelaying bracket."

"That's what I figured. I didn't have time to consult you; I had to use enough mile-seconds to be sure they wouldn't have boost enough to reposition on us."

"Yes, you had to." Libby looked worried. "I thought we were free of any possible Naval interference."

"They're not ours," put in Slayton Ford. "They can't be ours no matter what orders have been given since I—uh, since I left. They must be Venerian craft."

"Yeah," agreed Lazarus, "they must be. Your pal, the new Administrator, hollered to Venus for help and they gave it to him—just a friendly gesture of interplanetary good will."

Libby was hardly listening. He was examining data and processing it through the calculator inside his skull. "Lazarus . . . this new orbit isn't too good."

"I know," Lazarus agreed sadly. "I had to duck . . . so I ducked the only direction they left open to me—closer to the Sun."

"Too close, perhaps."

The Sun is not a large star, nor is it very hot. But it is hot with reference to men, hot enough to strike them down dead if they are careless about tropic noonday ninety-two million miles away from it, hot enough that we who are reared under its rays nevertheless dare not look directly at it.

At a distance of two and a half million miles the Sun beats out with a flare fourteen hundred times as bright as the worst ever endured in Death Valley, the Sahara, or Aden. Such radiance would not be perceived as heat or light; it would be death more sudden than the full power of a blaster. The Sun is a hydrogen bomb, a naturally occurring one; the *New Frontiers* was skirting the limits of its circle of total destruction.

It was hot inside the ship. The Families were protected against instant radiant death by the armored walls but the air temperature continued to mount. They were relieved of the misery of free fall but they were doubly uncomfortable, both rom heat and from the fact that the bulkheads slanted crazily; here was no level place to stand or lie. The ship was both pinning on its axis and accelerating now; it was never intended to do both at once and the addition of the two accelerations, angular and linear, make "down" the direction where outer and after bulkheads met. The ship was being pun through necessity to permit some of the impinging adiant energy to re-radiate on the "cold" side. The forward cceleration was equally from necessity, a forlorn-hope maneuver to pass the Sun as far out as possible and as fast as possible, in order to spend least time at perihelion, the point f closest approach.

It was hot in the control room. Even Lazarus had voluntarly shed his kilt and shucked down to Venus styles. Metal was ot to the touch. On the great stellarium screen an enormous circle of blackness marked where the Sun's disc should have een; the receptors had cut out automatically at such a ridiculous demand.

Lazarus repeated Libby's last words. " 'Thirty-seven minutes to perihelion.' We can't take it, Andy. The ship can't take t."

"I know. I never intended us to pass this close."

"Of course you didn't. Maybe I shouldn't have maneuvered. Maybe we would have missed the mines anyway. Oh, well——" Lazarus squared his shoulders and filed it with the might-have-beens. "It looks to me, son, about time to try out our gadget." He poked a thumb at Libby's uncouth-looking 'space drive." "You say that all you have to do is to hook up hat one connection?"

"That is what is intended. Attach that one lead to any portion of the mass to be affected. Of course I don't really know hat it will work," Libby admitted. "There is no way to test t."

"Suppose it doesn't?"

"There are three possibilities," Libby answered methodically. "In the first place, nothing may happen."

"In which case we fry."

"In the second place, we and the ship may cease to exist as matter as we know it."

"Dead, you mean. But probably a pleasanter way."

"I suppose so. I don't know what death is. In the third place, if my hypotheses are correct, we will recede from the Sun at a speed just under that of light."

Lazarus eyed the gadget and wiped sweat from his shoulders. "It's getting hotter, Andy. Hook it up—and it had better be good!"

Andy hooked it up.

"Go ahead," urged Lazarus. "Push the button, throw the switch, cut the beam. Make it march."

"I have," Libby insisted. "Look at the Sun."

"Huh? *Oh!*"

The great circle of blackness which had marked the position of the Sun on the star-speckled stellarium was shrinking rapidly. In a dozen heartbeats it lost half its diameter; twenty seconds later it had dwindled to a quarter of its original width.

"It worked," Lazarus said softly. "Look at it, Slayton! Sign me up as a purple baboon—it *worked!*"

"I rather thought it would," Libby answered seriously. "It should, you know."

"Hmm—— That may be evident to you, Andy. It's not to me. How fast are we going?"

"Relative to what?"

"Uh, relative to the Sun."

"I haven't had opportunity to measure it, but it seems to be just under the speed of light. It can't be greater."

"Why not? Aside from theoretical considerations."

"We still see." Libby pointed at the stellarium bowl.

"Yeah, so we do," Lazarus mused. "Hey! We shouldn't be able to. I ought to doppler out."

Libby looked blank, then smiled. "But it dopplers right back in. Over on that side, toward the Sun, we're seeing by short radiations stretched to visibility. On the opposite side we're picking up something around radio wavelengths dopplered down to light."

"And in between?"

"Quit pulling my leg, Lazarus. I'm sure you can work out relatively vector additions quite as well as I can."

"*You* work it out," Lazarus said firmly. "I'm just going to sit here and admire it. Eh, Slayton?"

"Yes. Yes indeed."

Libby smiled politely. "We might as well quit wasting mass on the main drive." He sounded the warner, then cut the drive. "Now we can return to normal conditions." He started to disconnect his gadget.

Lazarus said hastily, "Hold it, Andy! We aren't even outside the orbit of Mercury yet. Why put on the brakes?"

"Why, this won't stop us. We have acquired velocity; we will keep it."

Lazarus pulled at his cheek and stared. "Ordinarily I would agree with you. First Law of Motion. But with this pseudo-speed I'm not so sure. We got it for nothing and we haven't paid for it—in energy, I mean. You seem to have declared a holiday with respect to inertia; when the holiday is over, won't all that free speed go back where it came from?"

"I don't think so," Libby answered. "Our velocity isn't 'pseudo' anything; it's as real as velocity can be. You are attempting to apply verbal anthropomorphic logic to a field in which it is not pertinent. You would not expect us to be transported instantaneously back to the lower gravitational potential from which we started, would you?"

"Back to where you hooked in your space drive? No, we've moved."

"And we'll keep on moving. Our newly acquired gravitational potential energy of greater height above the Sun is no more real than our present kinetic energy of velocity. They both exist."

Lazarus looked baffled. The expression did not suit him. "I guess you've got me, Andy. No matter how I slice it, we seemed to have picked up energy from somewhere. But *where?* When I went to school, they taught me to honor the Flag, vote the straight party ticket, and believe in the law of conservation of energy. Seems like you've violated it. How about it?"

"Don't worry about it," suggested Libby. "The so-called law of conservation of energy was merely a working hypothesis, unproved and unprovable, used to describe gross phenomena. Its terms apply only to the older, dynamic concept of the world. In a plenum conceived as a static grid of relationships, a 'violation' of that 'law' is nothing more startling than a discontinuous function, to be noted and described. That's what I did. I saw a discontinuity in the mathematical model of the aspect of mass-energy called inertia. I applied it. The mathematical model turned out to be similar to the real world. That was the only hazard, really—one never knows that a mathematical model is similar to the real world until you try it."

"Yeah, yeah, sure, you can't tell the taste till you bite it—but, Andy, I still don't see what *caused* it!" He turned toward Ford. "Do you, Slayton?"

Ford shook his head. "No. I would like to know . . . but I doubt if I could understand it."

"You and me both. Well, Andy?"

Now Libby looked baffled. "But, Lazarus, causality has nothing to do with the real plenum. A fact simply *is*. Causality is merely an old-fashioned postulate of a pre-scientific philosophy."

"I guess," Lazarus said slowly, "I'm old-fashioned."

Libby said nothing. He disconnected his apparatus.

The disc of black continued to shrink. When it had shrunk to about one sixth its greatest diameter, it changed suddenly from black to shining white, as the ship's distance from the Sun again was great enough to permit the receptors to manage the load.

Lazarus tried to work out in his head the kinetic energy of the ship—one-half the square of the velocity of light (minus a pinch, he corrected) times the mighty tonnage of the *New Frontiers*. The answer did not comfort him, whether he called it ergs or apples.

8

"FIRST THINGS FIRST," interrupted Barstow. "I'm as fascinated by the amazing scientific aspects of our present situation as any of you, but we've got work to do. We've got to plan a pattern for daily living at once. So let's table mathematical physics and talk about organization."

He was not speaking to the trustees but to his own personal lieutenants, the key people in helping him put over the complex maneuvers which had made their escape possible—Ralph Schultz, Eve Barstow, Mary Sperling, Justin Foote, Clive Johnson, about a dozen others.

Lazarus and Libby were there. Lazarus had left Slayton Ford to guard the control room, with orders to turn away all visitors and, above all, not to let anyone touch the controls. It was a make-work job, it being Lazarus' notion of temporary occupational therapy. He had sensed in Ford a mental condition that he did not like. Ford seemed to have withdrawn into himself. He answered when spoken to, but that was all. It worried Lazarus.

"We need an executive," Barstow went on, "someone who, for the time being, will have very broad powers to give orders and have them carried out. He'll have to make decisions, organize us, assign duties and responsibilities, get the internal economy of the ship working. It's a big job and I would like to have our brethren hold an election and do it democratically. That'll have to wait; somebody has to give orders now. We're wasting food and the ship is—well, I wish you could have seen the 'fresher I tried to use today."

"Zaccur . . ."

"Yes, Eve?"

"It seems to me that the thing to do is to put it up to the trustees. We haven't any authority; we were just an emergency group for something that is finished now."

"Ahrrumph——" It was Justin Foote, in tones as dry and formal as his face. "I differ somewhat from our sister. The trustees are not conversant with the full background; it would take time we can ill afford to put them into the picture, as it were, before they would be able to judge the matter. Furthermore, being one of the trustees myself, I am able to say without bias that the trustees, as an organized group, can have no jurisdiction because legally they no longer exist."

Lazarus looked interested. "How do you figure that, Justin?"

"Thusly: the board of trustees were the custodians of a foundation which existed as a part of and in relation to a society. The trustees were never a government; their sole duties had to do with relations between the Families and the rest of that society. With the ending of relationship between the Families and terrestrial society, the board of trustees, *ipso facto*, ceases to exist. It is one with history. Now we in this ship are not yet a society, we are an anarchistic group. This present assemblage has as much—or as little—authority to initiate a society as has any part group."

Lazarus cheered and clapped. "Justin," he applauded, "that is the neatest piece of verbal juggling I've heard in a century. Let's get together sometime and have a go at solipsism."

Justin Foote looked pained. "Obviously——" he began.

"Nope! Not another word! You've convinced me, don't

spoil it. If that's how it is, let's get busy and pick a bull moose. How about you, Zack? You look like the logical candidate."

Barstow shook his head. "I know my limitations. I'm an engineer, not a political executive; the Families were just a hobby with me. We need an expert in social administration."

When Barstow had convinced them that he meant it, other names were proposed and their qualifications debated at length. In a group as large as the Families there were many who had specialized in political science, many who had served in public office with credit.

Lazarus listened; he knew four of the candidates. At last he got Eve Barstow aside and whispered with her. She looked startled, then thoughtful, finally nodded.

She asked for the floor. "I have a candidate to propose," she began in her always gentle tones, "who might not ordinarily occur to you, but who is incomparably better fitted, by temperament, training, and experience, to do this job than is anyone as yet proposed. For civil administrator of the ship I nominate Slayton Ford."

They were flabbergasted into silence, then everybody tried to talk at once. "Has Eve lost her mind? Ford is back on Earth!"—"No, no, he's not. I've seen him—*here*—in the ship."—"But it's out of the question!"—"*Him?* The Families would never accept him!"—"Even so, he's not one of us."

Eve patiently kept the floor until they quieted. "I know my nomination sounds ridiculous and I admit the difficulties. But consider the advantages. We all know Slayton Ford by reputation and by performance. You know, every member of the Families knows, that Ford is a genius in his field. It is going to be hard enough to work out plans for living together in this badly overcrowded ship; the best talent we can draw on will be no more than enough."

Her words impressed them because Ford was that rare thing in history, a statesman whose worth was almost universally acknowledged in his own lifetime. Contemporary historians credited him with having saved the Western Federation in at least two of its major development crises; it was his misfortune rather than his personal failure that his career was wrecked on a crisis not solvable by ordinary means.

"Eve," said Zaccur Barstown "I agree with your opinion of Ford and I myself would be glad to have him as our executive. But how about all of the others? To the Families—everyone except ourselves here present—Mr. Administrator Ford symbolizes the persecution they have suffered. I think that makes him an impossible candidate."

Eve was gently stubborn. "I don't think so. We've already agreed that we will have to work up a campaign to explain away a lot of embarrassing facts about the last few days. Why don't we do it thoroughly and convince them that Ford is a martyr who sacrificed himself to save them? He is, you know."

"Mmm . . . yes, he is. He didn't sacrifice himself primarily on our account, but there is no doubt in my mind that his personal sacrifice saved us. But whether or not we can convince the others, convince them strongly enough that they will accept him and take orders from him . . . when he is now a sort of personal devil to them—well, I just don't know. I think we need expert advice. How about it, Ralph? Could it be done?"

Ralph Schultz hesitated. "The truth of a proposition has little or nothing to do with its psychodynamics. The notion that 'truth will prevail' is merely a pious wish; history doesn't show it. The fact that Ford really is a martyr to whom we owe gratitude is irrelevant to the purely technical question you put to me." He stopped to think. "But the proposition *per se* has certain sentimentally dramatic aspects which lend it to propaganda manipulation, even in the face of the currently accepted strong counterproposition. Yes . . . yes, I think it could be sold."

"How long would it take you to put it over?"

"Mmm . . . the social space involved is both 'tight' and 'hot' in the jargon we use; I should be able to get a high positive 'k' factor on the chain reaction—if it works at all. But it's an unsurveyed field and I don't know what spontaneous rumors are running around the ship. If you decide to do this, I'll want to prepare some rumors before we adjourn, rumors to repair Ford's reputation—then about twelve hours from now I can release another one that Ford is actually aboard . . . because he intended from the first to throw his lot in with us."

"Uh, I hardly think he did, Ralph."

"Are you *sure*, Zaccur?"

"No, but—— Well . . ."

"You see? The truth about his original intentions is a secret between him and his God. You don't know and neither do I. But the dynamics of the proposition are a separate matter.

Zaccur, by the time my rumor gets back to you three or four times, even you will begin to wonder." The psychometrician paused to stare at nothing while he consulted an intuition refined by almost a century of mathematical study of human behavior. "Yes, it will work. If you all want to do it, you will be able to make a public announcement inside of twenty-four hours."

"I so move!" someone called out.

A few minutes later Barstow had Lazarus fetch Ford to the meeting place. Lazarus did not explain to him why his presence was required; Ford entered the compartment like a man come to judgment, one with a bitter certainty that the outcome will be against him. His manner showed fortitude but not hope. His eyes were unhappy.

Lazarus had studied those eyes during the long hours they had been shut up together in the control room. They bore an expression Lazarus had seen many times before in his long life. The condemned man who has lost his final appeal, the fully resolved suicide, little furry things exhausted and defeated by struggle with the unrelenting steel of traps—the eyes of each of these hold a single expression, born of hopeless conviction that his time has run out.

Ford's eyes had it.

Lazarus had seen it grow and had been puzzled by it. To be sure, they were all in a dangerous spot, but Ford no more than the rest. Besides, awareness of danger brings a *live* expression; why should Ford's eyes hold the signal of death?

Lazarus finally decided that it could only be because Ford had reached the dead-end state of mind where suicide is necessary. But why? Lazarus mulled it over during the long watches in the control room and reconstructed the logic of it to his own satisfaction. Back on Earth, Ford had been important among his own kind, the short-lived. His paramount position had rendered him then almost immune to the feeling of defeated inferiority which the long-lived stirred up in normal men. But now he was the *only* ephemeral in a race of Methuselahs.

Ford had neither the experience of the elders nor the expectations of the young; he felt inferior to them both, hopelessly outclassed. Correct or not, he felt himself to be a useless pensioner, an impotent object of charity.

To a person of Ford's busy useful background the situation

was intolerable. His very pride and strength of character were driving him to suicide.

As he came into the conference room Ford's glance sought out Zaccur Barstow. "You sent for me, sir?"

"Yes, Mr. Administrator." Barstow explained briefly the situation and the responsibility they wanted him to assume. "You are under no compulsion," he concluded, "but we need your services if you are willing to serve. Will you?"

Lazarus' heart felt light as he watched Ford's expression change to amazement. "Do you really mean that?" Ford answered slowly. "You're not joking with me?"

"Most certainly we mean it!"

Ford did not answer at once and when he did, his answer seemed irrelevant. "May I sit down?"

A place was found for him; he settled heavily into the chair and covered his face with his hands. No one spoke. Presently he raised his head and said in a steady voice, "If that is your will, I will do my best to carry out your wishes."

The ship required a captain as well as a civil administrator. Lazarus had been, up to that time, her captain in a very practical, piratical sense but he balked when Barstow proposed that it be made a formal title. "Huh *uh!* Not me. I may just spend this trip playing checkers. Libby's your man. Serious-minded, conscientious, former naval officer—just the type for the job."

Libby blushed as eyes turned toward him. "Now, really," he protested, "while it is true that I have had to command ships in the course of my duties, it has never suited me. I am a staff officer by temperament. I don't *feel* like a commanding officer."

"Don't see how you can duck out of it," Lazarus persisted. "You invented the go-fast gadget and you are the only one who understands how it works. You've got yourself a job, boy."

"But that does not follow at all," pleaded Libby. "I am perfectly willing to be astrogator, for that is consonant with my talents. But I very much prefer to serve under a commanding officer."

Lazarus was smugly pleased then to see how Slayton Ford immediately moved in and took charge; the sick man was gone, here again was the executive. "It isn't a matter of your personal preference, Commander Libby; we each must do what we can. I have agreed to direct social and civil organization; that is consonant with *my* training. But I can't command the ship as a ship; I'm not trained for it. You are. You must do it."

Libby blushed pinker and stammered. "I would if I were the only one. But there are hundreds of spacemen among the Families and dozens of them certainly have more experience and talent for command than I have. If you'll look for him, you'll find the right man."

Ford said, "What do you think, Lazarus?"

"Um. Andy's got something. A captain puts spine into his ship . . . or doesn't, as the case may be. If Libby doesn't hanker to command, maybe we'd better look around."

Justin Foote had a microed roster with him but there was no scanner at hand with which to sort it. Nevertheless the memories of the dozen and more present produced many candidates. They finally settled on Captain Rufus "Ruthless" King.

Libby was explaining the consequences of his light-pressure drive to his new commanding officer. "The loci of our attainable destinations is contained in a sheaf of paraboloids having their apices tangent to our present course. This assumes that acceleration by means of the ship's normal drive will always be applied so that the magnitude our present vector, just under the speed of light, will be held constant. This will require that the ship be slowly precessed during the entire maneuvering acceleration. But it will not be too fussy because of the enormous difference in magnitude between our present vector and the maneuvering vectors being impressed on it. One may think of it roughly as accelerating at right angles to our course."

"Yes, yes, I see that," Captain King cut in, "but why do you assume that the resultant vectors must always be equal to our present vector?"

"Why, it need not be if the Captain decides otherwise," Libby answered, looking puzzled, "but to apply a component that would reduce the resultant vector below our present speed would simply be to cause us to backtrack a little without increasing the scope of our present loci of possible destinations. The effect would only increase our flight time, to generations, even to centuries, if the resultant——"

"Certainly, certainly! I understand basic ballistics, Mister. But why do you reject the other alternative? Why not increase our speed? Why can't I accelerate directly along my present course if I choose?"

Libby looked worried. "The Captain may, if he so orders. But it would be an attempt to exceed the speed of light. That has been assumed to be impossible——"

"That's exactly what I was driving at. 'Assumed.' I've always wondered if that assumption was justified. Now seems like a good time to find out."

Libby hesitated, his sense of duty struggling against the ecstatic temptations of scientific curiosity. "If this were a research ship, Captain, I would be anxious to try it. I can't visualize what the conditions would be if we did pass the speed of light, but it seems to me that we would be cut off entirely from the electromagnetic spectrum insofar as other bodies are concerned. How could we see to astrogate?" Libby had more than theory to worry him; they were "seeing" now only by electronic vision. To the human eye itself the hemisphere behind them along their track was a vasty black; the shortest radiations had dopplered to wavelengths too long for the eye. In the forward direction stars could still be seen but their visible "light" was made up of longest Hertzian waves crowded in by the ship's incomprehensible speed. Dark "radio stars" shined at first magnitude; stars poor in radio wavelengths had faded to obscurity. The familiar constellations were changed beyond easy recognition. The fact that they were seeing by vision distorted by Doppler's effect was confirmed by spectrum analysis; Fraunhofer's lines had not merely shifted toward the violent end, they had passed beyond, out of sight, and previously unknown patterns replaced them.

"Hmm . . ." King replied. "I see what you mean. But I'd certainly like to try it, damme if I wouldn't! But I admit it's out of the question with passengers inboard. Very well, prepare for me roughed courses to type 'G' stars lying inside this trumpet-flower locus of yours and not too far away. Say ten light-years for your first search."

"Yes, sir. I have. I can't offer anything in that range in the 'G' types."

"So? Lonely out here, isn't it? Well?"

"We have Tau Ceti inside the locus at eleven light-years."

"A G5, eh? Not too good."

"No, sir. But we have a true Sol type, a G2—catalog ZD9817. But it's more than twice as far away."

Captain King chewed a knuckle. "I suppose I'll have to put it up to the elders. How much subjective time advantage are we enjoying?"

"I don't know, sir."

"Eh? Well, work it out! Or give me the data and I will. I don't claim to be the mathematician you are, but any cadet could solve that one. The equations are simple enough."

"So they are, sir. But I don't have the data to substitute in the time-contraction equation . . . because I have no way now to measure the ship's speed. The violet shift is useless to use; we don't know what the lines mean. I'm afraid we must wait until we have worked up a much longer baseline."

King sighed. "Mister, I sometimes wonder why I got into this business. Well, are you willing to venture a best guess? Long time? Short time?"

"Uh . . . a long time, sir. Years."

"So? Well, I've sweated it out in worse ships. Years, eh? Play any chess?"

"I have, sir." Libby did not mention that he had given up the game long ago for lack of adequate competition.

"Looks like we'd have plenty of time to play. King's pawn to king four."

"King's knight to bishop three."

"An unorthodox player, eh? Well, I'll answer you later. I suppose I had better try to sell them the G2 even though it takes longer . . . and I suppose I had better caution Ford to start some contests and things. Can't have 'em getting coffin fever."

"Yes, sir. Did I mention deceleration time? It works out to just under one Earth year, subjective, at a negative one gee, to slow us to stellar speeds."

"Eh? We'll decelerate the same way we accelerated—with your light-pressure drive."

Libby shook his head. "I'm sorry, sir. The drawback of the light-pressure drive is that it makes no difference what your previous course and speed may be; if you go inertialess in the near neighborhood of a star, its light pressure kicks you away from it like a cork hit by a stream of water. Your previous momentum is canceled out when you cancel your inertia."

"Well," King conceded, "let's assume that we will follow

your schedule. I can't argue with you yet; there are still some things about that gadget of yours that I don't understand."

"There are lots of things about it," Libby answered seriously, "that I don't understand either."

The ship had flicked by Earth's orbit less than ten minutes after Libby cut in his space drive. Lazarus and he had discussed the esoteric physical aspects of it all the way to the orbit of Mars—less than a quarter hour. Jupiter's path was far distant when Barstow called the organization conference. But it killed an hour to find them all in the crowded ship; by the time he called them to order they were a billion miles out, beyond the orbit of Saturn—elapsed time from "*Go!*" less than an hour and a half.

But the blocks get longer after Saturn. Uranus found them still in discussion. Nevertheless Ford's name was agreed on and he had accepted before the ship was as far from the Sun as is Neptune. King had been named captain, had toured his new command with Lazarus as guide, and was already in conference with his astrogator when the ship passed the orbit of Pluto nearly four billion miles deep into space, but still less than six hours after the Sun's light had blasted them away.

Even then they were not outside the Solar System, but between them and the stars lay nothing but the winter homes of Sol's comets and hiding places of hypothetical trans-Plutonian planets—space in which the Sun holds options but can hardly be said to own in fee simple. But even the nearest stars were still light-years away. *New Frontiers* was headed for them at a pace which crowded the heels of light—weather cold, track fast.

Out, out, and still farther out . . . out to the lonely depths where world lines are almost straight, undistorted by gravitation. Each day, each month . . . each year . . . their head-long flight took them farther from all humanity.

PART TWO

The ship lunged on, alone in the desert of night, each light-year as empty as the last. The Families built up a way of life in her.

The *New Frontiers* was approximately cylindrical. When not under acceleration, she was spun on her axis to give pseudo-weight to passengers near the outer skin of the ship; the outer or "lower" compartments were living quarters while the innermost or "upper" compartments were store-rooms and so forth. 'Tween compartments were shops, hydroponic farms and such. Along the axis, fore to aft, were the control room, the converter, and the main drive.

The design will be recognized as similar to that of the larger free-flight interplanetary ships in use today, but it is necessary to bear in mind her enormous size. She was a city, with ample room for a colony of twenty thousand, which would have allowed the planned complement of ten thousand to double their numbers during the long voyage to Proxima Centauri.

Thus, big as she was, the hundred thousand and more of the Families found themselves overcrowded fivefold.

They put up with it only long enough to rig for cold-sleep. By converting some recreation space on the lower levels to storage, room was squeezed out for the purpose. Somnolents require about one per cent the living room needed by active, functioning humans; in time the ship was roomy enough for those still awake. Volunteers for cold-sleep were not numerous at first—these people were more than commonly aware of death because of their unique heritage; cold-sleep seemed too much like the Last Sleep. But the great discomfort of extreme overcrowding combined with the equally extreme monotony of the endless voyage changed their minds rapidly enough to provide a steady supply for the little death as fast as they could be accommodated.

Those who remained awake were kept humping simply to get the work done—the ship's houskeeping, tending the hydroponic farms and the ship's auxiliary machinery and, most especially, caring for the somnolents themselves. Biomechanicians have worked out complex empirical formulas describing body deterioration and the measures which must be taken to offset it under various conditions of impressed acceleration, ambient temperature, the drugs used, and other factors such as metabolic age, body mass, sex, and so forth. By using the upper, low-weight compartments, deterioration caused by acceleration (that is to say, the simple weight of body tissues on themselves, the wear that leads to flat feet or bed sores) could be held to a minimum. But all the care of the somnolents had to be done by hand—turning them, massaging them, checking on blood sugar, testing the slow-motion heart actions, all the tests and services necessary to make sure that extremely reduced metabolism does not slide over into death. Aside from a dozen stalls in the ship's infirmary she had not been designed for cold-sleep passengers; no automatic machinery had been provided. All this tedious care of tens of thousands of somnolents had to be done by hand.

Eleanor Johnson ran across her friend, Nancy Weatheral, in Refectory 9-D—called "The Club" by its habitués, less flattering things by those who avoided it. Most of its frequenters were young and noisy. Lazarus was the only elder who ate there often. He did not mind noise, he enjoyed it.

Eleanor swooped down on her friend and kissed the back of her neck. "Nancy! So you are awake again! My, I'm glad to see you!"

Nancy disentangled herself. "H'lo, babe. Don't spill my coffee."

"Well! Aren't you glad to see me?"

"Of course I am. But you forget that while it's been a year to you, it's only yesterday to me. And I'm still sleepy."

"How long have you been awake, Nancy?"

"A couple of hours. How's that kid of yours?"

"Oh, he's fine!" Eleanor Johnson's face brightened. "You wouldn't know him—he's shot up fast this past year. Almost up to my shoulder and looking more like his father every day."

Nancy changed the subject. Eleanor's friends made a point of keeping Eleanor's deceased husband out of the conversation. "What have you been doing while I was snoozing? Still teaching primary?"

"Yes. Or rather 'No.' I stay with the age group my Hubert is in. He's in junior secondary now."

"Why don't you catch a few months' sleep and skip some of that drudgery, Eleanor? You'll make an old woman out of yourself if you keep it up."

"No," Eleanor refused, "not until Hubert is old enough not to need me."

"Don't be sentimental. Half the female volunteers are women with young children. I don't blame 'em a bit. Look at me—from my point of view the trip so far has lasted only seven months. I could do the rest of it standing on my head."

Eleanor looked stubborn. "No, thank you. That may be all right for you, but I am doing very nicely as I am."

Lazarus had been sitting at the same counter doing drastic damage to a sirloin steak surrogate. "She's afraid she'll miss something," he explained. "I don't blame her. So am I."

Nancy changed her tack. "Then have another child, Eleanor. That'll get you relieved from routine duties."

"It takes two to arrange that," Eleanor pointed out.

"That's no hazard. Here's Lazarus, for example. He'd make a plus father."

Eleanor dimpled. Lazarus blushed under his permanent tan. "As a matter of fact," Eleanor stated evenly, "I proposed to him and was turned down."

Nancy sputtered into her coffee and looked quickly from Lazarus to Eleanor. "Sorry. I didn't know."

"No harm," answered Eleanor. "It's simply because I am one of his granddaughters, four times removed."

"But . . ." Nancy fought a losing fight with the custom of privacy. "Well, goodness me, that's well within the limits of permissible consanguinity. What's the hitch? Or should I shut up?"

"You should," Eleanor agreed.

Lazarus shifted uncomfortably. "I know I'm old-fashioned," he admitted, "but I soaked up some of my ideas a long time ago. Genetics or no genetics, I just wouldn't feel *right* marrying one of my own grandchildren."

Nancy looked amazed. "I'll say you're old-fashioned!" She added, "Or maybe you're just shy. I'm tempted to propose to you myself and find out."

Lazarus glared at her. "Go ahead and see what a surprise you get!"

Nancy looked him over coolly. "Mmm . . ." she meditated.

Lazarus tried to outstare her, finally dropped his eyes. "I'll have to ask you ladies to excuse me," he said nervously. "Work to do."

Eleanor laid a gentle hand on his arm. "Don't go, Lazarus. Nancy is a cat and can't help it. Tell her about the plans for landing."

"What's that? Are we going to land? When? Where?"

Lazarus, willing to be mollified, told her. The type G2, or Sol-type star, toward which they had bent their course years earlier was now less than a light-year away—a little over seven light-months—and it was now possible to infer by parainterferometric methods that the star (ZD9817, or simply "our" star) had planets of some sort.

In another month, when the star would be a half light-year away, deceleration would commence. Spin would be taken off the ship and for one year she would boost backwards at one gravity, ending near the star at interplanetary rather than interstellar speed, and a search would be made for a planet fit to support human life. The search would be quick and easy as the only planets they were interested in would shine out brilliantly then, like Venus from Earth; they were not interested in elusive cold planets, like Neptune or Pluto, lurking in distant shadows, nor in scorched cinders ilke Mercury, hiding in the flaming skirts of the mother star.

If no Earthlike planet was to be had, then they must continue on down really close to the strange sun and again be kicked away by light pressure, to resume hunting for a home elsewhere—with the difference that this time, not harassed by police, they could select a new course with care.

Lazarus explained that the New Frontiers would not actually land in either case; she was too big to land, her weight would wreck her. Instead, if they found a planet, she would be thrown into a parking orbit around her and exploring parties would be sent down in ship's boats.

As soon as face permitted Lazarus left the two young women and went to the laboratory where the Families continued their researches in metabolism and gerontology. He expected to find Mary Sperling there; the brush with Nancy Weatheral had made him feel a need for her company. If he ever did marry again, he thought to himself, Mary was more his style. Not that he seriously considered it; he felt that a liaison between Mary and himself would have a ridiculous flavor of lavender and old lace.

Mary Sperling, finding herself cooped up in the ship and not wishing to accept the symbolic death of cold-sleep, had turned her fear of death into constructive channels by volunteering to be a laboratory assistant in the continuing research into longevity. She was not a trained biologist but she had deft fingers and an agile mind; the patient years of the trip had shaped her into a valuable assistant to Dr. Gordon Hardy, chief of the research.

Lazarus found her servicing the deathless tissue of chicken heart known to the laboratory crew as "Mrs. 'Awkins." Mrs. 'Awkins was older than any member of the Families save possibly Lazarus himself; she was a growing piece of the original tissue obtained by the Families from the Rockefeller Institute in the twentieth century, and the tissues had been alive since early in the twentieth century even then. Dr. Hardy and his predecessors had kept their bit of it alive for more than two centuries now, using the Carrel-Lindbergh-O'Shaug techniques —and still Mrs. 'Awkins flourished.

Gordon Hardy had insisted on taking the tissue and the appartus which cherished it with him to the reservation when he was arrested; he had been equally stubborn about taking the living tissue along during the escape in the *Chili*. Now Mrs. 'Awkins still lived and grew in the *New Frontiers*, fifty or sixty pounds of her—blind, deaf, and brainless, but still alive.

Mary Sperling was reducing her size. "Hello, Lazarus," she greeted him. "Stand back. I've got the tank open."

He watched her slice off excess tissue. "Mary," he mused, "what keeps that silly thing alive?"

"You've got the question inverted," she answered, not looking up; "the proper form is: why should it die? Why shouldn't it go on forever?"

"I wish to the Devil it would die!" came the voice of Dr. Hardy from behind them. "Then we could observe and find out why."

"You'll never find out why from Mrs. 'Awkins, boss," Mary answered, hands and eyes still busy. "The key to the matter is in the gonads—she hasn't any."

"Hummph! What do you know about it?"

"A woman's intuition. What do *you* know about it?"

"Nothing, absolutely nothing!—which puts me ahead of you and your intuition."

"Maybe. At least," Mary added slyly, "I knew you before you were housebroken."

"A typical female argument. Mary, that lump of muscle cackled and laid eggs before either one of us was born, yet it doesn't know anything." He scowled at it. "Lazarus, I'd gladly trade it for one pair of carp. male and female."

"Why carp?" asked Lazarus.

"Because carp don't seem to die. They get killed, or eaten, or starve to death, or succumb to infection, but so far as we know they don't die."

"Why not?"

"That's what I was trying to find out when we were rushed off on this damned safari. They have unusual intestinal flora and it may have something to do with that. But I think it has to do with the fact that they never stop growing."

Mary said something inaudibly. Hardy said, "What are you muttering about? Another intuition?"

"I said, 'Amebas don't die.' You said yourself that every ameba now alive has been alive for, oh, fifty million years or so. Yet they don't grow indefinitely larger and they certainly can't have intestinal flora."

"No guts," said Lazarus and blinked.

"What a terrible pun, Lazarus. But what I said is true. They don't die. They just twin and keep on living."

"Guts or no guts," Hardy said impatiently, "there may be a structural parallel. But I'm frustrated for lack of experimental subjects. Which reminds me: Lazarus, I'm glad you dropped in. I want you to do me a favor."

"Speak up. I might be feeling mellow."

"You're an interesting case yourself, you know. You didn't follow our genetic pattern; you anticipated it. I don't want your body to go into the converter; I want to examine it."

Lazarus snorted. " 'Sall right with me, bud. But you'd better tell your successor what to look for—you may not live that long. And I'll bet you anything that you like that nobody'll find it by poking around in my cadaver!"

The planet they had hoped for was there when they looked for it, green, lush, and young, and looking as much like Earth as another planet could. Not only was it Earthlike but the rest of the system duplicated roughly the pattern of the Solar System—small terrestrial planets near this sun, large Jovian planets farther out. Cosmologists had never been able to account for the Solar System; they had alternated between theories of origin which had failed to stand up and "sound" mathematico-physical "proofs" that such a system could never have originated in the first place. Yet here was another enough like it to suggest that its paradoxes were not unique, might even be common.

But more startling and even more stimulating and certainly more disturbing was another fact brought out by telescopic observation as they got close to the planet. The planet held life . . . intelligent life . . . civilized life.

Their cities could be seen. Their engineering works, strange in form and purpose, were huge enough to be seen from space just as ours can be seen.

Nevertheless, though it might mean that they must again pursue their weary hegira, the dominant race did not appear to have crowded the available living space. There might be room for their little colony on those broad continents. If a colony was welcome—

"To tell the truth," Captain King fretted, "I hadn't expected anything like this. Primitive aborigines perhaps, and we certainly could expect dangerous animals, but I suppose I unconsciously assumed that man was the only really civilized race. We're going to have to be very cautious."

King made up a scouting party headed by Lazarus; he had come to have confidence in Lazarus' practical sense and will to survive. King wanted to head the party himself, but his concept of his duty as a ship's captain forced him to forego it. But Slayton Ford could go; Lazarus chose him and Ralph Schultz and his lieutenants. The rest of the party were specialists—biochemist, geologist, ecologist, stereographer, several sorts of psychologists and sociologists to study the natives including one authority in McKelvy's structural theory of communication whose task would be to find some way to talk with the natives.

No weapons——

King flatly refused to arm them. "Your scouting party is expendable," he told Lazarus bluntly; "for we cannot risk offending them by any sort of fighting for any reason, even in self-defense. You are ambassadors, not soldiers. Don't forget it."

Lazarus returned to his stateroom, came back and gravely delivered to King one blaster. He neglected to mention the one still strapped to his leg under his kilt.

As King was about to tell them to man the boat and carry out their orders they were interrupted by Janice Schmidt, chief nurse to the Families' congenital defectives. She pushed her way past and demanded the Captain's attention.

Only a nurse could have obtained it at that moment; she had professional stubbornness to match his and half a century more practice at being balky. He glared at her. "What's the meaning of this interruption?"

"Captain, I must speak with you about one of my children."

"Nurse, you are decidedly out of order. Get out. See me in my office—after taking it up with the Chief Surgeon."

She put her hands on her hips. "You'll see me now. This is the landing party, isn't it? I've got something you have to hear before they leave."

King started to speak, changed his mind, merely said, "Make it brief."

She did so. Hans Weatheral, a youth of some ninety years and still adolescent in appearance through a hyper-active thymus gland, was one of her charges. He had inferior but not moronic mentality, a chronic apathy, and a neuro-muscular deficiency which made him too weak to feed himself—and an acute sensitivity to telepathy.

He had told Janice that he knew all about the planet around which they orbited. His friends on the planet had told him about it . . . and they were expecting him.

The departure of the landing boat was delayed while King and Lazarus investigated. Hans was matter of fact about his information and what little they could check of what he said was correct. But he was not too helpful about his "friends." "Oh, just people," he said, shrugging at their stupidity. "Much like back home. Nice people. Go to work, go to school, go to church. Have kids and enjoy themselves. You'll like them."

But he was quite clear about one point: his friends were expecting him; therefore he must go along.

Against his wishes and his better judgment Lazarus saw added to his party Hans Weatheral, Janice Schmidt, and a stretcher for Hans.

When the party returned three days later Lazarus made a long private report to King while the specialist reports were being analyzed and combined. "It's amazingly like Earth, Skipper, enough to make you homesick. But it's also different enough to give you the willies—like looking at your own face in the mirror and having it turn out to have three eyes and no nose. Unsettling."

"But how about the natives?"

"Let me tell it. We made a quick swing of the day side, for a bare eyes look. Nothing you haven't seen through the 'scopes. Then I put her down where Hans told me to, in a clearing near the center of one of their cities. I wouldn't have picked the place myself; I would have preferred to land in the bush and reconnoitre. But you told me to play Hans' hunches."

"You were free to use your judgment," King reminded him.

"Yes, yes. Anyhow we did it. By the time the techs had sampled the air and checked for hazards there was quite a crowd around us. They—well, you've seen the stereographs."

"Yes. Incredibly android."

"Android, hell! They're *men*. Not humans, but men just the same." Lazarus looked puzzled. "I don't like it."

King did not argue. The pictures had shown bipeds seven to eight feet tall, bilaterally symmetric, possessed of internal skeletal framework, distinct heads, lens-and-camera eyes. Those eyes were their most human and appealing features; they were large, limpid, and tragic, like those of a Saint Bernard dog.

It was well to concentrate on the eyes; their other features were not as tolerable. King looked away from the loose, toothless mouths, the bifurcated upper lips. He decided that it might take a long, long time to learn to be fond of these creatures. "Go ahead," he told Lazarus.

"We opened up and I stepped out alone, with my hands empty and trying to look friendly and peaceable. Three of them stepped forward—eagerly, I would say. But they lost interest in me at once; they seemed to be waiting for somebody else to come out. So I gave orders to carry Hans out.

"Skipper, you wouldn't believe it. They fawned over Hans like a long lost brother. No, that doesn't describe it. More like a king returning home in triumph. They were polite enough with the rest of us, in an offhand way, but they fairly slobbered over Hans." Lazarus hesitated. "Skipper? Do you believe in reincarnation?"

"Not exactly. I'm open-minded about it. I've read the report of the Frawling Committee, of course."

"I've never had any use for the notion myself. But how else could you account for the reception they gave Hans?"

"I don't account for it. Get on with your report. Do you think it is going to be possible for us to colonize here?"

"Oh," said Lazarus, "they left no doubt on that point. You see, Hans really can talk to them, telepathically. Hans tells us that their gods have authorized us to live here and the natives have already made plans to receive us."

"Eh?"

"That's right. They want us."

"Well! That's a relief."

"Is it?"

King studied Lazarus' glum features. "You've made a report favorable on every point. Why the sour look?"

"I don't know. I'd just rather we found a planet of our own. Skipper, anything this easy has a hitch in it."

2

THE JOCKAIRA (or Zhacheira, as some prefer) turned an entire city over to the colonists.

Such astounding coöperation, plus the sudden discovery by almost every member of the Howard Families that he was sick for the feel of dirt under foot and free air in his lungs, greatly speeded the removal from ship to ground. It had been anticipated that at least an Earth year would be needed for such transition and that somnolents would be waked only as fast as they could be accommodated dirtside. But the limiting factor now was the scanty ability of the ship's boats to transfer a hundred thousand people as they were roused.

The Jockaira city was not designed to fit the needs of human beings. The Jockaira were not human beings, their physical requirements were somewhat different, and their cultural needs as expressed in engineering were vastly different. But a city, any city, is a machine to accomplish certain practical ends: shelter, food supply, sanitation, communication; the internal logic of these prime requirements, as applied by different creatures to different environments, will produce an unlimited number of answers. But, as applied by any race of warm-blooded, oxygen-breathing androidal creatures to a particular environment, the results, although strange, are necessarily such that Terran humans can use them. In some ways the Jockaira city looked as wild as a pararealist painting, but humans have lived in igloos, grass shacks, and even in the cybernautomated burrow under Antarctica; these humans could and did move into the Jockaira city—and of course at once set about reshaping it to suit them better.

It was not difficult even though there was much to be done. There were buildings already standing—shelters with roofs on them, the artificial cave basic to all human shelter requirements. It did not matter what the Jockaira had used such a structure for; humans could use it for almost anything: sleeping, recreation, eating, storage, production. There were actual "caves" as well, for the Jockaira dig in more than we do. But humans easily turn troglodyte on occasion, in New York as readily as in Antarctica.

There was fresh potable water piped in for drinking and for limited washing. A major lack lay in plumbing; the city had no over-all drainage system. The "Jocks" did not water-bathe and their personal sanitation requirements differed from ours and were taken care of differently. A major effort had to be made to jury-rig equivalents of shipboard refreshers and adapt them to hook in with Jockaira disposal arrangements. Minimum necessity ruled; baths would remain a rationed luxury until water supply and disposal could be increased at least tenfold. But baths are not a necessity.

But such efforts at modification were minor compared with the crash program to set up hydroponic farming, since most of the somnolents could not be waked until a food supply was assured. The do-it-now crowd wanted to tear out every bit of hydroponic equipment in the *New Frontiers* at once, ship it down dirtside, set it up and get going, while depending on stored supplies during the change-over; a more cautious minority wanted to move only a pilot plant while continuing to grow food in the ship; they pointed out that unsuspected fungus or virus on the strange planet could result in disaster . . . starvation.

The minority, strongly led by Ford and Barstow and supported by Captain King, prevailed; one of the ship's hydroponic farms was drained and put out of service. Its machinery was broken down into parts small enough to load into ship's boats.

But even this never reached dirtside. The planet's native farm products turned out to be suitable for human food and the Jockaira seemed almost pantingly anxious to give them away. Instead, efforts were turned to establishing Earth crops in native soil in order to supplement Jockaira foodstuffs with sorts the humans were used to. The Jockaira moved in and almost took over that effort; they were superb "natural" farmers (they had no need for synthetics on their undepleted planet) and seemed delighted to attempt to raise anything their guests wanted.

Ford transferred his civil headquarters to the city as soon as a food supply for more than a pioneer group was assured, while King remained in the ship. Sleepers were awakened and ferried to the ground as fast as facilities were made ready for them and their services could be used. Despite assured food, shelter, and drinking water, much needed to be done to provide minimum comfort and decency. The two cultures were basically different. The Jockaira seemed always anxious to be endlessly helpful but they were often obviously baffled at what the humans tried to do. The Jockaira culture did not seem to include the idea of privacy; the buildings of the city had no partitions in them which were not loadbearing—and few that were; they tended to use columns or posts. They could not understand why the humans would break up these lovely open spaces into cubicles and passageways; they simply could not comprehend why any individual would ever wish to be alone for any purpose whatsoever.

Apparently (this is not certain for abstract communication with them never reached a subtle level) they decided eventually that being alone held a religious significance for Earth people. In any case they were again helpful; they provided thin sheets of material which could be shaped into partitions—with their tools and only with their tools. The stuff frustrated human engineers almost to nervous collapse. No corrosive known to our technology affected it; even the reactions that would break down the rugged fluorine plastics used in handling uranium compounds had no effect on it. Diamond saws went to pieces on it, heat did not melt it, cold did not make it brittle. It stopped light, sound, and all radiation they were equipped to try on it. Its tensile strength could not be defined because they could not break it. Yet Jockaira tools, even when handled by humans, could cut it, shape it, reweld it.

The human engineers simply had to get used to such frustrations. From the criterion of control over environment through technology the Jockaira were as civilized as humans. But their developments had been along other lines.

The important differences between the two cultures went much deeper than engineering technology. Although ubiquitously friendly and helpful the Jockaira were *not* human. They thought differently, they evaluated differently; their social structure and language structure reflected their unhuman quality and both were incomprehensible to human beings.

Oliver Johnson, the semantician who had charge of developing a common language, found his immediate task made absurdly easy by the channel of communication through Hans Weatheral. "Of course," he explained to Slayton Ford and to Lazarus, "Hans isn't exactly a genius; he just misses being a moron. That limits the words I can translate through him to ideas he can understand. But it does give me a basic vocabulary to build on."

"Isn't that enough?" asked Ford. "It seems to me that I have heard that eight hundred words will do to convey any idea."

"There's some truth in that," admitted Johnson. "Less than a thousand words will cover all ordinary situations. I have selected not quite seven hundred of their terms, operationals and substantives, to give us a working *lingua franca*. But subtle distinctions and fine discriminations will have to wait until we know them better and understand them. A short vocabulary cannot handle high abstractions."

"Shucks," said Lazarus, "seven hundred words ought to be enough. Me, I don't intend to make love to 'em, or try to discuss poetry."

This opinion seemed to be justified; most of the members picked up basic Jockairan in two weeks to a month after being ferried down and chattered in it with their hosts as if they had talked it all their lives. All of the Earthmen had had the usual sound grounding in mnemonics and semantics; a short-vocabulary auxiliary language was quickly learned under the stimulus of need and the circumstance of plenty of chance to practice—except, of course, by the usual percentage of unshakable provincials who felt that it was up to "the natives" to learn English.

The Jockaira did not learn English. In the first place not one of them showed the slightest interest. Nor was it reasonable to expect their millions to learn the language of a few thousand. But in any case the split upper lip of a Jockaira could not cope with "m," "p," and "b," whereas the gutturals, sibilants, dentals, and clicks they did use could be approximated by the human throat.

Lazarus was forced to revise his early bad impression of the Jockaira. It was impossible not to like them once the strangeness of their appearance had worn off. They were so hospitable, so generous, so friendly, so anxious to please. He became particularly attached to Kreel Sarloo, who acted as a sort of liaison officer between the Families and the Jockaira. Sarloo held a position among his own people which could be translated roughly as "chief," "father," "priest," or "leader" of the Kreel family or tribe. He invited Lazarus to visit him in the Jockaira city nearest the colony. "My people will like to see you and smell your skin," he said. "It will be a happy-making thing. The gods will be pleased."

Sarloo seemed almost unable to form a sentence without making reference to his gods. Lazarus did not mind; to another's religion he was tolerantly indifferent. "I will come, Sarloo, old bean. It will be a happy-making thing for me, too."

Sarloo took him in the common vehicle of the Jockaira, a wheelless wain shaped much like a soup bowl, which moved quietly and rapidly over the ground, skimming the surface in apparent contact. Lazarus squatted on the floor of the vessel while Sarloo caused it to speed along at a rate that made Lazarus' eyes water.

"Sarloo," Lazarus asked, shouting to make himself heard against the wind, "how does this thing work? What moves it?"

"The gods breathe on the——" Sarloo used a word not in their common language. "——and cause it to need to change its place."

Lazarus started to ask for a fuller explanation, then shut up. There had been something familiar about that answer and he now placed it; he had once given a very similar answer to one of the water people of Venus when he was asked to explain the diesel engine used in an early type of swamp tractor. Lazarus had not meant to be mysterious; he had simply been tongue-tied by inadequate common language.

Well, there was a way to get around that——

"Sarloo, I want to see pictures of what happens inside," Lazarus persisted, pointing. "You have pictures?"

"Pictures are," Sarloo acknowledged, "in the temple. You must not enter the temple." His great eyes looked mournfully at Lazarus, giving him a strong feeling that the Jockaira chief grieved over his friend's lack of grace. Lazarus hastily dropped the subject.

But the thought of Venerians brought another puzzler to mind. The water people, cut off from the outside world by the eternal clouds of Venus, simply did not believe in astronomy. The arrival of Earthmen had caused them to readjust their concept of the cosmos a little, but there was reason to believe that their revised explanation was no closer to the truth. Lazarus wondered what the Jackaira thought about visitors from space. They had shown no surprise—or had they?

"Sarloo," he asked, "do you know where my brothers and I come from?"

"I know," Sarloo answered. "You come from a distant sun —so distant that many seasons would come and go while light traveled that long journey."

Lazarus felt mildly astonished. "Who told you that?"

"The gods tell us. Your brother Libby spoke on it."

Lazarus was willing to lay odds that the gods had not got around to mentioning it until after Libby explained it to Kreel Sarloo. But he held his peace. He still wanted to ask Sarloo if he had been surprised to have visitors arrive from the skies but he could think of no Jockairan term for surprise or wonder. He was still trying to phrase the question when Sarloo spoke again:

"The fathers of my people flew through the skies as you did, but that was before the coming of the gods. The gods, in their wisdom, bade us stop."

And that, thought Lazarus, is one damn' big lie, from pure swank. There was not the slightest indication that the Jockaira had ever been off the surface of their planet.

At Sarloo's home that evening Lazarus sat through a long session of what he assumed was entertainment for the guest of honor, himself. He squatted beside Sarloo on a raised portion of the floor of the vast common room of the clan Kreel and listened to two hours of howling that might have been intended as singing. Lazarus felt that better music would result from stepping on the tails of fifty assorted dogs but he tried to take it in the spirit in which it seemed to be offered.

Libby, Lazarus recalled, insisted that this mass howling which the Jockaira were wont to indulge in was, in fact,

music, and that men could learn to enjoy it by studying its interval relationships.

Lazarus doubted it.

But he had to admit that Libby understood the Jockaira
better than he did in some ways. Libby had been delighted to
discover that the Jockaira were excellent and subtle mathematicians. In particular they had a grasp of number that paralleled his own wild talent. Their arithmetics were incredibly
involved for normal humans. A number, any number large or
small, was to them a unique entity, to be grasped in itself and
not merely as a grouping of smaller numbers. In consequence
they used any convenient positional or exponential notation
with any base, rational, irrational, or variable—or none at all.

It was supreme luck, Lazarus mused, that Libby was available to act as mathematical interpreter between the Jockaira
and the Families, else it would have been impossible to grasp
a lot of the new technologies the Jockaira were showing
them.

He wondered why the Jockaira showed no interest in learning human technologies they were offered in return?

The howling discords died away and Lazarus brought his
thoughts back to the scene around him. Food was brought in;
the Kreel family tackled it with the same jostling enthusiasm
with which Jockaira did everything. Dignity, thought Lazarus,
is an idea which never caught on here. A large bowl, fully
two feet across and brimful of an amorphous mess, was
placed in front of Kreel Sarloo. A dozen Kreels crowded
around it and started grabbing, giving no precedence to their
senior. But Sarloo casually slapped a few of them out of the
way and plunged a hand into the dish, brought forth a gob of
the ration and rapidly kneaded it into a ball in the palm of his
double-thumbed hand. Done, he shoved it towards Lazarus'
mouth.

Lazarus was not squeamish but he had to remind himself,
first, that food for Jockaira was food for men, and second,
that he could not catch anything from them anyhow, before
he could bring himself to try the proffered morsel.

He took a large bite. Mmmm . . . not too bad—rather
bland and sticky, no particular flavor. Not good, either, but it
could be swallowed. Grimly determined to uphold the honor
of his race, he ate on, while promising himself a proper meal
in the near future. When he felt that to swallow another
mouthful would be to invite physical and social disaster, he

thought of a possible way out. Reaching into the common plate he scooped up a large handful of the stuff, molded it into a ball and offered it to Sarloo.

It was inspired diplomacy. For the rest of the meal Lazarus fed Sarloo, fed him until his arms were tired, until he marveled at his host's ability to tuck it away.

After eating they slept and Lazarus slept with the family, literally. They slept where they had eaten, without beds and disposed as casually as leaves on a path or puppies in a pen. To his surprise, Lazarus slept well and did not wake until false suns in the cavern roof glowed in mysterious sympathy to new dawn. Sarloo was still asleep near him and giving out most humanlike snores. Lazarus found that one infant Jockaira was cuddled spoon fashion against his own stomach.

He felt a movement behind his back, a rustle at his thigh. He turned cautiously and found that another Jockaira—a six-year-old in human equivalence—had extracted his blaster from its holster and was now gazing curiously into its muzzle.

With hasty caution Lazarus removed the deadly toy from the child's unwilling fingers, noted with relief that the safety was still on, and reholstered it. Lazarus received a reproachful look; the kid seemed about to cry. "Hush," whispered Lazarus, "you'll wake your old man. Here——" He gathered the child into his left arm and cradled it against his side. The little Jockaira snuggled up to him, laid a soft moist mouth against his hide, and promptly went to sleep.

Lazarus looked down at him. "You're a cute little devil," he said softly. "I could grow right fond of you if I could ever get used to your smell."

Some of the incidents between the two races would have been funny had they not been charged with potential trouble: for example, the case of Eleanor Johnson's son Hubert. This gangling adolescent was a confirmed sidewalk superintendent. One day he was watching two technicians, one human and one Jockaira, adapt a Jockaira power source to the needs of Earth-type machinery. The Jockaira was apparently amused by the boy and, in an obviously friendly spirit, picked him up.

Hubert began to scream.

His mother, never far from him, joined battle. She lacked strength and skill to do the utter destruction she was bent on; the big nonhuman was unhurt, but it created a nasty situation.

Administrator Ford and Oliver Johnson tried very hard to explain the incident to the amazed Jockaira. Fortunately, they seemed grieved rather than vengeful.

Ford then called in Eleanor Johnson. "You have endangered the entire colony by your stupidity——"

"But I——"

"Keep *quiet!* If you hadn't spoiled the boy rotten, he would have behaved himself. If you weren't a maudlin fool, you would have kept your hands to yourself. The boy goes to the regular development classes henceforth and you are to let him alone. At the slightest sign of animosity on your part toward any of the natives, I'll have you subjected to a few years' cold-rest. Now get out!"

Ford was forced to use almost as strong measures on Janice Schmidt. The interest shown in Hans Weatheral by the Jockaira extended to all the telepathic defectives. The natives seemed to be reduced to a state of quivering adoration by the mere fact that these could communicate with them directly. Kreel Sarloo informed Ford that he wanted the sensitives to be housed separately from the other defectives in the evacuated temple of the Earthmen's city and that the Jockaira wished to wait on them personally. It was more of an order than a request.

Janice Schmidt submitted ungracefully to Ford's insistence that the Jockaira be humored in the matter in return for all that they had done, and Jockaira nurses took over under her jealous eyes.

Every sensitive of intelligence level higher than the semi-moronic Hans Weatheral promptly developed spontaneous and extreme psychoses while being attended by Jockaira.

So Ford had another headache to straighten out. Janice Schmidt was more powerfully and more intelligently vindictive than was Eleanor Johnson. Ford was forced to bind Janice over to keep the peace under the threat of retiring her completely from the care of her beloved "children." Kreel Sarloo, distressed and apparently shaken to his core, accepted a compromise whereby Janice and her junior nurses resumed care of the poor psychotics while Jockaira continued to minister to sensitives of moron level and below.

But the greatest difficulty arose over . . . surnames.

Jockaira each had an individual name and a surname. Surnames were limited in number, much as they were in the

Families. A native's surname referred equally to his tribe and to the temple in which he worshipped.

Kreel Sarloo took up the matter with Ford. "High Father of the Strange Brothers," he said, "the time has come for you and your children to choose your surnames." (The rendition of Sarloo's speech into English necessarily contains inherent errors.)

Ford was used to difficulties in understanding the Jockaira. "Sarloo, brother and friend," he answered, "I hear your words but I do not understand. Speak more fully."

Sarloo began over. "Strange brother, the seasons come and the seasons go and there is a time of ripening. The gods tell us that you, the Strange Brothers, have reached the time in your education (?) when you must select your tribe and your temple. I have come to arrange with you the preparations (ceremonies?) by which each will choose his surname. I speak for the gods in this. But let me say for myself that it would make me happy if you, my brother Ford, were to choose the temple Kreel."

Ford stalled while he tried to understand what was implied. "I am happy that you wish me to have your surname. But my people already have their own surnames."

Sarloo dismissed that with a flip of his lips. "Their present surnames are words and nothing more. Now they must choose their real surnames, each the name of his temple and of the god whom he will worship. Children grow up and are no longer children."

Ford decided that he needed advice. "Must this be done at once?"

"Not today, but in the near future. The gods are patient."

Ford called in Zaccur Barstow, Oliver Johnson, Lazarus Long, and Ralph Schultz, and described the interview. Johnson played back the recording of the conversation and strained to catch the sense of the words. He prepared several possible translations but failed to throw any new light on the matter.

"It looks," said Lazarus, "like a case of join the church or get out."

"Yes," agreed Zaccur Barstow, "that much seems to come through plainly. Well, I think we can afford to go through the motions. Very few of our people have religious prejudices strong enough to forbid their paying lip service to the native gods in the interests of the general welfare."

"I imagine you are correct," Ford said. "I, for one, have no objection to adding Kreel to my name and taking part in their genuflections if it will help us to live in peace." He frowned. "But I would not want to see our culture submerged in theirs."

"You can forget that," Ralph Schultz assured him. "No matter what we have to do to please them, there is absolutely no chance of any real cultural assimilation. Our brains are not like theirs—just how different I am only beginning to guess."

"Yeah," said Lazarus, " 'just how different.' "

Ford turned to Lazarus. "What do you mean by that? What's troubling you?"

"Nothing. Only," he added, "I never did share the general enthusiasm for this place."

They agreed that one man should take the plunge first, then report back. Lazarus tried to grab the assignment on seniority, Schultz claimed it as a professional right; Ford overruled them and appointed himself, asserting that it was his duty as the responsible executive.

Lazarus went with him to the doors of the temple where the induction was to take place. Ford was as bare of clothing as the Jockaira, but Lazarus, since he was not to enter the temple, was able to wear his kilt. Many of the colonists, sunstarved after years in the ship, went bare when it suited them, just as the Jockaira did. But Lazarus never did. Not only did his habits run counter to it, but a blaster is an extremely conspicuous object on a bare thigh.

Kreel Sarloo greeted them and escorted Ford inside. Lazarus called out after them, "Keep your chin up, pal!"

He waited. He struck a cigarette and smoked it. He walked up and down. He had no way to judge how long it would be; it seemed, in consequence, much longer than it was.

At last the doors slid back and natives crowded out through them. They seemed curiously worked up about something and none of them came near Lazarus. The press that still existed in the great doorway separated, formed an aisle, and a figure came running headlong through it and out into the open.

Lazarus recognized Ford.

Ford did not stop where Lazarus waited but plunged blindly on past. He tripped and fell down. Lazarus hurried to him.

Ford made no effort to get up. He lay sprawled face down,

his shoulders heaving violently, his frame shaking with sobs.

Lazarus knelt by him and shook him. "Slayton," he demanded, "what's happened? What's wrong with you?" Ford turned wet and horror-stricken eyes to him, checking his sobs momentarily. He did not speak but he seemed to recognize Lazarus. He flung himself on Lazarus, clung to him, wept more violently than before.

Lazarus wrenched himself free and slapped Ford hard. "Snap out of it!" he ordered. "Tell me what's the matter."

Ford jerked his head at the slap and stopped his outcries but he said nothing. His eyes looked dazed. A shadow fell across Lazarus' line of sight; he spun around, covering with his blaster. Kreel Sarloo stood a few feet away and did not come closer—not because of the weapon; he had never seen one before.

"You!" said Lazarus. "For the—— What did you do to him?"

He checked himself and switched to speech that Sarloo could understand. "What has happened to my brother Ford?"

"Take him away," said Sarloo, his lips twitching. "This is a bad thing. This is a very bad thing."

"You're telling me!" said Lazarus. He did not bother to translate.

3

THE SAME CONFERENCE as before, minus its chairman, met as quickly as possible. Lazarus told his story, Shultz reported on Ford's condition. "The medical staff can't find anything wrong with him. All I can say with certainty is that the Administrator is suffering from an undiagnosed extreme psychosis. We can't get into communication with him."

"Won't he talk at all?" asked Barstow.

"A word or two, on subjects as simple as food or water. Any attempt to reach the cause of his trouble drives him into incoherent hysteria."

"No diagnosis?"

"Well, if you want an unprofessional guess in loose language, I'd say he was scared out of his wits. But," Schultz added, "I've seen fear syndromes before. Never anything like this."

"I have," Lazarus said suddenly.

"You have? Where? What were the circumstances?"

"Once," said Lazarus, "when I was a kid, a couple of hundred years back, I caught a grown coyote and penned him up. I had a notion I could train him to be a hunting dog. It didn't work.

"Ford acts just the way that coyote did."

An unpleasant silence followed. Schultz broke it with, "I don't quite see what you mean. What is the parallel?"

"Well," Lazarus answered slowly, "this is just my guess. Slayton is the only one who knows the true answer and he can't talk. But here's my opinion: we've had these Jockaira doped out all wrong from scratch. We made the mistake of thinking that because they looked like us, in a general way, and were about as civilized as we are, that they were *people*. But they aren't people at all. They are . . . *domestic animals*.

"Wait a minute now!" he added. "Don't get in a rush. There are people on this planet, right enough. Real people. They lived in the temples and the Jockaira called them gods. They *are* gods!"

Lazarus pushed on before anyone could interrupt. "I know what you're thinking. Forget it. I'm not going metaphysical on you; I'm just putting it the best I can. I mean that there is something living in those temples and whatever it is, it is such heap big medicine that it can pinch-hit for gods, so you might as well call 'em that. Whatever they are, they are the true dominant race on this planet—its *people!* To them, the rest of us, Jocks or us, are just animals, wild or tame. We made the mistake of assuming that a local religion was merely superstition. It ain't."

Barstow said slowly, "And you think this accounts for what happened to Ford?"

"I do. He met one, the one called Kreel, and it drove him crazy."

"I take it," said Schultz, "that it is your theory that any man exposed to this . . . this *presence* . . . would become psychotic?"

"Not exactly," answered Lazarus. "What scares me a damn' sight more is the fear that I might *not* go crazy!"

That same day the Jockaira withdrew all contact with the Earthmen. It was well that they did so, else there would have been violence. Fear hung over the city, fear of horror worse than death, fear of some terrible nameless thing, the mere knowledge of which would turn a man into a broken mindless animal. The Jockaira no longer seemed harmless friends, rather clownish despite their scientific attainments, but puppets, decoys, bait for the unseen potent beings who lurked in the "temples."

There was no need to vote on it; with the single-mindedness of a crowd stampeding from a burning building the Earthmen wanted to leave this terrible place. Zaccur Barstow assumed command. "Get King on the screen. Tell him to send down every boat at once. We'll get out of here as fast as we can." He ran his fingers worriedly through his hair. "What's the most we can load each trip, Lazarus? How long will the evacuation take?"

Lazarus muttered.

"What did you say?"

"I said, 'It ain't a case of how long; it's a case of will we be let.' Those things in the temples may want more domestic animals—us!"

Lazarus was needed as a boat pilot but he was needed more urgently for his ability to manage a crowd. Zaccur Barstow was telling him to conscript a group of emergency police when Lazarus looked past Zaccur's shoulder and exclaimed, "Oh oh! Hold it, Zack—school's out."

Zaccur turned his head quickly and saw, approaching with stately dignity across the council hall, Kreel Sarloo. No one got in his way.

They soon found out why. Zaccur moved forward to greet him, found himself stopped about ten feet from the Jockaira. No clue to the cause; just that—stopped.

"I greet you, unhappy brother," Sarloo began.

"I greet you, Kreel Sarloo."

"The gods have spoken. Your kind can never be civilized (?). You and your brothers are to leave this world."

Lazarus let out a deep sigh of relief.

"We are leaving, Kreel Sarloo," Zaccur answered soberly.

"The gods require that you leave. Send your bother Libby to me."

Zaccur sent for Libby, then turned back to Sarloo. But the

Jockaira had nothing more to say to them; he seemed indifferent to their presence. They waited.

Libby arrived. Sarloo held him in a long conversation. Barstow and Lazarus were both in easy earshot and could see their lips move, but heard nothing. Lazarus found the circumstance very disquieting. Damn my eyes, he thought, I could figure several ways to pull that trick with the right equipment but I'll bet none of 'em is the right answer—and I don't see any equipment.

The silent discussion ended, Sarloo stalked off without farewell. Libby turned to the others and spoke; now his voice could be heard. "Sarloo tells me," he began, brow wrinkled in puzzlement, "that we are to go to a planet, uh, over thirty-two light-years from here. The gods have decided it." He stopped and bit his lip.

"Don't fret about it," advised Lazarus. "Just be glad they want us to leave. My guess is that they could have squashed us flat just as easily. Once we're out in space we'll pick our own destination."

"I suppose so. But the thing that puzzles me is that he mentioned a time about three hours away as being our departure from this system."

"Why, that's utterly unreasonable," protested Barstow. "Impossible. We haven't the boats to do it."

Lazarus said nothing. He was ceasing to have opinions.

Zaccur changed his opinion quickly. Lazarus acquired one, born of experience. While urging his cousins toward the field where embarkation was proceeding, he found himself lifted up, free of the ground. He struggled, his arms and legs met no resistance but the ground dropped away. He closed his eyes, counted ten jets, opened them again. He was at least two miles in the air.

Below him, boiling up from the city like bats from a cave, were uncountable numbers of dots and shapes, dark against the sunlit ground. Some were close enough for him to see that they were men, Earthmen, the Families.

The horizon dipped down, the planet became a sphere, the sky turned black. Yet his breathing seemed normal, his blood vessels did not burst.

They were sucked into clusters around the open ports of the *New Frontiers* like bees swarming around a queen. Once inside the ship Lazarus gave himself over to a case of the shakes. *Whew!* he sighed to himself, watch that first step—it's a honey!

Libby sought out Captain King as soon as he was inboard and had recovered his nerve. He delivered Sarloo's message.

King seemed undecided. "I don't know," he said. "You know more about the natives than I do, inasmuch as I have hardly put foot to ground. But between ourselves, Mister, the way they sent my passengers back has me talking to myself. That was the most remarkable evolution I have ever seen performed."

"I might add that it was remarkable to experience, sir," Libby answered unhumorously. "Personally I would prefer to take up ski jumping. I'm glad you had the ship's access ports open."

"I didn't," said King tersely. "They were opened for me."

They went to the control room with the intention of getting the ship under boost and placing a long distance between it and the planet from which they had been evicted; thereafter they would consider destination and course. "This planet that Sarloo described to you," said King, "does it belong to a G-type star?"

"Yes," Libby confirmed, "an Earth-type planet accompanying a Sol-type star. I have its coördinates and could identify from the catalogues. But we can forget it; it is too far away."

"So . . ." King activated the vision system for the stellarium. Then neither of them said anything for several long moments. The images of the heavenly bodies told their own story.

With no orders from King, with no hands at the controls, the *New Frontiers* was on her long way again, headed out, as if she had a mind of her own.

"I can't tell you much," admitted Libby some hours later to a group consisting of King, Zaccur Barstow, and Lazarus Long. "I was able to determine, before we passed the speed of light—or appeared to—that our course then was compatible with the idea that we have been headed toward the star named by Kreel Sarloo as the destination ordered for us by his gods. We continued to accelerate and the stars faded out. I no longer have any astrogational reference points and I am unable to say where we are or where we are going."

"Loosen up, Andy," suggested Lazarus. "Make a guess."

"Well . . . if our world line is a smooth function—*if* it is, and I have no data—then we may arrive in the neighborhood of star PK3722, where Kreel Sarloo said we were going."

"Rummph!" Lazarus turned to King. "Have you tried slowing down?"

"Yes," King said shortly. "The controls are dead."

"Mmmm . . . Andy, when do we get there?"

Libby shrugged helplessly. "I have no frame of reference. What is time without a space reference?"

Time and space, inseparable and one—— Libby thought about it long after the others had left. To be sure, he had the space framework of the ship itself and therefore there necessarily was ship's time. Clocks in the ship ticked or hummed or simply marched; people grew hungry, fed themselves, got tired, rested. Radioactives deteriorated, physio-chemical processes moved toward states of greater entropy, his own consciousness perceived duration.

But the background of the stars, against which every timed function in the history of man had been measured, was gone. So far as his eyes or any instrument in the ship could tell him, they had become unrelated to the rest of the universe.

What universe?

There was no universe. It was gone.

Did they move? Can there be motion when there is nothing to move past?

Yet the false weight achieved by the spin of the ship persisted. Spin with reference to *what?* thought Libby. Could it be that space held a true, absolute, nonrelational texture of its own, like that postulated for the long-discarded "ether" that the classic Michelson-Morley experiments had failed to detect? No, more than that—had denied the very possibility of its existence?

—had for that matter denied the possibility of speed greater than light. Had the ship actually passed the speed of light? Was it not more likely that this was a coffin, with ghosts as passengers, going nowhere at no time?

But Libby itched between his shoulder blades and was forced to scratch; his left leg had gone to sleep; his stomach was beginning to speak insistently for food—if this was death, he decided, it did not seem materially different from life.

With renewed tranquility, he left the control room and headed for his favorite refectory, while starting to grapple with the problem of inventing a new mathematics which would include all the new phenomena. The mystery of how the hypothetical gods of the Jockaira had teleported the Families from ground to ship he discarded. There had been no opportunity to obtain significant data, *measured* data; the best that any honest scientist could do, with epistemological rigor, was to include a note that recorded the fact and stated that it was unexplained. It *was* a fact; here he was who shortly before had been on the planet; even now Schultz's assistants were overworked trying to administer depressant drugs to the thousands who had gone to pieces emotionally under the outrageous experience.

But Libby could not explain it and, lacking data, felt no urge to try. What he did want to do was to deal with world lines in a plenum, the basic problem of field physics.

Aside from his penchant for mathematics Libby was a simple person. He preferred the noisy atmosphere of the "Club," refectory 9-D, for reasons different from those of Lazarus. The company of people younger than himself reassured him; Lazarus was the only elder he felt easy with.

Food, he learned, was not immediately available at the Club; the commissary was still adjusting to the sudden change. But Lazarus was there and others whom he knew; Nancy Weatheral scrunched over and made room for him. "You're just the man I want to see," she said. "Lazarus is being most helpful. Where are we going this time and when do we get there?"

Libby explained the dilemma as well as he could. Nancy wrinkled her nose. "That's a pretty prospect, I must say! Well, I guess that means back to the grind for little Nancy."

"What do you mean?"

"Have you ever taken care of a somnolent? No, of course you haven't. It gets tiresome. Turn them over, bend their arms, twiddle their tootsies, move their heads, close the tank and move on to the next one. I get so sick of human bodies that I'm tempted to take a vow of chastity."

"Don't commit yourself too far," advised Lazarus.

"Why would you care, you old false alarm?"

Eleanor Johnson spoke up. "I'm *glad* to be in the ship again. Those slimy Jockaira—ugh!"

Nancy shrugged. "You're prejudiced, Eleanor. The Jocks are okay, in their way. Sure, they aren't exactly like us, but neither are dogs. You don't dislike dogs, do you?"

"That's what they are," Lazarus said soberly. "Dogs."

"Huh?"

"I don't mean that they are anything like dogs in most ways—they aren't even vaguely canine and they certainly are our equals and possibly our superiors in some things . . . but they are dogs just the same. Those things they call their 'gods' are simply their masters, their owners. We couldn't be domesticated, so the owners chucked us out."

Libby was thinking of the inexplicable telekinesis the Jockaira—or their masters—had used. "I wonder what it would have been like," he said thoughtfully, "if they had been able to domesticate us. They could have taught us a lot of wonderful things."

"Forget it," Lazarus said sharply. "It's not a man's place to be property."

"What is a man's place?"

"It's a man's business to be what he is . . . and be it in style!" Lazarus got up. "Got to go."

Libby started to leave also, but Nancy stopped him. "Don't go. I want to ask you some questions. What year is it back on Earth?"

Libby started to answer, closed his mouth. He started to answer a second time, finally said, "I don't know how to answer that question. It's like saying, 'How high is up?' "

"I know I probably phrased it wrong," admitted Nancy. "I didn't do very well in basic physics, but I did gather the idea that time is relative and simultaneity is an idea which applies only to two points close together in the same framework. But just the same, I want to know something. We've traveled a lot faster and farther than anyone ever did before, haven't we? Don't our clocks slow down, or something?"

Libby got that completely baffled look which mathematical physicists wear whenever laymen try to talk about physics in nonmathematical language. "You're referring to the Lorentz-FitzGerald contraction. But, if you'll pardon me, anything one says about it in words is necessarily nonsense."

"Why?" she insisted.

"Because . . . well, because the language is inappropriate. The formulae used to describe the effect loosely called a contraction presuppose that the observer is part of the phenomenon. But verbal language contains the implicit assumption that we can stand outside the whole business and watch what goes on. The mathematical language denies the very possibility of any such outside viewpoint. Every observer has his own world line; he can't get outside it for a detached viewpoint."

"But suppose he did? Suppose we could see Earth right now?"

"There I go again," Libby said miserably. "I tried to talk about it in words and all I did was to add to the confusion. There is no way to measure time in any absolute sense when two events are separated in a continuum. All you can measure is interval."

"Well, what is interval? So much space and so much time."

"No, no, no! It isn't that at all. Interval is . . . well, it's interval. I can write down formulae about it and show you how we use it, but it can't be defined in words. Look, Nancy, can you write the score for a full orchestration of a symphony in words?"

"No. Well, maybe you could but it would take thousands of times as long."

"And musicians still could not play it until you put it back into musical notation. That's what I meant," Libby went on, "when I said that the language was inappropriate. I got into a difficulty like this once before in trying to describe the light-pressure drive. I was asked why, since the drive depends on loss of inertia, we people inside the ship had felt no loss of inertia. There was no answer, in words. Inertia isn't a word; it is a mathematical concept used in *mathematically* certain aspects of a plenum. I was stuck."

Nancy looked baffled but persisted doggedly. "My question still means something, even if I didn't phrase it right. You can't just tell me to run along and play. Suppose we turned around and went back the way we came, all the way to Earth, exactly the same trip but in reverse—just double the ship's time it has been so far. All right, what year would it be on Earth when we got there?"

"It would be . . . let me see, now——" The almost automatic processes of Libby's brain started running off the unbelievably huge and complex problem in accelerations, intervals, difform motion. He was approaching the answer in a warm glow of mathematical revery when the problem suddenly fell to pieces on him, became indeterminate. He abruptly realized that the problem had an unlimited number of equally valid answers.

But that was impossible. In the real world, not the fantasy world of mathematics, such a situation was absurd. Nancy's question had to have just one answer, unique and real.

Could the whole beautiful structure of relativity be an absurdity? Or did it mean that it was physically impossible ever to back-track an interstellar distance?

"I'll have to give some thought to that one," Libby said hastily and left before Nancy could object.

But solitude and contemplation gave him no clue to the problem. It was not a failure of his mathematical ability; he was capable, he knew, of devising a mathematical description of any group of facts, whatever they might be. His difficulty lay in having too few facts. Until some observer traversed interstellar distances at speeds approximating the speed of light *and returned to the planet from which he had started* there could be no answer. Mathematics alone has no content, gives no answers.

Libby found himself wondering if the hills of his native Ozarks were still green, if the smell of wood smoke still clung to the trees in the autumn, then he recalled that the question lacked any meaning by any rules he knew of. He surrendered to an attack of homesickness such as he had not experienced since he was a youth in the Cosmic Construction Corps, making his first deep-space jump.

This feeling of doubt and uncertainty, the feeling of lostness and nostalgia, spread throughout the ship. On the first leg of their journey the Families had had the incentive that had kept the covered wagons crawling across the plains. But now they were going nowhere, one day led only to the next. Their long lives were become a meaningless burden.

Ira Howard, whose fortune established the Howard Foundation, was born in 1825 and died in 1873—of old age. He sold groceries to the Forty-niners in San Francisco, became a wholesale sutler in the American War of the Secession, multiplied his fortune during the tragic Reconstruction.

Howard was deathly afraid of dying. He hired the best doctors of his time to prolong his life. Nevertheless old age plucked him when most men are still young. But his will commanded that his money be used "to lengthen human life." The administrators of the trust found no way to carry out his wishes other than by seeking out persons whose family trees showed congenital predispositions toward long life and then inducing them to reproduce in kind. Their method anticipated the work of Burbank; they may or may not have known of the illuminating researches of the Monk Gregor Mendel.

Mary Sperling put down the book she had been reading when Lazarus entered her stateeoom. He picked it up. "What are you reading, Sis? 'Ecclesiastes.' Hmm . . . I didn't know you were religious." He read aloud:

" 'Yea, though he live a thousand years twice told, yet hath he seen no good: do not all go to one place?'

"Pretty grim stuff, Mary. Can't you find something more cheerful? Even in The Preacher?" His eyes skipped on down. "How about this one? 'For to him that is joined to all the living there is hope——' Or . . . mmmm, not too many cheerful spots. Try this: 'Therefore remove sorrow from thy heart, and put away evil from thy flesh: for childhood and youth are vanity.' That's more my style; I wouldn't be young again for overtime wages."

"I would."

"Mary, what's eating you? I find you sitting here, reading the most depressing book in the Bible, nothing but death and funerals. Why?"

She passed a hand wearily across her eyes. "Lazarus, I'm getting old. What else is there to think about?"

"You? Why, you're fresh as a daisy!"

She looked at him. She knew that he lied; her mirror showed her the greying hair, the relaxed skin; she felt it in her bones. Yet Lazarus was older than she . . . although she knew, from what she had learned of biology during the years she had assisted in the longevity research, that Lazarus should never have lived to be as old as he was now. When he was born the program had reached only the third generation, too few generations to eliminate the less durable strains—except through some wildly unlikely chance shuffling of genes.

But there he stood. "Lazarus," she asked, "how long do you expect to live?"

"Me? Now that's an odd question. I mind a time when I asked a chap that very same question—about me, I mean, not about him. Ever hear of Dr. Hugo Pinero?"

" 'Pinero . . . Pinero . . .' Oh, yes, 'Pinero the Charlatan.' "

"Mary, he was no charlatan. He could do it, no foolin'. He could predict accurately when a man would die."

"But—— Go ahead. What did he tell you?"

"Just a minute. I want you to realize that he was no fake. His predictions checked out right on the button—if he hadn't died, the life insurance companies would have been ruined.

That was before you were born, but I was there and I know. Anyhow, Pinero took my reading and it seemed to bother him. So he took it again. Then he returned my money."

"What did he say?"

"Couldn't get a word out of him. He looked at me and he looked at his machine and he just frowned and clammed up. So I can't rightly answer your question."

"But what do *you* think about it, Lazarus? Surely you don't expect just to go on forever?"

"Mary," he said softly, "I'm not planning on dying. I'm not giving it any thought at all."

There was silence. At last she said, "Lazarus, I don't want to die. But what is the purpose of our long lives? We don't seem to grow wiser as we grow older. Are we simply hanging on after our time has passed? Loitering in the kindergarten when we should be moving on? Must we die and be born again?"

"I don't know," said Lazarus, "and I don't have any way to find out . . . and I'm damned if I see any sense in my worrying about it. Or you either. I propose to hang onto this life as long as I can and learn as much as I can. Maybe wisdom and understanding are reserved for a later existence and maybe they aren't for us at all, ever. Either way, I'm satisfied to be living and enjoying it. Mary my sweet, carpe that old diem!—it's the only game in town."

The ship slipped back into the same monotonous routine that had obtained during the weary years of the first jump. Most of the Members went into cold-rest; the others tended them, tended the ship, tended the hydroponds. Among the somnolents was Slayton Ford; cold-rest was a common last-resort therapy for functional psychoses.

The flight to star PK3722 took seventeen months and three days, ship's time.

The ship's officers had as little choice about the journey's end as about its beginning. A few hours before their arrival star images flashed back into being in the stellarium screens and the ship rapidly decelerated to interplanetary speeds. No feeling of slowing down was experienced; whatever mysterious forces were acting on them acted on all masses alike. The *New Frontiers* slipped into an orbit around a live green planet some hundred million miles from its sun; shortly Libby reported to Captain King that they were in a stable parking orbit.

Cautiously King tried the controls, dead since their departure. The ship surged; their ghostly pilot had left them.

Libby decided that the simile was incorrect; this trip had undoubtedly been planned for them but it was not necessary to assume that anyone or anything had shepherded them here. Libby suspected that the "gods" of the dog-people saw the plenum as static; their deportation was an accomplished fact to them before it happened—a concept regrettably studded with unknowns—but there were no appropriate words. Inadequately and incorrectly put into words, his concept was that of a "cosmic cam," a world line shaped for them which ran out of normal space and back into it; when the ship reached the end of its "cam" it returned to normal operation.

He tried to explain his concept to Lazarus and to the Captain, but he did not do well. He lacked data and also had not had time to refine his mathematical description into elegance; it satisfied neither him nor them.

Neither King nor Lazarus had time to give the matter much thought. Barstow's face appeared on an interstation viewscreen. "Captain!" he called out. "Can you come aft to lock seven? We have visitors!"

Barstow had exaggerated; there was only one. The creature reminded Lazarus of a child in fancy dress, masqueraded as a rabbit. The little thing was more android than were the Jockaira, though possibly not mammalian. It was unclothed but not naked, for its childlike body was beautifully clothed in short sleek golden fur. Its eyes were bright and seemed both merry and intelligent.

But King was too bemused to note such detail. A voice, a thought, was ringing in his head: ". . . so you are the group leader . . ." it said. ". . . welcome to our world . . . we have been expecting you . . . the (*blank*) told us of your coming . . ."

Controlled telepathy——

A creature, a race, so gentle, so civilized, so free from enemies, from all danger and strife that they could afford to share their thoughts with others—to share more than their thoughts; these creatures were so gentle and so generous that they were offering the humans a homestead on their planet. This was why this messenger had come: to make that offer.

To King's mind this seemed remarkably like the prize package that had been offered by the Jockaira; he wondered what the boobytrap might be in this proposition.

The messenger seemed to read his thought. ". . . look into our hearts . . . we hold no malice toward you . . . we share your love of life and we love the life in you . . ."

"We thank you," King answered formally and aloud. "We will have to confer." He turned to speak to Barstow, glanced back. The messenger was gone.

The Captain said to Lazarus, "Where did he go?"

"Huh? Don't ask me."

"But you were in front of the lock."

"I was checking the tell-tales. There's no boat sealed on outside this lock—so they show. I was wondering if they were working right. They are. How did he get into the ship? Where's his rig?"

"How did he *leave?*"

"Not past me!"

"Zaccur, he came in through this lock, didn't he?"

"I don't know."

"But he certainly went out through it."

"Nope," denied Lazarus. "This lock hasn't been opened. The deep-space seals are still in place. See for yourself."

King did. "You don't suppose," he said slowly, "that he can pass through——"

"Don't look at me," said Lazarus. "I've got no more prejudices in the matter than the Red Queen. Where does a phone image go when you cut the circuit?" He left, whistling softly to himself. King did not recognize the tune. Its words, which Lazarus did not sing, started with:

> *"Last night I saw upon the stair*
> *A little man who wasn't there——"*

4

THERE WAS NO CATCH to the offer. The people of the planet— they had no name since they had no spoken language and the Earthmen simply called them "The Little People"—the little creatures really did welcome them and help them. They convinced the Families of this without difficulty for there was no trouble in communication such as there had been with the Jockaira. The Little People could make even subtle thoughts known directly to the Earthmen and in turn could sense correctly any thought directed at them. They appeared either to ignore or not to be able to read any thought not directed at them; communication with them was as controlled as spoken speech. Nor did the Earthmen acquire any telepathic powers among themselves.

Their planet was even more like Earth than was the planet of the Jockaira. It was a little larger than Earth but had a slightly lower surface gravitation, suggesting a lower average density—the Little People made slight use of metals in their culture, which may be indicative.

The planet rode upright in its orbit; it had not the rakish tilt of Earth's axis. Its orbit was nearly circular; aphelion differed from perihelion by less than one per cent. There were no seasons.

Nor was there a great heavy moon, such as Earth has, to wrestle its oceans about and to disturb the isostatic balance of its crust. Its hills were low, its winds were gentle, its seas were placid. To Lazarus' disappointment, their new home had no lively weather; it hardly had weather at all; it had climate, and that of the sort that California patriots would have the rest of the Earth believe exists in their part of the globe.

But on the planet of the Little People it really exists.

They indicated to the Earth people where they were to land, a wide sandy stretch of beach running down to the sea. Back of the low break of the bank lay mile on mile of lush meadowland, broken by irregular clumps of bushes and trees. The landscape had a careless neatness, as if it were a planned park, although there was no evidence of cultivation.

It was here, a messenger told the first scouting party, that they were welcome to live.

There seemed always to be one of the Little People present when his help might be useful—not with the jostling inescapable overhelpfulness of the Jockaira, but with the unobtrusive readiness to hand of a phone or a pouch knife. The one who accompanied the first party of explorers confused Lazarus and Barstow by assuming casually that he had met them before, that he had visited them in the ship. Since his fur was rich mahogany rather than golden, Barstow attributed the error to misunderstanding, with a mental reservation that these people might possibly be capable of chameleonlike changes in color. Lazarus reserved his judgment.

Barstow asked their guide whether or not his people had any preferences as to where and how the Earthmen were to erect buildings. The question had been bothering him because a preliminary survey from the ship had disclosed no cities. It seemed likely that the natives lived underground—in which case he wanted to avoid getting off on the wrong foot by starting something which the local government might regard as a slum.

He spoke aloud in words directed at their guide, they having learned already that such was the best way to insure that the natives would pick up the thought.

In the answer that the little being flashed back Barstow caught the emotion of surprise. ". . . must you sully the sweet countryside with interruptions? . . . to what purpose do you need to form buildings? . . ."

"We need buildings for many purposes," Barstow explained. "We need them as daily shelter, as places to sleep at night. We need them to grow our food and prepare it for eating." He considered trying to explain the processes of hydroponic farming, of food processing, and of cooking, then dropped it, trusting to the subtle sense of telepathy to let his "listener" understand. "We need buildings for many other uses, for workshops and laboratories, to house the machines whereby we communicate, for almost everything we do in our everyday life."

". . . be patient with me . . ." the thought came, ". . . since I know so little of your ways . . . but tell me . . . do you prefer to sleep in such as *that?* . . ." He gestured toward the ship's boats they had come down in, where their bulges showed above the low bank. The thought he used for the boats was too strong to be bound by a word; to Lazarus' mind came a thought of a dead, constricted space—a jail that had once harbored him, a smelly public phone booth.

"It is our custom."

The creature leaned down and patted the turf. ". . . is this not a good place to sleep? . . ."

Lazarus admitted to himself that it was. The ground was covered with a soft spring turf, grasslike but finer than grass, softer, more even, and set more closely together. Lazarus took off his sandals and let his bare feet enjoy it, toes spread and working. It was, he decided, more like a heavy fur rug than a lawn.

". . . as for food . . ." their guide went on, ". . . why struggle for that which the good soil gives freely? . . . come with me . . ."

He took them across a reach of meadow to where low bushy trees hung over a meandering brook. The "leaves" were growths the size of a man's hand, irregular in shape, and an inch or more in thickness. The little person broke off one and nibbled at it daintily.

Lazarus plucked one and examined it. It broke easily, like a well-baked cake. The inside was creamy yellow, spongy but crisp, and had a strong pleasant odor, reminiscent of mangoes.

"Lazarus, don't eat that!" warned Barstow. "It hasn't been analyzed!"

". . . it is harmonious with your body . . ."

Lazarus sniffed it again. "I'm willing to be a test case, Zack."

"Oh, well——" Barstow shrugged. "I warned you. You will anyhow."

Lazarus did. The stuff was oddly pleasing, firm enough to suit the teeth, piquant though elusive in flavor. It settled down happily in his stomach and made itself at home.

Barstow refused to let anyone else try the fruit until its effect on Lazarus was established. Lazarus took advantage of his exposed and privileged position to make a full meal—the best, he decided, that he had had in years.

". . . will you tell me what you are in the habit of eating? . . ." inquired their little friend. Barstow started to reply but was checked by the creature's thought: ". . . all of you . . . think about it . . ." no further thought message came from him for a few moments, then he flashed, ". . . that is enough . . . my wives will take care of it . . ."

Lazarus was not sure the image meant "wives" but some similar close relationship was implied. It had not yet been established that the Little People were bisexual—or what.

Lazarus slept that night out under the stars and let their clean impersonal light rinse from him the claustrophobia of the ship. The constellations here were distorted out of easy recognition, although he could recognize, he decided, the cool blue of Vega and the orange glow of Antares. The one certainty was the Milky Way, spilling its cloudy arch across the sky just as at home. The Sun, he knew, could not be visible to the naked eye even if he knew where to look for it; its low absolute magnitude would not show up across the light-years. Have to get hold of Andy, he thought sleepily, work out its coördinates and pick it out with instruments. He fell asleep before it could occur to him to wonder why he should bother.

Since no shelter was needed at night they landed everyone as fast as boats could shuttle them down. The crowds were dumped on the friendly soil and allowed to rest, picnic fashion, until the colony could be organized. At first they ate supplies brought down from the ship, but Lazarus' continued good health caused the rule against taking chances with natural native foods to be relaxed shortly. After that they ate mostly of the boundless largesse of the plants and used ship's food only to vary their diets.

Several days after the last of them had been landed Lazarus was exploring alone some distance from the camp. He came across one of the Little People; the native greeted him with the same assumption of earlier acquaintance which all of them seemed to show and led Lazarus to a grove of low trees still farther from base. He indicated to Lazarus that he wanted him to eat.

Lazarus was not particularly hungry but he felt compelled to humor such friendliness, so he plucked and ate.

He almost choked in his astonishment. Mashed potatoes and brown gravy!

". . . didn't we get it right? . . ." came an anxious thought.

"Bub," Lazarus said solemnly, "I don't know what you planned to do, but this is just fine!"

A warm burst of pleasure invaded his mind. ". . . try the next tree . . ."

Lazarus did so, with cautious eagerness. Fresh brown bread and sweet butter seemed to be the combination, though a dash of ice cream seemed to have crept in from somewhere. He was hardly surprised when the third tree gave strong evidence of having both mushrooms and charcoal-broiled steak in its ancestry. ". . . we used your thought images almost entirely . . ." explained his companion. ". . . they were much stronger than those of any of your wives . . ."

Lazarus did not bother to explain that he was not married. The little person added, ". . . there has not yet been time to

simulate the appearances and colors your thoughts showed
. . . does it matter much to you? . . ."

Lazarus gravely assured him that it mattered very little.

When he returned to the base, he had considerable difficulty in convincing others of the seriousness of his report.

One who benefited greatly from the easy, lotus-land quality
of their new home was Slayton Ford. He had awakened from
cold rest apparently recovered from his breakdown except in
one respect: he had no recollection of whatever it was he had
experienced in the temple of Kreel. Ralph Schultz considered
this a healthy adjustment to an intolerable experience and dismissed him as a patient.

Ford seemed younger and happier than he had appeared
before his breakdown. He no longer held formal office
among the Members—indeed there was little government of
any sort; the Families lived in cheerful easy-going anarchy on
this favored planet—but he was still addressed by his title and
continued to be treated as an elder, one whose advice was
sought, whose judgment was deferred to, along with Zaccur
Barstow, Lazarus, Captain King, and others. The Families
paid little heed to calendar ages; close friends might differ by
a century. For years they had benefited from his skilled administration; now they continued to treat him as an elder
statesman, even though two-thirds of them were older than
was he.

The endless picnic stretched into weeks, into months. After
being long shut up in the ship, sleeping or working, the temp-
tation to take a long vacation was too strong to resist and
there was nothing to forbid it. Food in abundance, ready to
eat and easy to handle, grew almost everywhere; the water in
the numerous streams was clean and potable. As for clothing,
they had plenty if they wanted to dress but the need was esthetic rather than utilitarian; the Elysian climate made clothing for protection as silly as suits for swimming. Those who
liked clothes wore them; bracelets and beads and flowers in
the hair were quite enough for most of them and not nearly
so much nuisance if one chose to take a dip in the sea.

Lazarus stuck to his kilt.

The culture and degree of enlightenment of the Little People was difficult to understand all at once, because their ways
were subtle. Since they lacked outward signs, in Earth terms,
of high scientific attainment—no great buildings, no complex

mechanical transportation machines, no throbbing power plants—it was easy to mistake them for Mother Nature's children, living in a Garden of Eden.

Only one-eighth of an iceberg shows above water.

Their knowledge of physical science was not inferior to that of the colonists; it was incredibly superior. They toured the ship's boats with polite interest, but confounded their guides by inquiring why things were done *this* way rather than *that?*—and the way suggested invariably proved to be simpler and more efficient than Earth technique . . . when the astounded human technicians managed to understand what they were driving at.

The Little People understood machinery and all that machinery implies, but they simply had little use for it. They obviously did not need it for communication and had little need for it for transportation (although the full reason for that was not at once evident), and they had very little need for machinery in any of their activities. But when they had a specific need for a mechanical device they were quite capable of inventing, building it, using it once, and destroying it, performing the whole process with a smooth coöperation quite foreign to that of men.

But in biology their preëminence was the most startling. The Little People were masters in the manipulation of life forms. Developing plants in a matter of days which bore fruit duplicating not only in flavor but in nutrition values the foods humans were used to was not a miracle to them but a routine task any of their biotechnicians could handle. They did it more easily than an Earth horticulturist breeds for a certain strain of color or shape in a flower.

But their methods were different from those of any human plant breeder. Be it said for them that they did try to explain their methods, but the explanations simply did not come through. In our terms, they claimed to "think" a plant into the shape and character they desired. Whatever they meant by that, it is certainly true that they could take a dormant seedling plant and, without touching it or operating on it in any way perceptible to their human students, cause it to bloom and burgeon into maturity in the space of a few hours —with new characteristics not found in the parent line . . . and which bred true thereafter.

However the Little People differed from Earthmen only in

degree with respect to scientific attainments. In an utterly basic sense they differed from humans in kind.

They were not individuals.

No single body of a native housed a discrete individual. Their individuals were multi-bodied; they had group "souls." The basic unit of their society was a telepathic rapport group of many parts. The number of bodies and brains housing one individual ran as high as ninety or more and was never less than thirty-odd.

The colonists began to understand much that had been utterly puzzling about the Little People only after they learned this fact. There is much reason to believe that the Little People found the Earthmen equally puzzling, that they, too, had assumed that their pattern of existence must be mirrored in others. The eventual discovery of the true facts on each side, brought about mutual misunderstandings over identity, seemed to arouse horror in the minds of the Little People. They withdrew themselves from the neighborhood of the Families' settlement and remained away for several days.

At length a messenger entered the camp site and sought out Barstow. ". . . we are sorry we shunned you . . . in our haste we mistook your fortune for your fault . . . we wish to help you . . . we offer to teach you that you may become like ourselves . . ."

Barstow pondered how to answer this generous overture. "We thank you for your wish to help us," he said at last, "but what you call our misfortune seems to be a necessary part of our makeup. Our ways are not your ways. I do not think we could understand your ways."

The thought that came back to him was very troubled. ". . . we have aided the beasts of the air and of the ground to cease their strife . . . but if you do not wish our help we will not thrust it on you . . ."

The messenger went away, leaving Zaccur Barstow troubled in his mind. Perhaps, he thought, he had been hasty in answering without taking time to consult the elders. Telepathy was certainly not a gift to be scorned; perhaps the Little People could train them in telepathy without any loss of human individualism. But what he knew of the sensitives among the Families did not encourage such hope; there was not a one of them who was emotionally healthy, many of them were mentally deficient as well—it did not seem like a safe path for humans.

It could be discussed later, he decided; no need to hurry.

"No need to hurry" was the spirit throughout the settlement. There was no need to strive, little that had to be done and rarely any rush about that little. The sun was warm and pleasant, each day was much like the next, and there was always the day after that. The Members, predisposed by their inheritance to take a long view of things, began to take an eternal view. Time no longer mattered. Even the longevity research, which had continued throughout their memories, languished. Gordon Hardy tabled his current experimentation to pursue the vastly more fruitful occupation of learning what the Little People knew of the nature of life. He was forced to take it slowly, spending long hours in digesting new knowledge. As time trickled on, he was hardly aware that his hours of contemplation were becoming longer, his bursts of active study less frequent.

One thing he did learn, and its implications opened up whole new fields of thought: the Little People had, in one sense, conquered death.

Since each of their egos was shared among many bodies, the death of one body involved no death for the ego. All memory experiences of that body remained intact, the personality associated with it was not lost, and the physical loss could be made up by letting a young native "marry" into the group. But a group ego, one of the personalities which spoke to the Earthmen, could not die, save possibly by the destruction of every body it lived in. They simply went on, apparently forever.

Their young, up to the time of "marriage" or group assimilation, seemed to have little personality and only rudimentary or possibly instinctive mental processes. Their elders expected no more of them in the way of intelligent behavior than a human expects of a child still in the womb. There were always many such uncompleted persons attached to any ego group; they were cared for like dearly beloved pets or helpless babies, although they were often as large and as apparently mature to Earth eyes as were their elders.

Lazarus grew bored with paradise more quickly than did the majority of his cousins. "It can't always," he complained to Libby, who was lying near him on the fine grass, "be time for tea."

"What's fretting you, Lazarus?"

"Nothing in particular." Lazarus set the point of his knife on his right elbow, flipped it with his other hand, watched it bury its point in the ground. "It's just that this place reminds me of a well-run zoo. It's got about as much future." He grunted scornfully. "It's 'Never-Never Land.' "

"But what in particular is worrying you?"

"Nothing. That's what worries me. Honest to goodness, Andy, don't you see anything wrong in being turned out to pasture like this?"

Libby grinned sheepishly. "I guess it's my hillbilly blood. 'When it don't rain, the roof don't leak; when it rains, I cain't fix it nohow,' " he quoted. "Seems to me we're doing tolerably well. What irks you?"

"Well——" Lazarus' pale-blue eyes stared far away; he paused in his idle play with his knife. "When I was a young man a long time ago, I was beached in the South Seas——"

"Hawaii?"

"No. Farther south. Damned if I know what they call it today. I got hard up, mighty hard up, and sold my sextant. Pretty soon—or maybe quite a while—I could have passed for a native. I lived like one. It didn't seem to matter. But one day I caught a look at myself in a mirror." Lazarus sighed gustily. "I beat my way out of that place shipmate to a cargo of green hides, which may give you some idea how scared and desperate I was!"

Libby did not comment. "What do *you* do with your time, Lib?" Lazarus persisted.

"Me? Same as always. Think about mathematics. Try to figure out a dodge for a space drive like the one that got us here."

"Any luck on that?" Lazarus was suddenly alert.

"Not yet. Gimme time. Or I just watch the clouds integrate. There are amusing mathematical relationships everywhere if you are on the lookout for them. In the ripples on the water, or the shapes of busts—elegant fifth-order functions."

"Huh? You mean 'fourth order.' "

"Fifth order. You omitted the time variable. I like fifth-order equations," Libby said dreamily. "You find 'em in fish, too."

"Hummph!" said Lazarus, and stood up suddenly. "That may be all right for you, but it's not my pidgin."

"Going some place?"

"Goin' to take a walk."

Lazarus walked north. He walked the rest of that day, slept on the ground as usual that night, and was up and moving, still to the north, at dawn. The next day was followed by another like it, and still another. The going was easy, much like strolling in a park . . . too easy, in Lazarus' opinion. For the sight of a volcano, or a really worthwhile waterfall, he felt willing to pay four bits and throw in a jackknife.

The food plants were sometimes strange, but abundant and satisfactory. He occasionally met one or more of the Little People going about their mysterious affairs. They never bothered him nor asked why he was traveling but simply greeted him with the usual assumption of previous acquaintanceship. He began to long for one who would turn out to be a stranger; he felt watched.

Presently the nights grew colder, the days less balmy, and the Little People less numerous. When at last he had not seen one for an entire day, he camped for the night, remained there the next day—took out his soul and examined it.

He had to admit that he could find no reasonable fault with the planet nor its inhabitants. But just as definitely it was not to his taste. No philosophy that he had ever heard or read gave any reasonable purpose for man's existence, nor any rational clue to his proper conduct. Basking in the sunshine might be as good a thing to do with one's life as any other— but it was not for him and he knew it, even if he could not define how he knew it.

The hegira of the Families had been a mistake. It would have been a more human, a more mature and manly thing, to have stayed and fought for their rights, even if they had died insisting on them. Instead they had fled across half a universe (Lazarus was reckless about his magnitudes) looking for a place to light. They had found one, a good one—but already occupied by beings so superior as to make them intolerable for men . . . yet so supremely indifferent in their superiority to men that they had not even bothered to wipe them out, but had whisked them away to this—this over-manicured country club.

And that in itself was the unbearable humiliation. The *New Frontiers* was the culmination of five hundred years of human scientific research, the best that men could do—but it had been flicked across the deeps of space as casually as a man might restore a baby bird to its nest.

The Little People did not seem to want to kick them out but the Little People, in their own way, were as demoralizing to men as were the gods of the Jockaira. One at a time they might be morons but taken as groups each rapport group was a genius that threw the best minds that men could offer into the shade. Even Andy. Human beings could not hope to compete with that type of organization any more than a backroom shop could compete with an automated cybernated factory. Yet to form any such group identities, even if they could which he doubted, would be, Lazarus felt very sure, to give up whatever it was that made them *men.*

He admitted that he was prejudiced in favor of men. He *was* a man.

The uncounted days slid past while he argued with himself over the things that bothered him—problems that had made sad the soul of his breed since the first apeman had risen to self-awareness, questions never solved by full belly nor fine machinery. And the endless quiet days did no more to give him final answers than did all the soul searchings of his ancestors. Why? What shall it profit a man? No answer came back —save one: a firm unreasoned conviction that he was not intended for, or not ready for, this timeless snug harbor of ease.

His troubled reveries were interrupted by the appearance of one of the Little People. ". . . greetings, old friend . . . your wife King wishes you to return to your home . . . he has need of your advice . . ."

"What's the trouble?" Lazarus demanded.

But the little creature either could or would not tell him. Lazarus gave his belt a hitch and headed south. ". . . there is no need to go slowly . . ." a thought came after him.

Lazarus let himself be led to a clearing beyond a clump of trees. There he found an egg-shaped object about six feet long, featureless except for a door in the side. The native went in through the door, Lazarus squeezed his larger bulk in after him; the door closed.

It opened almost at once and Lazarus saw that they were on the beach just below the human settlement. He had to admit that it was a good trick.

Lazarus hurried to the ship's boat parked on the beach in which Captain King shared with Barstow a semblance of community headquarters. "You sent for me, Skipper. What's up?"

King's austere face was grave. "It's about Mary Sperling."

Lazarus felt a sudden cold tug at his heart. "Dead?"

"No. Not exactly. She's gone over to the Little People. 'Married' into one of their groups."

"*What?* But that's impossible!"

Lazarus was wrong. There was no faint possibility of inter-breeding between Earthmen and natives but there was no barrier, if sympathy existed, to a human merging into one of their rapport groups, drowning his personality in the ego of the many.

Mary Sperling, moved by conviction of her own impending death, saw in the deathless group egos a way out. Faced with the eternal problem of life and death, she had escaped the problem by choosing neither . . . selflessness. She had found a group willing to receive her, she had crossed over.

"It raises a lot of new problems," concluded King. "Slayton and Zaccur and I all felt that you had better be here."

"Yes, yes, sure—but where is Mary?" Lazarus demanded and then ran out of the room without waiting for an answer. He charged through the settlement ignoring both greetings and attempts to stop him. A short distance oustide the camp he ran across a native. He skidded to a stop. "Where is Mary Sperling?"

". . . I am Mary Sperling . . ."

"For the love of—— You *can't* be."

". . . I am Mary Sperling and Mary Sperling is myself . . . do you not know me, Lazarus? . . . I know you . . ."

Lazarus waved his hands. "No! I want to see Mary Sperling who looks like an Earthman—like me!"

The native hesitated. ". . . follow me, then . . ."

Lazarus found her a long way from the camp; it was obvi-ous that she had been avoiding the other colonists. "Mary!"

She answered him mind to mind: ". . . I am sorry to see you troubled . . . Mary Sperling is gone except in that she is part of us . . ."

"Oh, come off it, Mary! Don't give me that stuff! Don't you know me?"

". . . of course I know you, Lazarus . . . it is you who do not know *me* . . . do not trouble your soul or grieve your heart with the sight of this body in front of you . . . I am not one of your kind . . . I am native to this planet . . ."

"Mary," he insisted, "you've got to undo this. You've got to come out of there!"

She shook her head, an oddly human gesture, for the face

no longer held any trace of human expression; it was a mask of otherness. ". . . that is impossible . . . Mary Sperling is gone . . . the one who speaks with you is inextricably *myself* and not of your kind . . ." The creature who had been Mary Sperling turned and walked away.

"Mary!" he cried. His heart leapt across the span of centuries to the night his mother had died. He covered his face with his hands and wept the unconsolable grief of a child.

5

LAZARUS FOUND both King and Barstow waiting for him when he returned. King looked at his face. "I could have told you," he said soberly, "but you wouldn't wait."

"Forget it," Lazarus said harshly. "What now?"

"Lazarus, there is something else you have to see before we discuss anything," Zaccur Barstow answered.

"Okay. What?"

"Just come and see." They led him to a compartment in the ship's boat which was used as a headquarters. Contrary to Families' custom it was locked; King let them in. There was a woman inside, who, when she saw the three, quietly withdrew, locking the door again as she went out.

"Take a look at that," directed Barstow.

It was a living creature in an incubator—a child, but no such child as had ever been seen before. Lazarus stared at it, then said angrily, "What the devil is it?"

"See for yourself. Pick it up. You won't hurt it."

Lazarus did so, gingerly at first, then without shrinking from the contact as his curiosity increased. What it was, he could not say. It was not human; it was just as certainly not offspring of the Little People. Did this planet, like the last, contain some previously unsuspected race? It was manlike, yet certainly not a man child. It lacked even the button nose of a baby, nor were there evident external ears. There were organs in the usual locations of each but flush with the skull and protected with bony ridges. Its hands had too many fingers and there was an extra large one near each wrist which ended in a cluster of pink worms.

There was something odd about the torso of the infant which Lazarus could not define. But two other gross facts were evident: the legs ended not in human feet but in horny, toeless pediments—hoofs. And the creature was hermaphroditic—not in deformity but in healthy development, an androgyne.

"What is it?" he repeated, his mind filled with lively suspicion.

"That," said Zaccur, "is Marion Schmidt, born three weeks ago."

"Huh? What do you mean?"

"It means that the Little People are just as clever in manipulating us as they are in manipulating plants."

"What? But they agreed to leave us alone!"

"Don't blame them too quickly. We let ourselves in for it. The original idea was simply a few improvements."

" 'Improvements!' That thing's an obscenity."

"Yes and no. My stomach turns whenever I have to look at it . . . but actually—well, it's sort of a superman. Its body architecture has been redesigned for greater efficiency, our useless simian hangovers have been left out, and its organs have been rearranged in a more sensible fashion. You can't say it's not human, for it is . . . an improved model. Take that extra appendage at the wrist. That's another hand, a miniature one . . . backed up by a microscopic eye. You can see how useful that would be, once you get used to the idea." Barstow stared at it. "But it looks horrid, to me."

"It'd look horrid to anybody," Lazarus stated. "It may be an improvement, but damn it, I say it ain't human."

"In any case it creates a problem."

"I'll say it does!" Lazarus looked at it again. "You say it has a second set of eyes in those tiny hands? That doesn't seem possible."

Barstow shrugged. "I'm no biologist. But every cell in the body contains a full bundle of chromosomes. I suppose that you could grow eyes, or bones, or anything you liked anywhere, if you knew how to manipulate the genes in the chromosomes. And they know."

"I don't want to be manipulated!"

"Neither do I."

Lazarus stood on the bank and stared out over the broad beach at a full meeting of the Families. "I am——" he started formally, then looked puzzled. "Come here a moment, Andy." He whispered to Libby; Libby looked pained and whispered back. Lazarus looked exasperated and whispered again. Finally he straightened up and started over.

"I am two hundred and forty-one years old—at least," he stated. "Is there anyone here who is older?" It was empty formality; he knew that he was the eldest; he felt twice that old. "The meeting is opened," he went on, his big voice rumbling on down the beach assisted by speaker systems from the ship's boats. "Who is your chairman?"

"Get on with it," someone called from the crowd.

"Very well," said Lazarus. "Zaccur Barstow!"

Behind Lazarus a technician aimed a directional pickup at Barstow. "Zaccur Barstow," his voice boomed out, "speaking for myself. Some of us have come to believe that this planet, pleasant as it is, is not the place for us. You all know about Mary Sperling, you've seen stereos of Marion Schmidt; there have been other things and I won't elaborate. But emigrating again poses another question, the question of where? Lazarus Long proposes that we return to Earth. In such a——" His words were drowned by noise from the crowd.

Lazarus shouted them down. "Nobody is going to be forced to leave. But if enough of us want to leave to justify taking the ship, then we can. I say go back to Earth. Some say look for another planet. That'll have to be decided. But first—how many of you think as I do about leaving here?"

"I do!" The shout was echoed by many others. Lazarus peered toward the first man to answer, tried to spot him, glanced over his shoulder at the tech, then pointed. "Go ahead, bud," he ruled. "The rest of you pipe down."

"Name of Oliver Schmidt. I've been waiting for months for somebody to suggest this. I thought I was the only sorehead in the Families. I haven't any real reason for leaving—I'm not scared out by the Mary Sperling matter, nor Marion Schmidt. Anybody who likes such things is welcome to them—live and let live. But I've got a deep-down urge to see Cincinnati again. I'm fed up with this place. I'm tired of being a lotus eater. Damn it, I want to *work* for my living! According to the Families' geneticists I ought to be good for another century at least. I can't see spending that much time lying in the sun and daydreaming."

When he shut up, at least a thousand more tried to get the floor. "Easy! Easy!" bellowed Lazarus. "If everybody wants to talk, I'm going to have to channel it through your Family representatives. But let's get a sample here and there." He picked out another man, told him to sound off.

"I won't take long," the new speaker said, "as I agree with Oliver Schmidt. I just wanted to mention my own reason. Do any of you miss the Moon? Back home I used to sit out on my balcony on warm summer nights and smoke and look at the Moon. I didn't know it was important to me, but it is. I want a planet with a moon."

The next speaker said only, "This case of Mary Sperling has given me a case of nerves. I get nightmares that I've gone over myself."

The arguments went on and on. Somebody pointed out that they had been chased off Earth; what made anybody think that they would be allowed to return? Lazarus answered that himself. "We learned a lot from the Jockaira and now we've learned a lot more from the Little People—things that put us way out ahead of anything scientists back on Earth had even dreamed of. We can go back to Earth loaded for bear. We'll be in shape to demand our rights, strong enough to defend them."

"Lazarus Long——" came another voice.

"Yes," acknowledged Lazarus. "You over there, go ahead."

"I am too old to make any more jumps from star to star and much too old to fight at the end of such a jump. Whatever the rest of you do, I'm staying."

"In that case," said Lazarus, "there is no need to discuss it, is there?"

"I am entitled to speak."

"All right, you've spoken. Now give someone else a chance."

The sun set and the stars came out and still the talk went on. Lazarus knew that it would never end unless he moved to end it. "All right," he shouted, ignoring the many who still wanted to speak. "Maybe we'll have to turn this back to the Family councils, but let's take a trial vote and see where we are. Everybody who wants to go back to Earth move way over to my right. Everybody who wants to stay here move down the beach to my left. Everybody who wants to go exploring for still another planet gather right here in front of me." He dropped back and said to the sound tech, "Give them some music to speed 'em up."

The tech nodded and the homesick strains of *Valse Triste*

sighed over the beach. It was followed by *The Green Hills of Earth*. Zaccur Barstow turned toward Lazarus. "You picked that music."

"Me?" Lazarus answered with bland innocence. "You know I ain't musical, Zack."

Even with music the separation took a long time. The last movement of the immortal Fifth had died away long before they at last had sorted themselves into three crowds.

On the left about a tenth of the total number were gathered, showing thereby their intention of staying. They were mostly the old and the tired, whose sands had run low. With them were a few youngsters who had never seen Earth, plus a bare sprinkling of other ages.

In the center was a very small group, not over three hundred, mostly men and a few younger women, who voted thereby for still newer frontiers.

But the great mass was on Lazarus' right. He looked at them and saw new animation in their faces; it lifted his heart, for he had been bitterly afraid that he was almost alone in his wish to leave.

He looked back at the small group nearest him. "It looks like you're out-voted," he said to them alone, his voice unamplified. "But never mind, there always comes another day." He waited.

Slowly the group in the middle began to break up. By ones and twos and threes they moved away. A very few drifted over to join those who were staying; most of them merged with the group on the right.

When this secondary division was complete Lazarus spoke to the smaller group on his left. "All right," he said very gently, "You . . . you old folks might as well go back up to the meadows and get your sleep. The rest of us have plans to make."

Lazarus then gave Libby the floor and let him explain to the majority crowd that the trip home would not be the weary journey the flight from Earth had been, nor even the tedious second jump. Libby placed all of the credit where most of it belonged, with the Little People. They had straightened him out with his difficulties in dealing with the problem of speeds which appeared to exceed the speed of light. If the Little People knew what they were talking about —and Libby was sure that they did—there appeared to be no limits to what Libby chose to call "para-acceleration"—

"para-" because, like Libby's own light-pressure drive, it acted on the whole mass uniformly and could no more be perceived by the senses than can gravitation, and "para-" also because the ship would not go "through" but rather around or "beside" normal space. "It is not so much a matter of driving the ship as it is a selection of appropriate potential level in an n-dimensional hyperplenum of n-plus-one possible——"

Lazarus firmly cut him off. "That's your department, son, and everybody trusts you in it. We ain't qualified to discuss the fine points."

"I was only going to add——"

"I know. But you were already out of the world when I stopped you."

Someone from the crowd shouted one more question. "When do we get there?"

"I don't know," Libby admitted, thinking of the question the way Nancy Weatheral had put it to him long ago. "I can't say what year it will be . . . but it will seem like about three weeks from now."

The preparations consumed days simply because many round trips of the ship's boats were necessary to embark them. There was a marked lack of ceremonious farewell because those remaining behind tended to avoid those who were leaving. Coolness had sprung up between the two groups; the division on the beach had split friendships, had even broken up contemporary marriages, had caused many hurt feelings, unresolvable bitterness. Perhaps the only desirable aspect of the division was that the parents of the mutant Marion Schmidt had elected to remain behind.

Lazarus was in charge of the last boat to leave. Shortly before he planned to boost he felt a touch at his elbow. "Excuse me," a young man said. "My name's Hubert Johnson. I want to go along but I've had to stay back with the other crowd to keep my mother from throwing fits. If I show up at the last minute, can I still go along?"

Lazarus looked him over. "You look old enough to decide without asking me."

"You don't understand. I'm an only child and my mother tags me around. I've got to sneak back before she misses me. How much longer——"

"I'm not holding this boat for anybody. And you'll never break away any younger. Get into the boat."

"But——"

"Git!" The young man did so, with one worried backward glance at the bank. There was a lot, thought Lazarus, to be said for ectogenesis.

Once inboard the *New Frontiers* Lazarus reported to Captain King in the control room. "All inboard?" asked King.

"Yeah. Some late deciders, pro and con, and one more passenger at the last possible split second—woman named Eleanor Johnson. Let's go!"

King turned to Libby. "Let's go, Mister."

The stars blinked out.

They flew blind, with only Libby's unique talent to guide them. If he had doubts as to his ability to lead them through the featureless blackness of other space he kept them to himself. On the twenty-third ship's day of the reach and the eleventh day of para-deceleration the stars reappeared, all in their old familiar ranges—the Big Dipper, giant Orion, lopsided Crux, the fairy Pleiades, and dead ahead of them, blazing against the frosty backdrop of the Milky Way, was a golden light that had to be the Sun.

Lazarus had tears in his eyes for the second time in a month.

They could not simply rendezvous with Earth, set a parking orbit, and disembark; they had to throw their hats in first. Besides that, they needed first to know what time it was.

Libby was able to establish quickly, through proper motions of nearest stars, that it was not later than about 3700 A.D.; without precise observatory instruments he refused to commit himself further. But once they were close enough to see the Solar planets he had another clock to read; the planets themselves make a clock with nine hands.

For any date there is a unique configuration of those "hands" since no planetary period is exactly commensurate with another. Pluto marks off an "hour" of a quarter of a millennium; Jupiter's clicks a cosmic minute of twelve years; Mercury whizzes a "second" of about ninety days. The other "hands" can refine these readings—Neptune's period is so cantankerously different from that of Pluto that the two fall into approximately repeated configuration only once in seven hundred and fifty-eight years. The great clock can be read with any desired degree of accuracy over any period—but it is not easy to read.

Libby started to read it as soon as any of the planets could be picked out. He muttered over the problem. "There's not a chance that we'll pick up Pluto," he complained to Lazarus, "and I doubt if we'll have Neptune. The inner planets give me an infinite series of approximations—you know as well as I do that "infinite" is a question-begging term. Annoying!"

"Aren't you looking at it the hard way, son? You can get a practical answer. Or move over and I'll get one."

"Of course I can get a practical answer," Libby said petulantly, "if you're satisfied with that. But——"

"But me no 'buts'—*what year is it, man!*"

"Eh? Let's put it this way. The time rate in the ship and duration on Earth have been unrelated three times. But now they are effectively synchronous again, such that slightly over seventy-four years have passed since we left."

Lazarus heaved a sigh. "Why didn't you say so?" He had been fretting that Earth might not be recognizable . . . they might have torn down New York or something like that. "Shucks, Andy, you shouldn't have scared me like that."

"Mmm . . ." said Libby. It was one of no further interest to him. There remained only the delicious problem of inventing a mathematics which would describe elegantly two apparently irreconcilable groups of facts: the Michelson-Morley experiments and the log of the *New Frontiers*. He set happily about it. Mmm . . . what was the least number of para-dimensions indispensably necessary to contain the augmented plenum using a sheaf of postulates affirming——

It kept him contented for a considerable time—subjective time, of course.

The ship was placed in a temporary orbit half a billion miles from the Sun with a radius vector normal to the plane of the ecliptic. Parked thus at right angles to and far outside the flat pancake of the Solar System they were safe from any long chance of being discovered. A ship's boat had been fitted with the neo-Libby drive during the jump and a negotiating party was sent down.

Lazarus wanted to go along; King refused to let him, which sent Lazarus into sulks. King had said curtly, "This isn't a raiding party, Lazarus; this is a diplomatic mission."

"Hell, man, I can be diplomatic when it pays!"

"No doubt. But we'll send a man who doesn't go armed to the 'fresher."

Ralph Schultz headed the party, since psychodynamic factors back on Earth were of first importance, but he was aided by legal, military, and technical specialists. If the Families were going to have to fight for living room it was necessary to know what sort of technology, what sort of weapons, they would have to meet—but it was even more necessary to find out whether or not a peaceful landing could be arranged. Schultz had been authorized by the elders to offer a plan under which the Families would colonize the thinly settled and retrograded European continent. But it was possible, even likely, that this had already been done in their absence, in view of the radioactive half-lifes involved. Schultz would probably have to improvise some other compromise, depending on the conditions he found.

Again there was nothing to do but wait.

Lazarus endured it in nail-chewing uncertainty. He had claimed publicly that the Families had such great scientific advantage that they could meet and defeat the best that Earth could offer. Privately, he knew that this was sophistry and so did any other Member competent to judge the matter. Knowledge alone did not win wars. The ignorant fanatics of Europe's Middle Ages had defeated the incomparably higher Islamic culture; Archimedes had been struck down by a common soldier; barbarians had sacked Rome. Libby, or some one, might devise an unbeatable weapon from their mass of new knowledge—or might not. And who knew what strides military art had made on earth in three quarters of a century?

King, trained in military art, was worried by the same thing and still more worried by the personnel he would have to work with. The Families were anything but trained legions; the prospect of trying to whip those cranky individualists into some semblance of a disciplined fighting machine ruined his sleep.

These doubts and fears King and Lazarus did not mention even to each other; each was afraid that to mention such things would be to spread a poison of fear through the ship. But they were not alone in their worries; half of the ship's company realized the weaknesses of their position and kept silent only because a bitter resolve to go home, no matter what, made them willing to accept the dangers.

"Skipper," Lazarus said to King two weeks after Schultz's party had headed Earthside, "have you wondered how they're going to feel about the *New Frontiers* herself?"

"Eh? What do you mean?"

"Well, we hijacked her. Piracy."

King looked astounded. "Bless me, so we did! Do you know, it's been so long ago that it is hard for me to realize that she was ever anything but my ship . . . or to recall that I first came into her through an act of piracy." He looked thoughtful, then smiled grimly. "I wonder how conditions are in Coventry these days?"

"Pretty thin rations, I imagine," said Lazarus. "But we'll team up and make out. Never mind—they haven't caught us yet."

"Do you suppose that Slayton Ford will be connected with the matter? That would be hard lines after all he has gone through."

"There may not be any trouble about it at all," Lazarus answered soberly. "While the way we got this ship was kind of irregular, we *have* used it for the purpose for which it was built—to explore the stars. And we're returning it intact, long before they could have expected any results, and with a slick new space drive to boot. It's more for their money than they had any reason to expect—so they may just decide to forget it and trot out the fatted calf."

"I hope so," King answered doubtfully.

The scouting party was two days late. No signal was received from them until they emerged into normal spacetime, just before rendezvous, as no method had yet been devised for signalling from para-space to ortho-space. While they were maneuvering to rendezvous, King received Ralph Schultz's face on the control-room screen. "Hello, Captain! We'll be boarding shortly to report."

"Give me a summary now!"

"I wouldn't know where to start. But it's all right—*we can go home!*"

"Huh? How's that? Repeat!"

"Everything's all right. We are restored to the Covenant. You see, there isn't any difference any more. *Everybody is a member of the Families now.*"

"What do you mean?" King demanded.

"They've got it."

"Got what?"

"Got the secret of longevity."

"Huh? Talk sense. There isn't any secret. There never was any secret."

"*We* didn't have any secret—but they thought we had. So they found it."

"Explain yourself," insisted Captain King.

"Captain, can't this wait until we get back into the ship?" Ralph Schultz protested. "I'm no biologist. We've brought along a government representative—you can quiz him, instead."

6

KING RECEIVED Terra's representative in his cabin. He had notified Zaccur Barstow and Justin Foote to be present for the Families and had invited Doctor Gordon Hardy because the nature of the startling news was the biologist's business. Libby was there as the ship's chief officer; Slayton Ford was invited because of his unique status, although he had held no public office in the Families since his breakdown in the temple of Kreel.

Lazarus was there because Lazarus wanted to be there, in his own strictly private capacity. He had not been invited, but even Captain King was somewhat diffident about interfering with the assumed prerogatives of the eldest Member.

Ralph Schultz introduced Earth's ambassador to the assembled company. "This is Captain King, our commanding officer —and this is Miles Rodney, representing the Federation Council—minister plenipotentiary and ambassador extraordinary, I guess you would call him."

"Hardly that," said Rodney, "although I can agree to the 'extraordinary' part. This situation is quite without precedent. It is an honor to know you, Captain."

"Glad to have you inboard, sir."

"And this is Zaccur Barstow, representing the trustees of the Howard Families, and Justin Foote, secretary to the trustees——"

"Service."

"Service to you, gentlemen."

"—Andrew Jackson Libby, chief astrogational officer, Doctor Gordon Hardy, biologist in charge of our research into the causes of old age and death."

"May I do you a service?" Hardy acknowledged formally.

"Service to you, sir. So you are the chief biologist—there was a time when you could have done a service to the whole human race. Think of it, sir—think how different things could have been. But, happily, the human race was able to worry out the secret of extending life without the aid of the Howard Families."

Hardy looked vexed. "What do you mean, sir? Do you mean to say that you are still laboring under the delusion that we had some miraculous secret to impart, if we chose?"

Rodney shrugged and spread his hands. "Really, now, there is no need to keep up the pretense, is there? Your results have been duplicated, independently."

Captain King cut in. "Just a moment—— Ralph Schultz, is the Federation still under the impression that there is some 'secret' to our long lives? Didn't you tell them?"

Schultz was looking bewildered. "Uh—this is ridiculous. The subject hardly came up. They themselves had achieved controlled longevity; they were no longer interested in us in that respect. It is true that there still existed a belief that our long lives derived from manipulation rather than from heredity, but I corrected that impression."

"Apparently not very thoroughly, from what Miles Rodney has just said."

"Apparently not. I did not spend much effort on it; it was beating a dead dog. The Howard Families and their long lives are no longer an issue on Earth. Interest, both public and official, is centered on the fact that we have accomplished a successful interstellar jump."

"I can confirm that," agreed Miles Rodney. "Every official, every news service, every citizen, every scientist in the system is waiting with utmost eagerness the arrival of the *New Frontiers*. It's the greatest, most sensational thing that has happened since the first trip to the Moon. You are famous, gentlemen—all of you."

Lazarus pulled Zaccur Barstow aside and whispered to him. Barstow looked perturbed, then nodded thoughtfully. "Captain——" Barstow said to King.

"Yes, Zack?"

"I suggest that we ask our guest to excuse us while we receive Ralph Schultz' report."

"Why?"

Barstow glanced at Rodney. "I think we will be better prepared to discuss matters if we are brief by our own representative."

King turned to Rodney. "Will you excuse us, sir?"

Lazarus broke in. "Never mind, Skipper. Zack means well but he's too polite. Might as well let Comrade Rodney stick around and we'll lay it on the line. Tell me this, Miles; what proof have you got that you and your pals have figured out a way to live as long as we do?"

"Proof?" Rodney seemed dumbfounded. "Why do you ask —— Whom am I addressing? Who are you, sir?"

Ralph Schultz intervened. "Sorry—I didn't get a chance to finish the introductions. Miles Rodney, this is Lazarus Long, the Senior."

"Service. 'The Senior' what?"

"He just means 'The Senior,' period," answered Lazarus. "I'm the oldest Member. Otherwise I'm a private citizen."

"The oldest one of the Howard Families! Why—why, you must be the oldest man alive—think of that!"

"You think about it," retorted Lazarus. "I quit worrying about it a couple o' centuries ago. How about answering my question?"

"But I can't help being impressed. You make me feel like an infant—and I'm not a young man myself; I'll be a hundred and five this coming June."

"If you can prove that's your age, you can answer my question. I'd say you were about forty. How about it?"

"Well, dear me, I hardly expected to be interrogated on this point. Do you wish to see my identity card?"

"Are you kidding? I've had fifty-odd identity cards in my time, all with phony birth dates. What else can you offer?"

"Just a minute, Lazarus," put in Captain King. "What is the purpose of your question?"

Lazarus Long turned away from Rodney. "It's like this, Skipper—we hightailed it out of the Solar System to save our necks, because the rest of the yokels thought we had invented some way to live forever and proposed to squeeze it out of us if they had to kill every one of us. Now everything is sweetness and light—so they say. But it seems mighty funny that the bird they send up to smoke the pipe of peace with us should still be convinced that we have that so-called secret.

"It got me to wondering.

"Suppose they hadn't figured out a way to keep from dying from old age but were still clinging to the idea that we had?

What better way to keep us calmed down and unsuspiciou[s] than to tell us they had until they could get us where they wanted us in order to put the question to us again?"

Rodney snorted. "A preposterous idea! Captain, I don'[t] think I'm called on to put up with this."

Lazarus stared coldly. "It was preposterous the first time[,] bub—but it happened. The burnt child is likely to be skittish."

"Just a moment, both of you," ordered King. "Ralph, ho[w] about it? Could you have been taken in by a put-up job?"

Schultz thought about it, painfully. "I don't think so." He paused. "It's rather difficult to say. I couldn't tell from ap-pearance of course, any more than our own Members could be picked out from a crowd of normal persons."

"But you are a psychologist. Surely you could have de-tected indications of fraud, if there had been one."

"I may be a psychologist, but I'm not a miracle man and I'm not telepathic. I wasn't looking for fraud." He grinned sheepishly. "There was another factor. I was so excited over being home that I was not in the best emotional condition to note discrepancies, if there were any."

"Then you aren't sure?"

"No. I am emotionally convinced that Miles Rodney is tell-ing the truth——"

"I am!"

"—and I believe that a few questions could clear the mat-ter up. He claims to be one hundred and five years old. We can test that."

"I see," agreed King. "Hmm . . . you put the questions, Ralph?"

"Very well. You will permit, Miles Rodney?"

"Go ahead," Rodney answered stiffly.

"You must have been about thirty years old when we left Earth, since we have been gone nearly seventy-five years, Earth time. Do you remember the event?"

"Quite clearly. I was a clerk in Novak Tower at the time, in the offices of the Administrator."

Slayton Ford had remained in the background throughout the discussion, and had done nothing to call attention to him-self. At Rodney's answer he sat up. "Just a moment, Cap-tain——"

"Eh? Yes?"

"Perhaps I can cut this short. You'll pardon me, Ralph?" He turned to Terra's representative. "Who am I?"

Rodney looked at him in some puzzlement. His expression changed from one of simple surprise at the odd question to complete and unbelieving bewilderment. "Why, you . . . *you* are *Administrator Ford!*"

7

"ONE AT A TIME! One at a time," Captain King was saying. "Don't everybody try to talk at once. Go on, Slayton; you have the floor. You know this man?" Ford looked Rodney over. "No, I can't say that I do."

"Then it *is* a frame up." King turned to Rodney. "I suppose you recognized Ford from historical stereos—is that right?"

Rodney seemed about to burst. "No! I recognized him. He's changed but I knew him. Mr. Administrator—look at me, please! Don't you know me? I *worked* for you!"

"It seems fairly obvious that he doesn't," King said dryly.

Ford shook his head. "It doesn't prove anything, one way or the other, Captain. There were over two thousand civil service employes in my office. Rodney might have been one of them. His face looks vaguely familiar, but so do most faces."

"Captain——" Master Gordon Hardy was speaking. "If I can question Miles Rodney I might be able to give an opinion as to whether or not they actually have discovered anything new about the causes of old age and death."

Rodney shook his head. "I am not a biologist. You could trip me up in no time. Captain King, I ask you to arrange my return to Earth as quickly as possible. I'll not be subjected to any more of this. And let me add that I do not care a minim whether you and your—your pretty crew ever get back to civilization or not. I came here to help you, but I'm disgusted." He stood up.

Slayton Ford went toward him. "Easy, Miles Rodney, please! Be patient. Put yourself in their place. You would be just as cautious if you had been through what they have been through."

Rodney hesitated. "Mr. Administrator, what are *you* doing here?"

"It's a long and complicated story. I'll tell you later."

"You are a member of the Howard Families—you must be. That accounts for a lot of odd things."

Ford shook his head. "No, Miles Rodney, I am not. Later, please—I'll explain it. You worked for me once—when?"

"From 2109 until you, uh, disappeared."

"What was your job?"

"At the time of the crisis of 2113 I was an assistant correlation clerk in the Division of Economic Statistics, Control Section."

"Who was your section chief?"

"Leslie Waldron."

"Old Waldron, eh? What was the color of his hair?"

"His hair? The Walrus was bald as an egg."

Lazarus whispered to Zaccur Barstow, "Looks like I was off base, Zack."

"Wait a moment," Barstow whispered back. "It still could be thorough preparation—they may have known that Ford escaped with us."

Ford was continuing, "What was *The Sacred Cow?*"

"*The Sacred*—— Chief, you weren't even supposed to know that there was such a publication!"

"Give my intelligence staff credit for some activity, at least," Ford said dryly. "I got my copy every week."

"But what was it?" demanded Lazarus.

Rodney answered, "An office comic and gossip sheet that was passed from hand to hand."

"Devoted to ribbing the bosses," Ford added, "especially me." He put an arm around Rodney's shoulders. "Friends, there is no doubt about it. Miles and I were fellow workers."

"I still want to find out about the new rejuvenation process," insisted Master Hardy some time later.

"I think we all do," agreed King. He reached out and refilled their guest's wine glass. "Will you tell us about it, sir?"

"I'll try," Miles Rodney answered, "though I must ask Master Hardy to bear with me. It's not one process, but several— one basic process and several dozen others, some of them purely cosmetic, especially for women. Nor is the basic process truly a rejuvenation process. You can arrest the progress of old age, but you can't reverse it to any significant degree— you can't turn a senile old man into a boy."

"Yes, yes," agreed Hardy. "Naturally—but what is the basic process?"

"It consists largely in replacing the entire blood tissue in an old person with new, young blood. Old age, so they tell me, is primarily a matter of the progressive accumulation of the waste poisons of metabolism. The blood is supposed to carry them away, but presently the blood gets so clogged with the poisons that the scavenging process doesn't take place properly. Is that right, Doctor Hardy?"

"That's an odd way of putting it, but——"

"I told you I was no biotechnician."

"—essentially correct. It's a matter of diffusion pressure deficit—the d.p.d. on the blood side of a cell wall must be such as to maintain a fairly sharp gradient or there will occur progressive autointoxication of the individual cells. But I must say that I feel somewhat disappointed, Miles Rodney. The basic idea of holding off death by insuring proper scavenging of waste products is not new—I have a bit of chicken heart which has been alive for two and one half centuries through equivalent techniques. As to the use of young blood—yes, that will work. I've kept experimental animals alive by such blood donations to about twice their normal span." He stopped and looked troubled.

"Yes, Doctor Hardy?"

Hardy chewed his lip. "I gave up that line of research. I found it necessary to have several young donors in order to keep one beneficiary from growing any older. There was a small, but measurable, unfavorable effect on each of the donors. Racially it was self-defeating; there would never be enough donors to go around. Am I to understand, sir that this method is thereby limited to a small, select part of the population?"

"Oh, no! I did not make myself clear, Master Hardy. There are no donors."

"Huh?"

"New blood, enough for everybody, grown outside the body—the Public Health and Longevity Service can provide any amount of it, any type."

Hardy looked startled. "To think we came so close . . . so that's it." He paused, then went on. "We tried tissue culture of bone marrow *in vitro*. We should have persisted."

"Don't feel badly about it. Billions of credits and tens of

thousands of technicians engaged in this project before there were any significant results. I'm told that the mass of accumulated art in this field represents more effort than even the techniques of atomic engineering." Rodney smiled. "You see, they *had* to get some results; it was politically necessary—so there was an all-out effort." Rodney turned to Ford. "When the news about the escape of the Howard Families reached the public, Chief, your precious successor had to be protected from the mobs."

Hardy persisted with questions about subsidiary techniques —tooth budding, growth inhibiting, hormone therapy, many others—until King came to Rodney's rescue by pointing out that the prime purpose of the visit was to arrange details of the return of the Families to Earth.

Rodney nodded. "I think we should get down to business. As I understand it, Captain, a large proportion of your people are now in reduced-temperature somnolence?"

("Why can't he say 'cold-rest'?" Lazarus said to Libby.)

"Yes, that is so."

"Then it would be no hardship on them to remain in that state for a time."

"Eh? Why do you say that, sir?"

Rodney spread his hands. "The administration finds itself in a somewhat embarrassing position. To put it bluntly, there is a housing shortage. Absorbing one hundred and ten thousand displaced persons can't be done overnight."

Again King had to hush them. He then nodded to Zaccur Barstow, who addressed himself to Rodney. "I fail to see the problem, sir. What is the present population of the North American continent?"

"Around seven hundred million."

"And you can't find room to tuck away one-seventieth of one per cent of that number? It sounds preposterous."

"You don't understand, sir," Rodney protested. "Population pressure has become our major problem. Co-incident with it, the right to remain undisturbed in the enjoyment of one's own homestead, or one's apartment, has become the most jealously guarded of all civil rights. Before we can find you adequate living room we must make over some stretch of desert, or make other major arrangements."

"I get it," said Lazarus. "Politics. You don't dast disturb anybody for fear they will squawk."

"That's hardly an adequate statement of the case."

"It's not, eh? could be you've got a general election coming up, maybe?"

"As a matter of fact we have, but that has nothing to do with the case."

Lazarus snorted.

Justin Foote spoke up. "It seems to me that the administration has looked at this problem in the most superficial light. It is not as if we were homeless immigrants. Most of the Members own their own homes. As you doubtless know, the Families were well-to-do, even wealthy, and for obvious reasons we built our homes to endure. I feel sure that most of those structures are still standing."

"No doubt," Rodney conceded, "but you will find them occupied."

Justin Foote shrugged. "What has that to do with us? That is a problem for the government to settle with the persons it has allowed illegally to occupy our homes. As for myself, I shall land as soon as possible, obtain an eviction order from the nearest court, and repossess my home."

"It's not that easy. You can make omelet from eggs, but not eggs from omelet. You have been legally dead for many years; the present occupant of your house holds a good title."

Justin Foote stood up and glared at the Federation's envoy, looking, as Lazarus thought, "like a cornered mouse." "Legally dead! By whose act, sir, by whose act? Mine? I was a respected solicitor, quietly and honorably pursuing my profession, harming no one, when I was arrested without cause and forced to flee for my life. Now I am blandly told that my property is confiscated and my very legal existence as a person and as a citizen has been taken from me because of that sequence of events. What manner of justice is this? Does the Covenant still stand?"

"You misunderstand me. I——"

"I misunderstood nothing. If justice is measured out only when it is convenient, then the Covenant is not worth the parchment it is written on. I shall make of myself a test case, sir, a test case for every Member of the Families. Unless my property is returned to me in full and at once I shall bring personal suit against every obstructing official. I will make of it a *cause celebre*. For many years I have suffered inconvenience and indignity and peril; I shall not be put off with words. I will shout it from the housetops." He paused for breath.

"He's right, Miles," Slayton Ford put in quietly. "The government had better find some adequate way to handle this—and quickly."

Lazarus caught Libby's eye and silently motioned toward the door. The two slipped outside. "Justin'll keep 'em busy for the next hour," he said. "Let's slide down to the Club and grab some calories."

"Do you really think we ought to leave?"

"Relax. If the skipper wants us, he can holler."

8

LAZARUS TUCKED AWAY three sandwiches, a double order of ice cream, and some cookies while Libby contented himself with somewhat less. Lazarus would have eaten more but he was forced to respond to a barrage of questions from the other habitués of the Club.

"The commissary department ain't really back on its feet," he complained, as he poured his third cup of coffee. "The Little People made life too easy for them. Andy, do you like chili con carne?"

"It's all right."

Lazarus wiped his mouth. "There used to be a restaurant in Tijuana that served the best chili I ever tasted. I wonder if it's still there?"

"Where's Tijuana?" demanded Margaret Weatheral.

"You don't remember Earth, do you, Peggy? Well, darling, it's in Lower California. You know where that is?"

"Don't you think I studied geography? It's in Los Angeles."

"Near enough. Maybe you're right—by now." The ship's announcing system blared out:

"Chief Astrogator—report to the Captain in the Control Room!"

"That's me!" said Libby, and hurriedly got up.

The call was repeated, then was followed by, "All hands—prepare for acceleration! All hands—prepare for acceleration!"

"Here we go again, kids." Lazarus stood up, brushed off his kilt, and followed Libby, whistling as he went:

> *"California, here I come,*
> *Right back where I started from———"*

The ship was underway, the stars had faded out. Captain King had left the control room, taking with him his guest, the Earth's envoy. Miles Rodney had been much impressed; it seemed likely that he would need a drink.

Lazarus and Libby remained in the control room. There was nothing to do; for approximately four hours, ship's time, the ship would remain in para-space, before returning to normal space near Earth.

Lazarus struck a cigaret. "What d'you plan to do when you get back, Andy?"

"Hadn't thought about it."

"Better start thinking. Been some changes."

"I'll probably head back home for a while. I can't imagine the Ozarks having changed very much."

"The hills will look the same, I imagine. You may find the people changed."

"How?"

"You remember I told you that I had gotten fed up with the Families and had kinda lost touch with them for a century? By and large, they had gotten so smug and sot in their ways that I couldn't stand them. I'm afraid we'll find most everybody that way, now that they expect to live forever. Long term investments, be sure to wear your rubbers when it rains . . . that sort of thing."

"It didn't affect you that way."

"My approach is different. I never did have any real reason to last forever—after all, as Gordon Hardy has pointed out, I'm only a third generation result of the Howard plan. I just did my living as I went along and didn't worry my head about it. But that's not the usual attitude. Take Miles Rodney— scared to death to tackle a new situation with both hands for fear of upsetting precedent and stepping on established privileges."

"I was glad to see Justin stand up to him." Libby chuckled. "I didn't think Justin had it in him."

"Ever see a little dog tell a big dog to get the hell out of the little dog's yard?"

"Do you think Justin will win his point?"

"Sure he will, with your help."

"*Mine?*"

"Who knows anything about the para-drive, aside from what you've taught me?"

"I've dictated full notes into the records."

"But you haven't turned those records over to Miles Rodney. Earth *needs* your starship drive, Andy. You heard what Rodney said about population pressure. Ralph was telling me you have to get a government permit now before you can have a baby."

"The hell you say!"

"Fact. You can count on it that there would be tremendous emigration if there were just some decent planets to emigrate to. And that's where your drive comes in. With it, spreading out to the stars becomes really practical. They'll have to dicker."

"It's not really my drive, of course. The Little People worked it out."

"Don't be so modest. You've got it. And you want to back up Justin, don't you?"

"Oh, sure."

"Then we'll use it to bargain with. Maybe I'll do the bargaining, personally. But that's beside the point. Somebody is going to have to do a little exploring before any large-scale emigration starts. Let's go into the real estate business, Andy. We'll stake out this corner of the Galaxy and see what it has to offer."

Libby scratched his nose and thought about it. "Sounds all right, I guess—after I pay a visit home."

"There's no rush. I'll find a nice, clean little yacht, about ten thousand tons and we'll refit with your drive."

"What'll we use for money?"

"We'll have money. I'll set up a parent corporation, while I'm about it, with a loose enough charter to let us do anything we want to do. There will be daughter corporations for various purposes and we'll unload the minor interest in each. Then——"

"You make it sound like work, Lazarus. I thought it was going to be fun."

"Shucks, we won't fuss with that stuff. I'll collar somebody to run the home office and worry about the books and the legal end—somebody about like Justin. Maybe Justin himself."

"Well, all right then."

"You and I will rampage around and see what there is to be seen. It'll be fun, all right."

They were both silent for a long time, with no need to talk. Presently Lazarus said, "Andy——"

"Yeah?"

"Are you going to look into this new-blood-for-old caper?"

"I suppose so, eventually."

"I've been thinking about it. Between ourselves, I'm not as fast with my fists as I was a century back. Maybe my natural span is wearing out. I do know this: I didn't start planning our real estate venture till I head about this new process. It gave me a new perspective. I find myself thinking about thousands of years—and I never used to worry about anything further ahead than a week from next Wednesday."

Libby chuckled again. "Looks like you're growing up."

"Some would say it was about time. Seriously, Andy, I think that's just what I have been doing. The last two and a half centuries have just been my adolescence, so to speak. Long as I've hung around, I don't know any more about the final answers, the *important* answers, than Peggy Weatheral does. Men—*our* kind of men—Earth men—never have had enough time to tackle the important questions. Lots of capacity and not time enough to use it properly. When it came to the important questions we might as well have still been monkeys."

"How do you propose to tackle the important questions?"

"How should I know? Ask me again in about five hundred years."

"You think that will make a difference?"

"I do. Anyhow it'll give me time to poke around and pick up some interesting facts. Take those Jockaira gods——"

"They weren't gods, Lazarus. You shouldn't call them that."

"Of course they weren't—I think. My guess is that they are creatures who have had time enough to do a little hard thinking. Someday, about a thousand years from now, I intend to march straight into the temple of Kreel, look him in the eye, and say, 'Howdy, Bub—what do *you* know that *I* don't know?'"

"It might not be healthy."

"We'll have a showdown, anyway. I've never been satisfied with the outcome there. There ought not to be anything in the whole universe that man can't poke his nose into—that's the way we're built and I assume that there's some reason for it."

"Maybe there aren't any reasons."

"Yes, maybe it's just one colossal big joke, with no point to it." Lazarus stood up and stretched and scratched his ribs. "But I can tell you this, Andy, whatever the answers are, here's one monkey that's going to keep on climbing, and looking around him to see what he can see, as long as the tree holds out."